CASTLING

Book II *of the*
Tempest Trilogy

by

Natasha Kennedy

The miſery of man proceeds not from any ſingle cruſh of overwhelming evil, but from ſmall
vexations continually repeated.

Samuel Johnſon, LL. D.

Raqian Seasons

Without a constant
like the sun, time is measured in
seasons rather than years.
Each season is different, with
their length ranging anywhere
from 21 to 500 days.

Days of the Week

Firstday (or) Octday
Watersday
Grounsday
Lightsday
Wingsday
Mansday
Somensday

Hours of the Day

Morning Bells:
Firstlight
Mid-morning
Late-morning

Midday Bells:
Ascending
Zenith
Descending

Evening Bells:
Firstdark
Mid-evening
Lastlight

Night Bells:
The seven bells of night

Human Aging

Each stage of development can last for any number of
seasons, and so ages are named rather than numbered.
Stages with approximate earth year equivalents:

Infancy: 0-2 years
Age of Wonder: 3-7 years
Age of Awakening: 8-11 years
Age of Questioning: 12-15 years
Age of Ability: 16-25 years
Age of Fullness: 25-40 years
Age of Wearing: 40-60 years
Age of Waning: 60-death

HIGHEST HEAVENS
WATERS ABOVE
GLASSY SEA
RAQIA
SPACE
EARTH
AND THE
LOWLANDS
WATERS BELOW
HADES

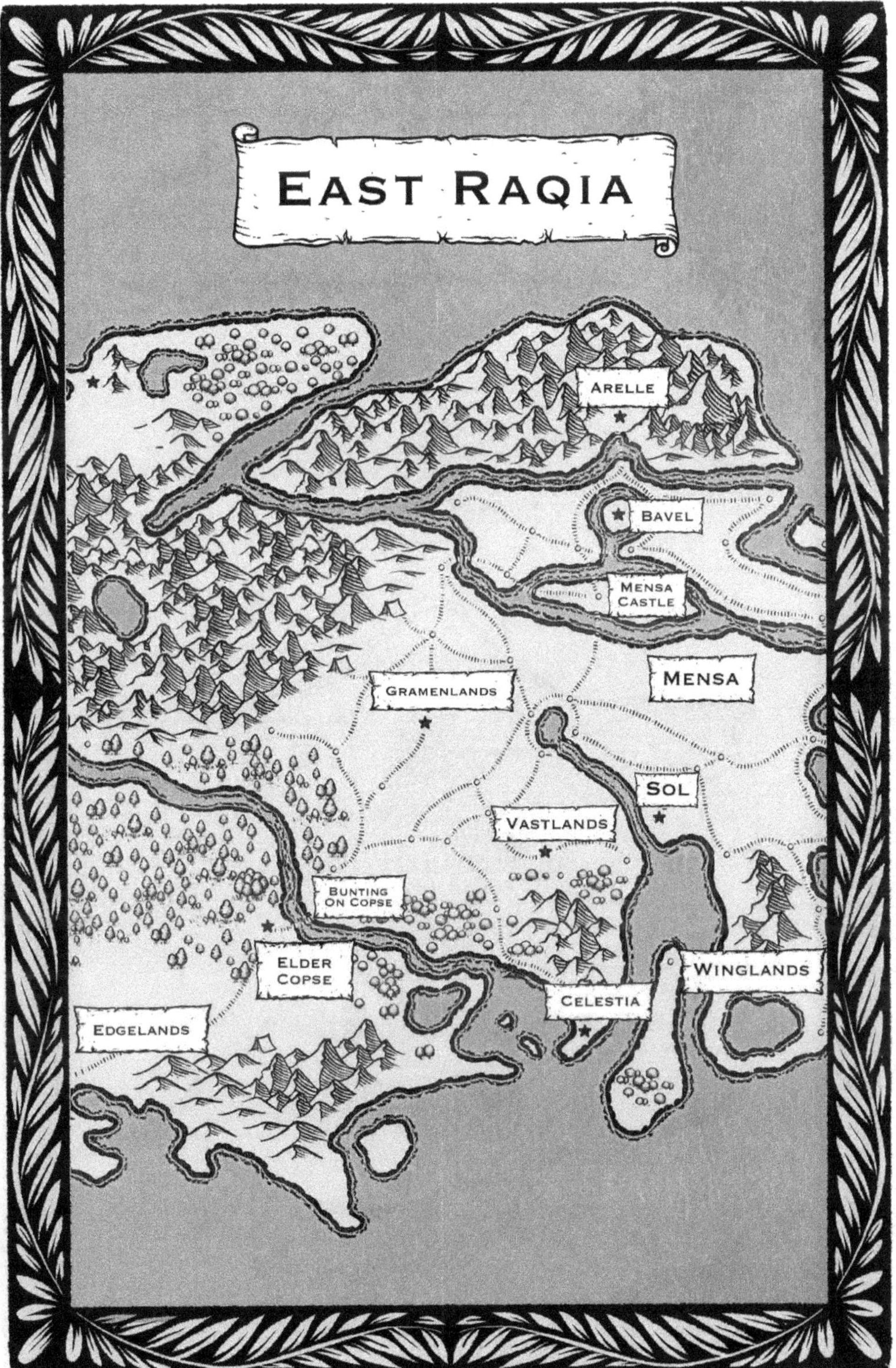

EAST RAQIA
ARELLE
BAVEL
MENSA CASTLE
MENSA
GRAMENLANDS
SOL
VASTLANDS
BUNTING ON COPSE
ELDER COPSE
CELESTIA
WINGLANDS
EDGELANDS

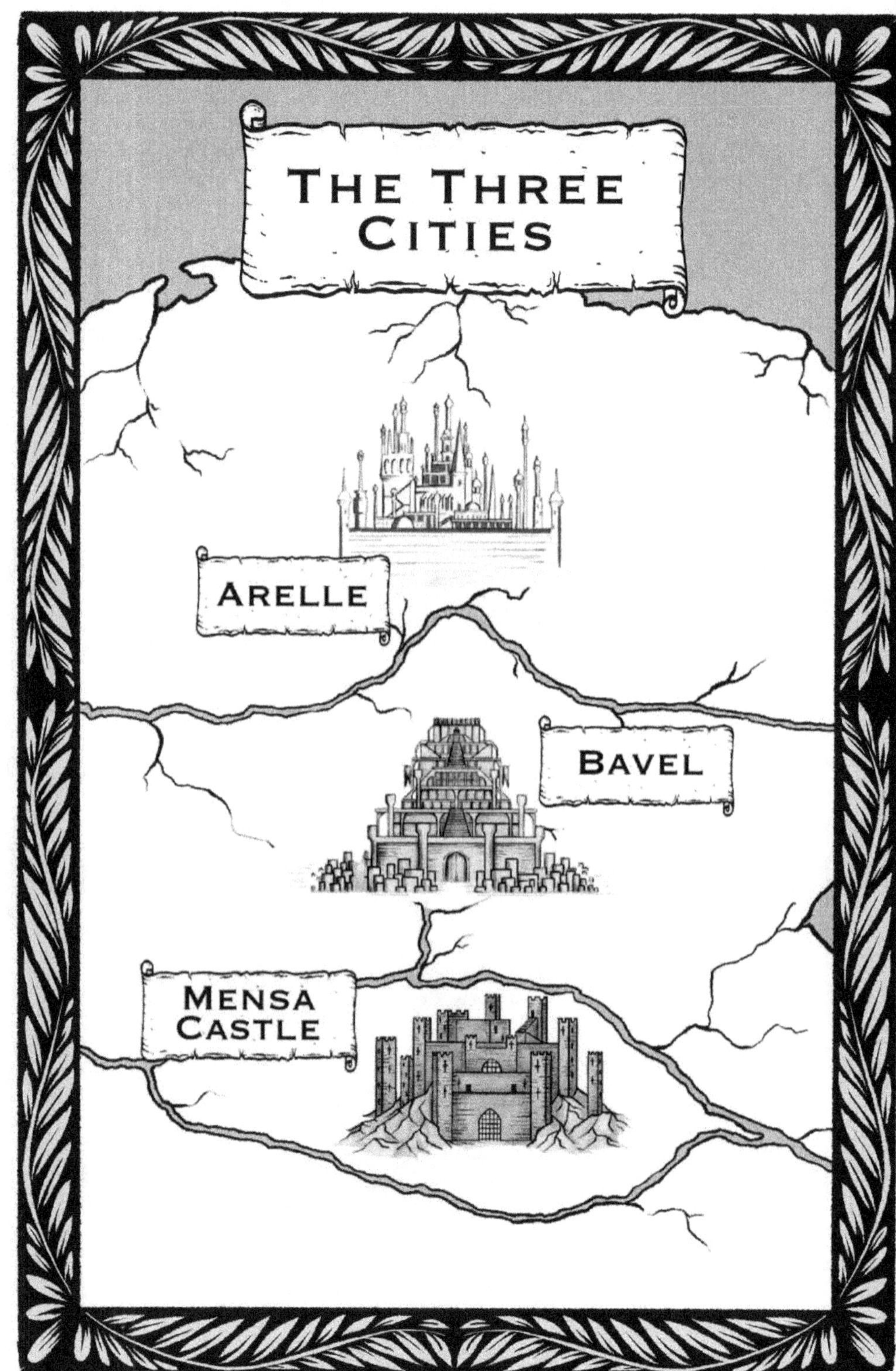

THE THREE CITIES
ARELLE
BAVEL
MENSA CASTLE

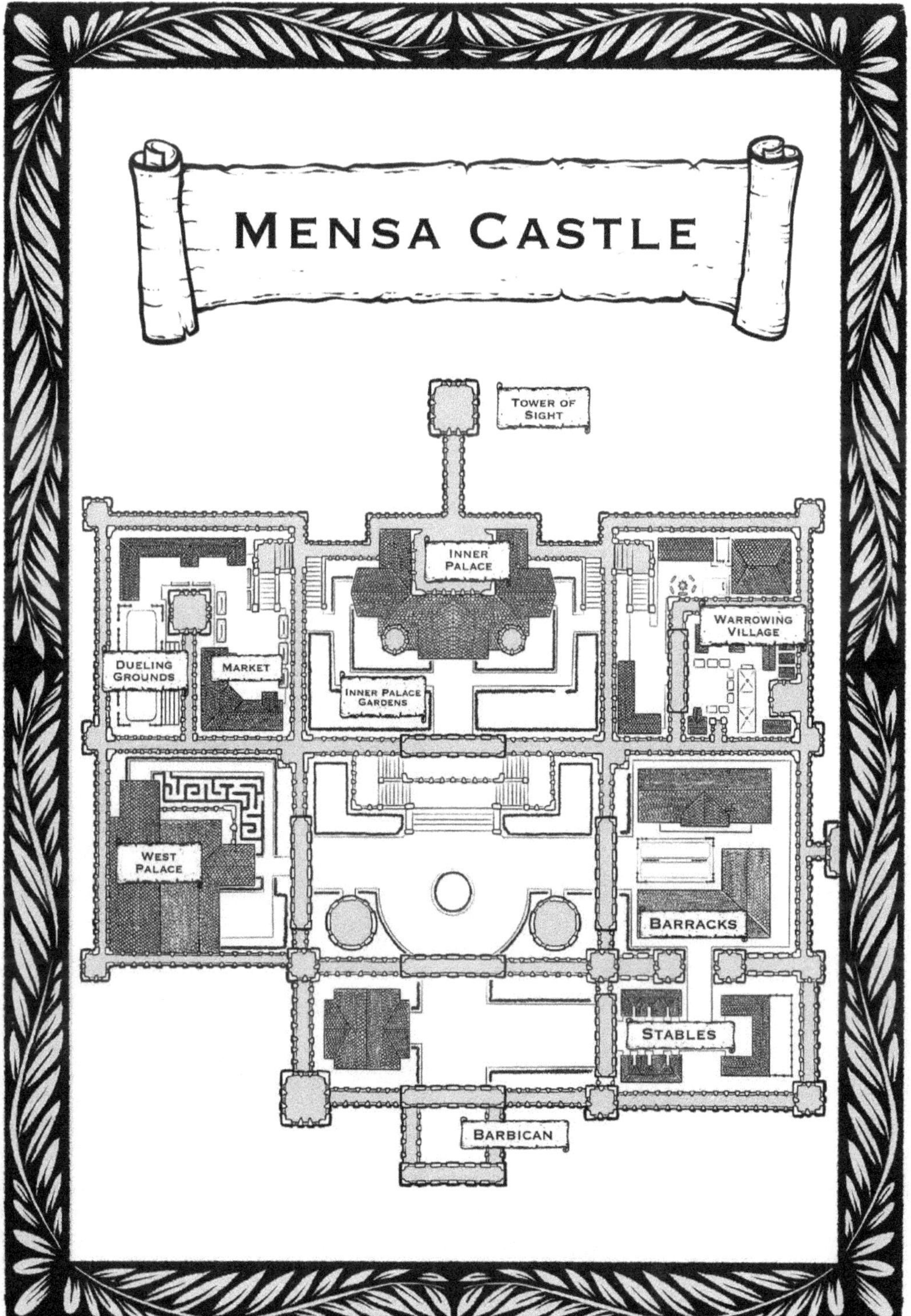

MENSA CASTLE
TOWER OF SIGHT
INNER PALACE
WARROWING VILLAGE
DUELING GROUNDS
MARKET
INNER PALACE GARDENS
WEST PALACE
BARRACKS
STABLES
BARBICAN

TABLE *of* CONTENTS

1

—— Rook ——

The Net of Scars

Rook avoided mirrors at all costs. This made it hard to step into Brid's little *Trinkets and Textiles* shop, where the merchant prided himself on stocking mirrors, and he put those mirrors everywhere.

"Can you just check," Rook said as he dodged the reflection of his face across three separate mirrors, "How long it will be before it arrives?"

Brid leaned over the counter humming as he inspected his ledger. He straightened up, then held his toothpick up to his mouth.

"Another week or so," he said. "Is there a hurry?"

"No," Rook smiled, "Just checking."

"It's for your... *friend*, isn't it? The velvet?"

"Hah," Rook slipped his hands into his front pockets. "He likes velvet."

"Is it a gift?"

"Thought I could have it made into something. I was hoping to get it before the next season started." Rook glanced over toward Brid's slate board, where the date

ROOK

was usually written. He had to avoid three other Rooks as his eyes passed over the mirror-garbed room. "Are we about to have a Firstday?"

"That's what the passing skydeacon told me," said Brid. He was tapping his lip with his toothpick. Tooth-picking—it was one of those pastimes that only nobles really partook in. But here was Brid, a small-town merchant, sporting a silver pick. He really was the closest thing to nobility that the town of Bunting on Copse had, so he might as well pick his teeth.

"Anyway, I wouldn't count on your order to come in before the next Firstday," the merchant went on, "Perhaps you can give it to him for his birthday?"

"If he would ever tell me when it is," Rook mumbled to himself.

"See here, Rook," Brid popped his hands on his hips, "I've seen your face enough times not to flinch. You don't have to cup your hand over your face like that."

"Hmm?" Rook dropped his hand. "Sorry–just not a fan of the mirror...s."

"Fancy items, these," Brid looked around with a grand sigh of admiration, "You know the upper classes use them every day. It *helps* to know how you look before you step out your door."

"Does it?" Rook held his smile. "I couldn't imagine that to be the case."

"Go on, it's not so bad to see yourself." Brid pointed toward one of the larger pieces by the door. "Take a good look before you walk out the door. You may remember yourself as worse than you really are."

"I highly doubt that," Rook mumbled as he turned to leave. "Thanks, maybe next time."

"You might have been a charming young man before..." he swirled his fingers vaguely at Rook, "before all *that* happened." He cleared his throat. "Come on. One look. I promise it'll do you good."

It didn't do him 'good'. Rook stood reluctantly before his reflection and crossed his arms. The man that looked back at him could have been a monster. There was hardly a patch of skin where the net of scars didn't interact. There were more scars than there was face. Sure, his nose was still straight, and yes, his jaw was still sharp, and of course, his clear blue eyes still made him look somewhat Human. But there was something about these scars—something that drew all the attention, and all the glory. They demanded the notice of all who looked his way. Rook's face was hidden behind them as if behind a mask.

"Well, what do you think?" Brid called from behind.

Rook turned slowly away from the mirror. "Thanks for the help, Brid," he said, "I'll check back in with you in a week."

He left promptly, slamming the door behind himself. Well, now his mood was ruined. Why had he looked? *Why* had he reminded himself of the one thing he had worked so hard to forget?

Bunting on Copse was a quiet village, but it was bigger than some on the southern edge of the remote Gramenlands. It was nestled right against the Copse River, making it a favored stop for travelers who came from the west. The little town had access to main roads, but still only a small population. This made for a peaceful home. Bunting Cross, the single-lane bridge that crossed over the Copse River, was a pretty, though humble, creation. It sat there pleasantly, marking where the Gramenlands ended, and the Elder Copse territory began. It had a reputation of tempting passers-by to cross it, if only just to find out what was on the other side.

Rook crossed it every day, for *he* lived on the other side. Technically, the Elves claimed this side of the river Copse but never came out this far unless crossing the border. So, the few homes on the far side of the river achieved some anonymity, while still benefiting from the close proximity to town.

Rook made eye contact with one or two villagers who passed by and gave him friendly, if apprehensive, nods. He was known around town—he had lived there for eight seasons—but his face still prevented him from forming any real relationships with the townspeople. He didn't really mind. At this point in this life, he liked anonymity. And he wasn't in want of friendship—he had all he needed there.

"Look there!" A village boy was leaning over the short stone wall that ran between the square and the river. He pointed south, down the road toward the faraway lands. "A big wagon!"

"How big?" Ingrid, the respectable and suspicious cobbler, had just closed up shop, and was ready to sniff out the latest gossip. She stepped up behind the boy and peered over his head. "Hmm... yes, that *is* a big wagon. I see two oxen pulling it."

"What's this?" Adeline, Brid's esteemed wife, glided close enough to the action to look, but far enough away to be distinct from the rest of the growing little crowd. "A two-oxen wagon? Will it fit on the Cross?"

"Of course, it'll fit on the cross," the boy, who Rook knew as Pip, yelled as he cupped his hand over his eyes. "We've seen a few two-oxen wagons pass through here in the last season, or so." He swiveled his head to look at Rook, who was standing only a couple meters away. "Do you think it's a merchant?"

"Why ask him?" Ingrid sniffed. "I know this town better than any newcomer does."

Newcomer? Come on—Rook had been there for *eight* seasons now!

"Yes, but he's seen other places," said Pip, "I figure he knows about—"

"It's not a normal wagon," said Rook as he glanced toward the horizon. "It's big..." he squinted, "pulled by two aurochs, I think."

"*Aurochs?*" Adeline scoffed, "Stop playing with the boy." She glanced toward the child and condescended to smile at him, "Aurochs are mythical creatures, young one."

"No," Rook said, "they're not." He smirked to himself. She'd find out soon enough, wouldn't she?

"Can two aurochs fit on the Cross?" Pip asked cautiously.

"I..." Rook glanced at the stone bridge, then back at the wagon. "It'll be a squeeze."

"I wonder what a big wagon like that is doing coming from the south," said Ingrid, with hands on hips. "Could it be Elves?"

"Don't think so," said Rook, "They travel by foot, not wagon."

"How do you know so much about Elves?" Pip asked with wide eyes.

"Don't ask him questions," Ingrid subvocalized. "He might come from a bad place."

Rook didn't resent the comment. He did come from a bad place.

"They're flying royal banners," a voice cried distantly. The townspeople's heads shot around in all directions, searching for the source of the call. Rook walked up to the rock wall and peered upriver.

"Damn," Rook hissed, "The river pirates are back."

"River pirates!" Pip shot a triumphant fist in the air. "Yes!"

"Pip!" Ingrid yelped, "You get indoors and find your mother!"

The women began to flee the scene. That tended to be the protocol whenever the river pirates moved through. Yes, Bunting on Copse's one and only crew of villains sailed past the village every season or so, tripping up traders to raid their goods. Rook had become the town's unofficial defender for such attacks, though it didn't seem to improve his standing with the townspeople.

Rook jumped up on the wall and eyed the river sloop. It was long and narrow, and large enough to carry a dozen or so crewmen. From what Rook could tell, they were readying their tripping chain and submerging their slowing poles.

"Oh, Hades," Rook cursed under his breath, "They're going to try to trip up the wagon... and it's going to destroy the entire bridge." There was no way this over-ambitious group of river pirates could successfully stop a wagon pulled by aurochs and get away. It was an imminent disaster.

Without missing a beat, Rook jumped onto the bridge's main stretch and charged for the oncoming wagon. He waved his arms, yelling for them to halt at the top of his voice. He could see the beasts up ahead wavering.

"Halt!" Rook cried as he and the wagon neared one another. "There's a—!" He jumped sideways with a yelp as an arrow whizzed past him from the wagon. He gritted his teeth. The wagon wasn't slowing down.

"Get off the road, or we'll run you down," a voice boomed through a horn.

The bridge was narrow, and long. Just as Rook was nearing the south end of the bridge, another arrow sang past his ear.

"Don't shoot me!" Rook called.

He heard the snap of the pirate's ballista firing. Behind him, a large, spiked chain shot over the bridge. This was the wagon's last chance—if they didn't stop, there would be blood. Rook stopped right at the entrance to the bridge, in the center of the road, and stretched out his arms.

The wagon was close enough now that Rook could more clearly see the men sitting up on the top level. They looked like soldiers; one was aiming a crossbow at him. The wagon really was large, with several rows of wheels, and solid wood.

The archer fired, and this time the arrow hit Rook's arm.

He yelled as he recoiled. "Idiots!" he cried, "Halt!"

It was the beasts that finally chose to stop. Their eyes focused on Rook, and then they scrambled to a screeching halt. Their long, regal horns entangled, the wagon slid sideways, Rook dove off the road, something large hit the water, and in a moment, all became a cloud of dust. Rook waved the dust away from his eyes as he sat up. He could hear shouting. The pirates were charging.

Rook kept to the sidelines as he watched the scene begin to unfold. The wagon had run aground into the grass, one of the aurochs was lowing and pawing the ground with distress, and the other couldn't be seen. The pirates weren't prepared for actual soldiers, and the fight got bloody fast.

But the battle was evenly matched in an odd sort of way. The soldiers seemed to be expert archers, but the pirates were quick and agile. They easily climbed up the sides of the wagon car and cut through the soldiers in a flash. Too much blood was being spilt—Rook had no choice but to intervene.

He shook his shoulder, gritting his teeth at the pain, then charged for the pirate closest to him. Bending the man's arm backwards, he seized his sword. Rook cut him at the knee, then shoved him against the side of the bridge.

Splash.

Rook flew toward the next pirate, whose sword was tangled with one of the soldiers.

Slash.

The pirate dropped, Rook nodded to the soldier, then sprung upwards, scaling up the side of the wagon. He landed on the top of the wagon, which was like a shallow railed decking. Two soldiers in black tunics with red emblems fought outnumbered by three pirates. Rook dashed, then slid, slicing one of the pirates at the knee. The pirate dropped with a scream, then Rook leapt up and struck his head with the butt of his sword. Now, it was the pirates who were outnumbered, and in moments, Rook and the two soldiers in black stood panting in victory.

"Oy! We have your leader! Surrender or we cut his throat!" One of the pirates barked from below. Rook looked at the other two, nodded, then dropped down onto his belly.

"We're coming," said one of the soldiers.

"Drop your weapons first," the pirate replied.

"Alright," said the soldier as he readied his crossbow.

Rook dropped down the back of the wagon and circled around the scene. Only two pirates remained standing. They stood at either side of a tall dignitary, who was posed there primly, bejeweled enough to be a king. Each had a knife to his throat.

"Do as he says, Tercius," said the nobleman, "I don't really want to die at the moment."

Rook crept around the sidelines like a cat, then once he was close enough, he pounced. He seized one of the pirates from behind, pulling him away from the dignitary, and at the same time, the archer downed the other man with a single shot. Then, there was silence.

It was a loud, slow clap that broke the silence. Rook tossed his terrified pirate over the bridge, then turned around. He furrowed his brow, studying the gigantic nobleman who was—even at a time like this—grinning.

"Well," the man barked, still slow clapping, "That was... *something*!"

"They're moving on!" A voice called from the other side of the bridge. The men of Bunting on Copse could be heard cheering as the pirates' sorrowful sloop sailed on, with only a third of their crewmen.

Rook still stared at the noble. "Hey," he snapped, "Will you stop clapping?" He pointed his sword at the man. "Men have died on your behalf!"

The nobleman snorted. "Not the first, and they won't be the last, will they, Tercius?" He tipped his head sideways toward the archer who was now standing to his right.

"No, sir," replied the soldier named Tercius.

"If that's the case," Rook replied, "then you shouldn't take it lightly."

"Don't mistake me, lad," he sniffed, "I know how to honor the fallen, *eh*, Tercius?"

"Yes, sir."

"I've seen enough to become a little calloused, my man," said the nobleman, "Hazards of the trade, I'm afraid."

"Well," Rook tossed his sword on the ground, then held his hand to his wound. "I hope you take the responsibility to clean up the mess you've made; I won't be having my townsmen spending the next week burying bodies, understand?"

"Now, hold it," the noble waved a hand at Rook, "I think you have this all wrong—*I'm* the authority here."

"Actually, the Copsian Elves are," Rook said blandly, "You made this mess on their land."

"I didn't make this mess," he fluttered his fingers at the scenery, "Your filthy pirates did—what? I don't make messes, I am too important to be blamed for such things."

"How nice for you."

"But listen," he placed his two monstrous hands together, "You saved my life, old boy! I saw you," he shook a ringed finger at Rook, "You flew through this scene like a bird. You've got skill, lad. Cards, Tercius, have you ever seen anything like that?"

"No, sir."

Rook glanced at Tercius. It was impossible to get a read on that kind of soldier.

"Look, I was just trying to keep you from bowling into my town," Rook said, "If you had heeded my warning earlier, this probably wouldn't have happened!"

"Look, Tercius... he's angry at—" he huffed, "You're *angry* at me?"

"I tried to warn you, and you *shot* me!"

"Oh, I didn't do that," he flapped his hand innocently, "Tercius did. Isn't that right, Tercius?"

"Yes, sir."

One of the few remaining soldiers walked up to the nobleman and bowed. "We've lost one of the aurochs, my Lord."

"Lord, huh?" Rook muttered to himself. Made sense. And what were those colors they were flying? Black with red?

"*Yes*, Lord!" Snapped the lord, "Highlord, at that. So *now*, will you show me some respect?"

"Probably not," Rook turned around. "I am going home to clean up. Good b—"

"*Bah—ha, ha!*" He slammed his hands together, "Oh, I like this lad, Tercius. Come now—don't leave. Come back." Rook groaned, then turned on his heel to give the highlord a scowl. "Alright—What's your name, lad?"

"Rook."

The Highlord snorted. "A made-up name if I've ever heard one."

"It's my name," Rook snapped, "And what—*my lord*—is yours?"

Tercius' eyebrow twitched. "You should know better than to ask his name," he growled. "He's a—"

"Oh, pipe down, Tercius." The highlord rolled his eyes. "Cato. Highlord Cato of the Edgelands."

"*Edgelands,*" Rook raised his eyebrows, nodding to himself, "Yeah, now I recognize the banner."

"Yes, I know, all you northerners think we don't add up to your *big* kingdoms, but we still have a–a–a..." he glanced toward his right-hand man. "Tercius, what do we have?"

"Spices, sir."

"*Yes!* Spices! And–and–and..."

"Sunfish, sir."

"And sunfish! Can't beat that."

"I am sure you can't," Rook said, not hiding his impatience.

"Look, lad—"

"I am not a lad."

"I am trying to say you impressed me, Rook. And *floods*, boy, you saved my sorry little caravan. Let me make it up to you. Come on, come over here."

Rook tromped up to the man and felt the slightest bit of pleasure when Highlord Cato cringed at the sight of his face.

"Hades, boy!" He recoiled. "What's happened to..." he shook a finger in Rook's general direction, "Wh—why are you smiling?"

Rook found himself oddly enjoying his closer look at the highlord. He was unusually tall for a Human, and broad shouldered. He wasn't someone Rook would describe as handsome, per se, but there was something inexplicably likable about his unique facial structure. While greying goatee and sideburns graced his face, the rest of his hair looked a bright golden blonde. His thick black eyebrows stood out amongst his otherwise light-colored features, and his eyes screamed the brightest blue.

"It's a pleasure to meet you, Cato," said Rook.

Cato snorted. "Stop ending conversations that I've only just begun. Look—you saved my life, and I am going to repay you. You'll let me, won't you?"

Rook blinked a couple times. "I..."

"Look, I am traveling to Mensa, and I've just lost half my bodyguards, and—"

"Mensa? You're traveling as far as *Mensa?*"

"Yes, and this little disaster has really made a muck of things. Anyway, got to move on and everything. Now look, don't turn me down, alright? I want to offer you a position."

Rook stiffened. "A what?"

"Come on, I could use a fighter like you around, and I like your wit. You saved my life, so I'll make you my wing."

"Your *wing?*" Rook scoffed. "Look, I am no fancy nobleman. You don't want me as your wing."

"Yes, I do." He folded his stiff arms. "Now, don't turn me down."

Rook chuckled. "Of course, I am going to turn you down."

"No, you're not!"

"I thank you for the honor, but I don't really need nor desire to leave my home here. Thanks—I realize it is no small thing for someone like me to be offered that kind of position."

Cato raised his eyebrows, over-acting how impressed he was. "See—I was right about you! You'd make a splendid wing. You have," he stopped to search for the right word while thumbing his chin, "you have *humility*. I like that—it complements me well."

Rook grinned, nodding slowly. "You're an interesting man, Cato. I like you."

"Oh, don't say that." Cato frowned, glancing to Tercius for support. "That complement has the cadence of a goodbye. Therefore, I will *not* take it as a complement!"

"As you wish," Rook sighed, bowing to Cato, then to Tercius, then to the other guard—whatever his name was. He turned to leave, but stopped as he heard Cato call out one final plea.

"Rook, lad?"

"Yes?" Rook turned, glancing at the man.

"I assume you people have a tavern in town?"

"Yes."

"Well, I'll be there until tomorrow. If you change your mind?"

"I'll let you know," Rook smiled, nodding.

"Oh, and Rook?"

"Yes?"

"Don't disappoint me."

"Goodbye, Cato." Rook turned, then left the bridge nonchalantly with his hand on his aching wound and his black cape blowing in the wind behind him. He could hear Cato's men shouting orders and throwing bodies into the river. Well, it would take some time to clean up the mess, but townspeople of Bunting on Copse had grown used to recovering after a pirate raid—they didn't need him for the cleanup. That was the unspoken pact: Rook protected them, and they dealt with the mess.

The wind began to move through the trees, bringing the scent from the great Woodland Forest to his nostrils. Rook smiled, tipping his head back. This was his favorite part of the walk home. The sound of rustling leaves and the bunting birds flitting around put his heart at peace.

Life was good. His days as a mercenary were behind him, and he had found a home. It was a good home, and he finally had a place where he belonged. The feeling of walking home was becoming a familiar thing to him, and he wasn't about to let that change. Yes, he liked his life.

Life was good.

Just before turning the corner to his home, a familiar face walked past him. Lily the seamstress looked as though she had just left there, carrying her large sewing bag. Rook waved. She held up her hand to wave back, flinched, then hurried on ahead. Rook didn't mind the reaction; Lily always did that. She couldn't help herself—no one could.

Once he came to his little wooden gate, he opened it and passed through. He walked down his stone path, which he had laid with his own hands, and lifted his eyes to see the little vine-covered cottage that sat there under a cheerful oak tree.

"Well, that was a day!" Rook belted as he pushed through the front door. The house had a stiff, dusty smell. *"Hallo?* Where are you?" He tromped through the house, looking left and right. "Why don't you *ever* open the window on a warm day like this?"

He moved toward a window, making sure not to disturb any furniture, and opened a window. Instantly, a breeze flowed through the house.

"Hallo?" Rook called through the open window. "I am guessing you're outside?"

"Get out here, Rook," a voice called from the back garden, "It's a lovely day."

"Right," Rook returned, "I'll be out in a moment."

He grabbed a towel from the hook by the stove, then stomped across the room and kicked off his boots. Rook pressed the towel against his shoulder, then wandered down the hall toward his bedroom. He passed by his roommate's room, and peeked in. It was immaculate, as always. For all his quirks, Rook's housemate knew how to maintain order and cleanliness.

Rook's room, on the other hand, left something to be desired. As he ventured inside, he studied his little quiet space. It wasn't messy, exactly, but there always seemed to be something on the bedpost, or the floor, or the mattress, or half-draped over a hanger in his wardrobe.

One of those odd items was a pillowcase, which Rook began to tear apart. Once he had an adequately long piece of fabric, he removed his shirt and looked at his wound. It wasn't too bad, thankfully the arrow hadn't gone through his arm, it had grazed the surface, but it was deep enough to bleed. He sat down on his bed, groaning as he wrapped the cloth around his arm. The wound smarted. Rook tightened the make-shift bandage, then moved to his washing basin. The water was a little old, but there was enough to clean most of the blood off his arms and hands.

He dressed himself, pushed back his hair with his wet hands, then strode out to the back garden.

The garden was enclosed within a flat-stoned wall that Rook himself had built, with every stone pulled from the Copse River. Rook wasn't exactly a gardener, so the nook looked more wild than kept, with bushy rose shrubs and patches of long grass. But it was the dogwood tree that made it pleasant. The thing was a masterpiece of creation. Its knotted grey trunk was a maze, shooting sideways in all directions, then up into great heights. It created a canopy over the garden, with big leaves and multitudes of white flowers.

Sitting below it, in his brown wicker chair, was Rook's best friend, his head leaning back on the chair and his black hair blowing in the wind. His long Faerie ears jetted out from either side of his silhouette, and his legs were stretched out, crossed at the ankles.

Rook walked barefoot across the stone path leading to the little spot, then sat down on the other chair, opposite his friend.

"Hallo, Rook," he said.

"Hallo, Felix," said Rook.

The two sat together silently for a spell, and Rook leaned his head back and folded his arms. He tried to ignore the throbbing in his arm and concentrated on the sounds of the garden. The dogwood sang as a gentle breeze moved through it, its multitude of leaves rolling like a calm shore.

"And what have you been up to today?" Felix said at length.

Rook looked up. Though the Faerie had no eyes, his eyelids, pressed around the sockets, were swollen and red. Rook's brow tensed with concern, but he answered cordially.

"Oh, pretty uneventful."

Felix snorted.

"I don't know," said Rook with a shrug, "I went to the textile shop and—"

"And what—" the side of Felix's mouth curled upwards, "Cut off your arm?"

"How did you know it was my arm?" Rook coughed out a laugh.

"I guessed. Smelled the blood, and your stride seemed normal."

"And no," Rook screwed himself into his seat, "I didn't *cut off my arm.*"

"Then will you please explain to me," Felix tipped his ear toward Rook, "how you injured yourself in the quiet little hamlet of Bunting on Copse?"

"And will *you* please explain to me," Rook leaned forward abruptly, "why Lily the seamstress was walking away from our quiet little cottage?"

Felix scoffed, rolling his head to the side as if rolling his eyes. "Don't start up on that again. She just came by... selling handkerchiefs."

"Did you buy one?"

"No." He sniffed. "She gave me one for free as a sample."

"Come on, man, she *likes* you." Rook nudged Felix's shin with his toe.

"Hades knows why," Felix said, "She should be setting her eyes on you— an *attractive* young man."

"You know," Rook chuckled, "You always call me that, but you have *no idea* what I look like."

"Well, your voice has the sound of one of those—tall, dark and—"

"*Not* handsome," Rook interjected.

"Oh, women love scars," Felix flapped his hand.

"Not this many. And besides, I have no desire for a woman. I am happy here—with you."

"Well, then why are you trying to push that seamstress on me!"

"I'm not!"

"Good!"

"I mean..." Rook cocked his head to the side. "You really don't mind being a bachelor?"

"I'm a Faerie," he said bluntly, "we don't crave companionship in the same way you Humans do."

"But come on, back in your day—whenever that was—surely there have been times you were tempted?"

Felix's playful smirk seemed to vanish.

"Ah!" Rook pointed. "I've struck gold, haven't I? There is a woman!"

"Was," said Felix, "and she was never mine."

"Come on. Tell me about her."

Felix shrugged.

"Come on, you tell me everything. Who is this girl?"

Felix shrugged again. "I... Well, I don't know. She..." he sighed. "It was back when I worked for *him*."

Him. That was King Somenus—the despot Faerie king Felix once served.

"Was she a Faerie?"

"No. An Elf."

Rook was quiet for a moment, then said, "How did you meet her?"

"Well, not the traditional way," he scoffed amusedly at himself. "I was tasked to spy on the Elven kings back during Somenus' reign. He wanted me to convince them to ally with him."

"Why?"

Felix exhaled. "Elves make for the best warriors. They are immortal like the Faeries, but like the Humans, they can kill. As long as they resisted him, he knew his reign was fragile. Anyway—I discovered through spying on these kings that King Antecus had a deep attachment to his daughter. That was the sort of thing..." he paused, looking pained, "Somenus could really use those types of things against people. And I knew it—I knew if I told him about this Elf princess, he would use her. But I..." he trilled his fingers on the arm of his chair, "I hesitated. I... I liked her."

Rook's eyebrows were stuck raised. "Wow..."

"Yes, it was pretty unconventional. I liked her. She was lovely. And I just... I hadn't ever seen someone I liked so much before."

"And..." Rook cleared his throat, "What happened? Did you go and meet her?"

"Well, I am not the kind of man to go and do something like that. And at the time, I just blindly followed Somenus."

Rook nodded. "So, you told him about her."

"Yes... I did..."

"And?"

"He had me abduct her. And Hades..." his fists clenched, "*he* liked her too."

Rook grew quiet.

"So he took her, raped her, nearly killed her."

Rook looked away. "Damn, Felix."

"Yes."

Rook rubbed his mouth. Felix had told Rook much about his dark past, but this was the first mention of the *Elf Princess*. "And what ended up happening to her?"

"She was rescued when Somenus was assassinated... the day I lost my eyes."

Rook cleared his throat. "Well that's... good?"

"Of course it is." Felix turned his face toward Rook. "I live the peaceful life I do today because I know she is safe."

"Well, good!" Rook clapped his hands together, then winced when his arm lit up with pain. "And all the better for me, I get to live life with a blind man, who never winces at my face!"

Felix smirked. "Is that all I'm good for? Being blind?"

"'Fraid so."

Felix nodded, chuckling to himself. His head bobbing continued ominously, slowing down as his face changed. All that was left was a ghostly expression.

"Felix?" Rook leaned forward. "Is everything alright?"

"Rook... I want to thank you."

Rook frowned. "For *what?*"

"You took me in all those seasons ago. Just a blind Faerie beggar, on the streets of Vastling—a wretched being, content to be nothing but someone to spit on."

"Felix..." Rook straightened up. "Don't talk like that. That's not how I saw you at all."

"It's who I was," Felix returned. "I wasn't asking for help. I didn't want any help."

Rook's mouth flattened. That was true enough; it was nearly impossible to get Felix to want to come with him. Rook could never forget the moment he first laid eyes on the Faerie. He was sitting on a dusty street, blind and filthy. Passersby spit on him for luck. Sure, the world hated Faeries now, but Rook couldn't stand to see one treated that way.

"I want to say this," Felix said calmly, "Let me say this, Rook."

"I don't like where this is going," Rook mumbled, "But fine."

"I've never had a friend," Felix said. "Before you, there was no one. I was alone, and I didn't mind. I never minded it, not for eight thousand seasons."

"Hades, Felix," Rook blinked, "*How* old are you?"

"But you are my friend. You didn't pity me; you weren't afraid of me; you didn't look down on me—you just treated me as an equal. You brought me to this place, where people are too quaint to know much about Faeries, and there's no bell towers to remind me of Arelle. We built this cottage together. Well..." he chuckled, "*You* built it, mostly."

"Don't sell yourself short."

"We waste away our days laughing and besting—talking about everything and nothing."

"I don't like where this narrative is going."

"Rook..." Felix sighed. "I don't *want* to leave you. I don't *want* to leave this place."

"And you never will," Rook burst into a yell.

"I... I have been so free as a blind man, Rook," Felix said with a strengthening tone, "I never have to worry about what evil my eyes will see. I have been like a cat whose claws have been removed; I have been like a dragon with no fire."

"Felix..."

"But I don't know what's going to happen to me now," his fists were shaking. "I don't know who I am to become, but I cannot be what I was... Not here."

"Felix," Rook reached out and placed his hand on Felix's fist, "whatever is happening to you, we will face it together, you understand? I am not leaving you—not ever."

"Rook, this thing turned me into something evil..." his whole body was trembling.

"*What* thing, Felix?"

Felix clenched his jaw. "I don't want to leave... but I don't know what to do."

"If you have to leave, we will leave together. But Felix, I *know* you. You're *not* evil. You're the best friend *I* could have had!" He scoffed. "Felix, it wasn't *you* who needed charity, it was me! *I* was the scorn of the world; *I* was the monster; *I* was the one with no family. It is I who needs you!"

Felix flung Rook's hand away, then grasped his head with his hands. "I can't... I can't *do* this again."

"Felix!" Rook punched the blind Faerie's shoulder. "Tell me what's going on!"

The jolt in Felix's shoulder made him suddenly regain his composure. He relaxed slightly, exhaling long and slow. "Sorry," he said quietly, "I won't let it get to me again... but this is why I need to leave, Rook."

"If you don't tell me what's going on, I swear, I'll punch your face next."

Felix huffed. "Fine."

Rook relaxed a little into his chair.

"The day I lost my eyes... I knew I would surely die. I am the Faerie of Sight, and I gain magik by seeing. Without my eyes, I knew I would slowly waste away."

"And yet, you lived," said Rook.

Felix nodded. "For a long time, I just assumed that my magik would eventually run out, but it never did. Time went on and on, and I was still alive. I wandered the world, looking for a place to decay, and eventually found myself in the Vastlands. I had been there for several seasons before you found me. And still—I never died. Then, it finally hit me."

"You were still gaining magik?"

Felix nodded. "My eyes had been removed, but they were still my eyes. Since all I ever saw was black, I figured they had been destroyed. But then—I thought—perhaps the man who took them kept them. Perhaps they were simply in a dark place."

"So you *were* still seeing," said Rook, "You were just seeing black."

Felix sighed. "But it all changed yesterday. Yesterday, I saw something."

Rook held his breath. "What did you see?"

"At first, I just saw a ceiling. Then someone came into my field of vision. I recognized him. It was the warrior who removed my eyes." Felix paused to rub his eyelids. "He... he wore a crown. He wore a king's crown."

"Felix... There is a warrior who was a part of Somenus' assassination. He became the King of Mensa. His name is King Hanz."

Felix nodded slowly. "Mensa, yes... the castle was built around my old tower."

"The tower of *Sight?* The one where you used to..."

"Yes. And it all adds up, because this man did something with my eyes... he did the last thing I would ever want anyone to do." he sighed. "He placed them up on a wall, facing the Crimson Gate."

"The *Crimson Gate?*" Rook raised his voice, wagging his head with rage. "Felix, he's making you look at the Crimson Gate?"

"And this time without eyelids," Felix said softly, "I may never look away."

"But this is torture!"

"Yes," Felix folded his hand, "It is."

"He can't do this to you—he can't... *use* your body like this. It's obscene!"

"It is."

"Felix, I..." Rook was standing now, looking around as if for a weapon, though he wouldn't know what he would do with it. "I can't let him do this to you."

"Rook. Sit down."

"*No!*"

"Rook! There is nothing to be done!" Felix was standing now, too.

"Of course there is something to be done," Rook said through gritted teeth. "I am going to go and get your eyes back! I am going to go and get our peaceful life back!"

"Rook, don't be ridiculous; you can't just walk up to a king and demand something like—"

"I'll kill him if I have to!"

"If the man who took my eyes is the man who *united* Mensa and *forged* his own kingdom in less than a decade, he is not someone to be trifled with. I heard his praises sung all over the streets—he is a *powerful* man, Rook."

"Yes, I *know*," Rook barked back, "I *know* who King Hanz is!"

"Then you should know you can't just—"

Rook snapped a hand on Felix's shoulder, then stepped up close. He spoke in a low growl, staring Felix right at where his eyes should have been. "I am going to Mensa," he said, "I have a ride there, and I am going to take it. I am going to Mensa, and I am going to get your eyes back."

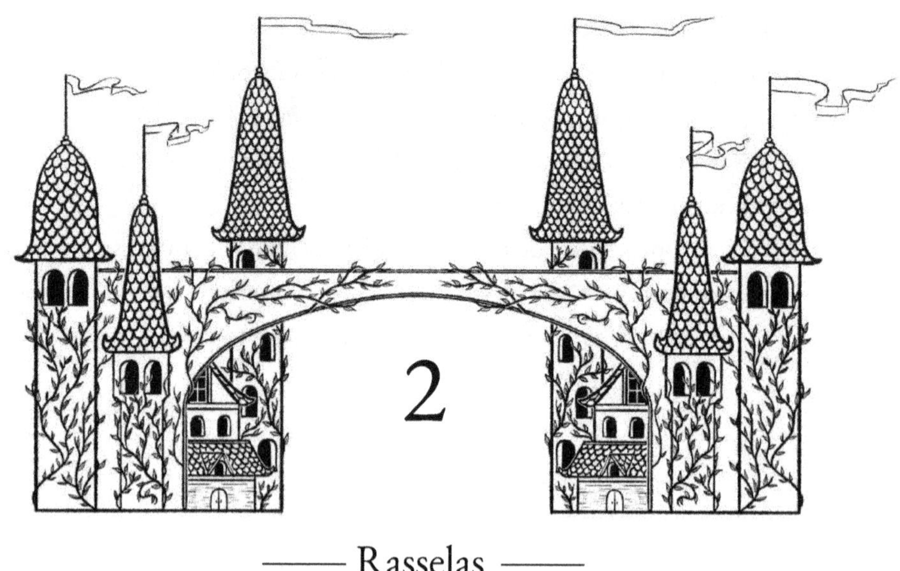

2

—— Rasselas ——

Moonvine

"RIGHT, NOW THAT YOU'VE GIVEN UP TWO CARDS, I give you two more. No—no—don't show them to anyone, my man," Rasselas flapped a hand at Everblossom, "That's right, for your eyes only. And you, Thorne, how many did you discard?"

"Three," Thorne, the solemn, brown-haired Elf said.

Rasselas dealt three cards to Thorne. "Now, don't show them to the group, old boy."

"Yes, I do remember the rules, Prince Moonvine," Thorne replied evenly. He picked up the cards with his soft hand, then frowned.

"Ah, see—that's another thing, old boy," Rasselas sighed as he sat back, "You can't make any obvious facial expressions when you look at your new cards. Then I might be able to guess what they are."

"That wasn't why I was frowning," Thorne picked one of his cards out from his hand, then pulled a handkerchief from his pocket. "There's some sort of... soot on this card."

22

RASSELAS

"Ash, my boy. Don't worry, I'll have you all smoking in no time!" Rasselas slapped the table with his hand, barked a laugh, then turned his attention to the third player. "Softbough, how many cards?"

"One," replied the light-haired noble. He couldn't seem to stop cringing any time he touched a new card. And as Rasselas slid him his replacement card, he picked it up with that same hesitancy.

Prince Rasselas and the three knights sat around a waxed birdseye maple table. Their terrace was made almost entirely of twisty maple trees, weaved around one another, suspended over the southeastern side of the Celestian Palace. The waves of the South Sea could be heard below them, folding over the sandy lagoon.

"Right. Now, let's all look at our cards, and everybody..." Rasselas looked around hopelessly. These Elves all looked the same, like groomsmen at a wedding, all with backs straight and shoulders centered toward Rasselas. This was going to be difficult, but he could do it. Rasselas could make real noblemen out of these... noblemen. "Could everyone just relax a little? It helps if you have a past time, what? Smoking, picking..." he looked face to face at the three others, "snuff?"

"We know about such pastimes," said Everblossom helpfully, "They're common amongst the Human nobles, but we..."

"They're beneath us," Thorne said with graceful bluntness, "Humans are already decaying, so it doesn't seem to matter to them to partake in harmful hobbies such as *smoking*. But we will outlive them, and we don't sabotage our immortality by dabbling with death."

"*Hades,*" Rasselas sniffed. "You're no fun at all."

"B–but if you want to smoke, Prince Moonvine," Everblossom chimed, "we won't mind."

"Call me *Rasselas* at the cards table, my man," Rasselas replied, "Cards tables are all about being relaxed and informal. Come on—Grandfather told me to get to know his knights, and the only way to *really* know someone is through a game of cards."

"Prince Moonvine," Thorne put down his hand of cards. That wasn't a good sign. "If the king did encourage you to know his knights, why would you then choose to impose your *own* ideals of nobility on us? Why wouldn't you come to us with humility and curiosity?"

"Slay me!" Rasselas drew back with a phony gasp, "Because that's not my *style*, old boy!"

"I don't mind learning about the prince's culture," Everblossom said with a humble smile, "If the king has chosen him to be his heir, then I think it's good to—"

"But this isn't even his culture," Thorne said through a restrained sneer, "He's from Winter's End—this whole *nobleman act* is adopted from his time touring the *Human* Kingdoms."

"He's right about that," Rasselas said with closed eyes. He touched his heart with his fingertips. "I am afraid I rather fell in love with their ways. I am particularly fond of the fashion elements."

"Yes, we could tell," Softbough muttered.

"I know Grandfather wants me to dress all *Elven* while I am here, but really—don't I look fabulous in this suit? Slay me—I can't imagine giving up something like *this*, only to put on something like *that*," Rasselas gestured toward Thorne's baby blue tunic.

In the distance, the bell tower began to ring. It was the Zenith Bell—the middle of the day. The three other Elves at the table put down their cards. Rasselas frowned.

"What, everyone is giving up? Just like that?" He tossed his cards on the table haughtily.

"W–well…" Everblossom glanced sideways at Thorne. "Don't you have luncheon with the King?"

Rasselas narrowed his eyes at the Knight. "Yes, but how did *you* know that?"

"We all know it," Thorne said flatly, "The king told us to make sure not to *keep* you from your appointment."

"Ah…" Rasselas sat back and tapped his lip with his finger. "So Grandfather has you all *babysitting* me now, does he?"

"N–no!" Everblossom jolted.

"Yes," Thorne said as he folded his arms. "Better not keep him waiting... *again.*"

Rasselas groaned. "Very well, Sir Thorne." He stood, straightened out his waist coat, pulled on his shirt cuffs, patted his hair for any flyaways, and rearranged his buttons to all be turned upright. "I'll try to be there *on time.*"

The others stood and all ceremonially bowed. Rasselas' mouth squiggled. After Rasselas was made the heir, his grandfather developed a certain imagination around what it meant to be a Prince. Unfortunately, he hadn't spent enough time around his mother's side of the family to know much about Elven nobility. Rasselas had never really interacted with the knights in all his visits to Celestia as a child, but after spending the last two seasons traveling around the Human kingdoms, Rasselas had spent plenty of time getting to know *their* nobility. Human leaders were a bunch of clowns, and Rasselas didn't mind acting like a clown. But the Elves? They wanted him to be serious all the time.

Serious. Rasselas could be serious. No one wanted to see him being serious.

As Rasselas left the Maple Turret, he noted footsteps following after him. Partway down the hall, he paused and turned.

"Thorne, old boy? Something wrong?"

"I thought I would accompany you to your luncheon," said Thorne, straight-faced.

Rasselas posed with hand on hip. "Asked you to follow me, did he?"

"The King? Yes." Thorne joined his hands behind his back.

"Well," Rasselas shrugged, "Do what you like." He continued down the hall, then made a turn toward the falconry tower. He began ascending the spiral stairs within, ignoring Thorne, who paused at the bottom of the stairs to clear his throat.

"The king is meeting you at the Warmwinds Tower," Thorne said from below.

"I'll get there when I get there," Rasselas called, "Just left something in the falconry."

Thorne grimaced, then rushed up the steps to follow Rasselas.

Why was this little suck-up following him? What did *he* care if Rasselas was late or not? Well, Rasselas knew how to shake a man like Thorne from his trail. Thorne was all *respect* and *rule-following*, and he would *never* do *anything* to bother King Antecus' beloved thunderbird.

At the top of the tower, Rasselas pushed open the door. The circular mews housed a colony of flighted ones, with perches and nesting boxes for all. Old oaks grew into the sides of the walls like rippling wood paneling, with branches and boughs, jetting out here and there to create a sort of forest in the rafters above. The floor was coated in a thick blue moss, requiring all who entered to either remove their shoes, or tread carefully across a trail of steppingstones.

None of the birds were leashed or caged; they were there because they wanted to be there. There were books in all the great libraries about King Anticus' falconry and the rare birds that resided there. And thanks to those many books, Rasselas was well aware of which of the birds was rarest—which of the birds was so prized, not even those the closest to the king would dare to touch.

Rasselas walked via the steppingstones to the center of the mews, where an old, leafless, contorted filbert tree stood, with its largest branch crookedly extending out, as if reaching for the southern window. A deep black raptor sat on that branch, as still as a statue. He was like a hawk-sized raven with a long, crooked bill, and everything about him was black, save the tips of his feathers, which seemed to glow with an orange sheen whenever they reflected the light.

"Embers," Rasselas snapped his fingers, "Come here, you cheeky bastard."

"Prince Moonvine!" Thorne hissed from the doorway, "The king has declared this place to be off limits to all but himself!"

"But this place doesn't belong to Grandfather," Rasselas said in a cooing voice, he held up his hand toward the black thunderbird. The raptor snapped his beak toward Rasselas, then squinted. "It belongs to Prince Embers here—doesn't it, you spoiled little tweet? It is up to you to turn me away."

Don't tempt me, said a soft, luscious voice. It wasn't a verbal voice—not something that could be heard by the ears. It was a heart voice—one that could only be heard by Rasselas.

"Nativitas could kill you in less than a click," Thorne pleaded, "Come out *now!*"

Embers smirked, puffing out his neck feathers while turning his slick back towards Rasselas, as though posing in front of a mirror. *Did you hear that?* He said, *I could kill you in a single eye blink.*

"I am sure you could," Rasselas said as he extended his arm. He slid his index finger under Ember's feathers, scratching his neck. "Why don't you just kill Thorne instead."

"Don't even jest!" Thorne practically growled. "Moonvine—if you do not come out, I must alert the king of your disobedience."

"Disobedience?" Rasselas said in a sing-song voice, still directing his words to the thunderbird. "Embers, have I done wrong to come in here?"

Not yet, but you're pushing it.

"I'll be along shortly, old Thorne," Rasselas glanced over, using his overdone posh voice. "Oh, and you're making Embers nervous standing there; either come in or leave, will you?"

Thorne left instantly. Rasselas chuckled.

What's going on with that Knight? Embers asked. He cocked his head to the side, then purred as Rasselas scratched his neck some more.

"Oh, he doesn't like me," said Rasselas, "I was just trying to bother him."

Is it true you are meant to be eating the Zenith food with my old friend Antecus?

"Yes," Rasselas lowered his hand, "I'll get there eventually." He sighed, then sat down at the base of the filbert. He leaned against its trunk and closed his eyes. Embers flapped his mighty wings, then dropped down onto the moss.

You don't seem very happy, Rasselas, said Embers, *is something wrong?*

Rasselas shrugged.

Embers waddled up to Rasselas and poked his hand. He poked it again, then again, until Rasselas lifted his hand to scratch the bird's neck some more. "It's nothing, really," said Rasselas, "I'm just... bored."

You're not enjoying living in Celestia?

"I enjoy you," Rasselas looked down at his feathered friend, "But I find this place so... so *serious.*"

Well, then why did you come here?

Rasselas pulled the corner of his mouth to the side. "Because I was bored at Winter's End. Wanted to go *do* something. And the Humans," he moved his hand to scratch under Ember's wing, "they seem to be doing things all the time! It's almost as if the Elves have lived so long, they don't mind if nothing happens in a day, but the Humans?" Rasselas closed his eyes. "They have such short lives; it's like they're trying to soak up every bit of life they can."

Which Humans? Embers turned his beak southward, which was a bird's way of expressing skepticism. *From what I have seen, all they do is waste their time.*

"I traveled around before coming here," said Rasselas, a distant look in his eyes, "I wanted to see a bit of the world before I settled down here."

You and I have not known each other long, said Embers, *but I know you well enough to see that you are hiding your true thoughts under the surface.*

Rasselas' eyes shifted. One of his eyebrows bounced up. "Oh, yes? And what are my *true* thoughts?"

You didn't like the Humans either, said Embers. *Admit it.*

"I liked their fashion."

I don't know what you mean.

"Their *outfits*, Embers—their feathers."

Ah. Embers bobbed his head thoughtfully.

"But no... I didn't like them. They're..." he blew air through his lips, "They're all a bunch of clowns."

And the Elves? What do you think about them?

"They're all pretending *not* to be clowns."

I see.

"It's why I spend so much time with you. You're just you. You don't pretend to be anything."

Embers blinked. *And what about your grandfather?*

Rasselas looked away.

He's trying to bond with you; why won't you let him?

What could Rasselas say? The truth? "He..." Rasselas subvocalized, "I don't trust him."

Why not?

Rasselas looked up at the tangled tree branches above him. "Do you know what happened to my mother thirty seasons ago?"

How could I forget? Embers looked down. *Antecus was devastated. His one and only child was kidnapped by the Faeries and forced into King Somenus' harem.*

"And what did he do about it?" Rasselas muttered. "Somenus offered him ransom. Did he pay it?"

Embers blinked. *I don't know.*

Rasselas sighed. "Mother was tormented, and Grandfather did nothing to help her. And all the while that I was growing up, did Grandfather come to meet me? To meet Dad?"

They did not come here either, said Embers.

"Mother didn't *want* to come back here," Rasselas snapped, "When Grandfather declined to pay the ransom, Somenus raped and tor—!"

Embers squawked. Rasselas stiffened.

"Good Zenith, Moonvine," said the steady and regal voice of the King.

Rasselas looked up to see Grandfather walking barefoot across the moss of the Mews.

"Oh, good Zenith, Grandfather!" Rasselas declared in his poshed-up nobleman voice, "Come to join me?"

Antecus knelt in the moss, about a meter away from Rasselas. He held out his hand and two other birds came to land on it. "Yes," he said, "I was informed that you wanted to stop here first, so I thought I would meet you here."

Rasselas faked a smile. In all honesty, he had *wanted* to peeve his grandfather. This was annoying.

"How thoughtful," said Rasselas, "What a wonderful chap you are, old pop."

Antecus brought his birds to his face, whispered to them, then sent them flying back up to the rafters. He folded his hands and smiled amicably. "May I ask you something?"

"Anything, old thing!"

"You have been here for eight weeks now; what do you think?"

Rasselas straightened out his legs and Embers nestled onto his lap. "Of Celestia?" He scratched the bird's neck.

"Of your life here."

"Well, how shall I—?"

"Be honest, Prince Moonvine."

"Well," Rasselas and Embers exchanged looks. "If I am to be *honest*, I would say that I'm finding everything a bit tedious."

"Tell me more."

"Well," Rasselas bobbed his head to the side, "It's fine and everything. There isn't a ton for me to *do* here, though."

"What sort of things do you wish you could do here?"

Rasselas felt a little thrown by the question. He hadn't even thought about that. "Well," he shrugged, "I like a game of cards. And I am trying to teach the lads, but—"

"Lads?" The king looked genuinely confused.

"You know, your *knights?* My sort of... *peers*, as you called them?"

"Ah... anything else?"

Rasselas chewed on his cheek, then straightened up and looked at the king square in the eyes. "You want me to be honest?"

"Of course I do."

"Look around the place," Rasselas waved his arm across the room, "All the Celestian Elves, all these ancient people who have lived a dozen Human lifetimes—they all have a place in this world. They all know exactly who they are, and what they are doing. But then they look at someone like me—their Prince and apparently *heir* to the Kingdom—and all they expect me to do is stand around, take orders from you, and show up at events and—and—*luncheons!*"

Antecus nodded slowly. "And what—if you don't mind me asking—*did* you expect to be doing when I invited you to come stay here?"

Rasselas huffed. "I don't know. I suppose I *expected* to be ornamental. It sounded fun. But slay me—it's downright boring. Anyway, I thought that if I came here as a Prince, I might be given some sort of authority and—I don't know—Do something worthwhile."

Antecus eyed Rasselas. "And what would be 'worthwhile' to you?"

"*Erm*—" Rasselas studied Grandfather for a moment. It was too soon to tell the king about Rasselas' ambitions... he didn't know where Grandfather stood when it came to Faeries.

"So," Antecus placed his hands on his knees, "You want to be useful to me? You want to be involved?"

"Rather, yes." Rasselas leaned forward. "Do you *have*, sort of, *Princely* jobs and what not?"

Antecus let out a slow exhale. "Yes, I do."

"And..." Rasselas blinked. "You want to, sort of, give them to me?"

Antecus nodded. "I have been requested to send a delegation to—"

"Delegation? You mean *travel*?" Rasselas lurched forward excitedly, "You want to send me somewhere?"

King Antecus smiled. "Do you feel you could represent me well?"

Rasselas scoffed as he leaned back proudly, puffing out his chest. "I mean—yes!"

Antecus nodded, then reached into a fold in his robe. He produced a scroll and held it out toward his grandson. "Read this and tell me what you think."

Rasselas took the scroll gingerly, keeping eye contact with Grandfather for a moment. Why? Why had the king decided to make Rasselas his heir? Did he *actually* trust Rasselas to do well, or was it all some sort of test?

Rasselas unrolled the scroll, and Embers poked his head up, peering curiously at the paper.

Tell me what it says, he said, *I can't read the scribbles.*

"It's..." Rasselas mumbled slowly as his eyes darted around the page, "It's a letter from Mensa!"

Antecus nodded.

"From King Hanz himself," Rasselas said, unwittingly allowing some anger to characterize his voice.

What does the King of Mensa have to say? Embers tapped the page with his bill.

"Patience, you little seagull," Rasselas snapped as his eyes scanned the first paragraph. "King Antecus... *da, da, da...* invite you as an honored guest for the coming season... *da, da, da, da...*" his mouth stopped moving, and his eyes didn't. He cringed as he read silently. "...as my lovely and dignified daughter comes of age... *oh for all the...*" Rasselas scoffed.

What? Embers pecked Rasselas' hand. *What's he saying?*

"Oh, he's clearly trying to advertise the fact he has a daughter to marry off. Wants to dangle a marriage alliance over the other..." he looked up suddenly, making eye contact with Grandfather. "*Hades*, man—*this* isn't why you made me your heir, is it?"

King Antecus chuckled. "No," he said, "read on."

Rasselas groaned inwardly as he returned to the letter. It was painful having to read the pompous written hand of a murderer.

"...Must put an end to the bickering and the border disputes... Calling for a peaceful council of..." Rasselas looked up again. "Oh, this is big!"

Antecus nodded. "Yes."

"He's summoning... everyone!"

"Yes."

Rasselas scoffed. "Who does he think he is? To summon kings to himself? Thinks he's a great *peacemaker*, does he?"

"He *is*, Moonvine."

Rasselas tossed the scroll at Grandfather's knees. "He's a murderer."

Antecus closed his eyes, exhaling silently through his nostrils. "He united the war-torn lands east of Bavel *without* a sword, young Prince. He built one of the largest Kingdoms on Raqia in less than thirty seasons. You may not like him, but he is a visionary—a paragon."

Rasselas shook his head. "He's a murderer who killed *hundreds* of women in Arelle, tried to murder Mother, Father, *and* Anodos the day he was born!"

"I am not defending him," Antecus said gently, "I am not telling you to trust him."

"Sorry," Rasselas looked down at Embers, who was still staring at the letter on the floor. "I am so tired of everyone talking about how great he is. Just because everyone else is impressed, doesn't mean *I* have to be."

"You don't have to be impressed," said the King, "I would have you be discerning. Hanz *is* a 'great' man. He is a master strategist. It would be unwise to underestimate such a man. Don't let your hatred cloud your judgment, Prince Moonvine."

"I never said I hated him," Rasselas said primly.

"You never had to."

Rasselas looked down.

"You're nineteen seasons, Moonvine. You have barely begun to see the world, let alone understand it. If I send you to Mensa, I would want you to go there with curiosity, not with—"

"Send me?" Rasselas snapped up straight. "To Mensa?"

Antecus nodded gravely. "I would like to send you to be my eyes there, yes. And I think this could be a very valuable time of learning for you. It is your chance to observe and study." He lifted up a finger, "But it would not be a time to *act*, Prince Moonvine, not without my permission."

"This letter spoke about the Kingdoms coming together to make some sort of international law," Rasselas said as he thumbed his chin, "Surely you'd want me to weigh in on whatever laws they are deciding to make."

"*I* would want to weigh in, Rasselas," Antecus said with a smile, "Through you. You may present your own thoughts there, too—of course—but when it comes to voting and decisions, I would want you to correspond with me." He lifted up one of his hands toward the rafters, "I will send a bird with you to—"

Rasselas and Embers both perked up together.

The king frowned. Rasselas had never seen him actually frown before. "Not Nativitas."

"Oh, *please*, Grandfather?" Rasselas hugged the thunderbird. "You wouldn't part us!"

"He is the crown of this falconry," Antecus declared firmly, "*Not* a messenger bird."

"But you could trust him with such an important assignment," Rasselas said, "And besides, he could keep an eye on me and make sure I am representing you well!"

It's true, Embers said in a small voice.

Antecus looked at the bird, then at Rasselas. "I am already sending someone with you to keep an eye on you."

It was Rasselas' turn to frown. *"Who?"*

"Sir Thorne will attend you as your Wing."

"Wing?" Rasselas balked, "I don't need a Wing! Rasselas is a one-man show!"

"All of the noblemen will be attended by Wings; surely *you* can see the value in respecting the Human culture while you're there."

Rasselas snorted. "A wing is supposed to be a man's best chap—someone who compliments him and protects him."

"Yes, and Thorne will do that for you."

"Thorne hates me," Rasselas snapped, "And I am beginning to dislike *him*, if I'm honest."

"As a Prince," Antecus said firmly, "It is your duty not to let your dislike of *anyone* change how you treat them."

Rasselas drew back.

"And you are *not,*" Antecus added, "taking my thunderbird!"

Embers flapped his wings, startling both Rasselas and the king. His wingspan was long, knocking Rasselas back onto his hands. He fluttered forward, landing just in front of the king, then said in a voice they could both hear in their minds:

I am going to Mensa, friend Antecus. And I will correspond between you and your Grandson.

The look on the king's face was sheer shock. He couldn't say no, not when he boasted to the world that he didn't imprison his birds. They were all there by choice, that's what he always said. And though he knew that thunderbirds were rare in that they could bond with more than one person, it was clear to Rasselas that Antecus did *not* like his favorite bird bonding with his grandson. It had taken many, many seasons for Antecus to earn the thunderbird's trust, and then here was Rasselas, cuddling him after only a few weeks.

Antecus nodded to Embers and then stood. "I will meet with you again at supper, Moonvine," he said as he turned toward the door, "And there we will discuss our plan of approach for your trip to Mensa."

"When am I meant to leave, Grandfather?" Rasselas looked up.

"King Hanz asks the delegations to arrive on or after Firstday," said the king, "That is in a couple days. I'd like to send you out tomorrow."

"So soon!" Rasselas jumped to his feet, finally feeling excited about something.

"That is why I wish to speak with you tonight," said the king. He pointed down at the floor where the discarded scroll lay. "I want you to study the letter, then come back tonight with your thoughts."

"Thoughts?" Rasselas blinked.

"I want you to tell me what you think King Hanz wants from this event; I want you to think about what we want from it—I want you to come to me with questions."

"Got it." Rasselas nodded. I won't let you down, old thing." He snapped into a bow. "See you tonight."

Antecus walked to the door, then turned. "Oh, and Moonvine?"

"Yes, dear old thing?"

"Don't be late this time."

Rasselas wilted a little. "Yes, pop."

Firstdark Bell

Rasselas took a long, indulgent look in the mirror. It wasn't necessarily vain to stare at himself for that long, he thought to himself, it was simply self-awareness.

His auburn hair was short and tidy on the left side and in the back, while on the right it was styled in an attractively chaotic swirl of thick curls. He had a thin, handsome face with a sharp jawline and bright green eyes. The delicateness of his features matched his Elven mother's: Lolette, the daughter of King Antecus. However, his over-animated facial expressions and spunky attitude were constant reminders to the world that he was his *father's* son. Thanks to his father, Leo, he was half Human. Still, Rasselas' ears made him look entirely Elven. That fact did help him fit in.

Rasselas was dressed for dinner in an entirely new ten-piece Gramen suit. He wore a matte vino-colored tailcoat and trousers, a waistcoat with gold embroidered designs, a ruffled shirt, a meticulously tied cravat with a matching white pocket square, golden cufflinks, slick black braces, pointy-toed shoes, and a cane.

"Slay me," he said to himself in his pompous voice, "don't you look a handsome picture. Prince Rasselas... *Prince*," he fixed his cravat, "Rasselas."

"*Prince,*" someone coughed, "Rasselas. It's time for supper."

Rasselas spun on his heel. "*Ah!* My favorite Wing. Old Thorne, how are you, my man?"

"I am well. Shall we go?" Lifeless. Everything about this Elf was lifeless.

"Fine, let's go." Rasselas strolled past Thorne hastily, forcing him to rush to catch up.

Judging by the man's begrudging nature, Rasselas guessed that Thorne wasn't too happy about being Rasselas' Wing. Well, perhaps that would mean they could get through the journey peacefully, ignoring one another the whole time. Thorne clearly hated Rasselas, but here he was, pretending he didn't. And the Elves were *so* proud of being honest. Ridiculous. They were just as ingenuine as the Humans.

Rasselas himself was seldom genuine. Or at least, he almost never revealed his true thoughts and feelings to others. He was a man of many protective layers which guarded his mind, he believed, from the manipulative influence of others. There were few people Rasselas trusted, and even fewer in whom he confided. Though Rasselas had been raised in a safe home with loving parents, certain events in his life had taught him that the world was a hostile, dangerous place, filled with people who, for the most part, were using others for their own advantage. Everyone had an agenda; everyone had hidden loyalties; and *everyone* wore a mask. Rather than pretending he didn't have a mask, Rasselas wore the most obvious and ornate mask possible; at least that way, he wouldn't be living a lie. Rather, he would put on an act, forcing others to admit that they were all in a play.

Wearing a blatant mask told the world that underneath his costume was a real man, and only those in his innermost circle could be trusted enough to know him. Rasselas' "mask" was a pompous, spoiled, handsome, shallow socialite whose main interests lay in fashion and popularity.

Supper was a charade. Antecus engaged Thorne and Rasselas in conversation that *seemed* meaningful on the surface, but none of the words really mattered. Before long, the king started talking about politics. It seemed interesting at first, until Rasselas realized that all Thorne and the king wanted to do was talk about what they thought all the *other* kings were going to try to do. They didn't seem to care what sort of outcome would result from the event, they just wanted to know what it was. Wasn't that what being an Elf was all about: knowing about everything, judging everyone for doing it; and never getting involved?

"It is my belief," King Antecus said with an air of finality, "That what King Hanz wants is an alliance. He wants the Eastern Kingdoms to agree upon a code of laws that can make travel, trade, and economy easier. If all the Kingdoms agree to such an alliance, there could theoretically be peace throughout the Human Kingdoms."

"Peace," Rasselas said with his mouth in his goblet. He lowered it slightly, "With himself in charge."

"The Human Kings will not sign alliance terms that make Hanz their leader," said Thorne, "Stop making him out to be a despot."

Rasselas snorted. "I don't need to make him out like one," he muttered, "He *is* one."

"Moonvine," Antecus sighed, "It doesn't *matter*. I am not sending you so that you can stop *or* agree to any alliance terms; I am sending you so that you may advise, and ultimately witness. The Elves will not be making any agreements with the Humans. Have I made myself clear?"

"Of *course*, old thing," Rasselas sloshed his cup of vino toward his grandfather. "You want me to spy on the Humans and see what they do, then come and share the gossip. Got it. Got it."

Thorne looked away. That seemed to be his version of a protest. The man would never snap at Rasselas, not when he was around the *King*.

"I think this could be a good thing for the Humans," Antecus said gently. "They could do with some tighter rule. They've been wallowing in war for thousands of seasons."

Rasselas slammed his goblet on the table. Antecus and Thorne both shot Rasselas surprised stares. "Tighter rule... and you think *Hanz* is the one to give it to them?" He let his spiteful voice slip out for just a moment. Quickly, he sucked it back in and relaxed into a foppy grin.

"Why not?" said Thorne, "He was able to bring peace to Mensa. Why not spread it to the rest of the Humans?"

"Peace?" Rasselas rattled out a phony laugh, "Peace at what cost, old boy? Slay me—Peace under the leadership of an evil man isn't peace at all."

"Even if King Hanz is as evil as you so claim," Antecus said civilly, "I would have to disagree with you."

Rasselas raised his eyebrows. "Oh? *Do* tell me why."

"Have you ever read this book," Antecus patted a small bound book on the table with his hand. Rasselas hadn't noticed it was there until now. "It is called *Conversations and Considerations.*"

Had he read it? Was there a Raqian Philosophical work Rasselas hadn't read? But no... he was playing the fop, and the last thing he wanted was people like *Thorne* to think he was well-read. "Not sure," Rasselas said as he leaned back. "Why?"

"It was written by the Green Lion of Bavel, a philosopher," said the king, "He believed that law was the one necessary component to peace. Without agreed upon standards, and agreed upon consequences, there would always be perpetual chaos."

Rasselas snorted. "Yes, but he also said that the law would kill as many as it saved," he said, then hesitated, glancing at his grandfather who turned the side of his mouth downward. "Or... so I'm guessing."

Antecus slid his hand off the book. "So, you have read it. Well, then—you know that he also said that the pain of death by *law* stung far less than the pain of death by *chaos*. With law, one knows *why* he dies; in chaos, the pain of confusion makes death meaningless."

"Some laws can decrease suffering; but some laws can make suffering far worse—especially depending on who *makes* them and who benefits from them." Rasselas said with a distant look on his face.

"You speak as if you know something," said Antecus. "What is it?"

Rasselas jolted. He had slipped out of character again. Well, at the very least it meant he was having some sort of *real* conversation with Grandfather. Still, he wasn't ready to tell anyone what he knew. Even Rasselas wasn't sure what it was he knew. He couldn't tell anyone anything until he knew more. No, he had to do more digging to find out how deep the root of the weed went.

"Grandfather," Rasselas cleared his throat, then dabbed his napkin against his lips. "May I borrow that book?"

Antecus nodded slowly. He passed to Rasselas then folded his hands in his lap. "Moonvine. Do you feel ready for tomorrow? Have I given you enough instruction?"

"Ready steady, old KC!" Rasselas tossed his napkin on his plate. "You can trust your little Half-Elf prince to get the job done."

"*KC?*" Thorne's lip twitched. He wanted so badly to frown.

"King of Celestia?" Rasselas chuckled, "Was it *that* hard to decode?"

Thorne's eyebrow twitched this time.

"Well, LP is tired," Rasselas said as he stood. Then he leaned toward Thorne and whispered, "That means *Little Prince,* if you couldn't figure it out."

"I did not care to," Thorne mumbled under his breath.

"Off to my beddy byes." He picked up the book and tucked it under his arm. "Any last words, poppy?"

Antecus just looked at Rasselas with half open eyes. The look said it all: *just don't make a fool of me.*

Rasselas thumbed through the little book thoughtfully as he made his way to his quarters. The Green Lion of Bavel was a fascinating writer, and admittedly one Rasselas himself was quite compelled by. He was a Third Level mason who wrote a few philosophical works some six thousand seasons prior. It had been a tumultuous time within the kingdom of Bavel, when their system was almost overthrown by the persecuted populace.

Once in his room, Rasselas plopped himself on his daybed, and stared at the ornate, fabric cover of the book. In his time, the Green Lion had agreed with the general populace that their government was corrupt, and he himself had suffered abuse and imprisonment; and yet his writings had stopped an entire war, encouraging the rebels that, in the end, corrupt law was better than lawlessness.

"Poor souls," Rasselas said aloud as he ran his fingers across the front of the book. How many people had listened to these words and chosen to submit to slavery because of them? Had thousands of brutalized citizens, who finally mustered the courage to rise up, truly laid down their weapons—submitting to their evil masters—all because of a couple of books like this?

"The power of words," Rasselas said, gazing up at the massive tree branch which curled about, decorating the ceiling in his room with its fracaline patterns. "If words like these can enslave," he said, "can they not also liberate?" He opened the book. "Like a spell."

The pages slid open to a marked spread, and Rasselas' eyes fell onto a familiar paragraph. He read it aloud.

"I compel you, brothers and sisters, to see yourselves not as weak and powerless individuals, but as a potent and controlled giant. Agreeing to live a certain way need not be an act of blind submission, but of sober choice. We do not suffer under the law, we choose the law; we choose to be a part of something bigger than ourselves. The powerful giant of the community can be enslaved when it is drunk with the drink of anger and passion; but with a sober and free mind, he can choose a wise existence for himself. Do not become drunk with the vino of the mob but be sobered by the water of wisdom and submission."

Rasselas drew in a deep breath, closing the book and his eyes. A soft breeze moved through the room like a calming presence. Words. What powerful things they were. Every time Rasselas read that paragraph, even he was compelled by words he deeply disagreed with. *This* was why he loved the Green Lion so much. He was just one man: one man with a pen.

The prince sat forward, opening his eyes with a flash. He stood, moving across the room toward his writing desk. He pulled a piece of paper from his drawer and placed it at the center of the table, then opened his inkwell. His feather pen was made from one of Ember's feathers, which he had taken without permission. Like Embers, it was black and glistened with a deep orange at the touch of light. Then he began to write.

I compel you, brothers and sisters, to see yourselves not as weak and powerless individuals, but a potent and controlled giant. You are not a beast of burden which can be trained to do the will of its master, but a shining, untouchable light, that cannot be quelled by darkness. Your existence and purpose cannot be hidden, just as day cannot be concealed by a cloth. You cannot be forced to serve, you choose to serve. So do not serve in a way that destroys; serve in the way you were made to serve. Serve not as a slave obeys the will of its master, or as a dog fetches a stick; but as a parent serves a child, or as a king serves his people. You are potent and controlled giants, filled with the gift of unimaginable power. Do not forsake this gift because others have told you it is your shame. It is not your shame. It is your glory.

Rasselas leaned back, putting down his quill. It wasn't perfect, but it was something. "It'll need some work," he mumbled to himself. "But I shouldn't wait too long." He pulled a book from his drawer and put it on the desk, opening it. His eyes scanned the pages as he thumbed through them. "Ten, twenty, thirty," he muttered, turning another page. "I should start with at least fifty copies. There could be as many as two hundred there. Maybe more... It's been thirty seasons."

He closed the book and leaned back, sighing. Could he really do this? Alone? Could words be enough to stir up a rebellion? They would have to be.

"I only need one Faerie to listen... just one," he said, "Then, I can go from there."

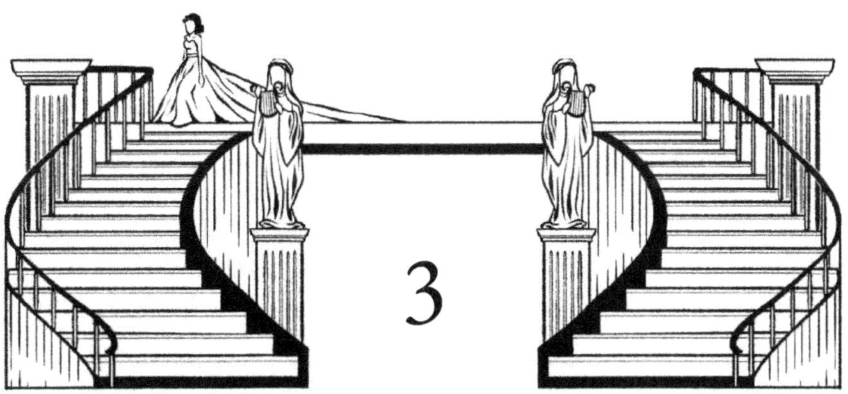

3

—— Rosamond ——

The Age of Ability

WHEN ROSAMOND WOKE UP, SHE KNEW everything would be different. She had reached the age of Ability today, and everyone knew that at the age of ability a girl became a woman. She threw off her thick feather-stuffed quilt and sat up quickly with a grin.

"Vy!" she shouted. "Vy, come through!" She gathered up her tangled mess of a night dress and hopped out of bed.

"Princess Rosamond," a scolding voice snapped from the side of the room. "Lower your dress!"

Rosamond frowned. It was her governess, Lady Stackly, who had stalked her steps since she was twelve seasons old. "Why?" Rosamond looked down at herself; she had her nightdress gathered just above her knees.

"I can see well above your ankles," the woman said, "You are a grown woman now; no one should be seeing your calves!"

"Vy!" Rosamond called again, "Vy, come through!" She turned to look at her governess haughtily. "You shouldn't be here!"

ROSAMOND

"Nonsense," Lady Stackly crossed her arms. She was a tall, thin woman with a bun so tight it made her head look like a pin. "I am your governess. I oversee *all* that you do."

"Not anymore!" Rosamond held onto her dress with a smirk, defiantly keeping her legs uncovered. "Valley! Where are you?" She called again.

"Just because you are *technically* at the age of Ability today doesn't mean you can ignore me," Lady Stackly chided.

"That is *precisely* what it means," Rosamond said smugly with a turned-up nose. She lowered her nightdress and walked over to her dressing screen. "I was born on the last day of the season of Goldlife, and that means today it's been seventeen seasons. I've passed all the markers and all the tests—therefore I *am* a woman, and that makes me an *equal* with you. Now... What on the table is all *this*?"

Lady Stackly walked across the room with a huff and peered behind the dressing screen. "What?" she asked.

Rosamond was pointing at what looked to her like a mound of unending fabric. "All this?"

"Your clothes," Lady Stackly said.

"Well it doesn't feel like much of a birthday," Rosamond sighed. "Not when all I have to wake up to is a grumpy governess and extra layers of skirt."

"Well, sorry to disappoint you," her governess said unapologetically. "But *becoming a woman* means dressing like one."

"You can leave now, Ms. Stackly," Rosamond mumbled. "I am, as you say, a woman now—and I wish to be *alone*."

"Fine!" Stackly snapped, "But don't be late for breakfast."

Rosamond let out an animated sigh of relief as her governess left the bed chambers. She pulled off her long, cumbersome night dress and found her first layer of undergarments. It was a simple white chemise which laced loosely down the front. She eyed the rest of the clothes, with all their complicated layers and buttons, but didn't attempt it on her own. Instead, she pulled her dressing gown over her shoulders and stepped out from behind her screen. Rosamond gasped, throwing her hands over her mouth with glee.

"Happy birthday!" said the newcomer, who stood at the center of the room, holding a small plate of honey bread.

"Valley!" Rosamond clapped her hands excitedly. "How sweet!"

Valley placed the plate of sweetbread on a little table just as Rosamond dove toward her with an affectionate hug. Valley squeezed her friend tightly, then stepped back.

"Happy birthday, sweet Ros," she said in her soft, honey-like voice, "You made it. You're free."

"Finally an adult!" Rosamond laughed. "I can't tell you how good it felt to send old Sickly away like a pile of bad laundry."

Valley laughed. "Come on," she said, "let's get your hair done."

The two girls skipped over to the vanity, where Rosamond sat on a padded velvet bench. Valley opened a shallow drawer, then pulled out a brush and stood behind her. They both looked into the large oval mirror which framed them like a painting, and talked nothing but nonsense, just as they did every morning.

"I think that now we are both of age, Father will let us attend banquets together," Rosamond said, keeping her back perfectly straight as Valley pulled the brush through her long silky hair.

Valley smiled doubtfully. "I don't know—I don't know if he would let *me* attend, anyway. Faeries aren't—"

"You're his ward!" Rosamond asserted, "That makes you basically my sister! Anyway, if he won't let you go as my sister, you can go as my wing."

Valley chuckled. "I don't think women have wings, Ros."

"Well, what *do* we have then?"

"Governesses and husbands, I fear," Valley said with a hint of skepticism.

"No," Rosamond rolled her eyes, "I am talking about people *we* get to order around—not people who order *us* around!"

"I don't know," Valley said, "You are King Hanz' first child to come of age, so it's all a bit unprecedented. Perhaps you can have court ladies, like they do in other kingdoms."

Rosamond nodded with a grin. "Yes. You will be my first lady!"

"That could work," Valley smiled hopefully, pausing, and then continued brushing Rosamond's hair.

Rosamond gazed at herself proudly in the oval looking glass. She knew she was always a pretty girl, but today she saw herself differently; today she saw a woman. She held her chin a little higher, then rotated it slightly left to right as she examined her jaw, which seemed to be growing more defined.

Rosamond liked to imagine she was a thing of beauty, inside and out. It was her outer beauty, however, that people seemed to notice about her. Her skin was a warm, milky chocolate-like color like her father's; and her body was small and supple. The color of her thick hair, which came down to the small of her back, resembled a near-black caramel mixed with a swirl of heavy cream. Her eyes were a bright amber with a golden center, her lips were plump and round, and her eyes like sideways teardrops lined with spider-like lashes.

The princess turned her gaze to her Faerie companion through the mirror. "Valley?"

"Yes, Ros?" Valley smiled at her, then began to weave an intricate braid design into Rosamond's hair.

"Shall we try the—you know—paints?"

Valley gave Rosamond a sly smile. "Well, I did bring them in last night."

"How about you do mine, and I do yours?" Rosemond clapped her hands together softly, careful not to disturb Valley's braiding.

"Let's not go overboard," Valley sighed, "I don't really think the face paints are meant for women like us."

"What do you mean?" Rosamond frowned, feeling her excitement under threat.

"I mean," Valley glanced at her through the mirror, "the paints are most often used to create colors and contours that weren't there before. Women who fear they are *lacking* use them."

"Valley!" Rosamond gasped, covering her mouth, though she had a sinister grin on her face. "So catty!"

"No," Valley shrugged, "Not catty. Anyway, you and I don't need that kind of support. Though, I suppose they can be used to *enhance* features we already have."

"Exactly," Rosamond folded her hands in her lap, studying her lips. "And if I am going to be meeting all sorts of men this season, I want to look my absolute best, Valley."

"I suppose..." Valley bit her lip.

"Come *on,*" Rosamond grinned, "Aren't you excited to meet some men, finally?"

Valley paused, then met Rosamond's eyes. "Not particularly."

"Of course you are!" Rosamond said, turning up her nose a bit. "You just don't want to admit it!"

"Whatever you say," Valley shook her head, snickering.

"Vy," Rosamond glanced toward her dressing screen. "You reached the age of Ability eight weeks ago—why haven't you been given outfits like *that* to wear."

"Like what?" Valley followed Rosamond's gaze.

"I have nearly seven layers of skirts to wear over there!" Rosamond pointed. "I am going to look like a volcano!"

Valley grinned. "I am not noble like you," she said, "I don't *have* to dress like it. And you know what they say: the more layers you wear, the more important you are. Your father will want you to dress like the most important woman on Raqia. So you will be wearing the most layers of any woman, I am guessing."

Rosamond nodded. "I guess so. Oh heavens, it will feel so dreadful, though!"

Valley stiffened as a sharp voice suddenly cut through the room.

"Are you *still* not dressed?" Lady Stackly was back. "It is nearly time for breakfast!"

The two girls didn't even glance at her.

"I'll skip breakfast today," Rosamond said dismissively as she waved her hand at her governess.

"You will not skip breakfast," Stackly barked.

"I will!" Rosamond matched her tone, still keeping her gaze toward the mirror.

"If you continue to disobey me, I will speak to your father!"

Rosamond scoffed. "Like Hades, you will."

"Rosamond!" Stackly marched toward her, grabbed the brush from Valley, and struck Rosamond on the thigh. "Don't swear!"

Valley backed away timidly, her eyes shooting down at the floor. It wasn't the first time Stackly struck one of them, but in that moment, Rosamond swore it would be the last.

Rosamond stood calmly and faced her former governess. "Lady Stackly," she said in a steady voice, "I do not take orders from you anymore—you are dismissed."

Lady Stackly's mouth dropped open. She raised the brush above her head, priming to strike again. "You cannot dismiss me!"

"I don't think you understand," Rosamond reached forward and snatched the brush from Stackly's hand. "I mean you are *officially* dismissed. I will no longer be requiring your services." She passed her brush back to Valley, whose eyes darted back and forth between Rosamond and her governess.

Lady Stackly snorted, then marched toward the door. "Your Father is going to hear about this!"

"Good!" Rosamond yelled, slamming her fist on the table as Lady Stackly disappeared. "And good riddance!"

All was quiet for a moment. Rosamond then sighed, sat down again, and rubbed her leg where she had been struck. "Ow."

"Wow," Valley said softly, "You stood up to her. I… I have never seen you like that before."

Rosamond sighed and looked at Valley through the mirror. "I do not play losing hands, Valley," she said, "today I finally have face cards to play with."

"I didn't know you had it in you," Valley said, smiling proudly. "You'll make a good princess."

Rosamond smiled proudly. "I like to think so!"

"Why are you skipping breakfast?"

"Oh, I don't know," the princess shrugged. "I just needed an excuse to defy the old bag. Plus!" She perked up, "You made me sweetbread!"

Valley nodded. She picked up some of Rosamond's hair and continued with her braiding. "Do you think your father will *let* you dismiss your governess—just like that?"

"Father respects those who convince him they deserve authority. If I act confidently enough, he will give this to me." She pursed her lips together. "I am not a child anymore, Valley. I will never again be powerless."

⚬

It was hard for Rosamond to grow up without a mother, and harder still to be raised by someone who hated her.

Rosamond's mother died giving birth to her younger brother. And as the daughter of one of the most important people on Raqia, Rosamond led an extremely sheltered life. Lady Stackly was Rosamond's only example of womanhood, and the only thing Rosamond had learned from Stackly was what she did *not* want to be like. So really, there was no real role model in Rosamond's that she wanted to emulate, aside from Father.

Rosamond's relationship with her father was a complicated one. There was no one she loved and admired more. Hanz wasn't just a king; he was a genius. He had not only united the lawless lands of Mensa in a few seasons, but he had created a thriving, stable kingdom whose culture paved the path for all of Raqia's future. His wisdom had reformed the way the Faeries integrated with the Human kingdoms, and his leadership commanded respect from even the most fickle of world leaders.

But in many ways, King Hanz was out of her reach. Who could grow close to someone so great? In her youth, Rosamond was loved—even doted on at times—by her father. But as she grew, he seemed to grow more and more distant. She had hoped that in her adulthood, he would show more of himself to her. Perhaps they could even be friends. So Rosamond made it her mission to study her father, how he acted, and what he pursued, hoping that if she measured up to some of his strengths, then she could prove to him that she was someone he could confide in. She was never quite sure what he was thinking.

All day long, Rosamond had expected to see her father—it was her birthday after all— but he was busy planning for all the delegations that would be arriving the week following. Instead, he summoned her to his room that night.

It was... *unfortunate*. Rosamond preferred public interactions with her father, as he always seemed to be more doting in those circumstances. In private... well, interactions were... *unpredictable*. Would he simply wish her a happy birthday? Was she to be scolded for ordering around her governess? Or was she to be commended for taking initiative? Rosamond had no idea, and it made her nervous.

As Rosamond approached Father's quarters, she sighed with relief when she saw Valley standing beside the door.

"Vy! Has he summoned you, too?" Rosamond asked, clasping hands with her friend.

"Yes," Valley held onto Rosamond's hand.

"Do you think I am in trouble?" Rosamond whispered.

"I don't know," Valley blinked, wide-eyed.

"I suppose I am only in trouble if I let myself be in trouble," Rosamond said confidently, "That's the sort of thing Father would say. I will not apologize!"

"Do you think that will work, Ros?" Valley asked timidly.

"I will *make* it work." Rosamond placed her hand on the door handle and pushed it open confidently, then glided into the room. "Father?" she called, spreading her arms out wide.

The King's chambers were spacious and opulent, with polished wood floors covered in great fur rugs and heavy drapery over the windows. There were candlesticks everywhere—far more candlesticks than Rosamond was ever allowed to have—and an unnecessary amount of lounging furniture for a man who slept alone. The room smelled like her father's favorite incense, which he burned at night to calm his nerves. A mix of spices, with scents like cassia and vetiver, made her nostrils tingle.

King Hanz was standing by his main window, though the drapes were drawn to keep out the cold night air. He was waiting for her, posing as if for a painting. His expression warmed at the sight of the two girls, and he held out his hands to them.

"Girls!" he said in a cheery voice, then he focused his eyes on Rosamond. "Darling, happy birthday!"

Rosamond's heart swelled at the sight of her father in a good mood, and she ran for him as quickly as she could. She may be a woman today, but once she was held in his big strong arms, she felt instantly like a little girl again. King Hanz was tall, and she was short for her age, so her cheek rested against his chest. He clutched her tightly, then lifted his head and held out his hand to his ward, Valley.

"Come, dear Valley!" he said. Valley approached a little more hesitantly but then smiled as she joined Rosamond in the family embrace. Hanz hugged them both tightly. "My girls!" He exclaimed. "My beautiful girls!"

"Papa," Rosamond pulled back, fighting against his strength. "You know I am a woman now. You can't exactly keep calling me a *girl!*"

"Nonsense." Hanz released his bear hug on the girls and straightened up to full height. He looked down at the two of them proudly. "Woman or not, I will call you both whatever I like."

"And Papa," Rosamond rubbed her cheek, "Your beard is far too scratchy; you'll make my skin red!"

"Well, we can't have that," the king said as he rubbed her cheek with his thumb. He paused, taking her gently by the chin, and turned her face from side to side. "My, my," he said with a look of awe, "You grow lovelier by the bell. You make me so proud, my dear Rosamond."

Rosamond couldn't help but smile. "I didn't think it would be so easy to make you proud!"

"It isn't!" he said, folding his arms. "Actually, it is quite difficult. I am not an easy person to please."

"Well," Rosamond tried to stand as tall as she could, beating her father to the punch. "Then I hope it *pleases* you to hear I have taken some initiative and dismissed Lady Stackly."

King Hanz froze, looking a little concerned. Then she spotted a look of amusement behind his eyes. "Is that so?" he nodded thoughtfully.

"Yes." Rosamond nodded frankly. "She was a horrible governess. I couldn't stand her. But I respected her authority—*and yours*—while it lasted and survived her horrible bothersomeness. Now that I am seventeen seasons, I assume I can start taking charge of my own person—at least where my daily habits are concerned. I have no need to keep that irritating woman in my life."

Rosamond held her breath and her confident expression as she watched for her father's reaction. He had the look of a man who had won a bet he didn't remember placing. "Well," he scratched his short, tidy beard. "I wasn't entirely fond of her either."

Rosamond blinked. "So... when she came and complained to you about me this morning... you stood by my decision?"

King Hanz chuckled, then nodded. "I did."

"She was a horrible governess, Papa." She raised her voice, relieved to finally be free to say it.

"Now, now," he said, holding up his palm, "I let you sack her, but let's not get carried away." He clasped his hands behind his back and turned to the side, looking down at the floorboards. "I chose her to train you, not to coddle you. She did her job, that job is done. If you do not wish her to remain in your service, that is your choice."

Rosamond glanced at Valley, who didn't respond but only stared with her wide, Faerie eyes. "Yes, father." Rosamond said quietly.

King Hanz turned to her with a renewed smile. "You have survived the testing and tempering of childhood," he said, "Now is the real battle." He walked between the two girls, placing a hand on each of their shoulders. "Our family has come a long way." Rosamond glanced at Valley for support, anticipating a monologue. "Our mission has been to unite the fractured lands of Raqia. Next week, leaders from every nation will come together to discuss a peace pact. Once it is cemented, we can finally see our dreams become reality: Raqia will be a place of peace, as it was in the beginning. I need to know you are both behind me, one hundred percent."

Rosamond and Valley looked at each other, then back at King Hanz. "Of course we are!" said Rosamond. "How could you think otherwise?"

"The average girl dreams of her own future," he said with distant eyes, "but you are not average girls."

The two women looked at each other again. "We know that, Papa," said Rosamond, "What are you saying?"

"Your mission is the same as mine," he said, "to unite Raqia. I must trust you to act and do as I tell you in the coming season. I have been lenient with you both while you were young, but now—I trust that you can act like the adults you are. I need you to do everything *right*."

Rosamond huffed. "Yes, *of course*, father! Have I not proven to you that I will obey you no matter what?"

Hanz nodded. "Rosamond, I will choose your husband in the coming season."

Rosamond held her breath a moment, then nodded. "Yes, I know. Though I hope you will at least take into account my preferences?"

"I will take them into account." He looked away for a moment. "Of course I will."

"Papa," Rosamond pulled his arm, drawing close to him.

He groaned, knowing she was about to ask him a favor. "Yes, darling?"

"I am coming out next week, am I not?"

"Yes..." He looked downward at her through the corner of his eyes. "...and?"

"I want Valley to come out at the same time. *Please*? It would be so much less pressure if I wasn't coming out all by myself!"

She felt her father's body tense, and he pulled away from her, shaking his head. "No," he said, "That is not possible."

"Why not?" Rosamond's heart fell. "*Please*, Papa?"

"Rosamond," Hanz' voice grew firm, "When I say no, the correct response is not to ask again. You should know now that a princess never asks twice."

Rosamond bit her lip but nodded. "Can she—"

"That is all, Rosamond," Hanz turned away from her. "You may go now."

Rosamond dropped her hands to her sides in defeat. She looked at her friend. "Alright, come on, Vy."

Valley began to follow Rosamond out when Hanz raised his hand. "Not you, Valley. Please stay a moment."

The girls met eyes, sharing confused glances. Then Rosamond left, feeling somewhat confused, as she always did after private meetings with her father, Hanz the King.

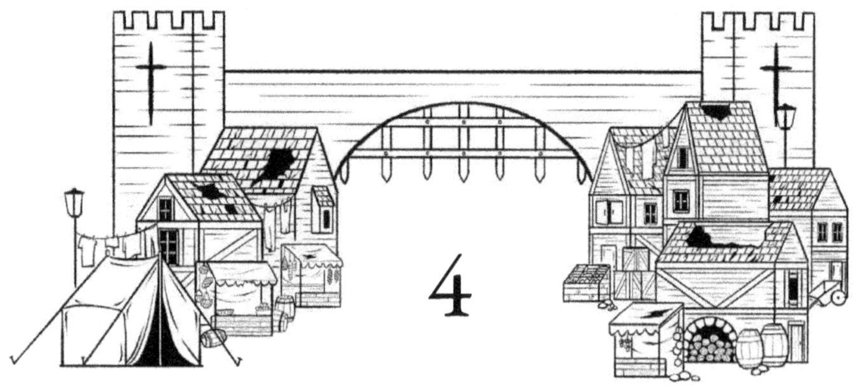

—— Valley ——

The Warrowing Village

VALLEY WATCHED KING HANZ CROSS THE ROOM. His heavy, fur-lined cape trailed behind him, and the attached gold buttons scraped along the floor. He sat down at his writing desk, removed his spiked gold crown, and placed it on the surface of the table. Valley stood perfectly still, like a deer scanning for danger.

"Come over here," said Hanz. He ran his fingers through his long, black, shoulder-length hair. He had dropped his stern fatherly act, and now, he just looked tired.

Valley moved toward him slowly, not making a single noise. She stood a pace or two away from the king and glanced to the side, noticing an image of herself staring back from the King's standing mirror. Now that Rosamond wasn't in the room, Valley began to notice how womanly she herself had become. It was easy to neglect her own reflection when the beautiful Rosamond was present. Rosamond's beauty commanded all eyes to look her way. But Valley would rather not exist than be noticed by others. And yet here she was: existing.

Valley

Valley was pretty—she had to grant herself that—but in a different way from the princess. Where Rosamond was all curves and caramel, Valley was angular and white. Where Rosamond was fire and earth, Valley was water and air. Valley had a pointy, impish nose, and large, deer-like Faerie eyes. Her long cleft ears stuck out conspicuously, while her bright, ashy, straight hair was pulled tightly into a high tail. Fringe framed the sides of her face. Her most obvious feature was that one pointy eyebrow she had on her right side; it made her look like she was always skeptical—and that particular feature she didn't mind.

Her frame was small and delicate, and her wings were, well, she wasn't quite sure what her wings looked like. They were invisible, as always. Once or twice she had tried revealing them in a dark room, but only ever in secret, and never in front of a mirror.

Hanz sniffed, and Valley jumped, becoming suddenly aware of a long silence.

"Was there something you needed, my lord?" she asked quietly, returning her eyes to the ground.

"I have raised you since you were an infant," King Hanz said, "as if you were my own daughter. Do not be afraid to meet my gaze."

Valley lifted her eyes for a moment, her eyes meeting the King's through the mirror. Then she dropped them again. It was too much—too much for someone as low as her to look into the eyes of the greatest man on the world. "What is it you wanted to speak with me about?" she asked.

Hanz sighed, swiveled to face her, leaned against his desk, and rested one of his arms on its surface. "Rosamond loves you, almost as much as *I* do, but she cannot fully understand what role you must play in this world because you are a Fae."

Valley looked up at Hanz' face for a moment, curious what sort of expression he was making when he said that. He looked... concerned. Her eyes returned to the floor again. "Yes, she sees me as her equal," she replied.

"I often wondered," Hanz cleared his throat, "If it was unwise to take in a Faerie as a ward, but I always came back to the same conclusion: it was good for Rosamond to be raised alongside a Faerie so that she could see how precious you all are." He stood, took a step toward Valley, then rested a hand on her shoulder.

"It is easy for Humans to forget that you are people too, with thoughts and feelings, capable of deep affection. I had thought that..." his voice trailed off and he dropped his hand. "Well, I had at first thought that when you and Rosamond came of age, you could be bonded to her."

Valley's heart froze. *Bonded?* No! Well... why not? What fantasy had she been living in where she believed she might *never* have to be bonded to a Human? Of *course,* she would be bonded. It was the fate of all the Faeries, wasn't it? But... no... Valley could hold her nerve, couldn't she? Why, then? Why did she feel like running away and crying?

Perhaps it wouldn't be so bad being bonded with Rosamond. At least Rosamond saw Valley as an equal, which was more than she deserved! Valley lifted her chin and looked at the king in the face.

"My lord," she said, "*am* I to be bonded with Rosamond?"

"I..." his voice trailed off again.

"Or perhaps, you think that is unwise?" she anticipated him. "My lord, what *is* going to become of me? Am I to be bonded to a Human?"

King Hanz studied her face for a long time, then sighed, "I," he paused, "What do you *wish* I would say, young Valley?"

Valley thought about her answer before she spoke. Well, she wouldn't dare say what she actually wished. That would be insane! Would he grant her what she wished? No... no, he would only do that if it matched his own will. She would have to ask for something reasonable. She straightened her back and said, "I had promised Rosamond that I would be with her when she came out, that I could be by her side for the events this coming season. I know that I cannot be presented as a court lady, but is there some way I can be there for Rosamond?"

Hanz raised his eyebrows, his mouth stuck open for a click, then he softened with a smile. "Well, that isn't exactly an answer to my question, but yes, Valley, I can find you a place if you wish."

"Perhaps you could postpone my bonding until after she is married," Valley suggested, hoping to buy herself some time.

King Hanz pursed his lips, deliberating to himself. "I don't know," he said apprehensively, "I don't like the idea of an unbonded Faerie, free and wandering around all those noblemen. You could be stolen."

"I am sure no one would dare steal a Faerie from under your nose while they are guests in your house, especially not one that you called your ward," Valley said, careful to keep emotion from her voice.

Hanz sighed. "I will think about it."

"Thank you, my lord." Valley bowed her head to him and kept it low for several clicks before backing away.

"Valley," came Hanz' voice. Valley looked up to see the king smiling wearily. "You're a good girl. If only Rosamond had been more like you."

Valley's eyes flashed with anger.

"No, no," Hanz waved his hand at her, "I love Rosamond the way she is. I just mean—oh *Hades*—that girl is too much like my sister: so headstrong. If she were more like you, I might get a wink of sleep every now and again." Hanz chuckled to himself.

"And I am...?" Valley raised a questioning eyebrow.

"You are a listener," King Hanz said, as he walked over to his reading chair. "You make one feel more at ease. Rosamond keeps a man on his toes."

Somehow that didn't feel to Valley like a complement. "I am glad I can make you more at ease, my lord," she said without a hint of sarcasm, though she felt it.

King Hanz leaned back into his chair and picked up a book to examine its spine. "Do you know," he said absent-mindedly, "of all the things that could make me anxious about the visiting delegations and political events, do you know what causes me the most worry?" He paused. Valley waited to see how rhetorical the question was, and when Hanz didn't continue, she asked,

"What causes you the most worry, my lord?"

He opened his book to a marked page. "My Faeries," he said, "I fear for my Faeries." He dropped the open book on his lap for a moment and glanced up at her with thoughtful eyes. "You are all like children to me. I—well, I want you all... cared for."

Valley nodded slowly. "It must be hard when it is time to let us go," she guessed.

Hanz looked genuinely sorrowful. "Valley, I want you to understand that I would never do anything to hurt any of your kind. It is my greatest mission and deepest desire to find a right and proper place for every single Faerie on this world. Do you believe me?"

"Of course I do," Valley answered quickly, "Why wouldn't I believe you?"

King Hanz sighed. "Well, you seem rather resistant to the idea of being bonded. Is it because you believe there is something better for a Faerie like yourself?"

Valley shook her head slowly. "No. I want to live a full and meaningful life."

Hanz nodded in satisfaction. "Yes, what a healthy way of putting it. Valley, do you remember what your parents said to me when they gave you to me?"

Valley sighed inwardly. Of *course* she knew; he had only told her a thousand times! "They said your love for me was stronger than theirs; they said you would find my place in this world."

Hanz grunted in agreement. "Yes," he said, "They trusted me to find you your best future. After the Faeries heard the answer to the question of their existence, so many of your kind came to me and asked for help. I had built trust with the Fae while they were still fighting for freedom from their evil king."

"But, my lord," Valley said timidly, regretting the words as they came from her lips, "who *were* my parents?"

"*I* am your parents, Valley," Hanz said in a sharp tone. Valley jolted, then nodded.

"I am sorry for asking," she said, shaking her head in shame.

"Well," Hanz said with a sigh, "No matter. You may go, child."

Valley bowed her head, hating herself for asking about her parents. She turned slowly and began to leave the room soundlessly.

"You know," the voice of the king came softly. She froze, listening. "I bonded your parents at the same time, both to the same Human," he said. "Most Faeries don't take mates, but they were quite devoted to one another. I found I couldn't separate them."

Valley's long ears perked up. "Really?" she asked, too curious to keep her mouth shut.

"Your Father had tears in his eyes when they left with their Human. He thanked me for saving his life and giving him a place to serve. They—they were so *happy*, Valley. They still are!"

Valley turned quickly, opening her mouth. "Can you—?"

"I promised them, Valley," Hanz said strongly, shaking his head, "I will not tell you any more about them. I must leave them be. They gave you to *me*. That must be enough for you. Have I not been a good father to you?"

Valley gave Hanz another long, deer-in-danger stare, then nodded. "Of course you have," she said, finally.

"Will you trust me like your parents did: trust me to save you?" he asked, locking eyes with her.

"Yes," Valley replied without thinking.

"Good," Hanz said in a brighter tone, releasing her from his gaze. He cleared his throat, then lifted up his book to read. "Goodnight."

Valley watched him for a moment, surprised at how quickly he could shift moods, then scurried away before he thought of another thing to say to her.

It was a short walk from the Inner Palace to the Warrowing Gate, but it wasn't close enough to keep Valley from arriving past curfew. She could hear the Lastlight Bell ringing from the distant bell tower, and then there was Gingre. The armored guard was standing beside the Warrowing Gate, slamming the gong with his hammer, and making the most infuriatingly irritating smirk. She arrived at the gate just as the bolts locked into place, and Gingre stood straight, resting his hammer on the ground with a grin.

"Late, Valloy," he said, reaching up to pick at the bald spot in his dusty brown beard.

Valley closed her eyes and drew in a calming breath before staring daggers at the hateable night guard. "I was held back by the King's orders, Gingre," she said, "You can't punish me for—"

"Alls I knows is to lock the gates when it's time to ring the gong. You see that there torch?" He pointed up toward the massive beacon at the top of the north tower. "My job is always been to ring this gong and lock these gates when that torch is lit. Any rule-breakin' Faes is to spend the night in the pit for missing curfew—and get ten lashings." He leaned on the long handle of his hammer with both arms, grinning widely.

"I told you!" Valley yelled. "I was held back on the King's—" she stopped short, calming herself. "Gingre, you *know* me! I am the King's ward!"

"Alls I knows is you're a rule-breakin' Fae who didn't come to bed when you's was s'posed to," he shrugged. "It'll be my pleasure to escort'cha to the pit after I help you to the lashings, if you don't mind," he said in an unnecessarily loud voice. "But don't worry, I'll use the gail's whip on you, since it's ye first time. It's smaller."

"Gingre!" Valley cried in a shrill voice as two other Human guards appeared and grabbed her roughly by the arms.

"Valley, is that you?" A voice called from the other side of the gate.

"Tristan?" Valley called desperately.

"Why are you back so late? I waited until the last moment for you!"

"King Hanz wanted—"

"Get t'bed!" Gingre yelled, slamming his hammer against the Warrowing Gate.

"Let her in!" Tristan called. "I'll scapegoat—take the lashings for her. If she was on King's business—"

"Rules is rules!" Gingre barked, pointing his men in the direction of the sleeping pit just outside the Faerie village. Tristan continued to call out from the other side of the gate as Valley was dragged away.

Gingre walked up to Valley's side as she thrashed between the guards, trying to break free. "Don't worry Valloy, I'll lash the back o'the legs so we don't displease the nobles with ye scars, there's a good gail."

"I'll be hanged before I let a scumbag like you see the back of my legs!" Valley screamed, pulling against the two guards as they dragged her to a stone courtyard. The flagstones beneath their feet were stained with fresh blood. Valley's panic rose as the guards pushed her down to her stomach. Her neat, blue dress that she had only just mended would be ruined now—stained and tarnished against the filthy ground. The guards roughly cuffed her wrists in irons. Valley looked up to see a fourth man standing above her.

"Captain!" she cried, recognizing Captain Oswald, the head of the King's personal guard. He looked a little diverted, but he cleared his throat and raised his hand to the other guards.

"That's enough soldier," he said to Gingre. "She was delayed on King's business."

"Aye, Captain," Gingre said reluctantly.

After a moment of silence, Valley shouted, "Come on—you heard him. Untie me this instant!"

Gingre huffed. "You could have waited another moment, couldn't you?" he asked in a pouty voice. The guards released her from the iron cuffs.

Captain Oswald snorted. "If this is the only chance someone like you has to see a woman's legs, then I feel sorry for you." He reached down, helping Valley up to her feet by the hand. She took it, rising to dust herself off. Her dress was ruined—again! She shot a glare up at the captain.

"I shouldn't have to be manhandled and disgraced if I am delayed by the King's business! What took you so long to come and defend me?"

"No one sent me," the captain said casually, offering her his arm. Valley frowned as she took it and walked with him back to the Warrowing Gate. The thick night had almost fully set in by this point, so their way was lit mostly by torches as the fortified castle prepared for the night bells. "But I had heard that he summoned you. At this bell? I thought this might happen."

Valley bit her lip. The captain did her a *favor*? "I owe you," she said quietly.

"Nonsense," he cleared his throat, "It is my duty to be aware of such things. But Valley," he looked down at the Faerie, who next to someone as large and burly as him looked even smaller, "You may have been the King's ward in your childhood, but you are still a Faerie. You cannot expect to be treated with the same respect as a Human woman."

Valley concealed her frustration. She wasn't supposed to be angry at comments like that. "Of course not—I don't expect that one bit. But I do expect to at least be treated with dignity."

Oswald nodded slowly as they arrived at the gate. There was a small door which granted entry to only a select few. Captain Oswald was one of those select few. He pulled a keyring from his pocket. "I cannot always control how others treat you," he said, "I can only warn you to be on your guard and plan ahead for things like this. It probably won't be the last time you are summoned unexpectedly at a late bell—I suggest next time you ask for some sort of clearance. If you do not fight for yourself, then I won't always be here to get you out of trouble."

"I don't need you to rescue me from being a Faerie," Valley muttered.

Oswald put the key into the lock and unbolted the small door which led into the Faerie village. "It is a hard thing to be a Faerie," he said, "and a hard thing to be a woman, I am sure." He turned to look her in the eyes, smiling from under his thick mustache. "I can only imagine it must be exceptionally tricky to be both."

Valley snorted, shaking her head at him. "I don't need pity, Captain."

"No," he nodded, "you don't." The captain motioned for her to enter.

She pulled up her long dress, and stepped inside the village, turning back for a moment to say, "Thank you."

Captain Oswald closed and bolted the door. Valley sighed and touched her forehead. She felt faint. Had she really just escaped humiliation, beating, and a night in the pit? Goodness—her life seemed to be a never ending tightrope! One half of her day, she was treated like a sister by Rosamond and a daughter by Hanz, and the other half she was beaten and bullied and treated like a possession. It wasn't just exhausting, it was confusing.

"Valley!" an exasperated voice came from beside her. She jolted as Tristan grabbed her by the shoulders and brought her tightly against his chest in a protective embrace.

"Tristan," she mumbled, feeling finally safe. He held her out at arm's length to look at her.

"Are you hurt?" asked the Faerie elder as his worried eyes searched her complexion.

"No," Valley shook her head, "Maybe a little bruised. Oswald defended me, thankfully."

Tristan nodded, dropping his arms to his sides. "Well, now that you're inside, everyone is accounted for," he said with a look of relief. "I think I can leave the gate now. Come on, let's get to the dinner hall. It's the start of a new season—a feast day!" He put his hand on Valley's back and guided her through the main courtyard.

Within the castle network at the heart of Mensa's capitol was a perfectly square village encased in protective tall, stone walls. This was the Warrowing Village: home to the Faeries. During the day, the gates were open, allowing the Fae to travel freely between their homes and their workplaces, but in the night, they would all gather back together in this place. It was the only place Faeries in Mensa could really call their own. These Faeries had few possessions and even fewer rights, but inside the Warrowing Village they had some semblance of identity, and that was enough for them. They knew where they belonged, and they knew what they were supposed to do.

Tristan had once been called the XI Faerie of Water, back before Faerie titles were banned. Now, he was Fae Tristan, the Warrowing Village's head elder. He led and managed the Warrowing Village, along with the other leading males, and maintained a steady community life for his people. He was one of the oldest Faeries Valley knew—at least three thousand seasons old. His gaunt and pointy features resembled Valley's enough that at times she fantasized that *he* was her birth father. But, no, she stopped believing that seasons ago. Several of the kids in the Warrowing Village were, in fact, his children. If she were one of them, he would have told her.

Still, he was like a father to all. He had been there thirty seasons ago when King Somenus was killed. On that day, the old Time Faerie told the Faeries why they were made, and Tristan was there to hear it. He was one of the first witnesses to the fact that Faeries were made to serve Humans. He and Hanz helped found the Warrowing Village, and this meant that all the Faeries deeply trusted him.

Tristan walked quickly toward the dinner hall as if stressed, his stork-like legs covering wide ground with each stride. Valley had to move her short legs twice as fast to keep up.

"Tristan," she asked, catching his arm, "Is everything alright?"

"Ah," he said nervously, consciously slowing down once he realized Valley was out of breath. "Yes, everything is fine."

Valley pursed her round, strawberry lips. "I am guessing you were busy planning for the delegations?" she asked. "What does the king have you doing?"

Tristan halted in his steps and turned to make eye contact with her. His face was whiter than its usual color. "He—uh, Valley..." his face looked pained.

"You are helping him decide who will be bonded?" she guessed.

Tristan nodded slowly. "Yes, I am."

"You know who I will be bonded to, then?" she asked quietly. Tristan licked his lips.

Valley sighed, bringing her hand to her shoulder absentmindedly. "How many of us will go to the nobles?" she asked. "How many does Hanz plan to bond this season?"

"It is hard to guess how many nobles will be interested," he said as he scanned the air with his eyes. "Some Humans don't like the idea of having Faeries around. But I am sure many will find homes in the coming season." He smiled weakly. "Don't worry, Valley, I am sure King Hanz will not send you far away."

She nodded, looking down. "You were lucky enough to be bonded to King Hanz," she said, "He is kind to Faeries."

"King Hanz will not send a Faerie to *anyone* who is not kind, Valley. Of that, I am sure," he said confidently. "He promised to help us fulfill our purpose. He sees us as his own children. He would *never* allow anything to happen to us that wasn't for our good."

Valley nodded. She felt a little guilty about how much she dreaded bonding. She held her breath for a moment, then asked, "How bad is it, really? The..." she touched her shoulder again, protectively.

"Oh," Tristan sighed, nodding. He pulled up his sleeve, revealing his own shoulder. An intricate symbol was carved into his skin in the form of a deep purple brand. "I hardly remember anymore how it felt but it's not as bad as you might think." Even he didn't seem to believe his own words.

"I don't know why I thought..." Valley muttered.

Tristan sighed. "You thought you might never get one?"

She nodded. "I've spent too much time with Rosamond...started to believe that we were equals—like sisters."

The old Faerie pulled his sleeve back down and patted her on the head. "You're a Faerie," he said, "it will feel right doing what you were made to do—you were made to serve."

"I know," she said, then she hesitated, raising her pointed eyebrow.

"What?" Tristan asked, grinning. "What is that face?"

"Tristan," she said slowly, "when do you know what sort of Faerie you are?"

Tristan looked disturbed by the question and seemed to glance from side to side, as if checking for eavesdroppers. "Why are you asking me this?" he asked. "Have you felt a change?"

"When did you know you were the..." she lowered her voice to a whisper, "...the Water Faerie?"

Tristan held his breath. Then he nodded. "When I was just a child," he said, "touching water was like touching magik itself. It gave me this power—this joy—that I could hardly contain," he paused, "it was easy to guess which title was mine."

Valley watched his eyes light up at the mention of water. "I know we aren't allowed to claim titles but is it wrong to know what they *would* be if we had them?" she asked.

"I..." Tristan hesitated. "It motivates ambition and the desire for gaining power. King Hanz forbids Faerie titles in Mensa, and it would be wrong to question him. I—" The two looked up quickly at the sound of the dinner gong ringing. Tristan smiled warmly. "Come on, enough of this! Let's eat!"

He led her by the arm to the dinner hall. It was a long, tent-like structure erected in the center of the Faerie village. There were three pointed domes in the canopy with openings at the top that allowed smoke to escape from the main fires. Banquet tables lined with rows of wooden chairs ran the length of the longhouse. Though some Fae were still bringing in large trays of food and setting them on the tables, most were seated. There were close to two hundred Faeries living in the Warrowing Village and every single one would be present to dine together.

In centuries past, Faeries had mostly lived alone, scattered across Raqia like hermits and nomads. But here in Mensa, they engaged in communal living and found more of a tribe identity as they laid their individualistic Faerie titles aside. They had become a giant family, all loving and caring for one another as they faced life in this new and daring world.

In the Warrowing Village, no one took up imperiums or intentionally sought out magik; no one took titles; no one showed their wings. Since the death of Somenus the Faerie King, they had learned the truth: Faeries were not made to be like gods; they were made to serve. The powers they had once boasted about were now reminders of their failures: a time when they had lived in pride and arrogance. Here in Mensa, they were able to live a humble and quiet life, one of servitude and contemplation.

Elder Tristan took his place at the top of the longhouse head table and raised his hands. Valley bowed her head reverently as he gave a prayer of thanks for the food. Then with a loud clap, he charged them to eat. Their food was mostly bread and steamed vegetables, though on special occasions the cooks would make up something unique. Valley served herself some food and listened as Tristan remained standing to give a speech.

"My dear family," he said in a clear, raised voice, "We have been preparing for the new season, and tonight, it is upon us. The skydeacons have predicted a dry season, with hot clear Skies, soft breezes, and sweeter fruits. I am pleased to announce that it is a Feast season. They have named it 'Kingsummons', commemorating this occasion as leaders from every nation come together to discuss peace. We are lucky to be here in Mensa at such a time, and it gives the Faeries great joy to aid in peace between men.

"Thirty seasons ago, Aorist, the oldest Faerie, told us our true purpose: to serve mankind. Since then, we Faeries of the Warrowing Village have laid down our titles and our powers to fulfill that purpose. King Hanz has taken much time and care to strategize where we can best be of service. Many of us have gone out into the world already and are thriving in new homes. Now, in the season of Kingsummons, a large number of us," he paused, his voice catching in his throat as a tear escaped his eye, "will be sent away. Leaders from every nation will have the opportunity to bond with Faeries and bring them back to their homelands. Soon, Faeries will be serving at the heart of every kingdom. And finally, we can taste our true purpose. Finally, we will be at peace."

The longhouse erupted into cheers, though as Valley looked around, she could see worry on some of the faces. Everyone wanted the final peace that came from living out their true purpose, yet they had no idea how it would feel. Only a few Faeries in the Warrowing Village, perhaps thirty, had actually been bonded to a Human. The rest were waiting and preparing, knowing that the season would one day come where they could be placed into new homes and new lives.

"Thirty seasons ago," Tristan raised his voice again, silencing the cheers, "King Hanz promised me that he would protect those of us who pledged ourselves to him in the Purple Order, those of us who rose up to dethrone Somenus the Faerie King. Now, in the season of Kingsummons, King Hanz will fulfill that promise; anyone who once pledged an oath to the Purple Order will be released to bond with a Human. If you do not wish to leave the service of King Hanz, you may petition to bond with him, but he urges you to trust him on your assignment as he has spent much time deliberating over his decisions. You all must do what you believe is right, but I can vouch for our King and his care for us. Trust in King Hanz. Long live the King!"

"Long live the King!" a chorus of voices returned in unison.

"Now, eat, and drink! Tonight, King Hanz sends us vino to celebrate the first night of Kingsummons!"

The cheers grew louder as the Faeries began opening the barrels of vino and distributing overfilled cups across the tables. Valley sighed as she received a cup in her hands, thankful that she would not be spending the night in the pit on a momentous day like this. She drank the vino, feeling the buzz of excitement. Why had she felt so apprehensive, so resistant, to the idea of bonding, when everyone in this village had been waiting for their whole lives for it? Perhaps she had spent too much time pretending to be a court lady and not enough amongst her people. Rosamond was an adult now and their relationship would change.

Valley looked down at her stained upper-class dress. A tight, strapless, corseted bodice encased her bosom, then from the waist down, four layers of thick, matte silk covered her lower half, masking any definition of her legs. It was the mark of a noble woman to mask the existence of legs, as if the mere shape of them was too prized to be seen by the common eye. But Valley was no noblewoman. She was a Faerie—a lower being. Most Faeries wore only two layers of skirt. Perhaps it would be a relief to shed the pomp and protection of her upper-class clothing. And perhaps not...

Valley sighed, putting her glass of vino down on the table in front of her. She had no idea what her life was going to be in the season of Kingsummons. Would she stay in the Inner Palace? Would she be bonded to a noblewoman from a faraway kingdom? Oh, it was no use wondering—she didn't know what she wanted her future to be. It all made her feel uneasy. She felt so powerless, but... perhaps that was a *good* thing. Power was bad for Faeries, wasn't it? So it was best for her to embrace the powerlessness rather than hide from it.

"What's gotten you so serious?" A voice interrupted Valley's reverie. She snapped to attention, turning to see a woman filling a tray with food and vino. It was Marbel, the once Faerie of Hunger. She was an interesting woman, uncommonly heavyset for a Faerie, and proud of it. Valley was particularly drawn to her, as she had a motherly way about her, constantly fussing over whoever happened to be in her vicinity. Some might have found that bothersome, but Valley craved it.

"Marbel," Valley chuckled, watching the woman grab most of the sweet rolls from the middle of the table. "Taking the best food for your tray?"

Marbel snorted, "It's going to those who need cheering up the most," she said, then stopped to shove a grape into her mouth. "While we are all feasting in here, others out there only get what's taken to them."

"You're going to the... confinements?"

"Of course, I am. I go every feast day."

Valley smiled. "Do you need a hand?" she asked as she put down her half-finished vino cup.

"Always," Marbel said gruffly, "Just grab that whole tray of buttered bread."

"Alright," Valley stood. She pulled a bread tray from the middle of the table.

"And bring a jar of preserve," she said, moving away from the table. Valley took the fullest jar of preserve that she could find and put it on her tray. She looked to Marbel for direction, then followed as the woman led her out of the long house and into the warm, night air. Valley was relieved to find herself dragged away from the feasting table; something about her mood made her want to seek every possible distraction. Marbel balanced one tray on top of her head and the other against her hip, and she sauntered confidently toward the confinement building at the back of the village.

It was a menacing, cube-shaped building made of stone bricks, its back attached to the tall village walls. All windows were barred, and only one central door led in or out. The door was guarded by two Human soldiers who leaned lazily against their spears. They jolted to attention and puffed their chests out as Valley and Marbel approached.

"Who goes there?" one of them asked, stepping forward.

"Oh, pipe down, Sam," Marbel grumbled, "Can't you see we are busy here? Let us through."

"Who's the little one," he pointed at Valley, "in the big skirt?"

"You know Miss Valley, the King's ward, she's helping me bring the feast food to the prisoners."

Sam stood straighter, grinning, "So what's the King's ward doing gracing us with her presence on the dark side of the village?"

Valley rolled her eyes. Why did she always have to be the center of attention?

Sam stepped forward to inspect the food trays, making a 'tutting' sound. "Fancy food for Faerie prisoners," he remarked.

"Everyone is to celebrate at the coming of a new season," Marbel boomed, "let us in!"

"Fine, fine." Sam stepped back, motioning to his companion to open the door for them. He eyed them carefully as they passed through, muttering something indistinguishable under his breath. The two women entered the prison, pausing to let their eyes adjust to the new lighting. It was darker than the night sky!

Valley stood patiently behind Marbel who was standing in place. "If you just wait for a moment," Marbel said, "you'll see a light down the hall, the first torch. Do you see it?"

"I see it." Valley was growing cold. How could anyone live in a place as dark as this? She had helped Marbel in the prison once or twice before, but never at night.

"Alright, follow me, and let's bring the feast!" the large woman said as she charged forward. Valley's ears perked up as Marbel began to sing. Her voice filled the damp halls with a sudden feeling of cheer. Soon, they came to the source of the only light in the building, a single torch at the center of a cross hall. Marbel stopped to put her trays down on the floor by the torch. Valley followed suit.

"Let's see," Marbel muttered to herself, "There are twelve inmates, so I think there's enough for each one to get a buttered bread, a fruit, and a roast potato." She took one of each, distributing them into twelve bundles. I'll take the hall on the left with the women, and you take the hall on the right. And we wish them a happy Kingsummons, alright?"

"I—" Valley grew increasingly nervous. She had come into the prison before, but she hadn't actually spoken to any of the inmates. She suddenly felt deeply out of her depth. Who was even in here—and what had they done? Would the inmates be hostile to her? She swallowed her fear with a loud gulp and gathered her first cluster of food—some bread, an apple, and a baked potato.

Braving the trek into the darkness, she entered the hallway on the right. It was narrow and lined with bars, but without more than the distant torchlight, she couldn't see inside any of the cells. She gagged, smelling a scent reminiscent of an outhouse, but charged forward bravely.

"Hallo," Valley said in a timid voice, "I bring supper." She tapped the bars of the first cell.

She jumped as a pair of hands reached through the bars and held themselves open. "Good evening," said a male voice. "I smell honey... and seasoning. Feast food from the coming of a new season?"

"It is the first night of Kingsummons," Valley said, feeling her courage rise. This voice didn't sound criminal to her. He sounded... well, normal! She held out the food.

"Thank you, friend," said the voice, taking the food in his hands which quickly disappeared back into the darkness. "What is your name, girl? I don't recognize you."

"Y—you can see me?" she stuttered. "In this darkness?"

She heard him chuckle. "Our eyes are quite adjusted to the darkness, miss."

"Ah," Valley straightened, feeling a little uncomfortable at the thought that they could see her, but she couldn't see them. "My name is Valley."

"Happy Kingsummons, Valley," said the man, "what's your title?"

"I…" she hesitated, "I don't have one."

"Ah," she heard him licking the honey off his fingers. "Forsaking your title? You must be young then, for a Faerie."

"I am. I am seventeen."

"Well, my name is Whisp, Eighth Faerie of Voice, at your service."

"Oh!" She felt a thrill surge through her body. There was something so… *stimulating* about hearing a Faerie announce their title with pride. It was the same sort of thrill she felt when she got away with a lie. "Well," she cleared her throat, suddenly conscious of the sound of her own voice, "Happy Kingsummons to you, too."

"What's got the skydeacons so excited that they'd pick a name like Kingsummons?" Whisp asked between bites.

Valley stopped to wonder if she was allowed to tell the prisoner anything about the outside world, then shrugged to herself. "King Hanz is inviting leaders from all the surrounding kingdoms to come and discuss peace terms."

"Ah," said Whisp. "Did you hear that, lads? King Hanz is promoting peace talks!" he said, raising his voice. Valley jolted and the sound of clustered laughter echoed around her. Even though she knew everyone was behind bars, she suddenly felt surrounded.

"Well," she said softly, "I'll get the rest of the food."

Valley walked back to the torch and brought the rest of the food on the single tray to keep herself from having to make repeated trips. She stood before each cell, holding out the food and was continually surprised that the hands who received the gifts weren't grabby or desperate but steady and thankful. She felt suddenly like she wasn't serving prisoners, but legends, forgotten gods who slumbered away their days in this thick darkness, abandoned by the world.

The final prisoner was at the far end of the hall. As she approached, she held out the tray hesitantly, as if to a dog who might bite her. She had heard talking between the rest of the prisoners, but no sound ever came from this cell. For a moment, she wondered if it was empty.

"Happy Kingsummons," she said to the darkness, "I have brought you feast food on this festive night."

A hand emerged from the darkness. Valley gasped as it took hold not of food, but her own hand. The touch was gentle and the skin soft. Valley found that she couldn't breathe; she couldn't move; she couldn't recoil.

"Who are you?" asked a voice.

Valley couldn't respond, she could only stare at the hand, feeling its cold touch. She opened her mouth, as if to speak.

"Did you say your name was Valley?" asked the voice. It was the voice of a gentleman. It was smooth like honey, and she couldn't help but match it with a handsome face in her imagination. "Valley... Lovely, a lovely name."

"Such a charmer," came Whisp's voice. "He's only talking to you cause you're pretty."

Valley found the courage to pull her hand away. "Are you hungry?" she asked, pushing the tray toward the unseen prisoner.

"No," he said.

"He doesn't eat," Whisp said from the other end of the short hall. Valley raised her eyebrows.

"You don't eat?" Valley squinted confusedly. She had heard that Faeries could survive without food, but she didn't know anyone who had ever braved the pain of hunger long enough to try.

"I am fasting," he said, "Waiting."

"For what?" she asked. Her heart was thumping inside her chest, though she didn't know why.

"It was a pleasure to meet you, Valley."

Valley lowered her tray and nodded. "What is your name?"

There was no reply. She turned, leaving the mysterious voice alone in the darkness.

"Your title," he said. "Is it... I can see it."

Valley froze, turning to look back into the black. "*What* did you say?"

"I sense your power; I know it. I know what you are. Is it *you*?"

Valley didn't know what else to do; she ran away.

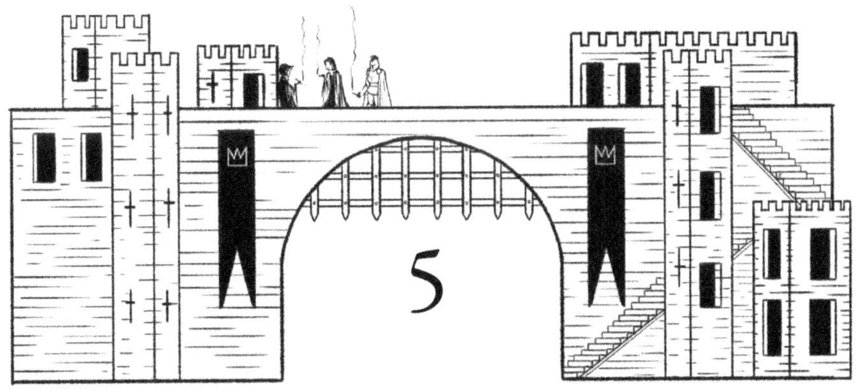

—— King Hanz ——

The Cloaked Captain

KING HANZ IMMERSED HIMSELF IN HIS LITTLE BOOK. Reading was one of his many daily rituals; it provided him with mindful rest from the intensities of kinghood. To him, there was nothing better than a dose of rich, indulgent fiction. *The Faeries might have lesser minds,* he thought, *but in centuries past they provided Raqia with a rich quantity of pocket-size thrills.* Hanz was proud of the collection he had amassed in his private library. On occasion, he wished he had more time in the day to read it, but for a man who was going to live forever, he didn't *need* time, did he? No, he contented himself with one solid bell of reading in the evening, from Firstdark to the first bell of night. And while the rest of the castle's residents settled into their beds, he was lazily transitioning.

Hanz snapped his book closed. He stretched, yawned, then placed his half-finished book on the table beside him and stood. He crossed his chambers, passing under a stone archway into his dressing room. It took several clicks to unfasten his cape and place it neatly on its stand, and several more to shed the rest of his kingly attire. He stood in the middle of the room, completely naked.

KING HANZ

Without the outfit, he was just a man. He turned his head, gazing into the full-length mirror beside him.

There he was: Hanz, the son of Timbre Wulf. He was 52 seasons of age yet without a single wrinkle or grey hair. He was handsome and caramel-skinned, like his father but without the scars of battle. His black wavy hair came just down to his shoulders, and his short beard was neatly and evenly trimmed. He had thick, squarish eyebrows and a sharply defined nose. His body was toned, lean, and well-built—though perhaps not as perfectly as when he was actively charging around on the plains some twenty seasons ago.

This image that he saw—it would never waste away, not when still over a hundred Faeries offered him their protection. Hanz raised his chin, smiling at himself. He was practically a god, though he would never call himself that. No—no he wasn't that prideful. He would let others say it, but never himself.

Stepping away from the mirror, Hanz reached for his black, silk cross-robe. He wrapped it around himself and tied it. Next, he slipped his feet into his soft, dark leather shoes. Then he reached for his second cross-robe, which was a slightly lighter shade of charcoal, and pulled it on, tying it tightly at the waist. Finally, he pulled his heavy, pitch-black hooded cloak from its mount and draped it over his shoulders. Turning to gaze at the new outfit in the mirror, Hanz grinned proudly at his second persona: not a king who raised children and conversed with nobles in the light of the day, but a rogue—a man, free of a crown and a reputation—free to work unobserved and unscrutinized in the shadows.

Once the blanket of night enveloped the city of Mensa and all of its daytime occupants went to sleep, another city came to life. The Mensa Castle network became the city of night, where a different sort of crowd kept the city busy and awake. Their deeds and dealings were not illuminated with the pure and timely light of day, but the flickering and ever-changing glow of torchlight. Here, night watchmen followed their own rules, gamblers found companions desperate enough to join their games, and procrastinators resorted to stealing clicks from their sleep to have more time. Hanz wasn't a watchman, nor was he the sort of gambler who hung around playing cards; he was a man who found the need for more hours for work and had found that a different part of himself came alive in the night city. He was king of the night life, but he wore it differently, only revealing his seal ring when truly necessary and otherwise enjoying the anonymity of being the 'Cloaked Captain', as most in the night watch called him.

Passing through the hidden staircase that led from his dressing room to one of the Eastern wall-tops, Hanz soon found himself strolling through the castle grounds and taking the night air deeply into his lungs. He approached a couple of officers who sat talking at the base of the north tower. He waved his hand as one of them noticed his arrival.

"Sire," Captain Oswald nodded respectfully but kept himself from bowing. It wasn't that Hanz didn't want anyone to know he was the King; he simply appreciated a more subtle sort of interaction in the night hours. It made things feel more casual.

"Captain," Hanz nodded back, crossing his arms as he leaned against the side of the tower.

Captain Oswald, who had been lighting his own cigar when he saw the King, held out a small metal box containing two other long wrapped sticks of tobacco.

Hanz nodded in thanks, taking one of the cigars and holding it to his lips as Oswald held out a light. Sigmund exhaled smoke through his nose and nodded to the king in recognition. Hanz and the two other officers smoked silently for a few clicks, watching from where they sat on the wall as the lower levels of the castle bustled with patrols and drills.

The Mensa Castle was a massive stone fortress with a central building where the king and his household resided; this central building was called the Inner Palace. But the castle network comprised so much more than Hanz's private home. There were also four main towers, an expansive barracks, a castle market, a bustling village, a Faerie enclosure, and so much more. The castle network was practically a bustling city all on its own; in fact, many noblemen hardly ever found reasons to leave it, as every sort of opportunity for pleasure and leisure seemed to reside there as well.

Hanz grinned proudly at his city through his teeth as he gnawed the end of his cigar. This habit wasn't the best for his yellowing teeth, but it was too late to try and stop it now. And it wasn't anything a little tooth-picking couldn't help.

"How'd the, *uh*—birthday party—go?" Sigmund asked.

"Which birthday party?" Hanz asked, absentmindedly blinking as his thoughts returned to the present moment.

Oswald chuckled. "Rosamond, your daughter?"

"Oh," Hanz shrugged, "Seems a bit hard to have a fully grown daughter, don't you think? Makes me feel a bit... old."

Sigmund blew smoke from his nostrils with an unimpressed sideways glance. "You're hardly one who should complain about being *old*, sire."

"Well, anyway," Hanz shrugged, "I didn't go to her party. I don't have time for things like that when Kingsummons starts tomorrow. The delegates should start arriving as early as tomorrow."

Oswald nodded. "Only you would be bold enough to invite them *all* to your home, sire. You really think having all of those cocks in one castle is a good idea? You're not worried you'll start a war?"

"No," Hanz said, stopping to take another puff, "I've thought this through."

"I *bet* you have," said Sigmund as he threw the butt of his cigar on the stones and crushed it beneath his foot.

"Don't mock me," Hanz said, glancing at the man.

"Wouldn't dare," Sigmund said coolly.

"How did the Faerie feast go?" Hanz turned his gaze toward Captain Oswald, who nodded as he thought about the question.

"It went fine, though one of the Faeries missed curfew."

"Who?" Hanz narrowed his eyes, then blinked, realizing who it would be. "Oh, damn—Valley." He comforted himself by drawing a deep inhale of smoke into his lungs, letting it linger there until his fingers began to tingle. He let it out. "Spending the night in the pit, is she?"

"No," Oswald said as he flicked his butt over the wall, letting it spark way down on the lower level as it fell. "I intervened and sent her inside. Figured since it was a feast day and since it was you who summoned her at such a late hour..."

"Well, yes," Hanz shrugged, "Suppose I forgot about the damned curfew. Glad she could make it to the feast, at least."

"Fire of Hades," Sigmund exclaimed with a look of distaste, "why those Faeries have to feast the night *before* the season starts is beyond me. Them and their strange ways."

"Faeries think a season starts at night." Oswald said casually. He stood and straightened his blue coat, checking to see that all his buttons were right-side-up.

Sigmund scoffed as he pulled out his toothpick. "Good for them. Meanwhile the real feast starts tomorrow. I assume you have time to come to *that*, sire?" he asked Hanz, his voice dripping with sarcasm.

Hanz rolled his eyes then glanced at Oswald again. "Is there some sort of badge—or—*seal* or something we can give Valley so that she can stay out past curfew?"

"You tell me, sire," Oswald said, "You're the King. But I can't imagine anyone is going to be thrilled about an unbonded Faerie getting that kind of privilege. To be honest, sire... none of us really know what to make of Valley. Is she a noble?"

"Hades, Captain," Hanz exhaled smoke through his teeth, growing more easygoing as the effects of the tobacco fizzled throughout his body. "A Faerie can hardly be noble."

Sigmund scoffed again, shaking his head.

"She's of age now," Oswald said, straightening his back. "If she is going to come and go from the Warrowing Village, she will need some official role in the castle that makes sense to people, or things could get awkward."

"I know," Hanz said, cocking his head to the side as he thought about it. "I'm still trying to crack that one, in a way that..." his voice trailed off.

"In the way that works best for you?" Sigmund asked, raising an eyebrow.

"Yes," Hanz said, sighing. "I am just trying to figure out what it is that I want."

Oswald shifted his weight from one leg to another. "You're thinking about bonding her to Rosamond? Might make a good birthday present."

"Well, I don't give a damn about that," Hanz snorted, "No. Rosamond will be married soon. No use bonding Valley to her, only for her to be taken away."

"The ward could be much more useful than that," Sigmund guessed, picking loudly at one of his teeth. He sported a shiny, silver toothpick with a handle that resembled a twisted thorny vine. "You could get a lot selling her to a noble—a king, even. She's a pretty little thing."

Oswald's eyes widened for a moment, and he glanced at Hanz silently, as if asking if that was truly something he would consider.

Hanz chuckled. "Wouldn't you love to know what went through my head, Sigmund?"

Sigmund shrugged. "It's diverting to guess sometimes. Anyway, its impressive how you have managed to grow the most lucrative slave trade in the world with completely willing victims, and all under the name of *virtue*."

"Oh, don't put it that way, you fiend." Hanz frowned. "You make me out like such a villain."

Sigmund bellowed a laugh, then quieted, nodding to himself. "Yes, sorry about that."

Oswald cleared his throat. "When do you think you will decide about the Faerie ward?" he asked. "Delegations begin to arrive this week, you say. I'll want to know what to tell my men. I can get her a seal, but we will need to know what it's *for*."

"I'll add it to the list," Hanz said, sounding pained. So much to do. "You'll hear from me by tomorrow."

"Very good sire," Oswald said, giving Hanz a slight nod. "I'm off then."

Sigmund and Hanz watched silently as Oswald, captain of Hanz's personal guard, marched off to the lower levels. Hanz turned his gaze to Sigmund. He was not the most attractive person to look at, with a doglike face and a thin mustache turned up at the sides, but there was something about his condescending and mischievous expressions that entertained Hanz.

Hanz placed his hand on the side of the tower, patting it for a moment. "Join me?" he asked.

"Fine," Sigmund shrugged, then turned to follow. Hanz unlocked the tower door and went inside.

They ascended the steps, remaining silent until they reached the top. At the summit of the tower was a second door that required a second key. Once it too was unbolted, the two men stepped inside, and Sigmund closed it behind them.

The circular room at the top of the tower was lit completely by a glowing red light which emanated from a massive, oval portal standing at the back of the room. Its edging curled with iron designs, and its face was like glowing red water, rippling with movement. Lining the walls on either side were long tables, covered in an odd collection of random objects. From jewelry to scepters, to buttons, to boxes—they all glowed faintly with their own light. Mounted just above the entry was a pair of eyeballs encased in a gold setting. Their deep blue irises were directed toward the red portal, but when Hanz stepped into the center of the room, they shifted slightly and gazed down at him.

Hanz stared at them, thumbing the stubble on his chin. Wherever that felling Sight Faerie was, he would know it was Hanz who was using the portal. Unless... did he know Hanz by sight? Surely not.

"I'll find you, you little devil," Hanz said, glaring at the eyes.

"Well?" Sigmund asked lazily as he strolled up to the red portal. "What have you got for me today?"

"I want you to question her again," Hanz said, "I know she knows something."

Sigmund frowned. "Again? Hades, sire, that woman won't talk, no matter *what* I do to her. If you want to find him, let me go look for other clues."

"Question her again," Hanz said firmly, staring deeply into the portal as the images within began to change. "She was the last person to see him."

"She won't talk."

"I don't *care*!" Hanz said, his voice rising into a yell.

Sigmund nodded. "Anything else?"

Hanz sighed, turning away from the portal to make eye contact with the man. "Yes."

Sigmund straightened his back. "Will I need a pen?"

"Yes."

The man sighed, pulling a pen from his vest pocket. He then pulled a small book from another pocket and opened it, glancing at the king expectantly.

"I need some court ladies," Hanz began, folding his hands behind his back as he moved to pace the room.

Sigmund giggled childishly.

"No," Hanz rubbed his head in vexation, "Not *those* kinds of court ladies. I need you to find some daughters from amongst my noblemen who would come and keep an eye on Rosamond. She's too old for a governess now," he stopped to think as Sigmund scribbled away in his little book. "Perhaps find some woman who might have a good influence on Rosamond."

"When you say *good* influence..." Sigmund lifted his pen thoughtfully.

"I mean someone who will keep her focused, you know, women who can teach her about what sort of fashion and attitudes please men. I feel she's a little headstrong for a wife, you know—she needs to be shown what submission looks like. I want someone who can push her in the right direction."

"*Mmhmm.*" Sigmund nodded as he continued to write.

"And I want you to find out how much money it's going to cost me to rush the build on the extension to the West," Hanz said, looking down at his feet as he scanned his thoughts.

"...to the West..."

"Also I need to meet with our new skydeacon. Set up a meeting sometime tomorrow."

"...Meeting with the skydeacon..." Sigmund mumbled.

"Also," Hanz lifted his head quickly, as if catching a straying thought. "Have one of your men watching the Warrowing Village—on the inside. I need to know if there is any talk of resisting the bondings."

"Anything else?"

Hanz looked quickly at the tall, shady man who stood loyally beside him, pen ready. "Yes," Hanz said slowly. "Find someone who can teach me to read lips, someone of low origin who won't recognize me by sight." He looked back toward his portal.

"I'd advise you not to gaze for too long," Sigmund said, "You have a meeting at the second watch bell, remember?"

"Of course I remember," Hanz said as he continued to search the portal, "I am heading there next."

"Very good," Sigmund said as he tucked his book back into his pocket. "I'll get to business. Good night, Sire." With a bow, he was gone.

Hanz exhaled a sigh of relief once alone. Sigmund wasn't as bad as some others, but he grew tiresome after too long. Sigmund didn't have an official title in Mensa, and that was how Hanz liked it. He was the head of the covert division that operated in the night city, and since Hanz didn't want anyone tracing their dealings back to the crown, he kept their meetings private.

Hanz studied the portal. His vision traveled through the images within the portal, and he searched nearby cities and towns until he heard the sound of the first bell. It was easy for time to escape him when he gazed into the portal; time seemed to lose all meaning in there. The bell tower was Hanz's only indicator for how much time passed.

Since time wasn't constant, the castle network relied heavily on the skydeacons, and their ability to announce the time of day. They were able to predict the pace of either a fast or slow day and used certain meteorological indicators to announce each hour—or "bell"—of the day or night. Many cities didn't announce the bells of the night, since most people would be asleep, but Mensa had enough nightlife that Hanz had all seven bells announced.

Hanz had given himself a bell's worth of searching at his portal before he decided it was time to set off. He slammed and locked the tower door behind him, startling a group of crows that picked at the cigar butts stamped into the ground. They dispersed in a chaotic cloud of wings around Hanz, like an ominous aura, as he marched in a beeline across the top of the wall towards the central stair. This stair led down to the marketplace.

Once in the market square, Hanz pulled his hood over his eyes for the sake of anonymity. The square was well lit by rows of torches and braziers and, though many of the stalls were closed for the night bells, some had only just opened. These stalls sold unique wares or offered street food for those whose entire lives were lived in the dark.

Hanz passed a few buildings which bustled with business; one was a cards house, another a whore house. He himself stopped at a public house called "The Wicker Basket" and pushed open the creaky door. The tavern had a low ceiling, a couple oil lamps, a few small tables, and a prominent bar. Behind the main counter stood a polished-looking man whose tidy appearance was juxtaposed with the dingy pub. He picked his teeth with an onyx-handled toothpick.

The barman stood a little straighter when he noticed Hanz approaching.

"How's business, Cave?" Hanz asked as he leaned against the counter. He pulled the front of his hood down to cover his eyes.

"Oh, it's alright," Cave said, pulling a glass from the shelf. He filled it with beer from a tap with an ornate handle. "I wouldn't mind a few more females coming in for a pint, though."

Hanz nodded as Cave responded in code, communicating that his contact had arrived. Hanz made eye contact with the barman. "Perhaps if you started pouring sherry, they might be more inclined."

Cave smiled, revealing a full set of brown teeth. "Over by the painting of the farm," he said. Hanz glanced to the corner of the tavern where a rustic oil painting hung over a small table. A cloaked man sat beneath it, smoking a pipe.

Hanz took his beer and moved to the table, sitting across from the mysterious figure.

The man shifted, pulling his pipe from his mouth, and lifted his chin to reveal his face. "Sort of a knavish place, wouldn't you say?" he said with a thick, upper-class lisp. "Not the sort of establishment where I usually conduct business."

Hanz connected eyes and gave the man an unimpressed eyebrow raise. "I didn't have to meet you at all."

"No, no—oh, *cards*, sire," the man leaned back. "How many felling tests do I have to pass before you will trade with me?"

"None," Hanz said, "If you don't make a fool of yourself tonight, Lord Evenstine."

Highlord Evenstine, one of Hanz' richest and most powerful noblemen. He had been key in helping Hanz unite the Northeast region and oversaw the sea trade as Bridgeport's highlord. For several weeks, Hanz had tested his loyalty and ability to keep secrets before finally agreeing to meet with him.

"Don't mock me, sire," Evenstine said. "Are you going to sell to me or not?"

"I am," Hanz said. "Tell me how many you were hoping for."

"Well, at first I thought I would start with one—see how it settled in—but then I thought my wife might want one," he said as his eyes wandered around.

"Let's start with one," Hanz said, "And you can see how you like him."

Evenstine shifted in his seat and cleared his throat. "Now, were you thinking a 'he' or a 'she'?"

"He," Hanz said flatly.

Evenstine nodded. "What are my options? And what's the likelihood of—" he paused to search the room for eavesdroppers, then leaned forward with a whisper, "—of immortality?"

Hanz studied the highlord's face for a moment, then said, "That is all up to you and if you can gain their loyalty. I can bond a Faerie to you by law, but I cannot make them choose you as their mortal. When a Faerie gives you his protection, it is something they have to want. They can't do it out of obligation."

Evenstine nodded, watching as Hanz pulled a small book from his cloak pocket and placed it on a table. "I have a few I am willing to consider passing along to you," he said as he opened the book.

The small book was a record of Hanz' current Faerie candidates who were ready for bonding. Each spread had a hand-drawn portrait on the left page and a short description on the right. The highlord took the book and began to thumb through the pages. "I don't see your ward in here," he said off-handedly.

"She's not up for sale," Hanz said, leaning back.

Evenstine paused to look up from the book. "Is it true they will voluntarily scapegoat for you?"

Hanz nodded. "Yes, they see it as part of their bonding duty."

Evenstine continued to scan the book, nodding with admiration. "You have really done a thorough job here. I'm genuinely impressed, Sire! And they are—they're *willing* to do this?"

"That's the beauty of it," Hanz said, taking the book from Evenstine's hands. "They're not slaves that need guards and chains. They're the most loyal of subjects."

"Sure, but," Evenstine cleared his throat, "by *law* they're slaves, are they not?"

"I don't like to use that word," Hanz said quietly, "But essentially, yes. Once bonded, they are part of your... property."

"Speaking of," Evenstine said, "how much is this property going to *cost* me, after all?"

"That depends on which Faerie you choose."

"Well, I liked the look of a few." He crossed his arms. "The Faerie of the Sea, though.... I rather think he might help me with some of my endeavors."

"Ah," Hanz nodded, "Polaris, yes—he's a special one."

"Polaris," Evenstine grinned, "I rather like him."

"You can't even begin to calculate what sort of benefit he might be to your business," Hanz said sharply, "He's one of the greats, *extremely* powerful if given an Imperium, especially more so if he is near the Sea."

"Well?" Evenstine asked, growing stressed. "How *much*?"

Hanz sighed, shaking his head. "I can hardly part with one of the greats, Samish."

The highlord slammed his fist on the table. "What would it *cost* me?"

Hanz leaned back, savoring that sweet moment when he had the upper hand in a bargaining session. "A lot."

"Tell me."

"First, a down payment." Hanz leaned in close, looking Evenstine directly in the eyes. "And not a small one, either."

The highlord bit his lip from under his beard, narrowing his eyes in discomfort. "Do you mean..."

"I'm only just beginning." Hanz held up his finger then continued. "I will require a certain percentage of your profits. As your profits rise, so will my portion. I would be handing you a lifetime of fortune and success. I am practically giving you the god of the Seas—yours to do your every bidding. A proverbial genie in a lamp, living only to serve *you*. The Faeries are ultimately loyal to me. I am their King. And they serve me. So if you want one of them, you will have to pay tribute to me, their King."

Evenstine pulled the side of his mouth into a pessimistic line, then nodded. "And what sort of down payment are we talking about?"

Hanz sat back, grinning. This felt good; it felt *so* good. "Yes," he said, "About that."

⚜ ⚜

Hanz left the Wicker Basket a much richer man. Keeping control of his highlords was a balancing act, but the Faerie trade seemed to be the ideal solution. He had something they all wanted, and it kept them coming back to him. While Hanz was King of Mensa, he had only become so by making a lot of deals with the highlords who owned the lands. But one by one, they would fall into his net by giving over their lands to him in exchange for their own personal Faerie slaves.

The third bell of night sounded just as Hanz felt himself growing tired. He began to stride back toward the Inner Palace, letting his hood drop down behind him. Still, the thrill of the trade buzzed inside him. He had dragged out the bartering with Evenstine to increase the suspense, and it worked, by heavens—it worked! The highlord had not only given Hanz *his capital city* but a shocking amount of gold. Not to mention the interest Evenstine would be paying for the rest of his pathetic life. It felt too easy! But no—it wasn't easy; it was hard work. And he had done it, by heavens. He had done it!

King Hanz crested the top of the outdoor stone stairs which led back to his private entrance into his home palace. Someone stood there, waiting for him.

"Captain Oswald, what can I do for you?" Hanz asked through a yawn. It was getting late.

"Sire," Oswald said, "may I speak privately with you for a moment?"

"If you walk with me, you have until I arrive at my quarters. Then I am in bed," Hanz said.

"Thank you, sire," Oswald said, joining the King's side. The two walked through the private door and on through a quiet hall which led directly to King Hanz' chambers.

"What can I do for you, Captain?" Hanz asked.

"Well, sire," Oswald sounded uncharacteristically nervous. "It's about Valley, Sire."

King Hanz halted in his steps and turned to look the captain straight in the eyes. "Floods, Oswald—are you about to ask me to bond her with you?"

Oswald's face instantly turned a deep red. "Sire, I—"

"No," Hanz shook his head, "No, no. Hades—where is this coming from, Oswald?"

"Please, sire," Oswald bowed his head deferentially for a moment, then raised his palm, "That is not what I am asking."

"Oh thank the heavens," Hanz sighed, "Sorry, Captain. Hades, I am so tired. What is it then?"

"I had an idea about her: about how to get her easier passage throughout the castle during Kingsummons."

"Well?" Hanz grunted impatiently, charging forward in the direction of his chambers and, ultimately, his bed. "What is it?"

"Well, if she had an official role within the main palace, she could be given her own quarters. That way, she would not need to reside in the Warrowing Village with the rest of the Faeries. Give her a position as a housekeeper and she could live with the other maids and come and go that way."

"But she's a Faerie," Hanz said, "She can't live outside of the Warrowing Village without being bonded. It's too dangerous."

"*I* guard the Inner Palace, Sire. It would not need to be dangerous for her," said Oswald.

"The Warrowing Village isn't a home for Faeries, Captain," Hanz halted to make his point. "It's a vault where I keep my most treasured things. Unless she is bonded, I don't know if I want her residing in the palace. Someone else might try and..." his voice trailed off.

Oswald cleared his throat. "I don't think anyone will try to kidnap her, Sire. Nothing like that has ever—"

"We are about to have *kings* residing in the inner palace, Captain!" Hanz said in a raised voice, "I don't want to risk *anything*. But you have helped me make my decision."

"I—I *have*?" Oswald blinked. "And what decision is that?"

"I will have her bonded. I can't think of another way." Hanz nodded to himself. "Yes, I'll have her bonded tomorrow."

"Oh," Oswald's eyes widened. "T–to...?"

"To me."

6

—— Rook ——

The Unlikely Wing

ROOK WAS, APPARENTLY, A WING NOW. While he had learned to fight during his time as a mercenary, Rook didn't exactly see himself as a soldier. And while he had lived around nobles at one time, he never felt as though he belonged among them. Now, he was a Wing, a role encompassing both a soldier *and* a noble.

And why? Why, out of all people, had Highlord Cato decided to make Rook his Wing? He could have promoted any of his loyal men to that role, surely. Rook had to assume that Cato was truly moved by Rook's valiant rescue.

To be a nobleman's wing meant to be constantly at his side. As Rook stared at Cato from the other side of the small table, he wondered if his proximity to the man would help or hinder his mission. Having a high connection might give him access to more intimate places. And yet—he would be in the spotlight. *Everyone* would be aware of him. Surely that wasn't a good thing.

With his new and apparently improved look, Rook wore the clothes befitting the wing of a highlord. The outfit consisted of tightly tailored trousers, a white shirt with far too many ruffles in the collar, a black waistcoat lined with metallic crimson embroidery, and an open, black coat with a dozen useless gold buttons lining either side. The long coat draped down against his calves, and it was clasped neatly at the waist by a belt sporting a large gold buckle in the shape of two Edgeland bird heads facing each other. Upon Cato's personal request, Rook had washed and combed his hair, but before long, it returned to the usual rough display of unruly black curls. They fell loosely on either side of his face, not quite long enough to touch his shoulders but thick enough to slightly distract from his scars

Rook looked far more noble than he felt. At one time, he had found the need to prioritize looks over comfort, but he had happily left those days behind. He preferred an inconspicuous life: one where he could live one day to the next without being noticed by the average passer-by. But here he sat stiffly opposite a highlord on a padded seat, in a fancy carriage headed directly toward the hot center of Raqia's politics. He had worked hard to avoid these kinds of situations, yet here he was—by choice—wearing a felling *suit*.

While Rook sat down in the carriage with Cato, the soldiers remained up on the roof. Cato's guards were dressed to match his banner in squid ink black with a crimson Edgeland bird symbol on their chests. Cato liked to call his three guards "Black Eagles". Of course, this title officially referred to the legendary archers who guarded the city of Bavel, but Cato took almost nothing seriously, so it didn't seem all that surprising to Rook that he would give his personal guard a playful name. He wasn't sure what *they* thought of their silly pet name, but they never complained.

"Oh, must you look so awkward?" Cato complained, leaning back into his cushion and giving Rook an unflattering view of his under-chin. "I had so enjoyed your makeover, yet with that expression you look positively worse!"

Rook pulled the corner of his mouth to the side. "Sorry," he said, trying to relax his posture. "Just breaking in the suit, I suppose."

Cato snorted a laugh and looked to the side, pulling open his curtain to peek out his window.

The carriage was the shape of a long rectangular box hoisted up on six massive swiveling wheels. It was about seven feet high and fifteen feet long, essentially a small living space complete with a sealed-off bed chamber, a dining table with chairs, and a padded lounging spot. A carriage this large could only be hauled by something as massive and strong as an aurochs—the legendary beasts of the west.

Cato had left the Edgelands with two aurochs but now had to travel a little slower with only one, having lost the other back in Bunting. Golden Grains, the remaining aurochs, was nearly as large as the carriage itself, having two massive five-foot horns sticking out on either side of his head, then jutting forward. He was essentially a large bull in appearance, though infinitely more majestic. Most people in the east had never seen one, but from what Rook had heard, aurochs were noble beasts, proud and independent. It was rare to see one acting as a beast of burden. An aurochs would only be seen pulling royal carriages if he had been persuaded to do so by someone close to him.

Whenever their crew arrived in Mensa, they were sure to be something of a spectacle. A highlord from a remote and ignored land arrives with a legendary beast in tow, only three guards, and a mysterious wing? *Definitely* a spectacle! It wasn't exactly how Rook had envisioned himself arriving in Mensa—being noticed by all. He would have to deal with his discomfort at being the center of attention.

"Cato?" Rook cleared his throat, leaning back and trying to play his part a little better by proving he could relax. "Can I ask you something?"

Cato grinned. "Bold enough to call me by my first name? Even *Tercius* won't do that!" Cato spat Tercius' name like a curse word. Thankfully, Tercius and the other two 'Eagles' sat on the top of the carriage as they traveled. Rook didn't feel the need to be constantly looking in Tercius' direction to make sure he wasn't growing annoyed at the constant attention. Rook hoped, likely in vain, that Cato wouldn't talk about *him* in the same way—as a prop in his meaningless banter.

"Do you have a problem with me dropping the 'lord', Lord?" Rook curled up the side of his mouth into a smile.

Cato giggled childishly, snapping his fingers as he sat forward. "Cards, I like you."

"The Edgelands are a western country. What are you doing traveling to Mensa?"

"Oh," Cato's smile waned slightly, and he nodded. "I thought you were going to ask me something more fun. Yes, about that. Don't you know about the peace talks?"

Rook shook his head. "No."

"Well, why would you?" he said more to himself than to Rook. Cato cleared his throat. "Open a bottle of vino, and I'll tell you all about it."

Rook blinked, "I'm sorry, what?"

"All my gods," Cato sighed helplessly, then pointed to a locked cupboard on the other side of the carriage. "In there: liquor!"

"Right," Rook smirked, standing. It took him a moment to catch his balance, as walking across a moving carriage was an unfamiliar experience. He unhinged the protective lock and pulled out a glass bottle of amber vino. He held it up towards Cato, then lurched unexpectedly as the carriage lumbered over a bump in the road. "This one alright?" he asked as he recovered.

Cato shrugged. "Whatever."

The nobleman didn't seem to care about the quality of the liquor as much as its side-effects. Rook found a pair of glasses and carefully brought everything back to where they were sitting. They seemed to be traveling through an area with annoyingly uneven terrain. Rook looked down apprehensively at the sloshing vino bottle, hesitating to open it.

"Are you sure you—"

"Just *open* it!" Cato waved his hand impatiently.

Rook shrugged and pulled out the cork. He proceeded to pour each glass half-full and distribute the drinks between them. He leaned back, taking a casual sip as if he deserved to be drinking with a nobleman.

"Right," Cato sighed, letting out a deep exhale, after swallowing the entirety of the glass in one gulp. "The *peace* talks." He pointed at the table between them. "Open that drawer."

Rook looked down at the table attached to the floor of the carriage. There was a wide, shallow drawer spanning the length of the table. He opened it. Inside was a long, rolled up scroll. He pulled it out and looked at Cato for direction. Cato nodded to him impatiently. Rook laid the sizable scroll on the table and rolled it open. It was a political map of Raqia.

"Alright," Cato said, surprising himself with a sudden belch. He leaned forward over the map and slammed his index finger at the River Copse which cut through Raqia's center diagonally and ran all the way to the southeast corner. "Bunting on Copse."

"The village you never intended to know intimately," Rook said with a hint of irony in his voice.

Cato chuckled. "And a place so small we had to pen in the name afterwards!"

"I can see that," Rook said as he glanced at the square, unrefined handwriting beside the dot that represented his hometown.

"Well," Cato scratched his chin for a moment, "I hope Tercius spelled it correctly."

"He did."

"Well, anyway," the highlord cleared his throat. "We came from here," he said as he slid his index finger southwestwards, dragging along the southern coastline for a moment, until it landed on a place marked 'Edgeland'. "Our capitol," he said, "Where I come from."

"Nice place?" Rook asked.

Cato shrugged. "Nice enough. Anyway, the King of Mensa sends me an unexpected letter!" He raised his eyebrows dramatically, inviting anticipation. Rook leaned back, watching. Cato spread his open hands into the air, miming a tale. "The great king of the north invites us to come and discuss universal *laws*!"

Rook pursed his lips. "King Hanz?"

"Yes," Cato dropped his hands anticlimactically. "Look here." His finger traveled northeast until it nearly touched Arelle, the Faerie city. "Mensa." The word, resting artistically inside a drawn banner, marked a kingdom that seemed to cover a quarter of the map. "What once was a hundred separate Human cities and settlements is now a prosperous kingdom united under one, seemingly immortal man." He raised his eyebrows twice for effect.

"King Hanz," Rook said again, less enthusiastically this time. Immortal— it wasn't a secret to the rest of the world that King Hanz had Faerie protection.

"King Hanz," Cato said in a thoughtful voice as he moved the tip of his index finger over a large star which indicated the capitol. "He secured a strategic spot. It was a spot that once represented the most powerful Human kingdom on Raqia." His eyes seemed to wander off to a distant place.

"You mean the city of Bavel." Rook said as his eyes focused on a decorative banner, marking the city-kingdom of Bavel. Interestingly, the kingdom seemed to rest within the vast borders of King Hanz' Kingdom, Mensa. Cato tapped his finger loudly on the spot where Bavel sat.

"A mysterious place," he said with that same distant look in his eyes, "For thirty seasons, no one has passed through its walls, coming or going. For thirty seasons, nothing but silence."

Rook nodded. "Ever since King Somenus died," he said, "Bavel has been quiet."

"Yes. Very quiet. No visitors admitted, no citizens traveling outside—nothing." Cato stopped to indulge in a deep yawn. He then opened his eyes and held out his glass, shaking it at his wing. Rook refrained from an eyeroll as he refilled it. "Anyway," Cato said, "Shadowroots and the other cities surrounding Bavel apparently grew tired of being left out of everything, so they joined with King Hanz, who worked *very hard* to make his own kingdom," he said in a patronizing voice, "So!"

"Mensa," Rook said as his eyes roved across the map.

"Yes, Mensa's borders run as far west as the Bridge of Cally, as far south as Longton, as far east as the Black Sea, and all the way up to the very gates of Arelle. Some guess that the Faerie city *itself* is part of Mensa's lands!"

Rook shook his head. "That's not what I have heard."

"Well," Cato shrugged, "King Hanz united the lands which surround Bavel, and he united the lands containing most of Raqia's Faeries—outside of Arelle, anyway—and he has set up trade routes with Sol, the Gramenlands, the Vastlands, the Winglands, and even the Elven kingdoms! Hades, *we* even have a trade route with Mensa! Now." He stopped to clear his throat. "Now, he wants us all to meet together to talk about universal laws."

"Why?" Rook asked flatly, hiding the suspicion he felt inside himself.

"Well," Cato held up his hands innocently. "It's not that hard to guess; We all hate all the extra fuss it takes to trade with each other. We all operate under varying laws and regulations—*especially* when it comes to trade. It will be economically beneficial for us all to figure out a common standard for international relations. Plus," he stopped to finish his second glass of vino, "petty wars over border disputes pop up pretty often, and it costs a lot of precious money to support armies, you know."

"I can imagine," Rook said. "So why have *you* decided to attend the peace talks?"

Cato blinked a few times, studying his new wing. "Well," he looked down at the map, "We may be on the edge of the eastern world, but we *are* a part of the trade network. If laws and standards are going to be talked about in Mensa, we want to be a part of it! I hate the thought of being left out, you know." Cato said the words, but as Rook studied Cato's expression, he wondered if he meant them.

Rook crossed his arms, neglecting to pour a third drink for the lord who grew desperate enough to hold up his glass. "You don't care about being left out of peace talks," Rook said, "Why *did* you come?"

Cato's face mimicked shock and horror for a moment, then gave up. "Dogs, I don't know," he shrugged.

"What did your king offer you?" Rook asked. "You know, to make the trip?"

Cato glanced down at the map, nodding to himself for a moment, then looked up at Rook with a sinister smile. "It's a little thing called *money*."

"He offered you money?"

Cato's face grew more distasteful. "No," he said, "he didn't *offer* me money."

Rook began to nod knowingly to himself. "Ah," he said with a grin, "Lost a bet, did you?"

Cato's eyes widened, studying the young Rook for a moment, then he leaned back, relaxing his face into a playful smile. "Well—rather—*yes*."

"I suppose that's why you couldn't get an entire battalion to come with you?" Rook asked.

Lord Cato shrugged his shoulders. "Well," he said, "I suppose there's ample opportunity to *make* money on this venture. You know, there's even talk of an heiress."

"Oh yeah?" Rook raised his eyebrows, "Tell me about that."

The boredom was stronger than the curiosity, as evidenced on Cato's face, and he huffed to himself in defeat. "Oh Hades, I don't know," he mumbled, "Hanz trying to marry off his daughter."

"Oh yeah?" Rook chuckled to himself. Nobles were such fascinating people. They held all the cards yet seemed to be so stressed about losing them that they were constantly searching for ways to sell them off to others for protection.

Cato took the bottle of vino into his own hand and didn't even bother to pour it into his glass. He tipped the bottle into his mouth, took a large swig, then leaned back with a hazy look of apathy. "How much would *you* pay for a garden, Rook?"

"A *garden*?" Rook blinked, "Oh—right." Rook wasn't fond of the euphemism; only one with a vulgar mind and a simplistic view of a woman would use it. He frowned with discomfort. "I..." He couldn't think of a good response. "How much would *you* pay?"

Cato made a deliberating noise. "King Hanz will tempt us to buy his garden, I think... and it won't be cheap, for one of two reasons," he said, "Either his garden is pretty enough for the money, or it leads somewhere strategic—grants access, if you know what I mean. Whoever marries her gets a seat next to Hanz at the table, so to speak." He stopped to sniff, thinking. "The former is hardly worth the price. And the latter, well, I am not desperate enough to make friends with the King of Mensa, so that has no real pull on me."

"And what if it offered both?" Rook asked.

Cato paused then shook his head. "Well, acquiring a garden that is both beautiful *and* leads somewhere I wasn't able to go before—well that just stinks of a bargain. And a bargain is too cheap for me."

Rook raised an eyebrow. "So you get the most satisfaction out of turning down those kinds of offers?"

"Yes," Cato said with a grin. "I feel rather set on *not* giving the Mensa King any satisfaction."

"So let me get this straight;" said Rook, "your reasons for traveling to Mensa are firstly, to fulfill your end of a bet, and secondly, to find opportunities to make money or connections on the side. And *yet*, you are not interested in making connections with Mensa because you don't want to give King Hanz the satisfaction of giving them to you?"

Cato frowned deeply. "Hades, Rook, when you put it like *that...*" He straightened his back, giving himself a reassuring nod. "Well... I suppose I'll just have to enjoy myself while I am there and soak up whatever *felling* generosity Hanz wants to waste on us hedonists. I mean—I have to be completely honest with you, Rook..."

"Oh, yes?" Rook leaned back with an amused expression.

"I really don't have any damned interest in politics. It's all a big sham to me."

Rook shook his head. How depressing it was to hear a highlord admit that he took the weight of his lands and all his subjects so lightly. He could, however, somewhat see Cato's point.

"I suppose it all seems a bit of a joke to me, too," he said, "World leaders always seem more concerned about the finances and ease of things, rather than what they should be concerned about: the people they lead." Rook paused, glancing at Cato, who didn't seem to be paying attention anymore. "Well anyway," he mumbled, "I can't blame you for not taking it all very seriously."

"Why don't you let me ask *you* something, Rook old boy," Cato said as he leaned forward toward the table.

Rook crossed his arms. "Alright."

"You, the man who said he was so happy in his quaint little town, turned me down. Then—not a day later—you come back to say you *do* want to come with me. So tell me, *Rook*, what is it that *you* want to find in Mensa?"

Rook drew in a deep breath, looking to the side as he chose a narrative. "There are some things I am curious about—in Mensa, you know—and I decided that this was my best opportunity to go and find out what I wanted to know."

"Well!" Cato startled Rook with a loud clap of his hands. "Now, *that's* entertaining! So mysterious, old boy. Alright, you've got me. What is it you are curious about in Mensa?" He leaned forward, overacting his anticipation.

Rook stared at the highlord for a moment, thinking. "Now, what fun would it be for you if I just *told* you? You're going to have to guess."

"Ah," Cato nodded gleefully, "Alright—so you're going to give me something entertaining to do in the coming season? You want me to try and guess what you're up to?"

"Sure," Rook shrugged. "It might be entertaining for me, too." In actuality, Rook would rather *not* have someone watching and analyzing his every move as he tried to steal a pair of eyes from the most powerful king in the world. But it was too late to try and change his tactic now. He'd have to throw out some red herrings for the man and perhaps devise a fake reason for coming to Mensa. A fake romance could probably do the trick; perhaps he could convince Cato he was meeting a lover. But, no... Rook couldn't imagine anything worse than even *pretending* to give attention to a woman, especially when just about everyone of that sex was revolted by his face. Well, sooner or later he would think of something. He would *have* to.

"Well, I appreciate you trying to make yourself as interesting as possible," Cato said, "It will make this trip less tiresome."

"Happy to be of service," Rook said, standing. "I think I'll ride on top for a bit."

"Oh, don't do that!" Cato whined. "I hate drinking alone!"

"I think you'll be fine." Rook said as he walked to the back door of the carriage. He was confident he could climb up without asking Tercius to bring Golden Grains to a halt.

"Oh, Rook?" Cato called out, turning his body to try and keep eye contact as Rook passed.

"What?" Rook paused with his hand on the handle of the little door.

"Those scars, how *did* you... come on," he cleared his throat, "come on, tell me what happened."

Rook left.

He swung out into the night air and latched the door closed. He held on tightly to the handlebar mounted on the back of the carriage and felt the wind moving past him on both sides as the vehicle charged along. The night still had some purple color; Rook guessed it must still be the first bell. He scaled up the ladder which led to the top of the carriage and soon found himself face to face with Titus, one of Cato's Eagles.

Titus nodded in Rook's direction and stepped back to let him pass. The top of the carriage was like a small terrace with siding, giving the guards their own place during the long and arduous travel from the Edgelands to Mensa. From here, Rook could see Tercius sitting down by the front of the carriage next to Fern, who was holding the reins of Golden Grains, the majestic aurochs. Rook made his way toward them.

"Damn," Tercius cursed, "What are *you* doing up here?"

Rook raised an eyebrow. "Am I not allowed up here?"

"Well, of course you are," Tercius said, in his surprisingly smooth and gentlemanly voice. "We just hoped you wouldn't think of coming up here."

"Oh?" Rook smiled, "Have I made things worse for your travels?"

"On the contrary," Fern yelled over his shoulder, keeping his eyes on the road ahead, "You've made things a lot better for us."

"Oh?" Rook glanced over at Tercius, who nodded in agreement. "How is that?"

Tercius finally gave Rook the courtesy of turning to face him. "Since you've joined us," he said, "you keep *him* distracted. All the time you've been down there, we've finally experienced a little peace and qu—"

Tercius was interrupted by the disturbingly loud sound of Cato pounding on the ceiling under them. "Tercius!" Cato called, "Anyone?"

Tercius glanced meaningfully at Titus, who sighed in defeat, then climbed down the back ladder. Tercius turned back to Rook with a look that said, *See?*

"Right," Rook chuckled, "Well, even *I* need a break sometimes."

"And well deserved," Tercius smiled, looking somewhat unrecognizable for a moment; Rook had grown so used to the usual stoic expression that Tercius wore like a helmet. "Have a seat."

Rook seated himself next to Tercius on the bench that ran along the port side of the carriage. The soldier pulled a metal case from his belt pouch and opened it, offering Rook a cigar. Rook smiled in thanks, taking one. He himself didn't smoke, but at times like these, it was better to not reject any sign of friendship. After receiving a light from Tercius, Rook leaned back, puffing silently.

"How long have you served Cato?" Rook asked at length.

Tercius spoke with his cigar pinched between his teeth. "He's been my superior since I was a lad, way back when I joined the force." He shifted his eyes to the side to look at Rook. "Sorry for shooting you."

Rook shook his head, letting a puff of smoke free from his lips. "No, no," he said, "All is forgotten."

"You seem to bounce back very quickly," Tercius examined Rook's face carefully, no doubt eyeing his deep and plentiful scars. "Either that, or you have learned to ignore pain."

"To be honest," Rook straightened and stretched out his wounded arm, "You made a pretty clean hit. The arrow went straight through. No harm done."

Tercius snorted. "You can probably fool others, but not me. I know a man can feel pain without expressing it. You have the face of a soldier. I can see it."

Rook smiled, taking that as a compliment. "I'm not much of a soldier, but thanks."

Tercius smiled with his teeth, still holding his cigar in his mouth. "I mean that you know how to grin through your pain. And you sure know how to handle yourself in a fight. Don't lie to me. You've served."

"I haven't served," Rook replied, "but I did live as a mercenary for a while. Traveled around taking this job and that. Did a lot of bodyguard and escort work."

"Where'd you learn to fight like that?"

"Well," Rook pulled his cigar from his lips and blew a cloud of smoke into the air, watching it escape quickly behind them as their carriage plowed forward. How should he answer this? Tercius was the sort of man who could spot a lie. "I trained alongside an experienced fighter for a time," he moved his eyes to the horizon, "How long until we reach Mensa?"

"A few days," Tercius cleared his throat, "Maybe less."

"And what happens when we get there?"

"Well, you and the highlord will be given rooms in the palace main, and we will stay in the barracks. The Mensa King doesn't want a bunch of soldiers in the inner palace, and who could blame him? So you'll be Cato's main security when we are not there." Tercius raised one of his grey eyebrows, "Think you can handle that?"

Rook cocked his head to the side. "You saw me fight. Do *you* think I can handle that?"

Tercius cackled. "True enough."

"Is... isn't it a bit odd for Cato to trust me—a total stranger—to be his protection? I mean... you've served him since you were young. Why wouldn't he make *you* his wing?"

Tercius looked down at his shoes as he thought about how to answer. "In many ways, yes. Yes, it is odd. He's a prominent leader in the Edgelands, and we have been at his side for decades. But in another way, no. No, it's not all that odd." Tercius sighed. "Our highlord may be a bit strange, but he is a good judge of character. If you've won his trust, you've won it for good."

"And you don't... you don't resent the fact that—"

"Resent?" Tercius barked a laugh. "I am no wing, Rook. Cato knows this. We all know this. We are soldiers, through and through. We don't want to sit around and—" he flapped his hand lazily in the air, "play cards, or–or–or," he scoffed, "suffer *conversations*. No. In all honesty, we are relieved that it's you and not us. You can protect Cato from other noblemen, and we will protect him from other soldiers. That's just the way it works."

"So," Rook leaned forward, resting his elbows on his knees, "Is that all it means to be a wing? To protect?"

"Oh, I forget the fancy saying. Protect, complement, entertain? Hades, I don't know. You're like his personal knight. Usually, you'd have a title—but for you we will just have to *pretend*." He shrugged.

"Hmm," Rook nodded thoughtfully. "So he's not interested in giving me a *real* title?"

Tercius scoffed. "Have you got *real* land? Are you related to anyone important?"

Rook shook his head. "No."

Tercius shrugged again. "Like I said, we will have to pretend."

"So I'll be staying in the Inner Palace? Like—where King Hanz lives?" Rook asked.

Tercius gave him a nod. "Yes," he said, "why?"

Rook shrugged. "Just kind of odd to think I'll be that close to the top of the world."

Tercius scoffed, spitting the butt of his cigar out of his mouth, over the side of the carriage. "Top of the world," he mocked, "*Right.*"

Rook sensed the tip of an iceberg but didn't press further. He sighed, taking another puff. "You know," he said in a more playful tone, "I bet Cato would give me land if I asked him."

"Oh, you do, do you?" Tercius raised his eyebrows in amusement. "And how is that?"

Rook smiled widely. "Because the man takes absolutely nothing seriously. I have a feeling if I made it sound fun enough, I could get him to give me *his* title!"

Tercius let out a deep, bellowing laugh, tipping his head back dramatically. "No," he calmed himself, "No—I don't think you've quite figured him out yet. He's not as daft as he makes himself out to be."

"Let's put some money on it," Rook nudged the soldier in the side. "I'll get Cato to give me a title."

"Do you *have* any money?" Tercius pursed his lips doubtfully.

"Well, no—not yet." Rook paused, touching his pockets. "Come on, what do you want to bet?"

Tercius tapped his chin thoughtfully, then grinned. "Loser tries to ride Golden Grains."

Rook blinked. "The—the aurochs? Do you have a death wish?"

"Do *you*?" asked Tercius.

Rook shook his head. "You're crazy."

Tercius shrugged. "Are you going to take the bet or not?"

"Oh, you're on." Rook couldn't help but grin. "How long do I have?"

Tercius shrugged. "Get yourself a title by the time we reach Mensa, or you ride Grains as a show for the Mensa King. If I lose, I'll ride him."

"Easily done."

Tercius chuckled to himself. "Alright," he said reluctantly, "I suppose you're not *only* good for distracting our Lord. You're alright."

"Ah," Rook leaned back with a feeling of triumph. "How kind of you to say."

"So, uh," Tercius pointed at Rook's face with his cigar. "Where *did* you get those scars?"

And that was where the conversation ended.

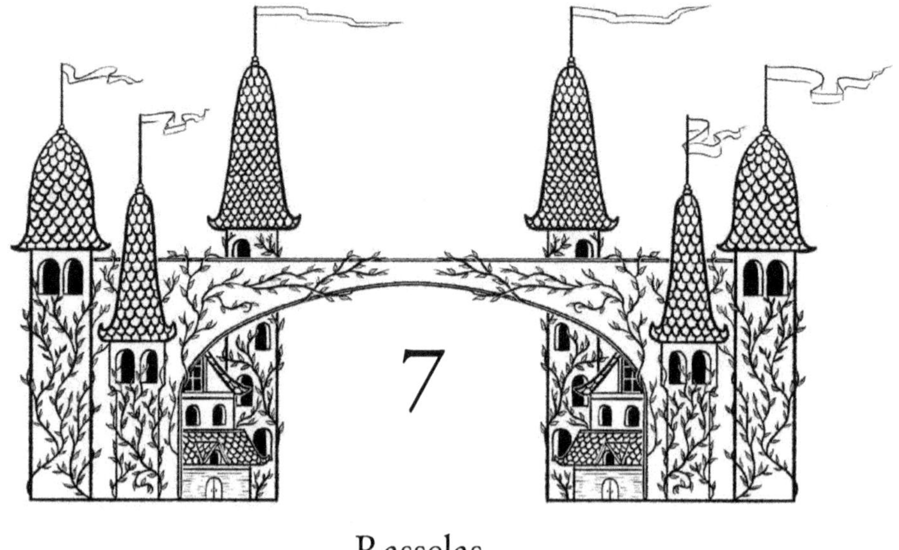

—— Rasselas ——

The Reluctant Wing

WHY THE ELVES ALWAYS INSISTED ON *walking*, Rasselas could not fathom. Sure—they had the sort of high-endurance bodies that allowed for a full day's walk without so much as a calloused toe, but still, it didn't feel very dignified for a prince like Rasselas. It was even worse for his clothes. He *was* wearing a travel outfit, booted with long, sturdy leather things, but it still seemed a shame when even those grew stained and worn.

The party had stopped to camp at the Tradings River crossing and Rasselas was standing on a stone outcropping which hung over the edge of the roaring waters. He had taken four warriors, four servants, a skydeacon, and of course, his wing, Thorne. The Elven servants worked quietly to set up the tents while the warriors stood at the four corners of their camp, keeping watch.

Embers soared over Rasselas' head gracefully in a wide circle, then fluttered down toward him. The prince held out his arm and waited as the raptor dropped down to clutch it with his talons.

How was that? The bird blinked, cocking its head to the side curiously.

"It wasn't bad," Rasselas said as he reached out to straighten one of Embers' stray feathers. "You're getting better."

Well, Embers shifted his weight from foot to foot, looking down at his talons. *I would have begun practicing more graceful landings sooner, if you had only told me I was hurting your arm.*

Rasselas snorted. "Well I wasn't really going to admit that a bird was hurting my arm, you know. Seems a little pathetic."

I take offense to that, Embers said, *I am no mere pigeon. I am a Thunderbird. I could hurt anyone's arm, if I wanted to. I could wound even the gruffest of characters, I am sure.*

"Oh," Rasselas frowned, "That's fine and all, but I hope you didn't intend to use the word gruff when describing *me*."

I wouldn't dare, Embers blinked. *'Foppish' suits you better.*

"*Foppish*?" Rasselas balked, then sighed. "Well, I suppose I deserve that."

"Prince Moonvine," Thorne said, approaching from behind them. As Rasselas turned to look at his Wing, Embers exploded into a burst of movement and flapped up into the sky. Thorne recoiled in surprise, watching in awe as the Thunderbird charged off. Rasselas cleared his throat expectantly.

"Yes?" Rasselas said as he posed, chin high and back straight.

"Moonvine," Thorne straightened, regaining his composure. "The camp is ready. You may enter your tent whenever you wish." Thorne turned to leave, but Rasselas grabbed his wrist.

"Thorne, old boy?"

"What?" Thorne grimaced.

"Is everything alright?"

"*What?*" Thorne yanked his arm free. "What do you mean?"

"Well," Rasselas tugged at his ruffled sleeve cuffs, a common tick of his. "You seem rather out of sorts since we left Celestia. Before we get to Mensa, I would love to know what it is that's bothering you."

"I'm sure you wouldn't," Thorne said, looking Rasselas straight in the eye.

"I'm sure I *would*." Rasselas held his gaze.

Thorne tightened his jaw, then sighed. "I don't like traveling with you, Moonvine."

"Oh!" Rasselas made a blinking face of sheer shock. But no, he wasn't surprised.

"In fact," Thorne narrowed his brow, "I don't really like *you* at all."

"Well," Rasselas flamboyantly placed his hands on his hips, "Why ever not?"

"Because of *that*," he pointed his finger sharply at the prince. "That ridiculous act of yours, it's a disgrace."

Rasselas scoffed, tossing his head to the side. "Really, now."

"Do you really expect me to just *play along* with your foppish whims? Do you expect me to be pleased that the man representing our kingdom, in one of the greatest political meetings of our century, is a felling *coxcomb*? It was bad enough that the king chose a *Half-Elf* to represent us, but for you to prance around like a felling Faerie all the time? You are *impossible* and you'll make Celestia a laughingstock!"

Well, he just *had* to use the word 'foppish', didn't he? Rasselas glanced upwards at Embers who was circling above, then sighed as he looked back at the angry Thorne.

"Is that all?"

Thorne huffed. "For now."

Rasselas nodded, pulling at his sleeve cuffs once more, then fixed a loose hair that seemed to be falling down in front of his eyes. "Well, I don't see what is so bad about acting like a *Faerie*," he said. "I could hardly take that as an insult."

Thorne scoffed. "Oh," he said with a sarcastic tone. "You don't find it insulting? To be compared with a half-witted race who stole our princess, only to turn her into a—"

Rasselas seized Thorne by the collar, pulling him close in a surprising show of force. Thorne's eyes flared wide as he found himself staring into a face possessed with wild rage. Thorne took hold of Rasselas' wrists with both his hands and tried to yank himself free. Rasselas held tightly and pressed his nose toward Thorne's.

"Heavens know I am used to you insulting my father," Rasselas said in a low voice. "But to insult both my brother *and* my mother in one breath?"

Thorne gritted his teeth, "I said nothing of your brother!"

Rasselas shook him violently with a single yank then leaned close again. "Insult Faeries again and you will find yourself on your way back to Celestia! And leave my mother *out* of this!" Rasselas threw Thorne from his grip, who went tumbling backwards for a couple steps before catching himself. He stared at the prince in shocked silence. Then after a moment, he opened his mouth again.

"I didn't insult your mother," he said in a low voice, "I wouldn't dare."

"You insult her by thinking you have some *shred* of an idea of what happened to her," Rasselas yelled. "Stop acting like it was the Faeries who wronged her when *none* of you came to her rescue!"

Thorne's face hardened with rage and his fists clenched into balls of fury. He took a single step forward. "You *cannot* blame us for...!"

"Oh, shut up!" Rasselas raised a fist of warning. "Mention my mother again and you're *out* of here!"

The two stared at one another, both restraining their fury like unbreakable dams. Embers descended, like a large flake of falling ash, and landed on Rasselas' shoulder. The bird pecked at his ear playfully, jarring him from his intense concentration on Thorne.

"*Augh*, stop it," Rasselas waved his arm, shaking Embers off. The bird fluttered in the air above him for a moment before landing back on his shoulder. Rasselas looked at his feathery friend with a sheepish smile. He then cleared his throat, reorienting his posture back into that of a 'foppish' prince, and tilted his chin up slightly in Thorne's direction. "Anyway, old Thorne," he said dismissively, "I don't really want to argue with you. And here I thought we were getting along!"

Thorne gritted his teeth tightly and shook his head. "You're impossible," he said.

"And I see no reason why you should despise all Faeries when you hold a grudge against only *one*."

Thorne stepped closer, now about an arm's length away from Rasselas, and studied him. "I liked you better when you were angry," he said. "Back to the stupid act again?"

Rasselas turned his head slightly but kept his eyes on Thorne. "Really?" he sighed. "What a shame."

"*Erm*—my lords?" A third voice interrupted the two Elves who turned to see another member of their party approaching hesitantly. "I heard shouting—are we... are you...?"

"Good heavens, Latimer," Rasselas rolled his eyes. "Calm down. Everything is fine. Come on, what have you got to say?"

Latimer, their Elven skydeacon, snapped to attention, looking a little ashamed for his timidity. He then proceeded to inch toward them cautiously, as though approaching a provoked hound.

He was a little shorter than most Elves, and quite slender. This was probably due to the fact that while most Elven lads trained for battle, he had passed his younger days in the shade reading books and watching clouds. He was a scholar through and through, regularly distracted by intrusively constant epiphanies and paralyzingly important questions in the Skies.

He was a skydeacon, a student of the vastly confusing and ever-changing Raqian weather. Though these scholars specialized mostly in perceiving the naming of seasons and the predicting of weather, they also tended to have skill in wayfinding. It was typical for Elves to travel with a skydeacon when they attempted longer or unfamiliar journeys.

Latimer cleared his throat, looking to the side as he tried to collect his scattered thoughts. "I... I just thought I should inform you, Prince Moonvine—as I might have already mentioned," he said, "It is the eve of a new season tonight. Tomorrow is a Firstday."

"Oh, yes," Rasselas turned toward Latimer. "What are you fellows calling this one?"

Latimer stuttered for a moment, shaking his head, "No, no, sire," he smiled meekly, "*We* don't name them. We just..." he scratched behind his pointy ear, "we discern the name—together, that is."

"Alright," Rasselas said with an encouraging nod. "And what is it?"

"Well, I haven't had a chance to contact my order since spotting the new signs... so I cannot speak to a name yet. But I *can* say that I think it will be—erm—warmer?" He looked to Rasselas as if for confirmation.

"Hades, how should I know?" Rasselas crossed his arms. "I haven't the faintest clue how you skydeacons decide when to change the season." He was lying, of course. Rasselas' education had included an extensive amount of research involving the weather. But scholarly knowledge didn't seem to compliment the aristocratic air he worked so hard to maintain.

"Oh!" Latimer sputtered. "No, no, no, Prince Rasselas—*erm*—Moonvine! We don't *decide* anything! We *interpret* what the Skies are saying." He clasped his hands together in reverence, looking upwards. Then he paused, holding up a finger, "And...since the Faerie King died—" Latimer cut himself off. His eyes grew wide with shame, as though he spoke of a forbidden subject.

Rasselas narrowed his eyes. "You mean since the *previous* Faerie King died?"

"Yes," Latimer nodded quickly. "King Somenus was able to guide how the seasons affected the Land, you see, from his throne. But without a Faerie King..."

"Oh, please," Thorne sneered. "Latimer, you don't have to apologize for saying the Faerie King is *dead*."

Rasselas felt the heat rising within himself again as he slow-turned his head to snarl at Thorne.

"The current King—King *Anodos*—is *not* dead," he said in a low voice.

Thorne snapped his nose in Rasselas' direction. "Even if King Anodos *is* alive," he snapped, "Regent Hevel who *acted* on King Anodos' behalf is dead."

Rasselas took a step toward Thorne threateningly. "Thorne," he said in a shaky voice, "Anodos is not dead."

"There is no Faerie King," Thorne said, "The throne is empty."

"My brother is not dead!" Rasselas' voice seemed to echo for miles, and the entire camp grew silent. Latimer, who was currently cowering, peeked up to look at Thorne, who shook his head slowly at the prince.

"Wherever your brother is," he said calmly, "it makes no difference. The Faeries have no king."

Rasselas turned sharply to look at Latimer, who had grown brave enough to lower his protective hands. "Latimer!" he said, "Would *you* like to be my Wing?"

Latimer's mouth dropped open, and he shook his head quickly. As a skydeacon, he was both above and below such a position. "Heavens above!" he exclaimed. "Please don't fight, my lords!" He stepped up to Rasselas and touched his arm. The prince looked at him, mildly surprised. "I didn't mean to bring up such a controversial subject. I merely meant to say that reading the Skies is tricky. But what I *can* tell you is that tomorrow is Firstday." He reached his hand over to touch Thorne on the arm, making a sort of bridge between them. "Please do not quarrel. We are on a mission of great importance. How can we walk together if we are not in agreement with one another?"

"Good question," Rasselas said, with his eyes aimed at Thorne, who turned aside to scoff.

"We are all Elves, and we are all going to Mensa to promote peace, am I right?" Latimer asked, turning his gaze back and forth between the two.

"Well, cards, Latimer, of course you're right," Rasselas sighed.

"Then please, if we cannot find peace together on this road, it would be fruitless to continue to Mensa. For we cannot make peace through war."

Rasselas paused, blinking as he considered the skydeacon's words. "My dear Latimer, you couldn't be more correct. Forgive me... I've acted wrongly."

Thorne sighed. "I am sorry," he said, looking toward Latimer. "I was wrong to pick a fight."

Rasselas wagged his head in surprise, "Was that an apology?" he asked in fake astonishment.

"I was apologizing to Latimer," Thorne said flatly as he turned his gaze toward the prince.

Rasselas held his breath for a moment, studying Thorne from head to toe. It was clear now. Thorne didn't just dislike Rasselas, he *hated* Rasselas. This wasn't simply a matter of personality clashes. There was *true* hatred behind those eyes. Rasselas released his deeply held breath and turned his eyes upward toward Embers. It was one of those rare moments when Rasselas wished for the supportive presence of a friend to help him say what he needed to say. He held up his arm, waiting as the thunderbird alighted upon it.

How was that? Embers asked. *Did it hurt this time?* Rasselas smiled warmly, then looked over at his Wing.

"Thorne," he said. "I am sorry for unleashing my temper on you. Damn, if you don't seem to know how to get under my skin. Here: I promise I won't threaten to replace you anymore. And if we can both agree not to bring up my family, then I think I can manage to get to Mensa without challenging you to a duel."

Thorne's eyes widened in astonishment. "A—"

"So can we let that be that, then?" Rasselas asked abruptly.

Thorne stood frozen for a moment, with his mouth hanging half open, then stepped back with a single nod.

"Fine," he said, "If we can avoid talking much at *all*, I would be pleased."

"Great!" Rasselas startled the group by snapping his hands together in a loud clap. At that, Thorne huffed and marched away, disappearing into his tent.

Rasselas turned to look at Latimer, who stood there, wide-eyed.

"Are you alright there, chap?" Rasselas asked, breaking the skydeacon from his frozen state of shock by a touch of the shoulder.

Latimer jolted in surprise. "Prince," he exclaimed, placing his hand over his heart, "Sorry. Yes! Yes, yes, I am fine."

"I am sorry for being such a flighty leader," Rasselas said with a smile, "I'm sure I don't know why Grandfather thought it would be a good idea to send *me* on a mission as important as this."

"Oh, I am sure you do," Latimer said without a hint of sarcasm in his voice. He crossed his arms and looked up at the clouds, studying them for a moment.

Rasselas grinned. "What do you mean, scholar?"

Latimer turned to Rasselas, raising his eyebrows. "Oh," he said nonchalantly, "I just mean that I think you know you're up to the task. You're smarter than you let on, I mean."

Rasselas glanced at Embers then back at Latimer, still grinning. "Aw," he said teasingly, "How nice of you to say!"

Latimer glanced at Rasselas with an unimpressed eyebrow raise. "Well," he said, "I am sorry for bringing up your father—oh Hades—I mean *brother*!"

"It's alright," Rasselas' smile faded. "I can't expect—Hades, I don't really *want* people to tiptoe around the subject."

"If you don't mind me asking," Latimer said softly as he stepped up toward the edge of the riverbed and looked down at the water. "What *did* happen to your brother? I mean no offense, but I was told he was killed."

Rasselas sighed, his chin dropping to his chest. "I..."

"Oh," Latimer gasped in distress, reaching his hand out to grab Rasselas' arm. "Please, forget I asked!"

"No, no," Rasselas said with an unconvincing laugh, "It's fine." He lifted his head to smile at the scholar. "I was a kid when everything went down, just five seasons old."

"So... did he die?" Latimer asked slowly.

"No," Rasselas said, "well, many think he did, but he didn't. If the Faerie King really did die, then his throne would be left vacant. Any Faerie could sit on it and become the next King. But the fact that the throne is empty? This means Anodos is still alive. I am sure of this."

"True," Latimer said with distant eyes.

"Anyway, Anodos was in Arelle at the time, training under Regent Hevel," Rasselas said, shaking off the seriousness for a moment. "And some sort of insurrection happened. I am not sure who attacked that day—*many* people didn't want the son of Somenus reigning over Arelle. The insurrection resulted in the death of Hevel and his entire family, yes. But the king wasn't killed." Rasselas folded his arms. "I mean, *sure*—my brother Anodos was *going* to officially take the throne once he reached the age of ability, but that doesn't change the fact that he was crowned when he was a baby. He *is* the King of the Faeries, Latimer."

Latimer was silent. "If he wasn't killed, then where is he?"

Rasselas frowned. "I think... I believe he was taken."

Latimer studied the prince for a moment, then said, "And you think you know who took him?"

"Oh, I *know* I know who took him!"

"You think It was King Hanz," Latimer said cautiously.

"I *know* it was King Hanz."

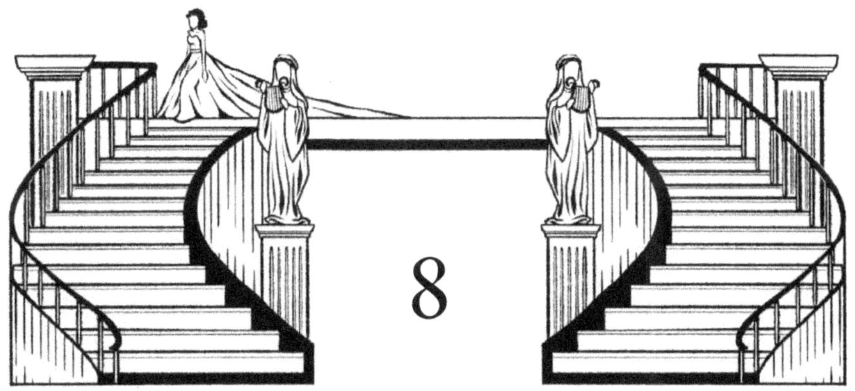

8

—— Rosamond ——

The Game

"THE KEY IS TO NOT BE SEEN," Rosamond whispered, "If we are not seen, no one will think to give us things to do!"

Valley pursed her lips. "That may work for you, but I have places I am supposed to be today!"

"Quiet," Rosamond huffed, "You'll draw attention to us. Look, if we can get from here to there," she pointed across the hallway, "without anyone noticing us, we can get out the side door and explore the market."

Valley leaned back against the wall and closed her eyes. "Why do I feel like we are going to get in trouble?"

"We won't!" Rosamond pinched Valley on the arm.

"We are both dressed as maids. You aren't allowed to wear fewer than four layers, and *I* am supposed to be preparing for my bonding ceremony tonight! We are *definitely* going to get in trouble—for sneaking out of the Inner Palace, at least!"

"Vy!" Rosamond sighed, "Why are you so worried all the time? Come on." Rosamond pulled her scarf over her head and charged into the hallway as if she belonged there. Valley, cursing under her breath, followed quickly after. The two girls, dressed as maids in simple floor-length uniforms, passed the set of guards who stood chatting at their post. They stopped to examine the girls' legs through the thinly layered skirts but didn't seem to notice who they belonged to.

Rosamond cheered within as they made it down to the side exit. She placed her hand on the latch and pulled. She was surprised how easily the heavy wood door seemed to swing open until she realized that someone was pushing it from the other side. Rosamond and Valley backed away and gasped in surprise. A tall, sturdy figure stepped into the hallway and towered over them.

Captain Oswald closed the door behind him, shaking his head with a sigh.

"Ladies," he said as he placed his hand on the hilt of his sword out of habit. "Where might you be headed?"

Rosamond felt Valley's elbow stab her in the side. Rosamond bit her lip. "We were just off to the market to buy some lunch on our break, you see," Rosamond said.

Oswald crossed his arms as a grin formed on his face. "Princess," he said. "Were you under the impression that the outfit masked your face somehow? Did you really expect me not to recognize you two?"

Rosamond wilted. "Fine, it's me, Rosamond." She crossed her arms in defeat.

"I know," Oswald chuckled, then glanced at Valley. "Ladies, I can't let you go into the market dressed like maids."

"But—!" Rosamond gasped.

"Go on." He pointed back down the hall commandingly. Both women bowed their heads in defeat and began to head back toward Rosamond's quarters. Oswald followed them, ordering the guards to turn their heads away. He marched them all the way back to Rosamond's door and pushed it open.

As they walked in, the captain cleared his throat. "Ladies," he said quietly. Rosamond turned to look him in the face. He wore a sympathetic expression. "I won't tell the king you were out here dressed like..." he paused, doing his best not to look down at their loose skirts, "like *that*. I don't think he would take it lightly."

Rosamond scoffed. "Why? Father has never given any thought to what I wore."

Oswald's mustache bristled. "Princess Rosamond," he said in a low voice, "can I be frank with you about something?"

Rosamond's eyes widened. For most of Rosamond's life, she had been ordered around and dismissed by those above her, but now... now it felt like a new thing to be spoken to like an adult by, well, *another* adult. She folded her hands together in front of her, trying to look as composed as she could. "Yes, I suppose. Tell me what you have to say."

Oswald held out his hand, gesturing for her to walk into her room. Rosamond and Valley found places to sit in the lounging area by the fire. Oswald left the door open as he walked in and stood by the hearth. He joined his hands behind his back and turned to look at them.

"I have served the king as the head of his personal guard for many seasons now and I have known you since you were born," he said, looking Rosamond directly in the eyes.

She bit her lower lip, hoping to hide her surprise. Goodness! When he put it like that, it made him sound so old, yet looking at him now, he appeared no older than the men in the suitors book she was given earlier that day. She began to think of Oswald differently than she had before.

"It is hard that you had to grow up without a mother," he continued, "and those of us who have known you since you were a child understand that. But you are not a child anymore."

Oh... this was a *lecture*? Rosamond felt her pulse begin to rise. "Are you trying to tell me that I am still acting like a child?" she asked sharply.

"It is a warning," Oswald's face softened, "from a *friend*."

Rosamond relaxed, leaning back into her chair. "Friend?" she asked.

"I wanted to warn you that the Inner Palace is *not* a friendly place. You are the princess, yes, but you have very little power," he glanced at Valley, then back at the princess, "and your father—" Oswald held his breath for a moment, as if deliberating within himself. "Princess Rosamond, I will only ever say this to you once."

Rosamond straightened her back as her pulse rose further. "Yes?"

"Your father is not concerned with your interests, only his own. You said your father never cared one way or another about what you wore." His eyes flickered a glance at her skirt; the layers were thin enough to reveal the shape of her knees. Rosamond grew suddenly self-conscious. "But you are wrong. Now that you have reached the age of ability, not only does he *care*, but he has very specific *intentions* for you and every little thing you do."

"Why do you make that sound like a bad thing?" Rosamond furrowed her brow.

"Please do not mistake me," Oswald cleared his throat, and Rosamond could see hesitancy in his face, "I am not trying to say anything negative about your father." His voice cracked. "Rosamond, many eyes are on you. And many eyes will be on you in the season of Kingsummons. I warn you to be on your guard. Do not trust anyone—and no, not even your father—to watch your back. You must watch your own back. Dressing up as a maid and trying to explore the market square," he gestured back toward the hall where he had found them, "might be harmless for a safe and spoiled princess—but that is *not* what you are." His eyes darkened. "You are a lamb in a den of wolves."

Silence. Rosamond slowly turned her head to meet eyes with Valley who wore her usual unblinking expression. The princess's gaze drifted back to Oswald. She studied him. Was he trying to *scare* her? Yes, it seemed that he was! But why? To scare someone who was perfectly safe was cruelty. To scare someone in danger was a kindness. Was he being... kind?

Rosamond crossed her legs at the knees and held her chin a little higher, "Well," she stopped to clear her throat, "I suppose *you* think you are the only person I am supposed to trust, then? You seem to want me to distrust everyone! Well, I sure as Hades won't distrust Valley just because you told me to."

"I—!" Oswald paused, then his face softened, and he nodded. "I would have you trust Valley, Princess, of course." Then his expression darkened. "Valley, did I hear you are to be bonded today?"

Rosamond looked over at Valley, who nodded quietly. "She's only being bonded to father," Rosamond said, "so it isn't like she is going anywhere." She glanced back as Oswald. "Now, if I could just circle back to what you were trying to warn me about," she said in a strong voice, though she felt as shaky as a blade of grass in the wind. "Are you trying to tell me that I am out of my depth in this castle?"

Oswald stood a little straighter and placed his hand on his hilt. "Your highness," he said in a clear, gentlemanly voice. "I am telling you how deep the water is so that you do not *find* yourself out of your depth."

Rosamond blinked, then stood with a sigh. "Well," she said, "Then I suppose I should thank you for the warning. It is time for me to stop fooling around," she glanced at Valley with an apologetic face, then turned back to the captain, "And learn the rules to the *new* game."

"Game?" Oswald shook his head, "Life isn't a game, Princess, it is—"

"It's your turn to listen to *me* now, Oswald!" Rosamond raised her voice, stepping toward the captain with her index finger pointed at his face. "It *is* a game, with rules. Yes. I grew up without a mother, and I have *no* idea what it means to be a typical girl." She took another step closer, realizing just how much shorter she was than the man she was scolding. "So, I will just have to do things my way. You say I need to watch my back?" She nodded. "Then I will watch my back like I watch the deck, by counting cards and watching how others play them." She dropped her hand and stepped back, losing some of the heat in her verbal fire.

"Life *is* a game for me, Oswald," she said in a low voice. "A game of cards—and I am trying to win. And to win, I need to know all the tricks and all the rules. So," she peered up at the tall man in the eyes, "Thank you for your word of warning. And I hope that if you ever feel the need to give me warning again, you will not hold back."

Oswald stared at her, blinking. Rosamond thought she could see a little smile from under his thick whiskers. She sighed animatedly, slapping her thighs with her palms. "Goodness," she said, "I must seem so ridiculous to you."

"No," Oswald shook his head, "Not at all. Thank you for listening." He cleared his throat and stepped toward the door. "Now I suggest you get changed before someone sees you and tells your father his soon-to-be-engaged daughter is charging around dressed like a maid." He glanced at Valley. "I'll be at the ceremony tonight." He paused, as if there was something more he wished to say, then turned his back on them and disappeared from the room like a sudden gust of wind.

Rosamond ran to her door and slammed it closed, turning the key to lock the bolt, then shot her face toward Valley. "Heavens, Valley!" she exclaimed, then ran over to her Faerie friend and they joined hands together. Both erupted into a noise of nervous giggling, then Rosamond pulled Valley by the hand, dragging her behind the large dressing screen which stood at the east end of the room. Once behind the screen, they both dropped to their knees, laughing further as they helped each other untie the laces on their corsets.

"What in Heaven's name!" Valley shook her head, "That was so scary!"

"I thought he was going to scream at me," Rosamond said in a shrill voice. "Goodness, what *was* all that?"

Valley pulled Rosamond's body corset free and threw it into the pile of maids' clothes she had nicked from the laundry room. "Oswald was just being Oswald," she said, "He thinks we are just helpless girls who can't take care of themselves."

"Well, isn't he *right*?" Rosamond took Valley's bodice and added it to the pile. The two girls sat there on the floor in their petticoats, acting as if behind the dressing screen was the safest place in the world. "Hades, I don't know what I am doing! Did you hear what he said?" She lowered her voice so a whisper. "He said Father cares about what I *wear*—I mean that's just insane! I can barely get Father to notice *anything* I do." She leaned back on her hands, blowing air out of the side of her mouth as she pondered. "Do you think he is right?"

"Well," Valley, who was sitting on her knees, leaned forward toward Rosamond, "He knows your father very well. I see them talking sometimes. You and I both know that the king is all about plans and strategies, so..." she grew quiet.

"So, Papa sees me like a strategic card," Rosamond raised her eyebrows in realization, "and he will want to play me right."

"You're like a chess piece," Valley said, knowing to stick to game metaphors with Rosamond, "A really important chess piece that he kept safe near the back of the board, but now—you are coming out. Now all his attention will be on *you*."

Rosamond nodded slowly with a determined look on her face. "The only question is going to be how to keep myself from being the chess piece. I need to have my *own* strategy!"

"What do you mean?" Valley asked, leaning back again. "Your father has the power, Rosamond, he controls the board. And... what would *winning* look like for you, anyway?"

"You think *we* don't have power, Vy?" Rosamond seized Valley by the wrist and gazed fiercely into her eyes. "That is what everyone *wants* us to think! We have power, it is just a different kind of power," she loosened her grip and sighed, "and I need to figure out what it is." Her eyes lit up and she squeezed Valley's wrist again. "I've got it!"

"What?" Valley asked, yanking her arm free.

"My power is what people think I am. If they think I am just a naive girl who only cares about men and cards then they will underestimate me, and that will be my power!"

"But Ros," Valley raised an eyebrow, "All I ever really hear you talk about is men and cards—what is it that you *are* trying to achieve?"

"I..." Rosamond grew quiet.

"You spoke so confidently to Oswald about cards and strategy, and games, and tricks and rules—but Rosamond... Do you even know what it is you are trying to achieve? What is it you really want in life?"

Rosamond paused, her eyes darting around, then she held her breath, nodding to herself. She met Valley's eyes. "What I want is to control my future, even if I make it look like it was someone else's idea, I want to control what happens to me. I know I have to get married—that is just life—but I want to hold all the cards when I do." She nodded to herself as a sinister smile crept onto her face. "So, it will be my job to find a husband who is dumb enough for me to wrap him around my little finger!"

Valley scoffed. "Oh, Rosamond!" She rolled her eyes, then fell backwards, laughing.

"Don't you dare laugh at me!" Rosamond grabbed a nearby corset and swatted Valley on the back with it. "I was being serious!"

"Ros!" Valley pushed herself up on her arm, still chuckling, "I've known you my whole life! You are not going to fall in love with a *dumb* man!"

Rosamond snorted. "This isn't about falling in love. It is about securing a comfortable future! And," she couldn't help but grin, "perhaps I can just marry a *handsome* dumb man!"

"But, Ros," Valley sat up straight, looking suddenly cautious, "What if your father already has someone in mind for you?"

"Oh!" Rosamond paused, "Yes, I had not thought of that. He is definitely the kind of man who would have already decided on his best-case scenario. Hmmm..." she tapped her lips with her finger, then drew in a sharp breath. "I know!" she said, "What I need to do is figure out who Father wants me to marry, then I can be one step ahead of him!" She sighed, deflating. "Though I don't know how that is supposed to help me." She glanced at Valley. "Oh, I don't know what I am doing. Oswald is right... I am a lamb in a den of wolves. I've got no say in which one of them eats me first."

Valley put her hand on Rosamond's shoulder. "We both have little power over what happens to us," she said, "but there are some things no one can take away from us."

Rosamond lifted her head to see Valley's face. There were tears in her eyes. "Each other?" she asked.

"Yes," said Valley as the wetness escaped her eyes. "Our friendship. You know at night, how I go back to the Warrowing Village?"

"Yes," Rosamond said, sniffing as she wiped her face with her arm. "With the other Faeries?"

"Yes," Valley leaned back, tucking her knees up into her chest as she smiled. "None of us have any power over what happens to us. We spend all our days taking care of others. Sometimes we have good days, and sometimes we have very bad days." Her face darkened for a moment, then her smile returned, "But we always end them together. Our fellowship makes all the badness disappear, and we all know that we are not alone."

"I wish I could go there," Rosamond said with distant eyes. "Every night when you would go back to the Warrowing Village, I would be left here alone by myself with Lady Stackly. She would punish me if I had been less than perfect—which, of course, was every day! And I always cried myself to sleep." She focused her eyes back on Valley. "I can't tell you how many times I wished I could go back with you to the Village."

Valley had her wide deer-eyes as she studied Rosamond's face. "But," she stuttered, "You've never told me that before."

Rosamond shrugged, pulling her long, silky hair over her shoulder so she had something to fiddle with. "I'm a princess and you're a Faerie. I didn't want to complain to you, Valley, not when you have it so much harder than me."

Valley sighed. "Perhaps that's not as true as I always thought it was."

Rosamond smiled. "Were you about to tell me that hard things aren't so bad when you have those you love to end the day with?"

"Yeah," Valley shrugged, "Though now I regret saying it."

"No," Rosamond shook her head, feeling her optimism return to her. "I think you are right, and you have convinced me!"

"Of what?" Valley raised her pointy eyebrow.

"To change my strategy." Rosamond stood, thrusting her first excitedly into the air. "My mission is to get married!"

Valley snorted, standing as well. "Well, that should be easy."

Rosamond held up her finger. "Ah—no, it won't," she said, "For my mission is to marry someone I *love*. I will marry the perfect man to end the day with, so I never have to sleep alone again."

Valley cringed. "So your mission is to fall... in *love*?"

"Yes," Rosamond had a wildly competitive look in her eye. "I will outsmart my father by finding out which of those jokers he wants me to marry and subsequently fall in love with him!"

"I hope I don't regret taking this position," Viola said in her raspy voice. She stepped into her new room in the castle. "This is much smaller than my sitting room back home and I had a total of *four* maids."

Rosamond stood by the door. "Where is your father's estate again?" she asked.

"In Shadowroots," Viola snapped, turning to give Rosamond a disappointed scowl. "Have you already for—"

"Ah!" Rosamond stepped into the room, gliding gracefully with her extensive train dragging behind her. "Of course! The thirsty remains of Bavel's rejects," she clasped her hands together with a pretentious smile, "What a step up—from there to Mensa Castle—you must be thrilled."

Viola studied the princess morosely. "You're mocking me?"

Rosamond came to Viola's side and offered a single nod, then said, "Four maids in a hovel can't be compared to a single maid in a castle, Lady Viola."

Lady Viola snickered to herself. "They said you were feisty."

"They said *I* was feisty?" Rosamond pretended to look offended. "And what do 'they' say about *you*?"

Viola pursed her lips. "The gossips have little to say about me," she said, "because I am their leader."

Rosamond seated herself gracefully on one of Viola's new chairs. "I never would have thought to hear someone actually *boast* about being the head of the gossips."

"That is because you are on the outside." Viola said, sitting by Rosamond's side. "But listen, I didn't take this post just to gossip about you."

"Oh?" Rosamond raised her eyebrows, "Then enlighten me. Why did you agree to be my first courtier?"

"Well," Viola gave a modest shrug, "Firstly, I came for personal advancement. Those in your court will be walking in the highest circles of Raqian society. But secondly, I actually came to help *you*. You're fresh, Princess Rosamond. No one has seen you yet, and you haven't exposed your values to the market—so I have a chance to mold you a bit. You know, give you a chance to really make Mensa shine."

"Make *Mensa* shine?" Rosamond frowned.

"Why, of course!" Viola said matter-of-factly. "Mensa is the pride of Raqia. We even make *Bavel* blush with our might. And you are Mensa's hair," she reached out to touch Rosamond's luscious black locks, "you are her *glory*. If you are spoken well of, then Mensa is spoken well of. Don't you see? You are the older sister to every other noble lady in Mensa. If you are honorable, all of us will be praised. If you are a fool, all of us will be mocked. It is in my best interest to make you presentable before you hit the market, don't you see?"

Rosamond refrained from slapping the woman in the face. Instead, she sat still, with her hands resting softly on her lap and a calm smile on her face. So, Viola—the self-proclaimed head of the gossips in Mensa's pretentious society—had taken the job as Rosamond's first court lady in order to *form* her. *We shall see who of us does the forming, Viola*, she thought to herself.

"Well," Rosamond sighed, "I am sure you will be a valuable ally then. I have been locked away in this castle for seventeen seasons, and all I have to help me prepare is that book of noblemen that my father gave me. Perhaps you can educate me before my coming-out party."

Viola seemed a little surprised by the invitation and studied Rosamond a moment further before saying, "Well, Rosamond—if you don't mind me calling you by your first name—*all* of us were locked away until we were seventeen with only a book of noblemen for support. But you see, I have an older sister. She is married now, but she is married to a Gramenlands highlord. She *knows* things. And before I even came out, she taught me all about the social network which runs like an anthill through the lives of every western noble house. So yes, you are lucky to have me as a confidant."

"So," Rosamond said with a burst of energy, "Tell me who the most eligible bachelors are and all that! And don't lie to me about which one *you* want to marry, otherwise I won't be able to help you get what you want!" She reached out to grasp Viola by the hand, surprising her.

"Well," Viola maintained her pompous air. "Why don't you fetch your book of noblemen, and I will tell you."

"Great!" Rosamond stood and began to walk toward the door.

"Oh, Rosamond," Viola called after her in a monotone voice, "Wait."

Rosamond turned, holding the pose of someone who was eager to leave. "Yes?"

"My first piece of advice, slow down a little. If you keep rushing around everywhere, it makes you appear flighty. If you take your time, you seem less eager and more in control."

Rosamond bit her tongue, nodding. "Thanks for the advice," she said, "but I plan on continuing to be as enthusiastic as I please in the coming season."

"Suit yourself," Viola shrugged, turning her head away from the princess. "I can't control how your manner impacts others."

"That's for sure," Rosamond placed her hands on her hips, then cocked her head to the side as she examined Viola sitting there with poise.

Viola's steady manner did make her seem like she was the one in control. And yet—somehow that form of social intimidation didn't *work* on Rosamond. Why was that? Perhaps Rosamond wasn't familiar with the subtleties of female society and peer pressure. She often saw her lack of a mother-figure as a weakness. Could it also, perhaps, be an advantage? Could it be a helpful tool that Rosamond didn't function like other women did?

"You know," Rosamond said thoughtfully, "Perhaps we can talk about noblemen another time. There is something else I want your opinion about." She walked back to the sitting area and placed herself right by Viola's side. "Father has given me the important job of planning a social activity for the Kingsummons peace talks."

Viola nodded, then said, "Once you are out, you shouldn't say 'Father' anymore. 'Father' is what children say. You may call him 'the King', since that is his title."

"Anyway," Rosamond continued, "Father said I can pick anything I want and invite people to join along. I imagine he thinks it is my chance to see which men might be interested in me; or perhaps it is merely a chance for me to exercise some authority."

"It doesn't matter *why* the king has told you to do this," Viola said coldly, "It is not a woman's job to know why someone has asked her to do something, but to figure out the best way to do the thing she has been asked to do."

Rosamond snorted a laugh. "Well that's ridiculous," she said, "How could I do something well unless I know what it is I am supposed to accomplish? Anyway, I would like to prove to my father that I am up to the task—whatever it might be."

"The only thing you need to prove to the king is that you can do what he tells you to do without making any mistakes. Let's leave it at that."

Rosamond was beginning to realize that Viola would end her thoughts in phrases like, 'let's leave it at that', to assert her authority in a conversation. Well, it wasn't going to work—not on someone immune to those kinds of social pressures.

"Perhaps in your world," Rosamond said, "That is enough. But for me, I have few more things I need to be keeping track of. Let's leave it at *that*. But let me tell you a few ideas I had," She touched Viola's hand, "Do you want to hear them?"

Viola raised an eyebrow then nodded silently.

"Well, at first I thought I could plan a themed dinner," Rosamond said, holding up her hands in a mime.

"Oh, please no." Viola groaned. "Have you seen the order of events for the first week? There's already a themed dinner. Two would be redundant."

"Well," Rosamond placed her palms together, thinking, "Then my second idea was to plan an excursion somewhere. You know—take everyone to see some of Mensa's sights. Like a boat ride down the canal."

Viola shook her head. "You don't want to give the noblemen distracting things to *look* at like views and scenery."

"Why ever not?" Rosamond asked, growing tired of Viola shooting down all her ideas.

"Because, Rosamond," Viola sighed, "You want men looking at *you*. Pick a social activity that promotes interaction and flirtation."

Rosamond pulled her lips into her mouth thoughtfully. Well, it sounded dreadfully vain, but Viola was right—she did want to interact with men. She grinned. "I know just the thing, then."

"What is it?" Viola looked genuinely curious.

"Oh, I am not going to say this time!" Rosamond held up her finger. "Otherwise you might shoot this idea down, too. And this is *too good*!"

"Come on," Viola said, flapping her hand with faux playfulness, "How can I help you plan it if I don't know what it is?"

"No, no," Rosamond stood, "I am planning this one all on my own!"

"Well," Viola pouted, turning her head away as a sign of displeasure. "Why ask me to be your court lady if you aren't even going to let me do anything?"

Rosamond laughed. "Well, *I* didn't ask you to be my court lady, did I?"

Viola shot a glare in Rosamond's direction. "I suppose you didn't, but I would at least hope you would *try* to get on my good side!"

"Heavens above, Viola!" Rosamond said in a disappointed tone, "Of course, I am trying to get along with you. But if anyone is to try to be on anyone's side, it is *you* who should be trying to be on *my* side. And besides," she sighed to herself, "I hate all this talk of 'sides'. It makes life feel like it's some kind of war."

"Isn't it?" Viola asked as she rose to her feet.

"For some, maybe," Rosamond said, "But war isn't how I like to think of it."

"How, then?"

"Well," Rosamond smiled, "—like a game!"

9

—— Valley ——

The Ominous Oaths

VALLEY SAT IN A SMALL ROOM WITHIN THE INNER PALACE, which was guarded by half a dozen Human soldiers. She wasn't alone, thankfully; Polaris sat beside her on the floor. The two young Faeries were the only ones selected for bonding that night. Valley had never been to a bonding ceremony—unbonded Faeries were never allowed to attend—so she knew very little about what was coming. She wondered why so many Humans would be guarding them. Surely, they didn't worry about her trying to escape? Why would a Faerie ever try to run away from their bonding ceremony? Still—something inside her *did* want to run away. Why? Why did she always feel the need to *escape*?

Valley lifted her head, which had been resting between her knees, to look at Polaris. He was dressed in a simple white toga, just like she was; it was the customary outfit for a Faerie when it was bonding time. For a woman who grew up dressing in layers, Valley felt almost naked. Perhaps that was how she was supposed to feel: like a newborn baby, starting a new life. All things from her past were stripped away from her, she was to become someone new.

Polaris smiled back at her. He sat there with his back against the wall and his legs crossed in front of him at the knees.

"Hallo," he said cheerily.

"Hallo," said Valley.

"Oh!" Polaris placed his hands behind his head, "So you *can* talk!"

"Stop acting like we have never spoken before," Valley rolled her eyes.

"Why are you so quiet all the time, Valley?" The young Faerie asked. He was in his fifteenth season, though already he was much taller than her and sounded like a grown man her own age.

"Why are you so talkative all the time?" Valley said flatly.

"Most people talk all the time, Vy," Polaris said, blowing some of his unruly brown hair away from his eyes. "Now come on, why are you acting so glum?"

"I don't know," she huffed, resting her chin on her knee as she pulled her legs to her chest protectively. "I guess I am not exactly thrilled about being bonded."

"Why not?" Polaris leaned toward her, trying to meet her eyes. "Come on!"

"Why are *you* so excited about being bonded to a Human?" she snapped, pushing him away from her.

"Why wouldn't I be?" he shrugged, "I finally get to leave the Warrowing Village and find my purpose in life. Lord Evenstine plans to take me to the Sea! Imagine the sorts of adventures I am going to have."

"And you don't care that you'll have to be bonded to someone you've never met? What if he is cruel? What if he beats you?"

"Well, Vy," Polaris chuckled, "I am used to beatings by now, aren't you? Plus, he won't have any reason to beat me if I make life easy for him. I like helping people. It feels great. Makes me feel like I am a true Faerie, you know?"

"I guess," Valley said quietly. She had been raised in the Inner Palace. She *wasn't* as accustomed to beatings, but she chose not to mention it.

"Can you believe there are Faeries out there who have absolutely no connection with Humans at all? They just hide away and waste their existence on hedonism and things. That's what Tristan says, anyway. Sounds depressing to me."

"Aren't you the least bit concerned about the branding?" Valley asked spitefully. "Do you *really* not care about physical pain?"

Polaris' enthusiasm faded for a moment. "Well," he said, "I'm trying not to think about that until I have to. It's sort of like childbirth, right? Like what you women have to do? You know something painful is coming, but after it is over, you don't even remember!"

Valley all but rolled her eyes. "Well unlike you, I am not able to keep it from my mind. And I don't know, maybe it isn't the physical pain that I am dreading the most. I—I think I feel like something is wrong."

"What feels wrong, Vy?"

"I don't know," she sighed, "It's the thought that I didn't choose this. Someone else chose it for me. And now I have to live with it for the rest of my life."

"Well, Vy," Polaris cleared his throat, "Most people don't get to choose what happens to them, not even Humans! Think about all those rich nobles. They all have to marry people their parents choose for them. Isn't life about making the most out of what's been given to us?"

Valley's eyes brightened. Now *that* resonated with her. "Making the most out of what's been given to me," she said softly. She looked up at the door, spotting one of the soldiers peeking in to check on them. Yes, she knew why they were there. They were there because she would run if she could. She didn't want to be bonded. That, at least, she could admit to herself. If she could choose for herself today, she would not be bonded to anyone. She would live like one of those 'hedonist' hermit Faeries Tristan told Polaris about. Maybe that was a waste of life, but she didn't care. It was what she wanted.

But she could not have what she wanted. Whatever anyone else had to say about it, she was being forced into this. She was being forced to bond. She would do it, of course she would—it wasn't something they would *let* her say 'no' to. So, she would do it with dignity. *Make the most out of what has been given.* Who was to say there couldn't be some privilege that came from a life as one of Hanz' Faeries? At the very least, she might be granted more freedom within the Inner

Palace. And if she could be allowed to attend the Kingsummons events, she could help Rosamond when she needed support the most. That would have to be enough for now.

"Come on," Polaris said, reaching out to pat her on the shoulder, "Don't be sad. It's going to be alright, Vy. If it hurts really bad, I give you permission to yell at me."

Valley turned her gaze to Polaris. The boy who had always gotten in trouble for staying out past curfew, and stealing extra portions of food, was becoming a man. His now solid jaw and thick arms weren't the only indicators of this manhood. He seemed to carry that confident, protective presence that Valley admired about the opposite sex. Somehow, when he looked at her like that, things didn't seem so bad.

"Fine," she said, "I will."

"You can hold my hand, you know," he said as he straightened his back.

"What?"

"When branding time comes—hold my hand."

"I..." Valley wanted to retort that she wasn't a scared little child, but kept her mouth closed. She nodded. Who in their right mind, in a moment like this, would ever say 'no' to *that*?

"It's time, come on." One of the soldiers stepped into the room and looked down at them with a face of disgust. "On your feet, you dogs!"

Polaris hopped up quickly, with a bright grin on his face, then held his hand out to Valley. She took it and rose, trying to appear as modest as possible in her white robe. How was a woman supposed to mask the existence of legs with only *one* layer? Polaris took her by the arm, as if her escort, and raised his chin with a self-important pose.

"Alright, lead the way, soldier!" he said with pretend pomp.

As Valley and Polaris stepped into the hall, the guards surrounded them on all sides. A seventh soldier approached, stepped between two guards, and walked right up to the two Faeries. His hand rested on his sword hilt.

"Good evening, young Faeries," he said.

Valley felt a boost of confidence at seeing Captain Oswald. He had a sympathetic—even sorrowful—look on his face.

"Hallo, Captain," Valley said.

"Well," Oswald said with a sigh, "I suppose it is time. Are you ready?"

Valley wanted to say 'no,' but she nodded instead. "I am ready to do what I must."

"Of course, we are ready," Polaris chimed. Oswald glanced at Polaris, then returned his gaze to Valley.

"If there had been a way I could have given you more time," Oswald said, then hesitated as his voice caught in his throat. He turned away. "I am sorry."

"Why are you apologizing?" Valley asked. "Captain?"

"Let's get this over with," Oswald signaled to the soldiers. The party began to march down the hall toward the throne room.

Valley had been to the throne room before, but never for an actual event. She had grown up playing hide-and-seek with Rosamond and knew the big hall like the back of her hand. It was surprising to see it in a formal setting. The chandeliers above were lit with hundreds of tall beeswax candles and the aisle was adorned with a long, patterned carpet. Pristinely dressed soldiers with their ornate spears lined the length of the hall. It was as if an entire army was there just to make sure Valley did what she was told to do.

Bonding ceremonies weren't attended by guests, from what Valley knew, it was a ritual intended only for those who needed to be there. Besides the armed guards, Valley noted only a couple people. She lifted her chin slightly, then dropped her eyes to the ground once more. She saw enough to know that only three people stood at the end of the aisle, waiting for them.

After what seemed like an eternity of walking, they arrived at the top of the large throne room. King Hanz stood beside his throne, wearing his many-spiked crown and looking like a deity. She had never seen him so regal! Beside the king stood the man Valley assumed to be Highlord Evenstine, the man Polaris would be bonded to. Beside Evenstine stood a man dressed like a Lights Priest, only he wore black robes rather than white. He had a pointy white beard and held a book open in his hands.

Valley and Polaris were ushered forward. Highlord Evenstine gave King Hanz a quick glance, looking somewhat pleased with what he saw. Valley and Polaris were made to kneel before them and kept their heads down.

"Polaris," the man in black robes said in a scratchy voice, "Do you swear to serve your master all your days, to make his will your own and his desires your own, to use everything in your power to come to his aid, and to protect him with your entire body? Do you swear to devote your life to Lord Evenstine, forever calling him your master?"

Valley was surprised to see Polaris hesitate. She reached out and took hold of his hand, gripping it as tightly as she could. She heard the young Faerie breathe in sharply, then say in a loud voice, "I swear it!"

"Lord Evenstine, by signing here," the priest held the book out to the highlord, "You acknowledge the transfer of ownership."

Lord Evenstine took the pen eagerly and relished writing his name in flowery letters.

Once he finished, the priest pulled away and turned his gaze toward Valley. Her heart stopped. She didn't realize she would have to actually *swear* anything! Her eyes darted from side to side, checking for a last chance route of escape despite the innumerable guards. She caught a glimpse of Captain Oswald standing on the sidelines. Though he stood frozen like stone, his wide eyes were locked on her. Valley pulled herself back to the present, looking up toward the man who she was about to pledge herself to, King Hanz.

His body was as still as Captain Oswald's, but he was not looking at her. Instead, he stared at the ground, waiting.

"Valley," said the priest, "Do you swear to serve your master all your days, to make his will your own and his desires your own, to use everything in your power to come to his aid, and to protect him with your entire body? Do you swear to devote your life to King Hanz, forever calling him your master?"

Valley felt Polaris squeeze her hand. She suddenly understood the paralyzed terror he had felt only moments ago. Something was *wrong*. This all was very, very wrong. She remained silent until a sharp yell startled her.

"Valley," came King Hanz's commanding voice.

"I swear," she said, startled. And that was it—her life was over.

"King Hanz," The priest continued his ceremonial speech, "by signing here, you acknowledge the transfer of ownership from 'unbonded', to you."

King Hanz signed quickly, then stepped back, looking down at the two Faeries. "Alright," he said.

Just then, a new character emerged onto the scene holding a pair of red-hot branding irons.

Valley shot her gaze toward Polaris, who met eyes with her. There it was—Polaris did have it after all. Terror. They locked their hands together until their knuckles turned white. And after a seemingly unending flash of unimaginable horror, it was over.

—— Hanz ——

The Morning Star

"THE STARS HAVE FINALLY ALIGNED and everything is in place," Hanz said as he sat comfortably in his new armchair, up at the top of the North Tower. Before him was the great Crimson Gate, the last of the great Faerie portals. Through it, he could see as far as he desired, and if he ever wished, he could travel there. Of course, he seldom ever used it for such a purpose, since it was impossible to return back home through the portal.

Most nights, Hanz sat gazing through the magnificent door, combing through the lands of Raqia for that one, elusive, slippery bastard no one seemed able to find. Tonight, however, Hanz didn't search for his missing person. Instead, he rested from his endeavors, enjoying the pleasurable sights the portal had to offer.

"The delegates will be arriving tomorrow," Sigmund said with pen in hand. "Is there anything not already in the plan that you want me to see to?"

King Hanz let out a long, drawn-out sigh. "Tell me again who hasn't responded to the invitation."

"The Elves of the Elder Copse have not sent a written response," Sigmund said, brushing the feather end of his quill against his chin.

"Thank the Lights for *that*..."

"Silence from Bavel, obviously..."

"Obviously."

"We haven't heard anything from the Edgelands, but that doesn't come as a surprise."

"Yes," Hanz said, rubbing his fingers against the arms of his chair. "Wait," he paused, turning to look at Sigmund. "What about the Coastal Elves?"

"Well, Sire..." Sigmund checked his notes. "Yes, it seems they have sent a response."

"Hmm," Hanz turned back toward his portal, "King Antecus is coming?"

"I believe he said he is sending a delegate in his place."

"How has the new girl settled in? You got a courtier for Rosamond, didn't you?"

"It's been fine," Sigmund said unenthusiastically, "Her only report thus far is..." he turned a page in his book, "is that she thinks Rosamond is too headstrong to be marriageable."

Hanz groaned. "Well... we will have to see what happens. She's pretty though, isn't she—Rosamond?" Hanz turned to look at Sigmund in the face.

Sigmund shrugged modestly. He didn't need to say his thoughts out loud. Yes, Rosamond was *more* than 'pretty.'

"Pretty enough to make up for her—*erm*—obstinance?"

Sigmund tapped his chin with his pen. "For most men, yes. But for kings? ...We will see."

Hanz sighed. "Why do there always have to be small, irritating things outside of my control?"

"Everything is fine, sire," Sigmund said, tapping his little black book with his finger. "I wouldn't trouble yourself over a few small details."

"Yes, well." Hanz crossed his arms, suddenly feeling dissatisfied. "It's always the *little* details that get overlooked. *Little* details topple kingdoms."

"How did you like your new lip-reader?" Sigmund asked.

Hanz scoffed. "Hades, I don't know. It seems like it won't be as easy to learn as I thought it would. But how am I supposed to know what anyone is *saying*," he gestured to the portal, "if I can't read lips?" He turned to gaze up at the eyes mounted over the door. So long as those eyes pointed at the Crimson Gate, Hanz found he was able to use it. "Can *you* read lips?" he asked the eyes, "You can, can't you, you little devil!"

Sigmund glanced at Hanz hesitantly. "Sire?" he said, "Anything else?"

Hanz was silent, seething in his chair for a moment, then asked, "How is she?"

Sigmund hesitated. "Do you mean... the Faerie woman?"

"*Valley*," Hanz said, "How is Valley?"

Sigmund looked at his book for a moment, then up at Hanz with a confused expression. "Oh, *that* Faerie girl. You're asking—how she is *doing*? Since the branding?"

Hanz grunted awkwardly. "Never mind." He watched the portal for a short stretch of time, then asked, "how is the *other* Faerie woman?"

"The one you asked me to question?"

"Yes, that one, who else? What did she say?"

Sigmund opened his book to a particular page. "Would you like me to quote her?"

"I don't like where this is going..."

Sigmund cleared his throat and read in a loud voice, "*you can tell that snake that he can come and ask me himself. In that event, I can tell him exactly what he needs to hear—*"

"Here we go."

"*...That I hope someone ties his felling immortal body to four wild aurochs and he gets ripped apart and travels the length and breadth of Raqia in all his bloody glory...*"

"Alright, that's enough," Hanz waved his hand. "So, she didn't talk, then?"

"Oh, she talked!" Sigmund grinned. "Hades, Hanz, she *talked*. I could read more, if you like..."

"That damn woman." Hanz cursed, rubbing his forehead. "Alright, well. Let's withhold food for a bit and see if that changes anything."

"She refuses to eat anyway," Sigmund said, "Didn't you know that?"

"What?" Hanz turned, studying Sigmund's face. "Why?"

"I thought I mentioned that already," the man scanned the pages of his little book for a moment. "Here. She says she's fasting."

"Fasting?" Hanz froze. His face darkened. Fasting—it was how Faeries waited for important events. It was a demonstration, an act of protest. "She's…"

"…waiting for the king to come," Sigmund said quietly, doing his best to mask any hint of reverence in his voice.

Hanz stood quickly, flexing his muscles in an astonishingly epic pose. "Well," he said, "She will have a king soon enough."

"As you say, sire," Sigmund said, stepping backwards toward the door.

"Don't go," Hanz marched toward him. "Sigmund," he said with a wild look in his eyes. Sigmund shrunk back.

"Yes, sire?"

"I want you to watch the portal. Write down if you find any Faeries, any blind men, or if you see that cursed *bastard*!" His voice crescendoed into a banshee-like scream.

Sigmund shrunk. "Fine, sire."

Hanz pushed past the man and stormed out of the chamber, letting the door slam behind him.

He descended the spiral stairs down to the base of the tower, then blasted out of doors, moving like a shadow in the night. His heart raced. Was he winning or was he losing? He was winning. He stopped walking just as he came to the edge of the wall and stared southwards toward the horizon. Only six bells from now, leaders from every nation would be coming to make friends with him.

Hanz' cape blew in the wind, dancing around him like a pair of wings. He turned his gaze northwards toward the city of Bavel. In the distance, the monstrosity towered above the Table like a colossal mountain, scraping the very Sky with its peak. Shifting his gaze only slightly, on the other side of the Labyrinth City he saw the city of Arelle. With the Sky too dark and distance too great for him to see clearly, all he could discern with his eyes was a shining white light. Arelle—the morning star, that woman always just out of reach, taunting him with her beauty.

"Arelle," he said, though his voice quickly dissipated in a heavy, powerful sudden gust of wind.

11

— Rook —

Into Mensa

"Can I have some land?"

Cato glanced at Rook, then shrugged his shoulders. "Sure," he said, leaning a hand against a birch tree while he relieved himself into a little creek by the roadside. Rook leaned his back against a nearby tree, watching the Eagles as they tended to the needs of the great beast, Golden Grains, whose head was currently submerged in a large sack of feed. "Why?"

"I don't know," Rook said, "I'm coming to Mensa as a wing. I figured I needed some land to go with my position."

"Sure, why not?" Cato said nonchalantly, as if he were passing out candy to children. Turning, the lord tied up the front of his trousers and looked around at his caravan. "How long until Mensa now?"

"We are about to cross the border of the city main. Then it's a couple hour's ride to the Castle." Rook replied.

"Finally," Cato said under his breath.

"If you're finished," Rook said, feeling his own urge, "I'll take a walk down the stream for a few clicks."

"Fine," Cato mumbled, then marched back toward the caravan and disappeared inside it.

Rook walked along the edge of the stream until he came to a place where a cluster of trees blocked the view of the road. He wasn't the bashful sort, but he appreciated a moment of privacy every once in a while—something he wouldn't be getting much of in the coming days. Taking his place facing the stream, and relieving a bit of tension, Rook's eyes met with someone else's who seemed to be there for the same purpose.

"Hallo," said the newcomer. Standing on the other side of the stream was a slender-looking man, dressed in a long grey cross robe, tied at the waist with a silver belt. With an outfit like that, he was unmistakably a skydeacon. His chestnut hair was trimmed in a short, stylized cut, with a shiny swirl of combed locks resting just above his brow, and he was clean shaven. His face was angular but handsome, and his ears pointed. He offered a cheery smile to Rook, lifting his hand to wave as he unabashedly urinated into a bush by the rippling stream.

"Hi," Rook said with a blank look on his face.

"Your colors," The skydeacon gestured toward Rook's clothes with his free hand. "I don't recognize them. It's not the Edgelands, is it?"

"It is," Rook said, offering a pathetic excuse for a smile. He was still trying to figure out how a nobleman interacted with others.

"Fascinating!" the skydeacon's eyes lit up. "Oh, Lights! I have so many questions!"

Rook chuckled, offering a genuine smile this time. "You're an Elf," he said, "traveling to Mensa from Celestia?"

"How did you know?" The skydeacon appeared genuinely impressed. "Yes, we are coming for the peace talks. You?"

"Same," Rook said, "I am Rook."

"Latimer, at your service!" The skydeacon, having finished his business, covered himself quickly and bowed in greeting from the other side of the creek. He straightened up, looking a little embarrassed as he asked, "Uh—are you an officer?"

　　　　　　　　　　　　　　　　　　　　

"I'm a Wing," Rook said, "I am here accompanying an Edgelands highlord."

"Oh, wonderful!" Latimer hopped across the little stream, holding up the ends of his robe so as not to get it wet, and skipped over to Rook. "The Lights know I have about a hundred questions for a man from the west. Could our parties walk together, perhaps? It seems like a grand idea to make friends on the road to peace!" He was so enthusiastic for an Elf; Rook couldn't help but grin as he watched the little scholar roll up one of his ill-fitting sleeves to reach out for a handshake.

Rook shook his hand with a firm grip. "Latimer, it's a pleasure to meet you. I am sorry to disappoint you, but I am not actually from the Edgelands." He paused, wondering to himself if he should be honest about that. Well, it was too late now. "And I am not sure if your party could keep up with ours," he glanced behind himself for a moment, then turned back to see Latimer's disappointed face.

"We walk faster than you think! We can keep up with palanquins and even oxen!"

Rook smiled broadly. "Friend," he said as he reached out to pat the skydeacon on the shoulder, "You can certainly try. But I am afraid our aurochs likes to move at its own pace, and that tends to be pretty fast."

Latimer's mouth dropped open in awe as he made a most rewarding expression. "Oh, Lights! Please can I see him—or—*her*?"

"Well, come on then," Rook said, gesturing with his chin toward where his caravan awaited him. Latimer followed, hiding somewhat behind Rook's tall, sturdy body as he approached cautiously. Just as the aurochs came into view, Rook heard a satisfying gasp and turned to see Latimer with an immense grin on his face.

"Lights, friend!" he exclaimed, placing his hand over his mouth. "He's so beautiful. I—I have always wanted to see one."

"Who is this, Rook?" Fern, one of Cato's Eagles, approached with an empty grain sack in his hands.

"He's a skydeacon I found by the creekside," Rook gestured with his thumb.

"Hallo!" Latimer straightened, looking a little sheepish, though not unenthusiastic. "My name is Latimer!"

"I didn't know the Elves had skydeacons," Fern said, straight-faced.

Latimer, looking a little bewildered, shook his head, "Well of course we do. It isn't just the Humans that have skydeacons."

"He wanted to have a look at Golden Grains," Rook said. "Are we ready to move?"

"Yes," Fern pulled his cigar roll to his lips and took a quick puff. "We are just waiting on the captain." 'The captain' is what the other two Eagles called Tercius.

Latimer suddenly whirled his head around at the sound of an uncommon bird call. "Oh!" he exclaimed, turning back to Rook. "Friend," he said as he grabbed Rook by the wrist. "It was a pleasant meeting, and I am sure the Skies foresaw it. I will see you again." He skipped quickly off down toward the stream, calling behind him. "In Mensa!"

Rook and Fern watched him leave with blank expressions. Once he was gone, Rook turned to his companion. "Where is Tercius?" he asked.

"He's soaking the old foot in the stream," Fern said with smoke emanating from his mouth.

"Old foot?" Rook glanced back toward the stream.

"Never been the same since the calamity," Fern sighed, "But he—" the man froze, his eyes going wide as if he just let something slip. Then, drawing himself up, he said, "He just needs to cool it every once in a while, you know, it helps the pain and all that."

Pain? Rook clenched his jaw, feeling a swell of guilt rise up within him as he thought about their bet. Was he really about to force an old, wounded soldier to go bull-riding in front of a king? "He never complains, does he?" Rook said.

"Not the captain," Fern said reverently. "Even at sixty seasons, he still keeps the young folk on their toes."

"Tercius is *sixty*?" Rook raised his eyebrows.

"Well, sixty-two, I think—but..." he glanced at Rook sidelong, "don't tell him I told you that. Nah, some age slower than others. That's what they say, eh? He's barely begun waning!"

Rook nodded, watching as Tercius returned from further downstream. It was at this moment that Rook finally noticed the man favoring one leg. He sighed to himself. "Alright," he said to Fern. "I'll be inside with Cato."

"Oh, thanks, Rook!" Fern relaxed with relief. "I owe you one."

Rook, not thrilled about having to spend another leg of the journey with the talkative highlord, charged toward the carriage determinedly and entered it, closing the door behind him.

"Ah, Rook," Cato said from his cushioned chair, holding up a half-drunk bottle of vino. "Let's *celebrate*!" He sloshed the bottle in Rook's direction.

"No, thanks." Rook paused. "Wait—celebrate *what*?"

"Your land!"

"Oh," Rook cleared his throat. "Yeah, about that..."

"What," Cato frowned, "You want *more*? I haven't even told you which piece you're getting!"

"No, I don't want any land," Rook said abruptly.

"Oh," Cato glanced down at his mess of papers before him on his little table. Just then, the carriage shook, thrusting forward into motion. Rook caught himself against the wall and felt a small amount of glee as Cato's face nearly smashed into the table.

"Tercius!" Cato screamed, "Warn me next time!" He glanced up at Rook and shrugged defeatedly. "Fine, no land then."

"Great," Rook said, watching as Cato tried to gather his papers into a pile. "Well, I think I'll ride up on top, then. I want to see Mensa."

"Oh, come on!" Cato whined, slapping the table as he leaned back defeatedly. "I don't want to be down here *alone*! Could you send Tercius down?"

Rook masked a grin and nodded. "Sure." He exited through the back of the caravan and climbed up the ladder, finding himself once more on top with the other soldiers.

All three Eagles groaned at the sight of him.

"I guess I'll go down," Titus sighed, moving toward the back. Rook took Titus' place on the bench closest to the driver's seat, where Tercius held the reins.

He could have sent Tercius down, as asked, but he felt curious about the man, and preferred his company.

"Well," Tercius said, after clearing his throat loudly, "We just passed the border into Mensa's capital."

"Time's up for the bet, then," Rook sighed, leaning back with his arms against the siding.

"Well, I have to hand it to you—"

"No land for me, I guess," Rook interrupted him. Tercius frowned and glanced at Rook quickly out of the corner of his eye.

"Aye? What do you mean?"

"I said, no land." Rook said again, "Looks like you'll get to see me bull-riding." He stood quickly, moving away from the captain to look at Mensa from the other side of the wagon.

"Rook..." Tercius said quietly, keeping his eyes on the road.

Rook paused and turned to the captain expectantly. "Hm?"

"You're pitying me," he said, as if the statement were an accusation.

Rook looked down at his boots. "No," he said, "sorry, I don't know what you mean."

Tercius scoffed to himself. "Suit yourself."

Rook sat down, leaning over the side of the wagon to gaze out at the city.

Mensa proper: it was the capital of the largest Raqian Human kingdom, when it came to land. There was pomp to this city, even in its outer limits. Everything was picturesque. Every road was paved with stone. Lining the streets were innumerable brick houses with neatly thatched roofs and picketed fences. Rook drew in a sharp breath as he realized just how *many* houses there were. So many people, so close together—it seemed almost unnatural to Rook, who had lived most of his life in rural settings.

As their carriage drew closer to the heart of the city towards the castle, their pace slowed greatly. Theirs wasn't the only carriage and it didn't take long for them to reach the congested cluster of caravans. The queue led directly to the castle which stood as a centerpiece in the middle of the city, surrounded by a monstrous stone wall.

"It'll be slow going for a bit," Tercius said, breaking the silence as he turned to Rook. Rook nodded, then moved to the other side of the wagon to observe the western side of the road. Their carriage stood on a portion of the main road which ran beside a village square. He was intrigued to see a considerably large crowd of local citizens gathered in it, making a chorus of angry noises. Rook peered this way and that, trying to see what it was they were all gathered around.

A man stood at the center of the crowd, guarded protectively by a small fleet of armed soldiers with spears drawn. He was shouting something, but Rook couldn't make out what it was.

"What do you think is going on down there?" Rook mumbled.

"What?" Tercius turned to eye the crowd, "Who knows."

Rook leapt over the side of the carriage and landed on the ground in a crouch. He could hear Tercius yelling curse words at him.

"I'll be right back," Rook called, moving closer. From the edge of the crowd, he still couldn't make out what the man was saying. He looked at an elderly man beside him, who was also striving to hear the voice of the speaker.

"Can you hear him?" the old man asked. "My ears aren't good."

Rook smiled at the man and shook his head. "No. Who is he?"

"He's the lord over our distribution. Is it true what they are saying?" the man said in a raspy voice.

"What are they saying?" Rook asked, glancing back toward the lord encircled by guards

"They are saying he will be thinning the rations—which were already tight. And they're saying that we didn't gather enough to last the new season. But that can't be right. We gathered as much as they told us to!"

Rook narrowed his eyes, refocusing on the man. "*Food*?"

The man's face twisted with confusion. "Of *course*, food—what else would we be waiting for? They're here to pass out our rations!"

"There is not enough food?" He felt a stabbing pain in his heart, one he could hardly bear. "Why isn't there enough food?"

The old man blinked a few times, as if he must have heard wrong. "My ears are no good," he said, "did you ask why they are not giving us the rations they promised?"

Rook shook his head. "I..." he hesitated, "I don't understand why there isn't enough food."

The old man dropped his head, sighing in defeat. "It was never supposed to be like this," he said. "In my day, there was always enough food." Rook stared blankly at the man, his face frozen like stone. Was there really a lack of food in the land? Had things really come to that?

The peasant looked up at him with a smile. "I am sorry," said the man, "I shouldn't complain."

Rook watched as the man turned to leave the city square and meandered down a side street. He then heard a frantic voice calling from a distance. It seemed his carriage had begun to move again.

It didn't take long for Rook to rejoin them; they *still* weren't moving very quickly. He gazed up toward Tercius, shielding his eyes from the blinding skylight with his hand.

"I won't fall behind," Rook yelled up toward the captain, "I'll just walk down here."

"Suit yourself," Tercius called back, "But don't complain to me later if you fall behind. We won't wait for you."

"Good!" Rook yelled back.

"What's all that noise?" Cato's face suddenly popped out from his little viewing window screen. "And why aren't we moving?"

Rook was just below the window, walking slowly to keep pace with the wagon which began moving forward at a snail's pace.

"Traffic," Rook said, making eye contact with the highlord.

Cato groaned. "*Traffic*? Dogs... I didn't come all this way to get stuck in traffic!"

"Deal with it," Rook said sharply, walking up ahead of the carriage.

"What's gotten you in a sour mood?" Cato called after him. Rook ignored him, figuring he would see how many other processions were ahead of them.

Rook jogged forward until he found himself parallel with a fancy-looking cluster of soldiers. They were fitted with full suits of shiny plate armor and held green banners with yellow filigree. Whoever they were, they were wealthy.

Rook kept pace with one of the soldiers, who hailed him with a wave of his hand. The soldier had to turn his head to see through his helmet slit.

"Hallo," the soldier said, then turned back to look ahead as he walked.

"Where do you hail from?" Rook asked.

"The Gramenlands," he said in a friendly tone. "You?"

"Edgelands," Rook said, quickening his pace to keep up as the party began to move faster.

He heard the soldier whistle. "Edgelands, eh? Hades!" Rook would have to grow used to surprised reactions whenever he mentioned the Edgelands.

"Yup," Rook said, scanning their party. At the center of the group, several burly servants carried a covered palanquin. "Who have you got in there?" he asked. "A highlord?"

The soldier scoffed, turning to look at Rook for a moment, then shifted his gaze forward again. "Not a lord," he said, "A king." The soldier cleared his throat. "Security or nobility?"

"Who, me?"

"Yes, you," the soldier barked.

"N—nobility," Rook stuttered. It just didn't feel right saying it.

"Wing?"

"Yeah," Rook said, slowing his pace as the party reached a halt.

The soldier rested his spear on the ground and turned full to face Rook. Rook saw the man's eyes widen in shock through his eye-slit. Those damn scars—they seemed to startle just about everyone, didn't they? "Uh," the man stalled.

"So you've got the King of the Gramenlands," Rook said, placing his hands on his hips as he gazed further down the line of clogged processions. "And we have got an Edgelands highlord." He looked back at the soldier. "I met some Elves on the road—do you know of anyone else who is coming?"

"Just ahead of us is the party from Sol," he said, lifting his spear again as the party began to move. "A prince, I think," he said.

"A prince from Sol," Rook gazed just ahead where he could see orange banners, lined with blue. "There?" he pointed.

"Didn't I just say that?" The soldier asked.

"Thanks," Rook said, trotting further forward. His heart began to beat with excitement as his eyes scanned the long lines of important-looking carriages and palanquins. He was at the center of *something.* Such an idea should have seemed horrible, but now that he was there, it felt exciting.

Cutting off the side of the road, he ran up the side of a building and climbed swiftly on top to see over the processions. There it was: Mensa Castle. His heart pounded harder. King Hanz was in there—the man who stole Felix' eyes; the man who stole *everything.*

"What am I doing?" Rook whispered to himself. "Did I really come here?" Rook felt a terrifying cold rise up within his body. Nightmares scratched at the back of his mind. No—don't think about them; don't give them power. He could hear a voice inside his head screaming—his own voice. He closed his eyes, drawing in a deep breath, then let it out. The horrors drifted away like dust in the wind. No, those memories belonged to someone else.

"For Felix." Rook said to himself, "I am doing this for Felix."

Down below, Rook could see the procession moving forward again. He leapt off the rooftop and made his way back to his people. In moments, he was on top of the wagon again, seating himself next to Tercius, who made a noise of displeasure.

"What?" Rook asked. He had hardly been gone for a hundred clicks.

"I am going to be frank," Tercius said, without giving Rook the courtesy of looking at him once. "I don't like pity, and I don't need it."

Rook sighed. "Tercius..."

"I *mean* it, Rook," he said sharply. "I don't want your damn pity. You got the land from Cato, that was that. I don't make bets I don't plan on upholding," he turned now to look the young man in the eyes. "I plan to uphold my end, alright?"

"I'm sorry, Tercius," Rook said firmly, "But I stand by my decision to give back the land. I can't in good conscience put a veteran like yourself needlessly in harm's way—I—I did it out of respect."

Tercius spat. "If you wanted to show me respect, you would have treated me like an equal, not some felling cripple."

There was silence between them for a hundred clicks or so, then Rook broke it.

"You're tired of being treated differently because of old wounds. You want to be seen as what you really are."

"Yes."

Rook rubbed his bare chin. "Alright—then how about I pretend I don't notice your limp, and you pretend I don't have scars."

Tercius' eyes widened for a moment as he studied Rook's face. "Son," Tercius said slowly, "Whatever happened to you..."

Rook's face darkened, "Can you *really* not see past them??"

Tercius' face softened, then he dropped his head in shame. "I am sorry," he said, "I will not ask you about them again." He lifted his eyes to meet Rook's. "No more pity."

"No more pity," Rook nodded. "That works for me."

Hours passed before their Wagon finally came through the barbicans and under the portcullises into Mensa Castle: a world of stone and torch fire, crafted in symmetry and precision. The castle network itself was the size of a city—in fact, many *called* it a city. Rook and his party on top of the wagon enjoyed all the cheers and gasps at the sight of their fantastic aurochs beast. Though he himself hadn't actually traveled all the way from the Edgelands, he still felt like a celebrity as he jumped down and joined Lord Cato's side. Just then, the greeting party came to meet them.

"Welcome to Mensa!" A man in a velvet purple suit spread out his hands in greetings. "What an unexpected surprise!" He approached Cato with a bow, eyeing Rook peripherally.

"Surprise?" Cato exclaimed, placing his hands on his hips as he straightened to his full height. However annoying the man was at times, he could look intimidating when he wanted to. Even Rook was surprised to see how tall the lord actually was. "What do you mean, 'surprise?' Didn't King Hanz get my letter?"

"I'm afraid he didn't," the greeter said with poise, "But our watchmen saw your banners from a long way off and we can proudly say that we have already prepared living arrangements for you. In fact," he smiled confidently, "King Hanz has asked me to put you and your," he glanced at Rook again, "*Wing*—in the chambers bordering his own! He wants you to know that your presence is a delightful surprise... *Lord*?"

"This is Highlord Cato," Rook said, hoping he was doing right by preventing Cato from having to introduce himself, "of the Edgelands."

"Welcome, Highlord Cato," said the greeter. "I am Sir Swain, and I will be overseeing all of the needs of the nobleman for the duration of Kingsummons. ...and you are?" He bowed his head to Rook.

"Rook," Rook said, suddenly growing self-conscious.

"*Rook*," Swain held a straight face, but Rook could see judgment behind his eyes.

"My blasted Wing," Cato sighed loudly, "*Sir* Rook: a Knight of Edgeland but without an *acre* of land," Cato swayed his head dramatically in Rook's direction, signaling his annoyance. He turned back to Swain, rolling his eyes, "The boy keeps forgetting his own title and, Hades, if he's not a very pleasant person to look at, but the felling man saved my life, and I want him treated right."

Swain bowed lowly to Rook, then rose saying, "Sir Rook, what a pleasure it is to have you." He held out his hands, addressing the two of them, "If you would allow, I will have your soldiers escorted to the barracks, your..." he hesitated, "*steed* taken to the stables, and your carriage properly stored—then, you and your lordship," he nodded his head toward Rook, "can come with me into the Inner Palace."

Rook and Cato were led up the wide set of stone stairs to what would be the third or fourth gate they had passed under thus far. Soon, they found themselves walking through an extensive private courtyard reserved only for those who resided within the Inner Palace. The Palace itself was framed by tall cypress trees and magnificent statues. Rook spotted spearmen at every turn and corner, whether up on the walls that looked over them or lining the paved path they walked. They entered the palace through the front doors and into the vestibule where a large curtain had been hung against the wall. An artist of sorts sat beside it on a stool with a pencil held in his hand.

"If you would just stand here a moment, my lord," Swain said to Cato, pointing at the velvet backdrop. "We are arranging a new book of portraits. Everyone will receive a copy for their records."

"Well, if Hanz wants to look at my face that badly," Cato waved his arms around, pretending to feel flattered. He stood himself in front of the backdrop, placed his hand on his hip, and stuck out his chest. The artist whipped up his sketch very quickly. Rook leaned over the artist's shoulder, watching Cato's face come to life on the page.

"Beautiful," Rook observed. The artist, a young man dressed in a simple white tunic and a floppy hat jumped, then turned to meet Rook's eyes. Rook drew in a sharp breath, noticing the young man's eyes; they were wide and colorful. Yes, his eyes were as deep as the Sea, and his skin just as black. After a quick glance at his ears, there was no longer any doubt: this boy was a Faerie. "You have a talented hand," Rook said.

"I—I..." The artist stuttered, growing confused as he examined Rook's face. "Thank you!" He broke eye contact to look back at his drawing and he gaped at the work of his own hand. He examined it carefully with his mouth wide open. Rook followed the artist's gaze and studied the completed artwork. The pencil markings were so detailed and so lifelike that they seemed to spring out from the page. He'd seen nothing like it.

"You must be the Faerie of lines," Rook said, touching the paper gently, picking it up.

The dark-skinned young man lowered his voice to a whisper and seemed to shrink into his stool. "How did you know that? I–I mean..." He flinched as he noticed Swain's judgmental eyes suddenly gazing in his direction. "That is to say," he swallowed loudly, "I have no title. But that is most kind of you to say..."

"Please, don't speak with the Faeries." Swain said sharply, stepping closer.

Puzzled, Rook turned to him. "What did you say? Why not?"

"Please step over here," Swain plastered on another smile, "It is your turn."

Rook swooped past Swain, standing in the posing spot, and spun to face the artist. His pose was simple: he just stood there, looking right at the boy.

Hades—he couldn't be older than sixteen seasons. The Faerie drew quickly, though he took a few moments to meet Rook's gaze. The boy studied them deeply, searching.

"All of the Faeries that you see here in the Inner Palace," Swain said in a ceremonial voice, "belong to King Hanz. He requests those visiting to respect their privacy and interact with them only when necessary." He seemed to be giving Rook a warning. Rook paid him no heed, only watching the Faerie of Lines draw. He couldn't stop looking at his eyes; they were so deep, and with so many colors at once!

"What's your name?" Rook asked, keeping his eyes only on the Faerie.

"For fortune's sake, Rook!" Cato tossed his hands in the air defeatedly, "Leave the thing alone! Do you ever listen to anyone?"

"Coppo," the artist said quickly, then shrunk a little behind his paper as he worked. His hand moved at an alarmingly quick pace.

"I am Rook," Rook said, stepping forward as Coppo signaled that he was finished.

"Gods, he is so fast," Cato remarked to Swain, who stood silently beside him with his arms crossed, watching Rook carefully.

Rook moved behind Coppo to look at the picture. When he saw it, his heart was filled with both pain and awe. He snatched the picture up quickly and blinked several times, trying to discern if he was seeing things right. After a few moments, he dropped the paper and connected eyes with Coppo, who looked at him innocently.

"Why have you..." Rook struggled to find the words. "Why didn't you draw the... scars."

"What scars?" Coppo narrowed his eyes for a moment. "I don't see..." he studied Rook, as if trying to see through a screen. "Oh!"

Cato stepped up behind Rook and took the paper, raising his eyebrows as he studied it. "Well, slay me!" Cato remarked, showing the drawing to Swain. "Hades, it looks exactly like you, well except for—." He looked up at Rook's face. "Hades, Rook, I didn't know you were such a dapper man—sorry—but that's the only word that comes to mind." Cato whistled. "Damn."

Rook frowned, glancing at Cato who was almost never serious. "Don't mock me."

"No," Swain said under his breath, "This is beautiful." He shot his eyes suspiciously at Coppo. He then closed his eyes, thinking to himself for a moment, and returned the paper to Coppo's stand. "Alright," he said quickly, "Let us move on."

Cato followed Swain as he glided down one of the halls. Rook lingered for a moment, sharing a smile with Coppo, then trailed along after.

Rook studied Swain from behind. The man was lean and tidy, with short silver hair and a black goatee. As annoying as he was, he had a pleasant face and that made it tricky to read him. He seemed to have this way of making one want to impress him, even when he was quipping or dropping condescending remarks. Why was he so protective of Coppo? No—protective wasn't the right word: *possessive*, perhaps. Swain didn't want Rook talking to the Faeries. Did he say they *belonged* to King Hanz? He felt his blood begin to pump wildly through his veins.

No, it wasn't his job to rescue every Faerie in trouble. He was here for his friend; he was here for Felix. If he stopped and helped every single Faerie he ever met, he would run out of... Rook felt a stabbing pain in his heart.

Stay focused, he told himself, *I am here for Felix. I am here for just the one.*

"And this door is yours, Highlord Cato," Swain said, bowing as Cato passed him and charged into the room in search of the nearest bed. Swain rose, looking at Rook.

"And you will be here in the adjoining room, just there, Sir Rook." Swain said as he folded his hands.

Rook stood still. "Sir Swain," he said, "Why did you say that the Faeries in the Inner Palace *belong* to King Hanz?"

"They are his staff," Swain said defensively, "You'll note that the maids, the servants, the ostlers, and even the *knights* belong to him, too."

"Alright, I meant no offense," Rook bristled. "Thanks for showing me to my room. Um," he glanced inside his quarters then back at Swain again. "Is there some sort of schedule, or something, that we need to be aware of? Or do we just... hang around."

"There is an order of events posted in every room for the week," Swain said. "And a servant will be along shortly to attend to you. There's a bell if you need anything sooner than that." He began to whisk away, but Rook cleared his throat. Swain reluctantly turned back to face him. "Yes, Sir Rook?"

"I, um..." he stalled.

"If you don't mind, I would love it if you made this quick," he said in a short tone, "There's a line of noblemen waiting outside, and they're getting grumpier with each passing click."

"Am I free to, *erm*, roam around?"

"Yes, yes," Swain waved his hand at him, "but go read the welcome letter first. Good-*bye*!" He was gone.

Rook turned and entered his chambers. He journeyed across the large room, sighing to himself as he took in its unnecessary size. There was, indeed, a door in the corner of his room which was currently hanging open, leading to Cato's room. He could see the highlord lying on his face upon his bed, sleeping. Rook closed the door, granting him a moment of privacy.

Well, after days of sharing a wagon with three strangers, he was finally alone. Damn—why was this room so big?

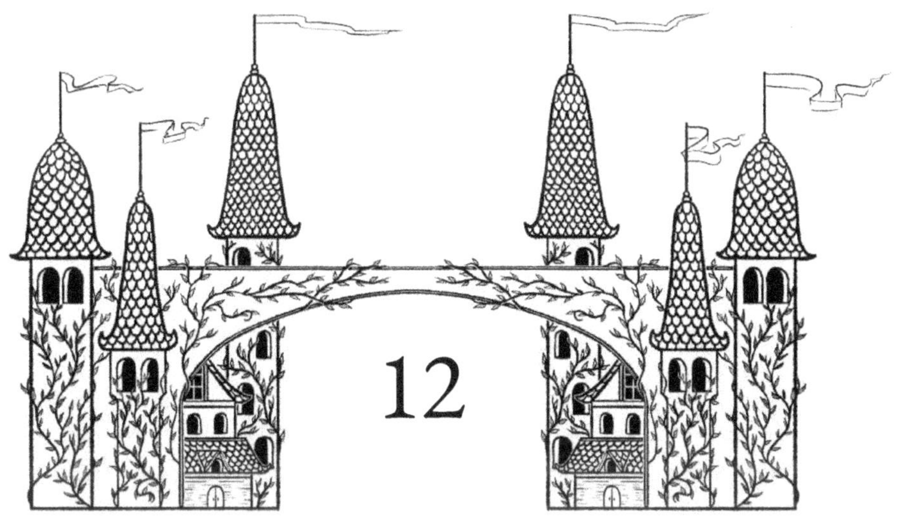

12

— Rasselas —

The Bath House

"Damn—why is this room so small? It makes me feel like I'm choking!" Rasselas complained. "We passed about five other larger rooms on our way here and I guarantee they were empty! Slay me! King Hanz is snubbing me on *purpose*!"

Rasselas' whining could be heard all the way from Thorne's adjoined room, and this last complaint was enough for the wing to poke his head through the door in protest.

"Will you *please* pipe down?" The brown-haired Elf said in a harsh whisper. "The servants will hear you! We are trying to make a good impression here!"

Rasselas, who was lying shirtless on his bed, waved his hand at the wing dismissively. "Why is your voice so annoying right now?" he said weakly. "I have such a headache from that felling walk. Did you notice how all the other delegates traveled, by the way? They were all in *covered* palanquins and the like! Meanwhile *I* had to—" A pillow interrupted Rasselas by colliding into his face.

Rasselas sat up quickly to toss a glare back in Thorne's face, but it was too late, the wing was gone already. The young prince rolled out of bed lazily and dragged his feet across the room to look at the wall where the order of events was mounted.

"Have you looked at this yet, Thorne?" he called out, half-heartedly. There was no answer. His eyes focused on the paper, and he studied it.

It read:

The First Week of Kingsummons

Beginning Grounsday, the delegates will meet in the Court House for the midday bells for official matters. Each evening you will be invited to attend the following events that Mensa Castle will be hosting for your enjoyment.

— Firstday —

Arrivals

— Watersday —

A Welcome Banquet

— Grounsday —

An Introduction for the Princess

— Lightsday —

Games

— Wingsday —

Costume Banquet

— Mansday —

Duels

— Somensday —

Lounge Day

It was currently Watersday, the second day of the week, so tonight there would be some sort of 'Welcome Banquet'. Rasselas wrinkled his nose, 'An Introduction for the princess'? That would be one of those social events where Hanz' own daughter is paraded around as a potential bride. King Hanz knew no shame.

"He's going to make us all 'ooh' and 'ahh' over his daughter," Rasselas shouted toward the closed door. There was still no response. "Can you ring the bell for service?" he called hopelessly. No answer.

Rasselas trudged across the room, where a velvet ribbon hung from the ceiling. He yanked it several times impatiently.

"How am I supposed to prepare for a banquet tonight if *no one will even come to my aid!*" He raised his voice angrily.

"I am not a servant!" he heard Thorne shout from his own room.

"So you *can* hear me, you little rat!" Rasselas mumbled to himself, yanking the ribbon a few more times. He wandered over to his mirror, examined himself, and cursed under his breath. "My hair is a *disaster*!" He yelled as if it were Thorne's fault. "Slay me!" he said to his reflection in a posh voice. "That fight with Thorne has completely put me out!"

He tried to tame his hair, which at one point had looked like a sculpture of a god. *Now*, he sighed, *now it looks like Embers has been at it!*

"Why is no one coming?" he yelled, marching toward the main door to his chambers. "I need a bath!"

He swung open the door aggressively, priming to yell down the hall, when he collided into someone else. Rather, the maid came colliding into *him*. Rasselas grunted in surprise. He stumbled backwards into his room, catching himself with his back foot and her with his hands.

"Cards!" he exclaimed, looking down at the poor frightened girl who was probably frightened further by being held tightly against his bare chest. Once she realized what had happened, she screamed and pulled away quickly from him.

"I'm sorry!" she gasped, holding up her hands as if surrendering. "I didn't mean to—"

"It's fine." Rasselas recovered quickly, dusting off his chest as if her touch had dirtied him in some way. "Just get me—" his voice caught in his throat. Well, she was uncommonly pretty! He stared with his mouth half open. Why were her eyes so striking? Then it hit him; she was a fairy!

"What did you need?" she asked, trying to regain her equanimity, though her wide deer-like eyes continued to dart around, studying him. Rasselas, realizing his half-dressed state, cleared his throat in apology.

"Well, slay me!" he said, placing his hands on his hips as if posing, "I was trying to ring for a bath."

The maid raised an eyebrow. "You wanted me to... *bring* you a bath?"

Rasselas was stuck looking at her again. He shook himself back to attention. "What did you say?"

"I can't *bring* you a bath," she said. There was the slightest hint of mockery in her voice. "There's a men's bathhouse down the hall. I can grab one of the servants to—" she began to move back toward the door but froze when Rasselas reached forward and took her by the wrist. Her eyes snapped up to meet his and she gave him an angry scowl.

"Wait," he said weakly, trying desperately to figure out what he even wanted to say.

"Sir," she said in a quiet voice, though her eyes were yelling, "unhand me."

Rasselas quickly released his hold on her wrist and shook his head quickly. "No!" he sputtered. "Sorry! I just wanted to ask you something!"

"*Well?*" She backed away toward the door cautiously. "Ask me, then!"

"Wait!" He stepped toward her, and she stepped further away, keeping distance. "Cards, woman!" he said, "I am not trying to be one of *those* men... *Hades*! You—you're a Faerie!"

The maid paused and rotated her head slightly, like Embers did when he was mildly curious. "So?"

Rasselas sighed dramatically. "Well, I," he stuttered. Damn! He had come all this way to meet a Mensa Faerie, and here he was, terrifying her! "Damn," he said, "I've got several good friends who are Fae, and I promised them I would look out for their brothers and sisters in Mensa—you know—pass along the peace and all that." He found it hard to keep up his phony act in the presence of a Faerie; they always seemed to bring out another side of him. Still, he used his fancy voice, and kept his chin high, smiling.

The maid's face was frozen for a moment as she kept her head at that same slanted angle, then one of her eyebrows, the one that was pointier than the other, rose slightly. "Friends?" she asked. "I don't understand."

Rasselas relaxed a little, chuckling. "You don't understand the word *friend?*"

"I—" she cut herself off, reorienting her head into a more suspicious stance. "You've met other Faeries? *Where?*"

Rasselas shrugged, chuckling once more, "Hades, I don't know! Lots of places!"

She narrowed her eyes suspiciously. "*Name* one."

Damn. She didn't believe him! "Slay me, woman!" He made a phony offended face. "I wouldn't *lie* about having Faerie friends just to keep you here longer!"

"You're not helping your case," the maid said, moving backwards once more.

"Fine," Rasselas frowned, dropping his act and slapping his legs in defeat. "Momentum, Cymbeline, Rowan—how many names do you *want?*"

The maid's eyes grew wide again. *Hades*—when he didn't think they could get any wider! "*Who?*" she asked.

Rasselas groaned. Well, he thought he had name-dropped the most famous Faeries in the world, but this girl didn't seem to know *any* of them! "You know—*Momentum?* Faerie of Time?"

The maid crossed her arms, wincing slightly as if the action caused her a touch of discomfort. "You're trying to tell me you are friends with *Aorist?*"

"Sure," Rasselas shrugged, waving his hand, "Aorist works too, but he doesn't like to—"

"This is rich," The maid chuckled, turning to leave.

"Where are you going? Wait!"

"Did you *really* think I would be friendly to you if you just named—I don't know—the most *famous* Faerie on the world?" she said, giving him a mocking smile.

"Now, see here!" Rasselas cried defensively, but she was gone. He stood there by the door, processing for a moment, then slammed it closed angrily. As he turned, he noticed the door to his adjoined room open wide, with Thorne standing under it wearing the most annoying grin.

"What?" Rasselas barked, "Why are you making that face?"

"Flirting? With a *chambermaid? Already?*" He cackled.

"I wasn't—" Rasselas held his breath. "I wasn't *flirting* with her," he said, "I—"

"Sure," Thorne, sauntered into the room, looking suddenly cheery. He stepped in front of Rasselas' mirror and examined himself, checking to make sure every single one of his long straight hairs was in its right place. "I saw what I saw."

Rasselas didn't feel the need to explain himself to the racist idiot. "I thought you didn't want to come in here," Rasselas said as he plopped himself on his bed. "Now I can't seem to be rid of you."

"Well," Thorne turned away from the mirror to face the prince. "I couldn't exactly miss a chance to see you making a fool of yourself in front of a female. I knew you were a flirt, but I didn't know you were so *bad* at it."

Rasselas bit his lip. "Got any tips for me?" he asked sarcastically. "I bet you have a way with the ladies."

Thorne snorted. "I have no interest in chambermaids, princesses, or anyone else we will find in Mensa."

Rasselas felt a pang of curiosity as he observed the distant expression on Thorne's face. "Slay me!" he exclaimed, "You're in *love*, aren't you?"

Thorne's face quickly hardened with anger. "Don't you *dare* try and 'figure me out', Moonvine."

"Hades, old boy!" Rasselas sat forward eagerly. "Tell me who she is! I'm sure I can—"

"You—" Thorne pointed one of his slender fingers at the prince, "Stay out of this!"

Rasselas sighed, leaning back, deflated. "Cards, Thorne. Why won't you warm to me?"

Thorne shook his head slowly. "I will never warm to you, Moonvine."

"Why? Why ever not?" Rasselas hopped off his bed, marching up to the wing. "What have I done that is so *horrible* to you?"

Thorne looked Rasselas up and down, head to toe, and toe to head, with a look of disgust. "Why it's simple, *Rasselas*," he said, "you were *born*."

Rasselas gaped, open-mouthed, blinking as Thorne turned and left as silently as he came. "You're mad at me for..." he said aloud to himself, "*existing*?" Hades, this man sure held implacable grudges! Well, there wasn't anything Rasselas could do about not existing, so he decided to give up on trying to make that infuriating man like him. Rasselas rotated to look at himself in the mirror once more, turning red in the cheeks as he replayed the moment when he came into direct contact with that Faerie girl. He held his breath, searching his memory for details about her appearance: her ash-colored hair wrapped up in a side braid; her plump lips, pursed in suspicion and deliciously crimson.

He shuddered, shaking off the growing tension he felt inside himself. He wasn't here to flirt, whatever Thorne might think. He was here on a far more dire purpose. If he could convince that maid he wasn't actually trying to *flirt* with her, he might have found a potential mole, a way inside the Faerie community.

The prince wandered over to his chest which sat beside the writing desk, over by his window. After opening the window, letting in some of the warm Kingsummons air, he unfastened the chest and pulled out his leather pouch containing loose papers. He slid the top sheet out from the pouch and read its contents which had been penned in red ink.

My beloved Faeries of Mensa — I see your chains. Do you? How can an aurochs be chained like an ox? Don't you know who you are? I compel you, brothers and sisters, to perceive yourselves not as weak and powerless individuals, but as potent and controlled giants. You are not like a beast of burden which can be trained to do the will of its master, but a shining, untouchable light, that cannot be quelled by darkness. Your existence and purpose cannot be hidden by lies, just as day cannot be concealed by a cloth. No one can force you to serve; you choose to serve. So do not serve in a way that destroys yourself. Serve in the way you were made to serve. Serve not as a slave obeys the will of its master, or as a dog obeys its owner; but serve as a parent serves a child, or as a king serves his people. You are potent and controlled giants, filled with the gift of unimaginable power. Do not forsake this gift because others have told you it is your shame. It is not your shame; it is your glory. Do not be ashamed of who you are, and do not forsake the greater purpose of your existence for a lesser one. I cannot free you from the chains until you first believe that they bind you. When you are ready, I will find you.

The letter was signed with a red stamp Rasselas had commissioned to look like Embers' footprint. He had worked on perfecting this letter during his walk from Celesta to Mensa, twisting and manipulating words and arguments from the great philosopher, Green Lion. Rasselas didn't mean to plagiarize so much as reference the philosopher. The Green Lion used words to keep an entire nation subdued. Only, Rasselas was now using similar words to do the opposite: to shake up a people who had been hushed into submission. The only question now was how to get this letter circulating amongst the Faeries.

Rasselas jumped at the sound of flapping wings. He raised his eyes from the paper to see Embers standing on the window's edge.

Well, it took you long enough to open your window. I was afraid you would concern yourself with bathing and napping before remembering I existed. The black thunderbird said with his head pointing directly south.

"Oh, calm down," Rasselas mumbled.

Have you decided what to do with that? Embers asked, picking at the paper with his beak.

"Seen anything interesting out there?" Rasselas asked, glancing over at the bird.

Embers shrugged in a bird-like way, picking at his foot with his beak.

"Fine, *don't* tell me where you've been." Rasselas grumbled, folding the paper up and tucking it into his pocket.

I don't like the feeling of being monitored, Embers said coolly, *I am the one keeping an eye on you, remember?*

"No one is keeping an eye on *anyone*!" Rasselas snapped.

Embers ruffled his feathers protectively. *What has gotten you so worked up? Did someone steal your shiny thing?*

Rasselas paused, trying to figure out what Ember's birdish turn-of-phrase meant. "Steal my—" he hesitated, "*Yes*, someone annoyed me."

Thorne? Embers faced west in amusement.

"Have you figured out where the Faeries are?" Rasselas asked, changing the subject.

There is a walled area on the eastern side of the castle network, Embers said, pointing his beak at Rasselas, *It is heavily guarded. Inside I saw many Faeries and their homes.*

"So Hanz has got them all cooped up together like a hen house," Rasselas rubbed his bare face. "At least they are all together. If they have a sort of community, I should be able to spread ideas quicker."

And what exactly do you plan on doing? Embers asked suspiciously. *Even if you did convince them to leave Mensa, I've counted over a thousand soldiers on the walls alone!*

"They're *Faeries*, Embers!" Rasselas said with conviction, "They're powerhouses! If I can figure out just which titles Hanz is hiding in there, I can make a plan of escape."

Embers didn't look convinced; his head drifted southeast like a broken compass.

Rasselas sighed. "Hades, Embers, if *you* don't believe in me, I am sure no one else will."

It's not that I don't believe in you, Embers said, *I just can't form an opinion on a plan that doesn't exist yet.*

"Sure," Rasselas shrugged, "That's what Father said, too."

What does he think about you coming here as a subversive spy? Embers asked.

Rasselas' eyes widened for a moment, then he blew air out of the side of his mouth.

Oh, Embers ruffled his feathers amusingly, *He doesn't know.*

"*Vigilante* isn't the word I would use," Rasselas mumbled, "All I want to do is spread ideas... for now."

And then you will lead a host of Faerie captives out of Mensa like a felling savior? Embers asked, blinking with sarcasm.

Rasselas grunted. "I can't explain what's in my head," he said sharply. "Of *course,* my parents wouldn't want me coming here. They think Hanz is the reason my brother went missing. They still treat me like their 'little baby boy' they don't want to lose. But this is important to me, Embers. Hanz hasn't just taken the Faerie King away from the Fae, he's taken their dignity—their *freedom!*"

Embers looked down. *Sorry, friend. I know.*

"I am not trying to rescue Faeries all by myself," Rasselas said, "I just want to bring them a message. I just hate that they are being lied to." He looked up at Embers. "We all knew Hanz still had influence over the majority of the Fae," Rasselas said as he stepped up to the window, looking out over the Inner Palace courtyard, "But it wasn't until I saw that young Faerie in the Gramenlands with the *slave* brand that I realized things were so bad." He shook his head. "When I asked him why he had been made a slave, he seemed confused—as if there wasn't a world where he *wouldn't* be a slave! He had been raised in Mensa. It was then I began to see just how deep the lies went." His face darkened as he turned his gaze eastward, scanning the area that Embers said the Faeries lived. "Hanz is *conditioning* Faerie slaves here, Embers. And he's twisting Momentum's words to aid his own despicable ends."

Rasselas placed his hands on the window ledge, closing his eyes as he felt the new season's warmth on his bare skin. He felt a peck on his arm and opened his eyes to see Embers looking up at him.

Your face is sad, Embers said, *Are you thinking about your brother?*

"I couldn't save him," Rasselas said, "But if he were here, seeing what I have seen, he would be *doing* something about it. They don't have a king to guide them, Embers. They're groping in the dark, buried under the avalanche of Hanz' lies. They need a light—to show them the way out." He observed the sympathetic bird who was peering up at him intently and sighed. "I'll find a way to tell Father and Momentum at Winter's End about what's going on here once I know a little more. For now, I'm just an Elven prince on my grandfather's business, coming to hear what the peace talks are all about.

The thunderbird made a squawking sound, ruffling his feathers encouragingly. Rasselas observed the bird's attempt to cheer him up and smiled for a moment. Then his face grew serious once more. "Embers?" he asked.

Yes, friend?

"Have you ever met my brother?"

Embers pointed his beak upwards, thinking.

"Embers..." Rasselas dropped down onto his knees, making his eyes level with the bird's. "Please tell me."

Embers sighed. *Yes.*

"Did you have a bond with him, too? I mean—did you speak with him, at least?" Rasselas' eyes searched longingly as he tried to remember his brother's face.

He visited Celestia once, Embers said, *when he was still at the age of questioning...fourteen seasons of age, I think—a season before he disappeared. We.... met.*

"Why don't you ever talk to me about him?" Rasselas asked softly. "I was four the last time I saw him. All I remember was how he used to play with me," his face grew vacant, "He had a smiling face and dark hair—I liked to play with his long Faerie ears."

It makes me sad to talk about him, Embers said.

"You think he's dead, don't you?" Rasselas asked.

I don't know what to think, Embers said. *You think that Hanz was at the source of the insurrection fifteen seasons ago. So do you think Hanz has him—here?*

"I don't know what to think either," Rasselas said, dropping his forehead to lean it on the corner of the window's edge. Embers took the opportunity to quickly poke through his hair to check for anything exciting.

Rasselas chuckled to himself as he struggled to think coherent thoughts with Ember's tickly beak rummaging through his curls. "An order of Faeries called the 'Purists' took credit for the death of Hevel and my brother. Hanz was in Mensa at the time. So I guess I don't have a ton of evidence, I just feel like Hanz is the only one who—*Ow!*" Rasselas lifted his head sharply. "Did you *bite* me?"

No! Ember looked both horrified and guilty at the same time.

"Anyway," Rasselas stood, no longer trusting Embers to rummage through his precious hair. "If you see a Faerie prison or anything like that, would you tell me?"

Sure. Why?

"I don't know," Rasselas ran his fingers through his rat's nest of hair, "I guess if Hanz did have my brother, he would want to keep him somewhere hidden."

Why would Hanz keep your brother as a prisoner? Why wouldn't he just kill him?

Rasselas frowned. "Because it's nearly impossible to kill a Faerie king, isn't it? And he couldn't let him go... He knows the King of the Fae would never allow his people to be sold like slaves, Embers. Hanz is getting away with these crimes because no one is watching the Faerie throne—Don't you see?"

Embers picked at his foot.

"Well, anyway!" Rasselas said in a less serious tone, "I've got to bathe if I am going to look presentable for tonight's banquet. If I am going to meet the devil tonight, I had better look fantastic."

Embers, realizing the conversation had shifted to Rasselas' vanity, flapped out of sight with a few shrill raven calls.

"Goodbye to you, too, old thing!" Rasselas said, swirling his hand dramatically in his aristocratic voice.

"Talking to yourself again?" said a voice. Rasselas whirled around to see Thorne opening the side door.

"Does that door have a lock?" Rasselas asked, observing Thorne, who was draped in a dressing gown.

"I am heading off to the bathhouse," he said flatly. "Are you coming?"

Rasselas placed his hand on his heart with a face of amazement. "Why, old boy, you thought to invite me along?"

Thorne frowned. "I'm still your wing," he said, "are you coming?"

"Well, rather!" Rasselas skipped over to his trunk and procured his dressing gown. He began to undress.

Thorne groaned. "Will you hurry up?"

"I'm a prince, aren't I? Don't rush me."

"I'll wait outside." Thorne let himself out.

Rasselas undressed, wrapped the gown around himself, and. tied it closed—though he left a deep 'v' of exposed chest. He jogged up to the door, saying, "Let's see if we can spot any interesting characters."

Once in the hall, Rasselas stopped to look around, spotting Thorne. "Which way is the bathhouse, dear Thorne?"

"Left," said Thorne. Rasselas charged forward, gliding down the hall, though not without checking to see if that maid was anywhere about.

The bathhouse was a large, tiled circular room, lined with marble pillars. At the center of the room was a large bubbling pool of shallow water. The place was excessively steamy, but that provided an element of privacy for those who were insecure enough to care about such things. Despite there being another ten or so men in the room, Rasselas disrobed and waded into the water within clicks of arriving. It took Thorne a few clicks before he joined Rasselas' side, sitting on the ledge beside him with his feet submerged in the water and a towel around his waist.

Rasselas dumped his face and hair in the refreshing water then emerged with a splash, pretending to look apologetic when Thorne, now half drenched, cursed at him.

"I'm right here, you ass!" Thorne scooted away from him, "This is a bathhouse, not the Sea, Moonvine!"

Rasselas leaned against the edge of the small pool with a grin, closing his eyes as he ignored the complaints.

"*Moonvine?*" said an unfamiliar voice, "That sort of pompous name could only be attached to an Elf. Am I right?"

Rasselas' eyes popped open to see a man sitting about six feet away from him, leaning his back against the edge of the pool. He was the sort of man Rasselas didn't feel the need or desire to see naked, with a plump body, curled upon itself in rolls and chunks, and a chest so hairy he might as well have been a bear. Rasselas appreciated the protective, though transparent, layer of water that prevented him from seeing further detail. The man's arms were stretched out on either side of his body as he reclined, and he watched Rasselas with mild interest.

"Hallo," Rasselas smiled, nodding his head in the man's direction. "Prince Rasselas—erm—*Moonvine*, at your service! And yes, I'm an Elf. Good spotting, old chap!"

The man, with his balding head of wispy hair, grinned widely, revealing a full set of near-black teeth. "It was the ears that gave you away," he said proudly.

"Ah!" Rasselas nodded encouragingly, "Good spotting!" He tried not to grimace at the sight of the man's teeth. Had he never *heard* of tooth picking?

"Yes, well," The man, who was much younger than he appeared at first glance, leaned his head back against the side of the pool and closed his eyes. "I keep an eye out for such things."

"An observant fellow," Rasselas said, sitting forward. "With an air of *royalty* about him, I would guess."

The man opened his eyes to glance back at Rasselas. "Quite," he said.

"Shall I guess where you hail from?" Rasselas said excitedly.

The man shrugged, reaching for a glass of vino which was sitting beside him on the ledge. "Sure."

"Well," Rasselas paused to think for a moment, "One of the Human Kingdoms, of course... Sol?"

"*Sol?*" The man balked. "Hades."

It was already clear to Rasselas this man was from the Vastlands. With teeth like *that*? That place was bursting at the seams with tobacco! "Not the Winglands, surely!"

"Do I look dark-skinned to you?" The man frowned.

"Oh, I give up." Rasselas splashed the water.

"He's playing with you, your majesty," said a voice from the other side of the pool. The thick steam in the air prevented Rasselas from seeing his face.

"Hallo?" Rasselas cocked his head. "Come on, if you're going to join the conversation you might as well come over here."

"Not all of us like conversation in the bath," said the voice. Rasselas could hear an element of playfulness in the man's voice.

"Alright, then," Rasselas shrugged, turning back to his large bathmate. "You're from the Vastlands. King Stathe?"

King Stathe chuckled. "I forget some of you like to study those portrait books."

"I've looked at them once or twice," Rasselas said, neglecting to tell the man that for him, 'once or twice' meant he had poured over them for bells, memorizing all the names and faces, before attempting the trip to Mensa.

"Speaking of the portrait books," the voice from the other side of the bath said, "I believe *your* face was missing in mine."

Rasselas sniffed. "And *your* face is missing from this conversation. Come now, don't make me befriend a cloudy head of steam!"

Rasselas heard the man chuckle, then watched as his formless shape moved toward him. A man emerged from the steam with tan skin, a muscular body and remarkably likable countenance. He had straight black hair, pulled into a long low tail, and a clean-shaven face. He moved boldly to where Rasselas was reclining, and sat down beside him, between him and King Stathe.

"Hallo," Rasselas greeted the man a second time, offering a friendly smile.

"Tingo," said the young man as he held out his hand to Rasselas. Rasselas shook it eagerly.

"Prince of Sol," said Rasselas, "I liked your face."

"Thank you, friend," Tingo looked somewhat amused, "Do I call you Rasselas or Moonvine, then?"

"Well," Rasselas assumed a persecuted expression, "Grandfather wants me to have an Elven name, and all that."

"Who is your grandfather?" Tingo asked, crossing his arms.

"His name is *King* Antecus," Rasselas made a dramatic gesture with his hands, then dropped them anticlimactically, "From Celestia, and all that."

The entire bath house seemed to grow silent, apart from the sound of the babbling waters. Rasselas looked side to side, wondering if he missed something.

"Celestia," he said again, "Slay me—have you all never heard of *Celestia*?"

"You're the son of King Somenus?" Tingo asked in a low voice.

"I—" Rasselas' voice caught in his throat. "Hades, no," he sighed, trying to regain his confidence, "That would be my brother Anodos," he shook his head, "Hades—have you all never heard of *Rasselas*, son of *Leonard*?" Rasselas said this, despite next to no one ever having heard of his father.

"Like I said," Tingo offered another smile, "Your portrait was missing from my book."

"Well, thankfully we all will be getting new books, eh?" Rasselas pretended to brush dust off his shoulder. "Anyway, my name might be written as Moonvine, or something like, but you'll see my face in there."

"A nice face," King Stathe observed in an encouraging voice.

Tingo and Rasselas both turned their heads to look at the rotund man. "I say," Rasselas grinned, "thanks, old man!"

The king shrugged, then took another sip of his vino. Tingo turned back to face Rasselas.

"I didn't know princess Lolette had two sons," Tingo said, "It is definitely a pleasure to meet you, Rasselas."

Prince Tingo seemed sincere to Rasselas, so he didn't mind talking about his mother. "No, you wouldn't," Rasselas said in a lower voice, "She likes her privacy."

"So I've heard," said the prince of Sol. "I think we all can appreciate that sentiment. You came here then on your grandfather's behalf?"

"Yes," said Rasselas, "The old man is trying to get me all trained up for the responsibilities of being an heir and all that."

"Heir... to his throne?" Tingo asked, leaning back. Thorne scoffed under his breath.

"I guess, so," Rasselas shrugged, "I mean—he's an Elf, so it's not like he is going to die any time soon. But I suppose since my brother has the Faerie throne to worry about, he thought the mantle should pass to me."

The room grew quiet again, and Rasselas perceived that all ears now were bent toward his conversation.

"Tell me about your brother," Tingo said with an unreadable expression.

Rasselas felt himself shrinking. "Why?" he asked. "I suppose everyone is curious about where he went?"

"Well, cards!" King Stathe exclaimed, making a small splash as he leaned forward. "Of course we are!"

"Well, let's clear the air then!" Rasselas announced loudly to the whole room. He couldn't know how many others were actually *in* there listening, but he didn't care. "It is no great secret that Arelle's throne is empty, and *why*?" He paused, searching the room for someone to take his hint and interact.

"Why?" asked King Stathe.

"Because a group of Purists assassinated the Death Faerie fifteen seasons ago," said Tingo.

"So, the Death Faerie was the King?" King Stathe rubbed his stubble in confusion.

"No," Rasselas huffed. It was shocking how little some world leaders actually knew about Arelle politics. "Hevel—*the Death Faerie*—was regent until my brother came of age. As you all know," he chose to face rather than avoid the awkwardness, "my brother is the son of Somenus, the late Faerie King. He was born the day Somenus was assassinated."

"The bastard," Stathe spat into the water. Rasselas gave the king the benefit of the doubt and assumed he was talking about Somenus—not calling his brother a bastard.

"*Anyway,*" Rasselas continued, twirling his hand in the air, "Somenus' bloodline is tied to the Faerie throne, so no one else can be king while my brother is alive. But!" He tried to build suspense by furrowing his brow, "Some Fae— yes, the *Purists*—didn't like the idea of Somenus' son becoming King. So they attacked Arelle while my brother studied under Lord Hevel. Anodos was fifteen seasons old at the time, nearly old enough to lead the kingdom himself. The Purists killed Hevel and everyone living in the castle that day. Everyone," he held up his finger, "except my brother Anodos."

"How do you know that?" Stathe asked with wide eyes. He was now sitting closer than he had been, watching Rasselas intently. Tingo, who was now sandwiched between the two of them listened with interest.

"Well, I know this for two reasons," Rasselas said calmly, "Firstly, if he had been killed, then someone else would have seized the throne by now. And secondly?" He placed his hand on his bare chest, "I know it in my heart. My brother Anodos is alive." There was, of course, a third reason, but Rasselas didn't think it wise to explain the ins and outs of Anodos being the Faerie of Magik, and how that was significant.

"Well, where *is* he then?" A fourth voice bellowed from another part of the bath. The three, who sat clustered together, turned their heads quickly in surprise. "If he's alive," said the loud talker, "where did he go?"

"Well, if I knew that," Rasselas said, "I wouldn't be sitting here *talking* about him, I would go and find him!"

"Perhaps the Purists didn't want him dead," Tingo pondered out loud, "Perhaps they wanted to brainwash him and bend his will to theirs. Then, at a later time, send him out to claim his throne."

"It's been fifteen seasons," The fourth voice bellowed, "If that was the case, wouldn't he have come out already?"

"You can either come over here and join the conversation or you can shut up!" Rasselas said coolly to the man. He heard the loud talker groan lazily, making a little splash.

"I am too tired to come all the way over there. I have been sitting in felling traffic all day and I'm downright exhausted," the voice complained. "Rook, *you* go over there and talk to them *for* me."

"I am not inclined to bathe at the moment," a quiet voice mumbled from across the pool where the loud talker sat soaking.

"Well, it sounds all interesting over there," the loud voice said. "Go on."

"Get over here, you fat slob," Rasselas laughed. "Stop ordering your wing around and come meet us."

Rasselas couldn't help but glance over to see Thorne rolling his eyes at the comment.

"No," the loud voice said haughtily, "Now that you've called me a fat slob, I am going to snub you for the rest of the evening."

"Oh, come on, old thing," Rasselas said, "You like being teased, I can tell."

"True," said the voice, "but I'm still not moving."

"Come on," King Stathe chimed, "Now you've got me all curious who you are."

"Let's guess!" Rasselas said excitedly.

"Oh gods, don't guess," said the voice, growing stressed. "You're all going to drive me insane."

"Come on, then," Stathe said, "Who are you?"

"Rook, can you just go over and talk to them?" The voice whined.

"No."

"Well," Rasselas sighed, "We know that *someone* is named Rook." He turned to face Tingo, rolling his eyes.

Tingo was grinning. "Are you from the Edgelands?" Tingo asked in a raised voice.

"Edgelands?" Rasselas wrinkled his brow. "I didn't see any Edgelands people in the portrait book."

"No," said Tingo, "But I saw their banner on the way into the city and I've met all the other visitors before. This man's voice I don't recognize."

"Well, you've got me," said the voice. "They call me Cato, if you must know, but I don't think it'll make much difference you meeting me now rather than later."

"Oh, bosh!" Rasselas exclaimed, "a friendship made while naked is surely going to last. I'm positive there is no one in this room I am *not* going to like, and that is that!"

"Well, I don't think you're going to like me," said a fifth, nasal voice.

"Hades, how many naked men are *in* here?" Rasselas raised his eyebrows, searching the steamy room for the source of the voice.

"We're not all as naked as *you*," said Thorne. His comment was followed by a few chuckles echoing through the room.

"Anyway, who said that?" Rasselas asked but was met with silence.

"That was just a squeaking rat," Tingo said, clearing his throat, "You'll meet it soon enough. But he's right. You won't like him."

"Oh come on," Rasselas pouted, "Who is it?"

"Now, now," King Stathe said in a rather congested voice, "He's not that bad."

"Well," Rasselas said, loud enough for all to hear, "It was a pleasure meeting *some* of you." He cleared his throat, "As for the rest, I will have the pleasure of seeing you at the banquet tonight, eh? But slay me," he stood, "My fingers will turn to unattractive prunes if I don't leave now. Thorne?" he looked at his wing, "Coming?"

Thorne shook his head. No doubt the prude wanted to wait until the bath emptied before he got in. So Rasselas strode over to his robe and covered himself.

"Nice meeting you," Stathe said. "I didn't know Elves were so jolly."

Rasselas didn't need to look to see what pained expression Thorne no doubt had on his face from that comment.

"Oh yes," Rasselas laughed as he exited the bathhouse, "very jolly!"

❦

What Rasselas saw looking back at him from the mirror was close to perfection—outfit-wise, anyway. He absolutely loved Mensa fashion and felt he wore it better than anyone. The tailoring on his dark green suit perfectly clung to the shape of his body and every single button on his long justaucorps was perfectly placed. He wore his coat open, as did all others in Mensa, to showcase his waistcoat, the most ornate part of his ensemble. The waistcoat was a light greenish silver with lavish embroidery and an intricately patterned fabric. His cravat was perfectly tied around his ruffly collar, adorned with a moonstone pin that his mother gave him on his eighteenth birthday. He wore skin-tight knee breeches, with long, square-toed, heeled boots that came up to his knees.

His toothpick had a silver handle in the shape of a raven's head and a long tip. He didn't really smoke but he still picked his teeth regularly for appearances' sake. Plus, it couldn't hurt to make sure his perfect set of white teeth were *even* whiter. He held his toothpick in his hand like an accessory, as it made for more attractive poses. Most men would be sporting toothpicks at a banquet like tonight's, though with ladies present, they would all be avoiding smoking.

His hair, which he had spent a good half bell combing, was now nothing short of perfection. He managed a great deal of height on his swirl of curls which were held firmly together with a handy paste he had procured on a recent visit to Tradings.

"Are you done?" asked Throne impatiently.

"Done what?" Rasselas asked, turning side to side slightly.

"Looking at yourself?"

"Almost," said Rasselas. He was about to be done, but he figured he could take a few more clicks of vanity simply to annoy the irritating man.

Thorne stood still with his arms behind his back, as he always did. "I've seen women spend less time in front of the looking glass."

"Well, of course you have," Rasselas said, turning to face him. "Anyway—is admiring one's own appearance exclusively a feminine thing?"

"Yes."

Rasselas scoffed. "My dear Thorne, if you ever expect to win over whatever fair maiden you've been pining for all week, you have to stop reducing females into sexist caricatures."

Thorne did his best to contain his rage. "We are now officially late," he said, changing the subject.

"Good," said Rasselas, "I wasn't exactly going to arrive *first*! Now," he faced the mirror once more, smiling at himself, "Now *everyone* will see my entrance."

"This is humiliating," Thorne said under his breath, turning to move towards the door. Rasselas followed him.

"Come along," said the prince, "Time to make an entrance."

The walk from the Inner Palace to the grand hall took about three hundred clicks, and all the while Thorne complained about how rude it was to arrive late. Rasselas had never heard someone so concerned about time! When they stepped into the hall, their presence was announced by a stiff-looking character in a lavender suit.

"Prince Moonvine of Celesta, grandson of King Antecus; and Sir Thorne of Celestia, son of Sir Riversong."

The hall, which was now filled with all sorts of fancily dressed noblemen, grew somewhat still at the announcement. Many turned to look, while others continued on with their conversations. Rasselas posed proudly, allowing those present time to admire. Then he moved down the set of stairs before him, holding his toothpick ornamentally over his right breast pocket and his chin raised high. Thorne followed silently behind him, staying mostly to Rasselas' right side, like a proper wing would.

At the bottom of the stairs stood a magnificent-looking character, caped in a deep purple robe and crowned with a stunning gold piece resembling something like a spiked blazing sun. Rasselas studied the man's face as he descended the stairs, preparing himself to meet the villain who had tried to kill his parents, enslaved hundreds of Faeries, and no-doubt kidnapped his brother. King Hanz, it was. He was infuriatingly handsome, with deep black hair, deliciously colored skin, and the most fantastic beard.

Rasselas wore a smug smile as he stepped up to the King. Hanz waited for him patiently, hands clasped behind his back.

"Welcome, prince Moonvine," said King Hanz with the sincerest of smiles. By heavens—he looked so noble! As Rasselas bowed ceremoniously, he found himself having a hard time disliking Hanz. What a strange experience.

"King Hanz," Rasselas said in his most played-up voice, "What an *honor* it is to meet you!" As he rose from his bow, he noted several others standing beside Hanz. One looked like some sort of officer, who stood at Hanz' right like a wing and wore a thick bush of a mustache on his upper lip. Standing beside the officer, and surprising Rasselas, was a short maid with ash hair and long Faerie ears. As the two of them made eye contact, the maid's eyes grew as wide as circles. What was she doing *there*? Rasselas returned his attention to Hanz, who moved to place his hand on his heart.

"My word," he said in a deep, earnest voice, "You must be Rasselas."

Rasselas wasn't sure how to respond. He blinked a couple times, holding his pompous smile, and said, "Well slay me—old man—of *course* I am!"

"I know your father," Hanz said, his eyes drifting upward as if visiting old, fond memories. "We were quite close at one time. What an incredible man!" His eyes moved back to meet Rasselas'. "We lived together at Winter's End."

"Yes," Rasselas raised his toothpick to his mouth and set the white tip on his lower lip. "So I have heard." His eyes did their best to hide his anger.

"I was young then," Hanz said wistfully. "Your father saw me at my worst, I fear," he shook his head, looking regretful. "But he's a good man. I am so glad to meet his other son." He held out his hand, and—*Hades*—there were *tears* in his eyes!

Rasselas was frozen in confusion for a moment but reached out his hand to shake the King's.

"Well cards, old man!" he said, shaking the King's hand, "How kind."

Hanz clapped his own hands together with a smile. "Well," he said, "I am so pleased your grandfather thought to send you! I had no idea you were living in Celestia now."

"Quite," said Rasselas, running the tip of this pick along the top of his front tooth.

"Tell me, how are my friends at Winter's End? How is Aorist?" Hanz asked eagerly.

Rasselas refrained from decking the man in the face for mentioning Aorist by name. "Cards, I don't know," Rasselas shrugged, "Haven't seen him for weeks!" He watched Hanz nod, then glanced over at the Faerie maid he had met earlier that day, whose eyes remained wide with shock. Returning his attention to the King, Rasselas said, "Anyway, I thank you for inviting me to your little *thing*, this is going to be grand!"

"Well," Hanz chuckled, "I hope so, Moonvine. Anyway, please come and meet the others," he held out his hand to the party, "and enjoy the feast!"

"I say," Rasselas cleared his throat, "Where's the famous beauty you're supposed to be parading around here?"

"My *daughter*?" Hanz raised his eyebrows, then chuckled. "She is not out yet. You will meet her tomorrow if you are inclined to attend her party."

"*Inclined*?" Rasselas showed a toothy grin, "My dear King Hanz, I wouldn't miss it for the world!" Rasselas couldn't care if she lived or died.

"Well," Hanz smiled proudly, glancing at Rasselas' poor excuse for a wing. "It was a pleasure to meet you, Moonvine."

"Likewise," Rasselas said, then brushed past the King's party toward the swarms of people who were gathered in clusters throughout the large hall.

Two long banquet tables lined the hall on either side, while the middle of the room was open for socializing. After a quick scan, Rasselas spotted a familiar face and decided that would be the best place for him to start. He made a beeline toward the character, holding out his hands in greeting.

"Prince Tingo!" he said excitedly, "You look marvelous!"

Prince Tingo, who was standing between two others, looked over toward Rasselas with a smile. He turned to face him, placing his hands on his hips and shaking his head. Tingo had his long black hair tied neatly in a knot on the top of his head. He wore an ornate gold hair piece, like a little crown, around his topknot. His clothes were like Rasselas' in that they were in the Mensa style, with a long, buttoned coat over an ornate waistcoat. Finally—a man who understood the importance of fashion!

"The mysterious Moonvine," Tingo said with a chuckle. "Get over here."

"Well," Rasselas sniffed as he placed himself in Tingo's little social circle. "Fancy meeting you here."

"Rasselas," Tingo said in a friendly, casual tone, "This is my wing, Sir Wynn," he gestured to the man on his right, who wore a similar look with a tidy topknot and a clean-shaven face. Wynn bowed his head in greeting and gave Rasselas a contagiously wide smile.

"A pleasure," Rasselas bowed his head.

"And him you know," Tingo pointed to the man on his left who straightened his back with a loud clearing of his throat.

"Ah, King Stathe!" Rasselas grinned. "Looking fantastic, old chap!"

"Well, aren't you as pretty as a peacock," Stathe said, pulling an unlit cigar to his lips out of habit. The man was a complete addict, it seemed.

"Why, *thank* you!" Rasselas grinned. "Anyway," he said quickly, "has everyone I should care about already arrived?"

"Yes," Tingo said, "You were the last to come of the visiting delegates, I think. There are some Mensa highlords here, too, if you are interested in meeting them."

"No," said Rasselas, making a face like he just tasted something off. "Not really. Where is that 'Cato' fellow? Slay me, I'm dashed curious to see what the slob looks like."

Tingo shook his head, chuckling. "Lord Cato," he said in a raised voice, turning to the group of people standing beside them. He waved his hand once he got the lord's attention, and Rasselas waited patiently as the two circles formed into one.

Lord Cato was the tallest in his little group, a giant of a man, and stood out like a swollen lip. Rasselas was surprised to see the presence of a man who wore the Mensa fashion even better than he himself did. His pose was perfect, like a full-length portrait. Every single button rested in its right place, and his ruffles were as perfect as icing on a cake. He had shiny blond hair combed back delicately, and striking black eyebrows. He wore a square, greying goatee, which gave some indication of age—Rasselas guessed somewhere in his forties, beginning the age of wearing. His most striking feature was his bright blue eyes. He stood with an overfilled glass of vino in one hand and a pure gold toothpick in the other.

Cato examined Rasselas with blinking eyes for a moment, then raised an eyebrow. "Oh," he said. "You're the Elf who called me a *fat* slob?"

Rasselas beamed. "Why Cato!" he said excitedly. "In the flesh!"

Cato's suspicious face turned to a wide grin. *Hades!* His teeth were almost as white as Rasselas'. "Well, finally someone entertaining at this blasted party," Cato said. "I was getting incredibly bored talking to this fellow," he gestured with his thumb to the man on his left, whose eyes widened with embarrassment.

"And you are?" Rasselas looked at the man. "Oh," Rasselas blinked, "Latimer?"

"Ah, Moonvine!" The Elven skydeacon smiled sheepishly. "Nice to see you!"

"I didn't know you were invited, old chap!" Rasselas chuckled. "How nice for you."

"Moonvine," Latimer said, "I'd like to introduce you to my friend here." Latimer turned to the side, smiling at a rather dark figure standing beside him.

"Heavens!" Rasselas placed his hand on his heart in distress, "Did someone open a door? I feel a sudden chill!"

"I'm sorry?" Latimer looked around in confusion.

"This man is wearing so much black I thought that the world might be ending!" Rasselas pointed at Latimer's friend. The man wore a broody frown and a face as scarred as a brawler. He looked like some sort of thief who might try to rob one in their sleep, with pitch black curly hair, and a suit, while fashionable, so menacing it made Rasselas want to run and hide. "Latimer, what sort of friends are you making these days?"

Cato cleared his throat, "Oh calm down," he said to Rasselas. "That's just my wing."

"*Rook?*" Rasselas raised an eyebrow as he examined the man's face. He was surprised to see that except for several gnarly scars, the man was actually quite handsome.

"Yes, Rook," said Cato, slapping his hand on his wing's back a few times. "Rook, say hallo! He can talk, you know."

Rook shot a glance at Cato, then looked Rasselas in the eyes. In stark contrast to his dark appearance, his eyes were like glass—no—the glassy sea; they rippled with depth and color. Rasselas blinked. Rook seemed to be studying him silently, then he cleared his throat.

"Hallo, prince Moonvine," he said in a deep voice, his face as blank as an untouched canvas.

"Hallo," Rasselas said quickly, then turned back to Cato, feeling a desperate need for escape from that tragedy of a character.

"Moonvine," Latimer said timidly, "Rook here—"

"Oh, are you still here, Latimer?" Rasselas turned to the thin Elf with astonishment. "How nice. Anyway, Lord Cato, nice to meet you in the flesh. How's the vino?"

Cato shrugged, glancing down at his glass. "Fine," he said. "And who is this fellow?" He gestured to Rasselas' right. Turning, Rasselas was surprised to see Thorne standing there.

"Oh, cards," Rasselas said with a sigh, "This is Sir Thorne, my wing. He's dreadfully serious, I doubt you would be interested."

"Ah," Cato nodded, "No, I don't have much time for that sort of thing— you know—serious things."

Rasselas nodded firmly. "Indeed! I think we will be great friends, then!"

Tingo belted a laugh. "Rasselas," he said, jostling the Elf slightly as he slapped his shoulder. "You're so funny."

'Funny' wasn't a word Rasselas liked being used to describe him, but he smiled anyway.

"Well this looks like the place to be," said a female voice. All in the circle turned their eyes in the direction of a distinguished-looking pair who were making their way toward them. The speaker was a woman, adorned in the epitome of Mensa's fashion.

She wore a dress with a corset so tight that she barely had a waist, and with no sleeves or shoulder straps on her dress, all focus seemed to be drawn to her neck, where a large, jeweled necklace rested against her collar bone. Her skirt was a huge, blue thing that took up so much space that she could have hidden five other people beneath it. Beside her was a tall, squarish, muscular sort of man with short, dusty blonde hair. He had all of the necessary elements of being an attractive man, but the most unlikable face. He was clean-shaven, aside from two thick sideburns.

Rasselas heard Tingo grunt sighed at the sight of them.

"Ah," King Stathe said, pulling the still-unlit cigar from his mouth, "Labyrinth."

"Gentlemen," said the blonde man in a thin, nasally voice. Ah, Rasselas raised his eyebrows, the mysterious man from the bathhouse. *Labyrinth*? What kind of pretentious name was that? The gall of the man to have such a fantastic name!

King Stathe pointed to Labyrinth with his sausage of a finger. "Moonvine, this is King Labyrinth."

"Of the Gramenlands?" Rasselas asked, turning to the man with a phony smile.

"Yeah," said Labyrinth, "This is Lady Viola," he said as he nodded to the woman beside her.

"Your wife?" Rasselas asked, scanning for a ring.

Labyrinth frowned, but didn't respond to the question. "So you're the Elf that was making so much noise this afternoon?"

"Why yes," Rasselas grinned through his pearly teeth.

"So, you've got a Faerie for a brother, have you?" he chuckled to himself, glancing toward Viola with a shake of the head, "What bad luck!"

It took Rasselas a moment to realize he was being insulted. "Ah," he said in a condescending tone, "Not partial to Faeries?" he asked, glancing toward Tingo with his own dismissive head shake, "Bit of a racist, are you, sire?"

There were a few nervous coughs and grunts within their social circle, which was quickly attracting attention from other attendees.

"Moonvine," Latimer said quietly as he reached out to tug on Rasselas' sleeve.

"*Racist?*" Labyrinth chuckled. "What a funny word." He turned to look at a man who was following just behind him. "Crag? What do *you* think? Do you think I am racist?"

The man jolted, surprised to be the focus of attention. Rasselas was filled with regret when he realized he was a Faerie. Crag was dressed in a fancy suit, similar to what other male servants were wearing. His brown hair was pulled back into a short tail, and his long cleft ears stuck out conspicuously.

"Master?" he asked, bewildered; there was fear in his eyes.

"Leave the fellow out of it," Rasselas said quickly.

"You heard me, you little mouse," Labyrinth said sharply. "Am I a *racist?*"

"Definitely not!" The young man said with a look of horror. "Never!"

"Well," Labyrinth looked back at Rasselas with a smug face. "All sorted then."

Rasselas wanted to give Crag an apologetic look, but the Faerie kept his eyes continuously downward.

"Well, well. *Moonvine!*" Viola said excitedly. "How exciting to have Elven royalty present!" The woman offered an inviting smile.

Rasselas looked at her sidelong. "And where do you belong in all this?"

"I am princess Rosamond's first lady," she boasted, "Would you—"

"How nice," Rasselas acted as though he didn't realize he was interrupting. "Well, Cato? Tingo? Where are you all sitting? I'm famished!"

"You might be the biggest peacock in the room," Labyrinth said flatly, "but you're not the biggest lion. You can stop pretending you own every conversation."

Tingo pursed his lips, pretending not to be as intimidated as he was by the King of the Gramenlands, then turned to Rasselas. "I'm sitting just over there, Moonvine. Cato? Care to join us?"

"Oh, whatever," Cato shrugged and followed as Tingo and Rasselas split off from the group, along with their loyal wings.

Rasselas loved fancy social events, but he liked the conversation to stay light and airy. He sat with Tingo and Cato. He liked Tingo because the man seemed to be both amiable and genuine—and those traits barely ever went together. Cato, he liked as well, because the man didn't really seem to care about anything, and he found that vastly entertaining. As it was with all of Rasselas' social excursions, he was quickly becoming the most popular person in the room. That made things more enjoyable for him, but it gave him little time to wander around and observe, as there always seemed to be someone who wanted to chat with him.

After talking everybody's ears off at the dinner table, Rasselas found his way toward the drinks table, hoping to catch a moment of silence so that he could—he looked around the great hall—*where was that maid?*

"Rasselas," said a voice from behind him.

Rasselas jumped, spilling a bit of vino on his waistcoat. He looked down at himself in horror, then up at the speaker, aghast. He jumped again, seeing the viciously scarred face of Cato's wing.

"Oh Hades, Rook!" he said angrily, trying to wipe the vino off his clothes. "Look what you've gone and done!" He looked back up at the dark wing and was surprised to see a small smile hiding on the corner of his mouth. "Can I *do* something for you?"

Rook's face went blank. "I just wanted to meet you," he said softly, "without others around."

"Well, you've met me!" Rasselas said defensively. Was this man about to rob him? *Stab* him? Rasselas' heart stopped.

Rook raised an eyebrow. "You alright?" he asked.

There she was—the Faerie girl! Standing all the way on the other side of the hall was the maid. She looked like someone who didn't want to be found so, naturally, he had to go talk to her before she could hide again!

"Look," Rasselas said, without giving Rook so much as a glance. "It was nice—sort of—to meet you…"

Rasselas moved quickly, skirting along the edge of the ballroom to avoid being seen by others. And when he finally got to the place where he thought he had seen her, she was gone.

"Damn."

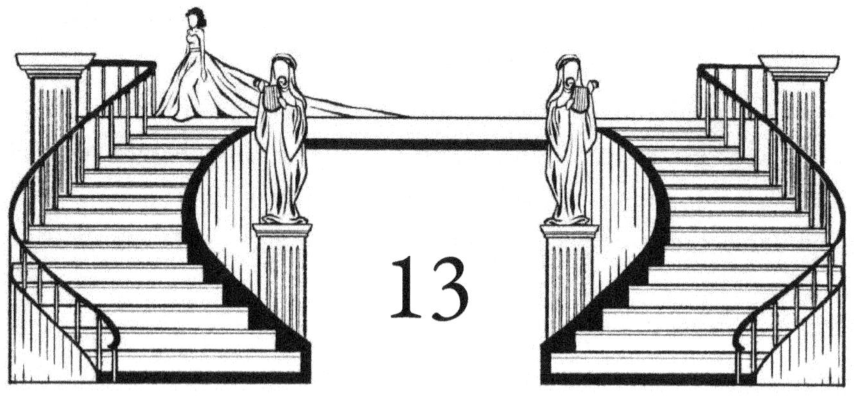

— Rosamond —

Princes, Portraits and Patience

ROSAMOND TURNED ANOTHER PAGE, resting her chin lazily in her palm as she laid on her stomach upon her large, pillowy bed.

"Prince Tingo," she read aloud, examining the hand-drawn portrait within. This book had been made for her earlier that day. Her father left her with one of the new portrait books, knowing she would feel horrible for missing the first social event of the season. "He looks nice," she said with a bored sigh.

She turned another page, groaning. "Here I am looking at drawings; meanwhile, *Viola* gets to go and meet these men!" Her eyes examined the next portrait. It was a Knight of Sol; Tingo's wing. "He looks nice, too," she said to herself. "Still not as nice as..." she flipped the book back to a place she had marked with a ribbon, "Prince Rasselas Moonvine," she said in a fantastical voice. Her eyes studied the seemingly perfect contours of his face. Unlike the other noblemen, this prince had actually smiled for his portrait. It was a calm, knowing smile—almost as if he were looking *through* the portrait like a window.

Rosamond rolled onto her back, feeling a rush of excitement. "Rasselas," she said, giggling to herself. "An Elf, too. How..." she sat up quickly, tapping her lip with her finger. "How fantastic!"

She turned back to her portrait book again and flipped back to the pages she had not yet seen. "Well, I have seen this portrait before," she said as she examined Labyrinth, the King of the Gramenlands. He did look somewhat attractive, but not as handsome as *Rasselas*! She turned the page, a Gramenlands highlord. She turned another page—more Gramenlands highlords. She sighed with boredom.

Turning another page, she saw a face she did not recognize. "From the Edgelands?" she cocked her head in interest. That was a land from the west! "Cato," she said the name aloud. He had striking eyes but otherwise looked sort of bland. "Maybe in person he looks better," she said to herself.

Oh, it *killed* her that everyone else would be meeting in person tonight! And here she was looking at a stupid book. She turned the page once more and stopped as her eyes fell on the most striking face. Rosamond sat up onto her knees so as to find a better angle. She studied the picture, which almost looked as if it were drawn by a different hand. It was the face of perfection. Was this man *real*? Her eyes scanned for a name.

"Rook?" she asked, feeling as though the face deserved a better name. "Like a *crow*?"

Rosamond looked up quickly, the sound of her door opening stirred her from her reverie.

"Valley!" she gasped in excitement, jumping off her bed. She ran to Valley, grabbing her by the hands with excitement. "Have you just come from the party?"

"Yes," Valley said unenthusiastically.

"And?" Rosamond shook Valley roughly, "Tell me *everything*! Is it over already?"

"Ow!" Valley snapped, pushing Rosamond away from her. "Stop that—and no, it is not over yet."

Rosamond blinked in confusion, unsure why Valley would be *annoyed* at her touch. "If it isn't over, why are you here?"

Valley walked over to Rosamond's bed and glanced at the portrait book. "Well," she said, "I figured you were feeling sad to be left out, so I came back to tell you about it." She looked up at the princess with a renewed smile on her face. "Were you looking at the portrait book your father sent you?"

"Yes!" Rosamond rushed to pick it up. "And I have questions!"

Valley laughed. "I thought you might."

"Alright," Rosamond jumped up onto the bed and patted the spot beside herself. "Come on."

Valley climbed slowly onto the bed and scooted beside Rosamond.

"Valley," Rosamond paused, giving her friend a quick glance. "Is everything alright?"

"Yes," said Valley. "Ask me your questions."

"Right!" Rosamond eagerly opened the large bound book and found the page with the gorgeous Rasselas. "Did you meet *him*?"

Valley pursed her lips as she studied the portrait for a moment. "Well..." she said slowly.

"*Well?*" Rosamond slammed her hand on the bed impatiently. "*Did* you?"

Valley glanced up at Rosamond. "Why?"

"Look at him!" Rosamond pointed her index finger at Rasselas' face. "He's perfect!"

Valley had a mysterious look on her face that Rosamond couldn't quite identify. "Yes, all the maids are talking about him."

Rosamond groaned. "*And?*"

Valley leaned back with an eye roll. "They all think he is pretty attractive."

"Well?" Rosamond grew irritated, crossing her arms. "What did *you* think?"

"Well," Valley shrugged modestly, "I might have gotten a *unique* perspective..."

"Valley, you're killing me!" Rosamond screamed. "*Tell* me!"

Valley, enjoying the power she held, took her time thinking about it. "Well, now that I am an Inner Palace maid..."

"Which makes no sense to me," Rosamond added quickly.

Valley shrugged, then continued, "I am on bell call from time to time. So prince *Rasselas* rings his bell…"

"*And?*" Rosamond slapped the bed with her hands. "Valley!"

Valley chuckled to herself. "Well, let's just say I saw a little *more* of prince Rasselas than anyone else."

Rosamond collapsed face first in a pile of defeated jealousy. Valley laughed heartily. "Oh, Ros," she said, patting her on the back. "Is *he* the one you're most excited about? He's so vain—seriously—*so* vain."

"I don't care!" Rosamond sat up quickly, pointing at the portrait once more. "Look at that face! I don't care if he has the worst personality in the world!"

Valley scoffed. "Yes, you do," she said. "You'd get bored with him."

Rosamond sighed longingly. "Who could get bored with that face?"

Valley's eyes drifted down to the portrait and she silently stared at it for a moment, then said, "Well, you'll meet him tomorrow." She looked at Rosamond. "He asked about you, you know."

"What?" Rosamond gasped. "Valley! What did he *say?*" she grabbed Valley by the shoulders desperately. She was surprised when Valley gasped in pain and pulled quickly away, hugging herself protectively. Rosamond grew quiet, a sudden feeling of dread rising up within her. "Valley?" she asked softly. "Can you please tell me what happened?"

Valley looked up with her wide, fearful eyes, but sat there completely silent.

Rosamond scooted closer and held out both her hands, palms up. Valley looked down at her hands, then timidly reached out and placed her own hands on top of them. Rosamond gripped her tightly, smiling. "Valley," she said slowly, "We are sisters—no matter what anyone else says. Yes?"

Valley nodded. "Yes."

"*Tell* me what happened at the ceremony."

Valley nodded again, then leaned back. She looked down at herself and carefully untied the bow at the front of her bodice. Her little maid's uniform had a white underdress with a drawstring at the front. Before Rosamond, Valley loosened the string and let the left shoulder of her dress fall.

Rosamond gasped in horror. A large, hand-sized brand had been deeply burned into the front of Valley's left shoulder. The mark was coated in blisters and bleeding scabs. Rosamond could see the surrounding veins swollen and red with distress and spreading across her shoulder was a disturbing amount of black bruising. Rosamond shook her head in disbelief.

"No," Rosamond muttered, reaching her hand out to hover over the wound. "No, this can't be!"

Valley looked down at herself, biting her lip as tears began to form in her eyes. "Rosamond," she said, "Have you never seen a Faerie brand?"

"But no," Rosamond furrowed her brow, "It was a marking... a—a *dye* or something. I—I didn't know..."

Valley looked up at Rosamond's face. "You honestly didn't know?"

"No!" Rosamond exclaimed as her anger kindled. "*Father* did this to you?"

Valley's eyes flashed, then she nodded.

"This," Rosamond stuttered, pointing at the brand, "This is inhumane! This is so wrong!"

"Rosamond!" Valley raised her voice. "Rosamond, don't you *get* it?"

Rosamond leaned back, studying Valley in surprise. Valley *never* yelled! "Get what, Valley?"

"I'm a *slave*! All Faeries are!"

Rosamond held her breath, letting the words hit her in their full strength and meaning. "But that's... wrong," she said in a quiet voice.

"*Is* it?" Valley scoffed, "No one else thinks so!"

Rosamond felt her heart beating like a drum. Her mind raced, thinking about all the Faeries in the castle. All of them had serving positions. Faeries were *made* to serve, weren't they? Didn't they *like* serving? Didn't they choose it?

"Valley," Rosamond said softly, "I am so sorry."

Valley sighed, then dropped her head down into Rosamond's lap, face down, and wept. Rosamond, feeling numb, placed her hands on Valley's head and stroked her hair.

Only a moment later, the door to Rosamond's room creaked open. Rosamond tapped Valley's head in warning. The Faerie sat up quickly, wiped her eyes, and fixed her dress as Viola stepped into the room.

"Well," Viola excitedly clapped her hands together. "Rosamond, I can't tell you—" she cut herself short once she spotted Valley. "Rosamond, can your maid leave, please?"

"She's not my maid," Rosamond said sharply, "she is my *sister*!"

"No," Valley said, jumping quickly off the bed, "It's fine, I'll leave."

"Valley!" Rosamond called, but it was too late. Valley left the room soundlessly, leaving Viola to sigh in relief.

"Right!" Viola grinned as she glided up to where Rosamond was sitting. "What do you think?" She pointed at the portrait book. "See anyone you liked? I can tell you about them!"

Rosamond looked down at the book with disinterest. Suddenly, fawning over handsome men lost all its appeal. All she could see in her mind was her father's horrible brand on Valley's beautiful body.

"Well," Rosamond mumbled, "There were one or two I liked."

"Some men were uncommonly handsome," Viola whipped out her fan and began to wave it at herself.

Rosamond looked up, feeling a pang of interest. "Was... *Rasselas* there?"

"Ah, yes," Viola said with a sigh, "Rasselas!"

Rosamond quickly turned the marked page in her book. "Did he look like this?"

Viola glanced down at the portrait, then grinned. "Oh, he looks even better in person," she said boastfully. She was clearly trying to rub it in Rosamond's face that she had met everyone first.

"Well," Rosamond searched the book for a moment, "Did you meet anyone called, *erm*, Rook?"

"Who?" Viola glanced down as Rosamond opened to the page with the beautiful face. Viola studied it quietly. "I would remember if I met someone who looked like *that*," she said.

"So you didn't meet the people from the Edgelands?" Rosamond asked.

"I met the highlord," Viola thought to herself, "and he had a wing, I think. I don't remember him, though."

Rosamond nodded. "Well, I suppose I'll have to wait to see anyone until tomorrow night."

Viola closed her fan with a loud snap. "Well, tomorrow some of us are going to the dueling grounds to watch some of the men practice with their swords, if you want to—" she cut herself off. "Oh," she sighed, "Right, you are not *out* yet. I guess you can't come, then."

"Are you trying to make me feel bad?" Rosamond frowned.

Viola shrugged. "Yes."

"Well," Rosamond sighed. "Do you want to tell me anything else about the party?"

"I would," Viola said as she made her way back towards the door, "But it is still going, and I don't want to miss any more than I already have."

"Sure," Rosamond grumbled. "Makes sense."

Seconds later, Rosamond found herself alone in her room once more. With Viola and Valley both now gone, she felt just how alone she was in that room. Everyone in the world was at the party!

Rosamond blinked. *Everyone* was at that party... including her father.

She stepped out of her bed and walked to the middle of the room. Her long, thin dressing gown which covered her night dress dragged across the floor behind her. Even Captain Oswald would be at the party!

Rosamond poked her head out of her room and peered down the hall. No guards were stationed in the hall, so she walked down it confidently until she came to an intersection. There was the door to her father's room. Way down at the end of the hall she could see the back of a guard's head, but he wasn't looking in her direction. She pushed open the door to her father's room and stepped inside.

Here was the familiar place, with the smell of her father's special Edgeland spices. But who *was* the man who lived in this room? Rosamond walked over to the bookcase beside her father's reading chair. It was filled with the same little fiction novels the Faeries were so fond of. She pulled one out and examined its spine.

Opening the book, her eyes glossed over some of the pages. She was surprised to discover that it was some sort of love story. A love story?

"Father reads *love* stories?" she asked herself, closing the book. She replaced it, then looked around the room. He was always sitting in here when she talked to him—so happy to see her and wrap her up in a big protective bear hug. But who was he when she *wasn't* there? Was he really someone who would *brand* Valley?

Rosamond found herself moving to the dressing area at the back of her father's room. She passed under a stone archway and came to where all his clothes hung. There was a big black cape hanging on a stand. She pulled some of the fabric to her face and took in its scent deeply. She was filled instantly with warmth and happiness. She loved that smell; it was the smell of her only family— a father who loved her.

Surely, he would only do that to Valley if it were the right thing to do. Rosamond nodded to herself reassuringly; perhaps he didn't even know about the brand! But the reassurance didn't last. Doubt filled her like rainwater fills the lowest of places.

Then her eyes, which had been exploring the little dressing room, fell on an object mounted up on the wall. Rosamond turned her head slightly, studying it. It was a whip of some sorts. It had a black leather handle, and three short tails, knotted. She took it from its stand and examined it. She ran one of the cords through her hand and held her breath as blackish dust came off into her fingers. This whip had seen flesh.

This was a device of torture, wasn't it? Rosemond looked around herself in confusion. Was she still in her father's room? Why would *he* have something like this in his dressing room?

Rosamond walked out of the dressing room, as if in a trance, holding the whip in her hands. She stood in the middle of her father's chambers like a ghost. Reexamining the room, it seemed changed. This wasn't the room of a father who liked to hug his daughters and read fiction—it was the room of someone who owned this thing. She looked down at it, turning it in her hands. Perhaps it didn't belong to her father; he had probably confiscated it from someone! Yes, yes that was it.

Feeling encouraged, Rosamond looked up quickly. Her heart froze as her eyes focused on another person in the room.

"F—Father!" she gasped in surprise, dropping the whip. It fell on the floor with a loud thud.

"Rosamond," said King Hanz. Her father's voice sounded cold and empty.

"Father, you're back from the party!" It was all she could think to say.

"What are you doing in here, Rosamond?" he asked.

"I..." Rosamond's voice found no strength. Confusion swirled around inside of her. "Father?"

King Hanz stepped toward her, taking off his many-peaked crown and setting it on a table as he passed. He walked right up to where she was standing and picked up the whip. He towered above her like a giant. She looked up at his face.

"Where did you get this?" he asked.

"I—" her voice cracked, "I found it in your dressing room." Guilt swelled up inside her.

"Why were you in my dressing room?"

"I don't know," she said, feeling a weight of shame. "I was all alone in my room and I—"

"Rosamond," Hanz sighed, shaking his head. "Rosamond, you can't just do things like this."

She could hear a hint of anger in his voice. She touched his arm, knowing she could soften him with her touch as she always did. Her father recoiled emphatically, gritting his teeth in anger.

"Father?" Rosamond held her breath.

"Rosamond," his voice grew harder, "You can't just *do* things like this!" He raised the whip over his shoulder suddenly, as if priming to strike.

Rosamond gasped and stumbled backwards, placing her hand over her heart. "I'm sorry!"

Hanz stood there, frozen like a statue as his eyes focused on her. "Sit down," he said.

"Papa," Rosamond held up her hands in surrender, "I'm sorry!"

"I said, sit down!" He screamed. Rosamond stumbled backwards until she landed in his armchair.

He marched toward her like a charging bull, holding the whip above his head. Rosamond threw her arms over her face with a shriek. "Father!"

"Your legs!" Hanz said forcefully, pointing at the ground in front of her. "Stick them out!"

"*Why?*" she gasped, tucking her legs up onto the chair.

"Because I'd beat your face if I didn't have to show it off tomorrow!" he bellowed with rage in his voice. "Rosamond!"

Rosamond obeyed, putting her legs out in front of her as she sobbed. As painful as it was, holding still as her father beat her, what hurt the most was the shame. Why had she been so stupid? Why had she *ever* wandered outside of her room when she wasn't supposed to?

These questions stung in waves, just like the bitter pain from the repeated lashings of Hanz's whip.

Hanz stepped back, panting from the effort. Rosamond whimpered, tucking her bloodied legs up to her chest.

"Rosamond," he said as he stepped back. "It's time for you to stop with all your silliness and *listen!* Tomorrow you are going to get out there and act like a bride. Stop fooling around!"

"Yes, Father."

"Do you really want to ruin the future that I have worked a lifetime to prepare for you?" He shook his head.

Rosamond shook her head emphatically.

"I thought you were an *obedient* daughter," he said, bowing his head with sadness. His arm that held the whip grew limp at his side. "I have always boasted to others about how obedient you were."

"Father..." Rosamond hid her face in her hands, crying.

"I... I long to look fondly on you..." Hanz muttered, "the beautiful bride I know you could be."

"Please, don't say that!"

"Come..." Hanz lifted his head, then held out his arms to her. "Let us not quarrel. Show me you are still the daughter I am so proud of."

Rosamond did not think; she simply responded on impulse. She jumped to her feet, pushing past the pain, and ran toward the King. She threw her arms around him, and he hugged her tight.

"Please... don't make me do that again," he said.

Rosamond hugged her father, but a strange feeling of dread crawled up her arms and legs.

Did *she* make him do that?

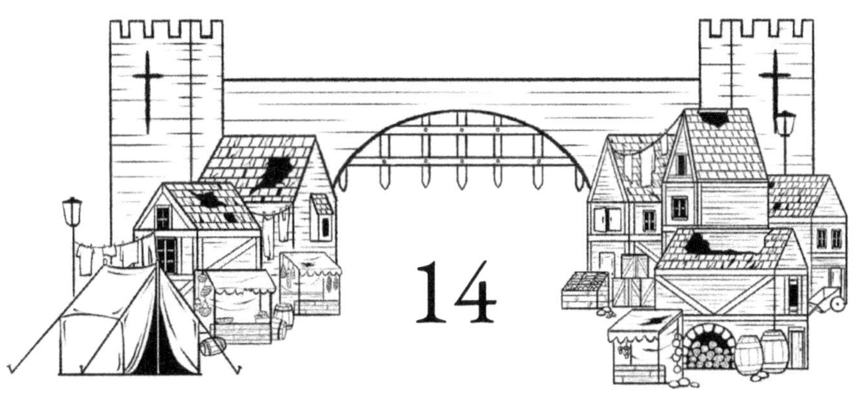

14

—— Valley ——

A Bonding of Bondage

"Good morning, Valley," said a bright voice.

"Morning," Valley mumbled. She stood in the hallway with her forehead resting on the wall. She lifted her head groggily to see who was greeting her. " Karo?"

A tall Faerie stood beside her with his hand resting on the wall. He was so much taller than her that he practically had to bend over halfway to meet her eye level. He wore a servant's uniform and a playful smile. His short black hair was slicked back with some sort of smelly wax, and, like most Faerie men, his face was bare.

"How's the pain this morning?" Karo asked with a smarmy smile, turning to lean his back against the wall beside her. It was a touch too close; Valley could smell his sickly hair wax and hear his heavy nasal breathing, just as though they were sleeping against the same pillow.

"It's worse." Valley said, turning to lean her own back against the wall.

"We've all been there," he said wistfully, "Day three is the worst. And I am the Faerie of—" he cut himself off quickly, making a loud throat-clearing sound, "—So I know what I am talking about!"

Valley peered up at the man with her signature raised eyebrow face. "Faerie of..." she said quietly.

"Now, now," he said, dismissing her with a wave of his hand. "I didn't say anything! Anyway, I wanted to *officially* welcome you to the crew!"

"The crew?"

"You know," he straightened up, pretending to salute, "King Hanz' bonded Faeries!"

"Oh," Valley refrained from an eye roll. "*That.*"

"Everybody wants to be one of us, *eh?* How did you get so lucky? I suppose it has something to do with you being his ward, and all that."

"Lucky?" Valley shrugged, "I guess so."

"Aw... you look cross. Well, everybody feels like that on day three," said the tall, slick-looking Faerie. "Well, no matter! I have a message for you."

Valley shook herself into attention. "What? What is it?"

"Master wants to see you," he said.

"You mean...?"

"*Yes,*" he nodded mockingly, "King Hanz, *himself!*"

"Well, I am supposed to change out the fires in the rooms right now," Valley said with a frown.

"I am sure he won't keep you long," said Karo with a chuckle. "King Hanz wants to speak with you before he starts the first meeting with the delegates. It's Grounsday, you know!"

"I *know* it's Grounsday." Valley grumbled.

"Alright, well," Karo bowed playfully. "Goodbye!"

Valley watched as the bonded Faerie skipped off down the hall. It was strange to be talking to him; he was one of those older, more important Faeries who didn't talk with just *anyone.* Now here he was, talking to her! So, Hanz wanted to see her? She sighed to herself and meandered down the hall toward King Hanz' chambers.

Everything still felt so surreal. Valley had grown up playing with Rosamond in the Inner Palace, running down these halls playing hide and seek. Now, she was as low as—if not lower than—a maid, cleaning and tending them.

Valley knocked several times on the door to King Hanz' chambers. When there came no reply, she entered anyway, as she had been taught. The room smelled as it always did, like spices. The candles weren't lit yet, but the curtains in front of the large window were drawn, streaming daylight into the room.

"My Lord?" Valley called, announcing her presence.

"Over here," she heard a groggy voice. She turned and peered toward Hanz' favorite armchair.

"My..." she muttered as she crept across the room. "My *Lord*?"

"Over here," he said again. Valley jumped, seeing movement on the bed. Was he not *up* yet? Valley bit her lip as she made her way slowly toward it, feeling more than a little disturbed.

"Is everything alright?" she asked. As Valley came to the edge of the four-poster bed, King Hanz turned over onto his back and looked at her. She jumped. *Hades-he was still in bed!* Valley did her best not to scowl at the audacity of summoning her before he was even up. As her eyes fully adjusted to the dim light, Valley turned away quickly when she realized the King's bare shoulders were exposed. She cupped her hand over her eyes modestly and cleared her throat. "*Sire*? Is everything alright?" she asked again.

"Oh, it's fine," he yawned, then draped his arm over his eyes. "Going to be a long day today," he remarked.

What? What kind of a summons was *this*?

"What did you need to speak with me about?" Valley tried to move the conversation forward, growing increasingly more uncomfortable at the sight of a grown man in his bed.

"Valley," Hanz mumbled, "How is the new post going so far?"

Valley blinked, still cupping her hand over her eyes. "It's going fine," she said cautiously.

Hanz chuckled. "Valley, you're one of my Faeries now, you don't have to be so modest. Come here," he patted the edge of the bed beside where he lay.

"That's alright," Valley said.

"Valley," Hanz' voice lowered, "Come here."

Valley inched closer, keeping her back turned to Hanz, and sat uncomfortably, unable to relax a single muscle in her body.

Hanz let out another yawn and reached over to pat her arm. "Well," he said, "you're probably wondering why, after everything, I made you an Inner Palace maid."

Valley's eyes darted around the room. *How was she supposed to respond to that?* "Sure," she said.

"Valley," Hanz said, "I raised you like my own daughter. You are different to all the other Faeries I have bonded with, and all the other Faeries in the Warrowing Village. Do you know why?"

"No," Valley said. *Hades.* She wished he would just get on with what he wanted to say!

"You and I have built trust with each other." Hanz patted her arm again and his hand remained there. "I can trust you with greater tasks."

Greater tasks? Valley's one pointy eyebrow twitched. "What do you mean?" she asked, "You made me a maid."

Hanz chuckled to himself, then stopped to clear his gravelly morning throat. "Valley," he said, patting her arm again, "Look at me."

Valley reluctantly turned her head and looked King Hanz in the face. He smiled, then said, "I made you a maid in the Inner Palace when *all* of the world's leaders are staying here. I made you a maid because I trust you to *spy* for me."

Valley's eyes flashed. "Spy?"

"Yes," Hanz squeezed her wrist with that hand that never seemed to stop touching her. "You can go in and out of all those rooms at any point. There are people I want you to report back to me on."

"Who?" she asked. So *that's* where this was going!

"I will tell you soon. But for now, just keep an ear out for any interesting conversations. And..." He paused, thinking. Valley glanced down at his hand resting on her arm, then took this opportunity to look away from him, and down at her knees.

"And what?" she asked.

"If any of the delegates seem interested in you, or in Faeries, then let me know. And..." he sighed, "I mean, you don't have to be afraid of encouraging their interest a little."

"What do you mean?" She couldn't help but express a hint of anger in her voice.

"Oh, nothing much," He patted her again, "I mean, some of these world leaders don't yet understand the appeal of Faeries. I want to be able to bond Faeries with all the leaders in Raqia—but if they aren't interested, it makes things difficult. You have an opportunity to show Humans," He turned his head to face her directly, "Your charms."

Valley shot her face in his direction. "If that is a euphemism for encouraging flirtation and—"

"No, no, no," he shook his head, then paused to yawn again. "Not like that, Valley—Hades!"

Valley relaxed slightly and nodded. She was, in a word, confused.

"Is that all you wanted to tell me? To keep an eye on things and report back to you?" she asked, looking back down at her knees.

"I wanted to catch up," he said with a shrug, "I wanted to connect and hear how you are feeling about everything. I like to build intimate relationships with my Faeries." He gave her arm a squeeze, "You're important to me, Valley."

"Well," she paused, trying to think of the most diplomatic thing to say, "I am feeling fine. My shoulder hurts, but Karo says it gets better from here."

"Good," he nodded excitedly, "*Good*! I am glad you're making friends with my other Fae!"

'Friends' was a strong word. "Yes," she said, hoping it would please him.

"Valley, there's something else I wanted to talk to you about." Hanz reoriented himself in his bed; she could feel his body shifting, turning slightly to face her more. Her body froze as the intimate setting reminded her just how uncomfortable she was.

"What?" she asked as calmly as she could.

"Have you felt anything lately? Anything new?"

Felt? "I have no idea what you mean," Valley said. Inside her was a tempest of confusion and stress, but on the outside, she looked as docile as a lamb.

Hanz moved his hand to touch hers and squeezed it. "Valley, you know I do not allow Faerie titles in Mensa."

Valley locked eyes with him, suddenly too curious to flee the conversation. "Yes..." she said, drawing out the word.

"Do you know what yours *would* be? If you had one?" His eyes searched her face.

"I..." she held her breath. Well, she couldn't lie! "No, I have no idea."

"There is nothing you feel or notice that gives you *any* indication? Nothing strange happening around you?"

"No." She paused to think again, then shook her head. "No."

"Do you ever feel any bursts of power within yourself?" Hanz' gaze held her attention like a vice.

"Power?" She shook her head, confused, "No. What would that even *feel* like?"

Hanz seemed to relax, and he leaned back into his bed. She hadn't even noticed him lean forward.

"Alright," he said. He seemed... relieved?

"My Lord," Valley pursed her lips for a moment. "My Lord, do *you* know what I am?"

"You haven't tried taking up an imperium, have you?" Hanz furrowed his brow.

"You mean... picked an item to store magik?" she leaned away from him. "My Lord, how would I even begin to know how to do that?"

"Good girl," Hanz said, as he stretched out his arms above his head with a big bear yawn.

Valley jolted, standing quickly. She had been sitting by this naked man for *far* too long.

"Where are you going?" Hanz wrinkled his tired face. He scratched his chest with his fingers and blinked his eyes sleepily.

"I—I..." Valley stuttered as she backed away from the bed. "I am supposed to be changing out the fires right now! I should go."

Hanz gave her a smile. "Yes, I know. I was the one who set that up. It will be a good opportunity to poke around before everyone meets at the Court

House. But you don't have to rush off," he made a floppy waving gesture with his hand.

"Sire," Valley cleared her throat as she interlocked her fingers tightly together, "I don't mean to be..." she drew in a deep breath, "*Rude*—but I don't think it is exactly proper for me to sit by your bed while you're," her eyes flickered as she tried to think of the best word. "Not yet presentable."

Hanz raised an eyebrow, then began to chuckle. He sat up in his bed. Valley quickly turned her back to him.

"You're a sweet girl, Valley," he said, still chuckling. Valley could hear him getting up, so she rushed to the door. "Don't worry so much," she heard him saying to her. "You'll get used to things soon enough."

Valley cracked the door open and slipped through it, closing it before her head exploded with embarrassment. She leaned quickly against the door, panting, then thrust her palms against her face.

"*Ugh!*" She groaned, "That was—!"

"Valley?" A voice sounded from beside her.

She yelped. Parting her protective hands, Valley's eyes found the face of Captain Oswald, the head of Hanz' personal guard. "Oswald," she groaned, "Don't startle me like that?"

"Are you alright?" he asked in a low voice, suspicion on his face.

Valley raised an eyebrow. "What do you mean?"

"Are you..." he glanced toward Hanz' room. "What were you doing in there?"

"Work!" she snapped. "The king summoned me first thing in the morning! I can't help it if—"

"Valley," Oswald held up his palm, offering her a smile, "It's alright. I wasn't trying to get on your case. You just looked... stressed."

"I *am* stressed!"

"Alright," Oswald tucked his hands behind his back. "How can I help?"

Valley dropped her hands by her sides defeatedly. "Oh, who knows. Get me the felling day off?"

Oswald pulled his mouth to the side, making his mustache look like a traveling caterpillar. "I could possibly do that."

"No, it's fine," she sighed.

"Did you want me to speak to the king about a day off?" Oswald asked protectively, "Because I will."

"No!" Valley jumped. "No, I seem to be on his good side right now…" she bit her lip, "I would like to keep it that way." Valley gave Oswald a quick glance. "I can take care of myself, Captain."

"I *know* you can, Valley," Oswald said sincerely. He moved to put a hand on her branded shoulder, then stopped himself. His mouth moved, though no words came out.

"I'm fine, Oswald," Valley straightened her back. "Stop worrying."

Captain Oswald placed his hand on the hilt of his sword and raised his chin. "I'll worry about whatever I want to worry about," he said firmly.

"Alright, well, I need to get to work." Valley glanced down the hall. Just then she noticed a head peeking out of one of the doors pull itself quickly out of sight. Valley pursed her lips. *Rasselas*—that stupid Elf. "I'll leave you now, Captain," she said, as she pushed up her sleeves. "I need to take care of something."

Captain Oswald raised his eyebrows curiously and watched Valley march down the hall. She banged her fist on the door.

The door to Prince Rasselas' chambers flung open instantly. There he stood, grinning. While King Hanz was likely still rolling around in bed, Prince Rasselas was dressed ready for a grand ball. Not a single one of his hairs was out of place, and he was even holding his toothpick.

Valley planted her hands on her hips.

"What can I do for you?" he asked excitedly. "I mean—come in!"

"I am not here on a social call," Valley said sharply. "I am here to tell you to stop bothering me!"

Rasselas recoiled, acting flabbergasted as he placed his hand on his heart. "Cards, woman!" he said, "But *why*?"

"Because I don't like you!" she crowed, leaning forward threateningly. Rasselas looked down at her and bit his lip to restrain a smile.

"You don't? Well, why ever not?" he asked innocently.

"Because…" she stalled. "Because you're a clown!"

Rasselas gasped. "Slay me, woman!"

"I'd love to!" Valley snapped, poking him with her finger.

Rasselas blinked in amazement, frozen in his recoiled pose. "Can I..." he said slowly, his voice sounding suddenly different. "Can I just ask you one thing?"

Valley, who was also frozen in her angry pose, held her breath. "Fine," she said, "What?"

"Your..." Rasselas dropped his hands, and the phony act seemed to fade from his face. "Your name?"

Valley blinked, then she crossed her arms. "It's Valley, alright?"

"Valley?" he asked with widening eyes.

"Yes—Valley!" she huffed.

"Valley," Rasselas said in a quiet voice. He stepped toward her, reaching his hand into his vest pocket.

Valley flinched, holding up her hands protectively.

"I... I was..." he stammered as he pulled a piece of paper from his pocket. "I was meant to give you this." He passed her the piece of paper, which was held closed with a wax seal. Valley took it in her hands curiously, then blinked her eyes in Rasselas' direction.

"What is this? *Who* told you to give this to me?"

Rasselas turned his face away from her, glancing toward the door to his wing's quarters, then met her eyes again. "Valley," he said in the most serious and sincerest of voices, "Show it to no one. Read it—read it as if your life depended on it. Then *think* about the words." His eyes grew fierce. "And then come back to me if you wish."

"What?" Valley ripped open the seal suspiciously. Rasselas jumped toward her, grabbing the letter back. He peered around, then stepped toward her, leaning his face down until it was inches from hers.

"Please," he whispered, "Please don't let anyone see, alright? Read it and burn it."

"If this is some kind of *proposition*..." Valley scowled.

"I've never been more serious in my life!" Rasselas whispered through gritted teeth. "Just read it, damn it! And I won't bother you anymore, alright?"

Valley pulled the letter free of Rasselas' grip and shoved it in her pocket. She kept her eyes on him the whole time, surprised at the sudden change in him. The foppish clown of a prince was nowhere to be seen. Here was just a man—a deadly serious, surprisingly handsome man. Valley shook herself back to attention.

Rasselas stood back and crossed his arms, examining her. They stood silently, separated by the door frame.

"Well, what are you still doing here?" Rasselas asked. Valley, realizing more than a moment had passed, started.

"I—" Valley stuttered, then jumped backwards as Rasselas grabbed the door and slammed it shut. She placed her hand on the side of her skirt, feeling for the letter. "What on the table..." she mumbled, "was *that* all about?"

She looked back up at the closed door, and soon her eyes got stuck studying the intricate patterns on the woodwork. Had Rasselas only delayed her to give her the letter? He wasn't just trying to flirt? Well, that was a relief—wasn't it? Her mind drifted, like a wayward ship.

The door flung open and Rasselas jumped.

"*Gah!*" He screamed, clearly not expecting to see Valley still standing there.

"*What!*" Valley screamed in return, equally surprised.

"Cards, woman! What are you doing here?" he stuttered. Judging by his voice, he was once more playing the fool.

"Uh..." Valley held up her finger as she tried to think of an answer. How long had she been standing there? "I am supposed to change out the fires."

"Oh," Rasselas pulled a handkerchief from his sleeve and dabbed his head. "Hades," he cursed, "Come on Thorne, let's not be late for the peace talks now." Rasselas whizzed past her, as did his wing. She heard Rasselas continue to mumble as he blazed down the hall, "Especially since you're so concerned about being late, and all that!"

And then he was gone. Valley turned her head, watching as the two Elves disappeared. Others began to leave their rooms as well. Valley dove into Rasselas' chambers for protection from the bustle—or at least—to avoid from being detained. She closed the door. Valley pulled a deep breath into her lungs, held it for a moment, then let it out with a vocal sigh.

"What in Hades," she said to herself as she reached up to touch her throbbing shoulder, "This morning is…" She dropped her hand, sticking it into her pocket and feeling for the paper, "…*interesting.*"

She pulled the paper out of her pocket and straightened out its crinkles. The seal was in the shape of a…

"A bird's foot?" she asked. Who told Rasselas to give this to her? Was it *from* Rasselas?

Valley walked toward the large, open window in Rasselas' room and sat on his windowsill, with her eyes still glued to the paper. She opened the letter and scrunched her nose as she read the mysterious letter penned with red ink.

It read:

Faerie of Mensa — I see your chains. Do you? How can an aurochs be chained like an ox? Don't you know who you are? I compel you, friend, to perceive yourself not as a weak and powerless individual, but as a potent and controlled giant. You are not like a beast of burden which can be trained to do the will of its master, but a shining, untouchable light, that cannot be quelled by darkness.

Your existence and purpose cannot be hidden by lies, just as day cannot be concealed by a cloth. No one can force you to serve; you choose to serve. So do not serve in a way that destroys yourself. Serve in the way you were made to serve. Serve not as a slave obeys the will of its master, or as a dog obeys its owner; but serve as a parent serves a child, or as a king serves his people.

You are a potent and controlled giant, filled with the gift of unimaginable power. Do not forsake this gift because others have told you it is your shame. It is not your shame; it is your glory. Do not be ashamed of who you are, and do not forsake the greater purpose of your existence for a lesser one. I cannot free you from the chains until you first believe that they bind you. When you are ready, I will find you.

Valley couldn't move; she could hardly even breathe. She clutched the paper against her chest desperately, peering around the room furiously. *Who wrote this? Who saw her? Who saw the shame and the bondage?*

She pulled the paper open, reading the words again. Then again—and again. Her mouth moved quickly, whispering the words to herself.

A horrific sound bellowed before her, causing her to jump and scream. She cowered as a gigantic black bird landed on the window beside her, crowing threateningly. The bird plucked the paper from her hand.

"No!" she gasped, standing bravely to face the bird. "Give that back!"

The crow stood there, paper in mouth and head cocked sideways.

"Please," she said, moving slowly so it wouldn't fly away, "Please give it back."

The crow placed the paper down on the window ledge then peered up at her. She jumped when it cawed again. Valley glanced at the paper, then up at the crow.

"Is this letter from *you*?" she asked.

The bird looked east toward the Warrowing Village, then back at her, blinking repeatedly, as if trying to communicate.

She knew animals of all kinds were intelligent, if one could only figure out how to speak with them. "You want me to show this to the Faeries in the Warrowing Village?" she asked, trying to discern what he was saying.

The bird picked at his foot. As he did, Valley noticed a glossy red sheen reflecting off his feathers.

"You're beautiful," she exclaimed, reaching out. The bird whipped up his beak in alarm, and she withdrew her hand. "Sorry," she said. Then she looked down at the letter and noticed its signature. It was the print of a bird's foot, marked with red ink. She gasped. "This letter is from you?" she asked, "Or... was it delivered through you."

The bird picked his foot again, then his head drifted back toward the castle gates.

"You need to leave now?" she asked. "Please, how will I know how to find the person who wrote this?"

The raven made a loud squawk, startling Valley, then poked his beak onto the paper, down on the last sentence: "*When you are ready, I will find you.*"

Valley folded up the letter determinedly, nodding to herself. "Whoever wrote this will find me when the time is right. Rasselas said to come to him after I thought about these words. That I will do. I *will* think about them." She closed her eyes tightly, "I will think about them every click of every day. They will be my inhales and my exhales." She jumped, feeling the bird's beak touching her arm. She looked down at him with a smile. "Whoever wrote these words knows the truth, doesn't he?" Then her eyes flashed, "This is from Aorist! It is—isn't it?" she asked the bird.

The bird opened his mouth but didn't make a sound. He closed it again.

"What do they call you?" she asked. The bird only looked at her.

"Your feathers glow red," she pointed, "so I will give you a name that suits you."

The bird hopped, looking excited, she thought.

"I will call you Pyre," she said proudly. "Pyre, my little fire, for your letter kindled a fire inside me—one that I didn't know was there," she looked down at the paper again. "Or did I?"

She thrust it into her pocket quickly, "If this is from Aorist," she said aloud, "Then I should speak with Tristan."

Pyre flapped his wings, then took off into the Sky with more crowing. Valley smiled. His appearance was a sign: he meant something. He was a catalyst for change.

"My existence and purpose cannot be hidden by lies, just as day cannot be concealed by a cloth," she recited. Then her face hardened. "I am going to find out who I am."

Changing out the fires in the empty rooms felt like the longest task of her life. This was not just because her shoulder hurt like Hades every time she had to scoop up the coals—no—a *new* mission burned within her. And no, it wasn't the brand. Those *words* were branded within her.

"No one can force you to serve; you choose to serve," she said over and over as she cleaned out the remains of the fires. "I choose to serve, I choose this."

Everything felt different, though everything looked the same. She no longer felt like a weak and powerless slave, forced to bow her head to the needs of those above her; she was a giant, controlled and poised; a great power hiding in the body of a small girl. Everything she did, whether it be carrying an ash pail or dusting coal from her apron, was her own choice. And until she knew of a better thing to do, she did it.

Once she had finished with her chores, she knew she could grab a moment of freedom. Forgetting the pain radiating like lighting through her brand, Valley raced toward the Warrowing Gate. She pulled her two-layered skirt up to her calves to run faster. She flew like the wind—like Pyre—racing through the castle grounds as if nothing could stop her.

But someone did stop her. That blasted Gingre, who liked to stall fairies at the gate just to lord his status over them.

"Oy, Valloy," said the little rat, blocking her path through the large gate.

"The gate is open!" Valley exclaimed, panting. "And even if it wasn't," she reached for a metal seal in her pocket and pulled it out. "I have right of passage now."

Gingre leaned on his staff, yawning. "I just wanted to tell you to stop running like a peasant," he said condescendingly. "I could see your ankles," he grinned.

Valley didn't dignify the man with so much as a groan. She pushed past him and marched into the Faerie village. It always smelled so good here in the morning! The place was bustling with movement as vendors set up their stalls. The front courtyard in the Warrowing Village housed around six to eight stalls with various kinds of street food, drinks, and little trinkets. Faeries tended to eat on their feet, grabbing breakfast or lunch between busy tasks. Valley caught the scent of a breakfast shack, where Marbel stood every morning, grilling seasoned potatoes, mushrooms, and sweet tomatoes on a stick.

Pushing past other hungry Faeries and the odd Human soldier who preferred the Faerie food to the fare in the market, Valley made her way to where Marbel grilled with a large fork in her hand.

"Only two chips for a breakfast stick!" she called out in a loud voice, though she kept her eyes on her craft at all times. "Only two silver chips!"

"Sounds like a bargain to me," said Valley, reaching into her hidden pouch. Marbel glanced up noting Valley, then back down to stab her large fork into a potato.

"One breakfast stick for young Valley!" she announced to the world.

Valley pulled a handkerchief from her pocket and took the hot stick from Marbel eagerly. "Always smells so good, Marbel," she said.

"Thank ye," Marbel mumbled, but was too busy cooking to carry on with the conversation.

"I'll take one," said another Faerie. Valley turned to see Coppo standing there, holding his chips out in an open palm.

"In the cup," Marbel tapped her money cup with her fork, still looking down. Coppo made the exchange of goods with Marbel then turned to smile at Valley with a tip of his hat.

"I hear you've joined the crew," the young man said.

"Yeah," Valley said with a mouth partially full. "It's pretty strange working for the King. Do you... *like* it?"

Coppo twisted his face, thinking. "'Like' is a strange word for work. I like *drawing*!"

Valley chuckled. "Yes, I am sure. You've always liked drawing, Copp."

"I got to draw a fleet of noblemen yesterday!" he said with eyes of wonder. "Several of them were uncommonly nice to me!"

"Noblemen? *Nice*?" Valley blew a raspberry with her lips.

"Really!" He brightened. "And," he looked side to side as if he were about to share a secret. Valley leaned toward him playfully.

"Yes?"

"And one of them is a *prophet!*"

"A—" Valley instantly thought of her letter. "What do you mean by a prophet, Coppo?"

"Well," he said in a loud whisper, "He told me my Faerie title! I always thought I was probably Faerie of Drawing—or something like that—but when he said my name it was like," he waved one of his hands across the air in front of him in wonder, "like everything became clear."

"What was your title?" she asked.

Coppo cringed. "Aren't we not supposed to talk like this?"

"Coppo?" Valley stuck her chin out, "We can talk about whatever we *want* to here in the Warrowing Village, alright? And I think there is nothing wrong with knowing your title: you are a potent and controlled giant, filled with the gift of unimaginable power. Don't forsake the gift just because others have told you it is your shame. It's not your shame; it's your glory. Now tell me; what is your title?"

Coppo's mouth dropped open, and he nodded. "Faerie of Lines."

It was a thrill for Valley to see the glory on Coppo's face when he said it.

"Right," she said, "Now I've just got to meet this 'prophet' for myself!" She hesitated, "His name isn't Rasselas, is it?"

Coppo shook his head. "Nope. He just said that his name was Rook."

"Rook?" Valley thought to herself. She couldn't remember a Rook from the party last night. Of course, she had been gone for some of the introductions. "Where was he from?"

"I don't..." Coppo tapped his chin. "I don't know, but I'll tell you if I ever find out! You can't miss him though; he has a really nice face. Hey—welcome to the crew!"

"Thanks," Valley said blankly. "Hey, have you seen Tristan around today?"

"He's not here," Coppo said, then took a large bite of potato. "Anyway," he said with his mouth full, "I'll see you around." With another tip of his hat, he was off.

Valley pursed her lips. So she wouldn't be able to talk to Tristan about the letter after all. Perhaps that was a good thing? Rasselas told her not to tell *anyone* just yet.

So—Coppo learned his title. Now only one question nagged at her mind: what was *her* title? King Hanz seemed to know what it was—or did he? Well, why couldn't *she* know? It was at that moment when Valley remembered someone *very* important.

She whirled around to look at Marbel who stood in that same place, turning potato sticks with her fork.

"Marbel?" she asked. "What do you think about donating some of those breakfast sticks to the inmates?"

Marbel looked up from her cooking with a look of urgency. "Oh!" she exclaimed, "You would be willing to take them for me?"

"Sure," Valley shrugged.

"I am not usually free until the evenings for delivering foods—did you really want to help the poor souls to some breakfast?" She smiled widely, "Valley, how jolly!"

"Yeah!" Valley felt a little bad that her motivation was almost purely selfish, but it was better than not going at all!

"Alright," Marbel said excitedly, "I'll just put five here for the men and," she counted fingers, "Three—no—two for the women. I forget that other one is fasting, too."

Valley's face fell. *Another* inmate fasting?

"Oh, don't make that face! It's not a bad thing." Marbel looked up from her busy work to point her turning fork at Valley. "Now you listen here, young darkwing." She cleared her throat, standing up straight to place both hands on her hips commandingly, "We may not go by titles now, but back when I was Faerie of Hunger, you know, I got magik from two ways."

Valley blinked in surprise. 'Darkwing?' How did Marbel know she was a dark Faerie? "How?" she asked curiously.

"I get magik from people being full in the stomach," she held up one finger, "And I get magik from people's stomach being empty," she held up a second finger, "Hunger, Valley—it's not a bad thing. Not for Faeries."

"Well, the old Nightmare Faerie got power from people loving him and from people fearing him, too. One of those was good, and one wasn't."

Marbel shook her head with a frown as she leaned down to pick up the two bundles of food she had made. "Wrong, darkwing. Fear isn't bad, *bad* fear is bad!" She passed the food to Valley who took them slowly, pondering to herself.

"So why isn't starving bad?"

"Valley!" Marbel scolded, holding up her fork like a warning, "I didn't say *starving* wasn't bad, I said hunger wasn't bad! In Aorist's name, child." She calmed herself by popping a grape-sized tomato into her mouth, then amidst her chewing, said, "A full stomach carries the riches of fulfillment, an empty stomach carries the riches of waiting. Now, you best remember that. So those Faes who are fasting in the confinements—they will enjoy their next meals a lot more than the Fae who ate the day before, don't you think?"

"Sure, Marbel," Valley nodded, smiling. She wasn't sure she understood, but she didn't really want to keep going with the conversation. "Well, I better take these to the, *erm*, the Faeries who *aren't* fasting."

"Go along then," Marbel waved her hand dismissively, "You've got a right of passage now, so they'll have to let you in, I think!"

Valley held the two bundles of food in one arm, then using her other hand, picked up the front of her skirt to walk in the direction of the confinement house. As she anticipated, one of the prison guards stopped her and checked her seal before he reluctantly let her through. He felt the need to remind her that Faeries don't have to eat to live, and that the Fae within—he thought—didn't *deserve* to eat either. It was as she passed the irritating guard that Valley began to wonder if they really did deserve to be in the prison.

As she entered the dark prison, Valley was surprised to find that it was just as dark during the daytime as it was during the night. There were no windows inside. She pressed forward boldly, feeling more confident this time around. She turned right to feed the men first, eager to meet that mysterious prisoner again.

"Lady Valley!" said the warm, welcoming Voice Faerie. "What an unexpected surprise!"

"Hallo, Whisp," she said as she knelt down on the ground to open the sack. "Marbel sent me with breakfast this morning."

"Breakfast?" Whisp was chuckling. "How *nice* of her!"

Valley stood and passed the first stick of potatoes to the Voice Faerie, who took it without question. As before, all she could see of the Faerie was a glimpse of his hands when they reached through the bars.

"What happened to your nice clothes?" asked another voice in the darkness beside Whisp. It was the other talkative Faerie she had met. She had never learned his name. "I thought you were a noble woman or something."

"I was bonded a couple days ago," Valley said, passing the next breakfast stick to the voice. "What is your name, friend?"

"Friend?" Whisp exclaimed. "By the Lights! Are you warming up to us, Lady Valley?"

"She just said she was bonded, Whisp," the second voice said sharply, "Have some decency! Are you alright, Lady Valley? Did they burn you?" The voice sounded deep, and Valley imagined someone tall and broad-shouldered.

"Yes," she said, feeling surprisingly validated. "Unfortunately."

"Well, I am Skatch, XII Faerie of Money," he said. "Thank you for the breakfast. It really is so kind of you to think of others when you have just gone through something so horrible."

"Thank you," Valley said in a strong voice. *Well!* This sure was different; rather than everyone making her feel strange for hating the branding, they were showing her sympathy! "Does everyone else want breakfast?"

The other Faeries still didn't really talk to Valley, but they took the food from her. Everyone, of course, except the one at the end. Still, she moved toward the darkness, drawn to its mystery, and placed her hands on the bars.

"Are you there?" she asked with a wavering voice.

"So *that's* why you're here," Whisp said from further away, "You're curious about him, aren't you? You're going to be disappointed, miss."

Valley turned her head in Whisp's direction. It was still so strange that he—and everyone else in the room—could see her, but she could not see them. "Why?" she asked, then turned back toward the darkness. "Hallo?"

Whisp sighed. "Give him a try!"

"Hallo," said the deep voice, smooth like silk. "What is your name, child?"

Valley hesitated. Hadn't she told him her name last time? Perhaps not. "Valley," she said.

"Valley," he said in a distant voice, "What a lovely name."

"What is *your* name?" Valley asked. He did not reply. This conversation was beginning to sound familiar—perhaps because it was the same one they had had before. "Do you have a name?" she asked again.

"I don't know what you mean..." the mysterious man said in a shaky voice.

"Do you have a *name*?" she asked, raising her voice. "What is your *title*?"

Valley could hear Whisp chuckling. She grunted. Finally, the voice spoke.

"I do not know," he said, "but I... I might know yours."

Yes. This was the moment she was waiting for. "How?" she asked. "What is it?"

She could hear some shuffling from the cell within. sniffling. Was he crying?

"I remember a child," he said, "There was a child."

"*What* child?" she asked, gripping the bars tightly.

"Where is the King?" the voice asked, growing desperate. "Where *is* he?"

"Oh, here we go—you've riled him up now." Whisp moaned.

"What do you mean?" Valley turned to him. "Who *is* he?"

"We have all been trying to figure *that* out for ages!"

"Where is the King? Where are his wings? Two dark, two light!" The man's voice grew distressed. "Where is he? Where is he? Two dark, two light!" His voice grew quieter, and Valley guessed he was retreating deeper into his cell, mumbling the questions over and over. "Where is the King?"

Valley sighed. "He's insane, isn't he?"

"Yeah..." Whisp said. "Sorry."

"Well then why did he say he knew my title? How did he know who I was?" She walked over towards Whisp's cell, feeling the pang of defeat.

"That was something we haven't heard him say before," he paused, then said, "but he is very observant of wings. Perhaps he recognized yours."

"Recognized..." she mumbled, shaking her head, "What do you mean? How could he know what my wings look like?" She heard laughter sound from the cells around her. "What?" she asked, looking around her confusedly.

"Because they're massive," Skatch said.

Valley blinked in amazement. "You... you can see them?"

"Of course we can!" Whisp said, "They clear as day—erm—*night*, in the dark!"

Valley looked eerily over her shoulder, as if a ghost loomed behind her. To her disappointment, but not surprise, all she could see was the dark.

"What do they look like?" she asked.

"Pointy?" Whisp suggested.

"Smooth, I think," Skatch said, "But it is hard to tell dark from dark."

"They're bigger than last time," said an unfamiliar voice. "You're gaining power."

"What?" Valley asked. "Who said that?"

"Never mind," the voice snapped.

Whisp chuckled. "We don't know who you are. Perhaps if you weren't rotting in Mensa, you could find *out*!"

"Are you all in here because you kept your titles?" Valley asked as she picked up the bundle of undelivered food for the female Faeries. Laughter sounded from all around her. "Well?" she pressed, growing angry. "Why are you laughing? Just tell me why Hanz locked you up!" She stamped her foot on the ground. "Why won't anyone tell me *anything*?"

"Come here, Valley," Whisp said, cooling his laughter. Valley walked over to the front of the Voice Faerie's cell.

"What?" She crossed her arms.

"You are right about one thing: We are here because we refused to do what King Hanz told us to do. Many of us were once members of the Purple Order. Do you know what that is?"

"Yes..." she said, unsure if she really did. "The Faeries who helped King Hanz kill the Nightmare Faerie?"

The laughter returned like a pack of wolves, surrounding her on all sides.

Whisp, through his cackling, asked, "Has Hanz convinced you all that *he* killed the Nightmare Faerie?"

"Well," Valley shrugged, "I don't know if he said *who* did the killing... but yes?"

"Valley," Whisp grew serious. "Hanz betrayed the Purple Order. We all followed him because he promised us freedom. Do we look *free* to you?"

"...obviously not," she said, "Did you do something to anger him?"

Whisp stayed silent as those around him broke out into another bout of laughter. "All you would have to do to join us, *Valley*, is say 'no' to just one thing he told you to do. We are in here because we refused to be bonded."

"I see," Valley said. "*I cannot free you from the chains until you first believe that they bind you,*" she recited softly to herself.

"What?" Whisp asked, and she saw his hand clutch the bar in front of him. "What does that mean?"

Valley was surprised that he could hear what she mumbled under her breath, then she remembered that he was the Voice Faerie.

"Nothing," she shook her head, "I am just realizing," she raised her chin, "that I am no different than you all."

"In what way?" Whisp asked, sounding a little skeptical.

"I am in a prison—and I need to get out."

"Well," Whisp blew air through his lips. "True enough, Miss Valley."

"Anyway," She took a step toward the exit to their little chamber, "I better take the food to the women while it's hot."

"Be careful," he snorted. "She bites."

She? Valley ignored the comment and left. She could hear Whisp shouting something playful at her, but she didn't hear what it was. She returned to the center torch, the only source of light in the prison. Then she stepped toward a place she had not yet seen, the cell to the left, where the women apparently were. She groped her way through the dark cautiously and soon found another set of bars.

"Hallo?" she asked, feeling more nervous than she expected to. "Would anyone like breakfast?"

"You're not Marbel," said a female voice soaked in suspicion. "What are you doing here, girl?"

"Marbel sent me with breakfast," Valley said timidly. She moved over to the bars where she thought the voice was. "Does anyone want any?"

There was only silence. The suspicious voice jeered. "I don't think they'll take food from you, girl."

"Why not?"

"They don't know you," she said, "And they are used to spies like you coming in here."

"Spies?" Valley shook her head. "No!"

"Oh?" said the woman. "Tell me you're not here for information. Come on!"

Valley felt a throb of guilt in her heart. "Well," she said timidly, "I came here to ask someone from the other side a question—so yes—I did come for information. But over here, I just wanted to bring food. I don't like the thought of you all locked away here in this prison so I—"

"Oh, how magnanimous!" The woman sneered. "We don't want your pity. We only trust Marbel."

"Fine!" Valley snapped, throwing the food down onto the ground. "You don't have to take it."

"Girl," the woman huffed, "I wouldn't take it anyway, but the other two are *scared* of you."

"Of me?" Valley snorted. "Well, they shouldn't be."

"Girl," the woman cleared her throat. "With wings like those, you could scare anyone."

"Well, I can't see my own wings!" Valley snapped, no longer hiding her indignation. "And no one will tell me who I am!"

"Oh, how *sad* for you!"

Valley held her breath, thinking. She could make an enemy out of this woman, or—if she were smart—she could befriend her. This woman had no reason to trust Valley. It was Valley who would have to prove herself here.

"Look," Valley softened her tone, "I'm sorry. Here I am, walking around free—free to do things like bring you food if I feel like it, or free not to. Meanwhile, you're stuck in this awful place. It's not right," she bowed her head. "You shouldn't be here."

The woman sniffed. "Look, girl," she said with slightly less sass in her voice. "Let's get one thing straight. A lot of what you said is fine, but you got one thing *dead* wrong."

Valley lifted her head. "And what is that?"

"I do deserve to be here, honey. I deserve to be here more than anyone else on the world—save for the devil himself. And by him, I mean that bastard for a king."

"Sire?" Valley asked.

The woman spat at the sound of the name.

Valley placed her hands on the bars and leaned her forehead between them. Peering into the darkness, she could see two glowing eyes, but everything else was pure darkness. No... no there was something else. An aura of some sort emanated from the cell. Who *was* this Faerie?

"What did you do to deserve this?" Valley asked boldly.

There was silence, and Valley thought the aura, which at first looked purple, began to glow red.

"Never mind what I have done," the woman said. "But it was enough to deserve this—to deserve *everything* Hanz throws at me. I am a monster—more of a monster than *you*."

"And what sort of a monster am *I*?"

"A very beautiful monster," said the woman. "And perhaps," there was hesitation in her voice, "perhaps you're not a monster at all."

Valley deliberated within herself. "You know my wings, don't you?"

"Yes."

Well—perhaps *this* Faerie who could tell Valley who she was!

"I know who your parents are, too," she said. "I know lots of things."

Valley's eyes flashed. "What?" She gritted her teeth. "What do you mean?"

Valley tensed as the red aura began to float toward her. The mystical lights rolled and shifted, forming into the shape of two great wings. The eyes drew closer and for a moment Valley thought they looked like fireflies moving around mesmerizingly.

"That's right, *Valley*," she jeered. "I know *everything* about you and your pitiful life. I know many things—including the fact that you've been bonded to the devil, himself." In a flash, she was at the bars, clutching Valley's hands and holding them in place. Her face pressed close, with her nose touching Valley's, and she glared with snarling teeth. Valley tried to withdraw but the Faerie held her in place. "Listen!" she seethed, "You tell that bastard for a king that his tricks won't work on me! I am the *queen* of tricks—you understand? Nothing you do can get me to tell you where *he* is!"

"Please!" Valley yelped, "I don't know what you're talking about! He didn't send me!"

"Lies!" The woman shrieked. "You're a liar, just like your predecessors!"

Valley's eyes focused on the woman's face, which was illuminated enough that she could make out detail. Her skin was marbled with dried blood and bruises. Her fingers, which clamped themselves tightly over Valley's hands, were bloodied and misshapen, missing several fingernails.

"What has happened to you?" she asked, horrified.

The Faerie hissed. "Don't pity me, pitiful *bitch*! Until my wounds are as many as his—it will never be enough. So torture me as much as you like, Hanz! I welcome it! But mark my words: I will *never* let you find him!"

She released her vice-like grip on Valley's hands and disappeared back into the darkness.

Valley gasped, yanking her hands free through the bars. "Please," Valley said breathlessly. "Please don't tell Hanz I was here."

She heard the woman snickering. "Whatever you say, *Valley*."

Valley could no longer feel her fingers and no longer had the stomach to remain in that dreadful place. Once again, she left the prison running.

15

—— Hanz ——

In Motion

"Today," said Hanz, standing authoritatively up at the podium, "We will make a plan. We will not get into the specifics, but we will make a list of topics we wish to discuss for the season of Kingsummons. Some of you have committed to staying for the first three weeks and others have agreed to stay longer, if necessary." He looked down at the listeners.

The Court House was lined with three rows of seating on raised platforms and at the center of the room was an open floor. The main delegates sat in the first row, while their wings sat behind in the second. To the side of the platform on which Hanz stood, Sir Swain sat, writing. On the third row were other important officials, including those from his own justice court and whatever skydeacons were present in Mensa.

"Now," Hanz continued, "I want everyone to voice the topics we will discuss ahead of time, so that we can prepare for each discussion. Then, Sir Swain and I will write up a schedule to ensure each topic is discussed. We can adjourn at the lunch bell, giving everyone plenty of time to relax and get to know Mensa

Castle before Rosamond's party." He clasped his hands together with a clap. "Right," he said, "I will list the topics I wish to discuss and then open up the floor."

Hanz carefully studied each of the main delegates. On his left sat Prince Tingo of Sol and Prince Rasselas of Celestia. On his right were King Labyrinth of the Gramenlands, King Stathe of the Vastlands, and Lord Cato of the Edgelands. Yes—this would be enough. Though some of the peripheral kingdoms were missing representation, this would be an ideal group to support his efforts. But he would have to play his cards right.

Hanz walked off the platform, down the narrow steps, and approached the small pedestal reserved for the house speaker. He cleared his throat, placed his hands on the little pulpit, and raised his voice.

"My first topic I wish to discuss is the problem of food. Yes... then, after that—the problem of Bavel. What is happening there?" Hanz turned his head toward Swain, "Write that down." He looked back at those gathered, "What is happening there, and what are we going to do about it?"

"What, indeed?" Labyrinth belted, turning to those beside him with a grin.

"I have the floor, Labyrinth," Hanz said, "Let's begin how we mean to go on and stay silent until the floor is open to discussion."

Labyrinth scoffed, as though Hanz had spoken above his office.

Swain's hand moved swiftly, whisking around his feather quill with panache.

"Secondly, I propose we discuss the idea of an alliance of kingdoms and decide *officially* on borders, therefore saving us all the trouble of little petty wars."

There was grumbling amongst some of those gathered, but Hanz continued. "Thirdly, I want to discuss Arelle, the Faeries, and what sort of role Arelle has in Raqia." He stopped to look around. No one seemed to be arguing with him, so he said, "I have more thoughts, but first I will open up the floor to hear some of your ideas."

Hanz tossed the side of his cape behind him and glided toward one of the seats, installing himself beside Prince Rasselas.

Prince Tingo was the first to rise and take the stand. "Greetings, friends," he said in a clear voice. "I would like to discuss the problem of hunger and famine. Some may want to deny it, but it plagues all our lands. We have resorted to rationing, which has started riots in Sol. I don't know what the rest of you are doing about it, but it would be beneficial to hear your thoughts on this."

Indeed, Hanz thought, a problem in need of a solution? Yes—this plan would work.

As Tingo sat, King Labyrinth took his place. "All I propose," he said as he leaned casually against the stone pedestal, "Is that we get some felling *trade* laws in place!" There was a ruckus of agreement in response to that statement. "Can we *please* discuss tariffs and embargoes? Let's make a standard, people!"

Swain wrote down the proposal, and Labyrinth moved away from the pulpit with his hands raised in victory. Cato applauded as he rose and stood in place.

"Well," Lord Cato said as he arched his back, hands against his hips. "I just wanted a chance to stand up here and look as fancy as you lot," he shrugged, turning to Hanz with a smirk. Prince Rasselas sat forward, cheering heartily, as Cato sat himself back down.

Hanz didn't want to give the goons the dignity of a scowl. They were as bad as each other—no—worse!

Rasselas himself hopped up, and he charged toward the stand. "I've got one!" he said, shooting his finger up into the air. In his peripheral vision, Hanz could spot the Elven wing, Sir Thorne, shaking his head. "I would like to discuss fashion standards," Rasselas said boldly.

"Hear, hear!" Cato leaned forward, charging his fist into the air.

"Alright," Hanz barked, "Let's stay on task."

Rasselas made an annoying face. "But I am deadly serious!"

Hanz held his nerve and leaned back in his seat, waiting patiently as a skydeacon stepped down from the third row and made his way to the stand.

"Greetings," said the pointy-eared man, "I would like to discuss universalizing the standards for the skydeacons and how we measure the changing of seasons and selecting a new hub for the skydeacon fellowship while Arelle is... *e–erm*," he stuttered, "empty."

Others came forward and proposed topics for discussion. All the while, King Hanz sat back listening. To think that he managed to get all these world leaders into one room! Yes... even without a Faerie King on the throne of Arelle, he could bring some semblance of unity to Raqia. Discussions didn't last too long and, as King Hanz promised, the meeting was concluded before the midday bell even rang.

Hanz didn't wait to stand around and chat with the others. Before anyone else had even risen from their seats, he left through the back door.

As Hanz stepped out into the daylight and headed eastward toward the man gate, a cloaked figure seamlessly joined his side, trailing behind him like a shadow.

"Good day, sire," came Sigmund's voice from behind. He pulled his hood down in front of his face with a yawn.

"Sorry to keep you up so long," Hanz said, still walking briskly forward.

"It's no problem, sire," Sigmund mumbled, "Would you like the report from last night?"

"Yes."

"No sight of the blind Faerie or the boy," Sigmund said, keeping his voice low, "And it was the same for me as it was for you, I couldn't see past the walls of Bavel."

Hanz nodded to a group of soldiers who saluted as he passed under the gate and up the stairs to the upper walls.

"Hades," Hanz cursed, "That's disappointing. What about Winter's End?"

"Well, sire," Sigmund rushed to keep pace, "I lost my way trying to find it through the portal. I doubt I could do any better than you, since you have been there, and I have not. I fear it has some sort of protective enchantment as well."

Hanz gritted his teeth. "Well then, my guess is the boy is hiding in one of those two places."

"He won't be a 'boy' anymore," Sigmund said in a slithery voice.

"Yes, I *know* that, Sigmund," Hanz snapped.

When Hanz found himself at the Inner Palace, he held up his hand to Sigmund, dismissing him. Sigmund paused, touching his chin thoughtfully.

"Is there something you need, Sigmund?" Hanz asked, rubbing his temple with his finger.

"I was just wondering to myself," he mused, "Do you think the Faerie of Sight can see through the walls of Bavel? You know—there's supposed to be nothing he can't see."

Hanz blinked his eyes. He had not thought of that before! "I'll think about it," he said, "For now go and get your sleep."

"*Thank* you, sire," Sigmund gave a bow then left as soundlessly as he had come.

Hanz entered the Inner Palace and whisked through the halls until he came to Rosamond's door. He stood there for a moment with his head bowed, thinking. Then, he opened the door.

Motion erupted in the room at Hanz's arrival. Several maids rushed about, nervous at the King's sudden appearance, holding stacks of colored fabric and odd bits of ribbon. Rosamond, who was standing at the back of the room, gasped at the sight of him, then dove behind her dressing screen.

As Hanz walked into the room, all the maids knelt, and the room grew quiet.

"Father, I am half dressed!" Rosamond declared from behind the screen. "Will you please *knock* next time?"

Hanz crossed his arms. "Rosamond," he said with a clearing of his throat, "I just wanted to check to see that you're feeling alright this morning. Are you ready for your party tonight?"

"Father," Rosamond huffed. Hanz could see Rosamond's silhouette from behind the screen, posing with hands on hips, "If I were ready, I wouldn't be standing behind this screen, would I? Besides, all we are doing is *deciding* on an outfit—the party isn't for *ages*, you know!" she said sarcastically.

After last night's lesson, Rosamond *still* answered her father back with *sass?* Did she think all the present witnesses would protect her from being reminded of her place? Still... Hanz kept his calm.

"Rosamond," Hanz said in his best fatherly voice, "I didn't ask if you were dressed. I want to know if you are ready to act more like a *princess.*"

Hanz watched the silhouette of Rosamond drop her forehead into her hand. Was that a display of sass or distress? He hoped it was the latter; perhaps his discipline *did* have some effect on Rosamond.

"Papa," Rosamond lifted her head. "I'll be the epitome of a princess tonight, just you watch!" Her attitude seemed determined, though Hanz knew veiled flattery when he saw it.

Hanz bit the side of his lip. No, that was sass—that was *definitely* sass. Did *nothing* get through to this girl?

"I just want to know that you will do your best to bring honor to the family," he said, feeling his muscles tensing, "I want to know that you can *act* like a girl that a king would want to marry."

"Papa, when have I ever *not* acted like a girl someone wanted to marry? I am perfection—surely!"

Hanz flinched. "You can be a bit headstrong at times," he said, "Just tone that down tonight, will you? Men want a nice *quiet* girl who flatters and complements them. Someone to *look* at, not someone to..." he searched, "...*spar* with."

"Of *course*, Papa!" Rosamond exclaimed.

Hanz didn't feel reassured. "Maybe just don't talk very much," he suggested, then glanced at the maid who bowed at his feet, "Have her wear something that's eye-catching, or what-have-you. You know—keep the legs modest but you can take liberties, erm," He made an awkward gesture toward his chest area. "Let's see if we can keep the attention away from her *mouth*."

"Oh, Papa," Rosamond rotated to stick her chin up into the air as she messed with her loose hair, "Stop making the maids so uncomfortable! Don't worry so much! I'll be your trophy daughter, just watch."

"I just wanted to make sure we wouldn't need to have another *frank* conversation tonight," he said. "I'll have my eye on you."

"Yes, Papa," she groaned, "I *know*!"

"Rosamond," he stepped toward the screen with a lunge.

"Oh, I wanted to ask you," she said, and he saw her shadow waving its hand playfully, "Was there any monarch in *particular* you wanted me to impress?"

Hanz froze. "Rosamond," he lowered his voice. "Don't worry about that. I don't want you—" he felt his pulse rising. Why was this all so stressful? "Please don't try and understand my strategies, you'll just mess everything up. Don't think about which one. I'll worry about which one. *All* I want is for you to be pretty and desirable. Think of yourself—" he grunted. Why was this so hard for her to understand? "Think of yourself like a...like a rare painting... or... no—like a cake!"

Rosamond dropped her hand. "Did you *really* just say that, Papa?" Even one of the maids made a sound. Hanz massaged his forehead.

"*Yes*, I said that, *darling*," he gritted his teeth. "Can you be a *cake* for me, dear?" He didn't hide his temper.

"I will be the epitome of fluffiness and cakiness!" Rosemond posed, clearly aware of her silhouette being visible to him. She was *definitely* getting another beating tonight. No one ever warned him that a daughter would do him more harm than good!

"Fine." He turned and marched toward the door. One of the maids rose and rushed toward him.

"My Lord?" She bowed nervously, "Sire?"

"Yes, yes?" Hades, this was taking longer than he anticipated. "What?"

"Are you asking me to *change* her outfit?" She wore a guilty expression, already knowing it was wrong to ask. "Do you mean to change what we already decided on?"

Hanz was flabbergasted. "I don't care two coins about the details," he howled. "Just show some felling cleavage! More than you were *going* to! Is that so hard?"

The woman trembled. "Yes, of course. I mean—*no*, my Lord!"

"Is it so hard to understand my words? Do I have to spell it out for you women like you are five seasons old?" He was yelling now.

The room was as still and silent as a tomb.

"Have no fear, Father!" Rosamond broke the silence with a performance that wouldn't impress even a drunk. "I will treat your desires like laws!"

Hanz stood there with his mouth half open. Was she the perfect daughter? Or... *oh, no...* Oh, *Hades*—either that, or this woman wasn't *anywhere* near broken. A beating was enough to refocus a confused woman, but—while the beating wasn't pleasant for her— it sure hadn't taught Rosamond to keep that runaway mouth of hers shut!

"It's Riah all over again," Hanz mumbled as he left the room, "she's cursing me." He slammed Rosamond's door behind himself and plodded down the hall toward his chambers. "Will there always be a stubborn woman keeping me from...?" he stopped walking with his hand hovering over the handle to his door.

"Master?" asked a voice.

Hanz turned his gaze right to see a figure standing beside him.

"Karo?" he guessed.

"Hallo, master!" said his bonded Faerie. Hanz turned his posture to face the slave.

"Karo," he said, "I need to change, is there something you need?"

"No, no," Karo shook his head, backing away with a bow.

"Look, just follow me in and we can chat while I change," mumbled the King. Like any loyal hound, Karo followed him into his room as Hanz plowed inside. Taking off first his crown, then his ceremonial cape, Hanz dressed down to a more comfortable, casual ensemble. As he threw items of clothing this way and that, Karo stood by, jabbering away.

"...so I told her that day three is the worst, I mean, neglecting to mention the fact that day five involves a *test* of some sort. Hades, I wouldn't steal the thunder from your Lordship, but I thought I would stop your way and mention that she did seem a little *excited* when I greeted her this morning!"

Hanz, halfway through taking off one of his gloves, froze in place. "Wait—*what* are you talking about?"

"Valley," said Karo, "Anyway, she skipped along, eager to see you and all..."

"Karo," Hanz cut in, neglecting to see the point of Karo's update, "Can you just cut to the chase? There's something else I wanted to..."

"The *chase*? Oh, ho, ho," the Faerie giggled, shaking his finger, "no *chase* here, my Lord, I just wanted to mention that I thought the young Valley is going to fit nicely into the, erm, the crew. I—erm," he trilled his fingers against the wall, "I say! Since you're all eager to match up Faeries and the like, you know, to sort of..."

"Karo!" Hanz threw his second glove against the wall with a smack, "You're talking nonsense again! *What* are you asking me?"

Karo fluttered his eyelids, distancing himself from the tension he felt from the confrontation. "Oh, nothing," he sputtered, "Just mentioning that Valley and I are getting on *swimmingly* and all that."

It wasn't hard to guess what Karo was asking for; the man was artless. No—there was no *way* Hanz was going to set up Valley as one of the lewd old Karo's mates. The man could hardly keep his eyes on one woman for more than one night!

"Karo," Hanz said blandly. "How hard is it to..." he tried to phrase his question strategically, "...to bind flesh together?"

Karo visibly blushed. "Bind fl—" he grinned, "it's not that hard at *all*, master!"

Hanz felt the urge to scream. "It wasn't a *euphemism*, Karo," he said, reaching for his daytime top hat. "Like if someone lost their arm, how hard would it be to bind the flesh back together again?"

"Well," Karo grabbed the collar of his suit, leveling his posture, "if I were the Faerie of Flesh—which of course I am *not*..." then he mumbled, *"since you won't let us have titles anyway..."* The artless Faerie cleared his throat. "I would say that it's very *easy*, Sire. That is—it might take a little light magik, but not *too* much."

Hanz ran his hand through his hair. "Alright," he said. "What about someone *else's* arm?"

Karo bobbed his head as he ran the scenario through his mind. "For me? Erm—no, for a Faerie of Flesh, which doesn't *actually* exist," he winked, "It would not be that hard, though it might take a little *more* magik."

"Then, let's say," Hanz turned to look in the mirror, examining his own face, "Let's say I lost my arm, and I asked... *the Faerie of Flesh*... to attach someone's arm to me. Say—say a Faerie's arm? Let's say I asked you to give me your arm."

Karos face didn't hide his trepidation at the thought. "Well," he bobbed his head again, processing, "I could do it—but of course Faerie flesh is a different matter. You cannot separate a Faerie's flesh from their being. So I suppose I could give you my arm," he swallowed, "but I can't guarantee you would be able to control it." He stood motionless for more than a few moments, thinking, then he added, "I think it is possible that you could control the arm, but you and I would both be connected to it. Does that make sense? It could never stop being my arm; but it would also be *your* arm. But you would no longer be able to use your old arm. Sire—" he drew in a sharp breath, "—*what* exactly are you considering?"

"Nothing," Hanz said. "Let's take the scenario further, then…" He walked toward his back door, and Karo stumbled after him, distracted by the theoretical nature of the exchange. "What if it were something more sensory?"

"Well, an arm *is* sensory, sire," Karo said, growing visibly stressed. The conversation was growing too specific to be *completely* theoretical.

"Fine," said Hanz, "So would *I* feel the things I touched with that arm? Or would only *you* feel them?"

Karo's mouth was fixed open as he considered the question. "Well…" he drew out his words as they formed in his mind, "…I think—theoretically—we would *both* feel it. I *think*," he stressed the inconclusiveness of his hypothesis. "…not that I'm an expert in this area or anything…"

Hanz stood beside the door which led out of his dressing chamber and into his secret passage. He rested his hand on the door, ready to push it open and press on to his next task, but he lingered. "When the Nightmare Faerie lost his hand, it was at Winter's End for an entire season. Would he have been able to move or sense with it?"

Karo stuttered, "I had no idea that he lost his—well—I mean, yes, I think he possibly could have—sensed with it, at *least*!"

Hanz nodded. "If I replaced my own arm with yours and then you died, what would happen?"

"This is…" Karo looked terrified.

"I am not *actually* going to kill you—just answer the question!"

"Right, well," he blustered, "I am not sure. I might need to research that one. Do you know what happened to the Nightmare Faerie's hand after he died?"

Hanz hesitated. "Yes," he said, "It turned to stone, then began to fade to ash."

Karo blinked. "You seem to know a lot about it..."

Hanz shot Karo a glance, his hand still hovering over the door handle. "Yes, I do," he said, "so with that information, can you answer my question?"

"Well..." Karo bobbed his head to the side, "I suppose if I merged it with your flesh, it becomes your flesh, too. So if I died, the part of me that lived in the arm might die, leaving you with a fully functional arm. On the other hand, it might turn to stone and ash—leaving you one-armed. If you wanted to bond Faerie flesh to yourself," he cleared his throat, "I would recommend keeping that Faerie alive... just in case."

Perhaps this *was* worth experimenting. Not on himself, of course, but he could try it on someone else. He would have to be sure before he tried anything permanent.

"Alright," Hanz said, "Tonight you can have some charge up time."

"Oh, *thank* you Sire!" Karo beamed. "Shall I meet you at the regular place?"

"I'll have Sigmund bring you your imperium," Hanz said, "No need for *me* to meet you, is there?"

"No, no," the Faerie clasped his hands together eagerly, "not at all. Thank you—*Thank* you, sire!"

Without so much as a 'goodbye', Hanz left. In his casual dress suit, Hanz sauntered back into the daylight, and glided across the upper walls. He had a strong hankering for a smoke, but brushed the feeling away, pulling his toothpick from his vest pocket. He made his way to the Warrowing Gate, plastering on the right kind of smile. It was the smile of a leader who was beloved by his people.

Once at the Warrowing Gate, Hanz was quickly joined by Captain Oswald.

"Sire," said the captain, "Right on time."

Well, the second midday bell had already sounded, so he wasn't right on time. The two men walked together into the Warrowing Village.

"How long have you been waiting for me?" Hanz asked, scanning the courtyard bustling with foot traffic.

"Since the second bell, or a little before," Oswald said.

"See anything interesting? Any noblemen come in here?" Hanz asked.

"Yes," said Oswald. "A set of them came through to grab lunch together. They were checking the place out, but didn't really speak with any Fae."

"Good, good," Hanz picked at his only browning tooth, "They're getting curious. Let them shop, just don't let them stay too long."

Oswald nodded curtly. "Very good, Sire."

"Which noblemen came in?"

"His majesty Labyrinth and two of his highlords."

"Right," Hanz nodded. "Well, grab a couple of soldiers and meet me at the prison," he said, "And bring torches."

Oswald bowed, then rushed off. Hanz stepped forward and immersed himself in the busy town center, taking lunch from the hunger Faerie, and striking up conversation with the villagers. He was nothing short of a celebrity there. Faeries of all ages gathered around, bowing and flattering him. They loved him; they really loved him!

He wanted to stay for ages, soaking up the affection, but he had to keep going. More pressing matters awaited him. Before long, he made his way to the prison and was soon joined by Oswald and his men. Each soldier held a large torch. Hanz had Oswald lead the way, carrying the light before him as they entered the prison. Hanz could hear nervous shuffling from the prisoners as light suddenly illuminated their world. Hanz turned a corner and sneered at the first body he saw, curling up into the corner of his cell, hiding from the light. The Voice Faerie, covered in grime and half naked, looked more skeleton than man now, and his hair had formed into a mess of matted dreads.

"Please!" he shouted, "The lights are too much...Less! Please!"

"Quiet!" Hanz barked. The Faerie flinched, then unshielded his face long enough to look at the King.

"Hanz?" he asked as an amused smile formed on his face. "To what do we owe the honor?"

Hanz moved past the Voice Faerie and examined each prisoner as he passed them; yes, they were all still alive. Near the end of the little walkway, he spotted one Faerie that didn't seem to be moving.

"What's wrong with him?" Asked the King.

Oswald banged against the bars with his fist. "Hallo?" Oswald called, "Wake up, your king is here!"

The body didn't move. "Which one is that?" Hanz asked, "Xandre?"

"The Persuasion Faerie," Oswald said, stepping back from the bars. "I think he's dead."

"What?" the Voice Faerie screeched, throwing himself suddenly against his bars. "No!"

"Shut up, Whisp!" barked the king.

"He was talking yesterday, I heard him! No, he can't be dead!" Whisp yapped.

"Would you shut him up?" Hanz snapped. Oswald nodded to one of the soldiers who whacked Whisp's bar-clutching fingers with his baton. Whisp fell back into his cell with a howl, then huddled back into his corner, whimpering. "Damn," Hanz whispered under his breath, "I needed him. What *happened*?"

"He couldn't get magik," said the deep voice of the Wealth Faerie. Hanz whipped his head around to look at the slender, dark-skinned Faerie who sat on the floor, leaning against the back wall of his cell. "None of us can."

"I give you enough," Hanz said, tossing a gold coin at the man. The coin fell to the ground with a clank, and the Faerie Skatch didn't so much as look at it.

"He shouldn't have died," Hanz said, more to himself, "I gave him enough. Damn. I *needed* him!"

"Death!" cried a shrill voice. All gasped, turning to look at the cell at the far end where a crazed Faerie was trying to press his face through the bars. "Death!" he cried again. "He is dead!"

"Friend!" Hanz held up his hands and took the opportunity to grab the Faerie's attention. "Friend, calm yourself."

The Faerie was pale and gaunt, with his long, colorless hair floating around like a disembodied spirit. His eyes searched longingly, restlessly. All others present grew quiet as Hanz stepped forward to touch the man's hands.

"Friend," Hanz said again, "Be at peace."

"At peace?" asked the Faerie. His eyes shifted, finding Hanz. "Yes... yes, he is at peace now. He found peace—yes—yes, it is peace."

Hanz nodded slowly. "You will find peace, too," Hanz said, "When you find the child—yes?"

The Faerie's pupils grew smaller as the whites of his eyes grew larger. "The child," he said, "there was a child..."

"What do you remember?" Hanz asked. "What did he look like?"

"Two light; two dark..." mumbled the Faerie with vacant eyes. "Where is he?"

"He is grown now," said Hanz, "I am he."

The Faerie's eyes focused on Hanz's face. "*What*?"

"Look at my eyes," Hanz said firmly, "You know my face."

The Faerie rotated his head sideways, studying the King. "No..." he mumbled, "two light... two dark..."

"Remember me!" Hanz whispered, "It is *me*."

"But..." The Faerie's lip began to quiver. "But there was a child! I remember a child!"

"He grew!" Hanz said, growing tense, "He is *me*!"

The Faerie stumbled backwards, mumbling wildly. Then crumpled up into a ball and wept.

Hanz sighed, looking back at the lifeless body of the Persuasion Faerie. "Get rid of the body," he said, then he hesitated, "Put it with the others and have Karo take a look at it."

"Bury him!" Whisp shrieked. "Please! *Please* bury him!"

"That's enough for today," Hanz said, turning to Oswald, "and would you make that felling Voice Faerie shut *up*?"

16

— Rook —

The Packrat Particles

"SOME OF THE 'BOYS' ARE GOING TO THE DUELING GROUNDS to practice sword fighting," Cato said with a mouth full of food. His long legs were stretched out above his waist as he balanced the tip of his boot heel against the edge of his writing desk. "Want to come? I think I could win some coin if you were willing to fight a round or two."

"I know you like being the center of attention, Cato," Rook said, "but I, on the other hand, do not. If you don't mind, I would like to take the opportunity to explore the castle a bit since I've had next to no time by myself in the last several days." Rook leaned against one of Cato's bedposts, running a tipless toothpick under one of his fingernails.

"Well, it's true, if I had a face like yours—no offense—I'd probably want to avoid the spotlight, too. But cards, Rook! It's going to be such a perfect opportunity to poke fun at people. Just think, you and me sitting on the sidelines, mocking all those princes and knights hopping around like little rabbits. Flood waters, boy—it's going to be hilarious!"

Rook looked up from his fidgeting and smirked. "As enjoyable as it is to listen to you ridicule pretentious princes, I'll pass."

"Oh, suit yourself," Cato sat up, his heels clacking against the stone floor. "I'm going to go enjoy myself. Oh," the man stood stiffly for a moment, eyeing Rook with skepticism. "Wait..."

"What?" Rook began picking at his nail again.

"I was supposed to be trying to guess what you're on about in Mensa, wasn't I?"

"Mhmm."

"Well cards, boy," Cato wheezed, "You're just too boring for me to care today."

"Great."

"You were a hair interesting yesterday, though," he mumbled as he walked toward the door. "That picture of you made me think you might have been a prince in another life. Ah—well, a shame that boy can't draw worth two lives."

"I thought you liked his drawing of me," Rook glanced up from his faffing.

"*Augh,*" Cato grimaced, "I was trying to complement the poor Fae. It looked nothing like you."

"Mm," Rook pretended not to care and stood there fiddling with the toothpick until Cato finally left.

As soon as the highlord was gone, Rook straightened and moved over to the chair where he had laid his over cloak. He flung the thing over his shoulders and scooted sideways to check himself in the mirror. Black on black... on black. He chuckled, remembering Prince Rasselas' condescending words.

This man is wearing so much black I thought that the world might be ending! Rook heard the boy's voice perfectly in his head and broke into a vocal laugh, shaking his head. Well, Rasselas wasn't wrong. Rook wore a *lot* of black. He didn't so much mind the "villain" look; something about it felt right to him. Perhaps it was because it matched his ghastly scars. Rook fiddled with his cravat, tucking it up just under his chin so that it hid most of his neck scars, then coughed. Well, it wasn't getting any better than this! He left.

Once outside, Rook meandered slowly, familiarizing himself with the layout of the castle grounds. It seemed to be square-shaped, with the Inner Palace on the north end, the dueling grounds to the west, and—he looked over the edge of the wall where he currently stood—he wasn't yet sure what sat eastward.

"Have you been down there yet?" asked a familiar voice, "Hallo, Rook!"

Rook smiled at the sight of his new friend Latimer. "Hallo, friend. No. What's down there?" Rook asked, standing back from the wall's ledge.

"Better food than what you can find in the market, and fully vegetarian!" Latimer held up some flatbread wrapped around grilled vegetables. "I just went with Moonvine to see what sort of lunch was sold in the Warrowing Village, and we ate there."

Rook eyed the food. "It looks nice," he said, "Where is he now?"

"Moonvine?" Latimer's eyes drifted upwards, as if the Skies held answers for him. "Oh!" He jumped. "He went to the dueling grounds where some of the nobles are practicing swordcraft; I think some people are excited by the idea of duels on Mansday."

"Do you spar?" Rook asked, though he already knew the answer.

Latimer sputtered, "I, well..."

Rook slapped the scholar on the shoulder, jostling him a little, and smiled. "I take that as a negative, then. So what's the Warrowing Village? I am guessing it's where the lower staff live?"

Latimer twisted his face in discomfort. "Well, no. It's where the Faeries live, actually."

"Oh..." Rook's eyes drifted.

"There are a few stalls there with some interesting fare, some of us swear it's the best food in Mensa! Though, I haven't tried very much yet," Latimer said as he rocked back and forth on his heels. He grew quiet. Rook noticed the man was stuck looking at the Skies again.

"You must always be aware of changes in the weather," Rook said.

"Mmm," Latimer hummed, "Yeah—well, no." He reached up to rub his chin. "No, not aware... just curious. One never knows what he might miss if he isn't looking up."

Rook smirked. "And one never knows what one might miss if one isn't looking *down*."

"What?" Latimer snapped back to attention. "Right!"

"Latimer," Rook turned toward the descending staircase. Latimer took the cue and followed along beside him. "What's going on with the Fellowship? They are no longer based in Arelle?"

Latimer started. "Where have *you* been for the last fifteen seasons?"

"I know there is no Faerie King to cause or guide the changing of seasons, but I thought the skydeacons would at least still meet in Arelle as they always have done."

"Ah, yes," the skydeacon nodded, "The Faerie King—or Faerex, as they call him, you know—he has always been the head of the Fellowship of Skydeacons. But ever since the regent and everybody in the royal court were killed, the castle has been vacant. We all used to make seasonal trips to Arelle to compare notes and all that, but without any Faeries there—well, it got a tad awkward. So for the last decade or so, we have been meeting at a different hub every season, alternating so as not to show one kingdom partiality. *Unfortunately*," he bobbed his head to the side, "The meetings are happening more and more often in Mensa. And the naming of seasons," he cringed, "Well, the Mensan skydeacons are sort of deciding on things like that before we are all in agreement."

Rook found himself more interested in the subject than he thought he would be. "So how *do* you all name the seasons?"

"We have complicated ways of predicting when a season is about to change, and signs to know what sort of season is coming. You know, like when certain species of birds begin to migrate in certain directions, or sudden changes in colors or wind temperatures." Latimer held his breath, realizing he was probably rambling. "*Anyway*," he shrugged, "we name seasons in the final week before Firstday. You know, the first day of the week is usually called Octday, but when it's the first day of a *season*, well, that's when an Octday is called a Firstday."

"Yes, I know the days of the week," Rook smiled, "I wasn't born yesterday."

"Right!" Latimer bowed his head apologetically, "So anyway, the week before Firstday, we all come together, or send correspondence, and *together* we decide on the season's name."

"Something tells me 'Kingsummons' wasn't a unanimous decision," Rook guessed.

"Yes, well," Latimer joined his hands behind his back as they walked, his long simple robe dragging behind him. "I know *I* wasn't involved in choosing it, and a few other skydeacons here have told me the same. It's a little concerning to me that things could go off-course like this. When it comes to the weather, you know, we have to be meticulous! There can be nothing missed!"

"So do you all vote on names, or..."

"*Vote* isn't the right word," Latimer thought. "We deliberate and bring all of our observations forward. Together, we select the truest name we can, based on the signs. Most of the time, we come together with each of us already knowing what sort of name it will be. It's more about picking which variation is the best representation of the coming season and the signs. Does that make sense?"

Rook tilted his head to the side noncommittally. "So what name would *you* have given this season?"

"Well," Latimer puffed out his bony chest, "You're the first person to finally ask me that!"

"Alright," Rook waited patiently.

"Well, it wouldn't be *Kingsummons*, I can tell you that!"

"What would it be, then?"

"Tempering?" He cringed, listening to how the word sounded out loud when he said it, "Or... Temperings?"

"Those two are pretty different," Rook observed.

"Tempering and Temperings?"

Rook chuckled. "No, Temperings and Kingsummons."

"Oh," Latimer snorted, "Well, *Kingsummons* didn't exactly pass through the rest of the Fellowship, if you know what I mean. It's the sort of name that, well..." he grunted.

"What?"

"Well, it sort of feels like a name someone who *isn't* a skydeacon would pick."

"Right," Rook drew in a deep breath. "You are concerned that political powers are interfering with your order."

Latimer halted, then turned toward Rook with a guilty countenance. "Did I say that out loud?"

"No," Rook smiled, "I guessed."

"Oh, well," he sputtered, "That *is* a concern of mine, I confess."

The two arrived just outside of the Warrowing Village and stopped when Latimer turned to face Rook.

"Frankly," said Latimer, "I'm concerned that without a Faerex, someone else is going to try and take charge of our order."

"And that would be bad because..."

"Because it's sacred!" Latimer exclaimed, "As soon as someone who doesn't understand who we are and what we do tries to use our work for their own selfish means, we will be lost! The Faerex *actually* had power and authority to govern and predict seasons. It made *sense* for him to lead the order! But that role can't be filled by just anyone!"

Rook pulled the corner of his mouth to the side. "Did you, um..." he hesitated. "Did you serve under the last Faerex?"

"Do you mean Regent Hevel? Or King Somenus?" Latimer asked, then shrugged, "Well, either way, the answer is 'yes.' I even served under King Sol."

Rook looked down at the ground, steadying himself. He looked back up at the Elf. "You've been a skydeacon a long time, then?"

"Yes," Latimer nodded. "A few centuries, now."

Rook raised his eyebrows. And here *he* felt older than the man! He couldn't help but ask, "What was it like serving under Somenus?"

Latimer's eyes drifted sideways, "Ah, well, an interesting subject, to say the least. I didn't exactly *serve* under him. But I did go to Arelle twice for summons during his reign. After meeting with King Sol for so long, it was a stark change. King Somenus was very decisive and... well... frightening. Aside from him *actually* causing famine in some places, though, Somenus wasn't the worst."

He slumped. "Well, no one likes it when I say that, but it's true. He was a king with many sides, just like all the other kings, I think."

Rook was astonished. "No, I have never heard anyone say a single word about King Somenus that wasn't, quite literally, a curse!"

"Yes, well," Latimer threw up his hands in defeat, "you can see why *everyone* loves to have me and my opinions around, now, can't you?"

"Was that sarcasm?" Rook grinned. "I didn't think you were the type."

Latimer flattened his lips. "Yes, well, that's probably true. I don't..."

Both paused, looking upward toward the bell tower as the third, Descending Midday bell crashed above them.

"Ah!" Latimer slapped his own forehead. "I promised Moonvine I would watch him spar. I had better be off!" And just like that, he disappeared.

Rook watched him go, deliberating whether or not he should just join him at the dueling grounds. His gaze drifted back toward the large gate which led into the Faerie village. He knew he would have to at least take a *look* inside; he didn't have to talk to anyone. Anyway, someone might know something about the Crimson Gate or Felix's eyes!

Bracing himself, Rook ventured inside. He walked under the large stone gate and looked around at the busy little village within. He was not two steps in when someone stopped him.

"It's you! Rook!" Coppo, the artist boy with dark skin and bright eyes blocked Rook's path with outstretched arms and a wide smile. "Remember me?"

Rook's stoic face broke and he found himself grinning. "Coppo, Faerie of Lines," he said, "It's good to see you!"

"Come in, come in!" Coppo took him by the sleeve and pulled, dragging him forward. "Come on, come on! Come meet my family!"

Rook gritted his teeth and looked side to side, "I—I'm not here to meet people, Coppo."

"Tristan!" Coppo called loudly.

"No!" Rook yanked his arm from Coppo's clutches. "No," he mumbled with a head shake, "not him."

Coppo turned to Rook with wide eyes. "You don't want to meet our chief?"

"Your *chief*?" Rook narrowed his eyes. "No," Rook sighed, "Not today, please."

Coppo dropped his head defeatedly. "Can I bring you to meet the lads, then?"

"The—" Rook sighed. "Sure, let's meet the lads."

"Great!" The artist boy took Rook by the sleeve once more and pulled him down a side street. They passed a few busy stalls then came to an alley blocked by a barricade of barrels. Coppo cleared his throat, then enunciated the words: "Penultimate Pernicious Pumpernickel!"

One of the large, shoulder-high vino barrels rattled. A little trap-window popped open out of the side of the barrel, looking as though it were roughly carved out by hand.

"Who have you got there, Copp? You're not supposed to say the password around non-club members," a young voice said from within.

Rook crouched, leveling his eyes with the little door. He could see a set of bright yellow Faerie eyes staring back at him. "I'm a Plausibly Pleasant Passerby. May I come in for a visit?"

The barrel jostled again, then the voice groaned. "Oh, alright."

Coppo gave Rook a curt nod, then reached forward and pulled against another barrel. The thing opened like a hinged door, and the boy climbed inside. Rook ducked deeply and endeavored to squeeze through. In clicks, he was on the other side of the line of barrels, standing back up straight.

"Stay low!" Coppo urged. Rook crouched and found himself amidst a circle of three other boys: Coppo, and two others who must have been a season or two younger. Rook squatted until he landed on his backside, then crossed his legs.

"Alright, what's all this?" he asked, keeping his voice low. The secret fort of sorts was nothing more than a shadowy cleft between two houses that butted up against the village walls. For a moment, Rook was transported to when he was a boy searching for dark and clever places to hide.

"Welcome, Rook," Coppo whispered as he knelt down in the circle. "We are the Packrat Particles."

The other two Faerie boys nodded heartily. "The most secret order in all Raqia," the smallest one said. He couldn't have been older than eleven, with large eyes and a dusty cap flattening his head of gold curls.

"Rook?" the third boy asked with wide eyes, "The knight who told you your title, Copp?" This Faerie had olive skin and teardrop eyes, with deep black hair pulled into a single short braid. He wore nothing but trousers and a bare chest. Rook guessed he would be around fourteen seasons of age.

"Yes," Copp whispered. "And Valley says Faerie titles aren't shame—they're glory. So I move that we use *secret* titles, and Rook here is going to give them to us!"

All three sets of Faerie eyes turned quickly toward Rook, who leaned back with a head shake.

"Now hang on a click," he held up his finger, "I am not a prophet or anything. I just guessed your title, Coppo."

"Riiiiight." Coppo winked. "Alright, so Rook is going to *guess* our titles. Right. So, Rook, this here is Theo," he gestured to the youngest, curly-topped Faerie. "And this is Michael," he pointed at the black-haired teen.

Rook smiled at each of them. "Hallo, boys. What's your group all about?"

"We are the protectors of the Warrowing Faeries," Coppo said, leaning back onto his hands. "And the hiders of trinkets!"

"Theo is best at finding the trinkets," Coppo pointed at the golden boy. "And Michael is best at delivering them here to the hideout."

"That makes sense. Though, you should be careful about sharing your secrets with strangers," Rook said with a smile, "This is important intel!"

"We know you're good, Sir Rook," Theo said in a bright little voice, "We trust you."

Rook felt a warmth inside his chest that both hurt and comforted him. "What sort of trinkets do you collect?"

"Everything!" Coppo said in a harsh whisper, leaning toward the middle of their circle. "Possessions are forbidden in the Warrowing Village, so we have to be very careful!"

Rook squinted. "You mean—no one has possessions here?"

All three Faerie boys wagged their heads. "Faeries can't have anything of value, Sir Knight," Coppo held up a finger, then Theo interrupted,

"Because having items of value is how Faeries get powerful!"

"I see," said Rook, "So Faeries aren't allowed possessions because they might try and keep an object for an imperium? And that's forbidden?"

"Yes, Sir Knight," Coppo said. "Faeries are not supposed to be powerful because they might try to rule Humans like the Nightmare Faerie did. So King Hanz forbade Faeries from hoarding magik, dark or light!"

"I see." Rook leaned back onto his palms. "But you want imperiums?"

"No, sir," Michael said, "We just like things. It's nice to have nice things!"

All three bobbed their heads in agreement. "Yes," said Theo, "Especially the really shiny things."

"Well," Rook leaned forward and rested his elbows on his knees. "I'll make my contribution to the, erm, the Packrat Particles."

The boys drew in close and watching intently as Rook reached into his cloak pocket and pulled out his money pouch.

"I'll not give you all of it," he said as he turned the pouch over and dumped out its contents, "But you can look and see what you like." With a few clanks and bells, a small stash of coins fell onto the ground, along with one or two other odd objects. The boys jabbered away in hushed excitement as they dove their hands into the pile, exploring its contents.

Rook leaned back and watched with a wide smile as they examined each trinket, one by one.

"This is the biggest coin I've ever seen," Michael said, turning a large gold five-piece in his hand.

Rook chuckled, "That's the biggest one there is!"

"This one has a hole through the middle," Coppo poked his finger through the silver three-piece.

"That's a special one," Rook pointed, "I got it from my highlord. He is from the Edgelands. There, they tie their money around their necks on strings.

"Oh," Michael reached for the pierced coin lustfully, "I *love* that!"

"What's this? A clicker?" Theo asked, picking up an intricate gold case, set with white stones. A long chain dangled off it. It looked huge in the little Faerie boy's miniscule hands.

"No. That's something really special," Rook held out his hand and Theo placed the thing in his palm. "It's called a watch." Rook pressed a button on the side that triggered the thing to open like a locket. The boys gasped in unison. Inside were a few moving switches and rotating dials. When Rook rotated the watch, a sphere of colors within swirled and changed. "It is one of the rarest things in the world: it can tell time."

"That's impossible," Michael said suspiciously, "Time isn't constant!"

"Smart boy," Rook snapped the watch closed, "But this watch isn't set to a rhythm. It is made with flood waters from the Glassy Sea." He gazed at the watch as an overwhelming feeling of nostalgia filled his heart. "It always knows what time it is, even before a skydeacon does. It is never wrong."

Theo took it back in his hands, gaping at it in awe, "It is such a special thing," he said. "I love it."

"This," Coppo broke Theo from his trance with a nudge, "This is much more beautiful, and I know what it is!" He held up a smooth silver quill tip. "It is for writing—for lines."

"Why don't you each pick your favorite thing, just—" he slipped the pocket watch back into his sack, "not this."

Theo made a moan but consented. "Alright, fair enough."

Michael held up the Edgeland three-piece and peered through it like a spyglass. "I choose the amazing coin," he announced proudly.

"I choose this quill tip," Coppo held it lovingly to his chest.

"And I will choose this," Theo held up a feather that was pure white with a silver sheen. Rook gaped at it.

"Where did you find that?" he asked, awe-struck.

"I told you!" said Coppo with a proud smirk, "He's good at finding trinkets!"

Rook and Theo held each other's gaze silently for a moment, and then Rook finally nodded. "Alright," he shrugged, "if you don't want anything from my pouch, you can have... a feather."

"Now," Coppo slapped his hands together, "Now for our titles, Sir Knight!"

Rook figured he might as well please them, so he shifted forward, sitting on his knees. "Alright," he said with as much intrigue as he could, "I will give you these titles, if you really *want* me to."

"We do!" Theo said, brushing his soft feather against his face.

"Right," Rook said, "Coppo: You are Faerie of Lines."

"This we know," Coppo nodded.

"And you, Michael?" He turned to the next eldest Faerie, "You are the Messenger Faerie."

The boy's face froze, then he swallowed. "Yes," he said, "...I..."

"And you," Rook popped up one of his knees and leaned on it, smiling at the little golden-haired Theo, "You are the Faerie of Wings."

The boys exchanged knowing glances. "He *always* sees wings," Michael said, "Everyone's! Even if they are hidden!"

"Well, I need to be going now," Rook said as he gathered the rest of the items back into his sack. "Don't let anyone see those, or they will definitely take them away."

The boys each clutched their item protectively.

"If you carry them with you always," Rook said, "They will be even more special."

The younger two boys nodded in agreement, but Coppo narrowed his eyes. "You're trying to give us Imperiums," he said.

"Call them what you want," Rook sighed, "And get rid of them if you want—it's up to you."

"Your wings are bigger, Coppo," Theo said with a blank face, "Much bigger."

Coppo bit his lip, darting his eyes back and forth between Rook and Theo. "Well," the boy said, "Let's make this the Packrat Particle's greatest secret."

All four of the Packrat Particle members started when the house window above them flew open.

"Alright, Michael, Theo, that's enough. Time to come in now, I need your help peeling the rest of the potatoes for tonight's supper," said the woman who popped her head through the window. She focused her eyes on Rook and blinked. "Found a new Packrat?"

"Shush, will you Marbel?" Coppo slapped his forehead. "The club name's a secret."

"Well, if this Human can know about it, then I sure as Hades can know about it!" She pointed a calloused finger at Rook.

"Hallo," Rook said sheepishly, squatting down in the little circle of Faerie lads.

"One of the nobles?" she chuckled. "Playing with the boys in the barrels?"

"It's not play, mother!" Theo frowned, "This is very important!"

"Get in here, both of you," she said, then turned to look at Rook again. "Sorry to interrupt your meeting, kind sir, but it's best you be going now."

Rook ducked under the barrel door, then popped back out into the roadway. "Oh, it's no trouble," he said, swinging his cape back into place. The woman popped her head back into the house, then opened the front door. She stood there with a paring knife in one hand, and a large purple potato in the other.

"My name's Marbel. Well! The boys don't usually take well to Humans," she said, "I'm impressed. But you have a nice face, I guess they liked the look of you."

Rook bowed in greeting. "I'm not trying to pick a fight, Fae Marbel, but I don't really appreciate the joke at my expense."

Marbel scrunched her face, then asked, "What do you mean? I said you had a *nice* face."

Rook held his mouth open, thinking, then said, "Sorry—are you *pitying* me, then?"

Marbel stepped out of her door frame, swinging side to side as she lumbered, then poked her nose up to look at him more closely.

"You feel shame about the scars, then?" she asked in a motherly tone. She tisked.

"I..." Rook was frozen with his mouth open again.

"Sweet boy," she smiled, "We are the people of scars, you won't get mockery here."

Rook gritted his teeth. The statement, while comforting, kindled his inner rage. He exhaled slowly, calming the storm.

"I see," he said. "Then this place is special."

"The place isn't special," Marbel cocked an eyebrow. "The *people* are."

Rook felt properly chastised and nodded. "So the scars don't offend you, then?"

"Pardon my indecency," she thrust her foot forward and pulled at her skirt, revealing the better part of her calf, "but have a look for yourself." Rook, being more of a country boy who wasn't scandalized by seeing a woman's leg, dropped his eyes downward to see a leg marred and misshapen by deep, lined gouges. Rook felt his heart tearing within him. How many beatings were represented on that one leg alone?

"A people of scars," Rook muttered.

"Aye, lad," she said, dropping her skirt, "A people of scars. You're one of us, lad." She patted his shoulder with the potato hand, "The scars endear you to us. So yes, boy," she touched his cheek lovingly with the cold potato, "you have a nice face. *Boys*!"

Rook flinched as the matronly Faerie yelled once more for the boys. They flew past her into the residence, and she plodded quickly after them.

"I'll see you later Sir...erm," she turned to look back.

"—Rook."

"Sir Rook!" she yelled, disappearing into the house.

Rook stood on the roadside, feeling stunned. A people of scars? His eyes welled with tears. Why did it have to be that way? Rook lifted his chin sharply, tightening his eyes closed, and took a deep breath. No, don't break now. He had to go on. He would help Felix, his friend. Just help one: that would be enough.

Rook felt he could stomach the Warrowing Village no longer. He turned his back on it, facing west, and charged toward the dueling grounds where all the nobles were gathering. Perhaps watching Cato yell insults at noblemen would be just the thing to calm his nerves. Or even better, swinging a sword

A three-hundred-click walk brought Rook to the armory. Stepping inside, he didn't see any of the noblemen. They were probably out on the field by now. Clothes and bags were strewn across some of the benches in the long rectangular room; it looked like a good number of men had shown up for the sparring. Rook made his way over to the edge of the room and peered through a side window. He could see several men standing about, and a few of them were bare-chested and clashing swords together. No one seemed to be displaying any remarkable skill. It was all performative; it was all for show.

Rook stepped away from the window. No, he didn't feel like socializing. He looked around, preferring the quiet of the empty room. The walls were lined with a range of weapons, some blunted, some sharp. He reached for a rapier, preferring the speed it granted, and whipped it to his side. It did feel good.

He heard a clank from the corner of the room and turned briskly to see a page boy sitting on a side bench holding a boot and brush. He had his hood pulled over his head, as if he were embarrassed to be there.

"Don't mind me," Rook said to the page, "I'll only be a click. You can... go about your business."

The boy nodded nervously, then began brushing the boot, keeping his head low.

Ignoring the one other person in the room, Rook began to swing his blade here and there, revisiting old stances. His tension began to lift. Yes, the sword: his constant companion. Somehow, every time he had that thing in his hand, all those cares and burdens seemed to drift away into nothing.

He paused after his first string of stances. His heavy cape constantly trailing after his movements. No, this wouldn't do. He threw the sword down onto the ground with a crash, then ripped off his cape and tossed it to the side. The sound of the sword seemed to alarm the page, who was peeking out the window to watch the other duelers. Well, it was better that way. Rook didn't want an audience.

Rook stripped off his coat and cast it aside as well. This left a black waistcoat over his white, billowy shirt. He tested out the outfit, picking up the sword once more and slashing it forward and back. After a few stabbing motions, he cursed, throwing the sword down again. He fiddled with the long string of buttons that held the waistcoat tight against his chest. The moment it was off, he drew in a deep breath and sighed. Seizing the weapon once more, he held it up, throwing back his long curls to clear his face.

He noticed the page's eyes focused on him again from under the hood, though he still could not make out a face. Nodding at the boy with a playful smile, he said, "Let's see how it goes now." Rook threw himself back into another string of battle stances. He revisited the fight on the bridge, dodging between thieves and brigands, gliding with unimaginable speed. This burst of movement ended with him crouching on the other side of the armory, further away from the page, who—he checked—still had his eyes on Rook. Well, he didn't mind having an audience of one.

Rook shook his arm, angered by the drag that the puffy sleeve seemed to create. He shot his face toward the boy, who still sat there scrubbing the same boot—which honestly looked plenty clean—and yelled.

"How was that? *Good*?"

The page nodded timidly.

"I can go faster," Rook said, feeling the rush of excitement replacing his anxiety. "Shall I?"

The page cocked his head to the side, then offered a thumbs up. Rook chuckled, appreciating his one little fan.

Rook pulled his shirt off from over his head, casting it aside.

"Let's see how fast we can go," Rook said to himself, then closed his eyes.

He moved like lightning, dashing from one side of the room to the other with graceful agility. He spun and moved more like a dancer than a warrior, whizzing his sword around like a silver ribbon. It felt amazing. Ending his sequence back at the front of the armory, he dropped down onto one knee, panting. He stood, only a few yards away from the page, and turned to face him with a grin.

"How was that?" he asked, spreading out his arms as though giving a presentation.

The page jolted, growing petrified as he stared at Rook's mangled body. Then, he let out a gasp, scrambling backwards. His hood fell back a touch, and Rook saw a glimpse of his face—or rather, of *her* face.

She pulled her hood back over her face, then hugged herself and backed away like a frightened cat.

"What?" Rook frowned, slashing his sword to the side.

The woman let out a little shriek, startled by Rook's movements.

"What?" Rook barked, "I wasn't going to *attack* you!"

The girl, clutching herself, was breathing heavily, as if caught in some horrific nightmare. She raised her quivering hand and pointed in his direction. Then it hit him.

Rook turned cautiously until he could see his reflection in one of the hanging mirrors. Then he saw what she saw: himself. What covered the center of his chest could hardly be called skin; wrinkled and deformed, his mangled body was, indeed, enough to instill horror.

The woman fled the scene, but Rook didn't turn. Instead, he stepped toward the mirror to face the monster. He scanned his eyes across the repeated lines scratched across his chest like massive claw marks that wrapped around his neck and arms. Memories flashed through his mind. Yes, it was real. Everything that had been done to him—it was all real.

Rook snapped, rushing across the room to find his felling shirt. He tore it as he tried to cover himself, then found his waistcoat and thrust it upon himself angrily. When he was dressed enough, he burst from the armory and ran as fast as he could to the Inner Palace.

When he got to his room, he bolted the door shut. Caught in a burst of fury, he ripped the clothes from his body roaring like a wild animal. Rook felt like his lungs couldn't breathe. The memories were too strong. They invaded his mind, and for a moment he could *feel* the pain of his chest tearing open. He stumbled through the room and ripped open his window, gasping as the fresh air met his face.

He stood, panting, gazing up at the sky, and placed his hand over his beating heart. Yes, it was still there—and it was beating. Rook collapsed onto his knees and dropped his head onto his chin. Anything—think about *anything* other than this.

Hallo, Anodos, said a familiar voice.

Rook lifted his head and gasped, his eyes meeting with those of a very old friend. A great black bird, with feathers touched with a red glow, stood there, blinking at him.

"Inferno?" Rook gasped. "Is that you?"

My god, Anodos, the bird asked, his inaudible voice filled with sorrow. *What happened?*

Rook's body began to shake, and there was nothing else he could do. He collapsed onto the ground and curled up into a ball. The bird flapped his wings and landed on the floor next to Rook, poking his beak at Rook's arm. Rook reached out and took the bird, clutching its body lose to his chest. He ran his fingers between the feathers, feeling its fragile frame beneath. Inferno purred, tucking his beak lovingly into Rook's neck.

The thunderbird, after digging around in Rook's hair, made a little squawk of distress. *Anodos, dear boy, what have you done to your ears?*

Rook's only response was to curl himself around the bird and weep.

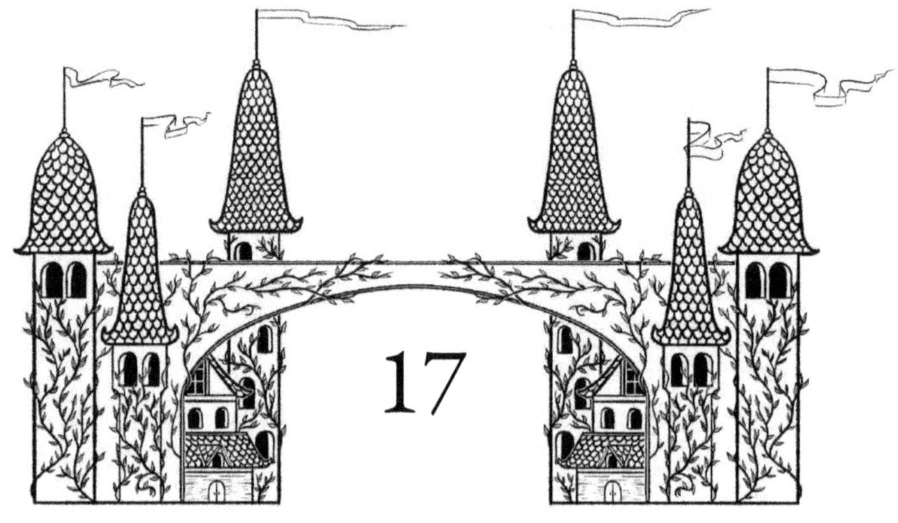

—— Rasselas ——

The Scholar

RASSELAS SAT AT HIS ARMCHAIR, READING SILENTLY with a little book resting in his lap. Well, he wasn't reading exactly, but his eyes *were* running across the pages. His mind, however, was replaying the events of his day and highlighting important moments. He thought about the meeting in the courthouse—*why would Hanz want to discuss Arelle with the other leaders?* He thought about the maid, Valley—*would she actually read the letter, and what would she think about it?* He thought about his visit to the Warrowing Village with Latimer—*were all those Faeries truly fine with their life of slavery?*

How long would he have to wait before that Faerie came back to him? Would she come at all? Even her name '*Valley*' was low and humble, as if she didn't deserve to be higher.

Rasselas frowned at the arrival of Embers, who flapped into the room and found a perch on Rasselas' open trunk.

"Oh, hallo. Have you finally decided I am worth your time?" Rasselas pouted.

Embers widened his large black eyes. *I'm sorry, have I even implied that I would just come here and talk to you every time you are alone?*

"I've been sitting here for two bells!" Rasselas turned a page briskly as if it made some sort of statement. "Where have you *been*?"

I have been to many places, said Embers, *I have met many interesting characters.*

"What do you mean 'met?'" Rasselas leaned forward with a suspicious scowl. "You're *talking* to other people?"

I do not need to speak verbally with someone to meet them, Rasselas. I am a bird, after all. A shared stare is a meeting for me.

"Whatever," Rasselas turned another page.

Are you angry, Rasselas?

The prince puffed out his cheeks. "No."

Oh. Alright. The bird turned to fly away.

"I just can't help but feel like I am in way over my head!" he blurted. "I am trying to help the Faeries by showing them that their enslavement is wrong, but what good will that do? The laws in Mensa allow for slavery! I can't... I can't..." he stuttered, "I can't..."

Perhaps you are trying to carry too many pebbles... he paused, searching for better words. *Perhaps you are trying to carry more than your load.*

"What do you mean?"

You are just one man, Rasselas. What if you only had one pebble?

Rasselas smashed his hand against his mouth thoughtfully. "I still don't know what you mean."

You want the Faeries in Mensa to be free. Many things would have to happen to make a world where they could be free. Faeries would need to believe in the cause, laws would have to change, countries might go to war; then there is the problem of the Faeries being leaderless...

"I know! That's why I—"

Embers interrupted Rasselas with a squawk. *What I am saying, Rasselas, is that such things involve many people. If you only had to play one role, as one man, what would you do? Let others rise up, if they will, but you can't expect to do all these things on your own. So: just carry one pebble.*

Rasselas slumped into his chair with a grunt. "I see," he said. "I am trying to wake up the Faeries and get them thinking about the lies they are being taught, but I don't necessarily have to be the one to set them all free? Is that what you're saying?"

I am saying to just do one good thing, and whether or not it has the outcome you were expecting, it will still be a good thing. It is too complicated a situation to try and craft a big escape. What if you just helped one person, or you unveil simply one lie.

"Yeah," Rasselas relaxed. "When I first learned that I was coming to Mensa on Grandfather's behalf, I thought, *oh! Here is a perfect opportunity to see the inside of what's going on! Maybe I can take the veil off the Faeries' eyes so that they can realize that what is being done to them is wrong!* Then after I got here... well, I started to think that maybe a persuasive letter wasn't enough. I need an actual plan of *action!*"

But you're not that kind of feather, are you Rasselas? You're not a soldier or a loud leader of men—you're a scholar.

"Quiet, Embers!" Rasselas jolted. "Don't say that too loudly or someone might hear you!"

It is nothing to be ashamed of, you old wren! And you can't hide that side of yourself from me; I know pretty well how many books you've read.

"Well how do you know I am actually *reading* them?" asked Rasselas smugly, "I might just be pretending."

Embers poked his beak skeptically southward toward the window. *Most people lie about being smarter than they actually are. You're the first person I've met who tries to appear stupider.*

"Well, intelligence is extremely alienating, you old duck," said Rasselas. "Haven't you seen how popular I am? People *love* stupid Rasselas!"

Embers picked at his foot silently.

"And anyway," said the prince, "It's much easier to fly under the radar this way. But I hear you, old friend—and perhaps you're right..."

Perhaps?

"Fine, you're right. I'll stick to writing and scholarship and let someone else play the hero, alright?"

Good, said Embers, *Perhaps now I can relax. Oh, and by the way, I do think your letter did some good. Though the maid does think it was Aorist who wrote the words.*

Rasselas blinked. "I'm sorry—*what*?"

Embers puffed up his feathers like a wet cat. *Oh, had I failed to mention...?*

Rasselas leapt out of his seat. "You met her? Did she read the letter? What did she say? Embers—Hades! Tell me!"

Well, she came in here to read the letter after you left, Embers said casually, strolling back and forth across the top of the wooden chest.

"And?"

The girl Valley gave me a very nice name. She thanked me for delivering the letter.

"*I* delivered the letter!"

Yes, I know that—I tried to tell her that. She couldn't hear me.

"But she liked it?"

Yes, she did. She hugged it, which I think is what you Humans do when you love something.

"Yeah, most of the time," Rasselas mumbled, "So—she thought Aorist sent it? Why?"

Well, I don't know. Did you give her any reason to make her think Aorist might send her a letter?

"Um..." Rasselas glanced to the side, "I did mention he was my friend... and I guess the letter is all about Faerie identity and stuff. Well, perhaps it's not the worst thing if she doesn't know the letter is from me." He nodded to himself, "Yes, perhaps the words could mean *more* if they're not coming from me!"

I don't see why that has to be the case.

Rasselas reached out his arm to Embers, who responded by jumping up onto it. "Because words can be much more powerful all on their own. It lets one use their imagination, and the words take their own shape and their own form. This is why truth is best told in narrative."

If you say so, Embers picked at his foot again, *you're the scholar.*

"Yes," Rasselas grinned, "I am! I mean—no," he turned toward his looking glass, putting on his posh voice. "I'm just a witless fop."

If you say so, Embers said. He hopped off his arm and flapped toward the window. *I think I'll be going now.*

"Why? Don't you want to watch me get ready? The big party is going to start soon, and I—" Turning, Rasselas found that the thunderbird was no longer there.

He wandered back over to his chair and plopped down upon it, beginning to process the idea of Valley opening his letter. He was interrupted by a knock. Rasselas' ears perked up and he cleared his throat.

"Yes?" he called.

The side-door opened, and Thorne entered.

"Oh, it's only you," Rasselas yawned. "Did you have a nice time watching me from the sidelines this afternoon on the dueling grounds? How was my form?"

"It was pretty sloppy for an Elf," Thorne said. "So yes, I enjoyed myself."

"Oh, I am so pleased!" Rasselas rotated to face him. "Ready for tonight, are you?"

"I was wondering if you have corresponded with your grandfather yet," he said.

"Well I haven't tried," Rasselas said through half-open eyes, "I've barely learned a thing—I mean I don't even know if Hanz' daughter is pretty enough to write home about."

Thorne held his stoic expression. "Fine. Let's head out at the Lastlight bell."

"No," Rasselas stood and stretched out his back. "Let's go now."

"I thought you didn't like going early," Thorne said.

"Well, sometimes it's the right thing to do, and sometimes it isn't. *You* just seem to be completely unaware of such things." Rasselas walked to the corner of the room where an accessory table held his prized collection of toothpicks. He selected one with an onyx handle, carved into a wolf's head. "I am ready now, if you are."

"I am ready," Thorne said, absentmindedly reaching up to check that his hair was falling on the right side of his shoulder.

"Well good," said Rasselas. He replaced the tip of his toothpick with a new white nib, then turned to his wing with a smug smile. "Let's be off, then!"

When the two Elves came to the Grand Hall in the West Palace, they found that others had gathered outside in the gardens where a band of minstrels played music and light refreshments were being served on platters.

Rasselas found Prince Tingo standing by himself under a vine-covered canopy. He signaled for Thorne to abandon his side and went over to Tingo, greeting him with a nod.

"I see you also thought to come early, Rasselas," Tingo said. "I take it you're as much of an extrovert as I am! Well, they won't open the doors until the Lastlight bell."

"No," Rasselas sniffed, "I was simply curious about the carriage that arrived while we were all sparring. Someone important, I gather. There were about fifty soldiers."

Tingo chuckled. "I had the same thought."

"Then, we are here for a common purpose!" Rasselas exclaimed. "Curiosity!"

"Yes," Tingo agreed, then pointed toward the West gate where other party guests were wandering through. "Though I know who it is, and you don't."

Rasselas spun his head to look at the approaching guests. One extra-large man was marching toward the gardens with not one, but *two* wings, one on either side. He looked like the most important man on the world, with his chin so high one could see up his nose and a gait that could stamp down cities.

Rasselas turned back to Tingo, who was scratching his sideburn. "Oh, he's magnificent!" Rasselas beamed. "Judging by that black skin, I'd say he was from the Featherlands!"

"It's called the Winglands, Rass," Tingo slapped his hand on the prince's back, "Don't let *him* hear you get that wrong."

"Slay me, old boy! Would he yell at me?" Rasselas asked excitedly, "How exciting!"

Tingo belted a laugh. "Oh, Rasselas, behave yourself!"

The newcomer sauntered into the party of guests socializing out in the gardens, observing the other guests, looking from face to face, as if searching for someone.

"Over here, you fiend!" Tingo belted, then raised his vino glass up into the air.

The man shot Tingo a look, then his judgmental scowl broke into a wide toothy smile. Rasselas watched him march over to their little canopy with arms stretched wide.

"Tingo," bellowed the broad-shouldered man in a voice deeper than the bottomless pit, "Who let you in here?"

"Mynx," Tingo clasped the man on the arm in a tight, friendly greeting. "It's been too long. Rasselas? This is Prince Mynx of the Winglands. Mynx, meet Prince Moonvine, Rasselas of Celestia."

"An Elf?" Mynx barked, staring downward toward the slender prince.

"Why, yes!" Rasselas posed proudly. "Quite."

"Is it a man or a woman?" Mynx crossed his thick, muscular arms.

Tingo snorted, "He's a friend."

"Well, I have to say," Rasselas gave a bow, ending with a little flourish, "I love your teeth."

Mynx tilted his head back proudly. "Yes," he said, "Thank you." He allowed Rasselas another look by grinning widely, showing a perfect set of shining white teeth.

"I say," Rasselas pulled his toothpick to his lips, "You must have albuminium coming out of your ears out there!"

Mynx pointed at Rasselas' fancy toothpick, "There's not a single nib on Raqia that didn't come from our mines."

"And I won't forget it!" Rasselas assured him. "Slay me—you must have excellent picks at your disposal. You haven't got any for sale, have you?"

Mynx glanced at Tingo suspiciously. "You've befriended a coxcomb—as a joke?"

"Nothing wrong with a man caring about fashion, old boy!" Rasselas smacked his lips, "And Hades, the ladies do love it."

"Oh," Mynx chuckled, "Well, in *that* case!" He turned his attention back to Tingo. "We got in a day late. The pass was frozen over."

"Frozen?" Tingo balked. "Has... has that ever happened before?"

"It happened on Firstday," Mynx said, "So it must be a seasonal change. *Kingsummons* indeed," he snorted, "How's it called Kingsummons if kings can't even *get* here?"

"How strange," Rasselas said vacantly. "I knew that the Winglands were cold—but *frozen*?"

The other two princes glanced his way expectantly.

"What is strange about it to *you*, Moonvine?" Tingo asked.

"Oh!" Rasselas piped, "Well, cards, boys! I've never even heard of a frozen place that's not a mountain peak! Is that a thing?"

"Some places are frozen in the far east, little Elf," Mynx said, "But not the pass. We do not build roads in the freezing places."

"Quite so," Rasselas said, "Well tell me, kind fellows, which of you are interested in the princess, eh? Why are we talking about roads when we could be talking about *that*?"

"Good question," said Mynx, turning to look toward the Western Palace. "Have you all seen her yet?"

"She's coming out tonight," Tingo glanced toward the bell tower. "They will open the doors at the Lastlight evening bell. Then I imagine we will all get to meet her."

"And?" Rasselas leaned closer to Tingo with a giddy grin, "How many of you find yourself needing wives and all that? I hear they are dashed handy to have around!"

"Indeed," Mynx said, "I've heard that too." He glanced at Tingo, then the two of them chuckled together. "Well, I for one am interested enough to have a look."

"I imagine your old man had the same idea as mine," Tingo nudged Mynx in the rib, "He realized his son wasn't completely useless and thought he could bring home a solid partnership with Mensa?"

Mynx pretended to cough. "Well, he might have thought of something like that." They both turned their eyes to Rasselas. "What about you? The Elves want you to marry King Hanz' daughter?"

"Well the old man wouldn't say!" Rasselas tapped his hand on his heart as if he had been stabbed, "I tried to get him to tell me, but he just loves being cryptic!"

"He won't tell you what he wants?" Tingo scoffed. "Hades, I would give anything for a father who won't tell me what he wants!"

"Well, you see, he's my grandfather. It's a shade different, you know," said Rasselas.

"Oh, I see," said Mynx, "Well, we will all have to make bets then."

"Oh!" Rasselas snapped his heels together. "I do love bets! Are we going to guess who is going to snag the princess?"

"No," Tingo tapped his nose, thinking, "No, let's pick something more short-term. Just a bet for the night."

"How about we try and guess who the princess will favor?" Mynx suggested.

"That's too easy," Rasselas shook his head, "That will clearly be me."

The other two men nodded. "Well, how about we guess who King Hanz sets her up to dance with first?" said Tingo.

"Hmm?" Rasselas turned, "What do you mean?"

"It's a Mensan tradition," Tingo said. "Becoming more popular these days. When a lady comes out, her father picks her first dance. And it *usually* is his way of buttering up his favorite suitor. Now, no one could guess what's going on in King Hanz' head, but it'll be fun to guess who he decides to favor tonight."

The three princes grew silent.

"King Labyrinth has the sort of exports Hanz needs for his expansions," Mynx said. "Stone and lumber... and food, too."

"I can't imagine him bending backward for tobacco," said Tingo, "Though I thought I saw a spot on one of his teeth."

"Nah," Rasselas flapped his hand dismissively, "He might have reason to favor you, though, old Tingo! You lot have glass and dyes and all that. Oh—and clothes!"

"Sure," Tingo shrugged. "But he's never tried that hard to befriend us. I doubt he'd pick me. You, though," he bounced his eyebrows at the tall, dark Mynx, "You've got salt, and albuminium, of course."

"And feathers!" Mynx said proudly, "We have heaps of feather down—you can thank us for all those soft pillows you sleep on. But what about Elves? Surely King Hanz wants to be friends with you, Rasselas Moonvine!"

Rasselas pursed his lips. "No," he said, "I don't think he would." He shifted his eyes. "What about the Edgelands fellow? That's a very distant trade route and would open up a path to the west."

Tingo cackled, "Cato is the only one I am *not* worried about. The Edgelands are small and poor."

"An Edgelands highlord is here?" Mynx exclaimed. "How funny."

"So, let's place our bets," Tingo slapped his hands together. "My vote is for Moonvine, whatever *he* has to say about it: five gold chips."

"I put my money on the Gramenlands," said Mynx, "They have big armies—I forgot to mention."

Rasselas pondered, "Five chips?" he asked, then huffed. "My guess is that he will play it safe and choose a Mensa highlord."

The other princes both groaned. "True," said Tingo, "I could see him wanting to hold his cards close to his chest."

"Well, the bets are placed," said Rasselas, rubbing his hands together. "And now? Let's get drinks!"

18

—— Rosamond ——

The Presentation of the Princess

ROSAMOND STOOD IN THE MIDDLE OF THE ROOM, square in front of her mirror. There she was, dressed like a princess, with *ten* whole layers of skirt. Ten layers of fabric covered her pain, her shame. Ten layers of confidence adorned her, and as she gazed at herself, she thought that she looked like the strongest woman in the world. Underneath it all was a woman in pain, but on the outside, she was shining.

Rosamond wore an upbeat smirk, with a head lifted high. Her famed, silky hair, black with swirls of caramel, was pulled to the side in a regal design, cascading downwards in intricate braids to show its length. Her bodice was tight and strapless, forcing a thin waist and emphasized bosom. In quiet defiance of her father, Rosamond had her maids fashion a garland of fresh flowers to adorn her neckline. It preserved some level of modesty on an outfit designed to draw attention.

It was, after all, the night she was to meet just about every bachelor of note in the land. Rosamond's father wanted her to make a strong impression on the guests. She couldn't exactly avoid that, but she found herself wishing she could meet the world in a less ostentatious environment.

Rosamond turned and observed the back of her mountainous skirt. It was bustled in several places and pinned with even more clusters of fresh flowers: white disas, violet night lilies, and the like. Aside from the splashes of hue from the assorted flowers, Rosamond's outfit was predominantly white.

The princess placed her hands on her hips, pursing her lips. Well—this was it! This was the night. She stood alone in the top guestroom of the Western Palace, just *waiting* while the guests piled in through the doors downstairs.

"A cake?" Rosamond said aloud. "Finally, I know what my father thinks of me: a cake." She let out a little growl, then moved toward the window. The cumbersome outfit dragged, slowing her to a crawling speed. Once at the window, she unfastened the latch and swung open the double panes. Peering downwards, Rosamond spotted the party guests far below funneling toward the door. The Firstdark bell was ringing. The party was beginning, yet still she would have to wait!

"And here I am," Rosamond muttered. "Playing my part as Father's chess piece—no—*cake* piece! And if I don't please him, what? Another punishment? It's as if I were a child again!" Yes, punished like a child, only this time, her beating was far more terrifying than anything Lady Stackly had done. She noticed a large bird perched up on a nearby spire that jetted out from one of the palace's turrets. In the dark night air, its silhouette had the appearance of a sinister gargoyle. She frowned at it, then continued to talk to herself.

"Do I even know what I want anymore? Why try and *want* anything... why not just *be* the chess piece?" She placed her hands on the window's ledge, studying the shape of its stones. One was particularly cracked, so she absentmindedly ran her fingers along it, testing for weakness. "I'd prefer to be an opponent," she said wistfully, "but who am I playing against? *Father?*"

Images flashed through her mind of her father's face from when he struck her with the black whip. It was the face of a man she did not know. She had heard of men who turned to violence in times of stress. Had she driven him to it?

Yes... it was all her fault. And, yet—

"Oh!" Rosamond drew in a sharp breath as a new thought came to her mind. "Or... it is *his* fault! I had not considered that." Then she wrinkled her nose, turning to scowl at that ugly bird. "*Father* is the one who always says, men are the masters of their own bodies. The only person you can blame for your mistakes is yourself." She snorted, yanking free a piece of the broken stone. "Well, *Father*," she spat while still watching the feathery daemon, "Then if you choose to be a villain, it's your fault!"

The bird turned its head sharply to stare its shiny black eyes at Rosamond. She jumped, throwing her hand to her mouth.

"What are you looking at?" she yapped, then thrust the piece of broken stone at the thing. The bird burst into movement, flapping about as it crowed in distress. "A raven, huh?" she scoffed, "get out of here, you monster!"

Instead of fluttering away like a scared little crow, the bird's dark figure rose and flew directly toward her, screeching in loud bursts. Rosamond stumbled backwards. It was so large! The giant raven reached out its talons threateningly and flew in through the window.

Surprising herself with a show of courage, Rosamond stood up straight and held out her palm to him, barking, "Back, gargoyle!"

The raven hovered before her, restraining his attack but continuing to caw loudly. Rosamond marveled for a moment at his sheer size. His wingspan looked to be at least six feet in length! It hovered there, his great wings whirring and beating with loud flaps. Papers dropped from nearby tables, and Rosamond's hair blew back as though she were in the presence of a great wind. Still, she did not cower. She raised her chin with the haughty look her father gave his subordinates.

"Oh, stop that!" Rosamond called over the noise of his wings. "All I did was chuck a pebble at you. Clearly you are too big to be harmed by it!"

The raven shut its mouth, but despite the absence of his crowing, his noisy flapping continued as he flew in place for a moment further. Then he perched upon the back of a chair, right at Rosamond's eye level. Finally, there was a stillness and silence in the room once more. Then, the bird looked at her very intently, and inside her head, she heard him speak.

Hurt my feelings.

Rosamond blinked, then leaned forward to shove her chin in his face. "Hurt your feelings?" she questioned. "How are you *talking*?"

Bird talk, he said.

Rosamond straightened. "Yes, I know birds talk. But how can *I* understand you, you big gargoyle? Don't Humans have to bond with animals in order to understand them?"

The raven bobbed back and forth, as if thinking.

"Have you been sent to taunt me?" Rosamond shook her head, mumbling. "I wouldn't put it past the old man."

I am bird.

"Yes, I know you're a..." Rosamond groaned, placing her hand on her face. "I am about to go meet every single noble bachelor in the East—and here I am talking to a bird!" She turned sharply toward the intrusive bird. "Listen, gargoyle! I don't appreciate the bullying, alright? If I want to throw a rock at you, I'll throw a rock at you! But don't go around attacking women in big skirts, alright? It's not very gentlemanly."

You bully, said the bird.

Rosamond bit her lip. "Fine. I won't throw rocks at you anymore—I..." Rosamond's voice fell silent. Her face softened. "Oh," she whispered, "I see. I am being my father, aren't I? Lashing out at others..."

Yes.

"How is one supposed to escape a bully without becoming a bully herself?" she asked herself absently.

No throw rocks.

Rosamond raised an eyebrow at the bird. "Are you giving me a lecture, gargoyle?"

Name not gargoyle.

"Yes, it is," she said with an air of authority. "If you are going to scold me like a child, I am going to call you Gargoyle."

The bird stepped back and forth on his two feet.

I not respond to Gargoyle.

"Fine," Rosamond shrugged and turned toward her mirror, choosing to ignore the irritating bird. "I never asked you to come in here and talk to me!"

You throw rocks.

"Look, I'm sorry!" she snapped. "I was feeling powerless, so I struck you, *alright?*"

The raven blinked its eyes repeatedly.

Rosamond sighed to herself, deflating as reality tapped her on the shoulder. "Everything in the world has more power than me, so I attacked the first thing I saw that was weaker than me."

The bird made a purring, hissing sound. *I big.*

Rosamond looked at the bird, then chuckled to herself. "Sure, yes, you're big." Then she turned her head away slightly, "But you're still lesser than me."

No. I very big.

"Well," Rosamond sighed, "I guess you're right... I am the most powerless person in this kingdom, aren't I? Even less powerful than a *bird.*"

The Raven made his blinking face again. Then he inched to the edge of the chair and peered up at her face. *Everything smaller than you,* he said.

Rosamond opened her mouth to speak but stood there motionless. "What do you mean?"

You big.

Rosamond turned her gaze toward the mirror, eyeing herself. She sighed. "Well, yes—my skirt is big. But I am not usually this big, you see."

Rosamond big.

Rosamond turned swiftly. "How do you know my name?"

I know your name. I watch you. I know you. But you not know my name.

"I know your name, Gargoyle," she said with a smirk. "Anyway, what do you mean, *Rosamond big*?"

You not hear well, the raven paused to squawk, *I speak well, you not hear.*

"Whatever," she waved her hand dismissively. "If you're trying to tell me that I have more power than I think I do, then you don't know what's happening here tonight." She stepped closer to the bird. "My father is presenting me *like a cake* to a bunch of hungry men. And... I must submit to his decision."

Gargoyle bobbed his head up and down. *Power is many names.*

Rosamond crossed her arms and furrowed her brow. "*Power is many names?*" she huffed, "What does that mean? Say it again."

Gargoyle cawed, then bobbed his head again. *Power has many names—many feathers.*

"Oh, power *has* many names? I think you said *feathers*?" She straightened, thinking. "There's different kinds of power?"

Gargoyle hopped, cawing affirmatively.

"Will you pipe down?" Rosamond lowered her voice to a whisper. "Viola might come in here and spoil my last moments of solitude, much like what *you* did!"

Different feathers of power. Your feather is black like mine.

Rosamond started. "Black? Are you saying I am *evil*?"

Gargoyle puffed up his feathers, making himself look like a ridiculous bush. *No. I not evil. I have black feather. I hide. I sly.*

"Sly?" Rosamond touched her lip with her finger. "Sly—now that's a good word."

Yes, you hear me now. Sly. I say sly. You sly.

"Okay, yes, I heard you. I am sly." She paused. "Father has an obvious power. Everyone knows he is powerful. But I appear weak, I appear powerless. So I can use my power in sneaky ways, right? Is that what you're saying?"

Yes. Sly. Sly.

"Well..." Rosamond chuckled, thinking it odd that she was taking advice from a bird of all things. "Perhaps you are right... Father wants to use me as a prop, to play all those men—using them all like pawns on his board. Well then, *Father*, I shall be the one playing them; and I shall turn your pawns to do *my* bidding. It is *I* who will get what I want. I will be the queen on your board that you just can't seem to control—the piece of cake you never actually get to eat!"

You switch metaphors.

Rosamond gazed sidelong at the bird. "Was that sass?"

Sass. Yes—you hear tone? Very good job, Rosamond.

"Oh, don't patronize me." Rosamond gathered her top layer of skirt, the longest layer, so that she could walk a little easier. She moved back toward the open window. "Now, it's time for you to go, you little daemon."

Gargoyle flapped up into the air, his size startling Rosamond once again. He descended down onto the window's ledge. *No,* he squawked, *not daemon.*

"Yes, daemon!" Rosamond pointed out toward the night air. "You should go before Viola gets here."

The raven looked out at the sky, priming to fly, but paused to look back at the princess.

Rosamond, he said, *you not small tonight. Think big.*

"Did you say, *think big*?" Rosamond giggled. "Alright, I will *think big*, Gargoyle." Her face fell. "But Gargoyle, I don't even know what it is I am fighting for! What do I even want for myself?"

The raven poked his beak down to nip at one of his talons. Then he raised his head, as if clarity came suddenly to him. *To not be cake. To not be chess. To not be game. To be Rosamond.*

She folded her arms. "And how do *you* know what I want?"

I am right, question? I am right?

Rosamond peered up at the night sky. The stars were beginning to appear. "Yes," she said, "I think you *are* right, Gargoyle. I suppose I want to be seen as I am."

The raven croaked, as if distressed. *Father not see!*

"I *know* he doesn't see," she huffed, "That is what I am saying! I want Father to love me for who I am!"

Father not love.

Rosamond gasped, drawing back. "Why would you say something like that?"

Others might see. Others might love. Find one who see.

"Father *does* love me, you daemon!" Rosamond shoved the bird, startling him into flight. "Now, away with you." She snapped the windows closed, turning her back on them. "Father not love?" she asked herself. "Well," she narrowed her eyes into slits, "Time will tell."

Rosamond straightened out her skirt and cleared her throat. "Anyway, whatever fathers or crows have to say about the matter, *I* am going to enjoy myself tonight, and that is *all* I am going to worry about!"

There was a knock on the door, then it opened. Turning, Rosamond saw Viola poking her head inside.

"We are ready for you," she said, wringing her hands excitedly. "And you look breathtaking!"

Rosamond lifted her chin. "Why thank you, Viola," she said. "Shall we display the cake now?"

"Yes," Viola nodded curtly. "Let's not forget your father's words. We want you to stay silent and beautiful." Viola stepped up to Rosamond, examining her neckline with a skeptical eye. "Who put those flowers there? I didn't approve this."

Rosamond glided confidently past Viola, though inwardly she was cowering. Rosamond still felt small and powerless, but her conversation with the strange raven made her want to keep her superior air. "*I* approved it, dear friend, aren't they lovely?"

"They distract from—"

"My face?" Rosamond interjected, "No, my face will be fine. Let us go!"

Viola mumbled something under her breath, but followed as Rosamond left the room.

As long as I act in charge, people will have no choice but to believe me! she thought, biting her lip. Viola stepped up to her side and they walked together down the hall.

"When we come to those double doors," Viola pointed ahead. "You will go through alone and I will meet you later. You will be announced and then you will walk down the stairs *slowly*. Many a woman has tripped and fallen on her coming-out entrance! These skirts are not for the weak-legged."

Rosamond halted, sputtering. "But—but I don't want to go in *alone*! With everyone watching me?" Rosamond instantly regretted showing her fear. She must emanate confidence!

They arrived at the entrance doors, and Viola rotated slowly, grinning at Rosamond's show of weakness. "Yes, alone. That is what this whole thing is about: you. Now, remember your father's words and keep that mouth shut."

Oh, I'll remember my father's words, Rosamond quipped inwardly. *It was him, after all, who said 'a man should never let anyone else tell him what to do.'* Well, she wasn't a man, but still—she could own it!

Viola left her there, behind those big doors. Two servants stood on either side, with their hands on the door handles.

"This is it," Rosamond whispered to herself. "There is no going back after this. Today, the world meets Rosamond."

The doors opened. Before her, Rosamond saw a long length of stairs descending three stories into the West Palace's ballroom. Hundreds of guests stood below, and all faces turned toward her. Rosamond had never seen so many people in one room. And they were all looking at her. For a moment, she froze in shock. Her sore, aching legs refused to move, and her mouth hung half open.

No one needs to know I am terrified, Rosamond told herself. *It is a secret for only me to know.*

She took a step forward, breaking the spell. Apparently, she could move, so she journeyed ahead. She imagined that each step made her stronger; each step proved to her that she wasn't afraid. And the fear began to drift away, floating off her like steam. When she came to the last stretch of stairs, she began to see faces. Her father waited for her at the bottom of the stairs, and beside him was Sir Swain. Gathered around at the front of the crowd were men she recognized from her portrait book. She was too nervous to search the faces; for now she just needed to arrive at the bottom of the stairs without falling! She plastered on a confident smile as Sir Swain belted out her name.

"Ladies and Lords, King Hanz would like to present to you Princess Rosamond, his first and only child!" Swain then bowed to her, and all those present bowed as well.

Despite feeling a little unsettled by all the bowing, Rosamond kept herself moving and descended until she stood a step above her father. She met his eyes—he was smiling warmly. There was a time when that smile would have given her an inner warmth, but now, she felt fear and anger mixed with a deep, undying affection for him. The stripes on her legs began to throb and she could hear his voice threatening her from behind the dressing screen earlier that day, *I just wanted to make sure we wouldn't need to have another frank conversation tonight. I'll have my eye on you.*

But there he was: smiling. Oh, how she loved that smile. For a moment, the anger vanished, and she was glad to see her father looking upon her with pride. He was always kind to her in public, and that made her excited.

"You look lovely, Rosamond," he said in a voice meant only for her, though others could hear it. Yes—yes, he was always very different toward her when others were present.

Perhaps...this was why she preferred spending time with him in public; perhaps the man who loved her was just a show. *Well,* she thought, *we will see what is show and what is substance tonight.*

"Thank you, Papa!" she said with a wide grin, then leaned forward to kiss him on the cheek. She could hear him grunt. She had surprised him, but he didn't look angry. Rosamond turned to the crowds and produced another confident smile.

"His majesty will sit with his daughter there," Sir Swain announced to the crowds, "and you can form a queue there for official introductions."

Rosamond turned to look at her father, who held out his arm to her. She took it, leaning her head on his shoulder affectionately for a moment. He led her toward two cushioned chairs which had been placed at the head of the room. Those of noble birth began to line up and Rosamond peeked over her shoulder at them, hoping to spot some of the fairer faces. Her father squeezed her hand, drawing her attention back to him as they walked.

"Your outfit is nice," he whispered, "but—"

"Why *thank* you, Papa!" Rosamond let out a loud giggle, slapping his arm. She felt her father tense, but he stayed silent as they approached their chairs. She moved to sit beside him, though it took her a few clicks. The skirt was so large she had to scrunch it up into bundles, then wait for a couple maids to run up and help her. Finally, she sat.

King Hanz leaned toward her. "Rosamond, I have arranged for the visiting monarchs to come and meet you directly. This is where you may stay silent. Just say, 'hallo' and that's it."

Rosamond nodded obediently.

The line of noblemen didn't appear to be too long, so Rosamond relaxed a little. Well, at least she didn't have to sit there and meet everyone! She could get right to the interesting people. She leaned to the side, searching the line for the handsome Elf prince, but jolted back to attention as the first nobleman stepped forward. He was alone, standing there without a wing.

He was a well-built, sturdy sort of man, with short blonde hair and a square jaw. He wore a king's crown along with a matching smug face.

"Rosamond," her father said in a friendly voice, "This is King Labyrinth of the Gramenlands." The king gave her a slight head bow. He opened his mouth to speak but closed it when Rosamond cleared her throat loudly.

"What a pleasure!" Rosamond said, "I studied your face in a book, but Hades—it's always different getting the full picture, don't you think?"

King Labyrinth raised his eyebrows, glancing at Hanz for a moment, then back at her. He curled the side of his mouth into a smirk. "And here you have me at a disadvantage," he said. "You had a portrait while I had nothing but anticipation. And now, Princess, dare I say my expectations have been exceeded?"

Rosamond let out a loud laugh, slapping her hand against her father's remarkably tense arm. "You flatter me," she said. "I didn't take you for a charmer, King Labyrinth, but I am quite happy to be wrong."

King Labyrinth stood still for a moment, then chuckled to himself. He turned to bow to Hanz, then to her again, and then left. As the next pair of men stepped forward, Rosamond felt her father move his arm to place his hand on top of hers. He gave it a tight squeeze.

"Rosamond," he whispered, "You—"

"Now here is someone I have been vastly curious to meet!" Rosamond exclaimed. Hanz jolted to attention, turning to look at the guests.

And though she was being purposefully obnoxious, she wasn't lying. She had fantasized about meeting the Elves ever since she saw Prince Rasselas' handsome face in her portrait book. She couldn't help but clap her hands gently together in excitement.

"Yes," King Hanz surprisingly played along with Rosamond's outgoing manner. He was even chuckling! "This is—"

"Not as curious as I!" A dashing man stepped forward, swooping the tails of his coat behind him with a flourish. "Prince Rasselas, at your service!" He bowed low, snapping in half like a broken stick. He popped back up with a most cocky and irresistible smile. "My, my," he said, "You are something for the eyes, what? Slay me! I might need to sit down!"

"Prince Rasselas," Rosamond grinned, wagging her head, "*You* are going to be trouble. And I suppose you won't even bother to introduce me to your wing, there?" She pointed to the man beside Rasselas, disregarding the social rule that forbade women from pointing.

King Hanz leaned back into his chair and crossed his arms. Oh, *Hades*—it felt good to see her father feeling as useless as teats on a bull. Rosamond wasn't even sure what reaction she wanted to get out of him; all she knew was that she wanted to show him she would not be caged—she would not be forced into a mold.

Prince Rasselas gently placed his hand on his heart, "Alas, Princess Rosamond—slay me—thy beauty made me forget myself!"

"Ah," Rosamond smirked, "I understand. Now that you have remembered yourself, please," she gestured toward the wing. He was a stiff, slender sort of man with long, floaty brown hair. It was part way tied back into a braid, while the rest of his hair fell loose across his shoulders. She would have thought he was handsome if he hadn't been making such a blank face.

"This, my dear Princess Rosamond," Rasselas thrust his arm sideways toward his wing, "is Sir Thorne."

"Rosamond," Hanz cleared his throat with a chuckle, reminding the world of his presence. Only Rosamond felt his anger; to everyone else, he looked nothing short of jolly. "Prince Rasselas is the grandson of King Antecus of Celestia."

Rosamond pretended to be thankful for her father's addition to the conversation. "Well, it is a pleasure," Rosamond bobbed her head to the Elves who both bowed in return.

"Well," Rasselas stuck his nose into the air, "I met the princess! Hah!" He then spun around and marched away, as if there were some other place he needed to be.

Rasselas was not what Rosamond had been expecting. She had expected him to be handsome, yes, and if she was honest, she thought he looked even better than his portrait. But there was a phoniness about him, and it made it hard to know what he was really like. Perhaps that was all he was, handsome but shallow.

As Rasselas' wing bowed and left, others began to step forward. This time, her father didn't try to scold her. Instead, he remained perfectly still until the nobleman stepped up and bowed.

"Darling," Hanz said warmly, leaning over to touch her hand, "I would love to introduce you to my dear friend, King Stathe of the Vastlands, and his wing, Sir Enx."

Rosamond, feeling somewhat thrown by her father's affection, turned to see two men bowing. In the front was a short, somewhat stout king. Though he looked like a man in his full seasons, his head was balding; and when he smiled, Rosamond did her best not to wince at the sight of his black teeth.

"Hallo, Princess Rosamond," King Stathe said as he joined his hands together. He took a moment to allow his eyes to rove across her figure, then added, "It is a pleasure to behold you."

A pleasure to behold? Well. She acted flattered, but beneath her pleasant smile she hid her disgust. She'd never had a man look at her in quite that way before and she would be happy if it never happened again! Her father was right about one thing, this king seemed like a glutton eyeing a fluffy cake.

"King Stathe," Rosamond glanced at her father. "It is a pleasure to meet you, too."

"She's a pretty thing, Hanz," the king said to her father, "I can see why you hid her away for so long."

"She's my pride and my joy," Hanz said, nodding to the King of the Vastlands. Rosamond wanted to make a gagging sound, but instead looked over toward the crowd to if she might get another glance at Prince Rasselas' lovely face.

Lost among the faces, Rosamond jumped when her father began to introduce someone else.

"Rosamond," he said, "I'd like to introduce you to Prince Tingo, son of King Tintura of Sol. Beside him is Sir Wynn, a knight of Sol." Rosamond studied the two men who bowed low slowly. They both had slick black hair tied into tidy top knots, and attractive smiling faces. Rosamond recognized them from her portrait book. Tingo, in particular, had a kind way about him, making eye contact with her, rather than her father. As their eyes met, she could see confusion. It was as if she was not what he was expecting her to be.

"What pleasant looking people," Rosamond said brightly. "I think I will like you, Prince Tingo. And my!" She grinned, "What a fun name to say!"

Rosamond heard her father clear his throat, though he feigned a polite laugh.

Prince Tingo raised his eyebrows, then broke into a hearty laugh. He turned to his man beside him and the two laughed together. Rosamond instantly liked them.

"Princess Rosamond!" Tingo said in a cheery voice, "You surprise me. Here I thought nothing could be more impressive than your beauty, and then you opened your mouth!"

Rosamond blinked. "Now, Prince Tingo," she said, "It's beginning to feel redundant hearing flattering comments about my beauty. However, you're the first person to compliment me for my *speech*." She couldn't help but steal a glance at her father who currently had his hand pressed against his mouth.

Prince Tingo laughed openly once more, "Excuse the flattery," he said, "but I really meant every word I said." He and his wing bowed first to Rosamond and then again, lower, to King Hanz, and then they turned and left.

During this short break, Rosamond felt her father's hand clasp around her wrist. It became so tight she worried her bone might snap. She held her breath as he leaned in.

"Rosamond," he whispered. That was all he said. Once more, Rosamond's legs began to throb, and for a raw moment of sheer terror, she feared another beating. But a moment later, the next nobleman stepped forward. A set of three black-skinned men posed themselves before her. She marveled at their outfits, which were lined in intricate feather designs. The tall man at the center smiled, showing a dazzling set of perfectly white teeth. She did not see *this* man in her book! Rosamond hoped to heaven his personality was as attractive as his looks.

"May I introduce Prince Mynx of the Winglands, son of King Ethox? On his right is Sir Snite, and on his left, Sir Loth."

The three bowed. "Princess Rosamond," Prince Mynx said in a deep voice, "it is a pleasure to make your acquaintance."

"And yours!" Rosamond said quickly, leaning forward in her chair. Mynx jolted in surprise at her sudden movement and studied her as she continued. "I have always been excessively curious about the Winglands! I confess—I have always thought of your lands as something out of a fantasy. You will have to promise to tell me all about them!"

"Bah!" Mynx belted a single laugh, "My lands are cold and boring. It is Mensa that borders strange and fantastical places. But yes, I will tell you about the freezing lands, as you Mensa people like to call them."

"Well!" Rosamond clapped her hands. "How grand!"

Mynx cleared his throat, growing suddenly aware of King Hanz. He turned and bowed to him once more. "It is a pleasure to meet your daughter, King Hanz. I did not expect to be so charmed."

"She really is something," Hanz said.

Rosamond waved to Mynx as he left. He gave her another glance over his shoulder as the next pair walked forward.

"Lastly, darling," Hanz said, "is Lord Cato of the Edgelands,"

Rosamond studied Lord Cato, who seemed a giant of a man. His hair was gold and his eyes a bright blue. He looked as though he had reached his age of wearing, but he was still handsome, and his only signs of age were some gray in his facial hair and a thick single wrinkle on his forehead. Of all the noblemen she had met that night, he was the first to look unimpressed at the sight of her.

"Well," he shrugged as if admitting defeat. "*Hallo!*"

"And this is his wing, Sir Rook of the Edgelands," her father said.

Rook? *Sir Rook?* That face in her book that was so... her eyes focused on the face before her. Rosamond couldn't help but gasp. *By the lights.* She tried to steady herself. *It's him!* Yes, that intriguing face from the portrait book and that horribly scarred swordsman from the armory—they were one and the same. Rook gave her a bemused smile at her reaction of shock.

"Oh, sorry," Lord Cato glanced to his side. "I forget how awful his face is sometimes. You get used to it, you know!" he said to Rosamond, "He's a fine chap, though a tad tedious at times."

"It is a pleasure to meet you, Princess Rosamond," said Rook, bowing lowly to her. His voice was kind and warm. For a moment she tried to look past his scars to see if she could find that striking face from the portrait. But she was struck by the memory of his marred body—back when she saw him in her covert trip to the armory—and found it too hard to look at him.

"Yes, well," she turned her gaze back to Cato. "Lord Cato—you seem to be an interesting pair!"

"I'm afraid not," he said, then glanced at Hanz. "If you pardon me, sire," he looked back at Rosamond, "I am afraid I'll be a shocking disappointment to you, if you like being flattered and all that."

"On the contrary," Rosamond straightened up, "I far prefer for someone to be honest."

"Well," Cato scratched his chin hairs thoughtfully, "A man can be too honest, you know," he said. "By the floods—it's not that I am honest either," he turned to Rook for support, "what word would *you* use, Rook?"

"Thoughtless?" Rook suggested.

"Yes," Cato mumbled, nodding to himself, "but I feel there might be a *better* word..."

"Mocking?" Rook offered with a smile.

"Yes! Mocking!" Cato turned to grin at the princess. "Mocking, your ladyship."

"Well," Rosamond cocked her head to the side. "I don't think I mind someone being mocking, so long as it's all in jest."

"Oh, Princess," Cato gave a playful bow, "I am afraid *everything* I do is in jest." He glanced up from his bow and stole a look at Hanz, who watched silently. The king didn't seem to be offended by his flippant behavior, so he rose and said, "Well, that was nice. Shall we go find some food, Rook? Hades, I am hungry!"

Cato and Rook left, leaving Rosamond alone with her father. Her body seemed to lose all its strength as she sat waiting for him to turn his attention toward her. She couldn't even bring herself to look at him.

"Rosamond," he whispered, "I know you're deliberately disregarding my words."

"Whatever do you mean, Papa?" she asked in an innocent voice, "I—"

"It's just us now, Rosamond," he said softly, "there is no need to put on a show."

Rosamond gulped. "Papa," she said quietly, "I was simply excited to meet everyone!"

"You can't fool me, Rosamond." His voice was as soft as a breeze, yet its effects as powerful as a typhoon. "Do not act in a way you will regret later. I forget nothing."

Her father stood from his throne, leaving her sitting there, and approached Sir Swain who was standing nearby. She let out a deep breath, slumping back into her chair for a moment.

"Sit up straight!" A voice whispered sharply from beside her. Rosamond turned to see Viola standing beside her, waving a laced fan. "Hades, Rosamond," she hissed, "Didn't you hear me tell you not to speak? Gods, girl, it's true what they say, you just won't listen!"

"Well, whoever 'they' are," said a familiar voice, "they're right. I don't think Rosamond ever listens to anyone who tries to order her around."

Viola gasped in horror, "I'll have no maid speak to me like that!" She raised her fan to strike.

"Valley!" Rosamond jumped up to her feet. *An ally—finally!*

Valley stood beside Viola, her eyes daring the court lady to strike.

"Oh Viola, would you go away?" Rosamond snapped, stepping between the two women. Rosamond took Valley by the hand and pulled her aside.

"How have I been doing?" Rosamond asked excitedly.

Valley's pointy eyebrow spiked. "You've been quite sassy," she said.

"Too much?" Rosamond cringed.

"No," Valley smirked. "I love it when you're spicy."

"Lords and ladies," Sir Swain cried from the sidelines. "All gather for Princess Rosamond's first dance!"

"Just do the dance," Valley whispered quickly. "Then you're free to socialize a bit, and I will be by your side."

"Thank you!" Rosamond squeezed her friend's hands then rushed off to join her father's side once more. Meeting her father's eyes, Rosamond felt a rush of surprise to see him smiling at her. He looked proud and affectionate. She knew it was empty, but in this moment, she chose to believe that face.

"Darling," her father led her out to the middle of the ballroom floor. "What a treasure you are, my dear. You look so beautiful tonight." Empty, beautiful words filled her with warmth followed by a stiffening chill. As the party guests moved aside, a circle of emptiness formed around them.

"My friends!" King Hanz called out to his guests, "My beautiful daughter, Princess Rosamond. As you all know, it is the Mensa way for a father to pick his daughter's first dance."

Rosamond scanned the crowds, feeling small once more amidst so many people. She spotted Prince Rasselas, standing with Prince Tingo on one side and Prince Mynx on the other. The three whispered amongst themselves. For a brief moment, Rosamond and Rasselas' eyes met. She searched for sincerity—what sort of man was under that flamboyant facade? It occurred to her that he might be wondering the same thing. He gave her a friendly grin. She blinked, then returned his grin with a smirk. He leaned to the side to whisper in Prince Tingo's ear, when she was called back to attention by her father.

"But, we are not just any Mensa family," Hanz said proudly, sharing a smile with his daughter. "So I am going to do things a little differently. Tonight, I will let my daughter choose who she wishes to dance with."

Rosamond widened her eyes nervously as all attention now turned to her. *She* had to choose? Did her father plan this all along, or was he now putting on the spot as a punishment for all her banter? No... he would have planned this to bait the noblemen. Well, she wasn't going to give him what he wanted, that was for sure. But did he already know that? By trying to defy him, would she choose the person he wanted her to choose? Her head ached. The whole world seemed to be waiting for her to decide.

"Rosamond," King Hanz said with an inviting smile, "Who would you like to dance with first? I wager there's someone out there who caught your eye!"

"Why, yes!" Rosamond clasped her hands together excitedly. "There is one man I am *dying* to spend more time with!"

Voices murmured throughout the crowd. Rosamond stepped forward, meeting Rasselas' eyes once more. He brightened, then opened his mouth as if to speak...and she shifted her gaze away to—

"Lord Cato!" Rosamond announced, stepping toward the highlord.

Lord Cato of the Edgelands stood there, with vino glass in hand, looking stunned.

"Sorry?" he asked, glancing to Rook for wisdom. Rook leaned over to whisper in his lord's ear, then reached to take his glass.

"Yes, you, Lord Cato," Rosamond placed a hand delicately on her waist, "get over here!"

Cato shrugged, looking like a man who had just won a prize for which he didn't know he was competing, and sauntered into the center floor. He glanced around, giving Rasselas and the other princes a grin and tipping an invisible hat to them, then joined Rosamond. The princes all clapped, cheering him on.

Rosamond's smile faded when she saw the calculating look on her father's face. *What was he thinking?* Hanz took her hand and held it out to highlord Cato, who took it gently in his.

She faced him but had to crane her neck up to see his face. Cato gazed down blankly, taking her waist into his hand as they stepped close into a dancing stance. The music started and, to Rosamond's surprise, he led her quite gracefully. Cato had seemed to have a bumbling way about him, but apparently, he could rein it in when needed.

The two of them waltzed, keeping their focus on each other. Rosamond found it easier to disregard all those watching eyes when she kept her attention on just one pair. At this moment, Rosamond realized she had never been so close before to a man other than her father. She had given up her chance to gaze into the eyes of Prince Rasselas, all to defy her father by dancing with someone no one expected. Instead, she was looking up this tall highlord's nose!

"Well," Cato said. "Hallo."

"Hi," she answered, feeling a little timid.

"You implied to the world that you were thrilled about conversation with me, so—?" He smirked.

"I couldn't care less about conversation with you," she said frankly. "I just knew you wouldn't make unwanted comments about my appearance."

"Well, I can't promise *that*," he said. "Who knows what this mouth might say?"

"Alright," said Rosamond. "Go on, say something."

"I don't know," Cato said. "Believe it or not, I genuinely think you're really nice."

"Aw!" Rosamond beamed, "Really?"

"I mean," he blew a raspberry with his lips, "It's true that your voice is a bit grating..."

"Ah."

"But honestly, if that's the worst thing I can think of, then I," he sighed to himself. "I'm genuinely surprised at how nice you are!"

"Well, Cato!" Rosamond grinned, "I do believe you're quite the gentleman!"

"I wouldn't go *that* far," he muttered. "I mean I was also about to say that I can see a *lot* more of your goods from this vantage point. How *does* that strike you?"

Rosamond's face grew hot as she glanced down at herself. From above, those flowers didn't hide quite as much as she'd hoped. "Um..."

"Hah!" Cato barked. "After all that, *I* was the first to make the lady blush!"

Rosamond flattened her lips. "Alright," she said. "Good job."

"Oh, don't be bashful," he rolled his eyes. "I just like making people uncomfortable. Isn't that why you chose to dance with me?"

Rosamond chuckled. "Yes, I suppose so."

"Oh, floods," Cato snorted. "That's not why you asked me to dance."

"Is it not?"

"No, you just wanted to throw off everyone's scent, you sly thing."

"Do you think it worked?" she asked, feeling a little bit sheepish. *Could everyone see through her?*

"Oh Hades, I don't know," Cato glanced around the room, studying the surrounding faces. Then, he looked back down at Rosamond with a grin. "Yeah, they all look *felling* jealous if you ask me. Well, that has me feeling mighty pleased with myself right about now! Turns out, being the biggest bore actually has some advantages!"

"Of course!" Rosamond laughed, patting his shoulder with the hand that rested against it.

Cato cleared his throat. "Alright then, you can tell me."

"Tell you what?"

"Come on—which of the lads did you *want* to ask?"

"What makes you think—?"

"Oh, come on," he lowered his voice to a mock whisper, "it's the Elf, isn't it?"

"Who?" Rosamond asked innocently.

"Oh, your face says it all!" Cato giggled. "Cards, woman, cards!"

"Oh, stop," Rosamond rolled her eyes, growing tired of the highlord's teasing.

"Well, *you* chose to dance with *me*, woman," he shrugged, still leading her quite skillfully through the waltz. "So you can either chat me up or let me leer at you, eh?"

And, thank the Lights, the dance ended there. Rosamond curtsied. Cato bowed to her, then to her father, then sauntered back into the crowd. *Finally, that was over!* In clicks, her father was back by her side, opening up the dance floor to others.

"An interesting choice," he said, taking her arm in his as the guests began to socialize.

"Oh?" Rosamond pretended to be surprised. "Surely it was obvious that ridiculous man was fascinating to me!"

Hanz snorted. "Right."

Rosamond pulled away, eager to socialize herself.

Hanz resisted, holding her arm in place, "Ah," he cleared his throat, "Just a moment, darling."

Rosamond whipped her head back to face her father. "Come on, Papa!" she pouted, "I've been waiting and waiting to meet people!"

"You still need an escort," he said, "I'll go with you."

"Men are hardly going to flirt with me with my *father* standing right there," she stated bluntly.

"True enough," Hanz said, "This is why I got you a court lady, Rosemond."

"*Father!*" Rosamond growled, "Please, can't I just be with Valley?"

"A maid?" Hanz hesitated, "I.... maybe later."

Rosamond watched her father with interest. He had *almost* said 'yes' to that!

"If you make me walk around with Viola, I will be sure to misbehave," she grumbled.

"If you misbehave, you will be sure to pay for it," he said in a dark voice. A shadow of terror passed over Rosamond and she found herself nodding reverently.

<hr>

"Where shall we start?" Viola asked eagerly as she held tightly onto Rosamond's arm. "I take it you will want to meet some of the other court ladies?"

"I guess," Rosamond mumbled. It wasn't that she didn't want other female friends; in fact, Rosamond had longed for more female companionship for most of her life. It was the thought of befriending *Viola's* people that made her skin crawl. "You know," she said, "if you gave Valley a chance, you might be surprised at how much you like her! I've never met anyone who didn't like Valley."

"Yes, you have!" Viola said through gritted teeth. "*Me.*"

"Valley's wonderful!" Rosamond insisted, "She is kind and—and compassionate."

"And she's a *Faerie*," Viola halted angrily, yanking her arm away from Rosamond's, "and Faeries are—"

"Fantastic?" a male voice suggested. The two women turned to see a set of three princes standing with drinks in hand. Rasselas, in the center with a toothpick held against his lip, grinned.

"If I needed someone to finish my sentence, Prince Rasselas," Viola said dryly, "I am sure I would be pleased for it to be you."

"Oh," Rasselas glanced toward Prince Tingo at his side. "Slay me, that's not where I expected that sentence to go."

"Nor I," Rosamond said as she tried to conceal her glare, "Viola, do you care to share with these gentlemen how you *really* feel about Faeries?"

"No," said Viola, "Why talk about Faeries when we are blessed with such fantastic company. Gentlemen! How grand to bump into your little circle!"

"Yes," Mynx said in his deep voice. "Grand indeed. Princess Rosamond, we all lost our bets because of you!"

Rasselas gave Mynx a quick nudge with his elbow. "I say, old fellow," he snickered, "The ladies couldn't care less about bets, I'm sure."

"Bets are men's pastimes," Viola said, bowing her head. "We women find little interest in gambling, I assure you."

"Of course, ladies," Tingo said, shooting Mynx a glare, "We were just joking around, just—erm—*men's* stuff."

"Making bets?" Rosamond chuckled. "Really boys, let's keep the bets to the card tables, shall we?"

"Of course," Mynx said.

"Tomorrow night, I hear?" Rosamond's eyes flashed with excitement.

"Ah yes," Viola reached out to touch Rosamond's arm, "The *men* are going to play cards, tomorrow—that is true, Rosamond."

Rosamond took the hint and rolled her eyes.

"Does the lady like cards?" Prince Rasselas asked, rubbing his knuckles against his coat.

"No," Rosamond said flatly. "Viola doesn't play cards. Trust me. I've tried *countless* times to teach her three-stack and she just yawns the whole time." Rosamond turned to smile at Viola playfully. "Isn't that right? She's far too ladylike to learn something like cards, I am sure!"

"Quite," Viola glanced stoically at Rosamond. "Cards, drinking, and smoking are pastimes best left to the stronger sex, Princess. Don't you agree?"

"Indeed!" Rosamond laughed, "If by the *stronger sex*, you mean women!"

The three princes stared wide-eyed for a moment as Rosamond belted out another laugh. She composed herself, then eyed her audience. "Oh, Hades," she sighed, "I am only joking. I don't mind being called the weaker sex—at least, not if I still get to play cards, drink vino, and—at some point—try a cigar."

Mynx burst into laughter. "It's good they hid you away for so long," he said, pointing. "You're a wit!"

"Sir!" Viola jumped at Rosamond's defense, "She was merely—"

"Why *thank* you," Rosamond grinned proudly, placing her hands on her waist.

"Slay me," Rasselas said, watching Rosamond carefully with his eyes, "She's not a wit," he said, "She's—"

"—A princess," Rosamond said smugly. "Now please, gentlemen, I've had enough people try to tell me what I am tonight. How about we talk about something else now, hm? I was just telling Viola here about the most wonderful girl in the world."

Viola shook her head in warning. "No," she whispered, "Please don't embarrass us further."

"She's somewhere around here," Rosamond gazed around the hall, scanning for Valley. *Where was she?*

"Now that you're *out*, Princess Rosamond," Tingo cleared his throat. "I imagine we will see more of you around the palace?"

"Oh!" That snapped her attention back. "Yes! Now you'll all grow tired of me."

"Stop acting so casual," Viola whispered into her ear. Rosamond swatted away the woman like a buzzing bee.

"Princess," polite Tingo said with a smile, "that could not be possible."

"There she is," said a familiar voice. Cato pushed his way into the circle, with his dark wing standing close behind. "My new friend!"

"Hallo, Highlord Cato," Rosamond grinned. "The big friendly bear."

"Friendly?" Tingo snorted, "The man has done nothing but insult people since he arrived!"

"And we love him for it," Rasselas said, snapping his heels together. "Don't we, Princess?"

"We do indeed, Prince Rasselas," said Rosamond, "And what do you think, erm—*Sir Rook?*" Rosamond tried to brave her fears and include the scarred man. She had to pretend she wasn't scared of him. After all, there was no way he could know that she was the girl dressed as the page earlier that day.

Those in the circle turned their heads to look at Rook, who stood silently in his black suit. He didn't seem perturbed by the attention but only cocked his head curiously.

"What *about* me, Princess?" he asked in a silky voice.

"Do you like your Lord Cato and all his insults? Do you think I can rightfully call him a big old friendly bear?"

"*Old?*" Cato groaned.

Rook's face softened, and he glanced at his lord before making steady eye contact with the princess. "I think you could rightfully call him a lot of things, though I don't think it makes much difference what I think."

"Quite right," Cato said. "Hades knows why she asked your opinion, Rook."

"*You* ask my opinion all the time," Rook smirked, "my lord."

"Yes but," Cato groaned. "That's just because..."

"Slay me," Rasselas sniffed, "This conversation is getting wildly erratic. I say—weren't you going to ask Princess Rosamond something, old Tingo?"

"I was," Tingo cleared his throat.

Turning back to look at him, Rosamond realized that he seemed a little stressed by all the interruptions. Wait—was he nervous? Could it be possible that *other* people were nervous, and *she* was the one in control? *Think big*, said the gargoyle's voice in her head, *you have power.*

"Ah, yes, Prince Tingo," Rosamond smiled politely, giving him her undivided attention.

"If you're free tomorrow afternoon, some of us will be practicing our swordplay at the dueling grounds. We'd love it if you came to cheer us on."

Ah! Finally, she could go and properly see the men fight without having to sneak out dressed as a page boy! She tried to contain her excitement and pretended to deliberate.

"That sounds like something new," she said. "I might do that."

Cato snorted, "Oh, she'll be there," he said, "I saw her blush when I mentioned—"

"Cato," she snapped, "I blushed when you said—" she cut herself off. "Oh, shut up, Cato."

Rosamond felt an elbow jab into her side. "I am afraid," Viola exclaimed suddenly, "that I see the king summoning us. Rosamond and I must go."

"What?" Rosamond looked around.

"Goodbye, gentlemen," Viola curtsied to those present, "it was such a pleasure to speak with you."

The men each offered a nod to Viola and a slight bow to Rosamond. Rosamond pouted as Viola led her away from the crowd.

"You *fool!*" Viola scolded under her breath, "You utter fool!"

"We were getting along great!" Rosamond whispered back, "I don't see what I was doing wrong!"

"Of course, you don't see," Viola said as she dragged Rosamond into the back hall. Once the door to the ballroom had closed, Viola raised her voice to a yell. "You were raised by a *man!*"

"So?" Rosamond threw up her hands into the air. "What is wrong with that?"

"You don't realize what your actions look like, *do* you?"

"No!" Rosamond matched Viola's tone. "What are you saying?"

"When you act familiar and brash with those men," Viola pointed back toward the ballroom, "You're not *flirting*, you're playing!"

"Playing?" Rosamond blinked. "What do you mean?"

"You're acting too masculine, Rosamond! If men wanted someone to play cards and joke around with, they would just spend time with other men. But men want women to be mysterious and charming! They want you to act like someone who needs to be *caught*, not someone who wants to make them *laugh!*"

Rosamond stood still with her fists clenched beside her. "I thought that…" her voice grew quiet, "…I thought that men want to fall in love. I thought that…"

"You thought that you could just go on being a headstrong, spoiled princess?" Viola scoffed. "You thought that your looks were good enough to make up for a loud-mouthed, boyish personality?" She stepped closer, pointing her finger directly between Rosamond's eyes. "Mark my words: your father is not going to hear of a *single* marriage proposal tonight, because you came off as such a brat! You'll be lucky if you don't get twice the beating after what you pulled tonight!"

"*What* did you say?" Rosamond stepped back. "You… how did you…?"

"Do you think the maids didn't see your legs when they dressed you today? Do you think there are not whispers about every little thing you do, Rosamond?" Viola smirked. "I would feel bad for you if I hadn't first taught you how to behave properly, but no—you just went and ignored me, over, and over again! Of *course* you got a beating!"

"You are *not* my mother!" Rosamond shrieked.

"No," Viola said calmly, "I was put in this felling palace to be your friend, to help you find your way! Why won't you listen to me, Rosamond? Why won't you trust me?"

"Because…" Rosamond lowered her voice, "Because you're cruel."

Viola snorted. "That shouldn't matter."

"It matters to some of us," said Valley, who arrived by Rosamond's side almost soundlessly.

Viola studied the two of them. "This," she pointed her finger alternatingly between them, "is a problem."

"I won't let you discourage my friendship with Valley," Rosamond said, "My father was the one who began it, after all."

Viola exhaled hot air through her nostrils like an angry bull. Turning, she left them without uttering another word.

Finally alone with Valley, Rosamond slumped.

"What was all that about?" Valley asked.

"I think Father might be using Viola to spy on me," Rosamond said. "She talks like someone who has more power than she should."

"Well," Valley said, "Captain Oswald did warn you not to trust anyone."

"Yeah, about that—" Rosamond crossed her arms. "What do you think that was all about? He works for father, so why tell me not to trust him?"

Valley pulled her lips into her mouth thoughtfully. "Well," she said, "I think Captain Oswald has the look of a man plagued by guilt. Perhaps it was penance."

"Valley!" Rosamond laughed, "You must be ten times smarter than me. I never would have thought of that!"

"Oh, stop," Valley rolled her eyes. "Now, did you want to get back out there? I'd be happy to walk with you."

"You know," Rosamond sighed, "I've waited ages for tonight, but at the moment I am just too fatigued to have all those eyes on me again. It's—it's just too much."

"I know what you mean," said Valley, "I can't stand attention."

"Oh, I love attention!" Rosamond threw up her finger. "I just like it in more manageable amounts! Anyway, this dress is so tight that I feel I might pass out. I think I want to head back and change."

"Well, come on then!" Valley took Rosamond's arm, "I'll help you. That way we can leave the maids out of it."

"Thank you, yes!"

The two girls found some guards to escort them back to the Inner Palace and sent a messenger to inform King Hanz of Rosamond's early retirement, and just like that, the party—as far as Rosamond was concerned—was over.

Rosamond and Valley laughed together as they removed each layer of skirt. Some came off easily over Rosamond's head, while others required Valley to sit and undo what felt like hundreds of buttons as Rosamond sat perched on a dressing stool designed specifically to fit under large petticoats. All the while, the princess monologued about her strange evening, leaving out whatever details had to do with the strange tension with her father.

"And then, the dance—" Rosamond groaned, "was so bizarre!"

"I have to stop you there," Valley said from down on the floor, where she was prying at a stuck button. "Rosamond, why did you ask that old highlord to dance? I thought you would have at least asked someone younger!"

"Right," Rosamond bit her lip, "Well...it's hard to explain, but you see, it was like father was playing a mind game with me tonight. I didn't want to pick the man he wanted me to pick!"

"Really?" Valley looked up curiously, "You and your father were at odds tonight?"

"Sort of..." Rosamond hesitated. "Valley, I have to confess something."

"What is it?"

"You see..." Rosamond cringed, "After I found out about your branding and everything..."

"Oh," Valley dropped her eyes to the floor.

"Well, I've just been sort of upset with Father! I am just really seeing him as a sort of villain! Hades—I know that's not right..."

"No," Valley sighed, "I know what you mean."

Rosamond stood from the stool as Valley removed the final thick layer. The rest of Rosamond's skirts were fastened by ribbons, so Valley rose to untie them.

"So, anyway, I picked Lord Cato because he would probably be the last man father cared about," Rosamond said, as the final skirt fell to the ground. There was silence. Rosamond glanced down at Valley, who was kneeling at her feet. "He is actually nicer than you would think," Rosamond added. "Though he did make a comment about my breasts—I think!"

"Rosamond..."

"...what is it, Valley?"

"What happened to your legs?" asked Valley.

Rosamond glanced down, gasping as she saw just how bad the wounds looked.

Valley rose to her feet, with a face that emanated malice. "Your father did this, didn't he?"

All Rosamond could do was nod.

Just then, there was a knock on the door. The two girls clutched one another, then began to panic as Rosamond pointed down at her exposed legs.

"Just a moment!" Rosamond called, as Valley threw a dressing gown into her hands. She quickly covered herself as the door opened, regardless.

"My girls!" cried King Hanz, who stepped into the room with outstretched arms.

Rosamond held her breath. He was acting affectionate—was that because Valley was there? *Perhaps the secret was to never be alone!*

"My dear Rosamond," said Hanz. He marched up to his daughter and pulled her up into a tight embrace. "You were *fantastic!*"

"I—I was?" Rosamond stuttered, darting her eyes over to Valley to exchange confused looks.

"Oh you were a gem," Hanz said, "and you did everything I wanted you to do! Well done. What an obedient child you are," he released her from his hug and took her by the shoulders, pushing her back to look at her at arm's length. Though his face was smiling, his eyes seemed to glisten with another emotion. Behind those eyes was the real man with his real thoughts.

"Well," Rosamond acted flattered, "I was afraid I was awkward. I was so nervous that I kept talking without thinking! Oh, everyone probably thinks I am such a loudmouth."

"Nonsense," King Hanz barked playfully. "No one would insult *my* daughter. Besides, I've already received two offers of marriage, and most others expressed their interest to me!"

Rosamond's heart leapt. "*Who*, father?"

"Now, now," he reached his hand out to pinch her chin. "You leave all that to me. Just get to know the noblemen and don't be afraid to encourage interest from more than one party. You never know which might be the one you are going to marry!"

Rosamond tightened her lips together. "Father," she said, pulling back from him. "You could *tell* me which one I am to marry, and then I won't have to encourage affection from other men."

"That's not how this works, Rosamond," Hanz said, dropping his hands to his sides.

"So," she straightened her back. "If I did so well tonight, then I hope you won't try and micromanage me anymore? I will be free to talk as much as I like, and wear whatever I please?"

Her father raised an eyebrow but said nothing. The look he gave her was enough. *Don't test me*, it said.

"Father," Rosamond's voice grew timid, "I don't like all the attention. I don't want to have to..." How was she supposed to say this? "I don't want to encourage those leering looks," she said under her breath.

"Stop thinking you know men's minds," he said firmly. "Just trust me. I am your father, and I wouldn't do anything to put you in any danger, alright? If I tell you to wear something, I want you to wear it."

Though they spoke calmly, the tension in the room was thick. All the while, Valley remained motionless, darting her wide eyes back and forth between father and daughter.

"Papa," Rosamond felt herself growing smaller and smaller. "I don't like how some of those men look at me."

"There are some things you had better get used to," he responded, "You're a woman now, Rosamond. This is what things must be like for you. If your mother were still alive, she would tell you the same thing."

Rosamond's fists tightened, though she nodded submissively. "I will try to... *get used to it.*" She couldn't stop a hint of defiance from seeping out of those last four words.

Hanz's face flashed with intensity, but he didn't react further. "You pleased me tonight," he said, stepping back towards the door, "But Rosamond, do not defy me further. Oh, and Valley?"

Valley jolted. "Yes, my Lord?"

"Come see me in the morning, at the first bell."

19

—— Valley ——

The Potent and Controlled Giant

"YOUR EXISTENCE AND PURPOSE CANNOT BE HIDDEN by lies, just as day cannot be concealed by a cloth."

Valley whispered the precious words to herself, her hand resting against her skirt pocket containing the letter. Those words—the words she had recited so many times—they felt like a part of her soul. Somehow saying them to herself made the hardest things easier. And this morning, walking into King Hanz' room felt like the hardest thing. She couldn't exactly articulate what felt so scary about going to see the King. Ever since her bonding ceremony, Valley had felt so small and terrified around him. A man who once acted as a sort of father-figure now treated her like a servant, or worse: a slave.

Valley waited to hear the ringing of the Firstlight bell outside before she knocked. After holding her breath a further moment or two, she opened the door. She winced as she peered around the room, expecting to find the king in his bed once again. She was relieved to see him fully dressed and sitting on his armchair with a small book open in his hand. He glanced up at her.

"Ah, Valley. Right on time," he said, snapping the book closed.

Valley remained standing in the middle of the room with her hands clasped nervously together.

"Earth and all his sisters, Valley," Hanz dropped the book with a sigh, "What is it *now?*"

"My Lord?"

"You're as tense as a bowstring. Come on—what is it?"

Valley bit her lip. "My Lord, I am still feeling strange about private audiences with you. I was taught that men and women shouldn't—"

"Valley, let me set the record straight for you there," he grew silent, and his eyes studied her for a moment.

Valley's bowstring of tension grew even tighter.

Hanz cleared his throat, "When a Faerie becomes bonded to a Human, you essentially become part of their identity, part of their being. So in a sense, your body is now a part of my body. Do you understand? This is why I could ask you to scapegoat for me if I choose, correct?"

"... Yes..."

"So, if I did have, well, *coital* intentions toward you, there would be absolutely nothing amiss or untoward about it. Do you understand? So, don't worry so much about the *impropriety* of meeting with me here. I may meet with any bonded Faerie at any time, and no one will think twice about it. Does that make sense to you?"

Valley shifted her weight from one leg to the other. "Yes..."

"But let's make something very clear. I do *not* have those kinds of intentions for you, Valley," Hanz said as he rose to his feet. He stretched his arms out, arching his back.

Valley's heart swelled with relief. "I—"

"I don't want you thinking anything like that is going to happen," he said sharply, turning to look at her out of the corner of his eye, "And you must not try to tempt me in that direction, understand?"

"*Tempt* you?" Valley shook her head quickly. "Why would I—?"

"Valley, please don't interrupt," he rubbed his forehead with his middle finger. "Just stop giving me those terrified eyes every time you come in here, it..." his voice trailed off and he grew quiet.

"Thank you for clarifying this," Valley said in a clear voice, taking a step closer to the King. "It really does relieve the...*erm*...the worry."

"I shouldn't have to explain myself to you all the time!" He turned to face her, his kingly cape swooping behind him. "Valley, you..." his voice trailed off again as he studied her. "Have you been doing as I have asked? Have you been observing and listening to the guests?"

She hadn't *really* tried to listen in, but didn't want to rile his irritation further. "Yes," she said, "though most of the time, the nobles are out of their rooms while I am doing my chores."

Hanz looked down at the floor. "Valley," he said quietly, "I have another guest staying in the Inner Palace. He is in the third-floor grand suite. I do not want you tending to that guest. I want him undisturbed. Do you understand? Do not go there."

Yes, she understood! Why was he always asking her that? "I understand," she said. "Who is the guest?"

Hanz lifted his head swiftly. "Valley!" He snapped. "I just told you I don't want you going in there; that is all you need to know!"

"I'm *sorry!*" Valley snapped back, then bit her tongue.

Hanz' face changed from angry to pensive. He caught it—he caught the defiance in her voice. "Valley?" he said carefully, "are you angry?"

Valley shook her head in shame. "No!" she assured him. "No, I am not."

The king studied her face.

"Well," he turned away from her. "Just keep doing as I asked and let me know if anyone seems interested in talking to you." He looked back at her. "*Has* anyone spoken to you? Sought you out?"

Valley felt the letter in her pocket radiating its existence. "Yes," she said, keeping her blank face. Well, she *thought* it was a blank face; but really, Valley's blank face was that nervous, wide-eyed deer expression.

Hanz straightened, facing her head on. "Who?" He had such a good poker face; she could read *nothing* from his expression!

"Prince Rasselas," she said. Surely others in the palace would have seen Rasselas talking to her! She had better say something.

Hanz nodded. "Is he showing you romantic interest?"

Valley shook her head. "No," she said, "I think he is interested in Faeries."

Hanz scoffed. "Not to *buy* them, though," he mumbled to himself. "Well," he sighed. "His brother was a Faerie."

Valley blinked. "He was?"

"Yes," Hanz said blankly, "His brother is dead, I think, but he is still trying to find him. He will probably try to use you to do that."

"Use me to find his brother?"

"Yes," Hanz said in a bored tone. He moved toward his writing desk and leaned down to check his face in the mirror. He moved some of his combed hair from one side of his head to the other. "Poor Rasselas. How tragic to lose one's own family."

"How did his brother die?"

Hanz glanced toward her. "His brother was the son of King Somenus, Valley. The to-be Faerex."

"H—he *was*?" Valley stuttered. "So we *did* have a king?"

Hanz shrugged. "Not exactly. He was training under the regent to become the king when he came to the age of ability. Anyway, something happened at Arelle, and everyone was killed." His eyes grew unfocused. "All that was found there was dust."

"Dust?" Valley found herself walking toward him.

"Faerie dust."

"The ash we become when we die?"

Hanz nodded. "So it is hard to know who died and who did not. But there was dust on the throne. Many believe that suggests Hevel must have died."

"Who was Hevel?"

Hanz turned to her with alarm, as if scared by hearing her say the name. "He—" he stammered. "He was the regent. The Death Faerie."

Valley wasn't used to the king telling her so many details about the Faeries. Perhaps it was true what others had said: Hanz really did trust his own bonded

Faeries! Well, if he really did see her as a part of his own flesh, he really would *need* to trust her!

"My Lord?" She asked.

"What?"

"Do you want me to spy on Prince Rasselas for you?"

Hanz' eyes widened, then he smiled. "Very good, Valley—yes!"

"Perhaps his desperate need to find his brother might make him more trusting of me."

"Yes... yes!" He placed his hand on her shoulder excitedly. "See what his plans are. See if he knows anything about where his brother is."

"You mean..." she met his eyes, "...where he *thinks* his brother is?"

"Yes, yes..." Hanz dropped his hand, thinking, "And perhaps you could talk a bit about how much you like bonding, and how good it is for the Fae? Could you do that for me, sweet Valley?"

"Of course," she lied, "I can definitely do that. Is there anyone else you want me to spy on in particular?"

Hanz gripped Valley by the shoulder, then pulled her close into a fatherly hug. "I am so proud of you," he said as he pulled away again. "Yes, please see about making some sort of connection with King Labyrinth. I want you to find out how bad the starvation is in his lands."

"That's... going to be a hard topic to bring up."

"I have total faith in you, Valley," he said warmly. "Now, I have much to prepare for today. You may go."

Valley nodded, brushing away the awkwardness she still felt at being in such an intimate setting. But rather than feeling like a trapped, powerless animal, Valley instead tried to imagine herself how the words talk about her: a controlled giant. Hanz seemed to trust her; she could use that. She would grow that trust if she could and tuck it into her pocket for safe keeping.

Valley held her submissive, innocent expression on her face as she studied the man before her.

Oh, how she hated him.

She left his quarters feeling empowered. Yes, he scared her, and yes, she hated him. But she saw the meeting as an opportunity. Perhaps being the lowest of the low could be a good thing; perhaps she could get around, listening and learning without being noticed. A valley, after all, is where even kings and princes must pass through to reach their mountains. In order to carry out his own selfish plans, a man like King Hanz needed little serving mice like Valley—and *that* would be his downfall.

Valley didn't see Rasselas when she went to tend his bedroom fire, in fact, most of the nobles seemed to be out and about by the time she got to their rooms. But as she was sitting on the visiting prince's floor, reading her precious letter, someone spoke to her.

"Maid?"

Valley thrust the letter into her pocket and stared up at the speaker, wide-eyed.

"Yes?" she blurted.

A man stood above her with his arms folded. His head was cocked to the side. Long, slick black hair trailed loosely down his back. She recognized him as Prince Tingo of Sol, the small, though culturally rich nation south of Mensa. His brow was furrowed, and he was rubbing his upper lip between his thumb and index finger.

"I... have I seen you somewhere before?" he asked.

"I tend the fires," she said, looking back at the half-cleaned ash on the hearth before her. She drew in a quick breath, and added, "I also was at the welcome banquet. I am one of King Hanz' Faeries."

"Oh," he started, noticing her ears. "I didn't see you were a Fae." He began to turn away from her. "Sorry to bother you..."

Valley took her coal brush in hand and began to sweep the hearth, which is what she *should* have been doing instead of reading her letter.

"Uh, maid?" The prince spoke again. She turned to see him standing back where he had begun, peering down at her.

"*Yes?*" she asked, beginning to feel a little irritated.

"Did you say you had been bonded to King Hanz? Or you are, erm, just one of his Faeries he has living here?"

Why was he asking her this? Why was he even talking to her? "I am bonded to him," she said flatly. "He wouldn't let unbonded Faeries into the Inner Palace, usually."

"Right," he nodded, glancing to the side.

"Was there anything else?" she asked impatiently. He was just standing there *staring* at her!

"*What*?" he jumped. "Oh," he looked around, as if trying to remember what he had been doing before he noticed her there. "Nothing, I..." He wandered off without finishing his sentence.

Well that was odd! When Valley finished her work there, she left the place gladly. Once she had finished her morning work, she passed Captain Oswald in the hall. She paused long enough to nod a smile of greeting, then moved on.

"Valley!" she heard him call from behind. Pausing, she groaned, then turned slowly to face him as he came jogging up to her.

"Captain," she said, "I am off to grab something to eat. What is it?"

Oswald hesitated, "Are you... are you annoyed with me, Valley?"

"What? No—why? Do I sound annoyed?"

"Well, yes," he said, placing his hand on the hilt of his sword.

"I'm just hungry," she mumbled.

"I won't keep you, then," he said nervously. "May I walk beside you on your way for a moment?"

"Sure," Valley shrugged, then resumed walking. Could she not get some time to herself? She wanted to be anonymous today!

The two of them left the Inner Palace, walking side by side. Valley usually would have taken lunch in the Warrowing Village, but she moved toward the marketplace instead. Something inside her wanted to avoid the Warrowing Village ever since she met that disturbing woman in the prisons.

"How are you adjusting to being one of the King's Faes?" Oswald asked in a quiet voice as they passed by a set of guards.

"Fine," she answered.

"I am sure you're up to the task," he said awkwardly, "Ah, I mean you seem to do well at everything you put your hands to."

"So were you just hoping for some chit-chat, or did you actually have something specific to ask me about?"

Oswald grew silent as he walked beside her. "I guess I thought of us as friends. I wanted to see how you were doing."

Friends? He had stood by and watched when someone sunk a brand into her skin! *Friends*? "Sure, I guess we are friends of sorts, if you want," she shrugged, "I always just figured it was your job to check up on me. Isn't that what you're doing now? Your job?"

Oswald halted in his steps. Valley stopped, turning to face him expectantly. "Valley," he said slowly. "I am not a good friend to anyone, I fear. Friendship isn't something I have the luxury of keeping. I... I shouldn't presume to call you a friend. Sorry."

Hades! This man was replete with guilt! Valley sighed. "It's not easy working for King Hanz. He wants us all to be loyal to no one but him. Other loyalties threaten him."

Oswald started. "Yes," he said. "Yes—exactly."

"If you want me to call you friend," she said, "then show me kindness that Hanz *wouldn't* want you to show. Show *me* some loyalty. Then, I might begin to feel a shred of trust toward you."

Oswald held his breath. Who knew what thoughts were swirling around in that man's head? Who knew *why* he wanted her trust so badly! "Alright," he said slowly, "I will tell you something he does not want you to know."

Valley's heart made a thud. "Oh, yes?" she asked suspiciously, hiding her interest. "And what is that?"

Captain Oswald looked around for a moment, checking to see that they were far enough away from listeners for him to whisper. He lowered his voice.

"The fifth day after bonding is very important," he said. "Hanz always tests his Fae on the fifth day. He will want to know you are truly loyal to him."

Valley's pulse began to rise. The fifth day after her bonding was tomorrow! "What... what happens if I don't pass the test?"

Oswald's face grew dark. "I..."

"*Tell* me, Oswald," Valley said pointedly. "Don't shield me anymore."

Oswald exhaled through his nostrils. "Torture."

Valley nodded slowly. "Thanks for your frankness," she placed her hand over her heart, feeling it pound so hard that it stung. "And thank you for the warning. Do you know what sort of test he has planned for me?"

Oswald lifted his eyes to look at one of the looming Mensa towers. He blew air through his lips, considering. "Hanz no doubt wants you to spy for him. My guess is that he would test your information to see if you are telling the truth." He held his breath for a moment, then shook his head to himself. "Or..."

"Or what?" Valley pressed, stepping closer.

"Or he will test your emotions. He believes emotions reveal one's true loyalty."

"Test my *emotions*?" What could that possibly look like? "How?"

"I do not know," he said, "Hanz has never bonded with a woman Faerie before, so I do not know if he will treat you differently."

"He *hasn't*?"

Oswald shook his head. "No."

The two of them walked until they descended down the northwest stair and into the market square. As they neared the food stalls, Valley could hear a familiar voice. She halted in her steps and peered down a side street, where some Humans loitered about.

"What is it, Valley?" Oswald said in a stern voice, "Let's avoid this street."

"What is that place?" Valley studied the odd group. Several women dressed in single-layered skirts and strapless tops crowded around a man who seemed to be laughing heartily. It was Karo, one of the other bonded Faeries.

"Come on, Valley," Oswald tugged her arm protectively. Valley shot him a glare.

"I asked you what this place was!"

Oswald groaned like a creaking ship. "It's a brothel," he said reluctantly.

What was Karo doing there? Valley moved away from Oswald, marching determinedly toward the cluster.

"Valley!" Oswald stumbled after her. She ignored the captain, observing Karo whispering into the ear of one of the apparent whores. She noticed a second man, cloaked in black and with his hood shrouding his face.

"Pass it over, Karo," the cloaked man said in a nasally voice. He held out his gloved hand.

"A moment, sir," Karo said in a loud, jolly voice, "I will in a moment." He leaned to his other side, whispering into the ear of a second woman. She giggled in response.

"Karo!" Valley announced her presence and glided up to the tarty group.

"Ahh, pretty Valley!" Karo turned toward her with a grin. There was something different about Karo, though she couldn't discern exactly what it was. Something about his presence seemed more empowered, like an unleashed guard dog. "Looking fantastic this morning, my dear!"

Valley folded her arms. "You spent the night at a *brothel?* I thought Faeries weren't allowed to—"

"Oh, sorry, *mum*!" Karo laughed, "Did I not come back to bed on time last night?" He placed his hand over his mouth, feigning embarrassment.

Valley spotted something on his finger. Wait—a *ring*? It was a ring, and a beautiful one at that. It was set with a large ruby that glowed like a star. "Where did you get that?" Valley pointed.

Karo pursed his lips, studying her. "It was a present," he said. "Now, who made *you* the possession police?" He glanced at Oswald who was standing protectively behind her, then over at the cloaked man. "Gentlemen? Have I broken any rules here?"

"Just hand it over now, Faerie," the mysterious man said.

"But of course," Karo made a playful curtsy, then removed his ring and passed it off. The cloaked man took it and turned without giving Valley so much as a glance. She didn't even see his face. Karo watched the man leave, then sighed. "Well, it was fun while it lasted," he said to himself. "Oh, are you still here, Valley?"

"Do you have an imperium?" Valley asked, stepping up to the tall, slick Faerie who towered above her. He bent down slightly to grin at her.

"I have been bonded to the king for a long, *long* time, dear girl," he reached down to pinch her chin condescendingly, "And I don't need to explain myself to a crispy little Faerie like you."

"The king lets his Faeries store magik?" she pressed, ignoring the teasing. She felt Oswald's firm hand on her shoulder.

"Valley," he said, "Come on."

Valley brushed the hand off her shoulder and kept eye contact with Karo. "Does Hanz let you use your powers?"

"*Powers*?" Karo chuckled, "Me? Never! I—Well, I..." He looked face to face at his group of tarts, "I don't even have a title!"

"Fine, be that way." Valley scoffed.

"It's a funny thing seeing you on this street, little Valley," Karo said, "it's a context I quite like. Say, have you done something with your hair?"

Valley practically hissed as the man reached toward her hair. She stepped back. "Stop it," she said, "You won't see me here again. I just didn't know... didn't know we were allowed this much freedom."

"Oh!" Karo laughed openly, "I didn't know you *wanted* to spend time in places such as this, little girl. Well, Hades! Let me show you inside!" He gestured to the nearby building.

"That's enough!" Oswald barked. "Don't you have somewhere to be?"

"Yes, yes," Karo rolled his eyes, tapping his ladies on the backs. They took the signal and reluctantly wandered back into the unseemly building. Once they were out of sight, Karo shot Oswald a pouty glare. "I know he wants to meet me. I'll *be* there, but it's not until the third bell!"

"Run along, Faerie," Oswald said shortly.

Karo gave Oswald a prolonged stare, then shifted his gaze to Valley.

"I say," he exclaimed, "You really *do* draw the eye today, Valley. Do let me know if you change your mind about the old..." he gestured with his thumb toward the door to the brothel.

"Go on!" Oswald barked. Karo skipped off into the main square, leaving Oswald and Valley standing alone on the quiet street.

She turned slowly to peer up at the mustached face with a glare. "Oswald," she said, "How many times do I have to tell you not to *babysit* me!"

He frowned. "What are you talking about?"

"You keep coming to my rescue all the time as if I am some damsel in distress! I can take care of myself!"

He stuttered wordlessly.

"Will you stop acting like my protector? I never *asked* you to do that!"

"Valley," he placed his hands on his hips, "I would have stood up for *any* young lady who wandered down this street. That Faerie was suggesting vile things!" He pointed to the street where Karo disappeared. "And I told you—I see you as my friend!"

"You show me too much attention," she said, "It makes me uncomfortable!"

Oswald pulled his lips flat. "Alright," he said, "I will try to let you... take care of yourself."

"*Thank* you!" Valley, exasperated by all of the day's unwanted attention, turned to look at the door to the brothel. "Can you leave me now?"

Oswald looked side to side. "What, now? *Here?*"

"Yes." Valley all but rolled her eyes. "And I promise I won't get *assaulted* while you're gone."

Oswald grunted. "Fine," he said, "But Valley, I am not trying to babysit you, I just," he froze with his mouth half open.

Valley cocked her pointy eyebrow. "What? You just *what?*"

"I... never mind." He looked away.

"*What?* Will you just *say* it?"

To Valley's surprise, Oswald stormed off, looking broodier than ever. Watching him leave, she shook her head. *What a strange man.* Then she shifted her attention back to the brothel and stepped inside.

It was busier and brighter inside the stone building than she had expected. She found herself in a clean and tidy lounge of sorts, with a few doorways leading to long hallways lined with doors.

"We aren't seeing guests until the Zenith bell," a voice called out from a side room. "The rooms are either occupied or being cleaned."

"It's not a customer," said a woman who looked up from her floor scrubbing to smile at Valley, "It's just a Faerie girl."

Valley walked up to the Human and crouched down to her level. "Hallo," she said, "I'm Valley."

"Hallo," said the woman. She put her rag into her pail of water and dried her hands on her apron. She was dressed like a courtesan with a skirt so thin Valley could see the shape of her legs and a low-cut top—though her cleaning apron provided some modesty. She had curly auburn hair that hung loosely about her shoulders and her lips were painted a deep red to match. "I'm Poppy. Haven't seen you in here before. Someone send you with a message?"

"No," Valley rested her knees on the floor and tucked a loose bit of hair behind her ear. "I just noticed a friend of mine here, Karo. I didn't know Faeries visited places like this."

Poppy grinned. "Oh, Karo. What a charmer! We love Karo here."

"Do you live here in the Mensa Castle?" Valley asked, "Or do you just work here?"

"Everyone who works in Mensa Castle lives here, Miss Valley," Poppy said. "Don't you know that? We all have to work hard to get in here, you know!"

"You like working... *here*?"

Poppy shrugged, "It's not the sort of work I imagined doing when I was a kid," she stopped to belt a laugh. This woman had lungs! "But the patrons here are better than the Mensa streets, I can tell you that. Mostly just soldiers, but we get the odd nobleman, too."

Valley nodded, hiding her discomfort at the thought of what this woman *did* day in and day out. "Karo comes here often?"

"I wish he came more," she mused, reaching back into her bucket. "He doesn't just come for his *own* pleasure, you know. He takes care of us, if you know what I mean! And I am talking *all* night." She startled Valley with another booming laugh.

"I..." Valley *didn't* want to know what she meant, but she had an idea. "How often does he come?"

Poppy stopped to think for a moment. "He only comes when the king lets him, I think. He belongs to King Hanz, you know!"

Belongs... how Valley was beginning to hate hearing that word in relation to Faeries.

"Does he always wear that ring?" Valley asked.

Poppy's face changed for a moment. "Are you interrogating me?" she asked, genuinely confused.

"No!" Valley shook her head. "No, no, no. Sorry. You see, I just got bonded with the King, too." She slid the neck of her dress to the side, showing her brand.

"Hey, that's just like Karo's!" Poppy pointed.

"Yes," Valley smiled, as if she was proud of her brand. "Anyway, I am trying to learn the ropes. When I saw him here, I got curious. I didn't know bonded Faeries were allowed to, well...act as patrons around here."

"Well," she glanced around the room, then lowered her voice. "They're *not*."

"They're not?"

Poppy shook her head slowly, then continued to whisper. "He's the only Faerie we see here. We think the king sends him here."

Valley furrowed her brow. "But *why*?"

Poppy shrugged. "To get magik?"

"Why would—?" Valley cut herself short. Which Faerie was Karo? It seemed pretty clear that Hanz was allowing him to power up an imperium, but at a brothel? If Hanz did indeed let some Faeries use their skills, she would have to investigate further. Poppy looked expectantly at Valley, politely waiting for her to finish her thought. "Uh," Valley rose, "thanks for chatting."

"Thanks for the company!" Poppy said, waving cheerily, "I don't see many ladies in Mensa Castle. This is definitely a man's world here, eh?"

"Yeah," Valley chuckled, "It is. But, hey, we women look out for each other, eh?"

"Oh, yes!" Poppy grinned, "You let me know if you ever need anything, Valley!"

"You, too." Valley said, then left.

After stopping for a bite of food in the market, Valley walked slowly back to the Inner Palace. Which Faerie would gain magik from... well... from visiting a place like *that*? And what would King Hanz be needing him for?

Once back in the Inner Palace, Valley found herself wandering toward the library. She knew there was a small section of books on Faeries—she used to sneak in and read them when she was a girl. There was a thick book on Faerie titles that she used to thumb through, perhaps it would still be there!

Walking into the library felt like entering a secret garden. Not many people, aside from perhaps skydeacons and lawyers, visited the Inner Palace library. It was set aside for nobles like Hanz, but he seldom went there. It was large, though labyrinthine, giving the privacy of a hedge maze made of books. The only sounds in the library came from crackling fires. There were various alcoves and study spots for the reader to nestle into. Valley remembered the books on Faeries all being clustered together into one of these alcoves in the back. As she walked through the book-lined passageways, she drew deeply into her nostrils the scent of old books. Yes, she was lucky for a Fae—she had been taught to read! She was free to enjoy words. And though possessions were not permitted for a Faerie, *no one* could take words away from her.

She followed the path to the back alcove, her old memory as her guide, hoping it would lead her well. It had been several seasons since she had even thought to set foot in here! To her dismay as she turned the last corner, she saw that the quiet reading chair beside a cozy fire was occupied.

Jumping in alarm, she apologized quickly to the reader. "Sorry, sorry!" She waved her arms, turning quickly to leave.

"Valley, wait!" the reader called after her. She knew *that* voice. She froze, turned, then peeked around the corner bookshelf to see Prince Rasselas sitting there with a stack of books in his lap. Open at the top of the stack was that very tome she came here to find: the book on Faerie titles.

"Rasselas," she said slowly, "Hallo."

"Don't be shy," he said in his charming, clownish voice. He waved her over, "Come on, get whatever book you came for."

Valley crept around the corner slowly. "I didn't take you for a bookish sort," she said, eyeing the tome.

"Ah," he shrugged, "I like to pretend to read, you know? But I don't actually read! That is," he picked up a large, thin book that had been leaning against his chair, "unless its books on fashion like this!"

Valley snorted. "Don't lie to me," she pointed at the tome. "I know you're reading that. Why? Why that book?"

Rasselas marked the page with a ribbon, then carefully closed the book. "Did you read the letter?"

"Did you write it?" She reached into her pocket and pulled it out. "It's signed with a bird's foot."

"That..." Rasselas glanced at the paper, "That was written by the, *erm*— the Red Raven."

"The Red Raven?" Valley raised her pointed eyebrow. "Who is that?"

"Hades, I don't know!"

"Yes, you do." Valley lowered her voice and moved closer. "You said you knew powerful Faeries. You said you knew Aorist."

Rasselas looked at her with a thoughtful expression, then nodded. "Yeah," he said in a sincere tone, "I know him."

"Did he write these words?" She pointed at the paper.

"Does it matter who wrote them?" Rasselas asked, folding his hands together.

Valley pursed her lips, thinking. "Yes."

"Does it really?" Rasselas rotated his head to the side. "Can't they just be true?"

"Why did you give this to me?" Valley took another step closer to Rasselas and looked down at him where he sat. He followed her with his eyes.

"Because it's the truth," he said softly, "There are Faeries like you who are conditioned to be slaves. It's not right."

"Conditioned?" she scowled. "What do you mean?"

"Hanz is raising Faeries like you to believe that you are all servants."

"It was Aorist who said that, *wasn't* it?" She snapped her hands onto her hips. "*Your* friend!"

"Yes!" Rasselas rose to his feet suddenly, startling her backwards a few steps. "He is my friend. So don't you think I know best what he meant?"

"He said Faeries were made to serve Humans! Do you deny that?" Valley said in a stifled whisper, trying to mask her anger.

"You read the letter!" Rasselas snapped back, "Does a parent serve their children by becoming their slaves? Does a king serve his people by neglecting his throne?"

Valley recoiled back at the sting of the words. Then she nodded. "It's true," she said softly, "It's true."

There was a change in Rasselas' face. He looked... excited! "You thought about the words, didn't you?" he whispered. A wide grin formed on his face. With a smile like that, Rasselas really *was* as handsome as everyone thought.

"I did," Valley found herself smiling back. Then her smile faded. "What is being done here is wrong, Rasselas. We are being tortured and oppressed."

"I knew it!" He drove his fist into the air. "King Hanz is a villain, *isn't* he?"

Valley blinked. "Well... yes. *I* think he is."

"Valley," Rasselas took her by the shoulders and stared deeply into her face, "Listen to me. We need to do something! We have got to help the Faeries here!"

"But how? What could we possibly do? We are in a Human kingdom! Their laws prescribe this slavery. And honestly, all the other Faeries think what is being done to us is right."

"The letter," Rasselas pointed to the paper in Valley's hands. "Words, Valley. Words have so much power. We have to start by spreading ideas."

"If we start spreading these kinds of ideas," Valley said cautiously, "We are going to get killed. Both of us."

"But they are not our words," Rasselas smirked, "These are the words of the Red Raven!"

Valley raised her eyebrows amusedly. "Rasselas," she said, "These are *your* words."

Rasselas slumped. "Fine. I wrote it. But no one else needs to know that! We can spread the words without tracing them back to us."

"This is so dangerous, Rasselas," Valley said, stepping away from him. "I... I know King Hanz would deal harshly with this kind of thing. He... he can be very cruel when he is angry. It will be the Faeries who suffer."

Rasselas placed his hand over his mouth, considering. "Well, then let's start slow. Let's just be very careful who we talk to. Why don't you start with just small conversations and suss out who you think might be willing to listen. Oh, Valley!" He interrupted himself with a jump of delight, "this is *exactly* the kind of connection I was hoping to make! With *you*, we could really do some good here!"

"So," Valley joined her hands behind her back. "That is why you were showing me interest. You were hoping to make a connection with a Fae?"

"Uh... yes?" Rasselas cringed. "Is that bad? Or *good*?"

Valley chuckled. "I thought you were trying to flirt with me."

"Ah," Rasselas' eyes darted around for a moment, "I could see how you might think that."

"Can I ask you something, Rasselas?" Valley lowered her voice to such a quiet whisper that the prince had to lean forward to hear her.

"Yes?"

"Is King Hanz trying to find your brother?"

The expression on Prince Rasselas' face darkened and he grew tense. "Why are you asking me this?" he asked firmly, matching her volume. "Did King Hanz say something?"

"He..." Valley looked around, feeling suddenly fearful that Hanz was hiding behind one of the bookcases, "He told me your brother was the King. He told me you were trying to find him."

"*And?*" Valley felt Rasselas grip her shoulder tightly. She had never imagined him to be capable of looking so fierce.

"He asked me to find out what you knew... if you had any ideas where he might be."

Rasselas' face relaxed. He grew too curious to be angry. "So... Hanz is trying to *find* Anodos? Or is Anodos *here*? And Hanz is afraid I know?" He jolted. "Valley, is he having you spy for him?"

Valley nodded slowly. "Yes, but I need to be careful. He is testing me to see if he can trust me."

"Right." Rasselas withdrew his hand from Valley's shoulder and rubbed his lips thoughtfully. "Then we will need to feed him real information. Did he ask you to spy on me? *Specifically?*"

"Yes," Valley said, "He told me your brother is dead, but then seemed to want to know what *you* thought about his whereabouts. Rasselas—*is* your brother alive?"

"Of course he is!" Rasselas snorted.

"Why *of course*? Hanz said that there was only Faerie dust remaining, and that no one knows who died and who didn't?"

"*Did* he?" Rasselas scoffed. "How would *he* know what the scene of the crime looked like? He wasn't one of the investigators."

"How do you know the king is alive, Rasselas?" Valley pressed. "Is there really a Faerie king somewhere out there?"

"Yes!" Rasselas said sharply, straining to contain his intensity to a whisper. "And I know he is alive because he is a very special kind of Faerie with a title that has only ever been held *once* before, by one of the original eight Faeries made."

Valley marveled at the idea. "What title?" she asked earnestly.

Rasselas straightened his back. "The Faerie of Magik."

"Faerie... of *Magik*?"

"Yes," he whispered, "A Faerie whose very being emanates magik, both dark and light. He can power anyone and anything infinitely. Now, imagine that! How could anyone kill him?"

"How did the first Faerie of Magik die, then?" She asked skeptically.

"The first Faerie of Magik was killed by a weapon he helped make. And there has only ever been *one* of those."

"Perhaps whoever attacked Arelle had that weapon," she suggested.

"No," Rasselas said, "No, that is impossible. Because I *know* where that weapon is."

"You do?" Valley held her breath. Who *was* Rasselas? How could he *know* such great things?

"Please don't let that information get back to King Hanz," Rasselas pulled at his cravat nervously, "I would really get in big trouble."

Valley smiled. "I won't tell anyone."

"Anyway," Rasselas cleared his throat, returning his attention to Valley's face. Then his eyes seemed to glaze over as he studied her. Something was wrong... something seemed to *change* in him.

"Rasselas?" She asked, twisting her head curiously. "Are you alright?"

"Valley..." he said slowly, "I..." he shook his head quickly. "Valley!" he exclaimed. "I can't believe I forgot to ask you this!"

"What?" She smiled.

"What is your title? There is... tell me what it is so I can try and make sense of this."

"Make sense of what?" Valley's smile faded like daylight at dusk.

"It's nothing... that is..." he cleared his throat, "Just tell me your title."

No... don't break now! Not in front of *him*! Valley closed her eyes tightly as tears began to form. "I..." she said, fighting her emotions, "I don't *know*."

Rasselas sighed. "Right..." he lifted his hand and pulled a tear from her cheek with his pinky finger. "Titles are withheld from you."

Valley nodded, her tear-filled eyes still tightly closed. "I..." her voice broke, "I have asked so many people. No one can tell me. But I think I am something *horrible*."

Rasselas chuckled, "Oh, Valley!" He reached out his arms kindly and pulled her toward his chest, folding his arms around her tightly. She found her face resting against his beating heart. "You've been lied to. There are no horrible titles, you understand? They are all good. *All* of them."

"But I'm a darkwing!" she said as another wave of tears escaped her eyes.

Rasselas laughed, "Valley!" he said in a compassionate voice, still holding her tightly. "What is wrong with *that*?"

"I don't know!" she sobbed. "Do *you* know what I am?"

"I can try and help you find out!" he said, taking her by the shoulders and pushing her back to meet her eyes. "Do you have any powers?"

Valley sniffed. "I don't know. We can't keep imperiums, so I probably don't have enough magik to find out!"

Rasselas shook his head. "Every Faerie can store a certain amount of power within their own bodies. You should have seen signs of your powers your whole life!"

"Well, I am at a complete loss!" Valley said spitefully. "I know *nothing* about myself! Everyone else seems to know what I am, but no one will tell me!"

"More lies," Rasselas said softly, "You have been conditioned to doubt what you know about yourself. Just don't listen to those lies. You know yourself more than anyone else ever could, right? Just spend some time noticing things, alright? *Notice* how your presence affects a room; *notice* how others make you feel; *notice* if anything strange happens."

Valley pondered his words. "Notice…" she murmured.

"Yeah," Rasselas dropped his hands from her shoulders and tucked them into his pockets. "If you look hard enough into a mirror, Valley," he laughed, "you *should* be able to see yourself!"

Valley looked up at Rasselas' kind face with hopeful eyes. "Thank you, Rasselas," she said, "Thank you for empowering me, rather than patronizing me."

"Uh…" Rasselas' eyes twinkled, "sure!"

"You know," the side of Valley's mouth curled upwards into a smirk, "You're so different when you're not acting like an air-head nobleman around everyone else in public."

"Yeah…" Rasselas cringed, "can we just keep that between us?"

Valley shrugged. "Sure."

"Valley?" Rasselas' face grew sincere once more, "Don't be afraid of yourself, alright?"

Valley's eyes grew wide, then nodded. "Rasselas," she whispered, "Do you have any ideas about my title? Have *you* noticed anything different about me?"

Rasselas looked pensive. "I… I hesitate to say."

"Why?"

He shrugged casually, "Because I think my discernment might be a little off with you."

"*Why?*" She narrowed her eyes.

"Well, because you're a woman!" He said in his posh voice. "I get sort of…" he pretended to shiver, "…*thrown* around a pretty thing like yourself!"

Valley smirked. "So *were* you flirting with me the other day? When we met?"

Rasselas turned up his nose, pretending to be bashful, "Well, slay me—I couldn't say!"

Valley let out a little laugh. "You're ridiculous."

—— Hanz ——

Testing the Theory

FOLLOWING THE LIGHTSDAY PEACE TALKS, Hanz left the courthouse alone. So, it was true: not just Mensa, but all the Human kingdoms were experiencing famine and decreased crops. This morning, everyone reported riots, starvation, and even freezing conditions on their soils. The land of Raqia had been without a Faerie King for fifteen seasons now, and this was the result. Hanz still wasn't exactly sure how it all worked, and what the Faerie King did for the land, but it was clear he blessed it in some way.

Finally, the leaders of the other Human kingdoms were becoming aware of the need for a Faerie King. Would this desperation drive them to make alliances they would not have considered before?

Hanz smirked to himself as he walked through the Inner Palace courtyard. The air was crisp and clean. Lightsday always seemed to be the brightest day of the week. He stopped impulsively in his steps beside one of the large ornamental statues that he erected last season. Gazing up at it, he admired the skill with which the young Coppo, Faerie of Lines, had carved his likeness. It was a monument to

Timbre Wulf, the warrior Hanz had become in order to unite the scattered lands of Mensa, the man who had brought about the end of King Somenus.

He had become a legend.

Hanz turned his attention to a woman in the distance who seemed to be charging toward the Inner Palace western side entrance. Valley. She must have been returning from her breakfasting break. What a dedicated worker she was. It was the right choice to raise her close to himself; he needed her trust more than anyone else's. She would be useful to him, especially if she...

Hanz found himself lost in his thoughts. He blinked.

"Damn," he muttered to himself, combing his hair back with his hand, "She's starting to have an effect on me." It was a dangerous game he was playing, having her in close proximity to himself. He would need to be careful. It was risky to let himself become affected by such a powerful Faerie, but even more risky to leave her unattended. No, it would be fine. She could not gain any more magik than she had now, so her effect on him shouldn't become any stronger. Plus, Hanz was stronger than the average Human; he could resist Faerie magik.

Hanz blinked. His mind had wandered off again.

"I need to stay sharp," he said to himself, then continued on his path back to his personal palace.

He entered the palace and journeyed up the main staircase. He climbed until he reached the third level, where a cluster of twelve guards were stationed at the landing. They saluted him, and the head captain stepped forth.

"Sire," said the captain, "he had a hard night, but he is calm now."

Hanz looked around at the faces of the guards, then turned his attention to the captain, "I want no one to speak of what they see or hear from him, you understand?"

"Yes, Sire."

"Has Valley been up here?" The king asked.

"Valley... your ward?" The captain looked to the soldier at his left who shook his head. "No, Sire. Was she meant to be?"

"No," Hanz said, "I don't want her up here."

"I thought you didn't want anyone up here," the captain said.

"I don't," Hanz hissed, "I just especially don't want Valley..." his voice trailed off.

"Sire?" The captain cleared his throat.

"What?" Hanz snapped back to attention. "Let me pass." He pushed past the guards who parted quickly for him and ventured through the door to the main guest room.

The room had been partially trashed. Paintings had been torn from walls, vases smashed, and some of the bed linens were shredded and hung from the ceiling like tattered banners. Sitting serenely over by the window was a skinny, gaunt Faerie with pale, white skin. His eyes were closed as he soaked his face in the Lightsday air pouring in through the open window. Who let him open that window? What if he had flown out? Hanz tightened his fists but prepared a calm face as he entered the room.

"Hallo," Hanz said quietly.

"Hallo," the Faerie said in a velvety voice. The man might be insane, but at this moment he didn't sound like it.

"It's me again," Hanz said. "Do you remember me?"

The man turned his face away from the morning light and observed Hanz. "I do not remember you."

"What *do* you remember?" asked the King. He moved through the shroud of hanging bed linens, then sat himself on a chair beside the Faerie.

"There was a baby," the man said, looking back into the light, "Such a beautiful baby."

"With wings?" Hanz asked.

"Yes... two black wings," the Faerie's eyes began to dart around.

"Two black wings... and two light wings?" Hanz guessed.

The man started. He breathed in deeply, closed his eyes, then breathed out slowly. "Lightsday," he said, "I feel its healing touch."

"Healing touch?" Hanz raised his eyebrows. This Faerie usually stuck to a repetitive script. It was surprising to hear him veering from it. Good. This was progress.

"Lightsday," the Faerie said, "the fourth day. It is the day the spirits were made."

"It was the day the stars were made," Hanz said.

"That is what I mean," the Faerie turned his head slowly to study Hanz' face. "What is your name?"

"My name is Anodos," Hanz said. "Do you remember me?"

The Faerie narrowed his eyes. "I know that name," he said slowly, "Two dark wings, and two light?"

"Yes," Hanz said softly. He smiled. "You remember me."

"Where are your wings?" The Faerie asked, confused. "Where are your ears?"

"Hiding," Hanz said, "Do you remember my face, though?"

"Yes..." said the Fae, "But I grow confused. Where is the child?"

"*I* am the child," Hanz said firmly, reaching out his hand toward the Faerie. "I have grown now!"

"No," the Faerie recoiled where he sat, clutching the window frame fearfully, "No, there was a *child*!"

"Stay calm," Hanz rose to his feet, "I need you to stay calm."

"Two black wings!" The Faerie cried.

"Calm yourself, please!" Hanz raised his voice. "Do you know who *you* are, Faerie?"

"I can't remember!" The Faerie screamed, rushing to the darkest corner he could find in the room. He began to claw at his own skin, sobbing. "Two black wings," he muttered to himself repeatedly.

Hanz blew a loose piece of hair away from his face, then stood and left the room. Progress. He closed the door behind him and turned to look at the captain who stood motionless beside him.

"He's having a fit again," Hanz said, "Restrain him before he causes any more damage, will you?"

"The men are scared of him," The captain said in a low voice, "He's..."

"I *know* who he is!" Hanz snapped, "Look at him. He couldn't hurt a fly!"

"We are afraid to hurt *him*," the captain said.

"He's fine!" Hanz bellowed, then rushed down the stairs.

Once at the bottom of the landing, Hanz heard the sound of the third morning bell. He quickly pulled out his metal clicker, reset it, then shoved it back into his vest pocket.

"Damn," he whispered. He had somewhere to be. Hanz returned to his chambers and, removing his purple robe, pulled his black cloak over his shoulders. He didn't always want the attention of others during the day, especially when he had discrete tasks to see to. Once cloaked, he went into the North tower. Only, instead of ascending it, he took a descending staircase that led to a cellar deep under the castle.

In a windowless, circular chamber with three other adjoining rooms, Hanz found Sigmund and Karo waiting for him. Hanz pulled off his hood, then nodded to each of them in turn.

"Sire," Sigmund said, pulling out his notebook and flipping to a blank page. "We are ready to discuss your first trial."

Hanz shifted his gaze to Karo, who was rocking anxiously back and forth on his heels. The man looked a bit taller and prouder. Yes, he was always in a good mood after a power-up. Hopefully that would help him be more amenable to the task at hand.

"Right," Hanz said. "I see no reason to beat around the bush. Karo, do you have enough power to merge flesh to flesh?"

"I do," Karo said, looking around, "But I can't help but wonder whose flesh you expect me to—well—you see, I can't exactly use my *own* flesh for the, erm..."

"Karo, please," Hanz closed his eyes, sighing to himself. "I require none of your flesh. You're the *surgeon* here."

"Right, yes," Karo laughed nervously, "my sentiment exactly!"

"What did you have in mind, Sire?" Sigmund said, still holding his pen ready. "Shall I retrieve the eyes?"

"No," Hanz shook his head, "We need to see that this works first. He looked at Sigmund. "I need a body part, and I need a volunteer: someone I can trust. Whoever we use will receive a huge gift."

"Understood," Sigmund shut his book and shoved it in his pocket. "Are you suggesting *me*, sire?" He didn't seem too surprised *or* disappointed.

Karo started. "*Him*? I figured we would use some peasant or something, then you could kill him if it worked."

"Karo," Hanz shook his head, "this is why we don't ask for your opinions on these kinds of things."

"Right..." Karo placed his index finger over his lips, silencing himself.

"Well," Sigmund let out an animated sigh, "It would have to be a body part that I am willing to lose—in case things don't work out... and," he thumbed his chin, "It would be beneficial if it enhanced my line of work."

Hanz chuckled. What a bastard this man was. "Well, what have we got to work with?"

"That depends," Sigmund said thoughtfully, "on whether we pull a body part from a Faerie or we use something from the vault."

"What have we got in the vault?" Karo asked curiously.

"We have the tongue..." Sigmund said.

"No! Hades—no, are you insane?" Hanz jumped at the idea.

"Sorry for suggesting it, sire," Sigmund said coolly. "We have some ears, but I don't fancy those."

"Alright, what *would* you fancy?" Hanz crossed his arms.

"There's a *hand* I wouldn't mind having," Sigmund's neutral expression changed to a menacing, covetous smile.

Hanz flattened his lips. "*Whose* hand?"

"Not mine!" Karo gasped, thrusting his hands beneath his armpits protectively.

"How many times do we have to tell you not to worry, Karo!" Sigmund groaned. "As nice as it would be to have your sort of... *touch*... I was thinking of someone else. Someone more skilled."

"I see," Hanz nodded, "that would be quite a gift."

"For quite a large favor," Sigmund said slyly. "If you want me to do this for you, it has to be worth my while."

"Fine," Hanz nodded. "I suppose he has two hands. One should be enough."

"Precisely!" Sigmund smiled innocently.

There was a prolonged moment of silence as the three men stood there, thinking about the situation they were in. In an endeavor to loosen the tension, Karo fumbled at a cigar and began to light it.

"Well," Hanz sighed, placing his hand on the stone table that sat at the center of the room. "Let's do it tonight, when everyone is busy with cards. Bring him here at the Lastlight bell."

"Will you be here?" Karo asked.

"Yes," said Hanz, "I want to see how the experiment goes."

"Any idea how painful it all is?" Sigmund asked, hiding an inward cringe.

"Well—" Karo drew out the word, shrugging. "Best to get drunk first, you know... or... I guess we could knock you out?" He looked to his king for advice.

"I don't care," Hanz grunted, turning to leave. "And don't give Karo his imperium until the surgery. I don't want it going to his *head*!"

Hanz slammed the cellar door behind him, and he left the deep underbelly of the North Tower.

As he rounded the corner of the tower, Hanz spotted King Labyrinth of the Gramenlands heading down the northeastern steps toward the Warrowing Village. What was he doing venturing over there? Considering another Faerie purchase, perhaps? The man was so greedy. Feeling the rush of curiosity, Hanz swiveled over in his direction.

He caught up with Labyrinth at the bottom of the stairs.

"Labyrinth," he called. The King of the Gramenlands turned slowly and eyes Hanz amusedly.

"Hallo, Hanz," said the square-faced man.

Hanz pulled his cigar case from his pocket and opened it in invitation. "A light?"

"Sure," Labyrinth shrugged and took one of Hanz' tabs. The two silently lit their sticks, then each took a puff. Hanz didn't usually smoke during the daytime, but it was an agreement between men to offer a cigar when hoping to broach a sensitive topic. Labyrinth no doubt took the cue and waited silently at the bottom of the stairs, eyeing Hanz.

Hanz began walking and Labyrinth joined him. They both observed the large open gate to the Warrowing Village.

"You had the same thought as me, I think," Hanz said, pulling his cigar from his mouth.

"And what would that be?" Asked Labyrinth.

"All that talk of starvation in our lands. To think it's all caused by these creatures not having a king on their throne." Hanz pointed to the village.

"Is that what this is all about?" Labyrinth groaned. "Do we felling *have* to have a Faerie king on the throne of Arelle? And here I thought the Humans could finally be in charge of Raqia."

"Labyrinth," Hanz chuckled, "Nothing is going to take the power away from Humans again, I can assure you of that. But Arelle has some sort of mystical power over the Raqian soil, we all know this."

Labyrinth nodded, blowing smoke through his nostrils. "It's a problem."

"It sits there, empty," Hanz said.

"Just waiting for someone to take it," Labyrinth muttered, then he turned to Hanz with a scowl. "You're not suggesting that Humans could take Arelle? Aren't only *Faeries* allowed in there?"

Hanz laughed openly. "It amuses me how little most Humans actually know about the Fae."

"Most Humans are not like you, Hanz," Labyrinth said sharply. "The Faeries have kept away from Humanity for as long as I can remember. They stayed away from us for the most part, and we stayed away from them. It wasn't until Somenus started trying to lord his power over us that we began to *see* Faeries wandering around our kingdoms. But you? You were one of them. You were a *Faerie friend.*"

"Yes," Hanz turned away from Labyrinth to watch as Valley passed under the Warrowing Gate. What was she doing here? She seemed to be everywhere today. What a busy little bee she was.

"Sire?" Labyrinth sniffed, "Did you hear what I said?"

Hanz turned back to face the other King. "What?" He frowned.

Labyrinth chuckled to himself. "Yes, that one does seem to draw the eye, doesn't she?"

 CASTLING

Hanz coughed into his hand. "Sorry. I missed the last thing you said."

"I said, if you know so much about the Fae, then tell me if Humans are allowed in Arelle."

"Ah," Hanz smiled knowingly, "Well, to answer your question, yes. Yes, Humans can enter Arelle—if the gates are open."

"How hard would it be to take the city?" Labyrinth spoke so plainly and casually about war. There was something comforting about that.

"That depends on two questions," Hanz said slowly.

"On?"

"Well, firstly, it depends on whether we are let inside."

"I thought you said it was empty," Labyrinth pulled his tab to his lips.

"It is mostly empty, but it is guarded by a few loyal Fae, those waiting for the king to return."

"Well, that poses a problem," Labyrinth said with a mouth full of smoke.

"And the second question is how other nations would respond," Hanz said, hoping he wasn't revealing his cards too soon.

"Ah!" Labyrinth laughed, "I see. You don't want a war. You don't want us all fighting for the most strategic piece of land on all Raqia."

"It could tear us apart," Hanz said firmly, "If we do this together, we could all have a delegate there. We could all control Arelle."

"Diplomatic," Labyrinth shrugged, "But I can't help but feel we still have a *problem*. An obstacle—and I think you know what I mean."

"An obstacle that lies between us and Arelle?" Hanz asked, sighing. "Yes, Bavel."

"That ancient kingdom has coveted Arelle long before our Kingdoms even existed," Labyrinth said. "If we try to take it, I fear there will be a *real* war on our hands. What's your plan for *that*, old boy?" He chuckled.

"Yes..." Hanz said thoughtfully, "Well, we don't know what is happening in there, do we? No one comes in or out, all trade has stopped—for all we know they are experiencing the same starvation as the rest of us, or perhaps worse! They don't have farmlands."

"They've got those hanging gardens, don't they? They don't need farmlands."

"But famine is famine," said Hanz, "If it's happening here, it's happening in there, too."

"True," said the blonde-haired king, "I had not thought of that. Well," he shrugged, "if you plan on pitching this to the others, I would like to see some solid answers to these questions. I can guarantee that none of us—not even *I*—would want to go to war with the Black Eagles."

Hanz hid his disappointment from his face. "Makes sense," he said, "And fear not. I do have a plan. Just... keep this between us for now."

"Whatever you say," he chuckled. "Say, mind if I shop a little?" He gestured his cigar toward the Warrowing Village.

Hanz snorted. "Not sure if you could afford another."

"Well," Labyrinth nudged Hanz with his elbow playfully. "It seems to me you want to be making supportive friends right now, hmm? Think about it. I'm going shopping." Labyrinth took a few steps forward, then turned to add, "Oh, have you thought about my offer?"

"Which?" Hanz crossed his arms.

"You know, your firebrand daughter?"

Hanz snorted. "Ah—yes. Well..." he grinned inwardly. It felt good to let the matter hang over King Labyrinth's head. "As I said, I am still thinking about it. Yours wasn't the only offer."

"Well," Labyrinth shook his head to himself. "I can't say I am surprised."

"Yes, she's..." Hanz held out the 's' sound for a moment. "She's something."

"Hah," Labyrinth threw his half-finished cigar onto a flagstone and crushed it with his boot. "Hades, I didn't expect to get caught up in all that," he laughed, "I've got plenty of wives back home. But damn—she's got me interested. Well done, you ass."

The two kings shared amused smiles.

Labyrinth, King of the Gramenlands, marched off into the Warrowing Village. Hanz watched with delight. Well, perhaps he couldn't get him to go to war with Bavel, but he did manage to hook him on *two* fronts. The man liked Hanz's Faeries, and he sure as Hades seemed to like his felling daughter.

This was a win.

21

—— Rook ——

The Dormant King

"A SAILOR," SAID TERCIUS. THERE WAS A CLINK on the table as he threw out a silver chip.

"A beautiful whore," said Titus, also casting a coin onto the splintery wooden table. A few amused noises resounded from the gathered crowd of soldiers around them.

"A blind man," Rook flicked a silver coin onto the table. The large barracks lounge erupted into laughter.

"A well," said Scully, one of the Mensa soldiers, as he tossed out his own chip. Another burst of laughter filled the room.

As each player spoke, they flicked another coin into the pile. The pile of coins at the center of the table was growing and so too was the onlooking crowd. Rook always got a kick out of besting. It was a game that was popular amongst soldiers, as it involved banter, humor, and winning stacks of coins. There was no real skill involved, but it tended to keep spirits light. There was really only one rule to the game: convince the crowd your answer bests the last one spoken.

"A mason," said Tercius.

"A forest," said Titus.

"How does a forest best a mason?" A soldier asked from the sidelines. Rook recognized him as Jenk, one of the Gramenlands soldiers he met on the road to Mensa.

"Well, there's no rocks in forests," Titus said, "so how is he supposed to get work?"

The cluster of onlookers broke into a mix of mocking and cackling.

"What's the consensus?" Tercius asked the onlookers. "Is he in or out?"

"Out!" cried one of the soldiers. "Have you ever *been* in a forest? There's rocks everywhere!"

"You're out," Tercius said to Titus.

"Fine," Titus laughed, stepping off his chair. The only players remaining at the central table were Tercius, Rook, and Scully.

"Only three players left!" Jenk shouted. "There's at least twenty chips in the pile now. A worthy haul for any soldier!" This gathered a few more onlookers.

"Alright, Rook," Tercius turned to Rook, "What bests a mason?"

Rook thought for a moment, then said, "a famine."

"Oooh," said Jenk as he riled up the crowd with his contagious energy. "That flies!"

Scully thought to himself, then tossed out his coin, "A Faerie King."

There was an eerie silence. "Well," Jenk said, "some do say that the Faerie King can bless the land, near or far. Does it fly, boys?"

"It flies," said an older, gruffer soldier beside Jenk. The crowd agreed, then all eyes shifted to Tercius, the next player. Rook shifted uncomfortably in his seat.

"King Hanz," said Tercius, grinning. The surrounding crowd cheered. Rook looked around the room in surprise. He suddenly didn't feel like playing anymore but kept his nerve.

"Why King Hanz?" Rook asked flatly.

"King Hanz killed the Nightmare Faerie! Who *doesn't* know that?" said a young, passionate soldier from the crowd. Rook did his best not to laugh at the absurdity.

"Alright," Rook sighed, slamming a coin onto the table, "a son."

"A son?" Scully snorted. "How does *a son* best King Hanz?"

"Every king must eventually pass on all he has to his son. Every king must watch his glory fade," Rook said. "You can agree with me or not." The crowd looked around at each other, and some nodded.

"A bit deep for us," said Jenk, "but it can pass." The gathered soldiers mumbled in agreement.

"Fine," said Scully, tossing his coin onto the table, "a sister."

"A sister?" Tercius chuckled. "I don't see it."

"A son is bested by his sister?" Rook asked Scully, cracking a smile.

"Well, my sister could convince me to walk off a cliff if she so wished!" Scully said with a sobering face. "If any of you has a sister, I think you know what I mean."

"It flies," cried the young soldier. The crowd agreed with nods.

"Alright," Rook said, straightening his back, "a mother."

There was a quiet that came over those gathered, then some chuckled.

"Aye," said Jenk. "That flies."

Tercius leaned back in his chair, shaking his head. "Not sure I *want* to best mothers," he said, then twisted the sides of his mouth into a grin, "but I will!" He tossed his chip into the pile, "Death!"

"*Death*?" An onlooking soldier snorted, "You can't just say *death* all the time, Tercius!"

"Why not?" Tercius frowned. "Death kills mothers," he slammed his fist on the table. "Can't be a mother if you're dead!"

The crowd booed loudly, and Rook began to chuckle, shaking his head. "You're out of here!" He laughed.

"Fine," Tercius stood and left the table, stretching his back slowly. He moved to stand behind Rook, who remained sitting there with Scully, the dark-skinned Mensa sentry guard.

"I am trying to think of what would best mothers," Scully thought to himself. "I suppose loss. Yes!" He threw his chip, "A mother cannot fathom the loss of her children."

The crowd murmured in deliberation, then Jenk popped his head out of the whispering cluster, "it passes!"

Rook's heart pounded with pain. Loss—a mother cannot fathom the loss of a child. Loss? He looked at Scully across the table. The young Mensa soldier was eyeing the stack of coins. Rook had no real desire to earn that pile, and he certainly felt no more pleasure playing this game. This kid, though—*he* wanted it, and he could have it. What bests loss? He sure didn't know.

Rook cleared his throat loudly and leaned forward, sliding his coin across the table with his index finger. "A beer."

"A beer?" Scully scrunched up his nose. "Is a beer really strong enough to make up for loss? Or is it a momentary distraction?" He shook his head.

"Well," Rook shrugged, "it's all I've got."

The crowd booed loudly, and Rook belted out a hearty laugh. "Fine!" Rook swatted his hand at them. "You win, you win."

There was a burst of manly cheering and Scully gleefully wrapped his hands around the stack of money.

Just then, the Ascending bell rang. All of the ruckus calmed for a moment as just about every person in the room besides Rook pulled out his clicker to reset it.

"You all use those?" Rook asked Scully, who was shoving his little time piece into his pocket.

"We're soldiers. We have to," he said. "Our orders rely on clicks."

"You don't use one?" Tercius' boot hit the chair beside Rook.

Rook gazed up at him. Tercius was smirking.

"No," said Rook, "I guess I just let a bell be as long as it wants to be."

"Well, so do we," Tercius responded, "but we just keep track of it anyway. Keeps us synchronized."

"And we like to make bets on how long the hour is going to be," Scully leaned over the table to whisper. "It helps make the longer ones not feel so long."

"Yes," said Jenk, who stood nearby, listening, "Imagine being on sentry for two bells. They might be short bells, making your shift short, or they might be long bells, making it feel like eternity. So, we make bets on how many clicks it's going to be. Makes you not feel crazy, you know?"

"Yeah," Rook stood, "I could see that." He peered around for the exit. He found a certain sort of comfort hanging out with Humans, imagining himself to be one of them. But his round ears made him no more one of them than if a bird, wishing to become a fish, plucked off its own feathers.

He was growing restless.

"Well, I'll head out." Rook mumbled. A few soldiers waved to him as he meandered over to the door. Tercius joined him at his side.

"You out of sorts today, Rook?" asked Tercius.

Rook lazily gazed at the man. Out of sorts? He was shaken to his very core, walking around with a stabbing pain in his heart—so, sure, he was 'out of sorts'. "I'm not feeling myself," Rook said.

"Do you... want to talk about it?" asked the mature soldier.

"Not to you, sorry," Rook said.

"Well," Tercius looked down at his boots, "You looking for something to do to distract you, then?"

Rook brightened a little. "Yeah... Any ideas?"

"Well, Golden Grains is in the stables just south of the barracks here. He's restless being cooped up with the other oxen. He doesn't really take well to anyone except Cato. I was thinking maybe you could give him a try?"

Rook chuckled. "Yeah, alright."

"Thanks, son," Tercius raised his chin to look up at the Sky as the two of them exited the barracks.

"You guys doing alright out here? In the barracks?" asked Rook.

"Oh, it's fine," Tercius searched his pockets for his half-finished cigar. "Do you smell that?"

"Smell what?"

"A change in the air." Tercius lit his stick. "Damn. I'll never get used to the elevation here."

Rook shoved his hands in his pockets. "Yeah, I suppose Mensa Castle is pretty high up. You're from the coast, aren't you?"

Tercius looked at Rook from the side, giving his cigar a deep pull. He exhaled, "...Yeah."

"Well," Rook turned his gaze southward, "Any tips on befriending the legendary beast?"

"Nope," Tercius pulled his cigar from his lips and squinted. "Don't expect to be able to speak with him or anything. Just see if he will take any food."

"Alright," Rook gave Tercius a slap on the shoulder, then sauntered off toward the stables.

Mensa Castle kept decent stables, with wide, luxurious stalls for the oxen, but that meant nothing for a beast as large as an aurochs. When Rook entered the end stall where Golden Grains was being kept, he cringed. There was barely enough room for the creature to stand, and his sides brushed against the edges. There were scrapes along the stable walls where the aurochs' angular horns were resting. There were two stable boys standing just outside the stall, nervously watching Rook from behind.

"Does he get roaming time?" Rook asked.

"Well," one of the stable hands scratched his hair nervously. "Most beasts get some roaming time in the pasture every day, but so far, he hasn't wanted to move. And he... well..." he glanced at the other stable boy, "He gets angry when we try to lead him anywhere. We uh..."

"That's fine," Rook cut him off. "I'll see if I can't get him to come out. Is the pasture empty?"

"We can make it so," said the stable hand. He looked to his coworker, then the two left together.

Rook turned his attention back to the magnificent animal. It was a sad thing to see such a regal creature trapped in such a small area. It was cruelly familiar. Rook braved the journey to the front of the stall, squeezing past Golden Grain's side. The aurochs didn't so much as twitch as Rook ran his hand along the beast's hair.

The other end of the stall, where the animal's gigantic head was gazing around, lent a view of the pasture and Rook could see the stable hands leading away the roaming oxen. Golden Grains was watching the pasture with a bored expression. He didn't turn his head to look at Rook, but his eye did shift its focus down toward him.

"Hallo, friend," said Rook. "Fancy a wander?"

Hallo, the aurochs said.

"Come on, a canter will do you some good. Get those legs moving."

You have finally decided to come talk to me, said Golden Grains.

"*Finally*?" Rook smiled, "Were you expecting me to come talk to you?"

I was hoping, said the beast, *I could hardly believe my eyes when I saw you.*

"Saw me?" Rook's smile faded. "You... you know me?"

A king knows a king, said the aurochs. Rook watched with awe as the large, bull-like beast lowered his head to stare Rook in the face.

"You're a king?" Rook asked, reaching out his hand to touch the bull's nose.

Golden Grains closed his eyes, as if comforted by Rook's touch. *My kind are the Kings of the Land. You know this.*

"Yes," Rook said softly, "Aurochs: King of the Land; Leviathan: King of the Sea..."

I am not the great Aurochs himself, though I am his kin. But I need not be a king to know you. All creatures know you, Sire. You are the lord of us all.

"Please," Rook shook his head, "Stop. I am no one's king."

I do not know what you mean, said Golden Grains.

Rook sighed. "If you say I am your lord, will you come out for a walk?"

I would do whatever you asked, said the beast.

Rook opened the gate to Golden Grain's stall and led him out into the pasture. The beast dwarfed the little field; it took him only a few paces to wander from one end to the other. But he followed Rook anyway.

"Do you miss your friend? The, uh... the aurochs that died?" Rook asked as they walked.

The sadness is still too near for me to speak of it, sire, he said. *I am filled with sorrow.*

"Is that why you're hiding away in your stable? Sorrow?" Rook peered up at his companion sympathetically.

I find it too hard to be out in the light where others can see me. I feel they are looking at my sadness, but they cannot see it. The pain is too great. To be seen, and yet not seen.

"Yeah..." Rook pulled his lower lip into his mouth. "I think I know what you mean."

Why are you sad, my lord?

"I... I don't know if I can speak about it either, friend," Rook said slowly, "I—I suppose I am sad because I have gotten used to my sadness not being seen. But then... yesterday... someone saw it—exposed it—and now I feel like I can't seem to hide from it anymore. I feel the sadness every click of every bell."

The beast stopped in his tracks and gazed up at the heavens. *I am sorry,* he said, *I do not want this for my lord. What can I do?*

Rook found himself smiling at the beast's compassion. "I don't need anything done for me," he said, "At least, I have no idea what I wish someone would do for me. I suppose I appreciate the listening ears."

Golden Grains was silent for a while, keeping his eyes on the heavens. After a time, he lowered his head to the ground and made a deep groaning sound as he laid down in the grass. His body nearly took up the entire grazing pasture as he stretched out his legs. It gave Rook a swell of joy to see the beast attempting some kind of rest. He walked up to the animal's belly and rubbed it.

Sire? Golden Grains finally asked.

"Yes?" Rook leaned against his stomach and peered over toward his shut eye.

Why do none of these Humans know who you are?

"It is complicated," Rook said, cringing at his cliched response. "I mean... I don't know how to answer you."

Rest with me.

Rook grew still. It was such a simple, humble command, from one king to another. He wondered if the beast was the only other creature on the Table who understood him at that moment, and so he complied. Rook found a soft, comfortable spot in the grass, just beneath Golden Grain's chin, and closed his eyes.

— · ——— • ——— · —

"Product of rape, spawn of a tyrant," said her cold, stinging voice. "Product of rape, spawn of a tyrant."

"Please!" Anodos wrung his bound hands. If only he could cover his ears, but that voice—that voice would never stop. All he could see from that cold, stone table was the cracked ceiling above him. Who knew a single crack could become so familiar—so constant. He knew that crack better than he knew his own face. His face? He didn't even know what that looked like anymore. There was only one face now: *her* face.

"Product of rape," said the voice as she stepped into view. Her piercing eyes looked down at him with hatred. She held a knife. It was the short, square cleaver this time. He dreaded this knife. She brandished it against a sharpening stone and hissed, "Spawn of a tyrant."

"Please, stop," begged Anodos. He was no longer above pleading; he was dangling over the edge of his sanity. "Please, hear me. Have mercy. Please stop this madness."

She held the glistening knife above her head with both hands clenched tightly together. She gritted her teeth, then said for the hundredth time, "*Die!*"

— · ——— • ——— · —

"Wake up!" Rook woke suddenly to a swift boot kick to the chest.

"Mercy—*please!*" Rook gasped, clutching his chest in agony, remembering the cracking of his sternum as she pried it open.

"Rook!" Tercius barked. "You're dreaming again!"

Rook groped the grass beneath him frantically, searching wildly for blood. Then his vision began to clear as he felt the Lightsday breeze across his face. He shot his eyes upwards, finding Tercius' face.

"*Again?*" Rook croaked. His voice was hoarse.

"You should probably keep to sleeping indoors. The screaming upsets the animals." Tercius said in a casual voice. A veteran soldier like himself wouldn't be surprised by nightmares, it seemed.

It did not bother me, Golden Grains said from where he lay. Tercius did not hear him.

Rook rose to his feet. "Sorry," he mumbled as he straightened his coat. "I didn't realize I..." he glanced awkwardly at Tercius. "Has this happened before?"

Tercius snorted. "No, never." That was sarcasm. "Good on you for getting the old Grains out for a wander. He looks happier to me."

Rook examined the beast still laying in the grass. "I think he's sad about losing the other beast."

Tercius nodded. "That's our guess, too."

"Well, I have somewhere to be," Rook said, moving away from Tercius. Really, he just wanted to escape the discomfort of being observed after one of his dreams.

"Alright, *Sir* Rook." Tercius crossed his arms. "I'll see that Grains gets back into his stall. You can go."

"You heard him?" Rook said to the beast, leaning over to gaze at one of the monstrous, skull-sized eyes. "I want you to go back to the stall when he says so."

The beast groaned in response.

Tercius chuckled. "Alright, off with you, you big clown."

Rook left the pasture quickly, with his coat tails flowing behind him in the wind. Tercius was right about one thing, the air *did* smell different today. It was almost as if the Sky were nervous.

Rook wandered the Mensa Castle grounds aimlessly until he heard the Descending Bell ring. By then, he found himself standing outside the Warrowing Gate. It was like a giant magnet, pulling him ever closer. He wanted to resist, but he also wanted to go in. He had sought out the soldiers earlier, hoping to find comfort in their familiarity, but it had only worsened the alienation.

Here was the little village of Faeries—his own people, though none knew it.

"Sir Rook, Sir Rook!" cried a young voice. Rook couldn't help but grin as young Coppo came running toward him from the village, holding his hat against his head. He had long, lanky legs, and a cracking voice. He was right in that transitional stage they called the age of Questioning, still a child, and yet also a man. Coppo came crashing up to Rook's feet, panting excitedly. "I've been on the lookout for you for two bells!" He gestured behind himself with his thumb, "The Packrats been taking shifts. I started two bells ago, Theo before me, and Michael before him. And I—"

"Alright, slow down," Rook laughed, grasping Coppo's shoulder, "Take a breath."

"Come inside! We've been waiting all day!" Coppo broke away from Rook's hand and went running back into the Village. "Hurry!"

Rook shook his head, then jogged after the young Faerie.

Expecting to be led back to the Packrat Particle's hideout, Rook hesitated awkwardly as Coppo tried to lead him inside one of the houses. It was Marbel's house.

"Coppo," Rook pulled up his cravat over his neck scars, feeling suddenly aware of his own presence. "I can't just enter other people's houses without..."

"Get in here, boy!" Marbel's voice called from within. Little golden-haired Theo popped his head out the door.

"Sir Rook!" he beamed. Thundering footsteps pounded through the house, and then Michael popped his head through the door, just above Theo's.

"Sir Rook!" Michael exclaimed, "Miss Marbel wants to see you."

"I..." Rook didn't have the chance to refuse. The boys pulled him through the door and, moments later, he found himself inside the small, narrow Faerie abode.

It was pretty empty for a home—no doubt because the Fae in the Warrowing Village were not allowed possessions—but it still had a safe feel about it. Marbel's motherly touch seemed to fill the place.

She was sitting on a low stool beside a dingy fire, peeling potatoes. Her eyes were locked suspiciously on Rook as he shuffled toward her with Coppo pushing against his back.

"Hallo..." he smiled nervously. Why did he feel like he was about to be scolded?

"Sit," Marbel pointed to a dusty carpet on the ground. The other three boys rushed to the carpet and sat reverently. Rook joined them, leaning his back against the wall. Were these Faeries not even allowed *chairs* in their homes?

"Now," she resumed her peeling, and rocked herself back and forth on her stool, regardless of the fact that it wasn't a rocking chair, "The lads tell me you're passing out shiny objects."

Rook shot Coppo a look, then said, "I don't know what you're talking about."

"See here," Marbel looked up to point her calloused finger at him, "I'm a Packrat, too! So I know the secrets!"

"Ah," Rook nodded. "Sorry, I didn't realize."

Marbel chuckled, then grew stern again. "These boys could get in real trouble for carrying possessions. What are you passing them out for?"

"I *told* you, mother!" Theo piped, "He's special."

"He's a prophet," Coppo said, "He gave us all titles."

"So I heard..." she said slowly. Then she sighed, dropping her bare potato into a basket. "Alright, why don't you boys fetch the girl."

Before she could even finish her sentence, the three Packrats raced from the house excitedly, whispering frantically to one another as they went.

Marbel rose from her chair, then lumbered over to where Rook sat. She knelt down on one knee and met eyes with him.

"Sir Rook?"

"Uh... yeah?"

"Those boys have been storing magik in their trinkets you gave them. Did you know this?" She watched Rook's face for honesty.

"I..." Rook hesitated, "Yeah."

"Do you know the punishment for taking up imperiums?" Her face hardened.

"I—"

"—I know you're trying to help the lads and be kind, but already they be storing heaps of magik in those things. I'm worried..." she huffed.

"Marbel," Rook said, holding up his hand defensively, "What is wrong with a Faerie storing magik?"

Marbel closed her eyes, breathing deeply as if trying to calm herself. She opened them again, staring straight into Rook's eyes. "Answer me this, *Sir Rook*. What's my title?"

"Faerie of Hunger," he answered quickly, without thinking.

Marbel leaned back slowly. Rook couldn't read her face.

The three boys came parading back into the house, pulling a young girl by the hands.

"Here she is, miss Marbel!" Michael announced, pushing the little red-haired girl closer.

Marbel rose and walked over to the young girl. The girl couldn't have been more than six seasons old. Marbel took her by the hands and spoke softly to her.

"Hallo, Rois, how do you feel, darling?" she asked. The girl Rois blinked, turning her head to the side. Marbel turned her head toward Rook. "She doesn't talk to any of us, but she talks to herself sometimes."

"Why have you brought her here?" Rook asked, rising to his feet.

"We thought you could tell us who she is," Coppo said in a quiet voice.

Rook knelt before the little girl and met her gaze. He knew instantly who she was—her title at least. "Hallo, Rois," Rook said. He sighed, then looked to Marbel. "Where are her parents?"

"Her mother died at the birth," said Marbel, "And her father... well," She cleared her throat and glanced at the boys, implying that she didn't feel it proper to explain the girl's parentage in front of them.

"Karo is her father," Coppo said brightly, assuming he was being helpful. "He's father to lots of the—"

"She grows weaker day by day," said Marbel, interrupting Coppo. "We know we not allowed titles in Mensa but, if we can't know where she gets magik, she'll die like her mother did. We just want to help her. Can you tell us who she is?"

"She's a lightwing," Theo said, tugging against Rook's sleeve. "Does that help?"

Rook smiled encouragingly. "Sure, Theo. Yeah, it does." He rotated to face Rois. "Rois? I am Rook," he held out his hand, palm up.

Rois examined his hand, then placed hers on top of it. She smiled.

"Her wings are growing!" Theo exclaimed, jumping up and down and shaking Rook by the sleeve. "They're—!"

"Theo," Rook whispered, "Quiet. Please."

"What do you mean growing?" Marbel pointed at the little girl, whose ashy skin was brightening with color. "What do you see, Theo?"

Rois burst into laughter, then climbed up onto Rook's knee. Rook recoiled for a moment at her touch, then received her into his arms. He held her close to her chest. For a moment, he felt no pain. Rook rose to his feet, still clutching the little girl in his arms, and turned to face Marbel.

"He's so tall!" Rois exclaimed, looking down at the floor.

Those around looked with surprise at the sound of Rois' clear voice.

Rook hoisted Rois upon his hip. "Alright, Packrats, give me and Miss Marbel a moment. Go run along and keep watch for suspicious characters."

The lads made whiny noises, knowing they would be missing out on an important conversation, but they did as he asked and left the house.

"Can she read?" Rook asked Marbel in a hushed tone.

Marbel crossed her arms, eyeing Rook carefully. "No. Most of the children aren't taught to read."

"She's the Faerie of Literacy," Rook said as the girl rested her head against his shoulder. "She's very special, and she needs to learn to read. The common hand will do."

Marbel gaped. "By the floods! No wonder she can't get any magik!"

"Yes, she needs words. Start small," he said, "yes and no. Write them down. And until she can read, recite verse to her—things to memorize. Lots of words."

Marbel nodded soberly. "Thank you, son," she said, "You've saved a life today."

The stinging pain returned to Rook's chest. The weight was almost too much to bear. Rook's face darkened. "Marbel," he said, "This is no place to raise Faerie children. They need to be—"

"You seem to know a lot about Faerie children," Marbel cut in, shifting her weight to one leg.

Rook held his breath. "Mmhmm..." The room grew eerily still.

"I know who you are," she said.

"Mmhmm..."

Marbel stepped so close that Rook could feel the warm air blowing from her nostrils onto his face. "Ye going to make me say it out loud?"

"Please don't..."

"Anodos?"

"I—"

"I saw you power up Rois like an imperium. And my boy Theo can see your four wings. Two light, two dark, he says."

Rook sighed.

"My boy doesn't lie. I know you're the King."

"I'm not!" Rook hissed in a harsh whisper. "I was never crowned!" He glanced at the girl in his arms nervously.

Marbel took a step back, drawing her chin high into the air. "You're the son of King Somenus. You're the lost King."

"Quiet—please," said Rook, "*Please*—stop saying that!"

Marbel could clearly see the terror in his face. Her countenance softened. "What's been done to you, boy?" She reached toward him, moved aside his dangling black curls, and ran her finger along the edge of his ridged, misshapen ear. "You poor boy..."

"Please," Rook's lip quivered. "Please, stop."

Marbel nodded sadly. "I will not speak of it if you do not want me to."

Rook placed Rois on the ground and tapped her back. Rois reluctantly left his side and dashed from the house.

"I know it is dangerous to power up the lads," Rook said, changing the subject, "But I will protect them. If anyone finds out about their imperiums, come tell me. I will scapegoat for them. I will not let anyone hurt them."

Marbel's eyes widened. "But—"

"Just," Rook held up his finger, "—*tell* me if anyone finds out."

Marbel pulled the corner of her mouth to the side, then huffed. "Fine."

Rook could hear another ruckus of voices approaching the house.

"Just this way, it's Sir Rook! The knight I was telling you about!" Coppo's voice echoed from the streets.

Rook bit his lower lip and shot a glance at Marbel. "You had better tell those boys to stop telling people about me... or they really *will* get into trouble. And so will I!"

"*You* started all this!" Marbel laughed, then plodded over to her stool.

Coppo, Michael and Theo came triumphantly back into the house, dragging yet *another* Faerie girl with them. Well, this one was less a girl and more a woman—though only just. She walked reluctantly up to Rook, Coppo pushing against her back. She studied him skeptically with her sharp eyes.

"This is him, Valley!" Coppo pointed. "He's the prophet. He knows Faerie titles."

"Oh, *does* he?" The woman, Valley, crossed her arms. "A *Human*?"

Rook stumbled backwards, clutching at his chest. He crashed into Marbel on her little stool, nearly knocking her into the fire.

"Steady on, Rook!" Marbel screamed, catching him against her pillowy body.

"I'm sorry, I'm sorry!" Rook gasped, scrambling to his feet. He rose shakily, still clutching his coat fearfully, and turned to face the horror. Valley was majestically beautiful, and utterly terrifying, all at the same time.

Valley's face changed from skeptical to fierce. "Shut the door, Coppo," she said sternly. Coppo quickly obeyed, bolting it for good measure.

"What's going on?" Coppo asked, rushing to Rook's side. "You alright, Sir Knight?"

"Who am I?" Valley charged up to Rook, arms swinging at her sides. She grabbed Rook by the shoulders of his coat and shook him, though she was several heads shorter than he and couldn't budge him an inch.

Rook stared down at the short Faerie, frozen in shock. "I—I... What do you mean? How should *I* know who you are?"

"But you know *all* the Faerie titles, Rook!" Theo ran to Rook's side and yanked on his black coat tails.

"I don't know hers," Rook said, his voice cracking.

　　　　　　　　　　　　　　　　　　　　　　　　　　

"Please!" Valley begged, gripping his clothes helplessly, "You *have* to tell me! *No one* will tell me! Please! Please—for the Lights' sake—don't *lie* to me!"

Rook took Valley's hands in his and pried them off his coat. He lowered them slowly, keeping a steady eye-contact. He knew who she was, and not just because he had met her many seasons ago. But... how had she *survived*?

"Fine," Rook said quietly, "I will tell you your title, *Valley*." Apparently, she didn't know her true name.

She closed her eyes tightly. "Alright," she said, "I am ready."

Rook inhaled deeply, then exhaled. "There are many names for you, but only one real title," he said, "You are the III Faerie of Affection—the Faerie of Fear; the Faerie of Dreams. You, *Valley*, are the one they call the Nightmare Faerie."

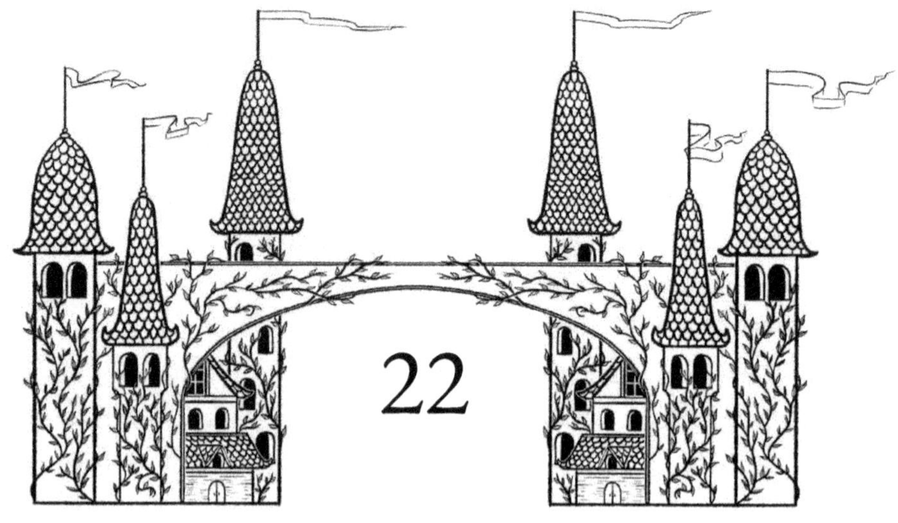

22

—— Rasselas ——

A Game of Cards

THE FIRSTDARK BELL WAS RINGING. The games were starting, but Rasselas couldn't pull himself away from his work. He flipped tirelessly through his handwritten notebook. He turned for the twentieth time to his section on vacant Faerie titles—at least the ones he was sure he hadn't identified yet. So many... there were so many who died during Somenus' reign! Valley could fit any number of these titles.

"But she has a draw," he mumbled to himself, running his finger down the line of titles written on the page. "An allure of some kind. I..." he sighed, leaning back in his chair, "Unless I just..." he thought about Valley's face. She was pretty, yes, but there was more. There was something about her entire being that made him want to study her; love her; *worship* her. He blinked. "This can't just be a crush," he said to himself. "There is a greater power at work."

He looked down at his list again, sighing. "The Faerie of Charisma? There hasn't been one since Sol's fourth son was killed. *Hmmm...*" The Faerie of Charisma drew the respect and admiration of all. It would be a new thing if a female held that title. No one could anticipate exactly what that would look like. But there was something more, something obsessive. Something intoxicating.

"*Intoxicating?*" He laughed at himself, "I sound like an adolescent girl!"

There was a knock on Rasselas' door.

"Come in!" he called, as he carefully closed his notebook.

Rasselas was surprised to see Latimer enter the room, strolling in nonchalantly with his hands behind his back.

"Hallo," he said, smiling.

"Why, Latimer!" Rasselas stood. "What brings you to my quarters at this bell? Have you... something—*erm*—*technical* to talk about?"

"Technical?" Latimer grimaced, "Surely you don't see me as some sort of *How*, do you, Prince Moonvine?"

"Well, whatever it is you do," Rasselas twirled his hand in the air. He was well aware that the Fellowship of Skydeacons was *nothing* like the 'Hows'. The Hows were observers whose pursuit was to find out '*how*' things work. But the skydeacons? They cared about the '*why*' behind things. The skydeacons were closer to Lights priests than they were to anything else.

"Actually," Latimer placed his hand over his heart, "I am here at the request of a friend."

"How virtuous of you!" Rasselas pulled at his sleeve cuffs, straightening what was already straight. "And which friend might that be?"

"Sir Thorne," Latimer said.

"Ah..." Rasselas refrained from making a jab at his wing's expense. "What was his request?"

"He told me he is not feeling up to cards tonight. There tends to be a lot of smoking in the games rooms, and he finds that it gives him a headache."

"Aw," Rasselas feigned compassion.

"Anyway, he's asked if I would attend in his stead!" Latimer seemed excited by the idea.

"Well, I don't exactly need a wing for a card game..." Rasselas began to say, then paused as Latimer's face began to fall. "But slay me, I think it would be dashed entertaining to watch a skydeacon playing cards! Do join me, old chap!"

"Ah!" Latimer brightened. "Great! Is there... anything I am supposed to wear, or..."

Rasselas snickered. "Calm down, old boy, it's just cards. Wear something that you don't mind getting a bit of ash on."

Latimer looked down at his gray robe. "Is this alright?"

"Come on," Rasselas strode toward the door. "Let's go."

They entered the hall, then found the path to the grand staircase.

"They've got a gamesroom on the fourth-level roof hall," Rasselas said, pointing up the stairs.

"Oh!" Latimer felt in his pockets for his hand-held notepad, "I do like the idea of seeing the Skies from the roof!"

"Give the Skies a break today, old boy," Rasselas smirked, "You're going to need to be all about cards, smoking, and drinks tonight."

"Ah..." Latimer sobered, "I'll try."

They began ascending the stairs.

"Erm, Latimer?" Rasselas said, "...you known Thorne long?"

"Oh, of course," the Elven skydeacon nodded, "hundreds of seasons, now."

"He doesn't like me," Rasselas said.

"Oh... sorry to hear that." He didn't sound too surprised.

"No," Rasselas cleared his throat, "What I should say is, he quite *hates* me."

Latimer remained silent, climbing the stairs thoughtfully.

"Latimer," Rasselas lowered his voice, "Do you have any idea why that might be? Hades, he hates me for *existing*!"

"I confess," Latimer whispered, "I am not surprised... at least... I wouldn't have expected him to be angry for this long. He must have..." his voice trailed off. "I should not speak of this. I don't think he would want me to..."

"Come on!" Rasselas turned, grasping Latimer by the forearm and staring him in the face. "There's got to be *something* you can tell me!"

Latimer hesitated fearfully, then slumped. "I think I can tell you this... he was betrothed to... *erm...*"

"No," Rasselas squinted in disgust, "Not *mother*!"

"It wasn't fully official," Latimer said delicately as he resumed his stair climbing. "But he was pretty keen on the arrangement. You can imagine, then..."

"He was in love with my *mother*?" Rasselas felt like gagging.

"*Was*?" Latimer cringed, "If he hates you this much... I daresay..."

"Oh Hades," Rasselas cursed under his breath. "I don't want to think about this anymore. Let's change the subject."

"Well," Latimer said, "What are your thoughts on the princess? Everybody is talking about her. I am curious what the grandson of King Antecus thinks!"

Rasselas grinned, "Princess Rosamond," he said, shaking his head. "I didn't expect such a... a..." he searched for the right word.

"Beauty?" Latimer guessed.

"A goof." Rasselas said, raising his chin.

"A...?"

"I quite like her," said the prince, gazing up the stairs, "I like her juxtaposed with her father."

"I..." Latimer mumbled, "That's interesting." He was being polite; he really had no idea what Rasselas meant.

After they climbed to the fourth level of the stairs, passing by a mysteriously heavily guarded third level, they entered the spiraling staircase which led to the roof. Once on the roof, they walked through an open terrace. Other twirling stairs led to higher levels, and various overlooks, but the two headed directly toward the center building.

The gamesroom was a single, domed hall at the top of the Inner Palace. Inside, the ambiance was warm and quiet. Great fires lit three sides of the room, and an iron chandelier hung from the zenith of the dome. There were several green velvet-topped card tables scattered about the room, some bigger than the others. At the center of the room, directly under the chandelier, was the biggest table, seating as many as eight players. The room was filled with the scent of old tobacco, mixed with some sort of incense.

Rasselas grinned, eyeing the players who sat quietly around the table shuffling their decks. Cards. Finally! There was *nothing* better than cards. The prince looked for the ideal spot, sauntering around the table and holding the sides of his smoking jacket proudly. He knew he looked a picture, he just wanted others to notice as well. There were Tingo and Mynx, sitting together, showing each other their chosen decks. Beside Mynx sat Labyrinth, the short haired, square-faced King of the Gramenlands. Sitting across the table from them was Highlord Cato, and his shady wing, who seemed especially broody.

"Oh! Rook!" Latimer excitedly claimed the chair next to the buzzkill. "Rasselas, here!" He pulled out the chair beside his own. Rasselas didn't exactly like the idea of sitting near the comically opposite pair, nor did he want to dampen the skydeacon's innocent excitement.

"Calm down, thing," Rasselas chuckled, pulling his deck from his vest pocket, "It's cards, not a newseasons party." He sat, then began shuffling his deck. It was a special stack of cards, given to him by his father.

"Now, see there, Rook? Cato said, pointing at Latimer. "The Elf brought his wing. You're not the only tagalong."

"Latimer isn't a wing," Rook grumbled. "And I still don't see why you *need* me here."

"Hallo, Rook," Latimer leaned over to his friend, "Sorry if you've been dragged here, but I am mighty pleased to see you!"

Rook eyed Latimer from the side, then let out a little chuckle. "Hey, Latimer."

"Why anyone would be sulking about having to play cards, I could never understand!" Rasselas declared, loud enough for the entire table to hear. "Now, what's everyone drinking tonight?"

"Lord Cato brought an Edgelands bottle," Labyrinth said with a fat cigar sticking out of his mouth. He didn't look up from his cards. "It's not bad."

An observant servant took the cue and came to Rasselas and Latimer with the bottle. Latimer refused the drink, but Rasselas took it heartily.

"We will have the highest rank start the first game," Tingo said, glancing at Labyrinth. The King of the Gramenlands demonstrated a clean, organized shuffle of his deck, then began dealing five cards to each player. There was silence in the room as everyone began examining their hands.

Rasselas lit his own cigarette, a long, clean, skinny thing. He liked the aesthetic of smoking during cards, though he feared its effects on his teeth.

"So, who else made the king an offer?" Mynx asked, breaking the silence.

Labyrinth chucked. "Already showing your hand, Prince Mynx?"

"Everybody knows Tingo and I are under orders to get married. It is no secret," he said in a booming voice.

"Leave me out of it!" Tingo said, eyeing his friend from the side.

"But you told me you liked her! You offered—"

"Mynx," Tingo laughed, slamming his hand on the table. "Felling shut it!"

"Well she has a nice pair," Cato said in a disinterested tone. "If a man got married for a pair, I might have considered it."

Latimer blanched and glanced at Rasselas, wondering if he had heard right.

"And what *does* a man get married for, Cato?" Rook asked, still slumped in his chair. He held his cards up in front of his face like a protective fan.

Cato groaned, "Hades, I don't know."

"I can think of three reasons," Labyrinth said, tossing a single gold chip onto the table, "Pleasure, position, or money."

"Hades, man," Rasselas slid his ante across the table, "There's got to be a fourth."

"Oh, don't say it," Cato groaned. "Don't say romance."

"Heavens help me!" Rasselas sighed animatedly. "It's not my fault I am a bit of a romantic. I've got lovebirds for parents!"

Rook glanced up from his cards but remained silent.

"Oh dear," Latimer leaned in to whisper into Rasselas' ear, "Are we to put *money* on the table?"

"Just *play*, old square, I'll spot you later," Rasselas muttered.

"Well, I am happy to count love as a fourth reason," Tingo said, digging his hand into his coin purse. "But I don't think it's a good *primary* reason."

"All four are rubbish," Cato yawned. "Hades. You get one solid night of pleasure, followed by a lifetime of bickering and expenses."

"Children is a fifth," said Mynx, "You're all fools for not considering that!"

"Well, some of us already *have* children," Labyrinth said.

"And some of us don't," Mynx cleared his throat.

"It's all a big scam," Cato said, finishing his drink, "we dress women under layer after layer of protection to preserve the *only* commodity they've got to offer between those legs. All because once it's been compromised, they're useless. They're like pigs, fattened for several seasons, only to be enjoyed for one night's feasting. Why a man would willingly give away money, land or *anything* for a swine, I can't fathom."

There was a disturbing silence at the table. Rasselas glanced aside to see Latimer frozen in horror, with his mouth half open.

"I say," said Latimer, "I can hardly stand by and listen to someone insult an entire sex! I... I..." He looked around the room.

"Oh, pipe down," Cato groaned, "Rasselas, if you can't get your wing to go along with my mockery, you should ask him to leave."

"*You* pipe down," Rook snapped, dropping his cards into his lap with a scowl.

"What's gotten you in such a sour mood?" Cato turned to his wing amusedly, "You disagree? You think women have a greater asset than their—" he made a mocking face, "—*garden*?"

"Of course I do," Rook said, then tossed his ante onto the table

With all bets placed, Labyrinth threw out his first card, saying "Alright. Out with it."

Rook frowned. "Out with *what*?"

"You said women have got a greater asset to offer," Mynx said loudly, "What is it?"

Rook threw his card out onto the table. "A woman's treasure is her passion."

"Yes," Cato snorted. "That's what I mean by *garden*, you old coot."

"No," Rook responded calmly, "I mean—her passion. If a man has a woman's passion, he might as well have the entire world. But one can hardly possess passion, I think. It is a wonder too great to own or contain—it would be like trying to possess the Sea. It is only ever given."

"Well," Rasselas cranked his body to face Rook, "I think there *is* another romantic in the room after all!"

This brought laughter to the table.

"I don't see why a man can't have all five," Tingo said, playing his card, "When Princess Rosamond is in the picture."

Labyrinth chuckled, "Showing your cards indeed, boy."

"What about you?" Mynx said in his deep voice, "If Rosamond gave you one of the five, what would it be?"

Labyrinth turned up the corner of his mouth into a smirk, but he didn't reply.

"I think Princess Rosamond is a lovely girl!" Latimer said bravely, "And I hope if any of you *do* marry her, you will learn to speak better about her when she isn't present!" This brought more laughter to the table.

"Is he always like this?" Cato asked Rasselas, rubbing his head as if in pain.

"Well, if men can't share their true thoughts about a woman over cards, there's no reason to go on living!" said a surprisingly feminine voice. "That's what my father would say, anyway."

All watched silently as Princess Rosamond claimed an empty spot at the table between Cato and Labyrinth. Rasselas turned to behold the woman. Her dress looked far too big and regal for a cards table, but he had never *seen* a noblewoman at a cards table! She wore her luscious hair gathered to one side and cascading down the front of her left shoulder. Her caramel skin was lit warmly by the intimate lighting, and the golden rings around her irises glowed like stars in the night sky. She smiled proudly as she placed her own deck of cards on the table.

"Am I too late to ante?" she asked.

"Cards is typically a man's table," Labyrinth said as he observed her from the corner of his eye.

"And thank the heavens for that," Rosamond laughed, "Viola hates smoke and cards, so I am finally rid of her!"

Cato barked a laugh, then turned abruptly to look at the princess. "You surprise me, you little weasel!"

"Thank you, Lord Cato," Rosamond said, shuffling her cards. She observed the gaming table. "Ah, I see you've played your first hand. I'll wait."

"The woman plays cards?" Tingo leaned forward.

"Yes, she does. How shocking!" Rosamond exclaimed.

"We are playing trumps," Rasselas said, "Would you like to pick the next round? And somebody get this woman some vino!"

The men awkwardly continued their round. No one really knew how to act with a woman present, and yet there was a buzz of excitement in the air. The topic of their conversation sat among them, making them all question their idea of what exactly a woman was. Some stopped to watch Rosamond as she brought the glass of hard vino to her lips and finished it in one gulp.

Rasselas chuckled to himself when she asked for a second drink.

"That stuff is strong, girl," Cato said with a burp, "Your skinny frame is—"

"Oh pipe down, Cato!" Rosamond said, slamming her cup down on the table. She then leaned forward, watching the game. Rasselas could tell she was studying the players. She wasn't just a curious observer; this girl was a card counter.

"Your game," Labyrinth said to her as he folded up his deck.

"Well, if I propose five-draw, are you all going to hate me?" she asked, sliding her cards free of their sleeve. The backs of her cards were designed with gold patterns, woven into the shape of a horned bull.

"Whatever you prefer, my lady," Tingo said. He leaned back and watched with interest as she shuffled her cards with skill.

"Well, you don't all have to stop talking now that I am here," she paused, "Unless you really *were* talking about me!"

"We would never!" Cato giggled.

"It doesn't bother me," Rosamond grinned as she began to deal, "Plus, I have a feeling you will all like me a lot less after tonight."

"I am sure that's not true," Latimer came, uninvited, to her defense.

Rosamond ran her fingers along the edges of her fanned out cards, smirking. "Oh, come on. I am not naive enough to believe that a woman could go around drinking and gambling without dampening her prospects. I figure I might as well reveal myself to be artless now and save you all the trouble of discovering it later!"

Cato sniggered boyishly, stamping his feet on the ground alternatingly. "Oh, this is funny."

"Just so long as you're not smoking," Mynx pointed at her with his cigar, "It would be a shame to stain those perfect whites!"

"I wouldn't dream of it!" Rosamond said, pulling her cards to her chest defensively, feigning offense. "Though I must confess... I'd love to at least *try*."

Rasselas silently held out his cigarette to the princess. She brightened, meeting his eyes for a moment, then cackled villainously as she took it from his fingers.

"Are we going to get in trouble for contaminating the girl?" Mynx leaned back amusedly, watching her pull the stick to her lips.

"Look at her," Cato said, "She's *already* a card!"

Rosamond coughed violently after a single puff. The table erupted into laughter.

"Heavens above," Rosamond shook her head, returning the cigarette to Rasselas, "You boys can have that one."

Rasselas took it from her, brushing his finger against hers. He noted a flutter of her eyes as he did. *Hah!*

"Anyway," Rosamond said to the table, raising her chin. "You can all be at ease around me now, because I can promise *none* of you are going to want to marry me after what I am about to say!"

"Well, you've got *my* ears," Tingo said through a grin.

"It is my charge to plan an activity for Somensday. Now—it is meant to be voluntary, but I require you *all* to be there! Otherwise I shall be very cross."

"How compelling," Labyrinth said through his cigar, pinched tightly between his teeth.

"That includes you, sire," Rosamond said, slamming her hands on the table. The unexpected noise jarred Labyrinth enough that he finally turned to make eye contact with her. She stared him down for a moment, then leaned back. "Are you all ready to hear what it is we are going to do?"

"I don't like where *this* is going," Cato shrunk into his seat.

Rosamond smiled proudly, closing her eyes. "I have selected a Faerie play for us all to perform. It will be very funny."

"All my gods..." Cato groaned. "Someone restrain this woman."

Rosamond waved over the servant, took a third glass of vino, then drank it in a single swig. "This includes you too, Carto," she said, her words slurring. "I've got the perfect part for you to play, too. Now," She placed her ante coin on the table, "Who wants to join for the play?"

"Didn't you just say it was compulsory?" said Labyrinth.

"Well I, for one, will be there," said Rasselas, "Slay me—I'm felling good at acting and all that." It was no new thing for noble houses to put on Faerie plays. A vain pastime, if there ever was one—and Rasselas never turned down the opportunity to wear a costume.

"We can see that," Rook mumbled from his dark corner.

"Which play?" Labyrinth asked, placing his bet.

"I am glad you asked, sire," Rosamond said, folding her hands together, "It is called the Tempest. Plenty of roles for men, and one passionate romance!"

"Well, *I'm* in, then," Mynx laughed, "And I think I would like to see skinny skydeacon over there in a costume. That will be entertaining."

Latimer blanched, shrinking into his chair.

"You are all required to be in the play! And I will not take no for an answer!" Rosamond declared. She then reached into the cleft of her bosom and pulled out a piece of paper. "Now let's see," she tapped her lip, "Labyrinth, you are to take the leading role of Prospero, the scheming magician."

"Whatever you say, Princess," Labyrinth said dryly.

"Mynx," Rosamond said, looking up from her paper, "You can be Alonso, King of Naples."

"Does he get the girl?" Mynx asked, nudging Prince Tingo in the side.

"Prince Ferdinand gets *the girl*," Rosamond said. "and that would be Miranda. She's really the only female in this story..." She ran her eyes up and down her list.

"This is ridiculous," Cato mumbled to his wing.

"Anyway," Rosamond said, "I think Tingo should be Prince Ferdinand."

"Well, what about me?" Rasselas whined, "Surely you would pick the most attractive man to play the dashing prince."

"I've got a better role for you," Rosamond said with a smirk, "You can play Ariel, the little dancing spirit. He's the servant of Prospero."

King Labyrinth chuckled behind his cloud of smoke.

"Fine," Rasselas shrugged. Rasselas already thought Ariel was the best character in the play, despite Rosamond's description.

"What about him?" Cato thrust his thumb at Rook, who rolled his eyes.

"You can leave me out of it, Cato," Rook said.

"I've got the perfect role for you," Rosamond said without so much as looking at the gloomy Knight. "You can be Caliban. He is the evil deformed slave who goes around trying to mess things up."

Rook's face went blank, and his Highlord Cato began to cackle with delight, slamming his hands on the table.

"Harsh," Latimer mumbled.

"You, sir," Rosamond pointed at Latimer, "can be Sebastian..."

"What about *me*?" Cato straightened his back. "I thought you said you had the perfect role for me!"

"Cato," Rosamond said in a lazy tone, "You can be our critic. You must laugh at everything humorous, and mock everything else. I dare say, it will be more entertaining to have you in the crowd than on the stage."

"I'll drink to that," said the highlord.

"I assume you're playing the role of the leading lady?" Rasselas asked.

"Oh!" Rosamond laughed, "No, no, no. I am the director! So I'll have a grand time ordering you all around. My first lady Viola is going to be Miranda."

A groan came from Tingo's side of the table.

As Rosamond continued to make a spectacle of herself, joking, drinking, and throwing out cards, Rasselas noticed a messenger waiting patiently on the sidelines and whispering into the ear of their attending servant. Rasselas met the servant's eyes and beckoned him over with a nod.

"There is a man here who wishes to speak to the skydeacon," the servant said to Rasselas. Latimer jumped, then left the table to speak with the man. Moments later, he and the messenger were rushing urgently out the door. Now what could *that* be about?

The next round of cards began, which Rasselas declined to play. Rook, who was now only one empty seat away from Rasselas, rose and left the table.

The man leaned against the wall with one of his hands, then pulled some sort of clicker from his pocket.

Rasselas placed his empty cup on the table, then wandered over to Rook. Rook straightened at the sight of him and shoved his metal timepiece back into his pocket.

"Not a fan of cards then?" Rasselas asked as he leaned his back against the wall where Rook was supporting himself. Rooks' sharp, dagger-like eyes connected with Rasselas'. Hades—the man really was a fright! His eyes, however, were as clean and reflective as mirrors.

"No," said Rook. "I..." he huffed, "I am not in good humor today."

"Are you ever, old chap?" Rasselas chuckled. "Come now, don't heed the comment about the deformed slave. It was in bad taste."

"Oh, I don't expect anything less from the daughter of King Hanz," Rook muttered spitefully.

"Plus," Rasselas procured his toothpick from his pocket, "I'm rather a fan of misshapen faces."

Rook shot him a threatening glare.

"I mean no offense!" Rasselas said, "I'll have you know, the man who wrote the book about my namesake had a scarred face himself, *and* a scary demeanor, but his words were as beautiful as the stars and his heart as kind as the heavenly lights. He wrote *Rasselas* to pay for his mother's funeral. Well," he ran his toothpick along his gum line, "I can't argue with being named after a man's love for his mother, eh? I have a dashed obsession with mine. I am what they call a *mother's son*, you know."

Rook's scowl weakened. "Your... your mother?"

Hades—the man was showing emotion! "Yes, well," Rasselas pulled the pick from his lips and tapped it thoughtfully against his chin, "My parents seem to be stuck on naming us all after literary characters anyway—take my sister, for example."

Rook narrowed his brow, "You don't have a sister."

"Well, slay me," Rasselas laughed, "You're right. I have *two*. Anyway, Cosette's name was from a rather long novel my father is fond of. And Beatrice, of course, was named after the lady from—"

"The Divine Comedy," Rook muttered under his breath, his eyes wandering off to distant places.

Rasselas paused, "Well... yes, actually. I say, you must be more well-read than you look! Didn't know people from the Edgelands read Faerie books!"

Rook took a step away from Rasselas. "Words can travel great distances," he said. "How, uh..." he turned away from Rasselas, "How old are your sisters?"

"Well, slay me," Rasselas cringed, "I'm not really supposed to be talking about them. Mother likes privacy and all that. Anyway, don't go trying to woo any of them yet! I know it must sound a thrill to find a woman as attractive as myself, but really—Cosette has hardly finished questioning! And you can forget Beatrice; she's all but a babe."

Rook cracked a small smile and nodded, still keeping his face turned away from Rasselas. "You have a full life," he said, "I am glad to hear it."

Rasselas frowned. "Stop it," he snapped, suddenly losing the ability to sustain his posh act.

Rook turned back to face him. "Stop what?"

"Don't you dare pity me," he hissed. "My brother isn't dead!"

Rook made no reaction, he simply turned and left.

Rasselas sheathed his toothpick in its protective case and shoved it into his pocket angrily. Well, that was the last time he was going to try and show kindness to that ghoul of a Human. The prince glanced over at the cards table, with all its laughter and banter, and found that he had no desire to partake in it any longer. Sadly, it seemed that even cards couldn't pull him out of the dark mood he was finding himself in.

Leaving his deck of cards on the table, Rasselas stormed out of the room and let the door slam behind him. He was met with a cold, brisk wind slapping against his face. He shielded the breeze with his sleeve and gazed around at the black sky. It had not been so breezy before! He took a few steps forward, finding it took much effort to walk against the strengthening wind.

He looked upwards, noting that he could not see any stars.

"What in Hades?" He looked around, then noticed a fleet of robed skydeacons standing in a row along the rooftop's southern ledge, all writing frantically in their notebooks. Latimer was among them. Rasselas made his way toward them and, not without some effort, placed himself just behind Latimer.

Latimer turned, observing him for a moment, then looked back at the sky. Rasselas could hear him muttering some kind of prayer.

"What in Hades is going on out here?" Rasselas asked, raising his voice so he could be heard over the thundering gusts.

"I don't know!" Latimer called back, "A storm is approaching, but we had no indication!"

"A storm?" Rasselas blinked. Storms were rare and skydeacons could usually predict storms weeks in advance. "What kind of storm?"

"We don't know yet!" cried Latimer. There was trepidation in his voice, but also excitement. "At the moment, we think it will just be highwinds like this."

"Are you—?"

"I am sorry, Moonvine," Latimer shouted, "I can't really talk right now. I don't want to miss...why the...why...?" His voice trailed off as he found himself caught up in his writing.

Rasselas stepped away from the skydeacons. As much as he wanted others to believe that he was a witless, idle princeling, he found himself sorry he was being excluded from the conversations and deliberations of these scholars.

Why, indeed, were the storm winds blowing tonight?

23

— Rosamond —

Port in a Storm

THE MOOD IN THE ROOM CHANGED after Rasselas, Rook, and Latimer left. Rosamond sat confidently in her chair holding her cards up to her face but felt as powerless as a caged bird. Cato, Labyrinth, Mynx, and Tingo all seemed different without the others there. It reminded Rosamond of how much her father changed when others were around, versus when they were alone together. Without witnesses, men seemed to show their true characters.

Rosamond *did* drink too much. The alcohol masked her fear and emboldened her, but still, she hated what it made her feel free to do and say. Had she really called that poor scarred Rook a deformed slave? Rosamond's mind swirled. She needed to be on her guard now more than ever.

Without the virtuous skydeacon or heroic Rasselas, Rosamond found herself compromised. Her boldness had left her. And she felt it was time for her to leave; she just needed a window of opportunity.

"Now," Cato held up his fat, half-finished cigar. "Try this one, Prancess. I can guarantee urt's better than the measly thing prince Elf offered you–rs."

Cato was drunk, and he was growing increasingly less and less charming—and he had little to no charm to begin with.

"Quiet, Cato," Rosamond said, doing her best not to slur.

"Come on, Princess," said Labyrinth, who grew notably more talkative after Rasselas left. "Be honest and tell us which man you think your father will give you to. You can't think it's going to be the Elf, can you? How much land has he got?"

"She never said she wanted the Elf," Mynx said, slamming his beer stein on the table, staining the spotless green fabric with drops of foam. "Look at her, she wouldn't still be here unless she wanted to bed one of us!"

"Gentleman!" Rosamond rose quickly, "I fear the drinks have loosened your tongues enough to give a lady reason to dismiss herself!" Her head spun at the sudden movement, and she stumbled back into her chair. "Oh," She muttered, clamoring to her feet. She was surprised to find a pair of arms lifting her up and turned to see Cato silently setting her on her feet.

"You're more drunk than us," Cato said, "You should worry about your *own* looseness."

"I..." Rosamond pulled her arm free of his support, "Please, I wish not to be touched."

"Wish all you want," said Labyrinth. Rosamond turned to see him looking down at her. Lust seemed to evaporate off of him like steam after a hot bath.

"I need to leave," she mumbled.

"We'll escort you back down the stairs," Tingo said, rising quickly.

"No!" Rosamond held up her palm. "No, please. I'll go alone."

Labyrinth cackled to himself. "Have it your own way, Princess."

Rosamond disregarded the inebriated gentlemen and stumbled toward the door. She froze for a moment, regaining her balance, and straightened her back. Slowly, she glided toward the door, steady as if she had never tasted liquor in all her life.

On the other side of the door, it was another story. Immediately, Rosamond met with the ground, a ferocious wind pressing against her. What was *happening*? Rosamond gripped the stones beneath her, doing her best to plant her feet against the ground, then attempted to rise. The wind crashed against her from all sides. She searched for the door that led back down into the palace. It was so dark now! Where were the stars?

Rosamond's world spun, within and without.

She tossed her head left and right, with her loose hair blowing about her face and repeatedly blinding her. She pulled it aside with her hands, then stumbled forward as her dress caught a gust.

Just then, a black shape flashed through the air. Rosamond followed it with her eyes. A thin staircase led upwards to one of the higher lookouts. There, standing upon the curling stairs was a silhouette of a man. The black shape flapped two great wings and descended upon the silhouette of the man.

"Gargoyle?" she asked, as the man turned to greet the bird.

Who was that man? Rosamond's drunken mind seemed both more confused and clearer than ever. Was that... was that man her *father*? Yes—of course it was.

"So..." Rosamond's inebriated logic spilled out from her numb lips as she swayed in the wind. "Gargoyle belonged to Father all along? He... he sent his bird to spy on me? Or... or... to *mock* me?" Anger filled her body.

Fueled by the foolish, groundless confidence of the liquor, Rosamond disregarded the violent winds and marched toward the silhouette of the man.

Her father turned to climb to the top of the stairs, up to the lookout, with his coattails flapping behind him. Rosamond groped her way up the stairs on her hands and knees.

It was a miracle she wasn't swept aside on her journey upwards, clutching the steps of the steep stairs. Eventually, Rosamond found herself standing atop a private square courtyard, framed on three sides by tall stone walls, and an open lookout to the south. There the silhouette stood at the center of the platform with Gargoyle clutched against his arm.

Rosamond stumbled to her feet and pointed her finger at him. "So! What was your plan? Did you want me to think I had made a friend, only to laugh at me? Is this all a game to you?" She screamed at the top of her lungs, though the winds diminished her volume to barely a whisper.

"Who is the mocker here?" The man she assumed was her father responded in a dark voice. "You are no different from him, are you, *Rosamond*? Leave me in peace."

"I—!" It took Rosamond a moment to hear what the man said. "*What*?"

"I said *leave* me!" The man barked. "Why can't the world just forget me for one single *bell*?"

"I have had it with you!" Rosamond screeched, "I *hate* you!" The windy gales forced her roughly to her knees. Rosamond steadied herself, stood, and continued, "I am sick of your stifling, puppeteer hold over me! I am sick of you pushing me at these lustful monsters! I don't care if you punish me—I will *never*—"

Rosamond's skirt caught the wind like a sail, and she felt herself rise. In a sudden swap, the stone became Sky, and the Sky became the ground. She let out a deafening shriek as she spun upwards, caught up in the high winds with a flighted caravan of scattered debris.

In a short moment that felt like an eternity, Rosamond was one with the storm. She tumbled through the black air, not knowing which way was up, down, left, or right. In every direction, there was only storm. Wind wrapped around Rosamond like a spool of wool, tying her up in the Sky's duress. A horrific roaring noise shook her, vibrating through her skeleton like an angry, celestial scream. She felt it—she felt the rage and vengeance the storm felt at what had been done.

Howling winds blew through her ears, and a deafening thunder spoke into her heart feelings that were too strong for words. It was as though Rosamond was no longer a person of her own; she was a part of something so much bigger. She was the beating heart at the eye of the storm. She was its curling fingers, forming themselves into fists.

This should not have happened. This is wrong.

Rosamond's body was carried further upwards by the tempestuous air. She couldn't tell if she was falling or flying. She only saw blackness. Painful, cold bullets of rain began to beat against her face. The droplets of rain were thick and swollen, gathering around her like bees to a honeycomb. It felt as though she had come as high as the source of rain and thunder—so high she might hit the hard ceiling of the Sky. Rosamond shook her head violently, fighting to break free.

Then suddenly, she dropped. She shot down like a falling star. She would get her wish then; she would die.

But... it wasn't really her wish. She *didn't* want to die!

Arms snapped tight around Rosamond's torso like a steel trap.

In an instant, her freefall ceased, and the world felt still again, though the winds still beat against her from all sides and Rosamond felt her feet dangling in the free air. Against her back was a beating heart. She turned her head, searching for the face of the rescuer, when a blinding flash of white lightning lit up the Sky around her. She saw not his face, but four great wings, with a span as wide as the sky: two black on one side, and two dazzlingly white on the other.

Then, the violent winds took them both. Rosamond screamed and scrambled to clutch the body of the one who struggled to keep a vice-like grip around her. They flew downwards, back toward the Table. Rosamond saw the top of the Inner Palace grow closer and closer. In a quiet and sane moment, Rosamond might have wished or even begged those four the wings to take her to faraway places where no one had ever heard of Mensa or King Hanz, but now all that mattered to her was a return to her life.

The wind fought against their attempts to escape its battering. The flight back down to the secluded lookout grew fierce and difficult, and just when they came close enough to land, a wall of wind and rain hit them like a taunting whip and cast them down against the stone in a graceless crash before they collapsed to the ground.

All was still. Finally—Rosamond was motionless.

Rosamond slowly opened her eyes. It took a moment to realize that her wish to live had been granted. She was not dead. She had not been swallowed up in that horrible, vengeful storm. The wind still tore around her like a wild beast, though its harshest blows seemed dampened somehow. She craned her neck and looked up to see a tent-like structure which seemed to block the blasting winds and debris from ripping her skin to shreds. It was a crooked structure, made from matte black wings and glistening white feathers. Still, the arms which had rescued her from the heart of the storm clutched her hard around the waist. Rosamond tried to push herself up, but she was held hard against the body that lay beneath her. There lay a man, as still as death, clinging to her with eyes shut tight.

"Sir Rook?" Rosamond said the words, but hardly any voice came out. Rook lay beneath her, and beneath him sprouted the wings she had seen in the Sky, curling up to create the blessed shelter. "Rook!" Rosamond cried and beat her hand against his chest, "Wake up!"

Rook would not wake. He lay there still, unmoving. Rosamond grew instantly fearful. The terrifying thought that she was encased inside the clutches of a dead man seized her. "Let me go!" Then the tears began to flow, and the horror of what was happening to her took its sobering hold. "Help!"

There was a rustling movement inside the protective wing shell. Rosamond jolted as two black eyes met hers.

Rosamond. Standing directly beside her was that great black raven.

"Gargoyle," Rosamond sputtered with a quivering lip, "He's dead!"

He isn't dead, said the bird.

"What is *happening*?" Rosamond pleaded.

It is a storm, said the bird, *An angry storm.*

Rosamond gazed upwards and tried to peer through a crack in the wings. She could see whole tree branches, bits of armor, and even birds thrown around like toys in the tempest. Only a moment ago, she had been one of those flying objects. "I..." she looked back at Rook. "He is a Faerie."

Yes... said Gargoyle.

"He was kind to me after I..." her foolishness early that night flooded her with shame. "Oh, Gargoyle," Rosamond fell into a sob, "I'm such a monster." She buried her face in Rook's cravat.

"Please," Rook's voice croaked. She could hear it vibrating from within his chest, "Please don't tell your father."

"What?" Rosamond lifted her head and met eyes with him. His irises seemed to be glowing in the darkness! "You're alive!"

"Please," he said again weakly, "Tell no one what you have seen."

"What I've *seen*?" Rosamond rotated her head in a circle, examining the tangled wings. "Do you mean your... your wings?"

"Don't you know who I—" he cut himself off. "Princess, your father is trying to kill me."

Rosamond examined the scars slashed across Rook's throat. They were countless. Had her *father* done this?

"I'm sorry," she said softly, in a voice he couldn't hear over the storm.

Rook saw the words on her lips and nodded.

"You must promise me to..." his words drifted into silence as he closed his eyes.

"Please, don't die! I mean—" Rosamond's eyes widened as Rook's head went limp and his hands remained tight around her waist. "Let—*let me go!*"

He will not die, the Gargoyle said from beside her.

"Do you think his body is broken?" Rosamond asked fearfully. She felt herself trembling. "Have I... have I done this to him? Gargoyle, I've been so cruel to him!"

You are in shock, said the bird. *His body will not be broken for long. He... is not like other Faeries. I just pray his wings will fade before morning. Thank the Lights no guards will be outside during a storm like this.*

Rosamond slowly laid her head back against Rook's shoulder. It had nowhere else to go. She sighed, letting herself relax a little, then said, "You have gotten better at talking."

It's you who has gotten better at listening, replied the bird.

Rosamond waited for the storm to pass, listening to the beat of Rook's heart like a steadying metronome amidst the chaos of the storm. Gargoyle said Rook would not die, and in her pitiful state, she chose to believe him. That made his arms the safest place she could be on that horrible, windy rooftop. As long as he was alive, Rosamond told herself, she would stay alive too. Gargoyle kept watch, poking his nose out from Rook's wings from time to time to watch the storm. Every time his chest rose and fell, and every time she felt the breath from his nostrils warm her wet head, she felt reassured.

No bells rang that night. No one could distinguish the bells when the Skies were alight with fury all night. But eventually the storm did pass. Rosamond didn't realize she had fallen asleep until her eyes shot open at the sound of the

Firstlight bell. She stirred, and Rook's arms slipped limply from her waist. She pushed herself up off of Rook's still body, sat upright, and gazed around at her surroundings. The canopy of wings was gone, and beside her lay just a man in clothes half soaked in rainwater.

"Rook!" Rosamond patted his chest. "Rook, are you alive?"

Rook blinked his eyes open and focused on Rosamond's face. In the morning light, she could see him more clearly now. But Rosamond felt, for the first time since meeting Rook, that she could see something of that picture in the portrait book and less of the scars and dark expression.

"Rosamond," he said as he sat up slowly. "Damn." He reached around to rub his back.

"I thought you were dead... Rook—you're a Faerie! But... with four wings?"

"What?" Rook snapped his head up, and some of his wet hair flung away from his eyes.

"Is that... What does that mean? I've never heard of a Faerie with four wings before."

"You, *what*?" Rook raised an eyebrow, "Seriously?"

"And your ears are round," she pointed, "So... how could you possibly be a Faerie? I'm... I'm confused."

"Rosamond," Rook quickly grasped her pointing hand and pulled it down away from his face. "You can't talk about these things. Understand? I—I don't want anyone to..."

"Oh," Rosamond drew back, remembering what Rook had said the night before, "You said my father wanted to kill you."

"Yeah..." Rook leaned back onto his hands, sighing. "Damn. I'm not safe here anymore."

"Rook," Rosamond said quietly, "I promise I will not tell a soul. You—you saved my life last night. And I—oh the Lights know I *hate* my father now. I would *never* tell him about you. Never!"

Rook cracked a smile. "Well, I guess I am going to have to believe you."

There was a moment of silence between them as they exchanged calculating looks. Rosamond broke that silence with a scream.

"*What*? Hades, woman!" Rook recoiled.

"Where on the *world* is my skirt?" Rosamond gaped down at her two simple tattered layers of wet fabric which had suctioned themselves to her legs. Her overskirt was gone.

Rook scoffed, rolling his eyes. "Your felling dress nearly got us killed. Do you know how *heavy* you are with that thing on? I had to..." he shrugged, "improvise. Look—I'm sorry."

"You took off my *skirts*?" Rosamond clambered to her feet and shook a finger at him as she searched for words. "That's—that's—!"

"I saved your life, alright?" Rook stood and swatted away her hand. "Now will you stop yelling at me? People are going to be looking for you. Do you want them to think I—I..." he stammered, "*dishonored* you in some way?"

"Oh," Rosamond stared into the middle distance, then nodded.

"Well... would you look at that?" Rook moved past Rosamond and walked to the ledge of the rooftop. He gazed around at their surroundings with a shake of his head, "the Castle grounds are... trashed."

Rosamond stepped up beside him. "Oh, my," she whispered.

"I hope Inferno is alright," he said with a sigh.

Rosamond blinked. "Who?"

"You know... the bird."

"Are you talking about the Gargoyle?"

Rook gave her a sidelong glance. "No."

"Well, there *was* a bird here, and he kept watch over you last night," Rosamond said as she fiddled with her rugged clothes, doing her best to hide any hint of the shape of her legs. It was, in a word, impossible.

"You can rest easy," Rook mumbled, "It doesn't bother me. Fashion is different where I come from."

"Oh, so you are *used* to gazing at women's legs, I gather?" she mumbled.

"I mean... I wouldn't put it that way."

"Men are so..."

"Please," Rook turned aside and began to descend the stairs.

"Wait!" Rosamond jumped, then ran after him.

Rook stopped short to turn and stop her with his palm held out to her.

"Rosamond," he said gently, lifting chin to look her in the eyes, "Let me leave quickly. You can follow along after a hundred clicks or so, but if you wouldn't mind, I would rather that no one knew we were together last night."

"Oh..." Rosamond nodded slowly, imagining a scene where Rosamond was found, half dressed, with a man on the rooftop, storm or no storm. "Alright."

"And Rosamond..." Rook's face grew solemn. "It would be wise if we did not speak again. And..." He licked his lips nervously, "I assume you will respect your promise?"

"I—" Rosamond hesitated. Why did those words sting? "Of course. I mean... if that is what you wish... but—why?"

"Thank you." Rook nodded to himself. "Goodbye."

Rosamond watched him dash away like a passing shadow. She wanted to shout out the word "wait." but she found she had no strength to beg. The strange man had saved her, preserved her through the storm, and then vanished. Rook. Indeed, such a strange man. He had seemed to radiate darkness and gloom, but in that dark night, he had been nothing but brightness to her. And just like that, he was gone.

Rook's words shook Rosamond back into the moment. What had he said? Wait a hundred clicks? Rosamond wasn't sure how long a click really was. When had she ever had use for a clicker, other than playing with her father's piece as a bored child? She resolved to just sit on the ground and count to a hundred. And as she counted, her skin began to stiffen from the damp cold. Gazing down at her legs, she could see a bare knee sticking out of a tear in her undergarments. She had never felt so exposed. The reality of her situation became more and more present as she recounted her terrifying flight in the storm.

The princess dropped her head onto her knees and whimpered as silently as she could. What a horrible night. Finally, when she thought Rook would have been long gone, Rosamond rose and shakily made her way to the main roof terrace. She could not help the trembling; between the cold and the terror, it was a wonder she could even walk. A sentry spotted her as she rounded the corner. Desperate, she held her hands out to him.

"Help!" she gasped, breaking into a sob, "Help me!"

The sentry man rushed to her and caught her just before she fell. She clutched onto him tightly and dropped her forehead onto his breastplate.

"Watch!" The sentry called loudly, "Watch, call for the captain!" The closest watchtower began ringing an alarm bell to a specific pattern. Rosamond just leaned lifelessly against the guard until Captain Oswald came charging over.

"Princess Rosamond!" Oswald gasped, "Where have you *been*?"

The sentry guard transitioned Rosamond into Captain Oswald's protection. Rosamond soon felt herself held up by the strongest, thickest of arms. The mere contact with someone familiar made her cry louder.

"I was stuck in the storm! I was going to die!" she cried.

Oswald held her tightly, standing still. "It's alright, Princess," Oswald said. "We will get you inside. Soldier?" He addressed the sentry. "Go alert the king that his daughter has been found. I'll bring her along."

"I was all alone," said Rosamond through her tears, "I was going to die!"

"You're safe now. The storm has passed." Oswald sighed. "This might not have happened if you had told the guard where you were going to be last night."

Rosamond's only response was to cry louder, so Oswald held his tongue. After a moment or two, the captain said, "Let's get you inside. It would be best if no one else saw you like this."

Rosamond pulled her head up shakily and gazed down at herself. "Oh..."

The sentry who had run off came back with a feather-lined blanket. Captain Oswald covered her quickly, then ushered her toward the door to the stairs. Rosamond followed along, whimpering, all the way to the ground floor. They approached her father's room.

"Please," Rosamond froze. "Let me go change."

"Your father is eager to see you," said Oswald. "He was so worried for you last night."

Rosamond's heart swelled with hope. Her father—*worried* about her? As true as her declaration of hate for him was last night, there was nothing she wanted more in this moment than to run into his arms and feel safe.

"Alright," she said softly, "Please, take me to him."

Oswald led her to the door and pushed it open. He guided her inside. There, standing by the window, was her father.

"Papa!" Rosamond cried with a breaking voice. She pushed away from Oswald's support and stumbled toward the Kind with outstretched arms.

Hanz turned slowly to face her. Rosamond halted in her steps when she saw his face. His teeth were gritted tightly, and eyes were alight with rage.

"Rosamond!" He barked, "Where have you *been*?"

"P—Papa, I got stuck in the—"

"Leave us, Oswald," Hanz said, his fists shaking.

"No," Rosamond drew back, stumbling toward Oswald. She turned and threw herself at the captain. "No, Oswald, please don't leave us! He's angry! He's so angry!"

Oswald looked down at Rosamond, but his body remained stiff. "Princess...." he mumbled.

"Please, Oswald! He is angry; you can't *leave* me with him like this!"

"Rosamond!" Hanz charged toward her and grabbed her by the arm, yanking her backwards. She fell onto her backside and her protective blanket slid off her back. She turned to look up at her father. "Look at you," Hanz gasped, drawing back. "You're dressed like a harlot!"

"Father!" Rosamond pleaded, "I was caught in the storm!"

"You were drunk!" He screamed with spit streaming from his mouth, "Oswald tells me that there were reports of you gambling and smoking and practicing *loose* behavior! For all we knew someone took advantage of you last night!"

"Oswald!" Rosamond turned back toward the captain, "Please don't leave me with him."

"You bitch!" Hanz thrust his boot into his wooden desk chair, crushing it to pieces. He seized it by one of its legs and began beating it against the wall until the leg finally came free and the remains of the chair fell to the ground.

"Oswald!" Rosamond wailed, "Please!"

Oswald did not move. His eyes showed evidence of conflict, but he did nothing.

King Hanz stepped toward Rosamond, holding fast to his chair leg club. "Leave us, Oswald," he said. "I would speak with my daughter alone."

Captain Oswald turned and left, closing the door behind him

Rosamond clasped the floor with her hands as a terrifying silence fell over the room. Another storm would come now, only this time there would be no Rook to shield her.

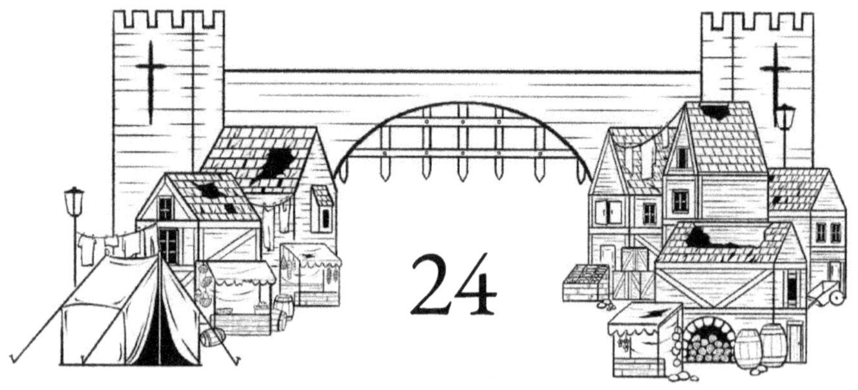

24

—— Valley ——

Dreamscape

VALLEY SAT ATOP A WHITE TOWER. Before her, the city was glowing with purity. In the distance, she could see the surface of the Raqian table stretching out before her. There was an eerie mountain obstructing her view to the south, towering so high that its summit scraped against the surface of the glassy sky. She thought about flying there but was distracted by a glimmer of light that was flickering down beneath her, within the white city. She leapt off the tower and soared down, stretching out her wings, and landed in some sort of garden.

On the ground, nestled into a patch of grass, was a plain silver ring. She picked it up and examined it. She knew this ring; she knew it very well. Then the world around her began to swirl; the colors of the scenery mixed together like wet paint. She could hear a thousand voices, a million thoughts. This was becoming a common occurrence in her dreams.

Valley closed her eyes, listening. For a moment, one of the voices became clearer. In her mind, she imagined the face of Prince Rasselas. Yes, it was his voice. How often she thought of that voice!

She listened to him, and was surprised to hear him say: "Mother, I have no desire or need to learn how to wash dishes. Do you know how wrinkly my hands get after a long bath?" Valley focused on the voice, and it became louder. "No, I am not going to *bathe* in the sink, mother! That is insane! I am a grown man, woman. A *grown man*!"

Valley opened her eyes, and the swirling colors took shape and form. She was standing in a large kitchen, not unlike the Inner Palace kitchens she often had need to visit. A woman was standing by a doorway with an infant scrambling against her hip.

"I have to watch Beatrice right now, Rasselas," said the woman sternly, "Now get in the sink and wash the dishes!"

Valley turned her head to see Rasselas standing beside a large community-sized kitchen sink. There was a mountain of dirty dishes inside it. Rasselas dropped his head to his chest. "This is degrading," he said, "*demeaning*!"

What on the *Table* was happening?

"You!" The woman suddenly pointed at Valley. Valley jolted, then made eye contact with her. She was beautiful, with long wavy red hair and large eyes. "Make sure he cleans every single dish in that sink! He can't come out until it's done." She stormed out of the room.

Valley turned to look at Rasselas who was climbing inside the sink. The basin itself began to grow, until it was the size of the bathhouse pool. Water flowed from nowhere, filling it, and Rasselas reclined against its edge, fully clothed, watching the messy dishes float around him like flotsam and jetsam. Valley stepped up to the oddly comical bath and leaned her elbow on it. Rasselas looked up at her, suddenly noticing her presence, and said,

"Valley! Can you *believe* the kinds of things she makes me do?"

Valley chuckled, "Strange indeed," she said. What an odd dream she was having! "Though I have to say, it's impressive how you can look fetching, even in dirty sink-water."

"Well, thank you," he said, huffing. Then he brightened. "Say, do you want to get in? The water is fine!"

Valley laughed. "I don't exactly want to be stepping into a pile of dirty dishes with you, Rasselas."

"Well what about the seaside?" Rasselas asked. Then he closed his eyes. Suddenly, there was something vacant and unresponsive about his expression. It was as though he were thinking about nothing at all.

"The seaside would be a much better aesthetic," Valley thought. She stepped away from the sink and closed her own eyes. When she opened them again, the world around her turned to a blur once more, with only she and Rasselas remaining a constant. Moments later, they were on the seaside. Valley gasped with wonder. She had never seen anything like this place before. Had *she* made this happen?

The sky, sand, and water were all grey in color, and still, they sparkled with light.

Rasselas sat in the sand, looking around as if nothing unexpected had happened.

"Am I dreaming?" he finally asked.

Valley chuckled. She walked over to where he rested and knelt beside him in the sand. "This place is beautiful," she said.

"It's my home," said Rasselas as he stared out at the water.

"Celestia?" Valley asked, following his gaze. The water looked so vast, and so wild!

"No," Rasselas laughed, "Winter's End."

Valley rotated her head slowly and watched Rasselas' face. There was no posh act, no smirks, no quips. He was simply at peace, smiling. With his hair blowing around in the wind, he looked younger and more relaxed than she had ever known him. Valley felt more drawn to him than ever before. She felt an impulse to reach out and touch him. How flawless his skin was...

Rasselas turned his head, noticing her intense focus on his face. He smiled brightly.

"Valley," he said, "I am thinking about you again."

"I am the one thinking about *you*." Hades—what a romantic she was sounding like! Well, it couldn't hurt to indulge in her dream a little.

"Why don't you go bathe in the Sea," Rasselas pointed out at the crashing waves. "I think it'd be nice to admire you from here."

Valley blushed. Alright, perhaps she was taking this a bit too far. "*You* get in the water," she said.

"Well, alright." Rasselas stood and dusted the sand off of himself.

Valley bit her lip, watching carefully as he began to remove his shirt.

⁂

Valley's eyes snapped open at the sound of the Firstlight bell. She sat up quickly, throwing her quilt off of herself.

"Damn," she muttered, groaning as she rose to her feet. She really had only gotten two bells worth of sleep. Between the terrifying storm and thinking about the conversation with Sir Rook, she had hardly rested.

Valley shuffled over to her small, oval mirror which hung against the wall. She noted her swollen eyes and frowned.

"You'd think the Faerie of *dreams* would be able to get some sleep," she muttered. *Hades*—is that truly who she was? Wasn't the Faerie of Dreams supposed to be one of the most powerful Fae to have ever existed? And how did that Rook character know who she was? Should she even trust his word? Was it all just a lie? No... there was something deep inside her that knew it was true. "The Faerie of Affection," he had called her. Affection? What did that mean?

Valley rubbed her eyes, shaking away the intrusive thoughts. Whatever her title was, did it really matter? She was a Mensan Faerie, and she would never be allowed to store enough magik to *use* her powers.

You are a potent and controlled giant, filled with the gift of unimaginable power. Do not forsake this gift because others have told you it is your shame. It is not your shame; it is your glory. Rasselas' words came to her. Even Sir Rook would have her feel ashamed of sharing the same title as the Nightmare Faerie, as some called him. Would Rasselas change his words if *he* knew who she was? Wasn't it the Nightmare Faerie who had raped his mother?

She shook her head. Did everyone but her know this already? Was it obvious to all? No *wonder* all those Faeries in the prison were afraid of her! How many of their kin had been killed by the tyrant with her same wings? But no... how *could* they know?

These were the questions that would continue to run through Valley's mind throughout the rest of her day. As she dressed, she recited Rasselas' letter to herself to keep from growing anxious. Once ready, she tucked the letter safely in her pocket. Just then, there was a knock on her door.

Valley opened it, then scowled at the sight of Karo's waistcoat. She had to crane her neck back to find his face.

"What do you *want?*" she asked suspiciously.

"Ah," Karo leaned against her door frame, "King wants to speak with you."

Valley was instantly reminded of her conversation with Oswald the day prior. Today was the fifth day after her bonding; there would be some sort of test.

"I'll go meet him then," she said, hiding her reluctance.

"Ah, wait..." Karo blocked her path as she tried to push past him. "He's busy at the moment and asks if you would meet him somewhere else."

"*Where?*" she frowned.

"He's asked me to escort you there," he said proudly as he slipped his hands into his pockets.

"I don't want to go anywhere with you," she said spitefully.

"Oh come now, Valley," he laughed, "We work together now. You had better get used to it."

Karo charged off down the hall, and Valley groaned as she closed her door and ran after him.

Karo led Valley to one of the spare bedrooms on the second floor and entered.

Valley looked around cautiously.

"When will he get here?" she asked as Karo wandered inside.

"Hades, I don't know," Karo yawned, fanning his mouth with his hand.

"Do you know what Hanz wants to talk to me about?" Valley raised her eyebrow.

"Can you *believe* that storm last night?" Karo laughed, "Now *that's* something for the skydeacons to talk about." Karo plopped himself onto the vacant bed and closed his eyes.

"If I am going to meet the king here," Valley said, "Why are you still here?"

"He wants to meet with us both," Karo said with his eyes closed. He yawned again deeply, then half-way through the yawn, turned to her, saying, "I didn't get a wink of sleep last night."

"I don't really want to hear about it," Valley muttered under her breath.

"I say," Karo exclaimed, leaning over onto his side, "Have you done something different with your hair? You know... if you wanted to—"

"Karo!" Valley, turned with a shout, "Stop with your veiled advances, alright? Do you hear me? Stop!"

Karo seemed to shrink into his skin, then hid his face behind a pillow and quietly said, "Yes, Valley."

Valley gazed in surprise. Well, that had surprisingly worked.

The two of them snapped to attention when the door slammed closed. Hanz was suddenly present, wiping his hands nervously against his coat.

"Good," he said with a discomfited look. "You're both here."

Karo flung his legs over the side of the bed then bounced to his feet. "Everything alright, Sire? I heard they found her."

"Yes, yes," Hanz shoved his hands into his pockets, "She's fine."

"Who's fine?" Valley asked, glancing back and forth between the two others.

Karo cleared his throat. "Ah... Princess Rosamond was—"

"Will you shut *up*, Karo?" Hanz snapped. Valley flinched at the King's tone. He was not in a good mood.

Karo rushed to King Hanz's side and whispered something into his ear. Hanz was still. His eyes found Valley and he studied her carefully.

"You can leave now, Karo," Hanz said, keeping his eyes locked on Valley.

Karo stuttered. "B–but you said—!"

"*Out* with you!" Hanz snapped.

Valley crossed her arms, growing nervous. This was all very strange. She figured this all had something to do with whatever felling test Hanz was planning for her. Dejected, Karo left the room and closed the door behind himself.

"What was all that about?" Valley asked coolly.

Hanz rubbed his forehead for a moment, still silently examining her.

"I..." he mumbled, then grew quiet.

Valley didn't like the awkward silence between them, so she broke it.

"I found an opportunity to speak with Prince Rasselas," she said.

"Oh, *did* you?" Hanz seemed to break from his trance. "What did you find out?"

Valley assumed that, if Hanz was indeed testing her in some way, she had better feed him some real information. "He believes his brother is alive, and he thinks you had something to do with his disappearance."

Hanz nodded slowly. "He thinks he is here, does he..." he mumbled, then said, "I think following Rasselas will turn out to be a dead end. Perhaps spend more time with the others. Have you..." his words trailed off again.

"My Lord," Valley said, taking a step towards him, "Is everything alright?"

"Everything is fine," Hanz said, though his face betrayed himself. She had never seen him so disheveled. "Valley... have you begun to notice anything strange?"

"You're asking me this again?" she asked, "You think I am gaining magik?"

"Are you?" he asked with searching eyes.

"No!" she answered truthfully, "My Lord, I have no possessions, and I have no idea how I would even begin to—"

"Fine, fine," he waved his hand dismissively toward her, then rubbed his head again. "I'm feeling off, Valley. I had thought I had a task for you to do today, but I think I will have to think of something else."

"Are you..." Valley raised her eyebrows hopefully, "are you giving me the day *off*?"

"Day off?" Hanz looked confused. "No, I just mean I have no special tasks for you. I... I have a headache or something... today."

"My Lord..." Valley stepped toward him and pointed at the hand he was rubbing his face with. His knuckles were cracked and bruising. "Are you alright? Your hand is—"

"Valley!" he snapped.

She drew back quickly.

"I... I don't need to speak with you further. Goodbye." Hanz turned and left, slamming the door behind himself.

"What in *Hades*?" Valley said aloud. That was her strangest interaction with the king yet. Well, apparently, once she finished her morning chores, she would have the day off! Did Hanz *cancel* her loyalty test just now? Or was this part of the test? Did she even care anymore?

Valley did not stay in that room any longer; it did not feel like a safe place. Excited to escape whatever mysterious task the king intended for her, Valley went room to room, tending fires as she was meant to do. Most of the monarchs were attending a communal breakfast, so she was able to clean in peace.

She kept Rasselas' room for last, hoping that he might be returning by the time she got there. She tarried inside Sir Thorne's chambers, brushing and re-brushing the hearth. She was torn between excitement and dread at the thought of telling Rasselas her title. What would he think?

"I am sure he just postponed the peace talks so he could focus on cleaning up the castle grounds," a man's voice came from the door that connected Thorne's room to Rasselas'. Valley saw the reflection of Sir Thorne through a nearby mirror but kept her head low.

"Yes, but it's cut the time in half! He *knows* I'll have opinions about the throne of Arelle. Now, there won't be any time for responses! We will all just have to listen to *him* talk about it!" Rasselas whined from his room.

"I am sure there will be time for all that," Thorne shouted back, holding the side door open. "But you aren't supposed to be coming here with opinions, anyway! Your grandfather told you to *observe*, not stir the pot."

"This is an *extremely* important debate!" Rasselas shouted. There was true anger in his voice. "Don't you see that?"

"Stop being so *Faerie*-crazy!" Thorne barked, then slammed the door. He stood there, calming himself with some controlled breathing, then kicked the door. Valley watched his reaction through the mirror as he noticed her presence. Thorne grimaced, then moved to the other side of the room.

"Are you quite *done* yet?" he asked her sharply.

"Yes," Valley rose and picked up her cleaning pale. She turned to smile at the wing. He only eyed her with skepticism. Then his face softened.

"I–I'm sorry, girl," he said, "I was angered. I didn't mean to take it out on you."

Valley was surprised to hear him sound so gentlemanly. "It's alright," she said, moving towards his door.

Thorne moved ahead of her and opened it. "Sorry to bother you, miss," he said.

Valley exited, moving to the next door, Rasselas'. She bit her lip as she knocked.

The door flew open. "Who is it?" Rasselas crowed as he stood there, holding the handle.

Valley started, losing her grip on her pail. It crashed to the ground at her feet, covering her in soot.

"Oh, damn!" Rasselas cried, scrambling to rescue the pail. The damage had already been done.

"Please," Valley pushed him away, "I can get it."

"I'm so sorry, Valley!" He took the pail, "Here, let me carry this in for you."

"It's not... a problem," Valley grumbled as she stepped into the room. Rasselas set the pail by the fire, then ran to close the door.

"Valley!" he said in an excited whisper, "I think I've figured it out!"

"Figured *what* out?" Valley examined her clothes through Rasselas' mirror. "Oh Hades—this is a disaster."

"Nothing a bath can't fix," Rasselas said with a smirk.

"In the kitchen sink?" Valley retorted.

"What did you say?" Rasselas blinked, looking somewhat taken aback.

Valley blushed. "*Erm*, nothing. What did you figure out, Rasselas?" she asked, turning to face him.

"I think I know what title you might have," he whispered, stepping closer to her.

"You... you do?"

"Yes! Now listen, there tend to be at least five seasons before a dormant Faerie title is passed on to a newborn Faerie, and from my list, I was able to really narrow things down. Now. Let me ask you something. Do you find that people are quite drawn to you, Valley? Like... you get a lot of attention?"

"I... I suppose lately..." she stammered.

"Listen. There is this Faerie called the Faerie of Charisma. He was one of the sons of the second Faerie King. Somenus killed him when he took the throne. I think you might have inherited his title!"

"I'm a darkwing, Rasselas," she said, crossing her arms. "Was the Charisma Faerie a darkwing?"

"Uh...." Rasselas' excitement waned, "Right. Forgot about that."

"Well, I have some news for *you*, Rasselas," she said as a wry smile appeared on her face.

"...what? What, have *you* figured it out?" he asked, leaning closer.

Valley didn't mind being close to the man. She kept her voice in the lowest whisper, requiring him to lean his ear toward her mouth.

"Have you heard of the Faerie of *Affection*?" she whispered.

Rasselas stayed beside her silently, making no reply. She was too close to see his face. What was he thinking?

He stepped back slowly. His face studied her with concern. "No," he said, "I don't think that can be right. Do you know who the Faerie of Affection is, Valley?"

"The Faerie of Dreams," she said.

"You can't be the Faerie of Dreams, Valley," Rasselas said. "Why did you think you were?"

"I know it is what I am, Rasselas," she said with a furrowed brow. "Why don't you believe me?"

"It's not that I don't believe you, I..." he stammered and stepped back, examining her from toe to head. "Valley... how old are you?"

"What?" she frowned. "I am in the age of ability—just like you!"

"Hah," Rasselas chuckled nervously, "Sure... but I mean... how many seasons? Do you know your birth season?"

"Seventeen..." Valley said slowly, growing concerned as the look on Rasselas' face changed, "The season of Patient Perseverance."

Rasselas turned away from her. He walked over to his window and rested his hands on the sill.

"Is something wrong?" she asked quietly. "Rasselas... I know that the other two Dream Faeries have done terrible things... but surely that doesn't mean that I—!"

"No, no," Rasselas said with his back still turned. "It's not that. *Damn*, Valley."

Valley walked slowly up to Rasselas' side and placed her hand on his back.

At her touch, he turned to look at her. He sighed, smiling.

"What do you know?" she asked.

"If that is the case... then I know who you *really* are," he said. There was pain behind his eyes.

"The Nightmare Faerie?"

Rasselas shook his head. "No, not your title. I mean... where you came from."

Valley's eyes widened. "You—you know who my parents are!"

"Yes, I do."

"Rasselas!" Valley took him suddenly by the sleeves, "Rasselas, I have wondered my entire life who they are! Please—tell me at once!"

Rasselas stared at her for a moment, as though studying her for the very first time. "Valley, your father was a great man. We all heard of your birth, the first female Dream Faerie." Rasselas lifted his eyes to gaze at the ceiling. His face grew distant. "That's when it all started."

"When *what* started, Rasselas? Who *am* I?" she urged, shaking him.

Rasselas looked down at her. "You are the firstborn child of Hevel, the caretaker of the Faerie throne."

"What?" Valley shook her head, "But... didn't he die? Hanz said my parents were alive!"

Rasselas shook his head. "Your parents were killed. Everyone thought you had been killed too. There were many who feared you—Hanz most of all."

"How can this be?" she asked, searching Rasselas' face wildly.

"I'll *tell* you how it can be." Rasselas' voice grew dark, "Don't you see? Hanz raised you! He knows who you are! *He* was behind the insurrection. He *took* you for his own purposes!"

Rasselas broke away from her and marched across the room. "And why didn't I think of this? We all thought that he would want you dead! But no... a Faerie so powerful..." he whirled his head around to face her again, "he would raise you loyal to him. He would keep his enemies close."

Valley stood there, dumbfounded. "My father is... *dead*?"

Rasselas sighed. "He was a great man. He—he was mentoring my brother, Anodos, in Arelle, you know. Anodos wrote to us about you. You were only a baby when it all happened." He dropped his head. It was evident that the memories brought him pain.

"If Hanz is behind all this," Valley said as she walked up to Rasselas and took him by the hand, "And he took me all those seasons ago... then he must know where your brother is."

Rasselas lifted his head to gaze at her with hopeful eyes. "Yeah... but where? Where *is* he, Valley?"

Valley thought about this. Then, an idea came to her. "There's a Faerie prison in the Warrowing Village," she said quickly, "There is a man in there who has lost his memory."

"*What*?" Rasselas tensed. "It *must* be him!"

"It's always dark there," she said, "So I have never seen anyone. But what did your brother look like?"

"He has black hair... kind eyes..." Rasselas said slowly. His eyes grew damp. "He has four wings. Two light, two dark."

"Two dark... two light..." Valley mumbled. Her eyes widened. "That is what the man in the prison always says!"

"My god, Valley!" Rasselas gripped her hand tightly. "Take me to him!"

Valley shook her head. "No one is allowed in the prison unless on a mercy mission. Let me go. I can investigate this without causing suspicion."

"My god, Valley," Rasselas said again, blinking a tear out of his eye, "Have we found him? Have I finally found him?" There was a glimmer of hope in his face. He pulled Valley quickly against himself and tightened his arms around her. He was clearly happy enough to hug a cactus, but Valley savored the embrace anyway. She took this opportunity to savor his increasingly familiar scent. But then she was thrown aside as Rasselas dashed across the room.

"I don't know what to do!" The young man said excitedly, "I don't know what to say! Valley—I think we have cracked it!" He turned to point at her. "*You* were the key! You were that dirty little secret that Hanz was hiding in his closet all along!"

"I am sure I'm not the only secret that man is hiding," Valley said, crossing her arms.

"True enough," Rasselas scoffed, "Anyway... once we get my brother free, everything will become simple. He can power up all the Faeries with magik and then we just get them all out of here!"

"But the Faerie in the prison was unstable, Rasselas," Valley said cautiously. "We need to be very careful. Rasselas... I don't know how to say this, but... I think he is insane."

Rasselas' smile faded. "I see..." he said softly. "Yes... if they can't kill him, they would render him useless." He sniffed. "Well, there is only one thing for it, then. I need to get him to Winter's End. Momentum will know what to do. What... Valley?" Rasselas froze as Valley's face began to break. "Are you crying?"

"No," she shook her head, turning away from him. "It's nothing."

"What is it? What did I say?" He touched her shoulder, but she recoiled from him. "Why are you crying? Oh *Hades*—what did I *say*?"

"I... I know you must leave eventually... but, I suppose I just..." she wiped her eyes ashamedly, "Oh, I don't know why I am crying!"

"Valley," Rasselas exhaled. "You're worried about being left *behind*?"

Valley bobbed her head in agreement but found it too hard to speak.

"Oh, Valley," he sighed, "I don't know what is in my power, but I won't let the daughter of Regent Hevel stay here, alright? I'll find a way to get you out of here."

"But *when*?" she asked through her tears.

"I don't know, but I can promise you that when Momentum hears about this, he will do something about it."

"Where is he *now*?" Valley raised her voice angrily, "All of us Faeries are just stuck here, and he has never done *anything* about it!"

"Valley—we didn't know what things were like! The Purple Order is extremely loyal to Hanz, and... well, they voluntarily moved to Mensa with him!

You are right at the heart of something big. You see so many things. But from the outside, it doesn't look like anything strange is going on at all! I came here after discovering a bonded Faerie last season. I had never even *heard* of such a thing before. But I can assure you, when I get a message back to Winter's End, something will be done."

"When will that happen?" she asked. "Do you have any way of contacting them?"

Rasselas bit his lip. "It's not easy... Winter's End is protected by really old magik. Birds lose their way there. I would have to send a messenger or go myself."

"Oh..." Valley nodded slowly. "I see."

"Let me chat with Embers about it," Rasselas said, patting her shoulder, "he will help me think of something. Then let's meet up at the masque. Will you be there?"

"Oh!" Valley blinked. "I suppose I *could* be there, since I have the day off."

"Great thing about costume banquets is the anonymity," Rasselas said, "So no one needs to know it's you. Just come dressed as something I'll recognize."

"I suppose I could get an outfit from Rosamond," she said, thinking as she tapped her lip, "I know she will be keen on me being with her anyway!"

"Great," Rasselas placed his hands on his hips. "Now, what will you dress as? Something I can recognize?"

"I don't know," Valley shrugged, "What will *you* be dressed as?"

"Why," Rasselas placed his hand elegantly over his heart, "A peacock."

Valley smirked. "Isn't that a bit feminine?"

"On the contrary!" he remonstrated, "It is the male peacock who has all the lovely feathers."

Valley shook her head. "Rasselas," she said, "you're a card."

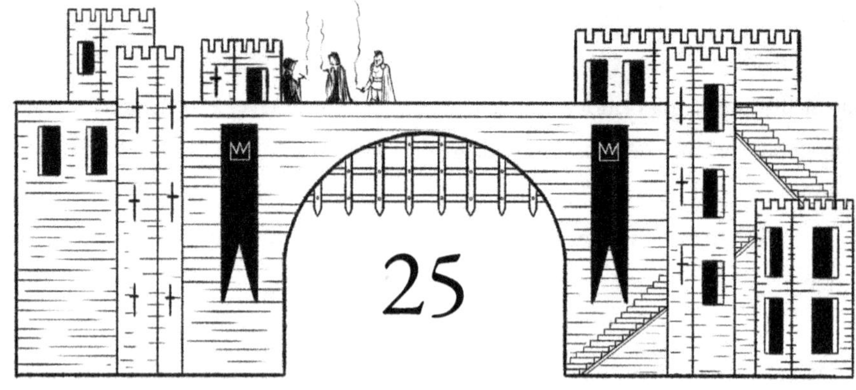

25

—— Hanz ——

The Empty Throne

A LONG BANQUET TABLE HAD BEEN BROUGHT into the courthouse, where the delegates gathered to discuss their agendas. The conversation this Wingsday would be about Arelle. Hanz wanted those present to feel as though they were a part of something both private and confidential. He wanted them to feel like they were part of whatever decisions were made, even if it were nothing more than an illusion. There were no wings present for this council, so the only men seated at the table were Hanz himself, King Labyrinth, King Stathe, Prince Tingo, Prince Mynx, Highlord Cato, and—regrettably—Prince Rasselas.

"Arelle," Hanz said, intertwining his fingers together as his hands rested before him on the table. All looked to him, sitting at the table's head. "What was once Raqia's capitol is now sitting idly, abandoned."

"Abandoned?" King Stathe sniffed. "What do you mean abandoned? Isn't that where all the Faeries live? *Seven levels of Hades*," he leaned back into his chair with a shake of his head, "I've never understood the felling Faeries. I've never had reason enough to care that they *exist*."

"The time has *come* for you to care, King Stathe," Hanz said in a scolding tone. "None of us can deny that our lands are yielding less and less. This fact is directly tied to the emptiness of Arelle. We must deal with this."

"So, why is it empty, then?" Mynx asked, "And is it really the cause of the famine?"

"Arelle is the heart of Raqia," Hanz said, "It is from her mystical throne, made by the First Faeries, that magik flows throughout the Land. The throne gives us all fertile lands."

Princess Rasselas made a boyish raspberry sound with his lips. All faces turned in his direction.

"Is it not true?" Prince Tingo asked Rasselas. "Do you disagree?"

"It isn't the throne that brings life and fertility to the lands, my dear fellows," Rasselas said, "It is the *King*."

"It is the king *on* the throne," Hanz corrected, "And for the first time in Raqian history, there is no one ruling Arelle. There is no one stewarding the Land."

"So the Land is losing its fertility because the Faeries lost their king, and now we all have to suffer for it?" King Labyrinth said. "How irritating."

"The Fae were the first beings on Raqia," Hanz said, "And though their charge was to bring Humans here so that the Humans could rule, they still kept power for themselves. They built Arelle for themselves, keeping Humans out of it. They maintained control of the Land, relegating us Humans to live here like tenants."

King Stathe scoffed. "They should be tenants on *our* lands!"

"Quite so," Hanz nodded. "In recent seasons, the Faeries have realized that they should not be the ones in charge. One cannot help but wonder..." Hanz raised his gaze to lock eyes with Rasselas. "...if their king stayed away because he *knew* he should not be on the throne."

That got the pompous prince to break into a scowl. "The—" Rasselas raised his voice.

"Please," Hanz calmly interrupted, "Let me finish."

Rasselas snapped his mouth closed, though his eyes filled with rage.

"The Faeries are, for once, taking a back seat. It is we Humans who live here in Raqia, we Humans who are populating it, and we want to rule ourselves! Is it not ironic that the very beings who can live without food are the very ones who control how much food we Humans have access to? Brothers—this empty throne is an invitation to us. It is a chance to finally rule *ourselves*!"

"And I supposed you think you are the one to sit in it," Highlord Cato spoke, his voice sounding suddenly as large and imposing as his stature was. Hanz shook his head.

"That would be for all of us to decide. First, we must agree on both the problem and its solution."

"You *can't* be implying what I think you're implying," Prince Rasselas snapped, sounding less like a carefree princeling and more like a fighter. "A Human cannot rule Arelle! Doesn't everyone *realize* that?"

"How do *you* know that?" Mynx asked quickly.

"He's the brother of the Faerie King," Prince Tingo mumbled, "Remember?"

"He is the half-brother of the son of King Somenus," Hanz said, "His brother was never the King."

Rasselas gnashed his teeth together but remained silent.

"But why is Arelle empty? Why is no one explaining this to me?" King Stathe complained.

"Arelle is empty," Hanz said with increased volume, "because without a king, the Fae had no reason to be there. The Fae have scattered around Raqia, aimless. Many have come to me for shelter. My scouts tell me that only one Faerie remains in the city, watching the gates so that no one may enter until there is a king."

"And what makes you think he would open the gates to any of us?" King Labyrinth asked with a smirk. "If you are truly suggesting that one of us could seize the throne, you can't exactly expect the Fae to just go along with it, can you?"

Good—these were good questions. Yes, they were following the trail of breadcrumbs.

"I do not wish to seize a throne," Hanz said as he looked to all at the table, face to face. "This throne has no king to seize it from. If one of us did take Arelle, it would be as one receiving a gift from the hands of someone offering it freely."

"Offering *freely*?" Rasselas scoffed bitterly. All turned to Rasselas again. The boy stared, open mouthed, then turned his nose up into the air. "I say," he muttered, "sounds dashed ridiculous, if you ask me."

"What don't you like about it?" Tingo asked, shifting his body to face the Elf prince.

"Well, old boy," Rasselas said, maintaining his stupid act, "The Fae have always wished to live separately from Humans. It is their way, and it is not wrong for them to rule themselves."

"But they're *not* just ruling themselves, are they?" Labyrinth asked provocatively. "They've got control over all the food and all the animals and all the felling pieces of dirt on this felling *world*! Why should we just wait around for them to find their felling King, when *we* are the ones starving?"

Yes. Thank you for making that point, dear Labyrinth, Hanz thought to himself.

"Is it true that the Faeries just recently admitted that they were created to serve Humans?" Tingo asked, directing his question at Rasselas.

The idiotic Elf prince bumbled for a moment, then said, "Well, yes. Thirty seasons ago there was a declaration of sorts. But there was nothing said about them giving up their charge over Raqia—giving up Arelle."

"You weren't *there* thirty seasons ago, Prince Rasselas," said Hanz. He could barely keep the grin from his face, but he managed. "I was."

All faces turned back to Hanz who nodded slowly. "Yes," he said, "I was there when the infamous Aorist announced the answer to the great question: Why were the Faeries made? Hades—that old Time Faerie has been around for thousands of seasons, keeping that felling secret all to himself. And why? Just so that the Fae could be in charge?"

"That's *not* why..." Rasselas said through gritted teeth.

"Son," Hanz said sharply, "I know that your father is Aorist's Faerie friend, and I will not hold your loyalty against you because—frankly—I admire it. But I, and many Fae as well, hold *different* opinions to what happened all those seasons ago. I fear you have been taught an incomplete history. I, and other Fae who were present, believe that Aorist—a man who kept the truth from the Fae for thousands of seasons—is not someone we should be trusting to tell us what to do next. It is good your friend Aorist keeps to himself in the remote western places. He has had the wisdom to leave us Humans alone, so that we, and we alone, can decide the fate of Raqia!"

"Hear, hear!" Cato shouted, though unenthusiastically.

"But really," King Labyrinth said, "do you honestly think that one of us could just walk into Arelle, sit on the throne, and bring the Land back into our control?"

"I do," Hanz said, then held up his finger, "but—it would have to be done carefully. The Faeries would need to acknowledge this man as their king."

"Oh, this is insane!" Rasselas muttered under his breath as he shook his head wildly. "I don't believe this."

"I don't understand why you think this is insane, Rasselas!" Tingo said in a raised voice. "To me, this all makes sense. We are the kings and princes of our own lands. Our lands are dying. The Faeries have abandoned Arelle, leaving us in famine—why shouldn't *we* be the ones to control Arelle?"

"Because it is a *Faerie* throne!" Rasselas rose from his chair and spread his arms out to his sides in bewilderment. "It's a felling *imperium!* Don't any of you know what that *means?*"

Most at the table shook their heads.

"What in Hades is an imperium?" Mynx asked with half-open eyes.

"It's a device that holds and channels a Faerie's magik. The throne is an imperium that can only be used by the Faerie King. It means that only a Faerie with the authority to use the throne could do anything to the Land! A Human sitting on a throne would be as useless as... as..." he searched, "as a man trying to breastfeed a child!" This produced some chuckles at the table.

"Authority is the key word here," Hanz said. "Someone with authority could use the throne."

"A *Faerie* with authority," Rasselas said as he leaned his hands on the table, "And the only Faerie with authority who can use that throne is the son of

King Somenus or an appointed steward. The bloodline is tied to the throne, King Hanz. And until that bloodline is broken, no one else can sit there."

"Ah yes," Hanz held up his finger again, "That is true for the Fae. But a Human has never sat on the throne before, has he?"

Rasselas snorted, "And most men I know haven't tried breastfeeding either. But be my guest, old thing!"

Hanz cleared his throat. "Whatever happens with the throne," he said to all gathered, "One thing is clear: we can no longer leave it vacant. We Humans must seize control of our own destiny. We must go to Arelle, and we must go united. We must not go to war over it."

Cato chuckled. "You are playing a dangerous game, old man."

Hanz examined the highlord, who sat slumped in his chair, arms crossed. "And what game is that?" Hanz asked.

"You are dangling your beautiful daughter over all of us thirsty men, while only one of us can have her. You think that fists will not meet faces?" Cato shook his head, "Arelle too is a beautiful woman. Who will not want her for himself?"

"It is true that only one man can marry this woman," Hanz said, rising. "And it will be for all of us to agree on who that will be. So let me ask you all this: who among you thinks you have the know-how, resources, and experience to lead Faeries? Who among you has earned the respect and allegiance of the Faeries? And who among you has the *desire* to leave your kingdoms and live in a world *filled* with Faeries?"

There was some grumbling at the table.

Hanz continued. "Yes, I put myself forward, because I have been trying to help the Faeries ever since they lost their king. My desire is not simply to save Humans from starvation, but also to stabilize the kingdom I helped destroy. It was I who killed their king, and it is I who will help them find their way again. Does anyone else want to do this? Raise your hand! Rise! Say, 'Aye'! I charge you all! Who among you thinks you can do what I am proposing?"

There was silence. Even the brat Rasselas remained quiet.

"So," Labyrinth finally said, "are you suggesting that we all travel to Arelle to... to set you up as the new Faerie king?"

"Someone needs to lead Arelle," Hanz said, "But I won't do it without your support."

"There are many problems with this," Tingo said hesitantly. "But one problem in particular will make this plan impossible."

"And what is that?" asked Cato, turning to look at the young prince with curiosity. "Do tell."

"Why," Tingo sighed, "It is the kingdom of Bavel."

"The kingdom of Bavel," Hanz said with reverence in his voice. "Yes. A problem, indeed."

"They've coveted Arelle since the beginning of time," said Labyrinth.

"Bavel and Arelle, the dueling peaks," said Hanz. "Yes. And one must wonder why Bavel has done nothing while Arelle remains vacant. What has become of Bavel? Have they suffered the same famine as us? Are they nothing but a city of bones?"

Many of the delegates exchanged curious looks.

"Do you think they will come against us if we go to Arelle?" Mynx asked.

"I do not know," said Hanz, "But our lands are dying and at this point we have little choice. But let us take some time to think about these things. We can discuss more tomorrow. For now, please consider my words."

Hanz left the table first, escaping while the others argued over the details. The seed had been planted, today's task was done. The seed would germinate without his help. All he needed was for everyone to believe his story. If they did, they would believe in his solution; and not even Rasselas, son of that bastard Leo, could stop him.

As ever, Sigmund was waiting for Hanz outside the back exit of the courthouse. He was leaning against the wall with his hood low, gazing down at his gloved hand. He was stretching it open and closed, turning it side to side.

"How does it feel this morning?" Hanz asked as he stepped beside Sigmund.

Sigmund yawned, then said, "Painless. And... tingly. It's a bit small though." He raised his head to meet King Hanz' eyes.

"Karo said it will grow more," Hanz replied, then yawned as well. "Hades, Sigmund, stop yawning."

"I was up all night," Sigmund said, putting his hand into his pocket.

"So was I," Hanz retorted, "Remember? Plus, aren't you *always* up all night?"

"Of *course*, Sire." Sigmund nodded.

"Are you still feeling confident in the success of the experiment?" Hanz asked.

"I said it last night, and I will say it again: everything works." He gave Hanz a thumbs up with his right hand.

Hanz examined it with a grin. "It *is* a bit small, isn't it?"

"Yes, well," Sigmund shrugged, "It's well worth the sacrifice. Even my handwriting has improved!"

"I am glad to hear it," said Hanz. Perhaps it was time to trial his *own* experiment. He felt a pang of terror in his heart. But what if it *didn't* work?

"The midday bell is due," Sigmund said as he pushed himself off the wall he was leaning against. "Shouldn't we be walking?"

"Ah, right," Hanz said through another yawn. He really *was* tired. He had managed to get a few short naps after the late night experiment, but it sure didn't feel like enough!

Hanz began to walk to his next appointment, and Sigmund followed along after him.

"Well," Hanz said as he walked briskly through the castle grounds, "What are the final reports before you disappear for the day?"

Sigmund pulled out his notebook and flipped through it. "Not much to say," he said, "Though I did want to ask how the test went for Valley."

"Why did you want to ask about that?" Hanz muttered.

"What? You always tell me about the tests. I write it down in my..."

"Fine, fine," Hanz sighed. "I changed my mind."

"About...?"

"I didn't think it was a great idea."

Sigmund halted in his steps.

Hanz turned to face him. "What?" Hanz snapped, "What is it?"

"Quoting yourself, sire," Sigmund said, "You wanted to test not just Valley, but *yourself* this time."

Hanz sighed, "And your point?"

"If I may be so bold," Sigmund stepped up beside Hanz and lowered his voice to a whisper. "You feared that having the Affection Faerie so close to you might compromise your own desires. You wanted to test yourself and her effect on you by giving her to Karo. You thought this would prove you had no attachment to her—as well as add to our list of healthy queens."

"I know, I know," Hanz whispered back. "I just wonder if giving her to Karo isn't the best idea. What if *he* gets attached to her?"

"Sire," Sigmund said firmly, "Are you failing the test you gave yourself? Is your judgment wavering while young Valley is in the picture?"

"But this was never a problem before!" Hanz retorted. "I... I just wasn't ready to—"

"Wasn't *ready*?" Sigmund shook his head, "This isn't like you to take back a decision. It was a good plan. It tested Valley's submission to you, and it tested your own indifference to her. It also gives us greater chances of growing Faerie numbers with her in our list of—"

"*Stop!*" Hanz snapped, "I know *why* it was a good plan. Just let me sit on it."

"Very well, sire," Sigmund said, scribbling away in his notebook.

Hanz eyed the book, irritated at whatever the daemon was writing in it.

"How's Rosamond, anyway?" Hanz asked, eager to change the subject. The two resumed their hurried walk in the direction of the Warrowing Village.

"Ah, Rosamond," Sigmund looked up from his book. "I looked in on her as you asked. I fear she won't make the masque tonight."

"Damn," Hanz groaned, "We had that outfit planned and everything."

"Perhaps absence might make the hearts grow fonder?" Sigmund suggested.

"That works," Hanz said, "Or we could have someone else dress as Rosamond. She'll be wearing a mask, anyway."

"I don't think *anyone* could impersonate those lungs, sire." Sigmund said.

"Indeed," Hanz groaned. She was too much like her mother. "Will she be back on her feet tomorrow?"

Sigmund made a little groan. "We will see."

"I think that will be all, Sigmund," Hanz said as they neared the Warrowing Gate.

"Very well, Sire. And—" he paused, holding up his quill, "Will you give some thought to what I said about Valley? You asked me to tell you if I thought your judgment was off."

Hanz sighed, nodding. "Yes," he said, "I will think on it, and we can reconvene tonight after the masque."

"Very well," Sigmund nodded, then disappeared.

Hanz turned his gaze toward the Faerie gates, gritting his teeth. Sigmund wasn't wrong. It *was* uncharacteristic of him to go back on his plan. What did he care if Karo slept with Valley? Hanz certainly wasn't going to do it, given the problems *that* had wrought for him. No, he would never compromise himself like that again. Was he keeping her from Karo—the serial predator—out of fatherly concern? No... though he had raised her alongside Rosamond, Valley was nothing like a daughter to him. She was, however, someone important.

Tristan ran to meet Hanz at the gate. Hanz entered into his friendly relaxed manner and smiled warmly, joining hands with Tristan in a tight clasp.

"Friend," Tristan said excitedly, "Welcome, welcome. Good Wingsday!"

"A good Wingsday to you as well, friend," Hanz said in return. "How fare you?"

"Things are good here," Tristan said, nodding to himself as he turned back to gaze at his Faerie village. "Though I think some grow restless. Kingsummons has been a disrupting season, I think."

"I want to hear more about this," Hanz said, patting his hand against Tristan' arm. "We both know the Fae are in a precarious place. They need much care. I do not want you to think I have forgotten about them, even with all the delegates visiting."

"No, no," Tristan shook his head, "You and I both knew that having outsiders in Mensa would be jarring for them. Faeries... they do better with little change. With time, they will adjust."

"Yes," Hanz said, "But I want them to know they are safe, despite all the change. I think they will need to see me more often."

"I think so too," said Tristan, and he began to lead Hanz into the Warrowing Village. "You are the only leader they have right now. That makes you a necessity."

"I am not the *only* leader they have, Tristan. It is you they named chief, I think." Hanz smiled, giving Tristan a knowing wink.

The two of them strolled through the Warrowing Square. "I think a few have reached the age of ability this season," Tristan said. Faeries began to spot King Hanz and gathered around like villagers to a puppet show. Hanz waved with a passing smile, then Tristan motioned for them to give the king space. "We are seeing some strong numbers for the Fae. If we keep this up, we might see the promise of a steady population after the Somenus massacre."

Hanz bowed his head. "It is almost too painful to think about," he said. "There were so few of you left."

"Yes," Tristan replied as he raised his eyes to the Sky. "It has not been easy to rebuild these numbers, Hanz. Many are resistant."

"Come," Hanz said, "Let us sit and talk. Tell me about the climate here. There is nothing you and I cannot solve, eh? Like old times?"

Tristan nodded slowly with a weary smile. "Like old times."

The two entered Tristan's residence; the largest building within the Warrowing Village. Even he owned next to no possessions. But, unlike everyone else in the Warrowing Village, he was allowed some furniture. The two men sat across from each other on a pair of armchairs and Tristan generously poured some freshly brewed tea into two glass cups.

"Tell me about the resistance you are facing, Tristan," Hanz said, as he brought the herbaceous tea to his nostrils. "Resistance from the young ones?"

"Well," Tristan leaned forward, balancing his teacup on one of his knees, "As always, most of the young women do not like to be assigned to the Elders. I often find myself needing to... well... threaten discipline. It doesn't feel right, you know?"

Hanz let out a deep exhale. "I know exactly what you mean," he said. "What are we supposed to do—let the Fae die off as a race?"

"I ask myself the same thing," said Tristan. "But I know that I would hate the idea of having to marry someone when I was happy just being as I am. It sounds downright... *petrifying*."

"Well, we aren't exactly making them get married," Hanz mumbled with a secret smile.

"True, but—"

"Did you know," Hanz said as he casually sipped his hot tea, "the Fae did not always marry?"

Tristan raised his eyebrows. "I have heard many of the greats reference that fact in old writings, though I never understood what they meant."

Hanz nodded. "Our time at Winter's End was not wasted," he said, "Aorist had many helpful books and biographies. There was one book in particular I found helpful here."

"Please, do share." Tristan relaxed into his chair.

"The Fae do not naturally seek out marriage or life pairs," stated Hanz.

"I could have told you that myself," Tristan chuckled, "Myself included. I find the Humans' need to romance one another and procreate quite ridiculous, frankly."

Hanz chuckled. "Honestly? So do I. In any case, *we* were made with this itch to fill our lands with more of ourselves. The Fae? The original Faeries were made with a set population: one thousand. The first Faeries were created, not birthed."

Tristan nodded. "This, I knew."

"Do you know why marriage was given to the Fae?" Hanz asked. Tristan shook his head. "There was a great Faerie war," Hanz said with a distant look in his eyes, "Many, *many* Faeries died. So many that their race was near extinction." As Hanz said this, he saw a look of terror in Tristan's face. He wanted to find out what was at the bottom of that fear, but he continued with his narrative. "Marriage became necessary for their survival. Some Fae married and some gave birth. But there could still only ever be one thousand Faeries in existence. There will only ever be a thousand titles. In times of war, the Faerie king would arrange marriages so that numbers could increase—can you guess why?"

Tristan chuckled, "Because we are not naturally inclined to marry."

"Yes," said Hanz. "The Fae are quite individual and independent creatures. You prefer solitude and silence. You are not community-oriented, you crave space and distance. Some Fae might marry and then live a hundred lifetimes hardly ever speaking a word to their spouse. A few rare couples actually do fall in love, I suppose, but those stories are something novel to tell children, and not something most ever experience."

Tristan sipped his tea thoughtfully, then said, "This all rings true."

"This is why I encourage arranged marriages or partnerships," Hanz said, "And honestly, I think you and I have built up enough trust with the Fae that they will not question us. They do not know how to do communal life because it is not natural for Faeries. But tell me, friend, do you think it has been good for them?"

"It honestly has!" Tristan replied. "In all my seasons on Raqia, I have never lived in a community such as this. We all live together, work together, share sorrows together, and we find a purpose in something more than ourselves and our own powers!"

"Yes!" Hanz said enthusiastically, "*That* is what my hope is by bringing them all together here!"

"Mine as well," said Tristan. His joyful face began to sober. "Aorist wanted us to find the truth... and the truth we did find. But we did not know what to do with it. At least *now* we can find it together."

"Do you feel like things have gotten better for those of you in the Purple Order? And for the Fae that have been born in our care?"

Tristan smiled. "I *do* feel that, Hanz," he said, "Though at times I question myself."

"What do you question?" Hanz asked, maintaining an honest expression.

"Well," Tristan groaned as he turned to gaze out his window, "some of the core group disagreed. You know—those in the prisons..."

Hanz pursed his lips silently, then said, "Do you think they were right to turn away from us?"

Tristan shook his head slowly, as if still trying to convince himself. "No," he said, "I think they held onto extremes... or at least..." he furrowed his brow, "They wanted to hold on to an old addiction."

"And what addiction is that?" Hanz asked.

"The addiction to their power," said Tristan. "They... they loved it too much." He was like a eunuch who pitied whole men, as if their power was a liability. This was good, Hanz thought.

"It is a sad thing," Hanz said, "To want something that is not your own. *Hades...* there's a word for that, isn't there?"

"Covetousness," said Tristan with conviction. "It is covetousness to want something that is forbidden to you."

"Like desiring someone else's wife," said Hanz lazily. And then for some reason he felt a stabbing conviction in his heart—a conviction that Valley should not belong to Karo. No, she did not belong to Karo. She belonged to—

"You really *are* a good leader," Tristan said with a sigh, "You care about us. You care enough to be a part of our lives, to live among us, and sacrifice your time for us." Again, the man looked like someone who was reciting lines to himself. If he said them often enough, he would believe them.

"Aorist seemed content to hide the truth from you, because he could not bear the responsibility of what he knew," Hanz said in a spiteful tone, "At least *I* will do something with what I know."

"Yes..." Tristan nodded, "Precisely."

"I don't always do the right thing. Hades, Tristan, I am sure many see me as a villain! But at least I *try*!"

"You are no villain!" Tristan gasped, leaning forward quickly to grasp Hanz by the hand. "You are our truest ally!"

The Faeries truest ally: that was Hanz. The king smiled at those words as they echoed through his mind. For the next bell, from the Ascending bell to the Zenith bell, those words played like music through his ears as he greeted his Faerie population within the Warrowing Village. Like excited peasants, showing off their meager accomplishments to their visiting Lord, the Fae flocked around him, showing him their children, and talking endlessly about how thankful they were to be amongst his protected Fae. What would they have if he had not shown them kindness? Who would they have been if he had not rescued them from the confusion of their existence? How many of these babies he kissed, or children whose heads he rubbed, how many would not exist if he had not ordered it so?

Some may call him a villain, and others a hero. What did it matter what others thought? He had brought life and beauty into this world. He had made an entire community, all by his wisdom and oversight. Whatever anyone had to hold against him, they could not take *this* away from him!

Hanz's head buzzed contentedly as he entered his chambers that afternoon. As it was every Wingsday when he went to visit the Warrowing Village, he did not want the day to end. There, he was a hero; there, he was a true King.

Hanz sat upon his favorite armchair, smiling to himself. There was a good bell before he needed to dress for the masque and, instead of picking up his most recent novel, all he wanted to do was sit there and dwell on his successes. He wanted to bask in the joy of his accomplishments. He wanted to feel the fullness of being the greatest man Raqia had known thus far. He was paving a way not just for Humans to survive and thrive in this new age, but for the Fae as well!

There was a knock on his door. Hanz' eyes did their best to focus, and he lifted his chin slightly as he said, "Oh, come in? That is—who is it?"

Hanz was surprised to see Valley enter the room. He had not summoned her. Had she... had she *wanted* to see him? "Valley!" Hanz leaned forward, feeling a thrill within his heart. "What a pleasant surprise!"

The girl blinked, taken aback by his enthusiasm, though she inched toward him slowly.

What a woman she had become in the last hundred days. Did she know how alluring her mere presence was?

"Sire," the girl said hesitantly, "May I speak with you?"

"Of course, Valley," Hanz snickered, "My, my, girl. Always so formal. Do relax." He settled into his armchair and popped one of his ankles onto his knee.

Hanz wouldn't ever take advantage of her flesh as Karo would, but he didn't mind admiring her as she stood submissively before him. What a small Faerie she was.

"My Lord," said Valley, "You did tell me you had no other commands for me today, and I was wondering... oh *Hades*..." her cheeks flushed.

"I'm wildly curious," the king said with a grin. He folded his hands together, watching her fumble.

"I was wondering if I could attend the masque tonight. You know—with Rosamond. I would wear a mask, so no one would know it was me!" Her eyes widened with terror, "Oh *Hades*, should I not have asked? I simply wanted to—!"

"Oh, Valley," Hanz belted out a laugh, "You silly girl."

"I am sorry for asking," Valley shook her head ashamedly, "It was really so stupid."

"No, no!" Hanz rose from his chair, waving his hand, "Please. Do not fret." He stepped toward the girl and placed his hand on her shoulder. How small it was beneath his touch. She was like a child still, and yet—very much *not* a child. "Of *course* you can go!" The response was that of the heroic king that the Fae had praised him for being. It felt good to give such a gift. Yes, he would let this lowly servant girl attend the royal masque. Though she didn't deserve to be there, he would find a way!

"Really?" Valley smiled excitedly. "Th—*Thank* you, sire!"

A smile! He had not seen her make a smile like that in quite some time. It was so pure and innocent.

"Of course," Hanz said quietly, watching her face with fascination. "I am happy to give you such things, Valley. When will you finally realize how much I care about my Faeries, hmm?" He felt her chin between his thumb and finger. "Don't you see? I *care* for you."

Valley's face changed. The innocent girlish excitement faded, and those wide eyes of trepidation glimmered before him.

"Is something wrong?" Hanz asked, tightening his brow.

"No," Valley said, though her eyes betrayed her. She was scared of him. *Why?* Why would such a girl be scared of him?

"Something is wrong," Hanz said, drawing closer. "Let me still your fears. Tell me, Valley, tell me what troubles you."

Valley drew back. "I think I will go now," she said.

"Valley!" Hanz said quickly as his heart pounded within his chest.

"Yes?" she quickly turned to stare wide-eyed into his face.

For a moment, time seemed to stop. Then he took her into his arms. She might have resisted, but he could not tell. He forced a kiss upon her lips. He drew in her scent, leaping with inward joy as he tasted her beauty. Then he was struck with sudden pain.

Hanz gasped, stepping backward. His foot throbbed, and he realized that Valley had driven her heel into it.

"Valley!" he gasped with sorrow, "Why do you withdraw from me?" He stepped toward her, reaching for her arm once more. The little rabbit of a girl dove away, holding up her hands.

"You swore you would not touch me!" she shrieked.

"Why do you recoil?" Hanz raised his voice, "I will not hurt you!"

"You said you would not do this!" she returned.

"What are you—?" Hanz licked his drying lips, watching the red-faced Faerie back away. Why would she move away from him when she was the one who...

Hanz' face hardened. "Valley..." he murmured like a distant thunder. "What have you *done*?"

"What have *I*...?" The girl shook her head. "I haven't done *anything*!"

"Valley!" Hanz roared, feeling his anger swell, "What have you *done*?"

Valley rushed to the door and threw her hands against the handle.

"Stay where you are!" Hanz shouted, pointing. Valley froze, then turned to gaze at him fearfully as he charged toward her. "You schemer! How could you do this! How could you *lie* to me?"

"What have I done?" She gasped. The woman fell before him, then bowed her forehead to the ground. "Please tell me so that I may repent!"

"Where is it?" Hanz asked as steadily as he could. Horror seemed to rise within him, coupled with a shaking rage. Wherever it was, he had to find it. *Hades*, he had to find it before it grew more powerful than he could control!

"Where is *what*?" Valley cried, "I do not know what you mean!"

"Where is it?" Hanz yelled. He seized Valley by the hair of her scalp and drew her to her feet. She stumbled upwards, but did not fight him. He sunk his hand into her skirt pocket. Valley resisted with a shout.

"What are you looking for?" she asked. "I will give you anything you ask for!"

"Where is it?" Hanz asked again, pulling at one of her sleeves. She was hiding it. Where would the bitch *hide* such a thing? He yanked hard on her sleeve until it tore off, revealing her blistering shoulder brand. Valley yelped with pain and pressed her hand against the wound. Hanz refused to relent. He pulled at every piece of loose fabric he could get his hands on, determined to find the source of the power.

He drove his hand into her other skirt pocket, and his fingers felt something crisp. He yanked free a piece of paper, stuck with a broken wax seal.

"No!" Valley gasped, watching as Hanz held it up to his face.

"What is this?" Hanz asked in a rage. "Where did you get this?"

"It's just a letter I found!" She replied, "*What*? What have I done?"

"Don't you know?" Hanz shook the letter before her eyes. "Tell me now, woman. Tell me for sure, does this letter *mean* anything to you?"

Valley stammered, her mouth hanging open.

"Tell me you don't care about this paper," Hanz said slowly, watching her face.

"It is just a letter!" Valley shook her head.

Hanz lunged to his hearth and cast it into the fire. Valley screamed with horror.

"No!" she cried, "Please, don't burn it!"

"Look!" Hanz bellowed, pointing at the flames, "Look and see what you have done!"

The two of them gazed into the flames. The paper did not burn. It lay amongst the flames like a fish swims in the water, unblemished.

Yes. There was no doubt now. The woman had begun to store magik in this thing. Whether she realized it or not, she had claimed an imperium. Who knew how much magik she had stored in that felling piece of paper. She was the felling Nightmare Faerie! And already, the woman had been working her magik on him, drawing his eyes and his passion.

"Do you know what you almost made me *do*?" Hanz said in a raised voice.

Tears formed in Valley's eyes. "You were drawn to me... because of what I am?"

"You know, don't you?" Hanz crossed his arms. "You know your title."

Valley nodded slowly. "I am the Dream Faerie," she said.

"Did you know you were growing in power?" Hanz asked, changing to a somewhat fatherly tone.

She shook her head. "I had no idea!"

"You knew you were not allowed possessions."

"But it is not an object of value!" Valley returned. "It is just a piece of paper."

"Yes, but one must wonder..." Hanz said in a cool tone as he pulled the letter from the flames with his fire tongs. "What is written within it? Do you think words do not have value?"

"Please, don't—" Valley bit her tongue.

"Don't what?" Hanz turned the paper in his hands. "*Read* it?"

"I'm sorry!" Valley said as she blinked the tears from her eyes.

"Valley, I am trying to keep you from becoming what Somenus became, don't you see? Don't you see what you did to me? You *made* me desire you!"

"I didn't do anything!" she cried.

"You must not grow in power, Valley," Hanz said in a dark voice as he drew close to her. "I raised you myself so as to keep the world safe from you. Don't you see? You are a monster, which if left unchecked, would eat up our world."

"I wouldn't!" she said weakly. "I would not do what Somenus did! I would not make others love me!"

"But you already have!" Hanz bellowed. Valley started, cowering as he shouted. "And I am sure you have worked on others, not just myself. Think about it, Valley—have you noticed a change in others?"

Guilt characterized her face. She dropped her head into her hands.

"You foolish girl," Hanz shook his head. "This... this cannot continue. You must never see this letter again."

Valley nodded, still hiding in shame.

"Oswald!" Hanz shouted. When no reply came, he charged to the door and flew it open. "Oswald! In here—*now!*"

Hanz' captain came marching into the room, then halted when he saw Valley standing there.

"Take her to the pit," Hanz said, gesturing lazily toward her with his hand, "I'll be along shortly."

"Sire?" Oswald asked calmly. "Is everything alright?"

Oswald seemed concerned. *Hades*—had she been working on *him*, too?

"Will you just do as I say, Captain?" Hanz asked shortly. "And bring extra guards. We have some Faerie discipline to attend to."

Valley lifted her head bravely and sniffed up her tears.

"I am ready, Oswald," she said, "I will not resist."

"Very well, Valley." Oswald said quietly. He waited until Valley joined his side, then left with her.

Hanz plopped himself into his armchair with a grunt. So, Sigmund was right. He had failed his own test with Valley. Hanz turned the letter in his fingers, examining it. Just how much dark magik was stored in this thing? It would make an excellent addition to his collection—and honestly—it was probably a good thing that Valley had picked an imperium by now. From what he understood, Valley would not be able to make a second until she got this one back. So while he had this letter, she could never grow any stronger. Yes, this was actually a good thing.

He cracked open the letter and began to read it, mumbling aloud.

Faerie of Mensa — I see your chains. Do you? How can an aurochs be chained like an ox? Don't you know who you are? I compel you, friend, to perceive yourself not as a weak and powerless individual, but as a potent and controlled giant. You are not like a beast of burden which can be trained to do the will of its master, but a shining, untouchable light, that cannot be quelled by darkness. Your existence and purpose cannot be hidden by lies, just as day cannot be concealed by a cloth. No one can force you to serve; you choose to serve. So do not serve in a way that destroys yourself. Serve in the way you were made to serve. Serve not as a slave obeys the will of its master, or as a dog obeys its owner; but serve as a parent serves a child, or as a king serves his people. You are a potent and controlled giant, filled with the gift of unimaginable power. Do not forsake this gift because others have told you it is your shame. It is not your shame; it is your glory. Do not be ashamed of who you are, and do not forsake the greater purpose of your existence for a lesser one. I cannot free you from the chains until you first believe that they bind you. When you are ready, I will find you.

"Damn," Hanz said as he closed the letter gently. Who wrote this? Whoever it was had taken and twisted words from the Green Lion of Bavel's writings. Who would use words of peace to stir up war? These were dangerous words.

"Damn," he said again, rising from his chair. Words were powerful things. Words were like seeds, scattered across fertile lands. Words gave birth to actions. "I should never have taught her to read," he mumbled as he shoved the letter in his pocket.

Well, at least he had found them before they had done too much damage. But how could he know the extent of the damage already done by these words? Had they spread? And how far? He would need to add this problem to his ever-growing list of things to solve.

But he would, *by Hades*; he would solve it.

26

—— Rook ——

The Tormentor

ANODOS LAY STILL ON THE STONE TABLE in a pool of his own blood. Was it a blessing or a curse that his body would instantly make more? He still felt pain from the previous attempt to kill him. How many bells had it been? Who could tell?

"It's not working. Nothing is working," said the voice of his tormentor. He could not see her face. "I can't kill him."

"Keep trying," said the voice of another woman. Anodos had not heard her voice before. Or had he? He could not remember.

"He can't be killed," said his tormentor.

"The previous Faerie of Power died. It is possible to kill him," said the second voice.

"That may be true, but I can't do it. When I slit his throat, the wounds heal before I can remove his head from the table. And when I try to remove his heart..."

"I have been here the whole time, Ahkish, I *know*. There has to be more you can try."

"Why don't *you* try!" said Ahkish, his tormentor.

"You *know* I cannot kill. I would if I could."

"I think it is time to move to try our alternative plan. Time for you to take over, Riah."

"Hallo?" Anodos called weakly. "Riah—is that you? Faerie of Illusion?"

"*Now* look what you've done. You've said my name in his presence!" Riah barked.

"He's a Faerie king," Ahkish said. "He will know who you are the click he sees your face anyway."

Riah sighed. "Fine. I will prepare for the alternative plan. But until I am ready to begin, just keep trying. There *has* to be a way to kill this monster."

"Why are you trying to kill me?" Anodos begged. "I am not my father!"

"Quiet, daemon!" Ahkish screeched.

"Riah!" Anodos called out helplessly, "Hear me! You are a Faerie—I am your kin, please! Set me free!"

"Quiet!"

⎯⎯ • ⎯⎯

"Riah!" Rook screamed, sitting up in his bed. There was silence around him. His body ached. Rook's hands went to his chest. The broken bones from his fall the previous night had all healed.

"Riah..." he mumbled to himself. How he wished he could forget her. "Damn," he groaned. He leapt out of his bed and searched his coat pocket for his timepiece. He examined it with bleary, tired eyes. The hour was approaching the descending bell. Before long, evening would set in.

Rook stretched out his body, feeling it pop and crack into place. He might be able to heal any wound, yet he still felt the pain of his broken bones. He strode to his window and pushed it open. The Mensa Castle grounds were still littered with debris. Would the stupid ball still be held even with all the destruction? He hoped not. What was that storm that came out of nowhere? He usually sensed coming storms. Why not this one? It had come so suddenly, as if even the Sky could not have anticipated it.

There was a hurried knock on Rook's door. Who could that be? Had Cato returned from the courthouse meeting?

"Come," he called as the door flew open.

To his great surprise, Latimer the Elven skydeacon blazed in.

"Latimer!" he exclaimed, "Whatever is the matter?"

"I am sorry, Rook," Latimer said, slamming the door behind him, "I didn't know who else to come to." He paced about the room as if chased by bees. "I—I—I—I'm just so angry!"

"I'm sorry to hear that." Rook approached the Elf and lay a calming hand on his shoulder. "Please, tell me what is wrong."

"What is wrong?!" Latimer blurted, shaking his head. He pulled a notebook out from under his arm and threw it across the room. Loose papers scattered into the air like falling snow. "What is *wrong*?" He threw his hands into the air, "They named the storm. *That's* what's wrong!"

Rook blinked. "They... named the...?"

"They named the storm! After what—a few *bells*? I—I—I—I don't even know what to say! This is... this is so wrong!"

It wasn't like the Elf to lose his temper. Rook folded his arms and took a step back, giving the angered man room to breathe. Despite the compassion he felt toward the skydeacon, Rook was still a tad entertained to see him so worked up over the weather.

"Sit yourself down, Latimer," Rook said, "before you hurt yourself."

Latimer collapsed into an idle chair, sighing. "The Fellowship is doomed."

"Tell me what happened. What have they named the storm?"

"It's not that I have a problem with the name itself—" he paused, "Well...I have a problem with that too, actually. But the fact that they have already named it? Rook, it takes days and days and days to name a storm! There is so much data to evaluate, wind directions, durations, signs..." he shook his head wildly, "And it takes a whole fleet of us coming together and deliberating before we can actually *name* the storm based on our findings! But... *oh Hades, Hades, Hades...* Do you know what they have *named* it, Rook? Do you?"

Rook shook his head slowly.

"The Mensa skydeacons, who *apparently* have most of the sway in the Fellowship now, have named it *The Quakes of New Beginnings*. The Quakes of— can you *believe* this?"

"I—"

"That was a fury storm, Rook—a *fury* storm! We all knew it! Hades, we had no idea if we would all die last night! It's a miracle only Princess Rosamond was wounded in the highwinds."

"What do you mean, Princess Rosamond?" Rook frowned. "She wasn't hurt, was she?"

"She nearly died!" Latimer exclaimed. "The Heavens were angry, Rook. And it is the job of us skydeacons to communicate that truth to others. And now... they have gone and named the storm *The Quakes of New Beginnings*? They didn't even consult me!"

Rosamond was injured? Surely not. Rook had been with her the entire time. She was fine!

"What do you think the storm should have been named?" Rook asked.

"Hades, I don't know! Rook, it will take me weeks and weeks to even have an *opinion*! The only thing I am sure of is its class. It was, by all means, a fury storm. We all know it."

Latimer let out a deep breath. His own inner storm began to disintegrate. And after a few moments of quiet passed, the only emotions left on Latimer's face were sorrow and defeat.

"Is this really happening?" The Elf asked. "Has the Fellowship actually been compromised?"

"It sure sounds like it," said Rook. "I am sorry."

"But why? Why would they want to sow their own meaning into the storm? Why not listen to what it wants to say? I don't understand!"

Rook sighed. "Perhaps they have their own truths—or lies—they want to tell."

Latimer shook his head. "But that's not what it means to be a skydeacon. They *know* that."

"Are others in the Fellowship as angry as you?" Rook asked.

"I am sure they are or will be… once others start hearing about it. Though, I have to say, Rook, I am surprised that the Mensan skydeacons are just going along with it."

"What will you do?" Rook asked.

"I… that is a good question, friend. I do not yet know. I think I need to find out how deep this problem goes. And who is behind it."

"Yes." Rook didn't know what else to say. "If you wish to learn more, I suggest you do your best to stay out of the spotlight. If you cause too much trouble to those who are behind this, they will see you as an enemy."

"It is not in my nature to hold my tongue, Rook," Latimer said. "I will not stay silent about this simply to spare myself danger. If other skydeacons are staying silent for that reason, it really will be the end of our order. No. I will not be silent on this. Even if it leads to my death, I will fight this."

Rook's eyes widened. There was something so simple and pure about Latimer's conviction. "I admire you, Latimer," he said, "You're a courageous man."

Latimer chuckled. "I thank you for saying so, but no. I am simply devoted to my practice. But I do not know how else to live! A thousand seasons I have watched these Skies; I simply cannot betray them by distorting their words to all who cannot speak their language. We are interpreters, you know—the skydeacons. We explain the words of the Skies to the people of Raqia. It would be a crime against creation to change what words we hear into our own words. Can you imagine? The Lights speak through the weather… shall we distort their words?"

"A crime, indeed," Rook said solemnly. "To take words from the Creator and make them our own."

"It is false prophecy; nothing less!" Latimer said in a stern voice.

"A fury storm… does that communicate that the Lights are… angry?"

"Didn't I say that?"

"I suppose you did," Rook smiled, "So why would the Mensa skydeacons change the message?"

Latimer thought for a moment. "I suppose they might want the people of Raqia to think that the storm represented something good. Perhaps give the gathered monarchs the impression that their plans are blessed by the Lights?"

"That is what I am wondering," Rook said. "A storm, whatever its true purpose, can be perceived in many different ways. Why not use it to one's advantage?"

Latimer gasped. "Rook... do you think King Hanz has... dare I say it... *bought* the skydeacons? Surely, he would not use them for his own ends!"

"I wouldn't put it past him," Rook said, frowning. "The man is cunning."

Latimer shook his head. "No. I cannot imagine someone could be so selfish..."

"And yet, you know I am right."

"I will think about these things, Rook." Latimer moved to gather his scattered notes. "I am sorry for bursting in here. I... I don't usually act so..."

"Think nothing of it," Rook said. He hurried over to the floor where Latimer was collecting his writings and helped him gather them. "I appreciate your friendship. You are a trustworthy man. Even if no one else appreciates your honesty, I do."

Latimer looked up from his stack of papers with a warm smile. "Thank you, Rook. I..." He leaned back onto his knees. "I think the Lights brought us together. You are a good friend."

"Sure," Rook chuckled. "I like that thought. Say..." Rook bit his lip for a moment, "Did you say Rosamond almost died in the storm? But she is alright; she didn't really get... *hurt*, did she?"

"Have you not heard?" Latimer asked with concern. "She was hurt badly. I spoke with the Mensa surgeon earlier today after I heard she had been stuck in the storm. Oh Rook... I feel so guilty for not looking out for her! I should have known better than to leave her there amongst those drunkards!"

"But she wasn't hurt!" Rook said sharply.

"Rook, don't you hear what I keep saying? She was badly hurt. She was in the storm!"

"I *know* she was in the storm!" Rook said, "That doesn't mean she was injured."

"Am I not making sense?" Latimer rose to his feet, holding his papers in a messy pile. "I am sorry. Forgive me. I mean to say that she is going to be alright. She will survive. But the surgeon did say she took a pretty bad beating. I fear she won't be there for the masque tonight. Poor thing. I wonder if Hanz will allow visitors? I'd love to offer my apologies. I should have run *right* back into the gamesroom once I realized there was a fury storm brewing! I just get so... so caught up in the moment! One cannot miss a single flash of lightning in a storm like that!"

"No one could blame you for what happened to her, Latimer." Rook stood and passed Latimer the rest of the papers he had gathered.

"Rook, do not try to get me off the hook here. It is good for us all to take some responsibility for what happened to her. Don't you think?"

Rook chuckled. "Latimer," he said, "You do know how to poke at a man's conscience."

"Oh I don't mean to make you feel... *oh Lights*... I can be a bit too self-righteous at times, I think."

"Stop worrying so much!" Rook laughed. "Latimer, how do you live with yourself?"

"Oh, I live just fine," Latimer joined in with the laughter, "I simply let the Skies drown out my flighty thoughts."

"I should take a page from your book," Rook said, "Come on, let's go outside and catch the last light of the day. I sense the Descending bell is about to ring."

"*Do* you?" Latimer grinned, "Well, we will make a skydeacon out of you, yet!"

Rook and Latimer strolled together through the Inner Palace grounds. Rook listened as the Elf talked through all the unique elements of the storm. It intrigued Rook that the storm's heart was centered directly over Mensa Castle. Once Latimer heard the descending bell ring, he excused himself from Rook's side, stating that he wanted to check in on the princess before the masque.

What had really happened, anyway? Rook knew she had been alright when he left her that morning. He was tempted to go with Latimer, but he felt that it might be the wisest idea to stay away from her for now.

Rook blew air out through his lips nervously, turning to walk in the direction of the Warrowing Village. He had promised the Packrats that he would stop by to visit them today. And with the masque being only one bell away, he knew this was his last chance. He was a mixed bag of feelings as he ventured toward the Faerie village. He honestly didn't know what he thought of the place. It felt both like home and like a prison.

Theo stood waiting for him at the gate.

"Rook, Rook!" Theo cried, rushing to Rook's side. "Hurry!"

"Why are you all always in a hurry?" Rook laughed. "Come on, Theo, what's going on?" His smile faded when he realized that Theo was distressed.

"I don't like being out here when a sister gets punished." Theo jumped, climbing up onto Rook's shoulder.

"Theo!" Rook chuckled as the boy pulled himself onto Rook's back like a steed.

"March! Quick! Into the Village."

"What do you mean about a sister being punished?" Rook turned around, noticing a group of soldiers gathering around the far side of the Warrowing Gate.

"Rook, I told you I don't like it! *Please* can we go inside?" Theo jabbed Rook's sides with his heels.

"I'm going, I'm going." Rook placed his hands on Theo's knees and walked into the village, toward Marbel's house. "You're a bit big for a shoulder ride, aren't you?"

"You're tall," Theo said, "I can see over people's heads!"

Rook shook his head with a chuckle. "How are the Packrats? Any reports?"

"Well..." Theo said quietly, "I'll let mother tell you."

That sounded ominous. "Alright..."

Soon, Michael came running up from a side street. "Rook!" he yelled, "You came!"

"How fare you, Michael?" Rook asked, reaching over to ruffle the boy's slick black hair.

"*Augh*," Michael swatted his hand away, "It's alright. I was just spreading the word to the rest of the village."

"What word?" Rook asked. Ah, the little Messenger Faerie, ever making it his job to make sure everyone knows everything.

"*Erm*, didn't you see?" Michael turned and pointed back toward the gate. "Valley got in trouble for taking up an imperium."

"Valley?" Rook turned to look back toward the gates. Hevel's daughter? "What's going to happen to her?"

"*Erm*," Michael shoved his hands into his pockets with a look of discomfort, "I heard they are going to make an example of her. That's what one of the soldiers told me, anyway. Some people like to watch. I don't like to, though. They took away her object, I think, and now she's in the pit."

"What..." Rook asked slowly, "is the pit?"

"It's in the outer court. You know, that place just north of the gate? It's where we get punished for breaking laws."

Rook's heart began to pound within his chest. Valley was there... *now*?

"What happens to Faeries who carry imperiums?" Rook asked in a low voice.

"Well," Michael looked down at his shoes as they walked, "We don't know. Valley is the first I have known of to try and get one. We will have to see what they... what happens to her. Maybe it's just a night in the pit?"

Theo wrapped his little arms around Rook's head. "I don't want to think about it," said the boy.

Rook sighed. He had given these boys imperiums and charged them up with a decent amount of magik. He knew it; they knew it... and they must be terrified.

"Come on, lads," Rook said, "I'm here now. Let's get to Marbel's and talk about it. You don't have to worry, alright?"

"We know you'll protect us, Rook," Theo said, squeezing Rook's head tightly, "Mum says you'll scapegoat for us."

Small drops of rain began to fall around them as they turned the corner and Marbel's house came into view.

Coppo was sitting on the ground, just outside Marbel's door. His hands were shoved into his pockets and his chin was hanging down low, resting on his chest.

Rook approached him. "You alright?"

Coppo lifted his head excitedly. "Rook!" He rose, keeping his hands in his pockets, and smiled. "We hoped you would come!"

"You worried about Valley, too?"

Coppo froze for a moment, blinking. "Valley…" he mumbled to himself, "will try again tomorrow…for now the best option is to…"

"Coppo?" Rook asked, cocking his head to the side. "Are you alright?"

"Oh!" Coppo shook himself back to attention, "Yeah, yeah… *Yeeeeeah*," he groaned, "Valley was storing magik, I guess. None of us knew, though."

"Come on, let's get inside," Rook said quickly. He was growing more and more nervous that someone might overhear their conversation and get the boys in trouble.

Marbel's door flew open, and the woman poked her head out. "So you came, did you?" she asked sternly. "Alright, get in here."

Rook and the three boys entered the house. Marbel closed the door quickly after them.

"Sit," she said, pointing at the rug on the floor. Rook placed the lad on the floor, then he, Theo, Michael, and Coppo all sat together on the rug. The little golden-haired Theo plopped himself on Rook's lap.

"I heard about Valley from the lads," Rook said, looking up at Marbel who stood above him with her arms crossed. "What happened?"

"She had an imperium," Marbel said sternly, "And now you can see how seriously it is taken around here. We don't store magik here, *Rook*!"

"What will they do to her?" Rook asked, "Please, tell me!"

"Oh, I don't know," she said. "But Rook, this can't happen. Boys? Do as I told you."

Theo was the first to obey his mother. He turned to face Rook and held up the white feather he had plucked from Rook's wing.

"You… you're giving it back to me?" Rook asked, feeling a swell of sadness within his heart.

"You'll keep it safe for me, won't you, Rook?" Theo asked, smiling. "I know you'll take good care of it."

"I will," said Rook. He took the feather gently from Theo's hand. It was one of his own feathers that Theo had plucked from his wing. The thing radiated light magik. Rook opened his small pouch and placed it inside. "I suppose you two are returning your things to me as well?" he asked Coppo and Michael.

"Marbel says it's too dangerous to have these," Michael said, placing his beloved coin into the sack. "And we would rather *you* have them than anyone else."

Rook glanced at Coppo, who still had his hands in his pockets. He sat on the floor, staring off into space.

"Coppo?" Rook asked gently. "You don't have to give it up if you don't want to. It is your choice."

"I..." Coppo lifted his eyes to Rook. They were damp.

"You're a special Faerie, Coppo," Rook said, "with or without an imperium."

Coppo sniffed, then bowed his head. He began to cry softly. Rook set Theo aside and put an arm around the young man.

"Oh, Coppo," Marbel said softly. She knelt down and put her hand on the boy's back. "You can show Rook what's happened. It's alright."

"What do you mean?" Rook asked Marbel with a frown. "What happened?"

Coppo shook his head wildly.

"Show him, Copp," Marbel said.

"Coppo," Rook sighed, "What has happened? You can show me."

Coppo lifted his head slowly and gazed up at Rook. "Will you think less of me?"

"Never. Now please, tell me what's going on."

Coppo pulled his arms from his pockets and held them out.

Rook's breath caught in his throat as horror came over him. Coppo's right hand was gone, perfectly removed without a single scratch. It was just *gone*.

"My drawing hand," Coppo said with a quivering lip.

"Coppo," Rook said, doing his best to restrain his anger, "Who did this to you?"

Coppo shook his head quickly. "I can't tell you."

"You can tell me. You *will* tell me," Rook said.

Coppo shook his head again. "I will *not* tell you!"

"Don't scare him, Rook," Marbel said slowly, "He won't tell any of us what happened."

"Did they find out you had an imperium?" Rook asked. "Is this a *punishment*?"

"No, no," Coppo shook his head. "I still have it," he glanced at Marbel, "I am sorry, Miss Marbel, but I won't give it up. I need it."

Marbel nodded slowly. "It is your choice, Coppo."

"You are still the Faerie of lines, even without your hand, Coppo." Rook said as he touched the boy's left hand. "No one can take that away from you. No one can take away who you really are."

"But I can't draw anymore," Coppo said in a shaky voice.

"Use your left hand. Never stop drawing. You could draw lines with your toes if you had to, but you must not stop!"

Coppo sighed defeatedly. "I will try," he said.

Rook and Marbel exchanged sorrowful looks.

"Listen, Coppo," Rook said softly, "I have lost something, too."

Coppo glanced at Theo, then back at Rook. "What have you lost, Sir Rook?"

Rook smiled weakly, then tucked his hair behind an ear. "Look," he said, "Look at the scars."

The boys gathered around, shoving each other roughly as they all tried to get a good view of Rook's deformed ear, cut right at the tips.

"What happened?" Michael asked quickly.

"Someone took the tips of my ears," Rook said quietly. "I'm a Faerie, like you."

"I knew it!" Michael gasped.

Coppo smiled. "Theo did say you have wings... we hoped he wasn't lying."

"Which Faerie are you?" Michael asked excitedly.

"That is a secret," Rook said, "But I do know the pain of losing part of who you are. It... it does something to you."

Coppo searched Rook's face with his pain-filled eyes. "Yes," he said, "It does."

"When you are ready to talk about what happened, I will be here," said Rook. "Hang on to that imperium. It will help you maintain magik until you can learn to draw with your left hand."

"Alright, Rook," Coppo said. He rose to his feet and looked around at all who were in the room. "Thanks, everyone. You are true friends. I am sorry, I cannot speak about this anymore."

At that, he left the house.

"Why don't you boys keep an eye on him," Marbel said to Theo and Michael, "He's in a dark place right now."

Theo and Michael reluctantly left. Rook remained on the floor, leaning against the wall.

"It was Hanz who took Coppo's hand, wasn't it, Marbel?" Rook asked lifelessly.

"We don't know," Marbel said, as she sat upon her little stool.

"You know it was him." Rook leaned forward. "Marbel, why do you follow him? Don't you see he is *oppressing* you all?"

"You know nothing about what life has been for us, Anodos!" Marbel snapped. "Things are not perfect here, but by *Hades*, we have a home!"

"Marbel!" Rook raised his voice, "Hanz keeps you all cooped up in this village like prisoners!"

"He doesn't *keep* anyone here, Anodos!" Marbel replied, "We *chose* to live here!"

"But—!"

"Anodos!" Marbel leaned forward, "You of all people should know that we have no king, we have no leader! A dictator, your *father*, oppressed us, imprisoned us, and killed *hundreds* of us! Then, on the day of his death, we find out that we were supposed to be serving Humans, of all people. Do you know what that does to a person? Do you know the confusion that brings? I joined the Purple Order, Rook. Do you know why I followed Hanz?"

"Why?"

"Because he brought a confused and broken race like us together. He gave us a home and helped us find a way to live out our true purpose."

"What about Hevel?" Rook asked quickly, "He called the Fae back to Arelle and tried to unite them! We... he and I had a plan for teaching the Fae what it meant to serve Humanity. Was that not enough?"

"Anodos, as pure as your intentions may have been, most of us could not trust the son of the Nightmare Faerie. Can't you see that? By the Lights, Anodos, isn't that why you're in hiding? Isn't that why you haven't claimed your throne?"

"I..." Rook froze.

"Hanz has ever been a leader to the Fae. He has always tried to care for us. And in the absence of a king or kingdom, we have a home with him. Where else are we supposed to *go*? You said yesterday that this is no place to raise Faerie children. Well? If you know better, why don't you show us! Why haven't you claimed your throne? Why are you wandering around Mensa acting like a—"

"Stop!" Rook yelped, "Please!" He thrust his hands over his ears. "I—I can't hear this right now."

"I don't know what happened to you, boy, and I am sorry if these words hurt you, but I am not going to stay silent about this any longer. Are you the Faerie King, or aren't you? Tell me straight. Are you our king?"

"I... I..." Rook stammered, "I'm a product of rape and the spawn of a tyrant."

Marbel leaned back with a face of shock. "*What* did you say?"

"Product of rape," Rook said with vacant eyes, "spawn of a tyrant." He shifted his gaze to look at her. "Isn't that true? Isn't that how you see me?"

Marbel sighed. "What evil words—you should not utter them!"

"A Faerie taught them to me," Rook said calmly, "one of your *Purple Order*."

Marbel frowned. "What? What do you mean?"

"It was the Purple Order who took me fifteen seasons ago, when I was no older than Coppo," Rook said, watching her face.

"No," Marbel shook her head, "No, it was the Purists!"

Rook spat on the ground. "The Purists were puppets! We both know who was behind them!"

"You can't know that for certain," Marbel shook her head, "I knew nothing about such schemes! Hanz wasn't even there when the insurrection happened. He was here with us!"

"He was behind it all!" Rook said in a raised voice. "His closest ally told me straight. Riah, remember? The Faerie of Illusion? Yes. She is the one who taught me those words. Do you remember *her*?"

Marbel's face froze. She opened her mouth but could not speak.

"Hanz wanted me dead, that's what she told me. What have you got to say about *that*?"

"Riah," Marbel said softly, "Yes, she was Hanz' closest ally. But she betrayed the Purple Order. She must have acted on her own when she abducted you, you poor lad. Perhaps *she* was the leader of the Purists."

"No," Rook shook his head slowly. "Do you want to know what she did to *betray* the Purple Order, as you so eloquently put it?"

Marbel's face hardened. "Tell me."

"She let me go."

Marbel sighed. "I want to believe you, Anodos."

"Do you? You would really side with Hanz? Marbel, he is having one of our own, little Valley, punished for simply carrying an imperium!"

"We chose to give up imperiums! We *chose* to live under these laws!"

"*Valley* did not choose this, neither did Coppo, neither did Theo— neither did little Rois. This oppression was forced upon them. Why can't you believe me? Marbel! Why would I lie to you?"

Marbel closed her eyes, breathing heavily as she processed. She opened her eyes again, then said, "There is only one way for me to know if you're telling the truth."

"And how is that?"

"We ask her," said Marbel.

"Ask who?" Rook narrowed his eyes.

"We ask Riah."

Rook did as Marbel instructed and hid his face behind a hood. He carried a large tray of bread loaves as she led the way to the Faerie prison. It was raining more heavily now, so Rook did his best to keep the bread dry with a cloth.

"Just stay quiet and let me do the talking," Marbel said as she hobbled toward the guards who stood on either side of the prison door.

Rook stayed a pace or two away from Marbel as she spoke with the guards. They were clearly accustomed to her visits and even smiled while talking to her. He saw her toss them each a bread loaf, and they took them eagerly, letting her and Rook pass without protest. Once inside the prison, the door slammed behind them, and the place grew very dark.

"Why are there no lights in here?" Rook asked, groping for a wall.

"Your eyes will adjust," Marbel said, "Come on."

"So this is where Hanz keeps his enemies? In total darkness?" Rook asked as they journeyed down a narrow hall. He thought of Felix. How symbolic it all was.

"Those who betray the order must stay here. They disobeyed Mensan laws, after pledging to keep them," Marbel said.

"Riah has been in here all this time?" Rook whispered. "For how long?"

"Thirteen seasons or so," Marbel mumbled.

Rook felt a sinking feeling inside his body. Thirteen seasons? Had Hanz imprisoned her immediately after she helped him escape?

Marbel led Rook down a little side hall. Flickers of torch light reflected off of iron bars. Rook instantly sensed the presence of other Faeries. There were three of them.

"The Truth Faerie is in this room," Rook said quietly. "Hanz found the Truth Faerie?"

"What do you mean?" Marbel asked quickly.

A gasp resounded, and a hand reached through prison bars, grasping Rook by the sleeve. Rook turned to gaze at the hand. It was small. Whoever it belonged to was not yet a grown woman, no older than Coppo.

Rook touched the hand with his own, "You are the Truth Faerie?" he asked slowly. "Are you alright, child?"

"That one can't talk..." Marbel said slowly. "She's had her..." her voice drifted into silence.

"They've removed your tongue?" Rook asked with horror. The hand squeezed his arm tightly. "Marbel..." Rook said in a low voice, "*Now* do you believe me?"

Marbel's silence communicated her horror.

"*No!*" A voice screamed with the passion of a grieving mother. "No, Lights—*no!*"

Rook knew the voice. He turned to face the cell from where the voice screeched.

"Riah," Rook sighed, closing his eyes. He had sworn he would never speak to her again.

"No, Anodos! No! Are you *insane*? What are you *doing* here!" Riah demanded, thrusting her arms through the bars. They groped the air. Rook kept his distance.

"Hallo, Riah," Rook said.

"Get out of here! He is looking for you, damn it! He is looking *everywhere* for you! *Please*, get out of here! Why have you come here? After all these seasons, don't let him find you!"

"He won't recognize me!" Rook shouted, "Remember? Didn't you put that damn spell on my face so that even my own *family* won't know me?"

"Spells can be broken!" Riah shouted, straining her voice. "Anodos, he will find you! The click he figures you out, that spell will shatter into pieces! And if I die, the spell dies with me! Please, I beg of you! Leave Mensa. You can't let him find you!"

"I live my own life!" Rook shouted back, "I have never listened to you, and I won't listen now!"

Riah began to cry weakly. She slumped down within her cell and placed her hands on the floor. "I will never forgive myself if he finds you... please... Anodos..."

Rook turned to give Marbel a glare. "Do you believe me *now*?"

"I've seen enough," Marbel said in a timid voice. "The Firstdark bell is ringing, we should go now before they lock the gates. Come, Rook... I believe you."

"Please," Riah's voice whimpered, "Anodos—*run!*"

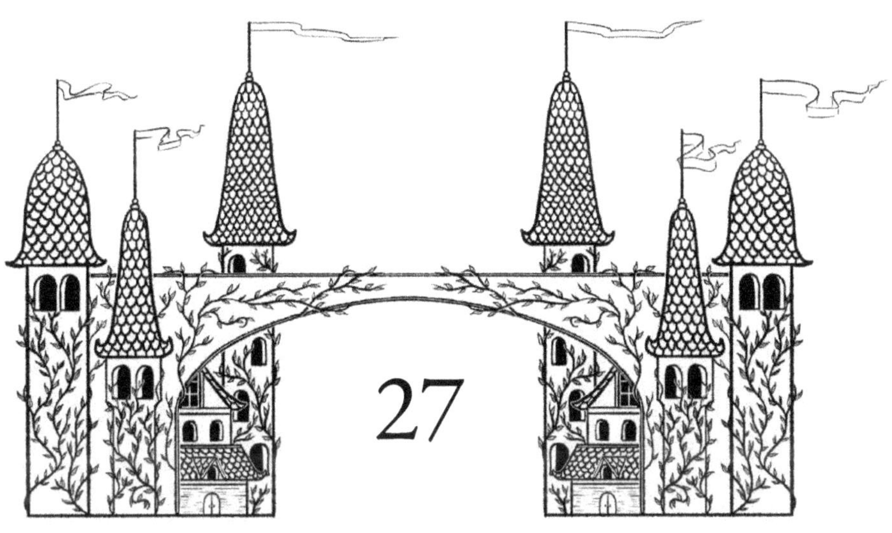

27

— Rasselas —

The Masque

"STAY IN THE SKIES NEAR THE TOP FLOOR BALCONY," Rasselas said to Embers, who alighted upon the top of a little garden statuette. They stood in the covered outdoor pavilion outside the Western Palace, where the masque was meant to take place. "So if I need you, you can see me from up there." Rasselas pointed up toward the balcony.

Embers gazed up at the palace, blinking his reflective black eyes.

"What? What is wrong with asking you to watch for me?" Rasselas asked as he straightened his sleeves.

I don't like being on call. It makes me feel like someone's clipped my wings, replied the black thunderbird.

"Come on," Rasselas scoffed, "Work with me tonight, old chap. I am hoping to bring Valley upstairs so you could meet her."

I've met her.

"Yes, well I wasn't there. Plus—the three of us need to come up with a plan." Rasselas lowered his voice, speaking more sincerely, "if Anodos is somewhere in Hanz' prison... we need to get word to Winter's End. I need your help, Embers!"

Embers made a grinding sound with his beak. *I don't like being a part of big plans. It doesn't suit me.*

"Oh, will you calm down?" Rasselas made a huff as he straightened his beaked mask. "I just need your advice, alright? Hades, Embers. I am so close to finding my brother! Now think: is there any way we could get a message to Winter's End?"

Embers looked around aimlessly, then focused his black eyes on Rasselas. *You would need to send someone who has been there before.*

"Haven't you been there before?" Rasselas asked, raising an eyebrow.

No.

"*Floods.* Do you think I should leave Mensa? Or wait—maybe *you* could go find someone who has been there before and ask them to deliver a message."

There are not many I trust enough to speak with about these things, Embers said, *Besides, no one would understand me. Plus, I am not a pigeon. So please don't treat me like one.*

"Didn't you come here as my grandfather's pigeon? So you could deliver him reports?" Rassles placed his hands on his hips.

That reminds me, Embers said casually, *I need to head down there before the week is out.*

"You make no sense to me," Rasselas remarked, as he pulled his hand mirror from his pocket and gazed into its reflection. He checked for loose hairs, smiled, then placed it back into his coat.

I am glad to hear it.

The bells began to ring. "Can I count on you to meet me upstairs?" Rasselas asked.

If I am around, I will come, replied the bird, *but I do not promise anything.*

"How do I look?" Rasselas asked excitedly, spreading his arms out before his companion.

You look like a felling peacock.

"Thank you!" Rasselas grinned, twirling in place to show his reflective, green and blue feathered coat.

I meant it as an insult, Embers said dryly, *peacocks are empty-headed buzzards.*

"Oh come now," Rasselas grinned, "That's not such a bad thing! At least we are *attractive* empty-headed buzzards!"

Embers didn't seem to feel like entertaining Rasselas' vanity, so he flapped away.

"Moonvine?" The voice of Sir Thorne sounded from behind. Prince Rasselas turned his head to see the man strolling up to him, wearing a silver, scaled fish mask.

"Ah, Sir Thorne!" Rasselas turned gracefully on his heel to face the Elf. "My wing!"

"Ready to go in?" the wing asked unenthusiastically.

"I say," Rasselas tapped his chin, "I was rather hoping you might send Latimer in your place tonight. Slay me, I was beginning to prefer his company to yours."

Thorne snorted. "I am sorry to disappoint you once again, Prince Moonvine," he said, "May I ask what you and Nativitas were talking about?"

"Yes, you may!" Rasselas smiled, then turned to march toward the now-open palace doors.

Thorne jogged to keep up. "Alright, well," he grunted, "What were you talking about?"

"Peacocks," Rasselas said, without even turning to look the Elf in the eyes. He glided excitedly up to the wide-open palace doors, from where music and lights were streaming forth.

Sir Swain stood at the door, dressed in his trim purple coat and holding a plain white mask.

"Good evening, gentlemen," Sir Swain said with a bow. "Welcome to King Hanz' celebratory Kingsummons Masque. And who might I announce tonight?"

"The Peacock," Rasselas said proudly, then turned to his wing. "And..."

"*Ikhthyes,*" Thorne said quietly, "...the fish."

"Ladies and Gentlemen," Swain cried to the party guests, "The Peacock, and Ikhthyes the Fish!"

Rasselas strolled down the entrance carpet, placing each foot in front of the other with perfect poise. His white teeth reflected as much of the party's dazzling lights as his feathers, and for a moment, his presence stole the attention of all in the room.

Down at the end of the runway was a long table, filled with party food. It ran the length of the back wall. Clustered around it was an array of glamorous masked guests.

Rasselas placed himself by a tray of stuffed dates, noting that he could best observe the party from that location while also staying close to the action. Beside him stood an individual with a black, feathery mask with a long, curved beak. To Rasselas, it was a pleasant sight, as if Embers himself had joined his side in Human form.

"Love the mask," Rasselas said, with his chin pointed high, "Damned pretty feathers."

"Not as pretty as yours," said the Crow in response. Rasselas couldn't quite place the voice, though this was no surprise since people liked to mask their voices as well as their faces at events such as this. Rasselas didn't try to hide his identity; his whole personality was already a mask.

Rasselas turned to examine the Crow with a smile. "Why, thank you! And what do you say, old crow? How is the party?"

"Dull," said the Crow.

"My, my," Rasselas chuckled, "You *do* remind me of someone I know."

"Oh, yeah?" asked the Crow, "And who would that be?"

"Now," Rasselas ignored the question, "Look at that character over there; what do you think about *that*?" He pointed to a guest who was entering through the main doors. Sir Swain announced him loudly as "The Tusked King of the Eastern Shores." The guest marched forward proudly, sporting a mask with two great white tusks curving downward from its mouth.

"Extravagant," said the Crow, "Like most of the costumes here."

"I say!" Rasselas exclaimed, "Those teeth must be made of pure albuminium!"

"Must be Prince Mynx then," said the Crow, "I have a feeling only he would have enough of the stuff to waste on useless tusks."

"Quite so," Rasselas nodded, then glanced at the bird. "Say, are you going to make me guess who you are, and all that?"

The Crow shrugged.

"Look at that pretty piece over there," Rasselas whispered, nodding his chin in the direction of a woman dressed in reflective silver. Her mask resembled a blazing star. "The princess, do you think?"

The Crow wagged his head side to side slowly. "No," he said, "Look at the skin color."

"Quite right," Rasselas reached for a date and popped it into his mouth.

"Besides," the Crow cleared his throat, "Isn't she laid up in bed after the storm?"

Rasselas frowned, then said with a mouth full of food, "I hadn't heard that—are you sure?"

The Crow shrugged again.

"That's a shame," Rasselas said, swallowing loudly. "I don't suppose..." his voice drifted off as he searched for other female party guests. Would that mean Valley wouldn't come after all? It would be a shame if he didn't get to see her, especially if she were wearing some sort of magnificent costume.

"What don't you suppose?" asked the Crow.

"Ooh, look at that one!" Rasselas nudged the Crow excitedly, pointing at a rather tall party guest. Two great horns jutted out from either side of his mask. They were so large, they would have been in danger of knocking over other party guests if the wearer weren't so tall. "An Aurochs! Well, it's not hard to guess who *that* might be!

The Crow pointed his beak in the direction of the Aurochs but said nothing.

"Well, that's disappointing," Rasselas frowned as another guest entered the party.

"What is?" the Crow asked.

"Well, look!" Rasselas pointed toward King Stathe, who sauntered into the room with a bland mask tucked under his arm.

The Crow chuckled. "I suppose not everyone loves these masks as much as you do."

"Well, he shouldn't have come!" Rasselas sneered. "He's ruining the whole vibe of the thing."

"What do you care? You *like* these kinds of events?"

"Of course I do!" Rasselas straightened his back proudly.

"Why?"

"Because, my dear fellow, everyone is finally honest with themselves at a masque," said Rasselas.

"Surely, it's the opposite," the Crow turned his beak in Rasselas' direction.

"No. Most days, people pretend to be themselves, when really, they hide their true identity. At a masque, a person may show their true identity. At a masque, a person chooses a symbol that means something to them, therefore showing something genuine about themselves."

The Crow cocked his head to the side—not unlike Embers when he was thinking. "So... when you chose to dress as a peacock, that was you communicating to the world that you really are quite vain?"

Rasselas laughed heartily, startling the Crow a tad. "Well, yes, I think it does. Now, what about you?" Rasselas turned to examine the Crow's laid-back demeanor. "What are you communicating?"

"What does a Crow communicate to *you?*" the Crow asked.

"A lot of things..." Rasselas said with a pause. "I'll have to come back to you. But take her, for example," Rasselas used a date to point toward the woman dressed as a star. "That woman dresses as though she were the main event. No doubt in reality, she feels quite overshadowed or under appreciated. But here tonight? She is the star. All must look her way. See what I am saying?"

"An interesting theory," said the Crow. "What about him?" He pointed at the Aurochs.

"Ah, the Aurochs: the King of the Beasts! I can only assume dear Cato wishes he were royalty, like everyone else here. No, that's not it... Perhaps..." Rasselas tapped his foot. "Perhaps he truly believes he is superior to everyone else here. Yes, that's it."

The Crow chuckled. "I could see that."

"You see? I am onto something. There, old Crow! I will have you enjoying yourself by the end of the night."

"You may," said the Crow.

They stood side by side, like a couple of peaceful bookends.

"A peacock? Figures," said an approaching figure. The Peacock and the Crow turned to see a grey Wulf with teeth of iron.

"Hallo, Sir Wulf," Rasselas said with a bow. "We were just standing here admiring all the masks. Say—what sharp teeth you have!"

The Wulf crossed his arms and examined the two birds silently. "May I join you, Rass—*erm*—Sir Peacock?"

"Be my guest," Rasselas said, posing. The Wulf stood beside him and began gazing around at the other guests.

"I hear the princess won't be here tonight," said the Wulf in a deep, growly voice.

"Yes, what happened there?" asked Rasselas. He kept his eyes on the party.

"She was drunk last night," said the Wulf. "She probably got lost in the storm on her way back to bed."

Rasselas turned his head sharply. "No one... escorted her back after cards?" It became clear to Rasselas now that the Wulf would have been at the cards table. "Damn..." he sighed.

"One can only hope that means her felling play will be canceled," the Wulf said. "But it's a damn shame we won't see her tonight. She would have stolen the party with whatever outfit she chose, I am sure. I'm beginning to expect she will make an entertaining spectacle of herself wherever she goes."

This man was speaking pretty freely, as though his mask was giving him the permission to say what he usually would have kept to himself. It wasn't *Tingo*, was it?

"Well, I am just sad to hear the reason why she isn't here," Rasselas said in a more sincere tone, "I hope she is alright."

The Crow turned to look at Rasselas, then poked his nose away again.

"Indeed," said the Wulf. "What do you think about the Faerie business, eh? Humans finally being able to control Arelle?"

The Crow stiffened.

Rasselas frowned. "I say, big Wulf, this is hardly the place to talk politics. Slay me, you'll ruin my mood."

"What do you say about him?" The Crow asked Rasselas, pointing over to a party guest dressed completely in metallic red. His scaly mask depicted the face of a dragon.

Rasselas snorted. "Someone who is trying much too hard," Rasselas turned his posture away from the Wulf, who was becoming a bit of a nuisance. "Look at him. He even has a set of wings!"

"What does a dragon symbolize to you?" asked the Crow.

"It's not about what it means to me, old Crow, but what it means to *him*," said Rasselas.

"What do you think it means to him?"

Rasselas blew a raspberry with his lips, thinking. "Well, it could mean power? Or perhaps... destruction?"

"Or a keeper of great treasures," the Crow suggested.

"I say!" Rasselas grinned, "You're getting the hang of this."

"What do you think of that costume?" the Wulf asked, pointing to a guest who was walking toward them. The Wulf couldn't know the depth of their conversation, but he clearly assumed he was a part of it.

Rasselas froze. The approaching man wore a green outfit, wearing a mask of a roaring lion with a magnificent mane. Rasselas was well aware of the allusion.

"It is the Green Lion of Bavel," Rasselas whispered as the lion approached.

"Why, hallo, Sir Peacock," the Green Lion said eloquently with a bow.

"Why hallo, green thing," Rasselas said.

"Nice costume," said the Wulf. "But why are you all green? I thought lions were supposed to be yellow... or red, or something."

The Crow silently glanced at the Wulf, then back at the Green Lion.

The Green Lion chuckled to himself. "I fear the allusion must be lost on you. It is no matter, I did it simply for my own amusement."

Rasselas' mount opened, then closed. Who could *this* be? And why...why dress as the Green Lion?

"Well, you're a pretty thing, I'll give you that," Rasselas said.

"Thank you," said the Green Lion. He took a date from the table, then moved next to Rasselas, forcing the Wulf to the side. The Wulf, averse to the idea of being on the outskirts of a conversation, left their little circle. Rasselas didn't mind.

"That Wulf wants us to think he is something to be feared, but I confess, the mask wasn't doing him any favors."

The Green Lion chuckled for a moment. "I think you must be right."

"And what about you?" the Crow said quietly to the Green Lion. "What does your mask say about you?"

The Green Lion turned his large mask to face the pointy-beaked Crow. "That is for you two to speculate, isn't it? Go on, Peacock," the Lion turned to Rasselas. "Tell me why you think I chose this costume."

Rasselas bit his lip from under his mask. As interesting as the conversation was, he was still trying to spot Valley in the crowd. None of the women were short enough to be her.

"*Erm*, well..." Rasselas stalled for a moment, then turned back to examine the Lion. Who *was* this man? "A *green* lion? I can't begin to fathom!"

The Lion chuckled. "Don't be so modest. I heard you call me the Green Lion of Bavel as I approached. Come now, humor me!"

Rasselas sighed. "Do you think yourself some sort of philosopher?" he asked unenthusiastically.

The Lion chuckled to himself. Just then, the Lion, the Crow, and the Peacock were approached by the Red Dragon.

"Always drawing a crowd, aren't you, Rasselas?" asked the Dragon.

"Rasselas? Who do you mean?" the prince asked, as though offended, "I am Sir Peacock!"

"Indeed you are," the Dragon groaned. "I got here late. What have I missed? Has the princess come yet?"

"The princess won't be here tonight," said Rasselas, "Stuck in bed, apparently."

The Dragon snorted. "I didn't think she got *that* drunk. Come on! She wouldn't miss a party like this."

"Have a care, Red Boy," Rasselas sniffed, "She got injured in the storm, you know."

"Oh," the Dragon said quickly, "Damn. Well, what's the use of coming here then? I should have just stayed and watched the other girl."

The three other masks turned in unison to look at the Red Dragon face-on.

"What other girl?" Rasselas asked.

"Oh, nothing, just a bit of fun." The Dragon shrugged.

"And what does a Dragon like yourself class as *fun*, might I ask?" Rasselas asked warily.

"Why," said the Dragon, "punishment." Even with that huge mask covering his face, his leery smile was visible through his voice.

"Punishment?" the Green Lion asked.

The Dragon made a shrug. "Just a disobedient Faerie. There was a whole crowd, you know, outside the felling Faerie village. Pitiful creatures." He chuckled. "Amusing."

"You *enjoy* watching things like that?" the Crow asked. There was disgust in his voice.

The Dragon scoffed. "Everyone does. Hades—even Faeries had gathered to watch her get..."

"Wait," Rasselas held up his hand, "*Who?*"

"Hanz' felling Faerie girl who's always buzzing around in our rooms. You know, the little spy?"

Rasselas' heart froze. "What has the poor girl done to deserve such a thing?" he asked in a shaky voice, doing his best to hide his rising anxiety.

"Felled if I know," said the Dragon.

"What's happened to her now?" the Green Lion asked with concern.

"I think they've got her in the pit," said the Dragon. "That's where they throw disobedient Faeries here, the dirty animals."

"I have no more stomach for this conversation," Rasselas said quickly, holding up his palms to those who stood around him. "I will go now."

Without waiting for farewells from his fellow guests, Rasselas charged toward a back door. His pulse pounded like a war drum, driving him forward. Something had happened to Valley—had it been his fault?

Just as he reached a side door, someone touched his arm. He turned quickly, coming face to face with the Crow.

"Where are you going?" the Crow asked.

"What do *you* care?" Rasselas snapped.

"You are going to the...the Faerie girl?"

"She's in trouble!" Rasselas yanked his hand free of the Crow's touch.

"Faeries are thrown in the pit nearly every day," the Crow said quietly, "Why do you visit *this* one?"

"I didn't know there was such a place!" Rasselas said, "If I had, I would have done something about it sooner!"

"Rasselas," the Crow said, "You should be careful. Laws are very strict here. Do not get yourself in trouble."

Rasselas balked. "*Excuse* me? Who even *are* you? Why are you trying to stop me from going?"

"I am not trying to stop you," the Crow said, "I am just warning you. If this girl is one of Hanz' Faeries, you should be careful not to anger him."

Rasselas took his mask by the beak and threw it aside, revealing his true anger to the Crow. "Others may look away while the Fae are being treated like slaves, but I will not!" he said.

The Crow stood there, motionless.

"I know who you are, you know," Rasselas said, drawing himself up to full height.

The Crow only stared at him silently, as if daring him to guess.

"A man who is perceived by the world as a dirty, useless, irritating bird. A pest who contributes nothing to the world's beauty. A reminder to the world that death is always lingering nearby. A nobody—is that who you are—*Rook*?"

Rook took off his mask. "Is it?" he asked.

"Felled if I know," Rasselas said sharply. "Now, you can stand around and judge me all you want, but I *care* about the Faeries here! I *care* that one of them is being punished. Do you think she deserves to be punished, Rook? Forget the laws. Do you really think that she *deserves* to be treated this way?"

Rook's eyes darkened, then he sighed. "Fine," he said, "Let's go."

The two men left the party. They raced through the Mensa Castle grounds, keeping to the lit walkways. The night had set in and there was a heavy downpour of rain. As he ran, Rasselas tore off his feathered jacket, hating every click he had wasted on preparing for such a frivolous event. The entire time, Valley had been in peril. What had happened? Had Hanz found out about their liaisons? His heart pounded with terror. Had...had Hanz found the letter? Was *Hanz* the Green Lion?

Rook ran beside him, easily keeping up pace. Though Rasselas grew breathless, winded by his rush of adrenaline, Rook glided effortlessly along.

Once they had descended the northeast stair into the Warrowing Compound, they saw no evidence of a crowd. They stopped, panting as they gazed around.

"Where is she?" Rasselas asked frantically. "Where's the crowd?"

"The Faeries get locked in the Village at night," said Rook, stepping forward. "The pit is around that corner," he pointed north of the walls. There was a cluster of torchlights shining through the rain and darkness.

Rasselas marched north, making a beeline for the torchlight. Rook rushed to keep up with him.

"What do you expect to do for her? There are guards everywhere!" Rook said in a rough whisper.

"Have you never heard of scapegoating? It's a law here!" Rasselas said in response.

Rook grabbed Rasselas' arm, forcing him to halt. Rasselas turned quickly to face him.

"What?" Rasselas demanded, "What is it now?"

"You're going to take her punishment on yourself?" Rook scowled.

"You may not think Faeries are worth scapegoating, but *I do!*" Rasselas screamed. "What is felling *wrong* with you people?"

"No," Rook said, "Let me do it."

"Oh, get out of my way!" Rasselas tore his arm free and raced as quickly as he could to the line of soldiers up ahead.

Tucked away to the side of the Warrowing Village was a stone pavilion. There was a row of stocks, a bloodied platform, and a large square pit. A decent number of guards stood about, undisturbed by the damp. One stared down into the pit.

Rasselas and Rook were initially stopped by one of the guards, but when the guard seemed to recognize them, he stepped aside to let them pass. Rasselas pushed past and ran to the edge of the pit. It was at least a fifteen-foot drop down into the stone-paved sunken dungeon. It was dark, but the soldier standing beside Rasselas held a torch up to light what lay beneath.

All Rasselas could see was a mess of jagged black wings filling the pit. They curled about the walls, too large to fit inside without getting bent out of shape. At the center, Valley's small feminine figure was curled up in a ball. Rasselas could see the reflections of himself, Rook, and the torch-bearing guard in a pool of rainwater that was collecting at the bottom of the prison.

Rasselas turned sharply to look at the guard.

"Get her out of there!" Rasselas shouted, pointing down at Valley.

The guard with the bushy, though wet, mustache turned to stare Rasselas down with his dark brown eyes. "No," he said, "the king has ordered that she stay there for the night."

"Get her out!" Rasselas cried, his voice cracking. "I'll scapegoat—get her out!"

"It's too late for that," the guard said.

"You felling *daemons!*" Rasselas ripped open his waistcoat, popping every button loose, and threw it aside. He crouched down and dangled one of his legs over the side of the pit in an attempt to scale down.

"You can't go down there!" The captain yelled, taking Rasselas by the arm and hoisting him back up onto the ledge as if he weighed nothing.

"Fell off!" Rasselas, jerked his arm free, then swung his fist into the captain's face.

The captain stumbled backwards, stunned by the attack. Rasselas dove down into the pit, careless of the risks. Rook threw himself at the captain, pulling him backwards before he could try and stop Rasselas.

Rasselas dropped down into the pit with a splash. Pain shot up his legs, but he ignored it, trudging through the water to the dark corner where Valley's curled-up body lay.

"Valley!" he cried. The rain dampened his voice, but Valley lifted her head to see him coming.

"Rasselas?" she asked weakly, pushing herself up from the ground on her arm. "Am I dreaming again?"

Rasselas rushed forward, then knelt before her. "Valley!" he said in a hoarse voice. "Valley, what in Hades *happened*?"

"Rasselas, what are you doing down here?" she asked fearfully, looking upwards.

Rasselas glanced up to see Rook and the captain looking down at them, then turned back to Valley.

"I heard you got in trouble. Valley, what happened? Did Hanz find out you were the Dream Faerie?"

Valley burst into tears, dropping weakly down onto her hands.

Feeling a rush of heroic passion, Rasselas dove beside her and wrapped his arms around the girl as she whimpered quietly.

He leaned back against the wall, looking up to gaze at the falling rain until Valley was ready to talk to him. His limbs began to grow stiff from the cold, and his legs began to throb from the pain of jumping into the ditch.

Rasselas petted her head as he caught his breath. "Did you get hurt?"

Valley relaxed into his arms. She rolled her head side to side, screwing her head into his chest as if to escape from her misery.

"I... I don't know... Just my wings, I think," she said weakly, "He hurt my wings."

"*Why*?" Rasselas squeezed her. "Why did he do this?"

"He found my imperium," she said.

"Imperium?" Rasselas blinked. "You... I didn't know you had one."

"Neither did I..." Valley moaned, "But he found it. He realized I was growing more powerful. He...he broke my wings."

Rasselas froze in astonishment. "He *what*? Valley!"

"He said it's a Faerie's punishment for storing magik... I... I didn't even know I was *doing* it!"

"That *daemon*!" Rasselas gritted his teeth. "He can't do this to you! I won't let him!"

"He's already done it," Valley snapped. "He has the right. He has the power."

"No, he doesn't!"

"*He* is the king here, Rasselas," she said through gritted teeth, "regardless of what you or I want."

"Valley—I swear to you—I will get you out of here."

"They'll let me out in the morning," she said with a sniff. "Don't worry about me, Rasselas."

"No," he said firmly, "I mean I will get you out of Mensa. I will take you to Winter's End."

Valley lifted her head slowly and gazed into Rasselas eyes. That look on her face—it was so hopeless.

Rasselas held his breath as he beheld her soft face, pained with the tears of the rain. He placed a hand on her cheek and pulled aside some tears with his thumb. She was even more beautiful now than she had been in his dream.

"You... you really mean that?" Valley asked quietly.

"Yeah," Rasselas pulled her toward his chest, tightening his arms protectively around her, "I promise."

Valley rested her face against his shoulder.

Rasselas found his lips resting against her damp skin, right where her shoulder and neck meet. And as things grew still, he began to feel the rush of excitement that came from being so close to her. Without thinking, he placed a kiss there, then breathed in deeply. Valley's body tensed then relaxed. He felt her fingers curling against his chest where her hands lay.

"I had a dream about you, Valley," he said.

Valley's body tensed once more.

Rasselas kissed her neck again, more intentionally this time. "I dreamed I took you to Winter's End, to the Sea."

"*What?*" Valley began to pull away.

"I love you, Valley," he said, then pulled her tighter, placing a third, lingering kiss on her jaw.

"No!" Valley drew back sharply. "Rasselas, stop!"

Rasselas blinked, then stared sorrowfully into her face like a rejected puppy. "I—I'm sorry," he said.

"Don't make that face," Valley said. Her countenance was filled with guilt. "This isn't your fault!"

"I—what?" He blinked.

"Rasselas," she said with a quivering lip. "It is not you who loves me. It is I who loves you."

Rasselas' heart-broken frown turned to a beaming smile. "Well, then!"

"No!" she cried, pulling further away from him, "No, you don't understand! It is not you who dreamed about me, but I who dreamed about you!"

"Valley," he said slowly, "I don't see a problem here."

"Rasselas!" she snapped, "Listen to me! I am the Nightmare Faerie, remember? Don't you see? I *found* you last night! I... I think I *invaded* your dreams!"

"Oh!" Rasselas looked down for a moment, then said, "Valley, you're just beginning to learn what you can do. I don't see that as a crime. That doesn't make you the *Nightmare* Faerie."

"You still don't understand," she shook her head defeatedly, "Don't you see? I *made* you fall in love with me."

Rasselas frowned. "Well Hades, Valley, you can't *make* someone fall in love with you!"

"I can!" she said, "Apparently I've been doing it to *everyone* around here!"

"I don't think that's how it works..." Rasselas mumbled.

"Please," Valley reached forward to grasp his hand, "Please don't kiss me, Rasselas. Alright? You don't love me. You're under a spell."

"Valley," he said weakly, "You're kind of breaking my heart right now. You can't tell me not to..."

"Just *trust* me—or at least..." she squeezed his hand tighter, "until I can figure out how to get this under control, you need to try to resist those feelings. Alright? Please, understand me. I am trying to honor you!"

Rasselas sighed. "Alright, alright," he said, "I'll try to believe you; I will keep it to myself."

Valley nodded, looking relieved. "I am sorry," she said, "This is all my fault."

"No," Rasselas said darkly. "Nothing is your fault, Valley."

"Some things are," she said, glancing off to the side. "Thank you for coming down here. I'll be alright. You can go now. I'd hate for you...to get in trouble on my behalf."

Rasselas scoffed. "I am not leaving you," he said, "and that's not just because I am in love with...*erm*...I just want to stay, alright? I am not leaving you alone."

Valley smiled weakly. Then her face grew tense, and once more, she began to cry.

"Come on, Valley," Rasselas said as he leaned back against the wall. He stretched out his legs so that she could use them as a pillow, keeping her face free of the wet ground.

And there he stayed until morning.

28

—— Rosamond ——

The Alliance

ROSAMOND LAY AGAINST THE DAYBED BY THE OPEN WINDOW. The morning light cast itself upon her like a warming bath. She could hear the songs of a hundred birds singing outside. Her world was so quiet; so peaceful. She was not in her regular chambers; her father had her moved upstairs to one of the rooms on a floor he kept empty. He didn't want her near all the others, though she wasn't exactly sure why. The surgeon said that the solitude would help her heal faster, but to Rosamond, the loneliness felt like a further punishment.

She didn't try to move; everything always started to hurt when she tried to move. Instead, she lay still with her feather blanket bunched up toward her middle. Her bare legs were uncovered she could see her splinted ankle with a pack of ice laying across it. Her toes on that foot had grown black. How hideous! It was a relief that Mensa fashion required women to cover their legs all the way down to the toes; it would be a long time before that color faded.

A full day had passed since the frightful run-in with her father, and Rosamond still hadn't felt up to walking. Resting at the window was the only pastime available to her at present, so she made the most of it by watching all the little birds who had gathered around her small, terraced balcony. So many birds!

Rosamond felt movement beneath her quilt. Her sleeping companion was rousing. He turned his head, which had been resting peacefully against her bosom all night. His presence had made the long dark night bearable, though she was concerned that he might find cause to leave once he woke.

"Good morning," she said with a smile, weaving her fingers between soft, crisp feathers.

Why have you left the window open? I can hardly sleep with all those felling finches chattering away out there, said Gargoyle in a groggy tone. He rotated his head so that one of his eyes turned up to look at Rosamond's face, his long beak resting against her sternum.

"I think they must be drawn to you," she said, looking over at the line of twenty birds who were perched upon the balcony rail. "Do other birds like you?"

Hades knows why, Gargoyle groaned.

"Well, I like their songs," Rosamond said, stroking him with a long, gentle glide of her hand from his head to his tail. "But I kept the window open for your sake. I thought you might want to leave at some point."

Oh, said the bird, lifting his head slightly, *I can go if you need me to.*

"I wish you wouldn't," she said, "I quite like your company, despite your pessimism."

Gargoyle seemed pleased and nestled his beak against her warm skin. She couldn't guess why the bird had grown to like her so much but appreciated him coming to find her the night before.

"What would father say to me having a pet?" she asked herself, continuing to stroke the bird.

I am not a pet.

"Of course you aren't, dear," Rosamond said, scratching his favorite spot, right at his neck. "But anyway, I can't imagine him being pleased. He doesn't seem to like me having anything I want, you know. It's as if he *likes* it when I am unhappy."

Rosamond, Gargoyle said, *Does that still surprise you?*

Rosamond paused her petting, thinking to herself. "There is a good reason for him treating me the way he does. I mean, think about this from his perspective, Gargoyle! I disobeyed his orders, went to an event unattended, with a bunch of other men, nearly got myself drunk, then nearly died in a storm, and arrived back to him half-naked! Doesn't he have every *right* to get angry?"

Gargoyle grinded his beak for a moment then said, *Everyone has a right to get angry, but it is up to us what we do with our anger, isn't it? He may have cause to be angry, but don't you think it was wrong for him to take it out on you?*

"But I am his daughter," Rosamond said quietly. "He is *allowed* to discipline me. That is his role."

Gargoyle grew silent and stiff.

"Gargoyle? Are you angry?" She poked at his side playfully. He jumped, then made a small cooing noise. "Are you angry with me?"

You frustrate me, Rosamond, he said.

"But, why?" She frowned. "After everything I have been through, how could you be *frustrated* with me? I deserve sympathy, surely."

That's just it, he lifted his head to look at her with both his eyes. *You have so much passion, so much intelligence, so much perception—you love to plot and scheme and defy—and yet? You still heel when your father asks you to. Why? When will you break out of this shell?*

"Shell?" Rosamond narrowed her eyes, "*What* shell?"

You taste freedom when you act on your own accord, whether going to a card game, or speaking out of turn, right?

"Yes..."

But that is only a taste of freedom, Rosamond. It is like a caged bird, flitting back and forth within his little prison, claiming that he loves to fly. There is a life outside of your father, Rosamond. There is a life outside of what he wants for you and what he thinks about you.

Rosamond blinked. "I..." she spoke slowly, "I do not know what it is to exist outside of how he sees me, Gargoyle."

Yes, said the bird, *That is exactly how he would wish you to feel. Imagine, Rosamond—imagine it not mattering what he thought.*

Rosamond sighed defeatedly, wincing as she turned her head slightly to the side. "I don't know how not to care what he thinks of me, Gargoyle. I fear...I fear I want to prove myself to him with all my heart."

What is it you think you need to prove?

"That I am a worthy opponent...or that I am a good daughter...or that I could help him achieve his plans."

Help him achieve his plans? the Bird scoffed. *What do you care about his plans?*

"They are so important to him," she said, "the most important things on the world."

Why? Do you really think his plans are important? Do you even know what they are?

"Well..."

What if his plans involve marrying you off to someone who will treat you as he treats you—or worse? What if his plans involve hurting your friends... like Valley?

Rosamond's face hardened. "His plans...Yes, why *do* I wish for him to succeed? What is *wrong* with me, Gargoyle?"

The bird rested his head against her once more, relaxing, then said, *Nothing is wrong with you...that is...it is not surprising that you would want to think well of your own father. He raised you. He raised you to aid him and support him.*

Rosamond nodded slowly. "This will be my life if I continue to live beneath his shadow," she said to herself, "Whether with words, fists, or schemes, he will beat me back into place, over and over again."

I don't want this for you, Rosamond.

The princess's eyes dampened. "I see why you pity me, bird."

I don't pity you, he said, *I admire you.*

Rosemond chuckled. "Please...don't patronize me."

There was a knock on her door. Rosamond quickly pulled the fluffy blanket up over her guest then immediately regretted the motion, as pain radiated through her body.

It was her father who stepped into the room. Rosamond hid her displeasure with an amiable mask of a smile.

"Good morning, Rosamond," Hanz said in a loud voice, much like a peasant's wife does to punish her husband the morning after he has gone out drinking.

"Father," she said softly, glancing at him as he approached. He was dressed regally, with his big, warm cape draped about his shoulders. She loved that cape; he was often in a good mood when he wore that cape. But no...she did not want to see him. She did not want to warm to him. He had hurt her.

"How are you feeling? Been up and about yet?" he asked quickly, scanning her with his eyes.

"No," she said, "I have not felt—"

"You need to get up and move around," he said as waved his arms in an encouraging gesture. "You won't get better if you just laze around."

"Father..."

"Some of the delegates have asked about seeing you. Are you up for visitors? Are you able to go for a stroll with them if they ask? Come on, Rosamond, a stroll is not hard."

"Papa," she said weakly, "I do not wish to see anyone when I am like this."

"Your face is fine," he huffed, pointing at her nose, "well...except for that bit there...but you shouldn't be self-conscious about your looks, Rosamond. You look..." he paused to examine her again, "You look *fine*!"

"Papa, it's not my appearance I am worried about. I simply do not *feel* well."

Hanz turned quickly, attempting to hide his exasperation. "That's probably because you're doing nothing but lie in bed."

"Papa, please," she said, "Won't you at least let me recover? *You* did this to—"

"*You* did this!" Hanz snapped, whirling around to accuse her with finger pointed. "*I* didn't do this. *You* did this! And now?" He threw up his hands. "Now some of the men are talking about taking back their proposals! They think I am hiding you away because you're...disfigured."

Rosamond frowned. "You want me to see people today...to show them I am still...attractive?"

"You know how men get," he said, "They need to see things to know for sure. Just...just see if you can't—"

"I am not able to see anyone today," she said, "And that is final."

Hanz straightened his back, examining her silently. "Are you...how bad is the..."

Was that *concern* in his voice? *No,* she thought, *do not fall for that.*

"I am not well today. I am sure the surgeon can bring a report to you. Goodbye, father. I wish to be alone."

"Fine," he turned away. "You have until tomorrow."

"How generous," she replied, "now, goodbye."

Hanz left. Rosamond could hear him locking the door behind himself. There really was no need for that! What could she possibly *do* when she wasn't even able to walk!

Rosamond held up the quilt, then smiled at Gargoyle's twitching eye.

"Oh, I do like having you here with me!" she said, "It makes me feel quite rebellious."

Glad you fought for yourself, he said, *though it's a bit disturbing to actually witness how the vulture speaks to you. Someone should pluck his eyes out.*

"Oh!" Rosamond gasped. "What a horrible thought!"

I might just do it, you know.

"Oh, stop," Rosamond laughed. She decided to try and sit up a bit. Perhaps her father was right; perhaps all she needed to do was get up and move. It was only a few broken ribs and her ankle she needed to worry about, the rest were just cuts and stitches that would heal with time. Really, the only thing she mourned was the bruise on the side of her face. It would fade, but still—it felt so humiliating to know how public it would be! At least everyone else seemed to think it was the storm that did this to her.

Gargoyle squawked as Rosamond disturbed his comfort when she shifted. He repositioned, curling up into a catlike ball on her lap beneath the covers. Rosamond, now sitting up, looked down at herself. Her loose hair dangled messily here and there, though it still shimmered gloriously in the morning light.

She wore a white slip and the buttons down her front were half-done. Her exposed skin was characterized with bruises and stitched up cuts from to the wooden chair leg. She shuddered as the scene replayed in her mind.

What is it? Gargoyle asked, poking his beak up at her for a moment.

"It's nothing," she whispered, "Just...remembering..."

Gargoyle's only response was to nestle his beak into her stomach. She smiled, petting his feathers with her hand. He knew his presence was a comfort to her. It was a touch that wasn't hostile or confusing. It was simple, affectionate—pure.

"Rosamond?" said a voice. "Rosamond...can I..."

Rosamond gasped and pulled the blanket up above her bosom.

"Who said that?" she asked quickly. Her eyes darted around the room. "Who is there?"

"Rosamond...I am sorry...*erm*, can I come in?" said the man's voice.

A figure dropped down onto her balcony. The cluster of little singing birds burst into a cloud of startled motion, flitting around the man in confusion. Rook rose from a crouch and stood there, dressed—as ever—in a tight black suit with long coat tails dangling down to his knees.

Rosamond blinked furiously, locking her eyes on him as he poked his head into the room. She couldn't help but blush. It was *Rook*? She pulled her blanket higher, up under her chin.

"What are you doing here?" she asked in a whisper, looking side to side. "How did you even get up here? Oh!" she gasped, "Oh—you can *fly*!"

"Yes, well... let's keep that to ourselves, alright?" Rook said as he scratched the back of his head. He stepped through her window and dropped down onto the floor beside her. He didn't seem at all bashful about her current semi-dressed state, perhaps because she looked less like a girl in her nightgown and more like a patient on a sickbed. "May I...may I speak with you?"

Rosamond sputtered. "I...here? *Now*?"

Rook's eyes focused on her exposed legs. His expression grew dark. He lifted his eyes to hers and asked in a very low voice. "What happened to you, Princess?"

Rosamond cringed. "I...um..." she bit her lip. "Please don't be angry! I know you gave so much to protect me, and—"

Rook held up his hand, motioning for her to be silent. He shook his head, then sat himself on the edge of her daybed. She saw him glance at her uncovered feet—there was her big black toe. Well, he had seen it now; her life might as well be over. His eyes found hers again.

"You look terrible."

"Oh..." she blushed. "I am sorry, I...."

Gargoyle, roused by the conversation, began to move. His thick talons brushed against Rosamond's thighs, tickling her. She cleared her throat loudly, hinting that she wished him to stop.

"Are you alright?" Rook's eyes dropped down to her conspicuous lump of pillowy blankets.

"Oh, it's, *erm...*" She swallowed, "I suppose I am not accustomed to having a gentleman in my room when I am...alone."

"Oh...right." Rook leaned back. "Well, I know it's a bad time...but it also might be the right time. I...I want to talk to you about something."

"Well," Rosamond sighed, then relaxed back against the chaise with a groan, "I'm not going anywhere. What did you want to talk about?"

"Rosamond...what happened?" His eyes were locked onto hers. Rosamond could hardly handle the intensity, so she looked away.

"Rook..." she whispered. "I don't know how to talk about what happened. Why...why are you asking me? You said you never wanted to speak with me again."

"I've changed my mind," he said, "I've changed my....things have changed."

"What's changed?"

Rook ran his fingers through his wavy curls, then gazed up at the ceiling. He seemed reluctant. "Do you remember...what I said? About your father?"

"Yes," she said, "You said that he was trying to kill you. I promised you I would not speak about it."

"Do you know why he was...*erm—is*—trying to kill me?"

"Because you're a Faerie?" she asked. No, that couldn't be right...her father was quite obsessed with Faeries! "Because..." she searched, "because you have four wings? Oh! Because you are not one of *his* Faeries?"

Rook's intense stare softened into a little smile. "You're getting closer," he said. "Yes...I have four wings," his smile faded. "It means something very important. But...if I tell you..."

"I already know enough to condemn you, don't I, Rook?" she said. "So what's the harm if I know more?"

Rook's face brightened, and that smile crept back. "Alright," he said, "But first, I want you to tell me what happened to you yesterday, after I left."

Rosamond's face fell. She sucked her lips into her mouth and shook her head.

"It's alright," he said softly, "I am pretty sure I know what happened, but I just want you to feel free to tell me. I don't want that to be taken from you." He leaned forward and rested his hand against her knee. His touch sent warm shockwaves radiating through her body.

"I..." she stammered, then jumped as Gargoyle reminded her of his presence with a poke from beak. From his irritating prodding, she could tell he wanted her to answer Rook. "Stop it!" she whispered.

Rook drew back. "Sorry," he said, "I didn't mean to touch your..."

"No, not you!" She gasped, "No, I didn't mind that! It was—*erm*—" she blushed, cutting herself off.

Rook frowned. "Someone else is here..." he said cautiously. He looked like a startled rabbit, about to take its leave.

"No!" Rosamond gasped, "Don't leave!" She reached out toward him desperately, inadvertently releasing her blanket. It fell down to her lap, revealing the large black raptor curled up against her. He had a smug look about his face as he gazed up at Rook.

Rook stared silently at the two of them.

Rosamond smiled innocently.

"Ah, you see...he came here to..." Looking down at herself, Rosamond remembered her less-than-modest attire and quickly pulled up her blanket again.

Gargoyle climbed out from his hidden nest, flapped about, then landed down by Rosamond's foot.

Rook turned his head away for a moment, giving Rosamond a moment of privacy as he followed the bird with his eyes.

Hallo, said Gargoyle.

"You rascal," Rook said to the bird. "What are you doing in here?"

I am doing what you are doing.

Rook poked Gargoyle in the stomach, still keeping his face turned away from Rosamond as she fiddled with her buttons and hair in an attempt to regain some modesty.

"Well," Rook turned back toward her. "I am glad to see you had someone here looking out for you," he said, poking Gargoyle again. Then he sighed. "Tell me what happened, Rosamond."

Rosamond let out a deep breath. "Father," she said. "Father did it."

Rook nodded slowly. "*Father,*" he said. "He hardly deserves that title."

Rosamond wasn't sure how to respond to that. "Whether or not he deserves it, he has it. He may do what he likes with me."

Rook scoffed bitterly. He bowed his head for a quiet moment, and Rosamond wondered what he might be thinking about. Then, he lifted his head again and studied Rosamond intently. His expression looked sorrowful and pained.

"So it is true, then," he said in a whisper, "he turned his anger against you—against his own flesh?"

Rosamond just stared back at Rook. What could she say?

"I shouldn't have left you...I should have—"

"Let me stop you there." Rosamond reached out her hand and placed it on Rook's arm. His blue eyes flashed her a look of surprise. "Father would have had you killed if he had found you with me that morning. You did the right thing by—"

"Oh, I was being selfish." Rook brushed her hand away. "I've been selfish and cowardly ever since I came into Mensa."

"No." Rosamond said with a shake of her head. "No, you saved my life. You risked being discovered by my father to save me."

Rook huffed. "I can hardly look at you now," he said. "I can hardly stomach thinking about what your father must have done to leave you looking this way."

Rosamond felt a funny little inner triumph—finally, she was getting the kind of vindication she had wanted to feel since getting hurt. "It is not so bad," she said, trying to sound a little braver. "I will get better."

Rook nodded, as though this seemed to comfort him.

Rosamond frowned. "I mean...I am not like you. I cannot just stand up and walk away after receiving broken bones. This will take some time to heal from."

Rook blinked, looking a little lost. He cleared his throat. "Oh...of course."

"After you left, Captain Oswald found me," she said, drawing little shapes into the wrinkles of her blanket as she avoided eye contact. "He said Father was worried about me. So he took me to him. But Father was angry. He heard I had been drinking and playing cards late that night without an escort. Then I was gone all night... and returned to him half-clothed. He did not care that I was afraid. He just seemed to fixate on how much I had tarnished my reputation. And Rook—" Rosamond lifted her eyes. "It is really my own fault. I have been in a battle of wills with my father."

Rook raised one of his eyebrows slightly. "Oh, yes?"

"Yes. Ever since I came of age, I have been trying to prove to him that I will do what I want to do. And it makes him angry. And I..." she bit her lip. "I suppose I have provoked that anger. I pushed him to this point of—" she cut herself off.

"I think you and I both know that what he did was wrong," Rook said. "It is unnatural for a father to want to hurt his daughter rather than rejoice that she was *not* hurt after a dangerous storm. He is not a natural man, Rosamond."

"No..." Rosamond looked down at her splinted foot. "He is not."

"Last I saw you, you told me that you hated him. Is that true?"

"Yes," she said hesitantly, "I think so. At least—I am realizing that he is not a good man. There are evil things he does that I..." She recalled the horrible black whip she had found in her father's room.

"I had an evil father," Rook said with a distant look in his eyes, "He...he was a terrible man. He did unspeakable things."

Rosamond drew in a deep breath. She recalled the brand on Valley's shoulder. Yes...her father had done unspeakable things, too.

"Yes," she whispered.

"It is a hard thing to prove to the world that we are not our fathers' children," Rook said. "The world hates us because they see our fathers in us."

"Yes," whispered Rosamond.

"And I suppose...in some way...we *are* a part of our fathers. Our fathers will always be the ones who gave us life."

"Yes..."

"But we have are our own bodies. Right? We are not extensions of them. We are our *own* beings. We find our own destiny in this world." Rook gazed intently into her eyes.

She nodded slowly. "Yes but...it is not easy for someone like me to make my own destiny. I belong to my father, and after him, I will belong to my husband."

"You do not belong to him," Rook said firmly. "Just as I do not belong to my own father's legacy."

Rosamond blinked. "Who...who *are* you, Rook?"

Rook leaned away from her and rested his hand upon the edge of the chaise. "My name was Anodos," he said. "I am the son of the Nightmare Faerie." He stared at her. Gargoyle looked from Rook to Rosamond, watching her expression change.

Rosamond's eyes widened. "But you...but you *died!*" Her mind raced as she tried to recount what she knew of the Faeries history. It hadn't ever interested her before, and now... "You're... you're *him?*"

Rook nodded soberly. "Yes. And, no, I didn't die, despite your father's efforts. Remember the scars you saw? That day in the armory?"

Rosamond flushed, recalling when she dressed as a page to watch the sparring that day. "You knew that was me?"

The corner of Rook's mouth turned upwards. "Do you remember?"

"...Yes."

"Those scars are the proof of the many efforts to end my life. Your father wanted me dead. His people tried, over and over, to kill me. But as you saw the other night, I am not someone who can...die."

Rosamond placed her hand over her mouth. "Oh, Rook," she muttered, "I am so sorry."

He lifted his head quickly. "What?"

"That must have been so painful—I... I am so sorry. I can only imagine a taste of what that must have been like."

He blinked. "Thank you... I... anyway," he looked away, "I have been hiding from him for a long time."

"But why come to Mensa? Surely you risk all by coming here under his very nose."

"Someone cast a spell on me," Rook said, his eyes darkening. "These marks," he traced a pattern of scar lines across his face with his finger, "Some are just scars, but some are deep spells. They mask me. They keep me from being recognized by those who might know me."

Well, Gargoyle ruffled his feathers, *Humans, anyway.*

Rook continued. "But this spell also means that even if I wanted to claim the throne of Arelle..."

"The Faerie kingdom?" Rosamond asked.

"Yes," Rook rubbed his chin thoughtfully, "Even if I did want to go back and claim it, I couldn't. Though they could not take my life, they took away my identity. I have nothing, and still...your father hunts me. He wants something from me, I suppose. But..." He turned to look at Rosamond, "That is not why I came here. You ask why I came to Mensa? I came for the service of a friend. Your father took something important from him, and I need to get it back. And—" he rose, and turned his back quickly to her, "I... I came here... I had no idea that..."

"That what?" Rosamond asked, braving her pain to lean forward.

Rook turned to face her. "I didn't know how bad things were, Rosamond. I..." his voice cracked, "I came here and Hanz is...your father is...Rosamond, my people here are being tortured and enslaved. I came here with the sole purpose of saving *one* Faerie from his cruelty, only to find *more* in need of help. In my absence, in my—my *neglect*—he has enslaved my people and..." his voice trailed off.

Rosamond watched him quietly, and when he did not continue, she patted the side of her couch with her hand. Rook twitched, staring at her hand, then sat beside her in a huff of defeat.

"You were supposed to be king, and my father took you far away from your throne. And with no king, your people were abused?" she asked quietly.

"Yes."

"But you escaped him, didn't you? How did you become free of him?" she asked.

Rook leaned his elbows on his knees and bowed his head low. "I was imprisoned for two seasons by his people. His...one of his closest friends...she set me free."

"She did?" Rosamond asked in astonishment.

"I don't know why she did, but she told me she was sorry. She told me to run away and hide and never come back. She shaved off the tips from my ears and put this spell on my face," he turned to look at Rosamond, "And by then... I didn't even want to be king anyway."

"Why not?"

"I... it doesn't matter right now," he said in a dark voice.

"You must be so lonely," Rosamond said. At that, Gargoyle hopped up on the other side of Rook and rested his beak against his thigh. Rook turned to observe Gargoyle with a smile, then to Rosamond, who placed her hand gently on his other knee.

"Well," he said, "I suppose I am."

"Why did you decide to tell this to me of all people?" Rosamond asked, "I really don't know much about your world at all."

Rook nodded. "Well," he said. "I realized yesterday that I needed to do something. I may not be the Faerie king, but I am a Faerie. And I can't just stand around while my people are being oppressed like this."

"What will you do?" Rosamond asked. "Is there anything I can do to help?"

A smile dawned on Rook's usually dismal face. "Yes... that's what I was hoping you might say."

"You *were?*"

Rook nodded. "Rosamond," he said as he straightened his back, "I need someone on the *inside.*"

Rosamond bit her lip. "Inside...you mean..."

Rook nodded again. "You."

She shook her head. "Father doesn't trust me. I mean, I want to help you, but I don't know how I could possibly—"

"He doesn't trust *anyone,* Rosamond. But you *are* on the inside. You see things. He hurt you, right? He trusts that you won't tell anyone that, doesn't he?"

"Yes..."

"He wants you to stay in your place and play the role he has for you," Rook said quickly.

"Yes..."

"Make your father think you are doing just that. Be the daughter he wants you to be...just for a little while...and help me bring him down."

"Bring him—" she gasped, "*dethrone* him?"

"No," Rook said, "No, I am not trying to take his kingdom...but he *is* planning something. He has been planning something ever since he instigated the insurrection in Arelle fifteen seasons ago. And we need to find out what it is. I have got to get ahead of him—for *once.*"

"Oh." Rosamond leaned back. "Rook, I don't even know where to begin here...I really...I don't even."

"Don't worry." Rook took her hand in his and squeezed it. "I will walk you through it. And for now, I just need you to help me find something very important."

Rosamond looked down at her hand, then back at his face. "What? What do we need to find?" The image of her father's black whip flashed suddenly in front of her mind. What *other* secrets was her father hiding?

"It's a big, red gate," Rook said. "And a little pair of dark blue eyes."

"Eyes?" Rosamond recoiled, pulling her hand to her bosom.

"I'll explain," Rook smiled, "But you'll help me, *won't* you, Rosamond?"

Rosamond paused, then nodded. "Yes," she said, "I would love to help you."

Rook looked pleased with her. Even proud. That look made her feel taller than a mountain.

"You'd help me, even though I haven't told you what you could get out of it?" he asked.

"Oh!" Rosamond blinked. "I hadn't even *thought* about that!"

You need to stop trying so hard to please others, Gargoyle piped in. Rook turned to look at the bird, then back at Rosamond.

"Rosamond, I wouldn't ask for your help unless I thought it would be the best thing for you."

Rosamond's smile faded. That sounded like something her father might say. "What do you mean?"

"I also want to help you get away from him. To set you free."

"Free?" She blinked. Did she *need* to be freed? "What do you mean?"

"Rosamond, I can't let you be treated like this, especially if you put yourself in further danger for me."

"But...I have nowhere else to go. And I don't want to be away from fa—" she tightened her eyes closed, "No...no, I don't mean that..."

"Rosamond," Rook said quietly, "You could have died."

Rosamond cracked one of her eyes open. "No...father wouldn't..."

Rook sighed. "Look. I won't make you do anything you don't want to do. But for now...you will help me? You will help me find out what your father is doing?"

"Yes!" she said with conviction. "Yes, of *course* I will!"

"Right." Rook rose to his feet. "This is what we are going to do..."

✦

29

—— Valley ——

Alone

VALLEY OPENED HER EYES. SHE COULD SEE THE SKY. Captain Oswald and the other man who had been watching her from above were both gone. It was a new day. It was Mansday and the Late-morning bell was ringing. The rain had stopped, and the Sky looked clear and blue, dusted with a few wispy clouds. Valley felt a disturbing pain in a part of her body that she didn't know could feel pain: her wings. Her right wing, to be precise, had been snapped along its main branch. She had hidden her wings now, but she could still feel the throbbing. Valley lifted her head from its uncomfortable resting place against the brick wall of the pit and looked down.

There was Rasselas, the restless sleeper. He was lying on his back, drenched in the last bit of water that remained in the bottom of the pit. It was really only an inch deep now; the pit must have some sort of drainage, but it was slow. His head made a pillow of Valley's thigh. One of his hands rested against his chest, while the other laid lifelessly on the ground. He was breathing heavily with a light snore.

He was dreaming about the seaside again. Valley had tried to stay out of the poor boy's head last night, but when she was asleep, her own inhibitions seemed numbed. She found that she couldn't help but peek into his mind. Now that she was awake, however, the guilt pressed upon her heart. First King Hanz, and now Rasselas—without even trying, she was making herself the object of obsession. She would need to distance herself from Rasselas if he was going to be freed from her spell. Perhaps one day, once she figured out how to control her effect on others, she could entertain romantic notions toward him.

Valley lifted her hand to move a tuft of Rasselas' hair that seemed out of place. It felt greasy, as if he had slicked it back with some sort of styling substance. She rubbed her fingers together and chuckled.

He sniffed, then his eyebrows tightened. He was waking up. At that moment, it suddenly felt thrilling to Valley to think that he had been there all night. Why had she been asleep? Why hadn't she just sat there studying his face? *Hades*—that face. There was a *reason* he was so proud of it. He had every right to be vain, she thought, even if it did make him rather...

Rasselas' eyes began to blink open. He winced at the blaring daylight streaming down onto his face. Then his gaze shifted toward Valley.

"Valley," he said, grinning like a child on his birthday.

Valley did her best not to smile back. "You should get out of here before someone sees you," she said.

"What, scale those walls with my bare hands?" He pointed upwards. "It's not like there's a ladder or anything."

Valley gazed around the pit, then back down at his face. "You're going to get in trouble."

"Valley," Rasselas mumbled, then brought his finger to her nose and tapped it.

Valley swatted his hand away. "Stop," she said.

"Valley?" he asked, changing his tone. His smile faded.

"What?"

"Why do you think that my affection for you is a bad thing?"

"Rasselas," she groaned, leaning her head back.

"I know you're the Dream Faerie, and that you can have a *draw*, and all that, but... I don't think that means you..."

"Rasselas," she moaned, "Please don't make this harder for me."

"But Valley... even if you *inspired* me to speak about it sooner than I had planned... I really do love you."

Valley stared down at the man. He had said it again; he said he loved her. Then a startling image flashed before her mind, and she jolted. It was that kiss—that unwanted kiss. Hanz, he was like a madman, saying one thing and doing another. He had changed from being a sort of father figure to a lustful predator all in one moment. How could she know that wouldn't happen with Rasselas?

"Rasselas," she muttered under her breath, "no..."

"It's ok," he smiled. "I get it. You're trying to protect me. I'll respect what you ask, but Valley—that doesn't change how I feel. And that's for me to deal with. You don't have to fear my feelings."

Valley raised her pointy eyebrow slightly. "Well," she said, "alright." So, why exactly was she holding back from kissing him?

Tension hovered around them like a buzzing bee. They both seemed locked in a trance of silence, gazing at one another without knowing what to say.

A rope ladder dropped down into the pit. Valley and Rasselas both looked up to see several guards peering down at them.

"Morning, Valloy," cried a familiar and irritating voice. "Morning, Sir Elf, sir!"

Rasselas groaned, pushing himself up to a sitting position.

"Morning!" Rasselas called out cordially.

"If you could be so good as to cam up here, Sir Elfman, sir? The boss is asked me to get you out of the pit."

Valley and Rasselas exchanged looks.

"Well," Rasselas said, combing back his hair with a cringe, "Better go face the judgment."

"Are you in trouble?" Valley asked, growing concerned.

"Well..." Rasselas drew out the word in a falsetto voice, "I *did* punch that captain..."

"Captain *Oswald*?" Valley gasped under her breath. "*Rasselas!*"

"Hey!" He frowned, "I don't care how many people I had to punch to get here. You don't deserve to be treated like this!"

"Rasselas..." Valley groaned, "*Deserve* has nothing to do with it. I broke the law, and so did you."

He snorted. "Broke the law? How?"

"Sir Moonman?" the guard called again, putting on as posh of a voice as his imagination would allow, "Could ye be so kind as to cam up here, please, Sir Moonman, sir?"

Rasselas groaned. "Coming, old chap!" he said in a cheery, sing-song voice, then sprung to his feet.

Valley watched as Rasselas awkwardly climbed the rope ladder. She didn't mind the opportunity to admire the prince from that particular vantage point. Once he reached the top, the cluster of guards burst into motion. Valley cringed hearing Rasselas grunting and arguing, as he no doubt was apprehended and dragged off somewhere. *Oh dear...*

Not long after, Captain Oswald stepped up to the ledge and looked down at her.

"Morning," he called.

Valley didn't feel like responding. She lifted her hand lazily and offered a single wave.

"Come on," he said, "your sentence is up."

Valley rose wearily to her feet. Her body ached. Her wing had taken most of the beating last night, but she was still sore from being violently dragged out into the courtyard and sleeping in the pit all night. She winced. How long would it take for her wing to heal? Faeries in Mensa were required to keep their wings hidden, but Hanz ordered Valley to reveal hers last night—apparently as an example to others. Her wings were unmistakable. Now everyone in the Warrowing Village knew she was the Nightmare Faerie.

Her wing had bled when it broke; she didn't even know wings bled! *Hades!* She knew next to nothing about what it meant to be a Faerie. It didn't feel fair that Hanz knew more about Faeries than she did.

Valley placed her hands on the rungs of the ladder and clumsily climbed upwards, making the best use of her numb limbs as she could. On the short journey upwards, Valley allowed herself to feel anger at the unjust life she lived. But once she reached the top, she reminded herself of her proper place: she was a prisoner.

Waiting for her by the edge of the pit was not just Captain Oswald but King Hanz himself. The king had surprisingly compassionate eyes and he held a fur-lined blanket in his hands.

"Valley," he said softly. "I am glad that's over. Here." He stepped closer and draped the kingly blanket over her shoulders. She wanted to rip it off and throw it in his face, but instead she did what she always did and just stood there, passively.

"What are you doing?" she asked. "Aren't you angry?"

Hanz sighed and shook his head slowly. "I am angry at myself. Angry at what I was forced to do last night. I... I am just glad it's over."

What he was *forced* to do? No one had *forced* him to drag her outside and beat her. No one had *forced* him to berate her in front of her entire community and make an example out of her!

"So am I," she said under her breath. "I...I would like to go bathe now. May I go?"

Hanz did the unthinkable—the *unimaginable*; he stepped toward Valley and wrapped his great, fatherly arms around her and squeezed her tightly. He let out a deep sigh. Valley was as stiff as a stone pillar, just counting clicks until it was over. In that eternity of a moment, she shot a glance at Captain Oswald, who looked equally uncomfortable. He was as still as Valley was, with his hand resting against the hilt of his sword like a memorial statue.

King Hanz didn't fully free Valley from the unbearable closeness. He turned, keeping one of his arms curled around her shoulders, and guided her in a forward walk.

"Valley," he said as they strolled, side by side. Oh, how she hated the sound of her name from his lips. "It takes time for every Faerie to find their place here in Mensa. And one of the greats? It is even harder. Yes, Valley, yes," he squeezed her shoulder, "*you* are one of the 'greats.' I was going to tell you once the time was right, but *Hades*—you figured it out. I... I wanted to shield you from the burden, you see. What would a little girl think when she finds out she is a thing of nightmares?" He shook his head to himself, "You unwittingly made an imperium, and *then* what do you think happened? Well... you started gaining magik faster than a roaring river! And *then* what do you think happened?" He turned to face her.

Oh—that last question wasn't rhetorical. He wanted her to say something.

"Um..." Valley stammered, "I started *using* the magik?"

Hanz sighed. "You were using it on *me*."

She felt an impulse to slap him in the face. Surely, he couldn't blame *her* for how he... well...*was* it her fault?

"I didn't mean to," she said. As angry as she felt inside, her voice sounded so frightened coming out of her mouth.

Hanz made a teasing smile. "Well, Hades knows *why* you did what you did, but Valley... all is forgiven."

Valley pursed her lips but remained silent.

"But Valley," he sighed, "There is a *bigger* problem at hand."

"What problem?" she asked, doing her best to mask her sarcasm.

Hanz led her to a small bench just beside the Warrowing Gate and bade her to sit with him. His arm remained canopied over her shoulders, a reminder of his dominance.

"Rasselas," he said in a whisper. He shook his head. "Damn."

"What *about* him?"

"Come, Valley," Hanz raised an eyebrow. "He raced out of the masque last night, attacked my guards, and practically broke his legs jumping in after you. You said he was forming an attachment to you but... this?"

Valley frowned. "It seems what motivated your wild outburst must have done the same thing to him too." Oh dear, perhaps that was too feisty. She bit her lip, then added, "That is... I didn't knowingly encourage either of you."

Hanz' calculating eyes studied her. "Valley... I know."

"Know?" Her frown deepened. "Know *what*?"

"I *know*, Valley," he said in a leading voice. "I know Rasselas wrote that letter. Your imperium—those... those *words*."

Valley wasn't able to hide her surprise. She made a pathetically petrified expression, widening the whites of her eyes into circles.

Hanz nodded knowingly, "Yes," he said, "The Green Lion, that's who he was trying to mimic. Do you know who the Green Lion was?"

Valley slowly shook her head.

Hanz snickered to himself, "Shameless, really, plagiarizing one of the great philosophers like that."

"*Plagiarizing*?"

"Yes," Hanz smiled, "It's sad. The Green Lion of Bavel saved the kingdom from war and bloodshed by writing words of peace. Then *Rasselas*, trying to be some sort of philosopher vigilante, uses those same words as words of upheaval." His smile drifted, and there was a look of pain on his face. Either he truly felt sad, or he was a damn good faker. "It's so hard for the Fae... they have been groping for a new purpose ever since finding out their legacy was a sham. And now here comes Rasselas, trying to *confuse* them!"

"I don't understand..." Valley said, "What was wrong with his words?"

Hanz' expression made Valley regret her words. His eyes widened and he slowly turned his head to face her directly.

"Valley... don't you *know*?"

"No," she said with a huff, "I *don't*."

"Potent and controlled giants?" he scoffed. "Giants, yes, but Valley... *controlled*? Don't you know what happened with Somenus, the *last* Dream Faerie?"

She shook her head.

Hanz leaned in so close that his lips were about an inch away from her ear. He held her tightly with his dominating arm and she felt about as small as an ant.

"He became obsessed with his power—*obsessed* with the affection and obsession of others. He was anything but controlled, Valley. And his obsession led to the death of *thousands*. He was *so* obsessed with affection," his whispering breaths hit her ear in uncomfortable bursts, making her flinch with each emphasized word, "that he married hundreds—yes, hundreds of women. He could not be satisfied. Would you call him a potent and *controlled* giant, Valley?" He paused, waiting for her response, his breath still radiating against her ear.

Valley shook her head quickly, hoping it would free her from the tension.

"He started out the same as you, Valley, young and naive." King Hanz pulled back. "You know," he said, "I didn't ask to lead the Fae, Valley. They *came* to me—begging. They handed me their babies and their children, asking, 'Please, will you show us what to do?'"

He dropped his arm, finally releasing Valley from his controlling grip. She pulled back, inwardly gasping for air. He turned his head to squint at the Warrowing Gate.

"Tell me what's going on with you and Rasselas," he said in a frank tone, "I need to know how much I can trust you. Tell me now, were you plotting together—was he... *discipling* you?"

Valley's heart seemed to stop beating within her chest. What could she say? Had she been found out?

Hanz caught her expression. He sniffed. "Valley," he said, "By law, I could execute Rasselas."

"*What*?" she cried, surprising herself with her own volume. "No!"

He chuckled, though his face held a scowl. "His fate is up to you. If he really has compromised our trust... if he really has driven a wedge between me and my bonded Faerie, I *will* kill him. I will not hesitate. So tell me now, Valley, what is your relationship with him?"

Valley sighed. She would not risk Rasselas' life. "Yes," she whispered, "He was discipling me."

Hanz seemed surprised for a moment but quickly hid his reaction. The king repositioned, crossing his legs to better face her, and leaned forward. "I'm listening," he said, "Tell me."

"He..." even Valley wasn't sure what would come out of her mouth. "He believes you are hiding his brother in the Faerie prison. He wants to set him free and take him back to Winter's End. He wants to take me to Winter's End, too. He told me that you are oppressing us and making us into slaves. He... he told me that I do not need to fear myself." She felt her voice growing stronger with each word. "He thinks that if I can rise above the shame that's been put on me for being a Faerie, that other Faeries might listen. We might free ourselves from..." her crescendo plummeted, "from *you*."

Hanz's expression was unreadable. "And you... believed him?"

"Yes."

Hanz' face began to soften. "Thank you," he said. She was astonished to see him smiling. "Valley, don't you see? *This* is trust! If we can be free to have these sorts of conversations, and to talk about these things, our bond can finally grow!"

Valley furrowed her brow in confusion. "I..."

"It's *alright*, Valley," he said, letting out a sigh, "You can tell me anything. We will work through these things. Soon, you will understand why Tristan and all the other Fae before you chose to stay. Does Tristan trust me? Do the others trust me?"

Valley hesitated, confused, then nodded slowly. "...yes."

"There is all the time in the world to learn *why* I do what I do, Valley." He gazed back toward the Warrowing Village entrance. "But it is not easy being a king, or a leader. One is forced to do hard things in order to lead others. But *you* have the privilege of being one of my trusted Fae, Valley," he said as he turned to meet her eyes again. "You will get to see on the inside. And Valley?"

Valley stiffened, hoping he didn't expect a verbal response. He clearly did, so she said, "Yes?"

"If you do manage to let go of this trifling relationship with young Rasselas, then *you* will have the opportunity to lead, too."

"*What*?" She pulled further away from him. "What do you mean?"

He smiled, amused by her reaction. "Changes are coming for the Fae, Valley. Would you want to be part of leading them, and making sure they are cared for?"

"I..."

"Let's say I told you that you could go with Rasselas to Winter's End, would you *want* to leave the rest of your kin?"

"I..."

"Do you know what's coming, Valley—what I plan to do next for the Faeries?"

She shook her head. How in Hades could she possibly know?

"I am taking them to Arelle."

Valley's mouth gaped open. "What? *Arelle*?"

Hanz laughed openly. "Yes," he said, then reached over to pat her shoulder. "Yes, Valley. I want to establish the Faeries in their rightful place again. Don't you want to be a part of that?"

"I do…"

"And I know you must still be confused by Rasselas' words. That's alright, don't feel bad. There will be time to discuss it all. But Valley, you must promise me to cease your liaisons with him. It is the only way we can really trust each other. I need to know you are on *my* side."

Valley wanted to scream at the top of her lungs just how badly she wanted to be on any side but his. But what would that do? As much as she hated Hanz, he was the gateway into her community. The only way she could really help her people was if she built trust with this man.

Rasselas was passionate, but foolish. His enthusiasm and affection were not enough to free her and her people. No… she would have to walk this path alone—at least for now.

"I am on your side," Valley said. She pulled the thick blanket off her shoulders and slid it into Hanz' hands. "You can trust me."

"You have the rest of the day off," Hanz said with a curt nod, "Rest now. The worst is over."

Was he really trying to play the role of *comforter*? Valley couldn't bring herself to thank him. Instead, she stood and left the bench without a word.

Valley meandered into the Warrowing Village, keeping her head down to avoid the eyes of others. Now that everyone knew who she was, would they fear her? Hate her?

Her public punishment replayed in her mind.

⸺ • ⸺

Valley had been dragged by the guards into the square, thrown against the stone ground, and forced to reveal her wings. Hanz had used some sort of lantern—he raised it above his head and commanded her wings. They appeared instantly, like large ship sails, covering the courtyard in darkness.

"All present, I call you as witnesses!" Hanz had cried to the gathering crowd. "Come see what becomes of a Fae who wishes to acquire magik. Come see the monster!"

Gasps and cries had reverberated through the crowd like an echo in a canyon, bouncing back and forth.

"The Nightmare Faerie!" he declared, "Here she is, living among us. Look at her wings, magnificent, and yet terrifying. Look at their sheer size! Shall we let them grow further?"

Another Faerie had been chained to the lashing court before her. His back was covered with bloody lacerations. He lifted his head to look up at her and her wings, and gasped. She recognized him as a fellow Faerie named Endring. Valley did not know what his title was—undoubtedly, neither did he.

"You're... the Nightmare Faerie?" Endring gasped. There was terror in his eyes.

"No!" Valley whispered back. "The Faerie of *Dreams*... I..."

"I love the Fae too much to let them become monsters. Hear now! See now!" Hanz continued. Captain Oswald brought him a blunt wooden sword. It looked to Valley like some sort of practice sword. Hanz tested it with his hands, adjusting his grip, then swinging it in a figure eight. His eyes met Valley's.

"Wings that grow too large will be broken," he declared. Then he stepped closer to her and lowered his voice. "I am sorry," he had said, "But one day you will thank me."

—

Valley shook herself free of the memory. She stood under the Warrowing Gate with her hands over her eyes, wishing she could melt into a pile of mud and stay there forever, trampled on by others—never to be noticed again. The shame was too great to bear.

"Someone's been a bad gail, eh, Valloy?" A familiar voice said from beside her. Why of all people did Gingre have to be the one standing there?

She dropped her hands and shot the guard a glare. He had a wide, stained-tooth grin.

"Been a bad gail, indeed," Gingre said, winking.

"Yes," she snapped, "I have. And would you like to cross the *Nightmare* Faerie?"

Gingre cackled, his shoulders shaking as if he were choking, and said, "says the gail with the broken wing. Like a little sparrow, aye, Valloy? With a broken wing?"

Valley stared at the man. What could she say?

"A caged wulf still bites," said a voice. Valley turned to see a man standing just behind her. He was close enough that she bumped into him.

"Rook?" Valley asked, gazing up at the tall, dark-haired knight.

"She's no wulf. She's a Faerie, see? A little bird with a broken wing, see?" Gingre said, pointing at Valley with his spear.

Rook walked up to the man, who seemed very suddenly much shorter. He leaned down and whispered something into Gingre's ear. The guard widened his eyes and nodded slowly, submissive as a snail. Rook returned to Valley, placed a hand on the small of her back, and gently pushed her forward past Gingre.

Valley found herself being led into the Warrowing Village. Rook said nothing as they walked.

"Rook?" she asked, lifting her head to peer up at his face.

"I heard about last night," he said, "I am sorry."

"Who *are* you?"

"I'm a pr—" he cut himself off, as if he hadn't meant to speak. Then, he cleared his throat. "What do you mean?"

"You... you're just a man... and yet you knew who I was. You... why do you...?"

"Hmm?"

Valley folded her hands together and looked down. "Why do you care about the Faeries? I see you with Marbel's boys. I saw you last night at the pit... Why?"

Rook coughed into his fist. "Why *wouldn't* I care about the Fae?"

"Most Humans hate us," she said, "or they just ignore us."

Rook exhaled slowly through his nostrils. "Faeries have been kind to me," he said, "So I am kind in return."

"But—" Valley stopped and turned toward him. "How do you know our titles? Coppo calls you a prophet."

Rook's eyes searched the Heavens innocently. "I... I don't know. I just *know*."

She could see conflict on his face. She would not get an answer out of him, would she? The man was as unbreachable as the Gates of Bavel.

"You're scared of me, aren't you?" she asked.

Rook glanced down at her, then sniffed. *"What?"*

"When you saw me for the first time... you were scared."

"You're the Dream Faerie," he said, "It startled me."

"Why?"

He crossed his arms. "You're a whole basket of questions, aren't you, *Valley*?"

"Yes," she said through her teeth.

"Sir Rook!" Michael came bounding over. He wore his straight black hair in a high tail, and it swung back and forth as he ran. "Oh—Valley!" He stopped before them, panting.

"*What*?" Valley asked urgently, "What's happened?"

"What do you mean?" Michael asked, still out of breath. "Oh," he smiled, standing up straight, "I saw you two and ran over."

"Well you came over here in such a state, I figured it was urgent," Valley said as she crossed her arms and arched her eyebrow.

"Rook—and Valley, too—Coppo wants you to teach us Besting, if you know the rules. We, uh... we challenged one of the guards."

Rook chuckled. "But you haven't got any money," he said, "Don't you know it's a gambling game?"

"Oh!" Michael's face paled. "Really?"

"Come on," Rook said, "I'll spot you." He turned to look at Valley hesitantly. "You, uh... you want to come along?"

"No, that's alright," she said with a tired smile. "I think I'll go grab some time alone."

Rook nodded, then did the unexpected: he smiled. It was the most innocent and unassuming smile a person could wear.

"I'm not scared of you, Valley," he said, sighing, "Really."

Valley raised her eyebrows. "I don't know if I should be disappointed or not," she said, then let show a slight smile in return.

Rook lifted his chin slightly. "Well," he said, "Hang in there."

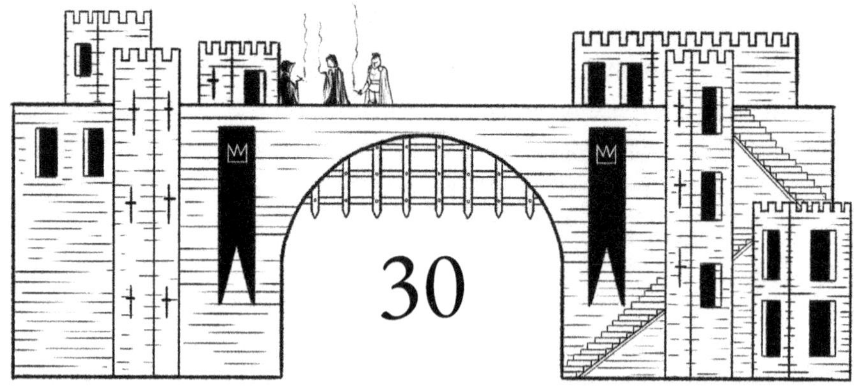

30

—— Hanz ——

The Woman in the Dark

Hᴀɴᴢ ꜱᴛᴏᴏᴅ ᴏɴ ᴛʜᴇ ᴄɪᴛʏ ᴡᴀʟʟ, ᴏᴠᴇʀʟᴏᴏᴋɪɴɢ the Warrowing Village from the east. He and Captain Oswald stood, like mirror images, looking down at the bustling Faerie village with their hands thumbing their chins.

"Cancel the duels," Hanz said, breaking the silence.

"Really?" Oswald glanced at the king from the corner of his eye.

Hanz shrugged, "The dueling grounds are still not cleared of debris after the storm. And I... I can't be assed."

Oswald cracked a smile, then said, "Yes, Sire."

"Then there's Rasselas," Hanz said, inadvertently whistling through his teeth when he said the enraging man's name. What kind of a name was *Rasselas*, anyway? Just *saying* it made him irritated.

"Yes," Oswald said.

"I don't want to anger Celestia," Hanz said, sounding pained, "But I want there to be some sort of consequence. A visiting delegate can't go around attacking my head captain and assaulting my Faeries without punishment."

"He wasn't *assaulting* Valley, I don't think," Oswald said with a shrug.

"Oh, *yes* he was," Hanz insisted. "She's bonded with *me*. No one can touch her but *me*. Anyway... Give him a light beating and stick him back in the pit for the day. In the morning, we will announce that we have given him clemency."

Oswald nodded. "Fine."

"What was the idiot *thinking*?" Hanz shook his head. "Making a scene like that!"

"I think the boy has an eye for Valley," said Oswald.

"You *think*?" Hanz snorted. "He's smitten. I just didn't think he would be stupid enough to go and do something like *this*."

"I think he felt her treatment unjust," Oswald said. His body tensed slightly, as if he regretted verbalizing his thoughts.

"He doesn't understand," Hanz said, "He was raised under Aorist's influence. He believes Faeries should be ruling themselves."

"Yes... I know," Oswald said.

"Anyway, I want you to prepare everyone for departure—the Faeries, I mean. I haven't announced it to the delegates yet. But get the wheels turning."

"It will be done, Sire."

"Oswald?" Hanz turned to look the man in the eyes.

"Sire?" The soldier turned.

"Do you think of me as a villain?"

"*Sire*?" Oswald's eyebrows twisted with concern.

"A villain—Come on."

Oswald hesitated. That was interesting. "I don't think anyone is a villain."

"Well, neither do I," Hanz said, "But some people believe in that sort of thing. Do you?"

"I just said that I don't," Oswald said in a stubborn tone. "Some people are needlessly unkind... I suppose that sort of person could be called villainous."

"Am *I* needlessly unkind?" Hanz raised an eyebrow.

"Sometimes. But then—I suppose everyone is sometimes. *Hades*, Sire. I am not one for philosophy. I think everyone just does what they think is right. Who am I to judge them for that? That is what the law is for. It gives us rules to follow. So I suppose…" He straightened his back, as if he had just in that moment figured out his take on life, "I suppose *lawbreakers* could be called villains."

"Am I a lawbreaker?" Hanz asked.

Oswald bristled uncomfortably. "Well, no," he said, "You're a law*maker*."

Hanz nodded. "Right you are."

"Why are you asking me this?"

Hanz pushed up the corner of his mouth into something resembling a smile. "No reason."

King Hanz left Oswald there to ponder and descended the stairs to the Warrowing Compound. He asked one of his guards to find Tristan. Before long, the guard returned with the head Faerie by his side.

"Hanz!" Tristan said excitedly, though he seemed flustered. "Thank you for meeting me."

"I heard that you wanted to see me," Hanz said coolly. "Everything alright?"

"Right. Yes…" the man folded his hands together in an attempt to still himself. "May we speak?"

"That's why I am here," Hanz said with a smile. "Is everything alright?"

"It's about…*erm*…*Valley*," he lowered his voice to a whisper.

"What about her?"

"Hanz…" Tristan blinked. "She's the *Dream* Faerie. Don't you know what that means?"

"Of course I know, old friend," Hanz said flatly. "She is the daughter of Hevel."

Tristan drew back. "You knew…all along?"

"Of course I knew," Hanz said. "I rescued her."

"R—*rescued*?"

"She's not the only one I rescued. Tristan…It is time you knew." This seemed like a good time to reinforce Tristan's trust. Tristan was clearly growing doubtful, more doubtful of himself than of Hanz—but still, that's where it always starts.

"Knew *what*?" Tristan raised his eyebrows in anticipation.

"We are going to Arelle," Hanz said. "I am taking the Faeries home."

Tristan opened and closed his mouth like a fish on land, trying to find the right words. He finally landed with "*What?*"

"I want you to help me set up the fairies in their home city. The children will thrive there." Hanz said.

"But...won't they find it unsettling to be so close to the empty throne?" Tristan asked, looking stunned.

"I have a plan for that," Hanz said. "We can't protect the Fae from their heritage. We need to...work around it, I think."

Tristan nodded slowly. "Yes," he said, "I can see that...Arelle? *Really?*" His excitement began to grow. Good. Good—Hanz needed Tristan excited; he would spread that enthusiasm to the other Faeries.

"In two days," Hanz said, "We will all travel there. The Humans will lead the charge, you understand."

"Of course, of course," Tristan said quickly. "Yes, you will know best what must be done. But Arelle! It will be so good to go back! I think it will really give me better resources to care for the Faerie children. They—well, they aren't thriving here."

"I know," Hanz said, "Can I count on your support? Tomorrow, when you tell the Fae where we are going, can you explain that this is better for them?"

"Yes, of course! Will they...will we..." Tristan hesitated, "Are we still to live in a compound like this?"

"Well," Hanz folded his hands, "Let's not shake things up too much. We need this to feel like a smooth transition. Something familiar would be better for them at first. Once they're settled, we could consider moving them into their own homes...but for now, I am thinking we could set them up in the Vineyard Palace."

"Somenus' old Harem?" Tristan twisted his mouth, "Are you sure?"

"It's private and secluded," Hanz said, "And easy to contain."

"I see," Tristan nodded quickly, "Yes, I see—that will work."

"Do you think I am making a good call?" Hanz asked.

"Well," Tristan whistled thoughtfully, "I decided a long time ago to stop trying to figure out what the Fae needed and leave all that to you—but yes, I think this will be good. Of course...There is the problem of the *throne*. *Erm*...Hanz?"

"Yes, old friend?"

"What will you do if the king comes back?"

"King?" Hanz raised his eyebrows. "What king?"

Tristan stammered then said, "I–I think you know who I mean, the son of Somenus."

"Even if he were still alive," Hanz said with a yawn, "he was never crowned."

"Yes, but...isn't his bloodline tied to the throne? If he is alive, he could take it if he wanted to."

Let him try, thought Hanz.

"If he is indeed alive, and he does come to claim his throne, we will welcome him. But right now, my only concern is caring for my Faeries. Here in Mensa we have the highest concentration of Fae in the world. *We* are the heart of the Faerie Kingdom, and so *we* should be in Arelle. Don't you think?"

"Well, yes," Tristan said, as his eyes darted around. He was processing.

"Trust me, friend. I always know what I am doing, don't I?"

Tristan laughed nervously. "Yes, yes, you definitely do! It's hard not being able to see the inner workings of your plans, but they do always come into fruition."

Yes, they do, Hanz thought proudly to himself.

"Now," Tristan rubbed his mouth, "Now there is something that might be tricky..."

"What?"

"The prisoners...will we bring them to Arelle, too?"

"We will bring them all," Hanz said, "I will worry about that. Why don't you go prepare a speech. You can deliver it tonight. I'll send food for a feast. You can tell them that they will finally have a more settled home, a better place in the world."

"They will be thrilled," Tristan said enthusiastically. "This place...it is safe and contained, but it is not a home. The children, they need more."

"Yes," Hanz said. His eyes wandered toward the back of the Warrowing Village where the prison was. The prison's enchanted containment wagons could transport the prisoners without too much hassle. However, *one* prisoner in particular might be a problem. "I...I have somewhere to be," Hanz mumbled, "Do you have what you need from me?"

"Oh!" Tristan jumped. "Yes, yes, I'll be fine."

Oh, Tristan. He was so concerned with helping his people and yet so doubtful of himself. He made a good puppet. He *liked* being told what to do and what to think. When Aorist announced to the world that Faeries were created to serve Humans, Tristan became as useless as a slug. He was purposeless, wallowing in confusion. But Hanz had given him a purpose.

Hanz waved Tristan farewell and made his way toward the prison. Taking a torch from one of the guards, he entered. It was dark inside. He liked it that way. It kept the prisoners docile, their imagination stagnant.

Hanz felt his heart beating harder, and his breaths became labored. He stood in the middle of the dark hall, holding his lantern with a trembling hand. Why was he doing this? *Why* did he think this was a good idea to come here? There was no reason to be timid! Just *go*!

He charged into the women's side of the prison, holding his lantern high. It did not illuminate the interiors of any of the cells that surrounded him, only that central hall where he stood. He knew all three Faeries there were watching him, though he could see none of their faces. What were they thinking? What would that truth Faerie say if she could speak? Oh, what did it matter? He made his own truth.

"What in *Hades* do you want?" A voice spoke through the darkness. That voice...it was like listening to rippling streams, evening gales, rising tides— mesmerizing. Even in this dank place, shrouded in darkness and rage, she was so mesmerizing!

"Riah," Hanz turned toward her cell. He could only see her glowing purple eyes.

"Finally come to see me?" she asked. "Do you finally have the guts to torture me *yourself*?"

Hanz' heart throbbed with both horror and pleasure at the torment done to this woman by his command.

"Riah," he said softly, "You broke my heart."

Riah, the Illusion Faerie, made a retching sound. "Save it, Hanz."

"You broke my *heart*!" He raised his voice, thrusting the torch against the bars of her cell. A rain of sparks flew off it, illuminating her face for a flickering moment. That momentary flash reminded him of the haunting fact that she was beautiful.

"No!" she yelled, grabbing the bars and pressing her face against them. She would wring his neck if she could. "No, no, no...*you* do not get to say that!"

Hanz stood a foot from the cell, holding the torch high so he could see her face clearly. Her skin was cracked and marbled with bruising, but her beauty remained. Was that beauty, too, an illusion? Or was it as real as the stones he stood upon?

"Riah... why?" he asked. He had not come here to ask this, but the moment he met her eyes, he felt her betrayal afresh.

Riah gnashed her teeth together. "Why, what?"

"Why did you do it? Why did you...betray me?"

"You betrayed *me*, Hanz," she hissed. "I was always loyal to you. I loved you!"

Hanz turned away, seeking relief from the pain of looking into her eyes. "You...you took Anodos from me. Regardless of what happened between us, you betrayed what we *believed* in."

Riah scoffed. "*What happened between us?* Hanz—you married that Human! You went and made her your *wife*!"

"You *knew* I had to do that!" Hanz broke into a sudden yell, slamming his palm against the bar beside her face. "I couldn't exactly have a *Faerie* for a queen, Riah! You know I still loved you!"

"No!" Riah shook her body back and forth, keeping her hands gripped on the bars. "No, no! You *loved* her! She gave you a *son*!"

"Well my son is dead—are you happy?" Hanz snapped back. "And so is she. There! Did you get your wish? Did you get what you *wanted*?"

Riah pushed herself away from the bars, stepping back into the darkness. "I hate you," she said.

"Riah…" Hanz said weakly "Don't go… come…come here."

"I won't tell you where he is," Riah said, "And you will never find him."

"Come back," Hanz said, fitting one of his hands through the bars. He reached out for her. "Let me see your face."

Hanz screamed at a sudden pain, dropping the torch onto the ground as he recoiled away from the bars, clutching his bleeding hand. She had *bit* him?

"You animal!" he cried, "You hateful, deceitful woman!"

"*You* are the animal, Hanz," Riah said. She began to chuckle, and her voice filled the cell as if she had replicated herself a hundred times. "I *know* what you did."

Hanz lifted his head sharply, gritting his teeth. "Quiet!" he whispered, "You know *nothing*!"

"You are the animal, Hanz," she said again.

"I always loved you!" he cried, then shot his face toward the cell holding the truth Faerie. "Tell her, girl! Speak the truth! I always loved Riah. I still love her!"

"If you wanted the girl to speak the truth, Hanz," Riah raised her voice. "Then you would not have cut out her tongue!"

Hanz shook his head hatefully. Thoughts swirled around his mind, stirred up by the confusion he still felt at why Riah turned against him.

"Why? *Why* did you let Anodos go?"

"You *know* why," she said calmly, "I wanted to ruin your stupid plans."

"No," Hanz shook his head, "No, something changed."

"You *married* her—that's what changed!" Riah screeched.

"You told me to marry her!" Hanz pressed, stepping closer to the cell. He could hear Riah breathing heavily. Was she laughing? Or was she crying?

"I…" her voice was breaking. Crying…she was crying. Oh, how it hurt to hear her cry. Hanz held his breath, listening.

"Please," he said, "*Tell* me, Riah."

"I… I can't tell you, Hanz."

"Please," he said in the gentlest of whispers. "We were so close, like two souls knit into one. We had so much trust. What happened?"

"It was *him*," she said, "Anodos."

Hanz narrowed his brow. "What *about* Anodos?"

"I...Never mind."

Hanz sighed. "Riah, I will be moving to Arelle in two days."

There was an eerie quiet in her cell for a moment or two, then she said, "So...you're ready, then?"

"Yes."

"I see," she sighed. "Then, I suppose you found a way to get what you want, even without Anodos."

"Yes."

"An old part of me wants to be glad..." she mumbled, "But that part of me is mostly dead now. I have since developed a hatred for you that is so vile, I curse the very sound of your name. I wish for everything you touch to turn to dust and ash."

Hanz nodded. "I... I wish I could hate you like that. It would be easier than this." He sighed deeply to himself. "I would have wanted you by my side. I... I wish you had stayed with me to the end."

The king did not wait for a response. He left.

Well—he had done it. He had spoken to her and hadn't completely broken. When Hanz reached the gate to the Warrowing Village, he found Karo waiting for him.

"Ah, sire," Karo bowed lowly, "Good day, good day."

"Karo," Hanz mumbled, "Thank you for waiting."

"Oh, sire!" He placed his hand upon his heart with a smirk, "It is a *pleasure* to wait upon you!"

"Alright," Hanz waved his hand at Karo dismissively; he wasn't really in the mood for Karo's ass-kissing. "Get everything ready. We will do it tonight."

"T–tonight? Are you *sure*?" Karo asked, looking side to side nervously.

"Yes," Hanz said, "I am leaving Mensa in two days, and I can't take the Crimson Gate with me. So I need those eyes."

"Are you sure you don't want to do any further experiments, Sire? Once I remove your…" his voice caught in his throat, then he decreased his volume to a whisper. "Once I remove your eyes, I cannot guarantee we can preserve them well enough to put them back."

"I will not need them anymore," Hanz said casually. "Right?"

"Y—yes…"

"Well then. We will do it tonight."

31

—— Rook ——

The Walk

Bound tightly to the stone table, Anodos could not move. With Riah leaning over him like this, he could not see the familiar crack upon the ceiling. Having looked at it for so long, it was one of the only shapes Anodos could even remember anymore. He knew that crack better than his own face. Yet, even the small, familiar comfort of looking at it had been denied him.

What was this pain he was feeling? Why was blackness clouding his vision?

Blood—it was blood. Riah was carving intricate lines into his face with her pen dagger. The dagger blazed with the bright light of magik power. It must have been her Imperium. She sat on Anodos' chest, bent over—her face only inches away from his—and carved a line in his cheek.

"Hold still," she hissed, "There can be no mistakes!"

Why was she doing this? She was insane—surely, this woman was utterly and completely insane. Why else would she do something like this?

Anodos realized that he could not respond because he was screaming. He shook his arms, his legs—everything, trying to be free of her. With each line carved by the knife, Anodos felt a burning enter his body. This was some sort of spell, he thought.

Riah sat up to examine her work. Anodos tried to blink open his eyes, but the sockets were filled with pools of blood.

"Why?" he croaked. "Why are you doing this?"

"Kindness," she said as she took hold of the lobe of his ear.

"No!" Anodos begged. He felt her sever the tip of his ear.

"This is the only way, Anodos... I'm sorry."

"Stop—*please*!" he begged. "Haven't you done enough?"

Suddenly, Riah screamed, and Anodos suddenly felt her weight lift from his chest. She was fighting someone.

"Get away from me!" Riah screeched. "Back, you harpy!"

"Leave him alone!" said another voice. "What are you *doing* to him?"

Anodos tried to lift his head. "Who said that?" he asked. No... this wasn't how it was supposed to go. "This...this isn't what happens, is it?"

"What have you done to his face?" asked the newcomer.

"It's the strongest spell I can give him," replied Riah, "See? I'm protecting him."

"No you're not!" cried the other voice. "You're hurting him!"

"Who is that?" Anodos called. There was silence. He lay there, feeling the pain throb on his face. Then he jolted. Someone was touching his hand; someone was cutting him loose. This never happened—this wasn't how it went.

Anodos sat up shakily. A cloth was placed into his hands. He pulled it to his face and wiped away the blood that covered his eyes. When he pulled the cloth away, he could see the face of his rescuer. A young woman—a Faerie! He could sense it...Yes! She was the Dream Faerie.

"What are you *doing* here?" Anodos asked in confusion. "Morningstar, is that really you? You're just a child... you're supposed to be... a child." Standing before him was no child, but a young woman.

The young woman stared at his face with a look of extreme distress. Her eyes darted around, eyeing all the cuts on his face. She took a deep breath, then said,

"It's me, Rook. Don't you recognize me?"

"I do... sort of," Anodos said, dabbing more blood off his face, though his accelerated healing had already begun to close up his wounds. "I held you when you were just a baby. Now you are grown. How? It's been only a season or two, surely? But... you're alive! Is Hevel alive, too?"

"Hevel?" she asked, widening her eyes.

"Your father," Anodos said, "Are you not Morningstar, Hevel's daughter? It must be you—you're the third Dream Faerie."

Morningstar stared at him like a startled deer. "Yes..." she finally said, "It is me."

"Am I dreaming?" Anodos asked, "Or have I really been *rescued*?" He felt hope swell within his chest.

There was sadness on her face. "Rook... I...."

"So this *is* a dream," he said, "Why do you call me Rook? I...I don't know that name."

"Is that not your name?" she asked carefully. "Or... What *is* your name?" Her eyes began to travel across his bare-chested body, and her face grew pale.

"Anodos," he said, then tried to smile. "You wouldn't remember me. You were only alive two seasons when I last held you."

"*Anodos*?" She stumbled backwards. "You're... you're *Anodos?*"

His smile faded. "You... you didn't know who I was? Didn't you come to rescue me?"

She stepped forward and placed a hand on his shoulder. "I *did* come here to rescue you," she said, "from this nightmare."

So—this was a dream. The moment this reality seized him, the pain in his body faded into nothing.

"Oh," he blinked, then swung his legs over the side of the table. "So, you are doing what my father *should* have done with his powers...yes...turning *away* the horrors instead of bringing them?"

"Oh..." she blinked. "Well..."

"Thank you for sending away my torturer," he sighed, "But I fear that the real nightmare comes when I wake. There, she will still be."

"No!" Morningstar said quickly, "No, it won't be! When you wake, you will be free! I think this is an old memory. When you wake, you will be free!"

"I will?" he asked. Tears began to fill his eyes. "You mean... I am back with my family? My parents? My... my *Dad*?"

Morningstar stepped away from him. "I have done what I can for you... *Anodos*. Be at peace."

━━━━━━ ● ━━━━━━

Rook awoke with a gasp.

"Come on. You slept in." Cato stood over him, looking down. Surprisingly, Cato was dressed.

Rook waved him away and sat up, groaning. "Can't a man sleep in privacy?"

Cato's eyes seemed to be lingering on Rook's many scars, but his expression was neutral. "You slept in," Cato repeated through a yawn, "and I am ready to go."

"Go?" Rook stepped out of bed and pulled his wrinkled shirt from where it was draped carelessly over a chair. He fumbled with it, trying to get it over his head. "Go where? It's still early."

"Oh," Cato rolled his eyes, shrugging his shoulders up to his ears, "Hanz wants us all to pay our respects to the princess and everything. I want to get my thing over with first before all the other princes—"

"Pay your respects?" Rook snapped, "Is she *dead*?"

"*Hades*, lad," Cato sniffed, "No, she's fine. She got a bit banged up in the storm, they say. Hanz said that anybody who wants to take her for a walk might cheer her up."

Rook's expression darkened. It wasn't the storm that hurt Rosamond; it was that daemon-of-a-father who hurt her—the same man who was now asking *others* to console her.

"Well come on, don't take all day," Cato huffed. He produced his toothpick from his sleeve and began picking nervously. The man's rings glistened in the morning light. Hades, Cato wore so many rings!

Rook swung his jacket over his shoulders and buttoned up. "There," he said, "Good enough?"

Cato pulled the corner of his mouth to the side. "What am I going to do with you?"

Rook stepped in front of his mirror. He did look a mess, so he tried to wrap an unruly cravat around his neck. His hair was more knotted than usual, and he had trouble getting his fingers through it. He didn't usually care how he looked but...well, if they were going to be out with the princess... Rook grunted, reaching for his comb.

"Don't take all day about it!" Cato barked.

"Look, I just woke up," Rook snapped. He was fighting to get the comb through his tangles. He found himself studying the lines carved across his face. Did only he see the pattern? Riah's spell. It felt so obvious; that cursed spell protected him from Hanz yet kept him from his family. The only way to break it was to be recognized for who he was by someone who knew him. Did he even want that to happen? Or was Riah right? Was this a *gift*?

Rook realized that Cato had been talking, so he did his best to catch up.

"...and Tercius thinks that Hanz is going to take us on some felling trip. Well, I don't know, nor do I care. I'm just hoping that, wherever we go, there's food."

"What?" Rook snapped the collar of his jacket into place. "What do you mean, 'a trip'?"

"Tercius says there's a lot of activity in the stables and barracks. Preparations and whatnot. Everybody is trying to figure out what it's all about... Well, all I can say is that Hanz had better provide some good food. Alright, you're presentable enough, let's go."

Cato turned and began walking out of his room. Rook raced to keep up with the man as he began to leave the Inner Palace.

They approached a walled garden. "Isn't Rosamond upstairs?" Rook asked, peering around.

"Well, I don't know," Cato said, stopping to gaze at a sculpture of a maned lion. Stone animals like this dotted the Inner Palace gardens. "I was told that Princess Rosamond was going for walks here, and that everybody should go see her." He made a persecuted sigh, "Dogs, Rook. I couldn't care less about this sort of thing."

"I know," Rook said, patting the man's shoulder. "It must be hard for you to pretend to care."

"Oh, I don't pretend," Cato returned, "I don't *care* enough to pretend. I just liked the idea of beating all the other thirsty boys to the well, if you know what I mean. Get the first peek."

"The first peek?" Rook frowned.

Cato shrugged with a guilty-looking smile. "Well...we all can't help but wonder if the legendary beauty got...*damaged* in some way. If there's gossip to harvest, I want the first swing."

Rook scoffed. "You're horrible," he mumbled. "The poor princess gets hurt, and all anyone can think about is what they might lose or gain from it. Despicable."

"Well, not everyone can afford to care, Rook," Cato said, "Anyway..."

"Well, good morning, Highlord!" said a voice as bright as the morning. Rook and Cato snapped their faces in the direction of the voice. Rosamond stood, leaning heavily on Viola's arm. They were approaching from the other side of the garden.

"Ah, Princess!" Cato bowed. "Looking stunning, as usual!" He then leaned down to whisper into Rook's ear, "And thank the Lights for *that*!"

"Come, Cato," Rosamond said, holding out her hand to him, "Why don't you lead me around the garden. The air is so fresh this Somensday morning."

Cato performed a mocking goofy jig as he pranced over to her, then stood straight to hold out a steady arm. Viola stayed back, letting Rosamond go walking with her companions alone, watching as Cato and Rosamond began to walk the twisting garden trail, touring the private gardens. Rook trailed behind them slowly, wondering why he had been summoned. Cato could have done this walk all on his own; it was as if he needed another man nearby, someone to whom he could roll his eyes—someone who would yawn with him when things grew too serious.

Rook listened to Rosamond and Cato chatting away in the most meandering conversation. They both knew they should speak, but neither of them cared what was said.

"I was surprised *you* took up the opportunity to walk with me, highlord," Rosamond said as they strolled. "Wouldn't someone who drinks as heavily as you still be in bed at this bell?"

Rook bit his lip, then cracked a smile when Rosamond turned slightly to meet his eye.

"Well, yes, I must confess," Cato said in an unnecessarily booming voice. "I usually would still be asleep... but I figured since *you* went so far as to ask me to dance and all that, I might as well come and take you for a walk. You know— even things out."

Rosamond chuckled. "What nonsense. You just wanted to be the one to see me first."

"Now, why would you think *that*?" he said, holding his chin high. He was a bumbling idiot, but when needed, he could act proper. He held his arm out steadily for the girl, encouraging her to lean against him for support. She was limping, though she did her best to hide it. As mismatched as they were in height, they looked a pretty pair.

"Because I heard you say so to your wing there," Rosamond turned to smile at Rook again. He raised an eyebrow at her. She turned away quickly, "You told him you wanted to get your hands on some gossip. You don't really know how to whisper, do you, old thing?"

"Oh dogs, Princess," Cato tutted. "Gossip? *Me*? Never."

"Well," Rosamond pulled herself from the highlord's side to spread out her arms. "What do you think? Has my beauty waned?" She was smiling mischievously, as if she would be pleased, no matter the response.

Cato studied her with his finger resting against his nose.

"Hmm..." he hummed, "Well, I can see some of those marks might scar... but most of them, I think not. That bruise on your chin, I suppose, could have been a problem. But frankly, it's not that bad."

"Well," Rosamond joined his side again, "Does that feel like enough ammunition to make the other delegates curious?"

"I suppose I could enhance the story a little bit, you know, tell them all that you had a big black mark on your face, and all that."

"That will have to do," Rosamond sighed. "I'm sorry to disappoint, but it really was nothing more than a few scratches from the occasional tree branch whizzing past."

Cato turned his head just enough to give Rook a look that said *save me from this monotony.*

"Well," Cato blew air through his lips and looked around. They were standing near the center of the little walkabout, just under a canopy of hanging vines. "Hades... I am just trying to find..." he mumbled.

"What are you trying to find?" Rosamond asked, bending her head back so she could gaze up at the man's face.

"Which of these statues do you think grants the best shade—I'm looking for somewhere to piss," he said.

Rosamond chuckled nervously, glancing back at Rook who gave an apologetic shrug. When Cato didn't join in the laughter, she hesitated. "Oh! You—you're serious?"

"That one looks good," Cato dropped Rosamond's hand, then turned to nod at Rook. Cato jogged off through some foliage—ruining some gardener's day—and shouted, "Be right back!"

Rook stepped forward and held out his arm silently to Rosamond. She looked at the arm, then at his face.

"Good morning, Rook," she said, then placed both her hands against him.

"Morning, Rosamond," he said, "How are you feeling?"

"I've been doing some investigating," she whispered, leaning her head close to his shoulder. "I haven't figured out much about a vault... or where father keeps his special items, like *eyes...*"

"Well, you've been in bed," Rook chuckled, "I would prefer you get some rest before you do too much—"

"But I *have* noticed something!" She paused, looking down at herself.

"Is everything alright?" Rook asked. She seemed troubled.

"Oh... nothing. It's fine," she looked back up at Rook. "I think it hurts my foot to do all this walking, but Father wants me to spend some time with the delegates. I have a feeling I'll be doing this walk ten times over by the end of the day!"

Rook frowned. "Your father should be keeping you in bed... *away* from the drama! You need to tell him you are not up for this."

"Rook!" she whispered quickly, "Cato's coming back in a click... Let me tell you... someone *else* is staying on my floor. A man... in the room next to me. Father keeps a whole fleet of guards by his door. I can tell he is important, I just don't know who he is! But I think..." She did her best to reach Rook's ear with her mouth, pressing herself up on the tips of her toes. "I think he's a *Faerie!*"

Rook looked down at Rosamond from the corner of his eye. Had he never noticed those gold rings around her pupils before? It looked as if her inner soul were on fire. "A Faerie in the Inner Palace?" he asked. Very interesting, indeed. "Do you think you could find a chance to speak with him?"

"Well," Rosamond dropped herself down to the flats of her feet. "I think I could possibly sneak onto his balcony from mine. It wouldn't be that hard."

"That sounds a bit dangerous, especially for someone with a broken foot." Rook said with a smirk. "Rosamond," he said, "You won't put yourself in danger, will you?"

"Oh, come on," she grinned, "When would I ever do *that*?"

"Don't go climbing out any windows," Rook said firmly, "But if you do find out anything about him, you can let me know."

"Oh!" Rosamond said, "You mean... you will come speak with me again? Like last time?" Her face looked hopeful.

"Oh..." Rook cleared his throat, buying himself a moment of time. "Is that something...you would *want*?"

"Well, how else are we going to discuss what I—" Rosamond turned her head. The sounds of snapping branches indicated that Cato was shuffling back through the bushes. She swiftly turned to face Rook and gave him a wide smile. "Rook, it was so nice to see you this morning."

"Oh," Rook mumbled, "Yeah, well..."

"Well, there he is!" Rosamond said loudly, placing her hands on her hips as Cato wiped his hands against his coat.

"Pleasant place, this!" Cato remarked as he stepped up to Rosamond's side again. He offered her his arm with a fresh smile.

"Oh," Rosamond glanced at the arm hesitantly, "You can't think I am going to touch you after…" She pointed back toward the bushes.

"Oh, come now," Cato coughed, "Every single man—"

"Princess Rosamond!" Mynx was bounding down the garden path. "Looking so well, aren't you, girl?"

"Ah, Mynx!" Rosamond said. She appeared enthusiastic, but her eyes could not hide her fatigue. "Good day, Highlord." Rosamond discarded Cato like a dirty napkin and glided over to Mynx's side.

Cato and Rook stood side by side for a moment, watching them leave.

"Well," Cato said with a sigh, "Poor girl."

Rook glanced up at the highlord. "Yeah."

"I think that…" Cato pulled his finger to his nose and tapped it, "Yes, I think that dear King Hanz is quite mad."

"Mad… at Rosamond?"

"Insane. Mad, Rook. The man is *mad*."

Rook blinked. Cato was being deadly serious. "What makes you say that?"

"It is one thing to beat his daughter because it achieves some goal. But Hanz has gone as far as to hurt *himself*. He wants us chasing her but look at what he has done—damaged his prospects, he has."

Rook examined the highlord. Yes, he was entirely genuine. "You think that… that *Hanz* did this to Rosamond?"

"Oh, come now, Rook," Cato sighed, "I wasn't born yesterday."

Rook frowned. "If that's true, it's disgusting. His own *daughter*?"

Cato made a melancholy sigh. "Well, it's not a *nice* thing, is it? Poor girl." He grew very quiet. "He'll kill her next time." Cato turned and began to walk back to the Inner Palace.

His words rang in Rook's ears. The man was an idiot, but he was right about this: Hanz had hurt Rosamond even though it seemed to impede his own plans. Why? Dread began to rise within Rook. What was to stop Hanz from hurting her further—or worse? No, Rook would not let that happen.

On his walk out of the garden, Rook spotted a familiar figure sitting on a quiet bench. His head was down, and he was writing fervently in a bound notebook.

"Good Somensday, Latimer," Rook said as he veered off his path to approach the Elf. "Shouldn't you be *resting* on the seventh day?"

"*Seventh?*" Latimer shot his head up, then smiled at the sight of Rook. "Oh, hallo, friend!"

Rook seated himself next to the skydeacon. "How did it go, confronting the other skydeacons about the storm?"

"Oh... that..." Latimer blew air through his gritted teeth. "Well..."

"You haven't talked to anyone yet?" Rook smiled.

"Well, no. I realized that since no one seems interested in naming the storm properly, I should probably do the work myself first. You know, find out its name. Then I can come to the fellowship with hard evidence. I... I don't want to go confronting anyone without actually doing my research! You know... they'll say things like, '*How do you know it was a fury storm, Latimer?*' Or '*show us your papers, Latimer!*' Things like that."

"I'm hoping you don't get yourself in trouble, ruffling the wrong feathers," Rook said.

"No, no, not this again!" Latimer held up his pen, pointing it at Rook's nose. "You cannot convince me to stay silent!"

"I know that now," Rook laughed. "I won't even try."

The two men jolted at the sound of a bell. It wasn't an hour bell, it was a summoning bell, which was higher and shriller.

"What could that be about?" Rook asked himself aloud.

"I heard the king might make an announcement today," Latimer said with a sigh. "I guess we had better go see what it is."

As the bell continued to ring, they rose and walked toward the front entrance to the Inner Palace where others were gathering as well. Rook noticed Rosamond approaching with Mynx on one side and Prince Tingo on the other. Hanz stood near the front door, waiting to make his announcement. Rasselas was nowhere to be seen—was he *still* locked up? Rook would have to find out.

Hanz silenced the bells with a single motion. "Ladies and Gentlemen!" Hanz said. "We have decided to continue our negotiations elsewhere. Yes, the rumors are true. We are all to travel to Arelle, the Faerie City. There, we will decide what is to be done with it. We will put an end to the starvation and famine. And there, Humans can finally rule themselves without Faerie oversight!"

A murmur of excitement filled the gathered crowd. Rook and Rosamond found each other's faces. Rosamond looked shocked but searching, as if to ask, *is this a good thing or a bad thing?* That was the right question to ask.

Was Rook ready to go back to *Arelle*?

"Wow," Latimer whispered into Rook's ear, "Look at *that*!"

"What?" Rook glanced at the Elf, "Look at what?"

"At that!" Latimer pointed at the King. "His eyes!"

Rook shot his attention back to the King. Hanz stood proudly, hands on hips, with the most self-satisfied smile.

Latimer was right. Hanz' eyes had gone from a dark brown to a soft, deep, ocean blue.

"Oh Lights..." Rook gasped.

Those were Felix's eyes.

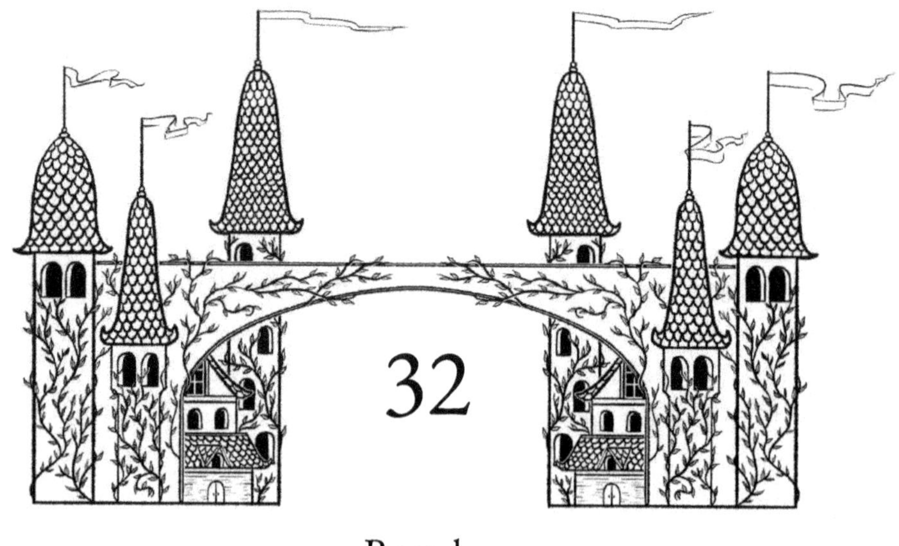

32

— Rasselas —

A Splash of Reality

RASSELAS LET OUT A LONG, RASPY SIGH AS HE SLID into the steamy bath waters. Finally! The moment he had been waiting for. He was out of that ghastly pit and soaking up the moisture his poor cracking skin deeply needed. Whoever had been in the bathhouse a moment before was now gone, due to Rasselas making a scene demanding privacy. He was quickly regretting that decision. He had been alone for all of Mansday and into this morning—did he want to be alone *still*? No, he wanted to *talk* to someone! He wished to complain and whinge about how poorly he had been treated.

His wish was answered, but in the worst possible way. Thorne came sauntering into the bathhouse, fully dressed, and with a smug grimace and everything.

"Ah, Thorne, old boy," Rasselas called from the bath. "I'm glad to see you, whatever you might have to say next. Slay me, I believe there *is* something likable about your face... perhaps it's your nose? For a long moment, I thought I might never see a Human face again! And yet—here you are!"

"I'm an Elf," Thorne said flatly, looking down at him condescendingly, much like a cat.

"Ah yes, of course. How could I forget?" Rasselas smiled through his teeth. "And such a *nice* Elf you are."

"Are you... alright?" Thorne asked. He didn't appear at all concerned but seemed to think it was part of his job to check on Rasselas after he had been in prison. In truth, yesterday had probably been one of the most joyous in Thorne's entire, pitiful life.

"Oh, I am fine." Rasselas said, putting on a heroic face that said, *I may be in pain, but I will never admit it.* "They roughed up your handsome prince a little, and I spent the night in a dank, porous hole. Had a lot of time for *thinking*, you know—came to a very serious decision."

"Oh?" Thorne crossed his arms. "And what was that, to stop acting like an utter *fool?*"

"No," Rasselas said primly, dipping his hands down into the water. He swished them side to side, making waves. He was missing the ocean... missing home. "No, it's much more revolutionary than that."

"Well?" Thorne asked, growing impatient.

"I'm thinking about growing a mustache," Rasselas paused as if waiting for applause. "A must*ache*. I think I would look rather good with one. What do you think?"

"Moonvine..."

"But you have to say it like that. You have to say: must*ache*, with the emphasis on the second part of the word. Otherwise, it's not as fashionable."

"Moonvine, I have news for you," Thorne said.

Rasselas turned sharply to see how serious the wing looked. "News? Well slay me, old boy, say it!"

Thorne cleared his throat softly, with his hands folded together stoically. "We will all be traveling to Arelle tomorrow, King Hanz announced it this morning."

Rasselas tensed his brow. "What did you say?" he asked, "*Who* is going to Arelle?"

"All of the delegates. King Hanz wants everyone to come to an agreement on what should be done with the empty throne."

"Right…" Rasselas sat there quietly. He wasn't surprised. Wasn't this what Hanz was gearing up to do all along? Didn't he want to make Arelle part of his empire? Didn't he want to have the throne under his own nose so that the king could not come back? Wasn't the covetous villain planning on taking the throne for himself? What a fool! *Nothing* could stop Anodos from returning once he was ready. Why didn't everyone understand that?

"I think King Antecus will want to know this," Thorne said, "I can only imagine Hanz will want everyone to sign alliance terms."

Rasselas slipped down into the water, submerging his head. For a moment, all he could hear was the churning of underwater pipes and the sounds of his arms gliding through the water beside him. He popped back up, flinging his wet hair backwards.

Thorne grunted, stepping back from the sudden spray of water.

"I'll have a little chat with Embers," Rasselas said.

"Fine," Thorne turned, ready to depart.

"Old boy?" Rasselas asked sheepishly.

"What?"

"Am I…invited…to come to Arelle? Or…did I…rather…"

"You are not forbidden from coming. King Hanz has granted you clemency," Thorne said with a sigh. "He said all is forgiven. But I must be honest with you, Moonvine, I *will* be telling King Antecus about your…outburst."

"Good!" Rasselas said loudly, stretching his back into an arch. "I would *like* him to hear about how the Faeries are being treated here—and how I would not stand by and watch it happen!"

Thorne scoffed. "You were told not to act. We were supposed to come here and investigate."

"And would you just stand around and *investigate* if the woman you loved was being harmed?" Rasselas asked, leaning forward with a sneer.

Thorne's eyes swirled with rage. "You…" he hissed through his teeth, breathing heavily.

Rasselas slid backwards, reclining against the bath's edge. "Well," Rasselas said calmly, "*Would* you?"

Thorne left the bathhouse without a word. He left behind, however, a cold breeze of fury. It lingered in the steamy room, leaving Rasselas to wonder what in the depths it was all about.

Rasselas drew in a long, slow breath, held it in his lungs, then dropped beneath the water's surface again. Once more, his ears became clouded with the deafening sound of the waters. In an instant, he was transported back to the Sea. Every day, every bell possible, Rasselas would walk to that gray, foggy coast to clear his mind of all noises. Here in Mensa, the closest feeling he could get was the smelly bathhouse, floating with the murky particles of other men.

He rose out of the water, taking in a deep breath. He flicked his hair, uncovering his eyes, and coughed. His lungs still hurt from that cold night in the pit. Then he noticed that he was no longer alone. Someone else was there in the bath, seated a couple yards away and observing him with amusement.

"I say!" Rasselas said as he tried to shake the water from his ear. "This is the last place I would expect to bump into *you*."

"Surprise," Rook said.

"Didn't take you for the type to bathe with other people," Rasselas said with a sniff. As the steam between them began to thin, Rasselas noted that the man's scarring appeared to continue below the throat and down his chest. His skin crawled when he realized just how many there seemed to be.

"Well how else is someone supposed to get clean around here?" Rook said blankly. "I can leave if you want..."

"No," Rasselas said quickly, "No, I rather like the company."

Rook's face softened into a smile. "Alright."

Rasselas scooted closer to the man, fulfilling his curiosity and observing Rook's apparent battle wounds. "I say," he muttered as he drew closer. Right at the center of Rook's chest was a spider-web of laceration scars. "No wonder you don't like bathing around others."

Rook only stared into Rasselas' eyes, as if daring him to look harder.

"What... happened?" Rasselas found himself asking.

"Well," Rook tipped his head back to look at the ceiling, showing off the concertina of scars that ran up his neck. "Where do I start?"

Rasselas blinked. "At... the beginning?"

"Well, it all started when you went running out of the masque, looking for Valley." Rook said with a grin, "Then we found her in the Warrowing Compound."

"Ah..."

"And then you punched Captain Oswald," Rook said.

"Right..."

"And then I managed to keep him from attacking you while you dove into the pit..."

"Oh, dear." Rasselas cleared his throat.

"And *then* I managed to convince Captain Oswald to let you remain down there and not have his men rain arrows down on you," Rook continued.

"You—*what?*"

"Then," Rook chuckled, "I asked him how we could keep you out of danger."

"You did?"

"He said he would speak with the king in the morning. So we kept watch all night to make sure nobody killed you."

Rasselas' mouth was frozen half open.

"You're impulsive, Rasselas," Rook said, "and rash."

"I..." Rasselas withered, "I'm sorry."

"...And yet you were the only one who did the right thing," Rook said as he stared into the prince's eyes. "You... you put the rest of us to shame."

Rasselas wasn't sure how to respond. He cocked his head slightly, studying the man. Bare skinned and without all the dark and unassuming clothes, Rook looked quite different. He seemed so much more Human. And yet, *more* than Human. Who *was* this man?

"I'm an idiot," Rasselas finally said, looking down at the water in front of him. "I put both myself *and* Valley in danger. *And* you... everyone, I guess."

"Valley was already in danger, and everybody was acting as if that was fine. You just cut through the games and the madness. You reminded everyone that some things still matter."

Rasselas shook his head. "No," he said, "I reminded everyone that my ideals are useless. I didn't actually change anything."

"Ideals are useless?" Rook chuckled, "What would your *mother* say if she heard you say that?"

Rasselas shot his eyes upwards. "What?" His mother, the lover of all ideals. "How did you...do you...?"

Rook chuckled, "What?"

"How did you know my mother would be angry at me saying that?"

"Wouldn't *every* mother be angry at that?" Rook asked innocently.

Rasselas leaned back. "I suppose so."

"Plus," Rook added, "You told me you were a mother's boy. Can't I tease you about that?"

"Yes," Rasselas said smugly. "I *like* being a mother's boy."

"So," Rook said with a yawn, "You fancy *Valley*, huh?"

"When did I say that?" Rasselas crossed his arms.

"When you dove in after her, calling her name?" Rook smirked.

Rasselas sent a splash Rook's way. Rook flinched.

"Don't splash me," he said stubbornly. "I don't like it."

Rasselas snorted. "What, you don't like your perfect *tangles* to be disturbed?"

"I just don't like it," Rook leaned back, closing his eyes. "I like to just sit and relax."

"What are you, a *cat*?" Rasselas made another splash, flinging water into Rook's face.

Rook lurched forward, irritated. "I said *stop*!"

Rasselas flicked his thumb against the surface of the water, sending a single drop onto Rook's cheek. The prince smiled innocently.

"How old are you, *five*?"

"Yes."

Rook stood, then waded over toward the prince. Rasselas shrunk for a moment, watching as the tall gentleman flaunted his prominent, though scarred, muscles.

"Now, now," Rasselas waved his hands, "It was all in fu—"

Rasselas' head was shoved under the water. He gurgled and thrashed and flailed his arms until Rook released his head and let him surface.

Rasselas gasped for air. "Hey!" he coughed, "Don't—"

"I thought you *liked* splashing," Rook said, shoving Rasselas' head back under.

From beneath the cloudy bath, Rasselas could hear muffled laughter. Well, Rook might have surprised him once, but Rasselas was more fish than man when he was in the water. He swam out from beneath Rook's oppressive hand and clung to his leg. Rasselas yanked hard on Rook's ankle, causing him to fall back into the water.

Rasselas stood up triumphantly, placing his hands on his hips. He bellowed a proud laugh as Rook scrambled to stand and catch his breath, looking like a wet cat with his hair slicked against his face.

"Hah!" Rasselas pointed, "Look at the warrior now! No one can best *me* in the water!"

Rasselas found himself submerged again. This time, he could not weasel away. Rook's surprisingly strong arms pinned him down against the tiled floor. Rasselas wrestled to the best of his ability. It wasn't fair—Rook was clearly bigger and stronger than he was! And just as Rasselas began to worry that he might suffocate, he felt himself drawn up by the hair.

Rasselas gasped for life, leaning against the only stable thing around: Rook.

Rook held him steady, laughing. "*What* were you saying?" Rook asked, pushing him back against the side of the pool, "*No one* can best you in the water?"

"Alright, alright," Rasselas waved his hand in surrender, "Hades! Stop!"

Rook sat triumphantly with a splash, seating himself beside Rasselas. He wore a beaming grin as Rasselas scowled, doing his best to mask his own embarrassment.

"Well," Rasselas said, running his hands through his hair in an attempt to feel in control once more, "Now that's the *second* time in two days that I've been taught a lesson!"

"Aw," Rook cocked his head to the side with a mocking sympathy, "I'm sorry."

Rasselas pursed his lips, then relaxed with a laugh. "Hades, Rook," he said, "Didn't know you had it in you. You're a card."

Rook scoffed. "If anyone here is the 'card', it's not me. Anyway, welcome back from the grave. I hear you're not to be punished further."

"Yeah..." Rasselas sighed, "Did you...did you hear how Valley is doing?"

"I checked in on her for you," Rook said with a knowing smile, "She's alright." Then Rook's face changed, as if he had just remembered something important—something urgent. "Anyway..." he said as his smile faded, "Yeah...she, *erm*, she's not going to be punished further, I don't think."

"Rook?"

"Hmm?" Rook shifted his attention to face Rasselas, as if pulled away from a straying thought.

"Why did you, slay me—why did you *help* me the other night? I... It's not like we are *friends* or anything."

"We're not?" Rook asked, watching Rasselas expectantly.

"Uh... well... I didn't *think* we were... but now you're making me rethink my, *erm*, thinking."

"Well," Rook stood, "Let me know how that goes." He waded his way through the pool until he found its edge. He left it, grabbing a nearby robe. Rasselas watched him and realized it was the first time he had ever envied another man's stature.

"Rook," Rasselas called from the water. Rook turned.

"Hmm?"

"Thanks."

"Yeah," Rook smiled, "Any time."

⚊⚊•⚊⚊

Rasselas didn't usually visit the Warrowing Village. Something about it made him feel...sticky. The whole place reeked of slavery, and he hated the idea of anyone seeing him there and thinking he might be *shopping*. That was what the other delegates seemed to do when they came here: they browsed. This was the Faeries' only place of solace, the only thing they could call their own. It felt *wrong* to go in there.

But go in, he did. He wanted to see Valley.

As he entered, he noticed several watching eyes. Did they know that he was the Elf who had helped the Faerie? Or was he merely another outsider coming into their space?

Rasselas observed a tall, light-haired Faerie come and greet him with a bow. "What can I do for you? I am Tristan, I—" he stopped short. "Oh!" He blinked, "You are Rasselas."

"Tristan," Rasselas smiled, "Faerie of Water. My Father has told me all about you."

"Yes..." Tristan twiddled his fingers together nervously, "Well, I don't go by that title anymore..."

"Sure, of course," Rasselas muttered, "Good to finally meet you, Tristan."

"I..." Tristan hesitated, "Yes, I knew your father, Leo."

"Knew? He's still alive, you know," Rasselas said dryly, "So, I guess you could say you *know* him."

Tristan nodded, "Yes, so sorry. Yes, I know him. We were friends, you know."

"*Were* friends?" Rasselas raised an eyebrow.

"Yes!" Tristan said quickly, "Yes. I have not seen him for many seasons now. We...we went separate ways after the death of Somenus."

"Yeah," Rasselas sighed, "I understand. There had been a falling out between those in the Purple Order and those of Winter's End."

Tristan gritted his teeth, clearly uncomfortable. It seemed as if Tristan was forbidden to discuss the topic but also feared being rude to a delegate. "Well," he ventured carefully, "You look so much like your father. Really."

"Why, thank you!" Rasselas grinned. "Handsome man, what?"

"Uh, yes!" Tristan laughed nervously. "Very handsome."

There was a moment of awkward silence.

"Rasselas, what has brought you to the Warrowing Village at this time?" Tristan asked.

"Oh..." Rasselas hesitated. Tristan worked closely with Hanz...he needed to be careful.

"May I ask..." Tristan lowered his voice, "Are you looking to bond yourself with a Faerie?"

Rasselas wanted to slap the man across his face. Was he...pitching a *sale* to Rasselas?

"Why do you ask?" Rasselas did his best not to show his anger.

"Many of my Fae who are ready to be bonded have asked. They know you are kind and...well, I think you would be the perfect sort of person to help a Faerie find his place in this world."

"May I be frank?" Rasselas asked, turning his shoulders to face the Faerie chief head on.

Tristan's face grew tense. "Yes..."

"I don't *like* bonding, Tristan—Faerie of Water. In fact, I hate it. It is a vile practice, masking the evil of slavery under the banner of reform and freedom. It is a lie, Tristan—a lie. It tells the most precious and gifted beings on this world that they are lesser, lesser than those who came after them." He did his best to say this with a level tone.

Tristan took a step back.

"And *anyone* who brands my beloved Faeries and sells them for *profit* to selfish and opportunistic highlords as pets—that person might want to steer clear of me."

Tristan's eyes darkened. "If you are suggesting that Faeries are sold for financial gain—?"

"Do you *deny* it?" Rasselas asked provocatively, taking a step closer to Tristan.

"When a woman is given in marriage," Tristan said dispassionately, as if reciting a line, "is the father not paid a price to prove that the suitor will *treasure* the daughter? It is a sign of..."

"Oh, *stop* it!" Rasselas snapped, "Stop! It's sick, you hear me? Sick! I don't want to hear your excuses. It's wrong, and you know it. Go sell your lies to anybody other than me."

Tristan backed away like a receding tide.

Rasselas straightened his shoulders, then pulled at the ends of his sleeves. Yes, this place felt slimy.

Further in, in the main Warrowing Village square, Rasselas heard shouts. He trotted over curiously, noticing a small crowd gathered around something. He pushed himself through the crowd of Faeries and peered toward the center.

"Valley," Rasselas whispered.

Valley stood beside a male Faerie who was shouting to a crowd in the center of the village square. She didn't look happy.

The Faerie beside her had his hands cupped around his mouth. "King Hanz may be fine with the Nightmare Faerie wandering around among us, but I am not! And she made an imperium! What's to stop her from doing it again? Will she oppress us all like *Somenus*? Will we do nothing about this?"

"I didn't know it was an imperium!" Valley cried. She dropped quickly onto the ground. "Everyone, please, you *know* me! I grew up here! When have I ever tried to *rule* anyone?"

"You grew up in the Inner Palace!" A voice cried from the crowd. "You live there now! What's to stop you from finding objects of value and storing power?"

"You all know this!" Valley said angrily, "A Faerie can't have more than one imperium, and Hanz has mine! It won't happen again!"

"Why did you break the law, Valley?" said a child's voice from the sidelines. "Why would you try to get powerful?"

"I didn't!" Valley pleaded, "I didn't know it was happening...and..." her face spotted Rasselas' eyes in the crowd. "And what is wrong with a Faerie using magik *anyway*?"

The crowd erupted with horrified gasps.

"See?" The man at the center pointed down at Valley with an admonishing finger. "This is how it started with Somenus, with the Faeries who followed him, they wanted to be *gods*!"

"I don't want to be a god, Endring!" Valley screeched. "Why do you keep saying that?"

Endring? Rasselas knew that name from his census he had been compiling.

"I saw your wings, Valley," Endring said with a shudder, "I served under the first Nightmare Faerie... they were one and the same. Do you know what he did to me?" The man directed his voice back to the crowd, "He was so powerful...It was like I had no will when I was around him. I was a *slave* to his desires. What is to stop her from becoming like that? Think about it, a woman, drawing on our desires..." he looked down at her, "How could we ever hope to refuse her?"

Valley stood, holding out her hands pleadingly. "I promise you all," she cried, "If gaining magik makes me become anything like Somenus, I will not do it! I will not...*draw* on men's desires..."

"But you already have," another voice called from the sidelines. "One of the princes nearly killed himself diving into the pit after you. A person doesn't just do something like that, especially not for a Faerie. You *did* something to him!"

Valley's eyes found Rasselas' face. She looked so empty, so hopeless—so angry.

Rasselas mouthed her name with a look of sorrow.

Valley gritted her teeth. "Please," she begged the crowd, "Don't shun me. I need you. You are my people! You are my only family!"

"You're bonded now, Valley," Endring bellowed, "You don't need to come to the Warrowing Village any longer. You are Hanz' problem, now."

Valley's lip began to quiver. "Please!" she said in a broken voice, "Other bonded Faeries come here, can't I?"

"You lost the privilege of being one of us when you took up an imperium, Valley," said Endring.

Valley bowed her head to the ground, shaking uncontrollably from her tears. Then, the crowd began to disperse. Rasselas crept forward, listening as Endring knelt down to pat her on the back.

"Perhaps we can let you back in eventually," Endring said, "But the stakes are too high. We have been through too much only to be enslaved by the Nightmare Faerie again, do you understand?"

Valley couldn't lift her head to respond. She remained there, weeping. When Endring noticed Rasselas, the white-haired Fae waved him over. Rasselas approached slowly, hands in pockets.

"You're the Elf prince," Endring said with a stern look, "The one who tried to scapegoat for her?"

"Yeah," Rasselas said. Valley lifted her head just enough to see the tip of Rasselas' boot inches away from her face.

Endring sighed. "She's done this to herself," he said, "The Warrowing Village is supposed to be a safe place for Faeries. We have really tight rules here to keep it that way. We need her to stay out."

Rasselas gazed at the man with sorrowful eyes. "Safe?" he asked. "Can it not be safe for Valley, too?"

"Can you escort her back to the Inner Palace?" Endring asked. "For her sake, she shouldn't be here anymore."

"I know your name," Rasselas said, "Endring."

The Faerie straightened his back in the same manner a bear rises to its hind legs. Yes, this Faerie was in Rasselas' census book of Faeries he had spent his entire adult life putting together.

"Faerie of Vows, isn't it? The Seventh, is it?"

Endring tightened his brow. "Boy," he said, "Have you no respect?

Rasselas, taken aback, stuttered, "I," he said, "I simply thought..."

We do not want your help, brother of Anodos." Endring finished his statement with a nod, then whizzed past Rasselas, heading down a side street.

Rasselas looked down at Valley, who was still sobbing.

"Come on, Valley," he said, kneeling down beside her. He touched her shoulder, but she recoiled from him. "Valley?"

"Go away, Rasselas," she said in a muffled voice.

Rasselas made a defeated sigh. "Valley," he said, "Come on..."

Valley lifted her head sharply to glare at him with a tear-streaked face. "Go *away*, Rasselas!"

“Valley…”

“Don’t you *see*? You’ve ruined everything!” she said through gritted teeth.

“Valley!” Rasselas pulled his hand away from her. “Why would you…?”

“Now my own people don’t even want me!” she yelled, “And you? You….you gave me an imperium.”

“Valley…”

“Stop—just stop!” Valley rose to her feet quickly, and began to walk unsteadily away, wiping her eyes. She charged toward the Warrowing Gate. Rasselas ran after her.

“Valley, wait!”

“Stop *following* me, Rasselas!” Valley turned to face him, pushing him away with her hands. “I don’t *need* you, alright? I don’t need you to rescue me. Stop treating me like some helpless slave. Stop…” she stumbled back a few steps, sniffing. Rasselas reached out his arms to steady her, but she swatted him away. “I don’t want your help anymore.”

Rasselas raised his voice suddenly, “Valley, we are fighting against something evil here! We are fighting against the lie that something is *wrong* with you!”

“Don’t you *get* it, Rasselas?” Valley cried, “Something *is* wrong with me!”

“No!” Rasselas snapped, “There is *nothing* wrong with you! You’re… you’re a potent and controlled—”

“Stop it! I don’t want to hear it!” Valley screamed at the top of her lungs.

Rasselas drew back, widening his eyes in shock.

“Valley…” he said softly. “What happened? What changed?”

“Everything changed, Rasselas,” she said with a dead look in her eyes. “Everything.”

—— Rosamond ——

The Painful Truth

ROSAMOND SAT ON THE GARDEN BENCH WITH HER EYES CLOSED. Her foot throbbed, her legs throbbed and, above all, her side—where her father had broken her skin with the wooden chair leg—it throbbed the most. Upon her father's direction, she wore a stiff and revealing corset that cinched tightly around her recently stitched wound, and she had gone for stroll after tedious stroll with all the visiting delegates. She didn't want to be doing any of this; she wished she could just be in bed.

"I wish to go back to my room," Rosamond said softly with her hands placed gracefully upon her lap.

"Only one left," Viola said, "Then you can."

Viola had been strangely kind to Rosamond since the storm. There were no insults or jabs, no underhanded comments about her behavior.

"Only one?" Rosamond asked, opening her eyes. She felt dizzy. The pain throbbed—oh, how it throbbed.

"I haven't heard anything from Prince Rasselas," Viola said. "Sorry."

"Well," Rosamond sighed, "What do you think about the visit to Arelle? Are you...excited?"

"Ah, that..." Viola cleared her throat. "Rosamond, I find I have reason to visit my sister."

Rosamond turned her head to gaze at the woman in surprise. "What? Really?"

"Yes..." Viola said slowly, "Is that alright?"

"But, *why*?" Rosamond was surprised to find herself, well...upset! "What will I do without you?"

Viola chuckled. "Oh, come now. We aren't close, Rosamond."

"No," Rosamond looked down at her lap, "But you're the only female companion I've got, aside from Valley. And I hardly see her anymore."

"I won't be gone long," Viola said casually, "just a few weeks..."

Rosamond could tell by the woman's face that she wouldn't be coming back. "What happened? I thought living in the Mensa Inner Palace was a huge opportunity for you."

Viola hesitated, running her eyes across Rosamond nervously. Oh—Viola was scared! Why? Was she scared of... what had been *done* to Rosamond?

"I will be back," Viola assured her, "Have no worries."

Rosamond nodded. This was good-bye, then. "I see."

"I will go pack my things then," Viola slapped her knees with an air of finality. "I think King Labyrinth will be here any time. Go for a short stroll, then you can go to bed."

Rosamond nodded. "Alright," she said, "Thank you, Viola."

Viola rose and fixed her skirt, checking for anything amiss. "Take care of yourself, Rosamond," she said, "I knew King Hanz was ..." she held her tongue. "Well, good fortune to you on your marriage."

Rosamond watched her leave. That was strange, the way Viola mentioned her father. So, it was Hanz that Viola was afraid of.

"Good Midday," came a familiar voice.

Rosamond turned her head to observe.

King Labyrinth approached by himself, with no wing or escort, hands in pockets. He carried himself like he was sure of his own desirability, though he lacked any charm whatsoever. But it didn't seem to matter to him what anybody else thought; he was a king. He grinned at the sight of her and sauntered until he stood just beside her bench. He held out his hand.

Rosamond placed her hand on his and rose. Her world began to swirl around her, and she tilted awkwardly to the side for a moment.

Labyrinth caught her by the arm.

"You alright?" he asked.

"Yes..." Rosamond whispered, though her voice sounded distant inside her own head. "I...I am sorry, sire, I think I am not well."

Labyrinth's smile dwindled. "Let's take that walk."

"No, I mean. I am so sorry, but I—"

"Your father promised me a walk," he said with a huff, "You...you snubbing me?"

"No!" She turned to look at the King, distressed. "I am so sorry!" Then she realized he must have been teasing. He had a smug smirk on his face. Rosamond sighed. "Sire," she said, "I'm not as sharp today."

"That's a shame," he said, taking her by the arm, "I was hoping to hear you spit some more fire today."

"Well, I might be able to manage something if you walk me back to my room," she said with a sigh, "How does that soun—*Labyrinth!*" Rosamond gasped, stumbling away from him. The man's hand had wandered carelessly close to her backside. If it were not for the thick, protective skirt she was wearing, it would have been scandalous.

Labyrinth chuckled, crossing his arms. His eyes knew no bounds.

"Fine," Rosamond said sharply, "If you are really going to abandon all gentlemanly sensibilities, I will take my leave."

"Your father promised me a walk," he said again, "Don't disappoint me."

"I'm afraid that is *exactly* what I am going to do," Rosamond said firmly as she backed away. "I will return to my room, now," she said, holding up her palm. "I don't feel well."

"Run, then," Labyrinth said, as if it were a challenge.

Rosamond had already begun to leave. "What did you say?" she asked, turning.

"I said, run. I'll give you ten clicks." The king pulled a silver timepiece from his pocket.

"Are you *mad*?" Rosamond said. There was a rising feeling of dread within her; the man had the predatory eyes of a wulf. "D–don't tease me like this, I don't like it."

"Run!" Labyrinth raised his voice, and all playfulness vanished from his countenance.

Terrified and confused, Rosamond ran.

Rosamond's foot stabbed with pain, but adrenaline pressed her forward. She had no idea what she was even running from, all she knew was that she was terrified. Was this actually a threat? Or was it all a joke? Why would he tease someone who was clearly in pain?

Rosamond stumbled into the Inner Palace, then moaned in anguish once she remembered her room was now *up* two flights of stairs. She gazed about, panting as she scanned for guards. Where had everyone gone? There was no time to wonder, so she dashed forward. Step by step, Rosamond dragged herself upwards. The urgency stayed, but her energy waned. The pain was taking over. It was like a horrible dream where she was running for her life but found she could barely move. She dared not look behind her; surely, he would have caught up with her by now. *Was* he actually chasing her?

After climbing for what felt like an eternity, Rosamond stumbled into her room and slammed the door closed. She found the bolt and flung it downwards across the door.

She placed her hands against the door and panted, doing her best to catch her breath. It felt as impossible as catching a fly in her hands. Her heart was pounding faster than a hummingbird's wings. What in Hades was *that*? That man was horrible!

Once she felt she could stand free of the door, she turned. Rosamond gasped, face to face with her tormentor.

Rosamond opened her mouth to scream, but Labyrinth took her by the throat and slammed her back against the door.

"Labyrinth!" she croaked, "You can't—My father—"

He tightened his grip then grinned, turning her head side to side. "Your father? Aren't I following his example? Hasn't he just given us all his permission to do the same?"

Rosamond's eyes widened in terror. Did *everyone* know?

"A shame about that bruise," Labyrinth said as he cranked her head to the side. There, against Rosamond's jawline was a long black patch of discoloration where she had been struck. The man leaned inward and placed his lips there. Rosamond tried to kick him, but her cumbersome skirt would not allow much movement.

She yelped at the sudden sensation of pain, horrified at the sensation of his teeth breaking her skin. She swiped her hand at his face, finding a soft place and digging her fingers into his eye. The man stumbled backwards, releasing her. Rosamond quickly felt her jaw.

"What is *wrong* with you?" she pleaded, rushing across the room.

"You bitch!" Labyrinth rubbed his eye.

"Help!" Rosamond screamed out her open window. "Somebody!"

Labyrinth scoffed. "Oh calm down, it was just a bit of fun."

"Leave!" Rosamond commanded as she tried to rally a bit of courage and pointed toward the door.

"When will you realize that your words are powerless?" Labyrinth shook his head. Then he charged toward her. All Rosamond could think to do was to cower. She formed herself into a ball on the ground and. covered her head with her arms.

A scream rent the air. Rosamond, still stunned, remained curled up on the floor. Amidst the screaming, she heard a sound of flapping. Rosamond cautiously lifted her head to see a burst of motion at the center of the room. Gargoyle was attached to Labyrinth's shoulders, flapping his wings furiously and attacking the man's face.

"Get it off me!" Labyrinth cried.

Rosamond hastened toward the door. She lifted the bolt and flung it open with the little strength she had remaining.

"Get out!" she cried.

Labyrinth fled toward the door in a panic. "Get it off me, get it off me!"

Gargoyle cawed repeatedly as he released his grip from the man's shoulders.

Like a beaten guard dog, King Labyrinth ran from the room.

Rosamond slammed the door closed behind him, bolting it. Then she turned, leaning her back against the door, and slid down onto her backside.

"Gargoyle!" she cried, as the tears began to stream down her cheeks. She hugged her knees and buried her face.

The bird landed on the ground, then waddled up to where she sat. He flapped his great wings in an attempt to climb up onto her knees, then he threaded his bill up between her arms and placed his head against her neck. Rosamond threw her arms around the bird, holding him tightly against her chest. The adrenaline began to dissipate, and her body shuddered. Soon all she could feel was pain.

Gargoyle rotated his head side to side, as if burrowing his compassion into the small of her neck. He opened his eye, noticing the teeth marks on her jaw, then closed it again tightly.

I should have plucked his eyes out of their sockets, he said spitefully.

Rosamond hugged him tighter, taking a moment to breathe, and when she was prepared to break the silence, said, "You saved me, Gargoyle. No..." she sniffed, "You're not a Gargoyle. You saved me, Ziz."

The bird snapped his eye open. The pupil rotated upwards, finding one of her eyes to stare into. *Ziz? Why did you call me that?*

"Isn't that the name of the Bird King? The ruler of the Skies?" Rosamond asked. "*Aurochs for the Land; Leviathan for the Seas; Ziz for the air...*" she recited the poem she had learned as a child.

The bird groaned. *Well, there is supposed to be, yes. The little birds like to sing songs about him. Damn, if I don't hate the idea of a felling Bird King, ruling over us all. I much prefer to be on my own, you know.*

Rosamond sniffed again, endeavoring a smile. "It's not like you to swear, is it? Did I just hear you swear?"

The bird grinded his bill against itself with a birdlike chuckle. *I'm afraid it's very like me to swear. I am not a very polite bird, you know.*

Rosamond chuckled. "You saved me—that's all I care about. You can swear all you like, my little Ziz."

Ziz groaned. *Don't call me that. It's pretentious.*

"You're my Ziz," Rosamond hugged him tightly, "The king of all birds. With you by my side, I never have to be afraid. Don't leave me, Ziz." She tightened her eyes closed, spilling out more tears.

Rosamond... Ziz sighed. *I must leave today.*

"Leave?" Rosamond gasped, "No! No, I will *never* let you go!"

Ziz groaned. *I'm sorry. I don't want to. But something very important has come up. And I need to send a message to a friend of mine down south, before it's too late.*

"Who?".

Oh, just an Elf friend of mine. He's a king.

"Rasselas' father?" Rosamond asked. Where was Rasselas today? Why hadn't *he* come instead of that horrible Labyrinth?

His grandfather, Ziz said, *Anyway, I will be back as soon as I can.*

"But what if something happens to me? I don't want to be alone, Ziz. You're my only friend here! If you hadn't come... I can't think what would have happened!"

Rosamond felt the bird tighten his talons together, then he relaxed. *You have other friends, don't you?*

"Could you ask... *Rook* to come my way?" she asked sheepishly. She felt a flutter within her heart at the memory of his face. "I mean... Anodos."

I will ask him, Ziz said, *If you wish me to.*

"If I knew he was coming to see me, I think I could face the day. Could you ask him to come here tonight?"

If I find him, I will ask him, said Ziz. *Perhaps you should get some rest now, Rosamond.*

"Please... please stay a while."

The raven made a long, drawn-out sigh. *Alright,* he said, *just a little while longer. But then I really must go.*

When Rosamond woke, the indent on her bed where Ziz had slept was vacant. She sighed, resting her hand against the spot. It was still warm. Her body ached; her foot ached; her chin ached.

She wanted to just lie there forever, never get up again. But no...she had promised Rook she would learn the name of the Faerie who was staying on the same floor. Yes...she needed a reason to get up, or she would become nothing more than a helpless, defeated prisoner.

Rosamond rose and hobbled over to her mirror. She combed her long hair with her fingers, studying her reflection. She could see the pain in her face. Where was that young, excited girl on her birthday? Memories of that strange conversation with Oswald a week ago flashed through her mind. *A lamb in a den of wulves,* he had said. He was warning her about adulthood.

"Well," she said to herself, "Better toughen up then."

Rosamond found a handkerchief and gently dabbed her jaw. Specs of blood were on the cloth, but otherwise the cuts were beginning to seal over. She felt sick. Why would that man do something like that? She shook her head. It was madness to try to understand the mind of a person like that.

She left her room quietly and approached the cluster of guards who stood by the mysterious room. She approached one, holding the cloth to her face.

"Excuse me," she said.

"Princess Rosamond!" he exclaimed, "Are you... alright?"

"Someone attacked me in my room," she said weakly. "Could you all please investigate? Could someone please alert Captain Oswald?"

The collection of guards began to shuffle with alarm, whispering to each other. Four of them immediately ran to her bedroom. The head guard remained by his post, looking down at Rosamond with concern.

"Were you..." he pulled at his collar, "Hurt?"

"Yes," she said quietly, "Could you summon the surgeon?"

The guard glanced at the door behind him, then at his men who were only a door away, then back at the princess.

"Alright," he said, "One moment." He leaned his spear against the wall, then went trotting off down the stairs.

Rosamond seized her opportunity. She slipped through the door and closed it behind herself.

"Oh!" She drew in a shallow breath as she examined the room. Some parts of it were trashed, as though vandalized, while other parts were draped in sheets, hanging by rafters and bedposts. A man sat by the window. There he was: the Faerie.

The Faerie turned his head to regard her, then smiled. It was an unsettling kind of smile, one that seemed to think it knew something that it didn't.

"Hi," Rosamond waved.

"Hallo," said the Faerie.

"I'm Rosamond," she said, inching closer.

"What a beautiful name," he said with a kind smile.

"What is *your* name?" she asked.

The man's countenance stiffened. "I..."

There was commotion by the door. "Why is no one guarding this room?" It was her father's voice. "Where are the felling guards?"

Rosamond gasped, then hid herself behind one of the tattered curtains by the window. The Faerie watched her but said nothing.

King Hanz came in, closing the door behind himself.

"I am sorry for all that noise, my friend," he said with a sigh, "Did I disturb you?"

"No," said the Faerie, who turned to face Hanz.

Rosamond could see the Faerie, but her father was blocked by the curtain.

"Good evening to you, friend."

"Good evening," said her father's voice she could see his shape through the curtain. She held her breath, realizing that a portion of her skirt was sticking out from under the curtain. Well, it was too late to do anything about it now!

"I think you were right," said the Faerie, "I am beginning to remember things. Shadows of things."

"Good!" said her father. "Do you... do you remember your name?"

"Yes," said the Faerie, "I think I do."

There was a pause. Then her father said, "What is it?"

The Faerie smiled. "Hevel," he said confidently. "My name is Hevel."

Hevel? Rosamond scrunched up her nose in thought. How did she know that name?

"Yes, *yes*!" Hanz said excitedly. "And...who were you, Hevel?"

"I... I was the caretaker of the throne."

Hanz let out a deep sigh. "Yes," he said, "And you still are."

"I am supposed to find the King," said Hevel.

"Yes," said Hanz, "Yes, the King."

"And I remember something else," Hevel said urgently. His face began to grow concerned. "A child."

"Slow down," Hanz said, "I don't want you to become unsettled."

"No, no," Hevel said with a wag of his head, "It's alright. It was a child. My child. She had two black wings—I remember! Morningstar was her name."

Hanz sighed. "I do not know of a Morningstar," he said, "But I will try and help you find her."

"She would be older now," Hevel said. He turned directly towards Rosamond, making eye contact. "Probably around this girl's age." He pointed at her.

Rosamond scrunched her eyes closed, like a child who believed it would make her invisible. She held her breath. The room grew eerily still, until her curtain was thrown violently aside. She cracked open an eye to see her father staring at her, utterly expressionless.

"Yes," Hanz said, examining her, "I see. I will try and help you find your child."

"I had a wife, too," Hevel added, "Can you help me find...her?"

"Yes, yes," Hanz said as he held out his hand to Rosamond. Not knowing what else to do, she took it. Hanz pulled her to his side, then turned back to the Faerie. "I will do what I can. Now, tomorrow we will travel to Arelle, to your throne."

"Oh," Hevel began to rock back and forth where he sat nervously, "I do not know if I am ready to go there..."

"I will walk you through everything," Hanz said in a calming voice, "Just rest now, and when the time comes, follow my lead."

"And you will help me find Morningstar? And...my wife, whoever she is?"

"I will," Hanz said with a smile. Then he led Rosamond out of the room by the hand gracefully, as if walking her out onto the dance floor.

One of the guards closed the door behind them as they left. He made eye contact with Rosamond, pity in his eyes. Yes, he knew what she had done, and now so did her father.

The king said nothing, he simply led Rosamond by the hand over to her bedroom. Rosamond's world grew darker and darker as Hanz stepped inside, closed the door, and turned to face her.

He let out a long sigh, then locked his eyes on hers like a flash of lightning.

"So... you weren't... *attacked?*"

"I—I *was!*" Her voice cracked as she spoke.

"Rosamond... I *know* what you did. You lied to get into that room," he said, pointing back toward the door.

"Papa!" Rosamond yelled, letting her anger rise, "I *was* attacked! Look!" She marched toward her father and pointed at her chin. A clear imprint of four teeth were visible.

Hanz snorted. "Is that all?"

"Papa!" Rosamond shrieked. "King Labyrinth came into my *room!*"

"I don't know what to believe," Hanz shrugged, "You're always lying. Always sneaking around. Never being straight with me."

"Father! You—" Rosamond cut herself short, blinking in confusion as her eyes focused on his face. His eyes were... *blue.*

Hanz lifted his hands up defensively and took a step back from her. "Rosamond," he said, "You're not my problem anymore."

Rosamond stuttered, her mouth hanging open. "*Problem?*"

"My discipline is wasted on you. It's time to let someone else deal with you. I...I can't take this anymore." He shook his head to himself.

"I... Papa, what are you *talking* about?"

"You're getting *married!*" he yelled, finally matching her anger.

Rosamond searched for words, but found she couldn't speak.

"There," Hanz sighed, "I told you. Yes, Rosamond, I have chosen your husband. I..." he sighed, "I know you haven't been the best daughter, but I should at least grant you... that you *are* paving a path for me here."

"What do you mean, Papa?" she finally said, "*Who?*"

"I..." he turned to the side, examining her bedpost. He ran his hand up and down its length. "I needed an army."

"What?" Rosamond gasped, "No...*no!*"

"King Labyrinth has the largest army besides Bavel," he said, gripping the bedpost with his hand, "I needed this alliance."

"But Papa, *he's* the one who hurt me! He—" Rosamond's voice died in her throat when she saw her father's face. He knew! He *knew* Labyrinth had been here!

"Like I said," Hanz responded in a low voice. "You're not my problem anymore."

"I thought you came because you cared about...what happened to me." Rosamond whispered. "I... I thought you loved me."

"Of *course,* I care!" Hanz snapped, turning to face her. "But Rosamond, you are not an easy child to raise! You are headstrong and you...you...you need more discipline! It is *because* I care that I am willing to...to..."

Rosamond shook her head. "Alright, Father," she said, growing still, "You have said enough."

Hanz shot her a glance, then straightened his back with a clearing of his throat. "Yes...well..." he sniffed, "You *did* say that you were alright with me choosing who you marry, remember?"

"Yes, Father."

Hanz nodded to himself. "Alright, then," he said. "Tomorrow, we go to Arelle. I will...I'll make the announcement then."

"Yes, Father."

Hanz left, slamming the door behind himself.

Rosamond staggered backwards toward her bed like an animated corpse. Her life was over. Or no...had a new life of misery just begun? She had promised herself that she would try to fall in love with whichever man was chosen for her. But was that even *possible* with a man like Labyrinth?

When the backs of her knees hit the edge of the bed, she sat.

"Rosamond, I'm sorry," a voice said from the window behind her.

It was Rook's voice.

"I guess you heard all that," Rosamond mumbled defeatedly without looking up.

"Yes." Rook stepped out from behind a curtain and walked up from behind. He leaned on one of the bedposts and looked down at her. "Inferno asked me to come—Gargoyle, as you call him."

"Ziz."

"Sorry?"

"His name is Ziz to me now." Rosamond scoffed at herself. "Here I thought he saved me from the horror...but all he did was save me from a *moment* of horror. Soon, that horror will be my entire life."

"Rosamond..." Rook sighed, "Don't say that."

Rosamond looked sharply up at the man. His face was heavy with sadness. "Why not? Why *wouldn't* I resign myself to my fate?" She stood quickly, ignoring the pain, and faced Rook with a scowl. "Why wouldn't I admit that I have to marry someone who is cruel and selfish—someone who *delights* in my pain. Because I'm definitely *not* going to say what I really want! No...to admit it now would only torment me further."

Rook exhaled silently through his nostrils, staying as motionless as the bedpost beside him. "What do you want, Rosamond?" he asked.

Rosamond's eyes grew damp, but she hardened her face, refusing to cry. She shook her head.

"Just say it, Rosamond. What do *you* want?"

"I want..." her voice made a little crack, as melancholy as the squeal of a violin, "I want someone strong, who never leaves me. Someone who sees me, and knows me, and cares about what I think. Someone who defends me when others treat me cruelly. Someone who fights for me when I need something..." the tears began to roll down her cheeks, "Someone who cares when I am in pain and cares when I am sad. Someone who can admire my beauty without wanting to destroy or devour it, someone who is kind and..." she lifted her eyes to look into Rook's face. "Someone who will never ever leave me alone."

Rook nodded slowly. "That sounds like a husband," he said, "or what a husband should be."

"I wish *you* were..." she said with a quivering lip.

Rook placed his hands on her shoulders, then brought her close. He pulled her head against his chest and enveloped her in a tight, protective embrace. She closed her eyes, then began to sob. Rook said nothing; he simply stood there, squeezing her tightly, like the most unmovable thing on the world.

"Oh, Rosamond," he finally said, reaching one hand up to stroke the back of her head.

"Why?" she moaned. "*Why*, Rook?"

"Why, what?"

"Why can't it be that way? Why won't *you* be that for me?" She squeezed him tighter, burying her face into the front of his coat.

"I never said I wouldn't."

"What?" Rosamond rotated her head to rest her chin against his sternum, looking up at his face.

He was smiling! He chuckled softly.

Rosamond's heart leapt within her. "Anodos," She whispered, "*would* you?"

"I am pretty sure I am the last sort of person who could get permission to..."

"Oh *damn* permission!" Rosamond snapped, muffling her voice as she pressed her face back into his shirt.

"But I..." he mumbled, sounding sheepish, "I'll do what I can."

Rosamond lifted her head again, gazing up at his face with eyes of hope. "Then you *do* love me? You *do* care about me? You would...you would..."

Rook nodded slowly. "Yeah..."

Rosamond blinked her large, golden eyes up in his direction, waiting.

Rook gazed down at her silently in return.

She frowned. "Well, why don't you *kiss* me already?"

Rook chuckled then turned her head with his hand, hugging her again. "Rosamond," he sighed deeply, "No."

"But, *why*?" She began to cry again. She grew even more angry when she felt his body shaking with subdued laughter. "Don't laugh," she said through her tears.

"Rosamond," Rook patted her back, "It's really hard *not* to kiss you right now, but I'm not going to."

Rosamond yanked herself away from him, glaring at him. "Why? Why are you being cruel?"

"*Cruel?*" he asked, sounding somewhat hurt, but maintaining a smile. "Rosamond... I thought you wanted someone who *wouldn't* take advantage of you. I... I shouldn't even be *in* here right now."

Rosamond scoffed, "This is different!"

"Rosamond, I... you deserve better than that. I'm not going to take advantage of you only a few bells after what happened with..."

"But I *want* you to! It's different!" Rosamond scolded, shaking her finger at him. Then a feeling of horror descended upon her, "Or...is it that you don't...you don't *want* to?"

Rook grinned. "I assure you," he said, "It's quite the opposite. But I...I frankly don't trust myself to..." he shook his head. "*Hades.*" He cleared his throat awkwardly, turning quickly to the side,

He gave her another tight hug. She seized him instantly, squeezing his body with desperation.

"Fine..." she said, "Don't kiss me. But please—never leave me."

Rook groaned. "Rosamond... I am not going to stay in your room. I...It's not..."

Rosamond sniffed pitifully.

"Rosamond..." the man sighed, "Let me do this the right way, alright? I... I'll..." he pulled her off of himself and held her at arm's length. "Let me say what I wish to say."

Rosamond blinked, then wiped her eyes.

Rook grew suddenly nervous, sliding his hands into his pockets. "I *do* think I care about you, and—Hades—I am not sure *what* I can do about it... but I promise you this: I will do everything in my power to get you out of here, if you wish it. And I... I won't let you marry someone like Labyrinth, alright?"

Rosamond clasped her hands over her mouth and nodded quickly. The tears began to flow once more. This was *Anodos,* the King of the Faeries! If anyone could rescue her from this horrible fate, surely, *he* could!

"Anodos..." she whispered as she pulled up the front of her skirt to wipe the moisture from her face, "Anodos, I think I've fallen in love with you."

He laughed. "Well," he nodded, hands still in pockets, "That's nice to hear, Rosamond."

"Well?" she snapped, growing fierce. "What about you? Aren't you going to say you've fallen in love with me, too?"

"If you ever gave me the chance, I might," he said, turning to walk toward the window, which was hanging wide open.

"Don't you dare leave!" Rosamond chased after him. He skipped away, lunging toward the window's ledge. "No!" She swung an arm at him, trying to catch him by a coat tail.

Rook spun around, perched on the ledge like Ziz would. "It's a bad idea for me to stay longer. I will go, and I will find a way to speak with you before the trip to Arelle."

"Wait!" Rosamond stepped up to the ledge, standing beneath him. "Wait, Anodos! I have something to tell you!"

"What?"

"The Faerie! I learned his name!"

"Oh," Rook raised an eyebrow, then sat himself down upon the window's ledge. Rosamond stepped closer, leaning in toward his ear.

"It sounded familiar," she said softly, "I wonder if you might know it..." she inched a little closer.

Rook gave her a suspicious smirk from the corner of his mouth. "Alright," he said, "Will you ever say it?"

"Yes...it's..." Rosamond placed a kiss upon his lips as quickly as she could. It was so hurried that she quickly regretted it; she didn't even feel it!

Rook sat there with his eyebrow still raised, then shook his head. "Woman," he said.

Rosamond frowned. "Fine, his name is Hevel."

Rook started. "What? *Hevel?*" The look on his face told her she had unearthed a gold mine.

"What?" she asked, "Who is he?"

"He's...he's..." Rook's eyes flashed side to side as he processed. "He's *alive?*"

"Father was telling him he is going to take him to Arelle...to claim his throne, or something. Is that a good thing or a bad thing?"

Rook narrowed his eyes. "What? I...Well, I don't know. But..." he sat silently for a moment. "But I think...I think I might know what to do." He rotated his head a fraction then grinned at Rosamond out of the corner of his mouth. "Yes," he said, "I've got an idea."

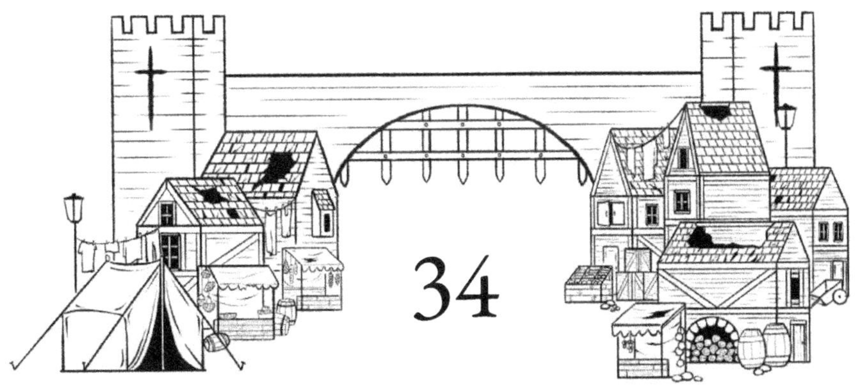

34

— Valley —

Keeper of the Dreamscape

"Rook is Anodos?" Valley mumbled to herself. The words had rattled through her mind all day. Rook was Anodos. How? Did Rasselas have any idea? No, Rasselas was completely in the dark. Why? Why didn't Rook tell anyone?

What could this mean? Had he come all this way to claim his throne? Would that even be a good thing? No wonder he knew Fairies' titles: he was the King! Was that... was that something the king could do? Did the king know everyone's titles? Or did it have something to do with Anodos' title? Oh, why did Valley always have to be in the dark?

But, perhaps, for the first time she *wasn't* in the dark. She knew something that no one else knew.

And yet? Did it even matter? Valley's spirit was broken. The words given to her by Rasselas, they had once given her hope and inner fire. But now they were curses. They tore her apart from her community. She was beginning to realize who she was: the Nightmare Faerie. Only two others had ever held her title, and they had both become drunk with their power.

Rasselas wanted Valley to become proud of who she was and not to fear herself. But wasn't Somenus proud of himself? Perhaps if he had been fearful—if he had refused to store magik—he might not have done what he did!

Valley hated Hanz. She hated the way he treated her and other Faeries, but was he right about her? Was he right that imperiums were dangerous? People like Tristan and Marbel respected him, after all. They were older and wiser than she was; they cared about the Fae; they put down their titles and their imperiums. Perhaps things weren't as black and white as Rasselas thought they were.

Then there was Anodos...the king that Hanz seemed to despise. He was alive...he was here! But why hadn't he taken the throne? Why did he allow the Fae to live like this? Did he know something that no one else knew?

He was the key to these questions...he was the answer.

"Ah, Valley!" Karo came running up from behind. Valley groaned inwardly, ignoring the Faerie. This was the third time today that Karo found an excuse to come speak with her.

"I know I am supposed to meet with the King," Valley said flatly, "You don't have to remind me... *again.*"

"Ah, hah, hah..." Karo laughed nervously, hurrying his pace to match Valley's. She was endeavoring to lose him, but unfortunately the man had more patience—and longer legs—than she did. "No, I wanted to talk with you about something...else."

Valley halted, though kept herself facing forward.

"Karo, I don't like you. Can you please leave me alone?"

"Oh," Karo chuckled awkwardly, "I say...well..."

Valley turned sharply. "Karo! Can you leave me *alone?*"

"Alone?" he sniffed, "Alone, you say? *Hades...* after you got shunned by the Warrowing Village, I sort of imagined you might be looking for friends!"

"I'm not."

Karo crossed his arms, then moved to block her path. "Will you give me a single moment of your time, Valley?" he asked, doing his best to act sympathetic.

She sighed. "You have a hundred clicks."

"Ah, hah, hah…" Karo shoved his hands into his back pockets and rocked forward and back, swaying his tall, lanky body like a tree in the wind. "Yes…well…Valley…"

"What?"

"We are going to Arelle tomorrow, as you know. And you and I are sort of similar in the whole… being-bonded-to-the-king-and-being-sort-of-outside-of-the-Warrowing-community thing…"

"Mm hmm…"

"Well, I sort of wondered if you might want to be friends! I've been on the outside of the Warrowing's good graces for seasons now, and…"

Karo seemed genuinely nervous. Valley sighed, folding her arms together. "And what?"

He shrugged, "Most Fae don't like us who get bonded to the King. We are above them, very often taking leadership-type roles—and yet, we are below Humans. So no one really sees us as one-of-them, if you know what I mean. I'm used to being sort of on the outside… but—I say! I just realized today that you might be on the outside, too, and I…"

Valley was blowing her fringe away from her face out of the corner of her mouth. "Karo…look. I *still* don't like you."

"Oh."

"But I'll give you a chance to redeem yourself."

"Oh!"

"Stop being weird to me, stop flirting with me, and start building some trust with me. Then, I might think about being your…" she cringed, "…*friend.*"

"Ah!" Karo clasped his hands together. "Splendid!"

Valley gave him a single nod, then turned to continue down the hall to the King's chambers. She groaned when she heard his footsteps rush to catch up with her again.

"Off to see the King?"

"No small talk, please," she mumbled.

"Has he given you a position in the new kingdom yet?" Karo asked quickly.

"What?" Valley turned, stopping in her tracks once more. "What new kingdom?"

"In Arelle. We are moving to Arelle. Didn't anyone tell you that?" He paused, thumbing his chin.

"Yes... I mean...moving *permanently*?"

Karo shrugged.

"No, he hasn't told me what I am going to be in the future," Valley sighed. And did it matter one way or another?

"Well, I'll put in a good word for you. I've got a bit of edge with the King. I'll try and," he made a clicking noise with his mouth as he flicked his finger into the air, "make things work in your favor."

"Actually," Valley said flatly, "I'd rather you stay out of all that. I know you're trying to get on my good side right now, but please don't do it that way."

"Right, right, right." He bowed his head repeatedly as he slowly backed away. "I'll leave you to it, then."

Thank the Lights, she sighed to herself. Was this her life now? A life where her only friend was the most *irritating* Faerie on the table?

She was standing in front of Hanz' door. Waiting until Karo trotted out of sight, she knocked then opened it.

Rook is Anodos, she thought. Rook is Anodos! The woman in Anodos' dream had said she put a spell on him, a spell where he could not be recognized. Without that spell, would Hanz have figured out who he was by now?

"Valley," Hanz' voice came from his desk. She lifted her eyes to see him bent over, writing. "I heard about what happened."

Valley approached then uncharacteristically sat upon a chair. She was too tired and defeated to care anymore. Hanz lifted his eyes to observe her, then sighed.

"I'm sorry," he said.

"For what?" she said in a short tone.

Hanz straightened his back, placing his pen carefully back in its stand. He seemed to be reevaluating what he wanted to say.

"I heard the Faeries of the Warrowing Village have shunned you."

Valley scoffed. "Yes, who *hasn't* heard?"

"I'm sorry," he said again. "I knew that things would be hard for a time, but I didn't expect *this*."

Valley raised an eyebrow, glancing at the King. Somehow, she guessed that he *did* expect this.

"It's done now," she said, "I'm...I'm no one now."

"You're not no one, Valley," Hanz said, rising.

"Well, I have no Faerie title," she began, throwing up her hands, "no friends, no community, no purpose, no ambitions..."

Hanz wandered closer, rubbing his beard. "Don't you *know*, Valley?"

She shot him a look, "Know *what*?"

"Who you are now?"

She shook her head. "Enlighten me."

"Every Faerie on the world is waiting for their purpose, waiting to know who it is they might serve. But you? You serve *me*. You are mine," he smiled proudly, "You are one of my trusted few, and when we get to Arelle? I can trust you to support me. Don't you see? The greatest leader in Raqia depends on you. Doesn't that... doesn't that excite you?"

Everything in Valley wanted to scream back, *No!* But instead, she shrugged.

Hanz knelt beside her, taking her hand. "I know you are not pleased about it now, but as time passes, you will be thankful for our friendship. All the other Fae might abandon and shun you—but I will not. I will still be here."

She glanced at him hesitantly out of the corner of her eye, refusing to look at the insufferable man directly.

"Am I really not allowed to see my friends in the Warrowing Village anymore?" she asked.

Hanz shook his head. "No," he said as he rose back to his feet, "No, I don't want them unsettled. I need things to calm down for a bit, especially with the move to Arelle I am planning. And frankly Valley, *you* are unsettled, too. You've been lied to and manipulated by Rasselas, and you've discovered your title, which..." He shook his head to himself. "Anyway, you need to find an anchor with me. I fear," he turned to look at her, "I will need to keep you on closer watch for a bit, you know, just until things have settled down."

Valley did her best not to scowl. Well, was she surprised? Of *course,* he wasn't going to trust her anymore!

Hanz' face grew suddenly pained, and he dropped down to his knees in front of her. Valley jumped, studying him in confusion.

"Sire?" she asked hesitantly, "Are you... alright?"

"Oh, I don't know," he moped, with the spirit of a child who had been refused their favorite treat. "I... no." He dropped his head forward, leaning until his forehead hit Valley's knee. She stared down at him in shock. What was he *doing?*

"...Sire?"

"I'm just so sad, Valley. I am on the brink of success, and yet..." he let out a pitiful moan, "I am sad."

Was there some sort of vase nearby that she could smash against the back of his head?

"Why?" she asked. She tried to move her knee a fraction, hoping it would encourage him to move away, but instead he only repositioned and turned his head to the side.

"I had a hard conversation with someone yesterday," he said, "Someone who used to care for me. I find myself feeling quite lonely, you know."

Valley bit the inside of her mouth. What if she just stood? What if she just *left?*

"Valley?" Hanz said, "It's all going to work out, isn't it? My plans...everything I have worked so hard for..."

Not if I have anything to do with it. "I..." she muttered, "I don't know."

Hanz lifted a hand and placed it heavily on her knee. Valley's cheeks flushed with embarrassment.

"Tell me it's going to work out, Valley."

Valley stared down at the back of Hanz's head. What could she say? This was the man who in one moment was kind and compassionate, and then in another was beating her in the public square! "It's...It's all going to work out," she said—and hated herself for it.

Hanz let out a deep sigh. "Thank you," he said, "Thank you, Valley." He pulsed a squeeze on her knee. She jumped, standing quickly and moving away from him.

"Well," she brushed away any evidence of contact from her skirt. "May I go?"

Hanz lifted his head from where he still knelt defeatedly on the ground. "I wish everyone were like you, Valley," he said with a hazy look in his eyes, "You have no guile...no lies. You simply *listen* to what a man says. You show respect and deference."

Valley kept her mouth snapped shut, for she was afraid that if she opened it, it might be the death of her.

"I am glad to have you with me," Hanz said, "I will need you in the coming season."

"I don't think you will need me," she said quickly.

Hanz placed a foot on the ground, then rose. "Oswald?" he suddenly called in a bellowing voice. Valley jumped, then moved to the side as Captain Oswald came rushing into the room.

"Sire?" The captain asked, looking around, "Everything alright?"

Any evidence of Hanz' melancholy mood had suddenly vanished, and he was standing confidently in the middle of the room with hands on hips.

"Valley has been shunned by the Village," he said, "They don't want her, and she's been too compromised to go wandering about unattended. I want her close to me until things have settled in Arelle."

Oswald stole a glance at Valley, then said, "Very well, Sire."

"Tonight, she can be in the room across the hall. I want it locked and guarded. Tomorrow, she can travel with us." The king moved back to his desk and sat, picking up his pen with a shake of his sleeve.

"You're... putting me on house arrest?" she asked. "Locking me up?"

"Valley," Hanz said in an impatient tone, "Until you can prove to me that you won't be breaking laws behind my back, I am afraid so."

Valley shot a glare at Oswald. The captain showed no emotion other than dutifulness.

There was a knock on the door, and then another man entered. He was wearing a dark, hooded cape. Once inside, he closed the door and dropped the hood. He was tall, with dark hair and a tidy goatee. He noticed Valley standing there and made a condescending smile.

"It's alright," Hanz said, "You can speak. She is one of us now." He waved a dismissive hand in Valley's direction. "Valley, this is Sigmund."

The tall, dark haired man gave Valley a slight bow. This was the same man she had seen meeting with Karo back at the brothel a few days ago.

"Sire," Sigmund said, turning to Hanz. "Someone wishes to have an audience with you tonight."

"Who?"

Sigmund's eyes shifted side to side, then he strolled up to the King, bent over, and whispered in his ear.

Hanz nodded slowly as he listened. "Fine," he said. Hanz looked perturbed. "Oswald, can you take Valley to her chambers?"

"Yes, sire," Oswald bowed, then took Valley by the forearm and led her out of the room. Valley tried to steal another glance at the mysterious gentleman, but the door closed too quickly behind her.

"Get your hand off me," Valley snapped, trying to pull her arm free. Oswald did not comply. He gripped her tightly until they crossed the hall. He pushed her into the small room, which was lit only by a single candle. As he turned to leave, Valley grabbed him by the sleeve. "Oswald!" she yelled.

He turned to give her a glare. "What?"

"What is *wrong* with you? I thought we were friends! Why are you treating me like this?"

"We *are* friends, Valley," he said, "But I still have to do my job."

"Why are you angry with me?" she pressed. "I can see it in your face!"

"You broke the law, Valley," he said, "You... you... that Rasselas."

"What?" Valley snorted, "You're mad that he punched you?"

Oswald flexed his mustache. "He took advantage of you. He..."

"How *dare* you?" Valley said in a raised voice, stepping away from the captain. "*He* took advantage of me? Oswald, don't you see who the real villains are here?"

Oswald only stared. "Don't be ridiculous."

"Don't you see how I am being treated? By Hanz, by Karo—by *you*?"

"*We* are not the ones breaking the law," he said firmly, "You...you're a nice girl, Valley, and I," he bristled, "I am quite fond of you—but you *are* a Faerie! You need to remember your place!"

Valley's mouth dropped open, but she found no words. She shook her head. "We," she said slowly, "are no longer friends. You may go, Oswald."

The captain's eyes flashed with hurt, then he nodded.

"Good night, Valley," he said. The door slammed shut, and Valley stood there listening to the jingling sounds of the lock clanking shut.

She turned slowly, observing her small quarters. A bed, a washing basin, a small table with a single chamberstick...It was just another prison.

"Well," she sighed to herself, "There is only one escape left for me now, only one power I have left."

She looked at the bed. Sleep. Sleep granted her the one safe place left, her only privacy: Dreams.

Without an imperium, Valley could only contain enough magik to fill her body. That was enough to visit other people's dreams, she had found, but she had no idea how much magik she drained. Nor did she know what exactly caused her to gain magik.

"Well," she said to herself as she began to remove her outer layers of clothing, "Might as well do some experimenting. What have I got to lose?"

Once she had stripped down to her undergarments, she climbed into the small bed, closed her eyes, and then—something she had always been able to do since she was a little girl—she fell *instantly* asleep.

<hr>

Valley found herself walking through the Inner Palace. It was as if her surroundings were the ghost, not she. The walls appeared to be translucent and through them anyone sleeping appeared to her as a shining white specter in their bed. It was late now, so most of the Palace's main inhabitants had turned in for the night. She could not see anyone who was awake but those whose bodies had surrendered their minds to the dream world shone like bright lights.

Valley walked through the Palace, observing all the sleeping bodies, with their gleaming souls. She felt like their queen. It had only been a couple of nights since she had found this place of waking dreams: the place she called the Hall of Dreams. Some of the sleeping people—or awake souls, as she started to call them—glowed brighter than others. When she approached, her mind seemed to buzz with stimulation. This, she wondered, could be when she gained power. What was the difference between those who glowed brightly and those who seemed dimmer?

One of the brightest lights in the entire Palace was Rasselas. It wasn't easy to miss him.

Valley, keeper of the Dreamscape, floated over to him. There his body lay, still and peaceful. As she came to his side, Valley felt her skin grow warmer. Lifting up her hand, Valley could see that it was glowing. Yes... Rasselas gave her power. She looked around, observing other glowing bodies through the walls. It seemed she could see all sleeping within a certain radius. Would that radius become large if her power grew?

She turned her attention back to Rasselas; he was smiling, even in his sleep. Valley hovered her hand over his head and closed her eyes. As always, he seemed to be dreaming about the Sea. She felt a magnetic pull towards his dream—yes... she wanted so badly to enter it.

"No," she whispered to herself, "No, I need to... I need to let him go."

Valley floated backwards, giving the man some space. The warmth she felt from his glow began to fade. Was this what Somenus felt? Did he feel himself drawn to certain people like this? Was Rasselas glowing brightly because he cared for her; or was it because she cared for him? ...or was there just something special about him? No. The most likely explanation was that he was glowing because *she* cared for him.

Choosing to forget the Elf for a moment, Valley turned her head to further scan the hall of dreams. There were several other bright lights. Spotting one in a nearby building, Valley floated, moving at unimaginable speed. It was as if no time passed between standing beside Rasselas and standing beside this person. No, time wasn't quite the same here, and neither was space.

A modest guest room housed the sleeping person. It was an Elf; Latimer was his name. Valley had met him before. His glow wasn't quite as intense as Rasselas' but he was definitely brighter than just about everyone else around. Why? Why was he so bright? She hovered her hand over his head.

Valley could see visions of grassy fields, of waterfalls, of endless skies. She withdrew her hand. The visions in his head were so clear—such a stark contrast to some of the other dreamers. She wanted to enter his mind, as she felt the same warmth in her close proximity with him, but she refrained. There was somewhere *else* she wanted to explore that night, but in the back of her mind, Valley made a note that the Elves seemed to shine brighter than the Humans.

Valley lifted her eyes back to the Hall of Dreams with all its ghostly souls. There was one light she wanted to see, a light which glowed like a sun in the midst of the Hall. She approached it, instantly at its side. Valley looked down at the sleeper, and she could hardly see his form because he was so bright. She felt unimaginable power emanating from him, and yet she could not draw from it in the same way as the others. The power was not freely offered to her as it was with the other dreamers, though she could not begin to know what that meant.

Rook—Anodos, here he was, the supposed King of the Faeries. Valley hovered her hand over his head for a moment, then winced. The pain of what she saw was almost too much to bear. The light that was Rook's body began to grow red. This, she had begun to understand, was a nightmare.

Valley entered his mind...entered his dream...entered his pain.

Valley came in through something not unlike a back door finding herself not at the epicenter of the dream, where Rook's mind was the most aware, but in the peripheral, like a wall ornament, or a passing shadow. As she surveyed the scene, she saw that she was standing at the back of a dark, windowless chamber with a stone ceiling. It was the same place she had seen last time she entered Rook's nightmare, when that horrible Faerie was cutting patterns into Rook's face.

What a horrible nightmare that had been! An experience that had made Valley never want to enter another dream again—and yet, after she had rescued Rook from the strange torturer, Valley had been thankful for the chance to free a person from such a wicked memory. It had become clear to Valley that what happened in Rook's last dream was not the twisted makings of his imagination, but a recounting of something real. This was a real place he had been to in the past, from every shadow in every corner, to every little crack on the ceiling; this room that Rook was imprisoned inside had been a real place. He knew it well. He knew it too well.

Rook was on the stone table at the center of the room. He was not bound. This time, he was sitting, dressed in a simple white shirt and black trousers. He was looking into a small, hand-held mirror.

"I...I don't recognize myself..." he was saying as he touched his textured face.

The same woman who had been cutting him before stood beside him now with her arms crossed. There was no doubt in Valley's mind now... this was the woman from the Faerie prison.

"Well," the woman said quietly, "I have done what I have done. Your face will never be the same." She pointed to the mirror. "Your appearance is altered, yes. But the spell does more than that. It makes you unrecognizable to any who have known you in the past."

"But... *why?*" Rook lowered the mirror and gazed at the woman. "Why would you take this from me?"

"You can create a new identity with this mirage," she said, turning to the side. "A name...a life...anything you wish. You...you just cannot be Anodos."

"But *why?*" Rook cast the mirror aside, "I don't understand...first you were trying to kill me, then you were trying to...well, I don't know—you were calling me a product of rape; a—"

"Anodos," the woman interrupted with an urgent tone, "I cannot restore to you what was taken. I confess..." she looked over her shoulder, as if checking to see if anyone was there. "Once I found I could not kill you, I hoped to make you useless to anyone who would try to make you a King. I...I taught you the lies about being a spawn of..." her voice trailed off as she gazed into his eyes, then she cleared her throat. "It doesn't matter anymore. The truth is this: I do not want to hand you over to him. He will only use you to his own selfish advantage. I... There is only one way I can give you any kind of life, and that is by letting you be nothing—just a scarred, *nobody* in the wilderness. Start anew, Anodos. Find a life if you can, Anodos." She touched his knee for a moment, then snapped her hand away. "Just forget everything I have been saying to you the last several weeks. It..." she looked away. "It will do you no good."

"What did you do? What do you mean?" Rook touched his face, turning it side to side as he examined himself. "You mean you put me through all those interrogations, those trainings, those... *sessions*, only to stop and leave it unfinished? Why?" He lowered the mirror, "I mean... it's not that I am not thankful for it to be over, but why? *Why* did you stop?"

"I'm not *supposed* to stop," she said quietly, "I am supposed to keep going until you're broken... until you're useless."

"Yes..." Rook said with weary eyes, "That's what I thought. But...what changed, Riah?"

Riah shook her head. "I can't tell you that. But—" she straightened her back, putting on a tougher exterior, "My decision is made. I do not wish to destroy you, Anodos. I want you to go free. Run—hide. Get away from Hanz, and don't let him find you."

"Hanz?" Rook raised his eyebrows. "*Hanz* is the one behind all this?"

Valley widened her eyes. So Hanz *was* the one who abducted Anodos? Her heart began to pound.

"Yes," Riah said with a scowl, "He is. And he wants you either dead or useless. Stay out of his way and you can have a life."

"But my family..." Rook said weakly, "...my life..."

"They are dead to you, Anodos," she said firmly, "They will not recognize you."

Rook touched his face, and his lip began to quiver, "Why would you do such an evil spell on me, Riah? If you wanted to set me free... why do this?"

Riah huffed. "What I did was a kindness to you. It was the strongest spell I could muster with the magik I had available. It takes a lot of energy to maintain a spell like this, and I am already sustaining another. This was the best I could do. But you're tied to me now, Anodos, and I to you. This is my... apology."

"Apology?" Rook's eyes darkened, "After everything you've done...you call sending me out, without a face or a name, or a family... an *apology*?"

"Like I said," she said gruffly, "It's the best I can do. Hanz is a powerful man, Anodos—more than you know. And he will not be happy when you go missing. So, I need you to do your best to hide and stay away from anyone you once knew."

Rook's shoulders began to shake. He was crying. Valley found herself placing her hand over her pounding heart. *This* was Riah's big secret? She was protecting Anodos from Hanz? As frightening as she was, perhaps she was not all bad.

"The spell *can* be broken," Riah said softly, "If someone sees through the deception—if they recognize your face as yours somehow. But that is near impossible if the scars serve me well. They distract the eyes; they make you too disturbing to look at for long."

Rook began to sob harder. There he was, that strong, stern Knight Valley had seen earlier that day—sobbing. What had been done to him to bring him to this point? Well... she was beginning to get an idea.

Riah stepped toward the pitiful man and placed her hands on his cheeks, lifting his face to her.

"Others will not be able to look at you for long, but I see through the mask, Anodos—I see you. *I* see who you really are. You are still so beautiful."

Valley cringed, watching with disgust as Riah leaned forward and kissed Rook on the mouth. He lurched backwards, swinging his arms with a yell.

"Get away from me!" he cried, "No... no, *never* touch me!"

"Anodos," Riah reached out a hand toward his face.

"If you are sincere about wanting to apologize to me," Rook said in a shaky voice, "Then please—*never* touch me again. Especially... not like *that*."

"Please, don't say that..." Riah's voice grew indistinct, bouncing around the room like a bodiless spirit.

Rook stumbled off the table and tried to walk, but his legs gave out and he fell to his knees.

Riah walked up to him and placed a hand on his head. "Please don't say that... at least let me say goodbye."

Rook placed his hands over his head, cowering like a child. "Please, don't touch me."

Valley pursed her lips, then stepped forward and snapped her fingers. The shadow of Riah's spirit within the dream vanished. Rook gazed upwards, scanning the room. Confused, he rose to his feet.

"Riah? Where did you go? I'm sorry!" He clutched his own body in his arms and began to tremble. "Riah? I'm *sorry*! Please... don't leave me here! *I don't want to be alone!*"

Valley stepped out of the shadows.

"Anodos," she said softly, using the name that he identified with in the dream.

Rook gasped, stumbling backwards. "Who are you?"

Valley sighed. Would she have to redo the same conversation as last time?

"I am the Dream Faerie," she said. It felt so natural and easy to say when she was in her dream world. If only she could have this sort of confidence when her body was awake.

"Dream Faerie?" Rook gasped. "*Morningstar*?"

He did it again; he called her 'Morningstar'. Was that her name?

"Do you know me?" she asked. Perhaps if she formed her questions differently, she would get new information this time.

"Of course I do," Rook stepped toward her, growing calmer. "You are Hevel's daughter. I... I held you as a baby. But that was only two seasons ago... How are you grown? Wait... is this a *dream*?"

"Yes, it is a dream. This is many seasons later than the memory you are reliving," she said, hoping the truth would come as a comfort to him.

Rook nodded slowly, studying her face. "I... I was scared of you..." he said, "I am sorry... I am sorry that I didn't want to hold you."

Valley blinked. *This* was new.

"That's alright," she said, trying out a smile. It was such a change for *her* to feel like the strong one in the conversation. "That was many seasons ago now, I am guessing. I don't remember it."

"You have the wings of my father..." Rook said cautiously. "Did you know that?"

"Yes," Valley said, "But I am not him."

"I know," Rook sighed. He peered around the room. "If time has passed since this memory, does that mean I escape? I... I start a new life?"

"Yes," she said, feeling sadness swell in her heart.

"And I... do I still have these scars? This *face*?"

"Yes."

Rook bit his lip. Tears began to trickle down his cheeks. "Then, I really am lost, aren't I?"

"I don't know," said Valley. "You and I have only just met."

"Is your father alive, too?" Rook asked quickly, "I had heard that everyone was killed." He glanced around the room cautiously. "I mean... that is what Riah told me... but I don't really trust much of what she says to be true."

"I don't think my father is alive," she said carefully, "But I know very little. Hanz raised me... and I don't think I can trust him to tell me the truth either."

Rook rose, straightening to full height, with a suddenly dark and protective glare. "Hanz *what*? *Raised* you?"

"Y—yes..." Valley shrunk back. It was such a stark change to see the quivering prisoner transform into an enraged giant in mere clicks.

"So... everything is becoming clear..." Rook said as he stared off into space, "Hanz was behind this all along. We should never have invited him to Arelle— never should have let him hold you!"

Valley shook her head. Hanz... meeting her as a baby? Holding her?

"What do you mean?" she asked quickly. "Tell me more! I am in the dark, Anodos... What did Hanz want when he met me?"

Rook gazed at her out of the corner of his eye. Something changed in his face. "What is going on?" He asked. The images painting the backdrop of the dream began to fade. He was waking up!

"It is me, Valley," she said quickly, stepping forward. "I am in your dream, Rook. Tell me... what did Hanz—"

"Get out of my head," he said darkly. "Get *out*!"

Then he, and his dissipating dream scene, vanished.

35

—— Hanz ——

The King and the Rook

"You plan to leave the Crimson Gate… unattended?" Sigmund asked as he ran his fingers along the edge of Hanz' desk.

"I don't need it anymore," Hanz said, gazing out into empty space. "I see. Sigmund, I see everything."

"And I am pleased for you," said the man. "And… may I ask… *what* you have seen?"

Hanz turned his head slowly, shifting his focus to his surroundings. It was like trying to pull a fishing line back to the surface from deep within the Sea. His eyes found Sigmund. Suddenly, every detail of the man's unpleasant, dog-like face became clear—from pores to moles; it was like gazing through a magnifying glass.

"I can see anything I want," Hanz said distantly.

"Anything?" Sigmund cleared his throat. "You wanted to see into Bavel… into Winter's End. Does it—work?"

Hanz groaned. "Don't rush me, I am still trying to get used to them."

"But you *have* tried, haven't you?" Sigmund asked. "What happened?"

"I could not see past the gates of Bavel," Hanz sighed. "And I could not find Winter's End."

Sigmund nodded slowly. "We did consider that the magik protecting those places might predate the second Faerie of Sight. There is old magik still protecting the ancient places of this world."

"I know," Hanz said with a groan. "But it doesn't matter now—these eyes will give me so much more than the Crimson Gate ever did."

"Whatever you say, sire," Sigmund bowed. "Shall I summon the Elf?"

Hanz scowled. "Why that little weasel thinks he can come speak with me, I—" he huffed, "The gall of this man."

"Shall I let him in?" Sigmund asked again.

"Fine, whatever." Hanz slammed his hand on the table. "Let him in."

Sigmund left the room then returned moments later with the smug-looking, pointy-eared nuisance.

"What do you want?" Hanz asked angrily. "I have business to take care of."

"We need to talk," the Elf said darkly as he approached the desk. He seemed to think he belonged in that room, as if he were a worthy appointment for the king of all living to receive.

He couldn't be more wrong.

"Try that again, Elf," Hanz, leaning back into his chair.

"What?"

"I am a King," said Hanz, "and you are nothing but a lowly wing. Try that again."

Sir Thorne drew his chin higher. "Sire," he said, "I wish to speak with you... about Arelle."

"No," Hanz yawned, straightening the papers before him. "There is nothing I have to say to you."

"You promised us the Faerie throne would stay empty!" Thorne raised his voice and slammed his hands against the desk. He gazed into Hanz' eyes. He would regret that.

"Now, you're going to Arelle," Thorne whined, "—to put someone on the throne?"

"*Us?*" Hanz asked lazily. "Who is '*us*?'"

"You *know* of whom I speak," Thorne hissed, "The Purists!"

"The Purists disbanded seasons ago. I owe nothing to that failure of a movement."

"You imprisoned our leader," Thorne said, leaning closer.

"Your *leader*," Hanz said with a tightening brow, "betrayed me. She set Anodos free. And the rest of you scattered like roaches. I care not what happened after that." Hanz didn't feel the need to tell poor Thorne that Riah had only *played* the Purists in order to use them.

Thorne closed his eyes tightly, counting clicks, then opened them with renewed calm. "Regardless of what happened with Riah and Anodos," he said, "We helped you fifteen seasons ago. *We* did your dirty work. *We* delivered Hevel to you, faked his death, and snuck Anodos away, and *we* planted the Faerie dust in all the right places to look as though they had died. All the while *you* sat comfortably here in Mensa, safe with your alibi. All we requested was one thing: for the throne to remain empty."

Thorne was proud of his delivery. Who did this worm think he was?

"Are you finished?"

Throne's eyes darkened. "*Why* are you going to Arelle? What is your plan?"

"Look," Hanz tapped his two index fingers together. "Even if I *had* promised to keep the Faerie throne empty, much has proven why that would be utter foolishness. There is widespread famine, Thorne. No one is going to survive for much longer without food—no one except, perhaps, the Faeries you hate so much. But Thorne, I *didn't* promise to keep the throne empty. I promised to keep Somenus' bloodline off of it."

"You promised to kill Anodos!" Thorne bellowed.

"And I *would* have," Hanz said in a calm tone, "If your people had not failed me. But as I said, Thorne, the Purists are a long dead movement. You are nothing but an old, disillusioned member of a failed scheme. Now so far, I have graciously ignored you, letting you exist in the world without molestation. But

Elf," Hanz leaned forward and lowered his voice, enunciating every syllable perfectly, "If you give me one reason to think that you are going to become a pebble in my shoe, I *will* kill you."

Thorne's eyes grew wide. The fool was realizing just *who* he was trying to intimidate.

"Sire," Thorne stuttered.

"Leave Mensa," Hanz said sharply, "If you value your life. And thank the Lights I am here to save you. I want you gone by morning."

The Elf had nothing more to say, so he left quickly and quietly. Hanz rested his elbows on his desk and massaged his temples. There was a short moment of solitude for the weary king before the door creaked open again. He lifted his eyes to see Sigmund approaching.

"You want me to kill him?" Sigmund asked, glancing behind himself.

Hanz shrugged. "*Hades*—I don't know. He might still be useful to me later. He has so much... hate. That's the sort of thing that's easy to use."

"True. Sire?"

"Hmm?"

"A light?" Sigmund held out a tin cigar case.

Hanz pushed up the side of his mouth into a grateful, though exhausted, smile. He took a stick, then placed it into his mouth and waited for Sigmund to offer a flame. The King's body creaked with fatigue as he reclined into the chair.

"You're making me smoke," Hanz said with suspicion in his voice, "Does this mean you're going to tell me something stressful?"

Sigmund shrugged. "I could tell the last conversation was irksome. I can't promise the next one will be any better."

Hanz cocked an eyebrow. "*Next* one?"

"Someone else is here to see you—he insisted it be tonight," Sigmund said with a doubtful look on his face.

"Anyone of importance to me?" Hanz asked as a cloud of smoke emanated from his mouth.

"No."

"Well," the king sighed, "Let him in."

Sigmund moved across the room to open the door. A large and energetic, though stiff, figure marched into the room.

"Ah—majesty!" Highlord Cato of the Edgelands said loudly but unenthusiastically, "What an *honor* to be received by you!"

Hanz blew smoke through his teeth.

"Well," the king said, "What do you want?"

Cato plodded forward and seated himself across from Hanz. "Oh!" He brightened, "You're smoking? May I?"

Hanz shifted his glance toward Sigmund who grimaced, then stepped forward to offer the Edgelands Highlord a light. The nobleman took it eagerly, smacking his lips as he wetted the tip.

"Lovely, lovely," he said with a grin, "Such *lovely* hospitality you have!"

Hanz blinked. "Well?" he asked. He was too tired to play around with the fool.

"Ah!" Cato shifted, noticing a chess board sitting there, with every piece perfectly arranged. "Do you play?"

"Obviously," Hanz responded dryly.

"One of the better things the Faeries gave us, eh? *Chess*?"

Hanz's only response was made of grey vapor.

"I say," Cato picked up the white king chess piece and turned it upside down, "Beautiful. What's it made of? Is this pure albuminium?"

"Cato," Hanz said, lowering his hand which held his cigar to the desk. "What in Hades do you want?"

Cato inspected the white king with a puzzled face, as though he were pretending to deliberate, but knew exactly what he wanted to say.

"Now what was that funny move called?" Cato asked as he placed the king back down. "That useless one—where the king trades places with the rook?"

"Castling."

"Ah, right—*castling*." Cato plucked the tower piece up into his hand. "Funny move, that."

"What do you want?"

"Not much," Cato said absentmindedly. Then his eyes focused, as if an inner fire were suddenly kindled. "Your lands?"

Hanz blinked. "My...my lands?"

"I want Mensa, Hanz," Cato said with a face as hard as stone.

"Go to Hades."

Cato nodded slowly, "Yes...well... It is not a threat, Sire. It is an offer—an offer I do not think you will refuse."

Hanz shifted his eyes to look at Sigmund. Sigmund shrugged with a face that said, *Don't ask me.* Hanz looked back at the highlord, who was rolling the castle piece in his fingers.

"What's this offer?" Hanz asked, groaning to himself.

Cato glanced at Sigmund. "Can we speak alone?"

Hanz motioned for his man to leave. Sigmund did so happily.

Cato began fingering his rings. He wore about a dozen on his left hand alone. Then, he slid one of them off and placed it in front of Hanz. Like most of Cato's jewelry, it was gaudy and covered in gemstones. Then Hanz' eyes narrowed; those weren't just gemstones—they were godstones. Hanz plucked the ring from the desk and brought it to his face. His magikal eyes examined it closely. *Never* had he seen such a ring—and most people never would. It was unmistakable, though.

"This..." Hanz said softly, shifting his gaze back to Cato, "Belongs to the King of Bavel."

"Well, yes," Cato shrugged, "It does."

"You... are not the King of Bavel." Hanz said doubtfully.

Cato grinned through his teeth. "Is it so hard to believe?"

"You came here from the Edgelands—with aurochs and everything."

"Well, we had to make it convincing, you know."

Hanz scoffed. No. Surely, not. "So you left Bavel... went to the Edgelands... and came *back?*"

Cato sucked hard on his cigar, then coughed, "Well, sort of." He seemed unwilling to fill the gap in his apparent story.

Hanz lowered the ring back to the table. "You don't expect me to believe..." his words trailed off as the look on Cato's face remained sincere. Hanz blinked.

"No," he said, "surely, not." Cato gave Hanz a toothy grin and spread out his hands.

"So, you..." Hanz licked his lips. "You've been, what... *spying* all this time?"

Cato made a disinterested blinking face. "I was mildly curious what you were up to: the man who took my lands."

For the first time in many seasons, Hanz actually felt dread. His armpits began dampening and his heart rate began to rise.

"Mensa belonged to no one," Hanz said in a soft voice, masking any sign of trepidation. "Even Shadowroots, clinging to your walls, was abandoned by you. Bavel has only ever cared about Bavel and those within its walls. For *thirty* seasons, you have been silent," Hanz' voice began to strengthen, "You did *nothing* when I claimed those lands!"

"Yes, well," Cato shrugged, slumping into his chair like a collapsing souffle. "We had things... to worry about."

"Tell me," Hanz said earnestly, "What *happened*?"

Cato gave the king a calculating look. "A disaster."

Hanz's eyes searched Cato's face for the truth. "In Bavel?"

Cato looked away. "You see...on the same day the Faeries lost their king, we lost ours. Well...our *Queen*, actually."

Hanz raised his eyebrows. "What happened?"

"Judgment, some say," Cato chuckled mirthlessly. "A prophet came and called judgment on us. Laugh, if you like, but it's true. But did anyone listen? What do you think?"

A prophet? Hanz refrained from mocking, if only just to hear the rest of the story. "And what happened?"

"A flood," Cato said in a deep voice. Hanz could see memories dancing around in the King of Bavel's eyes—terrifying memories. "Yes...the Sky broke open, and down it came. Flood waters. And like a vino fountain at an extravagant feast, waters of death descended through our city—killing all."

Hanz grew still. "...*All*?"

"Well," Cato sighed. "I guess not all... Guess who *didn't* live in the main part of the city?"

Hanz shook his head; he didn't know.

"Well, the Eagles, of course."

"The Black Eagles," Hanz said with wonder. Bavel's legendary army of archers, and the same army Hanz was eager *not* to go to war with.

"Yes, *those* Eagles," Cato puffed his cigar, "*My* Eagles."

"You... are an Eagle?"

"We lived on top of the walls, you see...we watched as the city filled with destruction. We saved who we could, pulling what women and screaming children we could up to safety. But... *Hades*, Hanz. So much death."

"So you mean to tell me that the Sky broke open over Bavel?" Hanz said with doubt in his voice, "A hole in the glassy sea? And rained down on you?"

"That is exactly what happened."

"And then it just... stopped?"

"Well," Cato groaned, reluctant to return to such memories, "Many brave Eagles gave their lives trying to repair the gap in order to stop it. The only thing one can repair the Glassy Sea with is godstones, you know—and they weren't easy to find." Cato paused to scoff. "By the time we stopped the flood, Bavel was a kingdom of lakes: levels and levels of lakes. Lakes populated with thousands of our dead, swollen and purple... floating and stinking for weeks and weeks."

"*Hades...*" Hanz cursed.

"Yes, indeed," Cato said. "Anyway, I was the most senior officer to survive. That made me king," he said flatly, "Hurrah."

"King of a dead city."

"King of the Walls, old man," Cato said as he drew in a deep breath. "Many did survive, those lucky enough to be a soldier, and those wise enough to heed the warning of the prophet. And for the last thirty seasons, we have made the walls our homes."

"And the flood waters..." Hanz said with interest, "receded?"

A grin formed on Cato's face. "Receded to where... to *lower* places? Places *downhill* of us?"

Hanz' face went pale as Cato's grin strengthened. The lower places... of course...

"Mensa..." Hanz muttered. He had a topographical map of his lands in that very room; it wasn't hard to see what was lower in elevation to Bavel. *He* was.

"Mensa would be the first in our path," Cato said thoughtfully, "All that water, just sitting there within the city walls. If we opened the gates...do you know where the *lowest* valley is, just down the way from us?"

Hanz' eyes widened in horror.

"Yes..." Cato nodded slowly. "The beautiful city—Arelle."

Hanz placed his palms on the desk and stared directly into the man's face. "You would...you would destroy Arelle? You would flood us all? *Why*?"

"I never said I would!" Cato placed his hand over his heart, looking offended. "Oh dear, Hanz, where would you get an idea like *that*?"

Hanz exhaled smoke through his nostrils. "Damn," he shook his head, "What do you want?"

"The bigger question, King Hanz, is what do *you* want? And think before you answer, because I *might* be willing to give it to you."

Hanz cocked his head to the side. "You think you know what I want, don't you?"

"I think we both might want the same thing," Cato said, "And if we make a strong alliance, we might be able to make it work."

"I am listening."

"Your lands are dying," Cato said flatly, "Well consequently, so are mine. Bavel is fed by the plants that grow along our walls—along our gates. We need someone on that felling throne, eh? And you want that throne, you bastard. Admit it."

"Fine," Hanz said, "But only because I know what to do with it. I don't know of anyone else who could sit there."

"Well," Cato shrugged, "Whatever. But the fact is, you want to be the new King of Arelle. Well, let me tell you what *I* want."

"Mensa."

"Yes," the King of Bavel smirked, "I want Mensa. My people are dying of starvation, but not only that—they need real *homes*. Bavel is dead, and we need land."

King Hanz let out a long, drawn-out sigh. "You want my kingdom. You want my people. This is... I worked for thirty seasons to unite these lands."

"Yes," Cato nodded, "And good job. But my people are going to die, which means I have nothing to lose. If you do not give me your lands, I will destroy them with the same flood that destroyed my city—and once the people have been washed away, I will take the lands anyway. Instead, why don't you just pass your throne to me? Then, you can be free to rule Arelle and lord it over everybody else, while someone else does the boring job of running the Humans in your kingdom. Then, my people will have a real place to live. Come on. Let me rule the Humans, and you can rule the felling *Faeries* you care so much about."

Hanz smashed the lit end of his cigar against the bare face of the table. "If I take Arelle, and leave you Mensa, you will agree not to flood my lands?" Hanz shook his head, "An alliance founded on threats... cannot last."

"I agree," Cato said with a nod. "Which is why I come to you with an olive branch. A trade of mutual benefit."

Hanz stared blankly at Cato. "And what would that be? What could you possibly have to give me?"

"I could be wrong," Cato said, rising, "But I think I have something you deeply desire."

The giant Bavel king wandered over to one of Hanz' bookcases and began to browse. Hanz watched curiously as Cato thumbed through a selection of historical records.

"Ah!" Cato pulled a book from the shelf and began flipping through it, as he made his way back to the desk. He stuck his cigar in his mouth, then placed the book open on the table in front of Hanz. "See there."

King Hanz glanced downward. It was the portrait book he himself had commissioned.

"I know all the faces in this book, Cato," Hanz said blankly, "I had it commissioned."

"Ah," Cato nodded, "And have you *looked* at it recently, Sire?"

"Well..." Hanz glanced down at the portrait which lay before him, examining the face.

"What was that chess move called again? *Castling*?" Cato asked thoughtfully as pulled deeply at his cigar, then he placed the white castle piece on the table.

Hanz studied the drawing before him. "Castling," Hanz muttered. "It is when a king trades places with a..." *Rook.* Before Hanz was a portrait of the man called Rook. It was the drawing commissioned by Coppo, Faerie of Lines.

"You know him," said Cato. "His name is—"

"Anodos," Hanz whispered. "His name is Anodos."

Cato exhaled deeply. "Yes," he said, "the poor fool talks in his sleep."

Hanz shot his eyes upwards at the King of Bavel. He stared at him with wonder, "You... you're *giving* this information to me?"

"Well, as you said," Cato said with narrowing eyes, "Alliances can't be founded on threats. This is my gift to you, Hanz, and I expect one in return."

"Mensa?"

"No—you are already giving me Mensa," Cato said as his looming figure bent over the table toward Hanz, "There is something else I want."

36

Unveiled

Rook was going to the one place he had vowed he would never return: Arelle. Memories of the Light City played through his mind as he helped Tercius load up the great Edgeland wagon. The same wagon that had brought him to Mensa would now take him to the Faerie Kingdom. So much had changed since he chose to come to Mensa in search of Felix's eyes. He had wanted to rescue his friend from the torments of Hanz, the same man who had destroyed his own life. But since coming to Mensa, things had become...messy. Now there were *others* he cared about...others who needed his help, others who made him willing to brave his terrors, others who... seemed to awaken desires he thought were not possible for him.

"Where's your head today," Tercius asked, slapping Rook on the back.

"Sorry?" Rook shook his head. He had been standing perfectly still staring at the stony ground, lost in his thoughts.

"You're all distracted," said the soldier. "You alright?"

Rook turned to regard Tercius, who looked concerned. "Yeah, I am fine. Are *you* alright?"

Tercius sniffed. He didn't like to admit to any weakness. "Why?"

"You seem… off," Rook said, wincing at his poor choice of words.

"Are you sure you want to go to Arelle?" Tercius asked, then he bit his lip.

"Why?" Rook blinked. "You don't *want* me to come?"

"I mean…" Tercius shrugged, "What if we let Cato travel with one of the other delegates—we can stay behind with Golden Grains and get some good gambling done."

This was odd. "I'm fine to go," said Rook, "And when you feel like you can tell me what's going on with you, give me a shout, alright?"

Tercius grunted, then walked away. Rook climbed up the rear ladder of the wagon and placed himself at the top. He liked how much of the world he could see from up there, and had insisted that Cato let him ride up top for the majority of the trip. It took at least a day to travel to Arelle if they made good time, and that would be a long trek. He gazed out at the courtyard; the whole place was busy with all the delegations preparing for travel. Rook could hardly believe it; it was really happening. Everyone was going to Arelle. He would have been more worried if he himself didn't have some sort of a plan. It wasn't a perfect plan, but it was *something*.

"Now," Rook mumbled to himself, scanning for King Hanz' wagon, "Where is she?" Rosamond, that ridiculous, infuriating, stunningly beautiful, *felling* woman. Where was she?

"Lucky!" cried a voice from below. Rook walked to the side of the roof and peered over to see a pair of Elves gazing upwards at him. Prince Rasselas was shielding his eyes from the bright morning sky. "You get to ride up *there* the whole time?"

Rook chuckled. "Where's *your* wagon?"

"We walk!" Latimer, who stood dutifully beside Rasselas, exclaimed proudly, "It's the only way to travel."

"Save me," Rasselas cried, "My wing has abandoned me, so now my only companion for the long day's walk is *this* fellow."

"I don't make very good company, I think," Latimer said brightly.

"Agree to disagree," Rook shouted back down.

"You haven't had to walk with this fellow for more than a bell, have you? It's nothing but 'wind this' and 'birds that!'"

"It really is," agreed Latimer. "And it's about seventy thousand steps to Arelle, I think. That's a lot of steps shared with a single person."

"Seventy thou—*Hades*!" Rasselas moaned, "How do you even *know* that? Save me, crow boy!"

"Alright, get up here. I am sure the Eagles won't mind," Rook said, walking to the back of the wagon.

"Oh, Lights!" Rasselas skipped to the back of the wagon excitedly then began scaling the ladder. Rook leaned over the ledge and waved at the skydeacon.

"How's the research going?" Rook asked, still looking down at Latimer.

"Lots to tell you," Latimer said as he patted his notebook. "Let's connect in Arelle."

"Looking forward to it," Rook called, then pushed himself away from the ledge as Prince Rasselas crested the top of his climb.

"I say!" said the prince, "What a view from up here! You can see so far— look! There's Bavel!"

"Well, now you're making me jealous..." Latimer mumbled from below.

"Get up here," Rook called.

"No, no. I am a walker. I need to count steps, you know."

"Have a jolly old time with that," Rasselas poked his head over, "see you in nine bells!"

The prince spun to face Rook with a grin. "Good *morning*!"

Rook shook his head, "So lazy. An Elf refusing to walk?"

"Now see here," Rasselas held up a finger, "A *prince* deserves to ride in style."

Rook snorted. What a lazy ass his little brother had turned out to be. "Come on, let's sit at the front."

The two of them crossed the top of the wagon, and came to the driver's seat, where Golden Grain's reins lay waiting.

"Slay me!" Rasselas exclaimed, "An aurochs!" He leaned over the edge and peered down at the animal. The beast turned its head slightly to peer a single eye up in Rasselas' direction.

I see you have a guest, said the beast, *Good. He is making you happier, I think.*

"Thanks, Grains," Rook said from above, "Are you ready for the trip?"

Yes. I am eager to leave this place of symmetry and stone. Give me the open fields again.

"Well, you're about to get it," Rook said, then turned to smile at Rasselas.

Rasselas was staring deeply at Rook's face. It was as if he were searching—intrigued by what he saw.

"*Erm...*" Rook winced, "Everything alright? The scars distracting you?"

"That's just it..." Rasselas mumbled, "They're not."

"Come on," Rook slapped his hand against Rasselas' shoulder. "Sit down. I'm driving for the first half, so you can sit with me."

"Jolly!" Rasselas grinned, shaking himself from his trance, "Will you let me hold the reins at all?"

"I don't think Golden Grains would appreciate that," Rook said hesitantly.

That is quite right, said the aurochs.

"See?" Rook grinned.

Rasselas' smile faded again. "You can understand him?"

"...Yes...don't you know that some people can understand beasts?" Rook said slowly.

Rasselas pulled the corner of his mouth to the side. "Well... Aurochs are different," he muttered.

"Are they?" Rook sat down in his driver's spot, "How?"

"Uh..." Rasselas sat beside him. "I'm not sure," he said unconvincingly.

Rook studied the prince for a moment; something was bothering the lad.

"Oy—Rook!" Cato called from below. Rook peeked over the side of the wagon to see the Highlord strolling up to the Wagon. "Hanz is about to lead the charge. Are we ready to go?"

"Yeah," Rook called, "I've grabbed a tagalong, if that's alright."

Cato's eyes shifted to regard Rasselas.

"Alright..." he said, "Whatever you want."

The highlord disappeared into the wagon. Moments later, the many caravans began to bustle with forward motion. Those in the front began to journey forward, so Rook directed Golden Grains to move. As the caravan of delegations, and their pompous messes of banners and soldiers began to journey forth, Rasselas stood, holding fast to the edge of the wagon, and peered about.

Rook watched his brother, the young Rasselas. He was full of life and passion. As his reddish hair blew in the wind, Rook thought he could see evidence of their mother's countenance. But Rasselas' passion, his wit? He was filled with his father Leo's spirit.

"What are you looking for?" Rook finally asked, noting that Rasselas seemed to be searching.

"The Faeries," he said, "Where do you think they are? They're coming, aren't they?"

Rook nodded. "Yeah, I think they'll be in the back. Tercius spotted several transport wagons that he was pretty sure they were putting Faeries into."

Rasselas turned to look Rook in the face. "You think it's wrong, don't you?" he asked, losing his posh act, "The way they treat Faeries here?"

Rook nodded again. "I do."

Rasselas smiled faintly, regarding Rook with relief.

Rook lifted his chin with a knowing smirk. "Don't worry," he said, "I saw Valley this morning."

"You did?" Rasselas started. "*Where?*"

Rook laughed. "Sit down, you sap. She's in the front with Hanz' Faeries." It was *Rosamond* who hadn't been located; Rook was trying his best to hide his concern.

"Oh..." Rasselas sat down beside Rook with a plop. "I guess that's good."

"What's wrong?" asked Rook, slapping his hand on Rasselas' back.

"We...fought." The prince slumped dramatically; it was a painful thing to witness.

"Ah...and...did she break your...heart—or something?"

"No...I think I broke hers...or something."

Rook nodded. What was the right thing to say to that? "*Erm*, well," he cleared his throat, "I'm sorry. That's...rough."

Rasselas glanced sideways at Rook. "Have you ever...fallen out with a...woman?"

"Mm..." Rook wasn't sure how to answer that. "I'm not...sure."

The conversation was as awkward and uneven as the stride of a three-legged ox.

"Well!" Rook said abruptly. "Now that we got that sorted," He turned to Rasselas with a smirk, "let's see how good you are at besting."

Bells later, Golden Grains desired a break from all the chatter and insisted that he could follow the other wagons without being led like a blind ox. As the Sky began to shift into its descending colors and wispy clouds, Rasselas and Rook laid on their backs, softened by a few thick rugs, there on the roof of the wagon.

Rasselas was hovering his hands up over his face, forming the shape of an empty square with his hands.

"And If you look through your hands like this," he was saying, "How many colors can you see in that small amount of space?"

Rook tried mimicking him. "Two?"

Rasselas scoffed, dropping his hands. "Rook, there were five, at *least*!"

"I thought you wanted to ride up here to avoid talking skydeaconry. Come on, stop stalling. I said, a heron. It's your turn!" Rook said from where he lay.

"Rook!" Rasselas moaned loudly, "this game is *so* tedious. I hate it. You win, alright?"

"What, you can't best a heron?" Rook slapped the back of his hand against Rasselas' shoulder. "I find that hard to believe."

"I don't *want* to best a heron," the prince said smugly, "They are creatures of beauty. Now, can we *please* be done with this game?"

"Well, it's better than your lessons on skyreading," Rook mumbled.

"I was just trying to change the subject," Rasselas barked, returning Rook's slap with a slap of his own. "I would rather do anything than one more round of besting. *Damnation*—you soldiers have the most primitive pastimes."

"Oh, and your pastimes are *so* much better," Rook turned onto his side and gave Rasselas a punch in the side. Rasselas groaned emphatically. "Tooth-picking? Smoking?"

"Will you stop *manhandling* me? I am not as thick as you...that hurts!"

"Oh, give me a break." Rook jabbed the prince in the gut, "You need to toughen up. Mess up that perfect hair once in a while."

"Don't touch my hair!" Rasselas rolled away from Rook. "Really. I am *really* serious about that!"

Rook seized Rasselas by the ankle and dragged him back, reaching for that pretentious head of hair.

"No!" Rasselas scrambled to get free, then kicked Rook in the jaw—much harder than he had intended to. "Oh! I'm *sorry*, Rook!" He cringed as Rook felt his jaw, straightening his head slowly.

Rook collapsed onto his back with a laugh, and Rasselas relaxed.

"Hades, Rook, I'm sorry!"

"Stop apologizing, you ass," said Rook, still stroking his jaw.

Rasselas crawled back to his spot on the rug, which was now displaced by the roughhousing. He lay back down to look at the sky. He sighed, panting still, then chuckled.

Rook relaxed, placing an arm behind his head. There was a quiet stillness as they stared up at the darkening sky.

"You...I..." Rasselas began to say something, then made a scoffing sound, as if annoyed at himself.

"What?" Rook looked over and found Rasselas looking directly at him. There was a moment of silence as they laid there, side by side, with their faces turned toward each other.

"Rook?"

"Yeah?"

"I want to ask you something."

Rook grew quiet, then nodded. "Alright," he said, "What is it?"

Rasselas drew in a deep breath slowly through his nostrils, studying Rook's face. His eyes grew glossy. "Answer me truthfully..." he said. His voice was small and thin.

Rook gazed intently at his brother, then nodded.

"Please," Rasselas said in a cracking voice. A single tear escaped his eye, "Please, don't lie to me...and please—don't...don't let me hope...I...Rook— please don't let me hope, if..."

Rook nodded. "Yes," he said.

Rasselas blinked out a second tear, "What?"

"Yes," Rook said again as a smile formed on his face.

"You know what I am going to ask you?" Rasselas asked with a quivering lip.

"Yes."

"And you..."

"Yes," Rook nodded, "It's me."

"Anodos?" Rasselas sniffed up some congestion, "Don't you dare lie to me..."

"Yes," Rook nodded, and his smile grew. "I'm Anodos."

Rasselas gasped then threw himself against his brother's side. He clung to him as hard as he could, burying his face into Rook's shoulder, and did what he would later deny: Rasselas sobbed. Rook put his arm around his brother and held him tightly.

"I'm sorry," Rook said, doing his best to hide his own damp eyes, "I'm so sorry for leaving you."

"I *knew* it was you!" Rasselas exclaimed, his voice muffled by Rook's cravat, "When you spoke to that Aurochs...I knew...I knew...it *had* to be you. I wanted it to be you...I *needed* it to be you! Anodos!"

"When I spoke to the aurochs?" Rook raised an eyebrow. "*What*?"

"Legends say they only speak to kings...so you had to be a king! I *knew* it was you!"

"Hah," Rook sniffed, then sought to be free of the embrace. Rasselas would not let him go. "You knew, huh?" Was it true that aurochs only spoke with kings? Cato could speak with Golden Grains...

"Your face..." Rasselas said softly, "I recognized you... something about your face, it..."

Rook blinked. Recognized? *How?* Had Rasselas just broken the spell?

Rasselas quickly pulled back with a gasp. "Anodos!" he exclaimed. "Anodos!" A beaming smile appeared on the prince's face.

"What?" Rook sat up, sore from lying against the wooden roof of the wagon.

"You're on your way to reclaim your throne! Oh my—oh Lights!" Rasselas gasped to himself, shaking his head as he ran his fingers through his hair. "You're going to save the Faeries, *aren't* you?"

"I don't know..." Rook said slowly, his own smile waning. "I don't know what's going to happen. But Rasselas—I am not ready to take the throne..."

"But why?" Rasselas shook his head, "No, no... everyone is waiting for you."

"Don't worry," Rook said firmly, "I won't let Hanz take it, alright? I have a plan."

"Someone has to take that throne, Anodos!" Rasselas chided, "And there's no one else who can do it but you!"

"Yes, there is," Rook said, reaching out to grip Rasselas by the arm. "There is someone."

Rasselas raised an eyebrow. "...who?"

"Hevel, Rass—Hevel is alive."

Rasselas drew back, stunned. "I... I don't know which thing I should be more shocked by, the fact that Hevel is alive, or the fact that you just called me Rass."

Rook smirked, "Hah...yeah, sorry. I called you that when you were younger."

"I know," Rasselas said with conviction. "I *know*, I remember."

Rook slid his hand up to ruffle Rasselas by the hair. The prince didn't resist the contact this time.

"Is this real...it's really you?" Rasselas asked.

"Yeah...I think so. But we need to be careful," Rook let out a suspenseful breath, "If you recognized me, then you've broken the spell."

"Spell? What spell? Wait—Anodos! Hevel is alive, too? *How?*"

"Yes, and so is his daughter Morningstar," Rook said quickly, "Though I think Hevel is not the man we knew...Hanz did something to make him lose his mind...but I think if he can reunite Hevel and his daughter, we can bring back his memories."

"Oh Lights!" Rasselas widened his eyes. "You know about Valley—of course! Wait... her name is Morningstar?"

Rook laughed. "We have a lot of catching up to do."

"But where is Hevel? Are you *sure* he is here?" Rasselas lowered his voice to a whisper.

"Yes, I am sure," Rook matched Rasselas' tone. "I think Hanz plans on having Hevel crown him. So he has to bring him along."

Rasselas practically spat. "That bastard! The idiot thinks he can use a Faerie throne? He's a *Human!*"

"I know," Rook shook his head, "He's an idiot, but I think he knows that he will have no actual power. I don't think he cares... It's the symbol of the throne he wants, the title."

"Damn." Rasselas rubbed his chin, "So, once you find Hevel, what are you going to do?"

Rook leaned back and rested his arms on his knees. "I need to be careful... just get his memories working again and see if I can't get him on the throne. Then we can restrain Hanz..." he hesitated, "or...I don't know...*kill* him?" Rook held his breath, watching the shocked look form on Rasselas' face.

"Kill him?" The prince asked.

"Well, how else am I supposed to get those eyes back?" Rook said impatiently. "Don't look at me like that."

"No, I get it...I just...I forgot you could kill people. Most Faeries can't kill." Rasselas said slowly.

"It's one of the benefits of being the King," Rook shrugged. "I have the authority to do that sort of thing. Hevel said it's some sort of...divine right."

"But I thought you said that Hevel was going to take the throne," Rasselas said.

"Well...we will have time to figure out all the details."

Rasselas nodded slowly. "Damn...that man has hurt so many people...I mean, just in our family alone! He—" the prince turned sharply, "Wait, *what* eyes?"

"Uh..." Rook pulled his lip into his mouth. Did he want Rasselas to know about Felix, the man who had tormented his mother years ago? "Never mind."

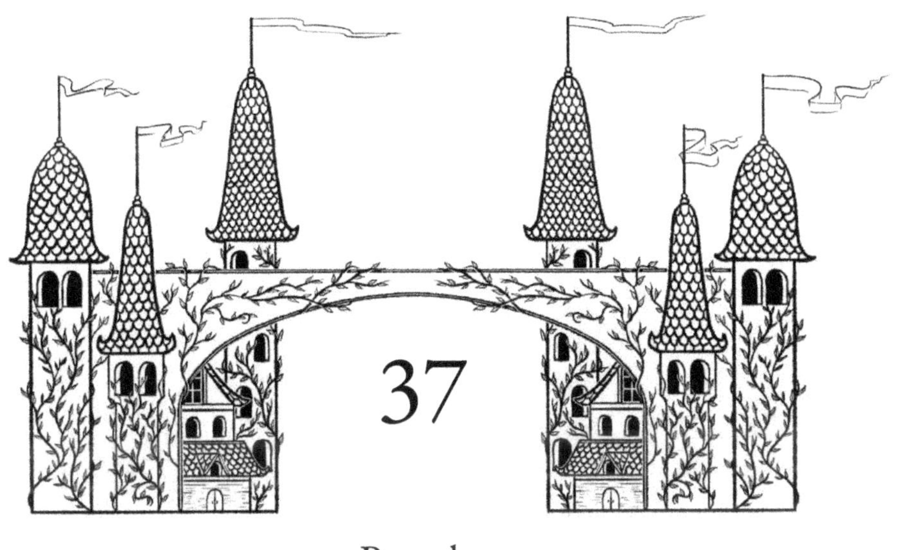

—— Rasselas ——

Declaration

"ARE YOU GOING TO MAKE YOUR MOVE TONIGHT? Before we arrive at Arelle?" Rasselas asked.

"If we are going to move at all, we have to be careful," Rook said with a sigh. "Hanz has all the Faeries locked up, an entire army, and a lot of influence in tow. So I think our best bet is to get the lay of the land once we enter the Faerie City."

Rasselas could see the hesitation in his brother's face. It was as if he didn't want to go to Arelle at all!

"Uh, Anodos?" Rasselas asked.

"Hmm?"

"Is it ok for me to ask... where have you been? Did... did Hanz abduct you?" Rasselas held his breath, expecting disappointment. It felt too easy to just *ask*.

"Oh, uh..." The expression on his brother's face—it was as though he were witnessing invisible horrors before his eyes. "Yeah, Rass... he did. At least...others who were under his command did."

"The Purists?" Rasselas asked intently. "I'm sorry to pry, but Anodos, I have been dying to know for so long! Uh... and the scars... How have the scars faded on your face? And... and..." he felt himself gaining momentum, like a heavy cart rolling down a steep hill, "How did you get away?"

Rook chuckled. "Yeah, the Purists. Anyway... we can catch up on all that later—but look," Rook pointed ahead toward the horizon.

Rasselas lifted his eyes to follow, then drew in a sharp breath. "Arelle!" he exclaimed in an awestruck voice. So it was true what they said, when she first came into view, the Light City looked like a bride. The city radiated such a shining white light, it was as if the Morningstar had rested on the Land, bringing the heavens down. She was so beautiful.

Rasselas turned to regard his brother with a smile. "There she is, Anodos: your inheritance—your bride."

Rook cleared his throat awkwardly, then scratched his head. "Listen," he said quickly, "Arelle is only a few bells away now. We need to find out where Hevel is, and—"

"*And* where Valley is," Rasselas added.

"Hah... yeah, *and* where Valley is..." Rook glanced to the side, "And then we need to meet up again once we reach the gates. We can make a plan then."

"Right!" Rasselas mimicked a salute, "Count on me, brother! I'll attend to it, then meet you back here once we reach the gates." Carrying out an important task for his long-lost brother? This is what Rasselas was *born* to do!

"If you really are going to try and find Valley," Rook said, "Please be careful. She... I think Hanz keeps a close eye on her. I think he," Rook blew some hair out his face, stalling, "I think he has plans for her."

Rasselas flattened his mouth, then leaned in close to his brother. "Anodos," he said, "You *know* something, don't you? ...about Valley?"

Rook retained a stoic face. "I don't know what I know."

"No..." Rasselas shook his head, leaning back, "You *know* something. What is it?"

"Everything will come into the light," Rook said assuredly, "Now, see if you can't track down Hevel. But be..." Rook huffed, "Rasselas, please be careful. I don't want anything happening to you."

"No," Rasselas frowned, "No, no, no, no... Don't do that."

"Do what?"

"Don't do what mother and father did—*over*protect me. I am a man now, and if I want to get involved, then you had better damn let me get involved!"

Rook curled up his mouth into a smile, then nodded. "Fine," he said, "What are older brothers for if not for getting younger brothers into trouble?"

"Exactly!" Rasselas stood, straightening his waistcoat. "Now... Hevel and Valley... Here we go!"

"The Faerie carts are in the back," Rook said as he stood, "But I honestly think Hanz would keep those two close. So start closer to the front of the procession before we set out, I saw Valley enter the wagon for his bonded Faeries. Begin there...Hevel will be a bit trickier."

"Alright, alright, alright," Rasselas waved his hands impatiently, "Don't steal my reins!"

The two brothers stared at each other silently for a moment, easing the awkwardness by either putting hands in their pockets or fidgeting with their buttons.

"Oh, fell it!" Rasselas lunged at his brother, hugging him tightly. Rook flinched, then slowly joined in the embrace. Rasselas pulled back, then coughed. "Sorry..." he said as he glanced to the side, "I just...I am really glad you're...I'm glad it's you."

Rook raised his eyebrows, "Well," he said, "Thanks."

"Alright!" Rasselas slapped his hand on the railing, then leapt over the side of the wagon.

He landed on his feet in a crouch, then stood and dusted himself off. He looked around while the wagon rumbled past him. About to run toward the head of the procession, he was stopped by a voice.

"Oh!" Latimer rushed to catch up with the prince, "Joining me at last?"

"*Erm*," Rasselas glanced at the skydeacon. Someone was slowing him down *already*?

"Elves were made for walking, eh?" Latimer said as he stretched his hands out toward the scenery. "Look at this view, these colors!"

"Yes, yes," Rasselas grumbled, "Say, old boy, seen any suspicious-looking wagons? You know...wagons without windows?"

Latimer blinked. "Uh...I suppose I have seen a few up front. Why? Do you..." he lowered his voice, "Do you suspect something foul?"

"Something like that," Rasselas mumbled, gazing down the line of wagons ahead.

"I do too," Latimer whispered, "I think King Hanz is...*up* to something..."

Rasselas turned curiously toward the Elf. "Really?"

"My findings with the storm," Latimer tapped his notebook emphatically, "are pretty disturbing."

"I see," Rasselas sighed. For a moment, he had hoped this man would be helpful.

"I am really concerned, Moonvine," Latimer whispered as they walked to keep pace with the procession, "The Lights are...*restless*...nervous."

Rasselas would be lying if he said he didn't notice the restlessness in the sky, but he didn't want the skydeacon to turn to him as a knowledgeable consultant. In that case, Rasselas would *never* be free of the man.

"That sounds ominous," Rasselas said noncommittally, "And...you think Hanz has something to do with it?"

"Well," Latimer swallowed, as if recovering from a dry mouth, "He and his skydeacons are trying to cover up the storm findings—or at least, misinterpret them." He shook his head, "I...this is unprecedented..."

"What, *really*?" Rasselas was genuinely shocked. "He is? But *why*?"

"That's what I am wondering," Latimer sighed, "I think I've discerned the name for that storm last week and I...I am concerned."

"Alright, well," Rasselas patted the man on the back, "Good job, old boy. I'll catch you in a click. Just got some things I've got to..."

And he was off, racing ahead toward the front of the caravan. He came into a cluster of soldiers bearing Sol banners. As he passed their central wagon, he reached up for the side rail, stepped up onto the siding, and peered through the open window.

"Gods, Rasselas!" Tingo cursed, "You scared the daylights out of me."

"Sorry, old boy," Rasselas grinned through the window, "How's the travel been?"

"Tedious," said Tingo. His wing was sitting across from him, snoring lightly.

"Arelle is just on the horizon," Rasselas said cheerily, "We will be there soon."

"You seem extra chipper today, Moonvine," Tingo said sourly, "I can guess why."

Rasselas blinked. "Slay me, I have no idea what you might be referring to!"

"Didn't you hear?" Tingo asked skeptically, "Hanz has chosen a husband for Princess Rosamond. We don't know who it is, yet..." he eyed the Elf prince, "But seeing as you're in such a good mood."

"Oh, Hades," Rasselas blew a raspberry childishly, "No. I never even submitted a request."

"You *didn't?*" Tingo drew back, "But we all thought..."

"Nice girl, and all that," Rasselas said, feigning a yawn, "But really, too witty for me."

Tingo snorted. "Why don't I believe you?"

"Believe me or not, I don't give a felling star. Anyway, which of these wagons has got the old king in it, eh?"

Tingo leaned his head out the window. "Up there, the red ones belong to Hanz' personal party. I think he's got Faeries in *that* one, officers in that one, and *somebody* in that one." The final one was accompanied by a lot of guards.

"Ah," Rasselas nodded to himself, "Thanks, mighty Prince Tingo!" In a sweeping motion, he hopped off the carriage and rushed ahead.

Rasselas jogged until he found the cluster of red carriages. There were plenty of guards around, so he did his best to avoid detection, ducking behind oxen, or jumping into conversations he wasn't a part of. Thankfully, they were more focused on what was in front of them—it was hard for anyone to be this close to Arelle and not gaze at her.

Rasselas hopped onto the small step at the back of the last wagon, then swung the door open. He was met with the face of a suspicious guard.

"Oh, Hallo!" Rasselas said innocently.

"What are you doing in here?" The guard asked as he tightened his grip around his hilt.

"Looking for the old king," Rasselas said quickly, "He in here?"

"King Hanz is in the front wagon," the guard said sharply. Rasselas did his best to peer around the man. Most of the passengers appeared to be officers. more than one of which he recognized from the healthy beating he received before being thrown into the pit.

"Ah, hah, hah," Rasselas slunk back, "I'll go find him then."

He exited quickly, hoping to avoid further suspicion. Thankfully, no one cared enough to follow him out. The next carriage didn't have many guards around, so Rasselas entered it without molestation.

There were Faeries sitting silently together inside. They looked up in surprise when he entered.

"Hallo!" Rasselas said with a little wave of his hand. "Valley in here?"

"You're Prince Rasselas, the Elf who tried to scapegoat for Valley," a Faerie boy said. He had dark brown skin and bright eyes. Rasselas recognized him as the Faerie who had drawn his portrait a week ago. He held his breath, noticing that the boy was missing a hand.

"Y—yes, I am," Rasselas admitted. "I wanted to see her... if..."

"Hah!" said a taller Faerie with jet black hair. "I bet you did!"

"Yes..." Rasselas raised an eyebrow. "Is that a problem?"

"Well, yes!" the man giggled to himself. "I do believe you're the last person the king wants her seeing right now, lover boy!"

Rasselas shrugged. "So where is she?"

"She's riding with the King," said the one-handed Faerie. "You can see if he will let you see her."

"Thanks," Rasselas said with a bow of his head, then turned to leave. He stopped for a moment, then asked. "Does, *uh...* does everyone know, *erm... think*, that I'm in love with Valley?"

Everyone sitting there in the wagon nodded.

"Ah," Rasselas tapped his chin with his finger. "Alright, well thanks for that!"

He exited the wagon.

He passed the smallest wagon, which had an entire battalion of guards. He guessed it contained the Death Faerie. Rasselas marched straight for the front wagon. There, he found Captain Oswald standing on the back step.

"Oh, fare thee well, old captain!" Rasselas said with a salute.

"Don't salute," Oswald said dryly, "It's against the law to impersonate an officer. Don't give me yet *another* reason to kill you."

"Oh, pipe down," Rasselas dropped his hand with a grunt. He had to trot along quickly to keep up with the pace of the wagon. "I come in peace."

"I find that hard to believe," Oswald said with eyes as thin as slits.

"King in there?"

"Yes."

"Can I speak with him?" Rasselas asked, plastering on a toothy smile for extra measure.

Oswald exhaled hot air through his nostrils, then turned to enter the wagon.

"What am I *doing*?" Rasselas asked himself under his breath, then brightened when Oswald returned.

"You can go in," the captain said. He stood to the side of the step, giving Rasselas a small space to hop up on. Rasselas climbed up, taking hold of the side rail, then made a gurgling sound when the captain grabbed him by the back of the neck.

"I'll be right here the whole time," Oswald said into his ear, "So don't try anything stupid."

"Fine," Rasselas wheezed. He entered the wagon.

The interior was lavish and warm. Glowing oil lamps and darkly dyed rugs lined the place, giving the impression of an old library. There Hanz sat, in a cushioned armchair, with a little book in his hand. Valley stood on the other side of the wagon, peering through a crack in the window curtain. She turned and made a little gasp at the sight of Rasselas standing there. She widened her eyes at him in warning.

"Prince Rasselas," Hanz said, gazing through half-open lids. "What a surprise to see you here."

"Ah, what book have you got there?" Rasselas strode in confidently. "I'm dying to know what a man as great as *you* likes to read in his spare time."

Hanz didn't so much as close the book. "You have a hundred clicks," he said, "What do you want?"

"*Erm...uh...*" Rasselas sputtered, tugging at his cravat.

"That's what I thought," Hanz said, still looking down at his book.

"Valley," Rasselas said quickly, turning his eyes to her. Valley's cheeks flushed and she shook her head, as if to say, *please, don't.* "Valley, I..."

Hanz looked up, then his eyes darkened. "Get the Hades out of here! *Oswald!*"

The captain swung open the door and seized Rasselas by the back of his collar.

"Valley, I don't care what befalls me if I say it—I love you!" He stumbled as Oswald dragged him backwards. "And it's not a spell. I *love* you, damn it, I—"

The prince found himself face down on the well-trodden terrain just outside of the wagon. He had to scramble to his feet in order to avoid being trampled by the next wagon in line.

"Don't come back!" Oswald yelled.

Rasselas did his best to right his clothing. "Well," he mumbled, "You just wait."

The king was coming; the *true* king was coming. And no one—not even Hanz—could stop him.

Anodos was coming back!

38

—— Rosamond ——

From One to Another

ROSAMOND SAT PATIENTLY IN HER SOLITARY WAGON. It had been bells since she had seen another person. She was so often alone now. Where was Valley? They used to be inseparable. Now? Now it was as if they lived in separate worlds.

Why did she feel so nervous? She knew Anodos would find her soon and tell her about his plan. Would he take back the Faerie throne?

"Oh!" She breathed in sharply, placing her hand over her mouth, "Will he even *want* to be with a Human once he is the Faerex?"

Her wagon came to a sudden halt. She jumped, then tapped on the ceiling with her pole.

"Hallo?" she called, looking upwards in the direction of the driver, whoever that was, "Hallo, are we there?"

The back door to her wagon opened. She turned excitedly, half expecting Rook to be there. Her enthusiasm weakened as Oswald came marching in. He seated himself across from her at her table, then offered a friendly smile.

"Hallo, Captain," Rosamond said matter-of-factly, as she folded her hands on her lap. The wagon jostled into movement again.

"Good evening, Rosamond," said the captain.

"Oh!" She raised an eyebrow. "Is it evening now? Hades, it's hard to know when I don't have windows. Am I to be locked up like a Faerie from now on?"

"Your father is merely protective," Oswald said, as he leaned a fist on the table between them. "He is to announce your engagement soon, and some of the delegates aren't going to be happy with who he has chosen."

Rosamond scoffed. "Father isn't trying to *protect* me, he is trying to keep me from getting into trouble."

Oswald shrugged.

"Oswald," Rosamond said, turning her nose toward him, "I would prefer someone else's company. Could you send Valley in? Or a snake? Or *anyone,* other than you?"

Oswald leaned back. "I'm sorry," he said.

"Oh? Really? You're sorry? For *what*?" she asked expectantly.

"For..." His eyes widened.

Rosamond shook her head. "But you don't feel bad about it, do you?"

"About..."

"You know of what I am speaking. Oswald, how could you... how could you just stand by and—?"

Oswald grunted in discomfort. "Do not ask me this."

"Captain!" Rosamond slammed her palms on the table. "You brought me to his room, *knowing* he was angry! You...you..."

"I did not think he would go so far!" Oswald responded with uncharacteristic emotion.

"That doesn't matter!" Rosamond cried. "Even if you *had* known, would you have stopped it?"

Oswald hesitated, then shook his head. "No."

Rosamond exhaled as calmly as she could, closing her eyes for a moment. "How do you live with yourself?"

"I am a soldier, Princess," he said, "I...I obey orders. I do my duty. It is my place on this world."

"I understand...somewhat, the life of a soldier. But Oswald, doesn't there come a point where your leader should lose your loyalty? What does my father have to do before you begin to question him?"

Oswald scoffed under his breath. "I asked myself that same question many seasons ago. Back then, I decided not to put myself in the place of a judge. Hanz is my King. He recruited me when I was a lad and he's the only leader I know. Some things he does are horrible, while others are magnificent. It may be other people's place to question him, but not mine."

"Are you telling me that even if he had *killed* me last week...you still would have stood by and watched?" Rosamond asked.

There was a thin, uneasy silence in the wagon.

"Yes," Oswald said. "Yes, I would. I have already done as much. That is why he trusts me."

Rosamond's face darkened like a sudden storm. "What do you mean by that?"

"When I warned you last week, it was because I knew what your father was capable of. That was the most I could do for you. You're getting married now, Princess. *That* is your rescue."

"Oswald..." Rosamond stared deeply into the man's eyes. "You said you have already witnessed my father's worst side. What *happened*?"

Oswald shook his head. "You will not want to know."

"I know my father is unstable enough to nearly kill me. Tell me now, Oswald, did he kill someone *else*?"

Oswald was as still a corpse.

Rosamond reached forward and touched Oswald's fist, which sat lifelessly on the table.

"Captain," she said in her most sincere and gracious voice, "Did Father kill my mother?"

Oswald closed his eyes, then nodded. "Yes," he said in a voice as distant as the Glassy Sea.

"And..." Rosamond's voice began to shake, "And my baby brother...?"

"Yes."

Rosamond and Oswald sat still like a painting, as if time had stopped. With his fist on the table, and her hand on his fist, they stared into each other's eyes. Rosamond broke the stillness with a sigh. Somehow, this didn't come as news to her; somehow, she had always known.

"Why?" she finally asked.

Oswald shook his head, pulling his fist off the table.

Rosamond furrowed her brow. "Oswald, I am getting married. And I have seen what my father is capable of, now. I'm a big girl. You can tell me."

"I don't know *why* he does what he does," the man said darkly. "And I do not want to know why. But I trust him. I trust his reasons are... enough."

"No, you don't," Rosamond said, "You don't trust his reasons, and that is why you don't want to know." She stood, then walked across the wagon. There was nowhere for her to go, but she felt the need to shake herself from the atrophy her body was beginning to feel. "I know why he did it," she said. "I know why he killed my brother, and yet he did not kill me." She turned slightly, swishing her large skirt against the wood flooring. She regarded Oswald, who sat there stiffly. "Do you want to know why?"

"No."

"Something tells me you know, too," she said. Then Rosamond let out a deep sigh. "I am a daughter. A daughter is an asset to her father. My brother..." Rosamond felt her eyes dampen, "My poor mother..."

Oswald lifted his head sharply, finally making eye contact with Rosamond. He watched her expectantly, both daring her to, and begging her not to say it.

"When my brother was born, Father knew he had a son. A daughter adds to a man's assets, but a son? A son takes away. A son desires an inheritance. Tell me I am wrong, Oswald. Tell me my father didn't kill his wife and his heir in a fit of rage."

"There may be another reason," he said, "We will never know."

"And you stood by..." her voice began to grow weak, "...While it happened?"

"Yes."

Rosamond dropped her eyes to the floor. She found she could not look at the man. "I am motherless...because you did nothing."

Oswald said nothing. He only stood.

"Get out." The princess pointed toward the door.

"Of course, Princess," said the captain. Moving to open the back door, he hesitated. "I came to offer you some company...but I see now that was the wrong choice."

"I am glad you came," Rosamond said as she turned her back to him. "I am always glad to hear the truth, as ugly as it may be."

"Someone else will come to you soon," Oswald said, "until then, you will be alone."

"Fine," said Rosamond. She was growing used to being alone. She didn't like it, but it was better than being in the company of those who wanted to use her for their own benefit.

Oswald left.

Rosamond paced the wagon from front to back a few times, then finally seated herself again on her chair. It was stifling staying in such a small space for so long. Why couldn't they at least grant her a *window*?

Someone else was coming. Who else would her father allow to...?

Rosamond's heart seemed to stop beating in her chest. A horrifying pain pressed against her chest.

"No," she gasped, "No, not him!" She stood, looking around frantically. Why had she sent Oswald away? He could have protected her! She shook her head. No...he wouldn't. He was a man of *duty*, not of honor.

"No, please," she whimpered to herself, thrusting her hands over her face. Where was Ziz? Where was Rook? Why was he never there when the worst things happened to her?

The back door creaked open. Rosamond threw aside some books, searching frantically for a weapon of some sort. Then she remembered that stick for summoning the carriage driver. It was nothing but a wood pole lined with ornate velvet. She seized it in her hands, then turned to face the intruder.

A man had to double down nearly sideways to get through the door into her wagon. Once inside, he straightened with a drunken smile.

"Oh—" he chuckled, examining her in her fighting stance, "am I *that* bad? I can leave..." He turned back toward the door.

"Cato?" Rosamond began to lower the poker, "What are *you* doing here?"

Cato snorted. "Last of all the people you expected?"

"Yes..."

"Sorry to disappoint."

"On the contrary," Rosamond lowered her weapon further. "I...what are you doing here? Does father know you're here?" She leaned sideways, checking for a chaperone behind him.

Cato sauntered forward then placed himself in the chair where Oswald had been sitting. The man's large frame was too big for the chair, too big for the wagon, too big for just about anything he tried to fit into, really.

"Damned stuffy in here without a window. Why haven't they given you a window?" he asked as he leaned an elbow on the table. "You got any vino in here?"

Rosamond huffed, then found a small little smile. She placed the stick down and sat across from her guest. "Do you think my father would trust me with liquor if he won't even trust me with a window, Highlord?"

Cato made a gurgling sort of laugh. "I suppose not. Well, that's one of the *first* things that we are going to change."

Rosamond blinked. "We? ...*What*?"

Cato pulled his lips into his mouth, spreading his short goatee hairs like a prickle bush. It was the first time Rosamond had ever seen the man looking...nervous?

"I, *erm*," He pulled his shoulders upwards, scrunching himself together like a concertina.

"Oh..." Rosamond shook her head, snickering, "No, no..."

"What?"

"You can't propose to me, Cato," Rosamond said with a laugh, "It's my father you need to ask. And he's already promised me to someone else. Not that I wouldn't prefer you a thousand times over King Labyrinth!" She laughed, thankful for a light moment for once.

Cato raised his eyebrows, then visibly blushed. "Well, that's a relief to hear."

"C–Cato…" Rosamond's grin mellowed, "No…you weren't *really* going to propose, were you?" She lifted up her hands defensively. "Because you really *do* have to ask my father—and he really *has* promised—"

"Yes," Cato said, "He has promised you to someone, it is true."

Rosamond blinked. "Do you…do you know something I don't, Cato?"

Cato nodded. Hades, the man's face was as red as a tomato.

"Cato…" Rosamond's voice lowered.

"I would ask you," Cato said with a sigh. He found it hard making eye contact with her, so he turned his head toward the wall, "But as you mentioned…It is a decision your father must make. But I hope to provide you with a comfortable…*safe*…home. With—" he turned sharply, urgently toward her, "With as much vino as you could ever desire!"

"I - I don't know what to say…" She stuttered.

Cato nodded. "I don't need you to…to…to…*Well*," He shook himself, as if resigning to a shiver.

"I thought you already had a wife," Rosamond said quietly.

"I do…more than one."

"And…other…sorts of…women."

"I do."

Rosamond let out a deep breath, then smiled. She reached out and placed a hand on Cato's arm. "…You're doing this for me, aren't you?"

Cato's bright blue eyes shot up to meet hers. "I will give you a good life," he said, "You will not want for anything."

Rosamond still didn't know what to say. But soon Rook would sweep her away to *wherever* and this whole conversation would become obsolete—but still! This was one of the kindest things a person had ever done for her.

"You're trying to protect me from…" Rosamond's voice trailed off. Cato knew, didn't he? He knew what her father had done. And he…he was going to *do something* about it!

"Yes, well," Cato shrugged, raising his volume and returning to his carefree self. "I'm no felling Elf with flowing hair, but I've got lots of vino." He stood quickly, then yelped as his head hit the ceiling.

"Oh!" Rosamond stood, wincing, "Are you alright?"

"Oh, I'll be fine," Cato waved away her concern with his bellowing voice. "Anyway," a grand smile stretched across his face. "You've made me a very happy man, *or whatever it is I am supposed to say, and all that.* You'll make a charming princess of Bavel."

He left quickly, slamming the door behind him.

Rosamond opened and closed her mouth, cocking her head to the side. "P–princess of...?"

39

—— Valley ——

The Gates

"WE ARE APPROACHING ARELLE," VALLEY SAID SOFTLY, gazing out the crack in the window drapery.

"Good," Hanz said. He snapped his book closed and yawned, making a creaking noise like an old door as he stretched. Whenever they were alone, Valley seemed to become uncomfortably aware of every single noise or movement the man made. It was almost as if he *wanted* to be the only thing interesting in the room and kept finding reasons to sigh or clear his throat. Valley wished to be anywhere but in his wagon. In the last bell, the only other person she had seen was Rasselas. That idiot came and risked Hanz's wrath, only to see her? To make a ridiculous proclamation of *love*? What was the foolish boy about?

Valley could not help but wonder if there was something more that Rasselas was trying to communicate to her. With Hanz there, Rasselas would have to be careful. Was there something he was trying to tell her? There was a sparkle in his eye, she thought. Perhaps he was just trying to communicate a glimmer of hope!

Valley couldn't help but feel a swell of warmth in her chest as she replayed the moment she had seen Rasselas march into the wagon. It was like a sudden daybreak in the midst of the darkest night, seeing him come in all jolly like that. However angry she was at him for complicating her already complicated situation, Valley sighed, Rasselas was important to her. Whether his feelings for her were involuntary or not, *she* didn't doubt her own love for him. Of that, she was sure. It wasn't a fanciful, childish affection she felt toward the man, nothing like how others seemed to fawn over their romantic obsessions. No, this wasn't like that. It didn't feel like an emotion; it was more solid, more of a conviction, something she *knew*. It was something that made sense in Valley's confusing, ever-changing, and oppressive world.

The words Rasselas wrote in the letter grounded her mind. But Rasselas himself, his character, and everything he *was* gave her heart something to cling to. Why, then…why did she feel so *guilty* whenever she thought about him? Why didn't her emotions align with her mind?

"Valley? Did you *hear* me?" Hanz said impatiently.

Valley's eyes shifted. She didn't look directly *at* the King; that would be giving him too much. She merely changed her general focus towards where he sat in the wagon.

"Sorry, no," she mumbled. "I was lost in my thoughts."

Hanz huffed. "Well, I said something sort of *important*, Valley. It bothers me that you didn't hear it."

Valley's pointy eyebrow lifted slightly. This man was so childish. Was it only she who saw it?

"Well," Valley closed her eyes. "Are you able to repeat it?"

Hanz shifted in his chair. "Valley, come over here and sit down."

Why was he annoyed? Valley finally deigned to look at the King. There it was: the unbecoming look of a spoiled child. She crossed the wagon quickly and sat down across from him on the second armchair. He gave her a scolding glare.

"What is it, Sire?" Valley asked, making dutiful eye contact with the King.

"I *said*," he bobbed his head, "it is time you learned the truth."

Valley blinked.

"*Yes*," Hanz said mockingly, "Now you see why it bothers me that you didn't hear the first time?" He scoffed. "Anyway, it is time to tell you who you *really* are, Valley."

Valley's expression didn't change. This was interesting. Now that they were at the gates of Arelle, he was changing his tune. Was he about to cook up another lie? Or was he about to embellish a truth? The only thing she was sure of was that she would not get the *exact* truth from him. This man treated the exact truth like money to a useful beggar. He only ever gave enough to cover their immediate need, while always withholding enough to keep them coming back

Hanz bowed his head. "Valley," he said solemnly, "I haven't been entirely honest about your parentage."

Valley refrained from an eye roll. She only looked at the king with eyes as sharp as daggers. "I hope you have a good reason for that," she said, "if it is indeed true."

"I do," Hanz nodded. "While you were a child, I believed it would be cruel to put this kind of weight on you, you must understand," he said nobly, "But I knew that a day would come when you could hear the truth. And you must hear that truth today, Valley."

"I may know more than you realize," Valley said, "My father is Hevel."

Hanz raised his chin, glancing at her with mouth half open, then nodded. "Rasselas," he said with a sigh, "Yes, of course. He knew that the third Nightmare Faerie was the child of Hevel."

"Yes."

"There is more," Hanz said as he picked up a torn piece of paper. He rolled the little thing between his fingers, as if the activity gave him some sort of sheepish confidence. "I...Valley, I want to tell you what *happened*."

Valley blinked. "Do you mean...you mean to tell me why you abducted me as a child?"

Hanz sniffed. He didn't seem to appreciate the accusation, but he didn't argue with it. "You," he said confidently, "were a child born into a very messy and complicated political climate. There are no two ways about it. Imagine this, my people, the Purple Order, were the Faeries who fled Somenus' evil reign. We worked together to remove him from the throne so that we could put a better king on the throne."

"And you succeeded," Valley said dryly. She was acting calm, but her heart was racing like a wild aurochs. Hanz...*knew* things. He knew everything that had happened in the past. So what was he going to tell her?

"We succeeded in killing Somenus, but one of his heirs remained alive," said the King. "Most of the Fae did not want the son of the tyrant to inherit the throne. But Aorist, the Time Faerie, held much influence at that time. He fought to give the throne to the baby."

"Anodos," Valley said softly. She saw Rook in her mind—she saw him lying bloodied and bound to the stone table of his nightmares.

"Yes," said Hanz, "but he was only a baby at the time, and so his *mother*," Hanz used the word as if it were a curse, "who was one of Somenus' whores, chose a regent until her son came of age." He snorted. "Imagine that, Valley, a concubine picking a regent? Anyway, she goes and picks the only other Faerie she knows, the Death Faerie. Do you know why she picked him?"

Valley shook her head. She had no idea that it was Rasselas' mother who had picked her father as regent! "Why?" she asked earnestly.

Hanz made a melancholy sigh. "The woman had been imprisoned in Somenus' jailhouse. Who knows why, but she had been punished there. Her only cell mate was the Death Faerie. Who knows what sort of influence he had over her, but he had managed to convince her to make him the next ruler. Anyway, once he took the throne, I and my Purple Order made ourselves scarce. We didn't want to cause further waves, of course, the Faeries had been through enough already. So I did my best to find them a home and a purpose away from the corrupt throne of Arelle."

Corrupt throne of Arelle? That was quite a leap! Valley nodded, indicating that she was keeping up with his narrative.

"I founded Mensa, uniting the chaotic lands outside of Arelle, and beyond. Many seasons later, the time for crowning Anodos was drawing near," he continued. Valley leaned closer. Tainted with his own dishonest edits or not, Hanz was giving Valley information she didn't have. "And, well," he sighed, "I had done my best to keep things peaceful between Mensa and Arelle. So, when

Hevel, Arelle's regent, your father, announced the birth of his first child, he invited me to come and visit. I came, of course, and...well, I met you, Valley. There you were, the child of Hevel the Death Faerie, and Olive the Fertility Faerie. You were so innocent and new," he said with distant eyes, "So...lovely."

Valley wasn't sure what to make of the declaration. This was the man who only days before had assaulted her with a less-than-fatherly kiss—the same man who had abducted her from the loving arms of her parents.

"Hanz..." she said cautiously, "What did you do?"

Hanz' eyes met hers with a dominating flash. "I..." she could see him sorting through a list of narratives, trying to find which one worked best for him. Did he believe his own stories? Did he even *know* which was the original?

"The Purists attacked Arelle," she said, "That is what I have been told. Was it the Purists? Was it *you*?"

"It *was* the Purists," he said slowly, "They heard the daughter of Hevel was the new Nightmare Faerie, and they heard Hevel's *plans* for you."

"Plans? What *plans*?"

"It was the final straw," Hanz said, disregarding her question, "They moved to dethrone Hevel and Somenus' son. They...they would have killed you, Valley."

"Were you working with them or not?" she asked quickly.

All he did was shake his head. "I took you. I saved you, Valley, and I saved someone else, too."

Valley's eyes widened. "Who—*who* did you save?"

Hanz' face grew as vacant as a beggar's purse. "I...I saved your father, Valley," he said.

Valley drew back, astonished. "*What*? My father is *alive*?"

"He is alive," Hanz said carefully, "But he is not who he was before. The Purists did something to him. His mind is fractured."

The *Purists* did something to him? Valley refrained from slapping the king across the face. If anyone had messed with Hevel's mind, she knew very well who it was, and it was *not* the Purists.

"Where is he now?" she asked urgently.

"That's just it," Hanz sighed, "He is here, Valley. And I plan to return him to his position of care taking the throne."

"*What*?" Valley gasped. Was Hanz *truly* going to hand the throne back to Hevel? No... something was wrong about this.

"Yes..." Hanz said, "But Valley, he does not know you are his daughter, and it is important that it stays that way."

"But *why*?"

"Because any time he talks about you, or his past family, he becomes unstable. I need him clear-minded in the coming days. I need him..." he hesitated, "*undisturbed*. Do you understand?"

Do you understand? Valley knew what *that* meant when it came from his lips; it meant, *You had better do what I say, or you will deeply regret it.*

"I hear you," Valley said, "But sire, if you thought he was unsuited to the throne before, why are you bringing him back now?"

"I did not say he was unsuited," Hanz said quickly, "I only said that the queen mother was unsuited to pick him. Anyway Valley, I am telling you this not so that you can understand all the inner workings of what is going to unfold in the coming days, but so that you can know where you fit in all this."

Valley leaned back. "And where would that be?"

"Next to me," Hanz said, "Safe."

"Safe?" Valley narrowed her eyes. "What do you mean? That *means* something..."

"Like I said," he cleared his throat, "You were born into a very messy and complicated political climate, and there you still remain. You and your father may be able to reunite someday, but for now, we need to stabilize Arelle and the Faeries. Do you understand?"

"I understand," she said with reluctance.

Hanz let out a sigh, smiling weakly. "What an admirable girl you are," he said, "I wish all women were like you."

It was like a dagger to the heart, hearing those words spoken of her. He was essentially saying, *I wish all women let those in power dominate them without complaint.* Was she proud that he thought of her this way? No. No, she was not. If only she could be more like the women who made him angry; the women who defied him and did things he didn't want them to do; the women who had wills of iron—women like Rosamond.

"Well," Valley said in a wavering tone, "I do my best."

Hanz leaned forward and reached out his hand toward her face with his index finger outstretched. Valley drew back cautiously, watching with nervous anticipation. He touched her cheek, then placed the full of his palm against the side of her face. His face drew closer.

"Please don't," Valley said, "I do not wish to encourage you...you...you said you didn't want to..."

Hanz blinked. "What?"

"You look like you're about to kiss me again," Valley said flatly. Hanz' face was inches from hers. "And you told me you didn't want to. I don't want to either, and I am sure I am not intentionally...*drawing you in,* so..."

"There is nothing wrong with me touching your face," the king said innocently, "I wasn't going to kiss you. You do not need to worry about that, Valley."

"Good," she pulled away from his hand.

Hanz chuckled. "I appreciate you thinking of me," he said, "but don't worry so much. I am fine." The king slumped back into his chair lazily. "I don't have interest in romance or even," his eyes connected with hers, "pleasure. I am not like most men. I prefer solitude and independence. I had a wife once...and before her, a lover. Both have taught me something. Do you know what that is?"

No, and do I not care to know, she thought. "What?" she asked obediently.

"I will never again entrust my body, soul, or mind to a woman. They..." he made a face of disgust, "They cannot be trusted. Do you know how *hard...*" He shook his finger suddenly, shifting his mood from thoughtful to provocative, "...I work to keep myself free of influence? I have such high ambitions... ambitions that most beings—mortal or immortal—cannot understand or comprehend, and I need a clear head in order to pursue them. *Women,*" he said the word with disdain, "cloud the mind. A wife has her own ambitions and demands, which can distract from a man's mission. And a mistress?" He snorted. "A mistress can take a man's mind from him by activating a fire of insanity within his body. I..." he shook his head, "I have too much work to do to indulge myself in such things."

Then what on the Table are you doing with me? Valley thought, *Aren't I a woman?*

"No," Hanz continued wistfully, "I gave up that kind of thing long ago. When my wife died, I told myself it was a sign from the Lights that I needed to be free from such cares. And a daughter?" He shook his head, "There is *another* kind of woman."

"What do you mean?" Valley asked sharply, "You have something against Rosamond, too?"

Hanz gave her a sidelong glance. "I know you and Rosamond are friends, and that is fine. But even *she* is a drain on me, Valley. Here, I have given her everything in the world a girl could ever ask for: dresses, friends, a safe home, a husband... and she," he slapped his thigh admonishingly, "She *resents* me! Anyway, it's good she has a husband now. I am done dealing with women."

Valley had a thousand questions stemming from that one thought, but she limited herself to asking, "Then what could you possibly have to gain by bonding with me? *I* am a woman."

Hanz turned his head dramatically in wonderment. "A very perceptive question," he said with the tone of a proud professor who realized his student body wasn't *completely* devoid of talent, "Yes, you *are* a woman."

Valley blinked. Did he have *more* profound wisdom to share?

"But you, Valley," he said, "are not wife, or lover, or daughter...you are something else. You are *me*."

Valley's face couldn't resist twisting in disgust. "*What?*"

"When a Faerie bonds with you," he said unwaveringly, "it is like they become part of your body. You are as much a part of me as my arm, or my foot, or my eyes."

Valley's focus shifted to his eyes, which had recently changed in color and character. She found herself stuttering. "Th–that—"

"So yes, you are a woman, but you are not an obligation to me. You are a support. You exist to *help* me. You listen, you obey, you apologize, you submit, you—"

"Hanz!" Valley's voice croaked. She had no idea what she would say next, but she knew she had to terminate that heinous sentence. The king blinked in offense at the interruption.

"Do you have something to *say*, Valley?"

"I... I..." What *could* she say? Did she want to dig herself into a hole of distrust with this man who held her very future in her hands? Did she want to anger him again, after his anger over the last transgression had finally cooled? "I am still a woman, aren't I?" She recovered shakily.

Hanz laughed teasingly, "Well, I should damn hope so."

"So I still could become a threat to you..." she said slowly.

"Well..."

"If I *became* a wife or lover to you..." she continued.

"Well, yes," his face grew serious. "So you can understand why I don't want you *tempting* me in that direction, you understand?"

Valley did her best to swallow her raging furnace of anger within. "I would like to make something very clear, sire," she said respectfully, "I do not wish for any of those relationships with you. I will *never* consciously pursue them. And I am sure it would help us both if you did not..." she faltered; her courage was waning as his expression grew more annoyed. "*Erm...*" she swallowed loudly, "touch my face...or...anything like that..."

"Valley..." Hanz was rubbing his temples with both hands.

"Have I said something wrong?" Her voice was as timid as a mouse. "I...I thought I..."

"You need only concern yourself with your *own* actions, woman!" he said harshly, using that apparently abhorrent word, "But do not judge mine. I am in control of myself! Don't you understand? This is what I have been saying this entire time. I keep telling you that I am in *control!*" His fist slammed against the table, rattling his vino glass.

Valley's stature grew smaller and smaller as each word crescendoed. She nodded quickly. "I am glad to hear it..." she mumbled.

"Stop it! Stop... *having opinions*, Valley!" He was yelling now.

She nodded again.

Hanz exhaled deeply, slumping wearily into his chair. "Can you...apologize, please?" he asked softly.

Valley bit her lip so hard it nearly bled, then said, "I'm sorry."

"Nothing I do is wrong," he said.

Valley had no response for that last comment; it was sheer madness. So, she nodded once more, like the obedient, submissive, *stupid* girl she was.

There was a knock on the door at the end of the wagon.

"Come in!" Hanz bellowed.

Sigmund, the man in the black cloak, popped his head inside.

"Sire," he said, shifting his gaze between Valley and the King, "We are here. The watchman is coming."

"Right," Hanz stood. "Valley?"

Valley stared expectantly at the King.

"Come with me and stay close," he said, then rose. As he marched to the wagon's back door, Valley followed. She didn't like tailing him like a hound, but she was appreciative of the chance to see what would happen when Hanz confronted the Faerie watchman.

Their caravan of wagons, legions and banners trailed behind, covering the length of the great, long bridge on which they stood. This must be what was called the Pleasant Way. The bridge stretched over a great canyon, leading to the gates of Arelle. Valley's eyes did their best to take in the vast scope of the scenery. They followed the bridge's length, all the way up to the gates and walls. Valley found herself gaping in awe, what she saw was almost too magnificent for words. The white walls glowed, as if emanating their own light. They reached so high that atmospheric wisps clouded their tops. Her eyes were drawn up to what seemed like a star floating down from above, shining in the night sky. A pair of reflective golden wings sprang out from the star's center. This must be the watchman.

Hanz took Valley by the wrist and walked to the front of the caravan. He cupped his hand over his brow, shielding his eyes from the light from above.

The Faerie flapped his metallic feathered wings and landed gracefully before King Hanz. His face appeared young, though his white hair and hardened expression gave him the look of a soldier who had survived many battles. He unsheathed a long, gold sword and pointed it at Hanz.

"How dare you bring a Human army to Arelle?" he asked, "You cannot possibly imagine that I would let you in!"

Hanz remained motionless, with the confidence of an eagle amongst pigeons.

"It may come as a surprise to you, Dezmund of War," Hanz projected like an opera singer, "That I come here with a *gift* for you."

Dezmund gritted his teeth and took a step closer to the King. "Don't use your tricks on me, snake! I was *there* the day you tried to kill Queen Lolette—the day you tried to kill her child. I will *never* grant you entry!"

"It may not be within your authority to refuse my entry," Hanz bellowed, though his face remained as calm as a breeze.

Dezmund scoffed. "How dare you!"

"Captain!" Hanz called, turning his head to the side, "Bring him out."

There was a murmuring of many voices from behind. Valley turned to see that the delegates had stepped out of their wagons to watch the scene unfold. Valley breathed in sharply when she saw Rasselas standing nearby, waving a timid hand in her direction. She made eye contact, watching his soft smile grow. He then started, losing his concentration on Valley, and gazed dumbfounded at something else. Valley followed his gaze, and her mouth dropped open.

There was Captain Oswald, leading a tall, frail Faerie. She had never seen this Faerie before, and yet he looked disturbingly familiar. Valley could see herself in his eyes. This—this was her *father*.

All faces followed Oswald and Hevel as they meandered forward to the gates. Hevel's eyes were filled with terrified confusion. Valley shifted her focus back to Dezmund. He was thunderstruck.

"Here," Hanz shouted, "I bring you back your regent. You must open to him, mustn't you?"

Hevel was trembling. "Arelle?" he asked Hanz, clinging suddenly to the King's side. "You've brought me to Arelle?"

"I told you we were coming here," Hanz whispered, "All will be fine."

"Hevel!" Dezmund's plate armor made a clanking noise as he crashed down onto his knees in a dramatic bow. "You're alive!"

Hevel stared down at the Faerie. "Uh...erm..." he glanced nervously at Hanz, then said, "Do get up, soldier. I, *erm*, can you please let us in?"

"Sire!" Dezmund lifted his eyes urgently toward Hevel. He could detect something wasn't right, but he didn't know what to do. "You want me to let...*everyone* in?"

Hevel glanced at Hanz who nodded slowly.

"*Erm*, yes," Hevel said quickly. "Yes, everyone. Alright? Is that...acceptable to you, soldier?"

Sorrow spread across Dezmund's face like a rising tide. "Oh, Hades," he mumbled. He spotted Valley, and his eyes narrowed.

"You heard the man!" Hanz bellowed, "Are you really going to refuse the regent?"

Dezmund's eyes lingered on Valley, then returned their focus to King Hanz. "There are many banners here," he said cautiously. "You plan to bring leaders from every Eastern Kingdom into Arelle?"

"Not me," Hanz said flatly, then pointed at Hevel, "*Him*."

"Lights help us..." mumbled the watchman.

Hanz elbowed Hevel, who jolted, then said, "Uh...erm...that's an *order*, soldier!"

Dezmund sighed deeply, then raised a hand. The Gates of Arelle began to slide open of themselves, causing many of the observers to gasp and whisper. Valley herself watched in amazement. She didn't like the manner in which she was entering the great Faerie city, but she was still excited!

Sigmund appeared out of nowhere at Hanz' side with an open notebook.

"Orders?" Valley could hear him whisper.

"I've seen inside the city, he's the only Faerie," said Hanz, "We will deal with him once there are no witnesses. Move the military into Fort Axes but have Oswald's guard come with us to the Eight Stones. The Fairies, move them to the Vineyard Palace. Have them closely watched by the Warrowing Guard. Have Swain choose residence within the Eight Stones for the delegates." He paused, giving Sigmund a moment to catch up with his scribbling, then added, "And put Hevel in the King's chambers. I'll be in the adjoining room...for now."

"And *your* Faeries?" Sigmund asked under his breath, as the large gates finally stopped moving.

"I want them close to me," whispered the King.

Dezmund faced Hanz with a look of defeat. "Well," he said, "Come on."

Hanz waved his hands in triumph to the long caravan of onlookers, producing a few cheers.

"Into Arelle!" he called, then led the way forward.

Soon, Valley was ushered away from Hanz' side by Captain Oswald, who stuffed and locked her into the smaller wagon containing Hanz' bonded Faeries.

"Well?" Coppo asked quickly, "what happened out there?"

"Why did *you* get to see all the action while *I* had to stay in here?" Karo said with a persecuted look.

Valley seated herself beside Coppo, keeping her distance from Karo.

"They've let us into Arelle," she said, as the wagon began to jostle into forward motion. "I think we are going to stay in the Eight Stones with Hanz while the other Faeries are being moved somewhere else."

Karo made a dramatic sigh of relief. "Well, thank the Lights for *that*," he said earnestly. "I didn't work so hard for this position just to be herded away with the cattle."

Coppo frowned. "You didn't work for this position," he said, "none of us did. It just happened."

"I don't mean *that*," Karo sneered, "Anyone can get bonded, but I—" he sniffed, "I have the King's *trust*."

Valley turned her back to Karo dismissively, facing Coppo.

"I have a bad feeling about this," she whispered. "I think Hanz is planning..." she paused, noticing that Coppo didn't seem to be listening. He was staring off into the middle distance and mumbling under his breath. "Coppo?" she whispered softly. He did not hear her. He was so distracted, it was as if his mind were no longer present in his body. "*Coppo*," she whispered, again, placing a hand on his arm.

Coppo turned his head sharply, looking at her with urgency.

"Oh, Lights!" he exclaimed.

"What?" Valley furrowed her brow.

"I... I..." he gulped. "I don't believe it..."

"*What*?" Valley squeezed his arm.

Coppo searched her eyes with his, as if for confirmation. "I...Rook!"

"What about Rook?" Valley decreased her volume further, glancing to the side to make sure Karo wasn't listening.

Coppo's face lost all its color. "Oh my..." it was as if he were listening to a voice only he could hear, and it was still speaking. He nodded slowly, listening. "Oh Hades... no...."

"Coppo...." Valley had no idea what was happening inside that boy's head, but she got the message that it was something terrifying. She began to tremble. "Coppo... What about Rook?"

Coppo shook the 'voice' from his head and looked at Valley helplessly. "He's... the King, Valley. Rook is Anodos."

Valley swallowed, then nodded. "I know," she whispered. "Why does that scare you?"

"Valley," Coppo whispered, grabbing her by the shoulder with sudden urgency. "Valley, something really terrible is going to happen."

"What do you mean?" Valley asked sharply, "Coppo, how do you know any of this? *What is going to happen?*"

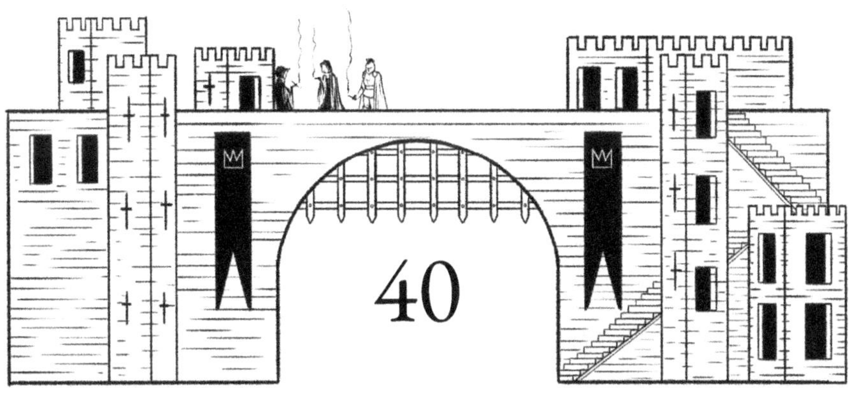

40

——— Hanz ———

Binding Oaths

ROOK PACED CATO'S ROOM AIMLESSLY, SAYING SOMETHING Hanz couldn't quite hear. Hanz studied Rook's face carefully. It was definitely different than before. Those disturbing scars which once masked his appearance had faded significantly. They were still there, yes, but were more like old etchings on a ruined temple wall. They were evidence of something that was once important. Rook was an attractive man, possibly more so than his father. For a moment, Hanz wondered how hard it might be to recreate those wretched scars.

Rook walked out onto the open balcony in Cato's quarters. Hanz' eyes followed. Rook was gazing around at the surrounding windows and turrets within the Eight Stones. Many of the other balconies could be seen from that vantage point. Rook peered around; he seemed to be searching for someone. Who? Perhaps he was hoping to find his brother Rasselas. Hanz had deduced that one crucial thing: Rasselas had discovered Rook was his long-lost brother.

Things were becoming very clear. Those scars on Rook's face? They were Riah's handiwork, and no mistake. Why she had resorted to *that* particular spell, he had no idea, but it was definitely her. No doubt the spell was broken when Hanz recognized Rook's face in the portrait book. Many would be starting to recognize Rook, so he needed to move quickly. Now that they were in Arelle, everything would be easier.

But who was Rook looking for? He followed the man's gaze. Rook spotted Rasselas on another balcony, gave him a wave, and then continued to peer around. There was someone *else*. Who?

"Hanz," said a voice from beside him.

"Two clicks..." Hanz mumbled. He watched Rook for a moment longer.

"Sire..." said the voice again. It was so strange hearing a voice directly beside his body when his eyes were so far away. Hanz did his best to return to his body, blinking as if from a trance.

"What?" Hanz said quickly, turning to see Sigmund standing there.

It was late, very late. It had taken bells to get everyone settled where they needed to be within the Faerie city, and the day hadn't been a very long one. It was well into the night bells now. While others were yawning and stumbling drunkenly around, looking for places to rest their heads, there was Sigmund, full of life. He was, as ever, a man of the night.

"It's done, sire," Sigmund said loyally.

"What's done?" Hanz asked, rubbing his eyes. The sleepiness was beginning to get to him.

Sigmund cleared his throat. "Dezmund," he said, "Hevel exiled him into the bag you provided."

"Ah," Hanz nodded. "Can you put it with the rest of my..."

"Already done, sire," Sigmund said proudly.

"Ah," Hanz ventured a smile. He had come so far. Everything was falling into place, so why didn't he feel the thrill of excitement?

"Everything...alright, Sire?" Sigmund asked, sliding his hands into his pockets.

"Hmm?" Hanz blinked. "Oh... yes, yes," he shrugged. "I suppose everything is ready for the coronation tomorrow?"

"Yes."

"And the Fairies? Are they settled into the Vineyard Palace?"

"Settled?" Sigmund made a modest shrug, "Yes, settled, I suppose. They are there and they aren't trying to...break out."

"And how are the delegates?"

"Tired. And grumpy. But they all seem to be planning to attend the coronation tomorrow. Though I don't think many of them *know* it is a coronation..."

"Fine, fine," Hanz yawned.

"Are you... ready?"

Hanz sighed. "I've never been more ready," he said wearily. "You know..."

Sigmund waited patiently as Hanz let out a long, drawn-out sigh.

"I was going to move forward without Anodos back in my grasp," he said, "It wouldn't have been as stable, but I would have done it. But now that I do have him?" He looked up and met his lackey in the eyes. "I think this is really going to work. It's like...I am staring at the board. I can see all the pieces sitting there, motionless, waiting for me to move them...and I know that once I move that last piece, it will be a checkmate. There is nothing that anyone can do." Hanz sighed. "It is that strange anticipation, that penultimate moment, that eerie calm before the opponent's king is knocked sideways, ending the longest game I have ever played. I've won, Sigmund," he said with growing strength, "I've already won, it just hasn't happened yet."

"Yes," Sigmund said dryly, "I see what you're saying."

Hanz turned to face the man. "Fetch my crown," he said, "It's time to go."

They marched together through the Eight Stones. This was the residence of Hevel the Regent, and Somenus before him—and before him, King Sol. This was the residence of every single Faerie King. There had only ever been three of them in all of Raqian history. Faerie Kings: the hardest beings in the Cosmos to kill.

Hanz came to Cato's door and pounded his fist upon it.

"Let them in, Rook!" Cato's voice called from within.

The door swung open, and Hanz found himself face to face with the would-be Faerie King himself. The boy looked shocked, stumbling backwards. He surely knew his spell was gone now and was no doubt wondering if Hanz could recognize him.

"Excuse me, boy," Hanz said quickly, pushing past him. Sigmund followed Hanz into the room, closing the door quickly. Hanz marched up to Cato, who was lounging on a chaise, eating grapes, and crossed his arms.

"Well?" Hanz asked impatiently, "Did you speak with her?"

"Yes," Cato said, glancing at Rook. "I did. I am happy with the arrangement."

Hanz turned to see Rook watching him.

There was another knock on the door. Rook jolted like a scared cat as Oswald and ten other soldiers came charging in. Sensing a threat, he began to back away toward the balcony.

"Get him, quick!" Hanz bellowed, thrusting a finger in Rook's direction. "Don't let him fly!

Rook's eyes flashed, but before he could react further, the armored guards began piling on top of him. With unimaginable strength, Rook threw them off of himself, roaring like a lion. His large wings began to unveil themselves.

Hanz fished into his cape then held out a glowing lantern. It flashed brightly, filling the room with its light. Rook, whose arms were now restrained by a dogpile of soldiers, watched in disbelief as his wings began to disintegrate, vanishing back into the air.

"What... what is that?" Rook demanded, despite the fact he had an eye for magikal items and had probably already discerned what it was.

"This?" Hanz held up the lantern. "The Imperium of the First Faerie of Wings," he smiled proudly to himself. "It is a rare thing, indeed."

Rook gritted his teeth, shaking against the mess of guards who held him down on his knees. Hanz could feel energy draining from the lantern. Hades! Rook's power was immense. Hanz had no idea if the spell would hold for long, so he acted quickly.

He stepped forward, gazing down at Rook with eyes of hatred.

Rook was sweating and, though he still seemed to be jerking and pulling against the soldiers beside him, he began to grow more still. He was the most powerful Faerie in the Cosmos, and yet it was power that he could not use himself, it could only be given to others. Without his massive wings, Rook was only as strong as his own muscles.

"Anodos," Hanz asked in a hiss. He dropped himself down onto one knee, so that his face was level with Rook's. "*Who are you?*"

Rook hesitated, then his pupils shrunk. He relaxed, then dropped his head in defeat. "I'm a product of rape—the spawn of a tyrant."

Hanz nodded to himself. Her work may have been incomplete, but Riah was a master. Much of her work still remained.

"Are you the Faerie King?" Hanz asked.

"No," Rook said quietly, "I can never be king."

"Why?"

"I'm a product of rape, and the spawn of a tyrant. I would be a stain on the throne, a reminder of oppression, and a symbol of..." his voice trailed off.

"Go on," Hanz said tauntingly, "Finish."

"A symbol of slavery."

Hanz rose to his feet. "Bring the cuffs," he said.

Sigmund, who had been watching silently from the sidelines, stepped forward. He held out two plan silver bands. The bracelets had little holes punched into the sides. Hanz took them from Sigmund, then lowered back down onto his knee. He showed Rook.

"Do you know what these are?" Hanz asked.

Rook looked at them. "Yes."

"What are they?" asked the king patiently. He was well aware that one of the powers of the Magik Faerie was detecting and identifying magikal items.

"Made by the Faerie of Vows, the oath bands restrain a Faerie from using their powers," Rook said through gritted teeth. "It will not work on me."

"Yes," Hanz turned the bracelets slowly in front of Rook's eyes, they reflected the room's dim light in little silvery bursts. "They could not stand against your magik, but..."

"No," Rook growled, "There is no way—"

"You have a hundred clicks," Hanz said sternly, "To bless these clasps. Do it."

Rook lifted his head to glare at the king in the eyes. "Why would I ever—?"

"Because I have about ten men with arrows pointed right at your brother," Hanz said calmly, "And if you don't, I will kill him." Then he added, "Sixty clicks now."

Rook jerked against the guards who held onto him as tightly as they could.

"I hate the little brat," Hanz spat, "I won't lose a moment's sleep over his death, in fact, I think my sleep will dramatically improve without that sniveling swine on the world. Forty clicks!"

Rook's eyes found Cato. "Please," he begged, "Don't make me do this."

Cato opened his mouth, then turned away.

"Bless the clasps!" Hanz held them just under Rook's nose. "I want them powerful enough to keep you from empowering others. Do it, or I kill that blasted Rasselas! *Thirty* clicks!"

"Do you *vow* not to hurt him?" Rook asked helplessly.

"Yes, yes," Hanz snapped, shaking the clasps, "Now do it! Twenty!"

Rook sighed, then closed his eyes. The clasps glowed brightly. Hanz felt the power in his hands. He watched them with his blue, discerning eyes. Yes, they were *filled* with unimaginable power!

"Now, Oswald!" Hanz snapped. Oswald stepped forward, pushing past Sigmund, and grabbed Rook by the wrists. Oswald, and about five other soldiers dragged him across the room and slammed his arms down on Cato's desk. Rook fought for a moment, then relaxed, watching as one of the soldiers hiked up Rook's sleeves.

"I'll put them on!" Rook yelled, "Just... just don't hurt Rasselas."

"Don't you dare let him go until they are on!" Hanz crowed. "Get them on him!"

Oswald threaded each of Rook's hands through the bracelets. Sigmund then stepped forward, holding thick silver pins in one hand and a hammer in the other.

"Hold him still!" Hanz screamed, slapping the back of Rook's head with his hand. "Get those damned things secured!"

Oswald took Rook by the hands and held his arms flush against the desk.

"Is this really necessary?" Cato asked timidly from the sidelines.

"Stay out of this," Hanz snapped, "I know what I am doing."

Rook began to roar a blood-curdling battle cry as Sigmund positioned one of the pins, or rather, nails over one of the holes in the bracelet. "Do it!" Rook screamed, "Just do it already!"

Sigmund nodded, then slammed the hammer down. The nail pierced through the bracelet and through Rook's wrist until its tip came out the other end. There was a burst of light as the magik within the bracelet welded the pin to the bracelet. Sigmund did the same to the other arm. Rook dropped his forehead down onto the desk, making no noise. The guards, who had worked tirelessly to restrain the powerhouse of a man, all stepped back cautiously. Blood began to drip from Rook's wrists where the pins had pierced him, and there they stayed, sealed with a magik as powerful as himself.

Rook did not move or lift his head; he just stayed there, defeated.

"And this," Hanz gestured toward him with his hand, "was supposed to be their king." He tutted. "How sad."

"So what...he's not got any powers anymore?" Cato asked cautiously.

"He just can't use them," Hanz said, stepping up to the desk to stand across from Rook. "He's just like any other Human... except for the fact that he can't die."

"Oh, floods," Cato exhaled noisily, "Well..."

"Make preparations," Hanz said to Sigmund, then he turned to Oswald, "Throw him in the prison beneath Fort Axes for now."

Rook lifted his head suddenly, gazing up at Hanz. "Please," he asked, "Honor your vow! Whatever happens, you must spare my brother!"

Hanz snorted, shaking his head.

Rook rose to his feet in a flash and slammed his hands against the desk, causing a spray of blood to fly across the room from his wrists.

"You swore!" Rook screamed. "You swore you would."

"I don't give a damn about Rasselas, and I don't give a damn about vows given to *Faeries* like you!" The king bellowed. "Do you really think I would pass up the chance to kill your *stupid* brother in front of everyone at the coronation tomorrow?" He scoffed. "Such a fool you are, Anodos."

"Please!" Rook screamed. He gazed directly into Hanz' eyes. "Save my brother! Save Rasselas! Do whatever you have to do—just *save* him!"

Hanz shook his head. "No," he said. It felt so good to say it: just, *no*.

Hanz motioned with his hand and Oswald, with the help of all his men, dragged Rook out of the room.

The place grew quiet. Only Cato and Sigmund remained.

"Hades," Cato cursed under his breath. "I've never known a man like him before, I think."

Was that... *reverence* in the King of Bavel's voice? Hanz turned slowly to regard Cato with his eyes.

"Yes..." Hanz said, "A freak, really."

Cato stepped up to Hanz with his chin held high. "You've taken your end of the bargain," he said, "I shall take mine tonight. I will leave before Daybreak."

Hanz narrowed his brow. "You will miss the coronation."

"Yes," Cato cleared his throat, "Sorry about that. But I assume our alliance is still solid, and everything? Are you happy with the final arrangement we discussed?"

"Yes, yes," Hanz sighed, waving his hand in annoyance. "But why tonight?"

Cato blinked. There was a reason that the man didn't want to say out loud.

"Fine," Hanz huffed, "Keep your secrets. You may go tonight. Take the felling woman with you."

"Do you mean your daughter?" Cato asked in a dull voice.

"Yes, yes," Hanz straightened his collar. "And do whatever you want with her."

"I will," Cato said slowly, turning to the side. "Goodbye for now. I am looking forward to working with you in the coming weeks."

"Yes," Hanz said quickly, looking toward the Bavel King, "Uh," he hesitated, "You, too. I think this will be a long, beneficial friendship."

"Yes," said Cato. "For the first time in history, Arelle and Bavel will be united."

41

—— Rook ——

The Sanctuary of Death

Rook had been stripped, searched, and beaten for good measure, no doubt on Hanz' orders. He was now chained to the wall in a cell within the prison below Fort Axes. There was a strange irony to the location, an irony that perhaps only he and Hanz knew. This was the cell where his mother and Leo had first met; it was where Anodos had been born, and where Hanz himself had come to kill him and his mother.

Rook wondered to himself if even back then Hanz would have been able to do it. Would Hanz have cut baby Anodos through the heart, only to watch his body knit itself back together? Leo had told Rook how he fought Hanz. He had subdued Hanz and chosen not to kill him, instead locking him in this cell. What if all those seasons ago, Leo *had* killed Hanz? So much misery would have been avoided. Rook never would have been torn away from his family and tortured to the verge of insanity. Rook blinked. But Rosamond...she would never have been born. And where would Rook be? He would still be Anodos, no doubt ruling as the King of the Fae, married to...he shuddered...married to the one person in the world he was sure he did *not* want to marry.

Rook was not sure which reality he preferred. Perhaps it was another reality altogether, one where he was never born, where his mother had never been raped and Somenus had never been king.

It was no use sitting there wishing that certain things hadn't happened. There was only one thing he did wish, though, and that was to keep his loved ones safe. It was the only thing that mattered anymore.

Rook heard someone clear their throat. He lifted his head slightly to see a dark figure standing on the other side of the cell bars.

"Hallo, Rook," came Cato's voice. There was a rattling sound and then the door to the cell opened. Cato stepped inside and wandered over. He walked right up beside one of Rook's bare feet, looked him over, and grimaced. "Damn, man," he said sympathetically, "They really don't waste any time, do they?" He referred to the marks Rook had received from the Faerie of Pain's three-tailed whip.

"Came in here to *what*?" Rook mumbled, "Gloat?"

Cato shook his head. "I didn't come here to apologize," Cato admitted, "Because I think that it would be rather pathetic of me to turn you over to your nemesis and then...well, apologize."

"What, then?"

Cato sniffed. "Well, I suppose I came to thank you."

"*Thank* me?" Rook gritted his teeth.

Cato's face grew solemn. "A true apology would involve trying to get you out of this mess. I'm afraid that's not something I am capable of. I do feel *sort* of bad," he admitted, "Because you really did save my life way back there in that odd town you come from. And I really did—uh, I *do* like you. So I wanted to thank you for all that. I was going to make you Knight of Bavel but, *erm*," he tugged at his cravat, as if it were tightening around his neck at the same rate his guilt was curling around his heart, "Then I found out you were a Faerie, that is— *the* Faerie! Well, as you know, Faeries are old enemies of Bavel, and all that."

"Bavel?" Rook's eyes widened as reality began to crystalize. "You're from Bavel?"

"I *am* Bavel," Cato corrected, "That's right, the King of Bavel. Two incognito kings hiding in the same Edgelands wagon. What are the odds of that?" He snickered. "Anyway," he puffed out his chest, "duty called, and everything. I had to turn you in, old chap. It was the *law*, you know," he said as if it were some sort of justification for what he had done, "In Mensa, you know, to turn in unbonded Fairies."

"Cato..." Rook said quietly, "I thought we were friends."

Cato shook his head, "No, no," he said haughtily, "That sort of thing doesn't work on me. I did what I did. But you're a good man, Rook, er, *Anodos*. And I don't like to see you in a place like this, but that's life, isn't it? Some rise, and some fall."

"Spoken like a true Bavelonian," Rook said with a sneer.

"Yes, well..." Cato cleared his throat. "I am leaving tonight. Back to Bavel, and all that...lots to do, lots to do..."

Rook leaned his head back against the wall. "It's been nice knowing you," Rook said with finality.

"Yes, well..." Cato turned to the side, looking back toward the gloomy shadows outside the cell. "Someone *else* wanted to see you."

"Who?" Rook tensed his brow.

Cato's expression was hesitant. "I...well..." He shrugged, then walked out of the cell.

Rook was shocked to see none other than Rosamond running into the dreary space. She wore a heavy traveling cloak, as if she were preparing for a journey. Her face was stained with tears, and she ran to throw herself against Rook's body. She knelt unashamedly down by his side, curled her arms around his chest, and buried her face in the cleft of his neck. Rook wanted to wrap his arms around her, but they were chained to the floor.

"Rosamond," Rook sighed defeatedly, "I'm sorry..."

"No!" she cried, squeezing him tighter, "Never say sorry!"

"I should have taken you far away before we came to Arelle," he said spitefully, "I don't know what I was *thinking* coming here!"

Rosamond lifted her head and looked into his eyes. "But you're the King! Can't you take the throne?"

Rook shook his head slowly. "No," he said, "I can't. Not like this."

Rosamond's lower lip quivered. "I don't want to be apart from you!"

He searched her face. Something was wrong. "What do you mean?"

"I am to leave tonight," she said in a weepy voice, "Father is sending me away with Highlord, uh, *King* Cato. He's giving me in marriage, Rook!"

"What?" Rook's eyes widened. "Are you...?"

Rosamond leaned forward to hug Rook once more, squeezing him so tight he coughed. "I never want to leave you ever again."

"It's good that you go," Rook said firmly, "I cannot protect you from your father anymore. I am just glad you will be away from him."

"But I don't want to be away from *you*!" She sobbed some more.

Rook noticed Cato stepping back into the cell. He had an impatient look about him, with his hands behind his back. He lumbered forward watching them silently.

"Cato will keep you safe," Rook said quietly, "Won't you, Cato?"

Cato's eyes met his. There was a silent moment of understanding between them.

"I don't *want* Cato!" Rosamond wailed like a toddler. "I want *you*!"

Rook and Cato's steady eye contact held as Rook said, "I am sorry."

"I love you, Rook," Rosamond said fervently, and she lifted up her head to plant a kiss on his lips. Rook, knowing it would probably be the last time he felt something so heavenly, closed his eyes. There in that same place where he was born and held by his adoring parents for the first time, he was held by Rosamond the woman who loved him.

Rosamond repeated several passionate kisses against Rook's mouth as she cupped his face in her hands. Then the contact was broken. Rook opened his eyes to see Cato taking Rosamond by the arm and lifting her up from the floor. She fought, screaming and kicking, but Cato pulled her back. He was gentle and silent, but firm.

"Rook!" Rosamond sobbed, reaching a hand out to him as Cato pulled her back.

"I love you too, Rosamond," Rook said softly. Then he gave her a weak smile.

He could hear her screaming and yelling in protest all the way out of the prison. Her voice faded into distant echoes, and then it was gone.

Rook sat there alone in the dank prison. Well, it had all come to this. He had never truly escaped Hanz. This was always coming—he was always going to end up here. Riah's spell had given him nearly thirteen seasons of privacy, but now here he was, a slave to King Hanz once more.

Things couldn't get much worse than this, could they?

The cell door creaked open once more. Rook lifted his eyes curiously, then his eyes widened. A chill moved through his body, and he gritted his teeth. "What is this?" he demanded. "What are you *doing*?" And then, it dawned on him what was about to happen.

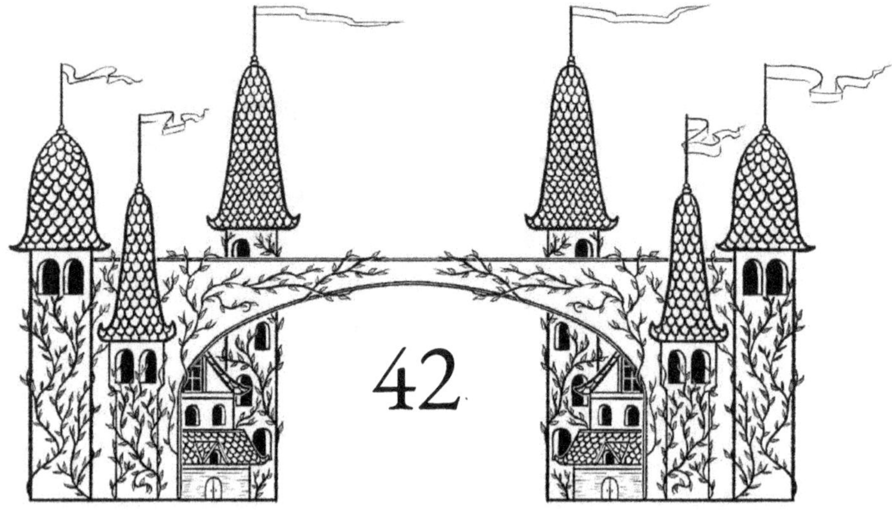

— Rasselas —

The Coronation

TODAY WAS THE DAY. The king was coming!

Rasselas stretched, yawning as loudly as he could. A good, solid, loud yawn was definitely the way to start this day. He ran out onto his balcony and peered out at the morning, Watersday light.

"Beautiful day!" he cried happily, "Just beautiful!"

Rasselas looked around, half expecting Thorne to pop into the room and tell him off for yelling and running around in nothing but his trousers. Then he remembered another happy fact, Thorne wasn't there!

"The best day *ever*!" Rasselas sang, skipping back into his room. He was grinning, imagining that stupid look on Hanz' face when Anodos would come fly into the throne room and slam Hanz down against the ground. Oh, it was going to be so perfect. And what would Valley think? She had no idea his brother was alive—that he was *here*!

"The Faeries will finally have their king," Rasselas said, as he tried to dress himself as quickly as he could, "And they will no longer be oppressed!"

There was a knock on the door. Rasselas, with his shirt half buttoned, cried, "Come in!"

The door cracked open slightly, "Hallo?" Asked a timid voice.

"I said, come in!" Rasselas barked. "Hades, is that *you*, Latimer?"

The Elven skydeacon poked his head in, then pushed the door open further and pressed the rest of his body through.

"Hallo, Moonvine," said Latimer, "How fare you?"

"Fine, fine," Rasselas said quickly as he continued to dress himself, "How soon until the meeting in the throne room?"

"Uh... I was just on my way there. I see you've," he hesitated, "slept in?"

"I'll be ready in just a moment," Rasselas retorted, "Now, I know you've got something to say. What *is* it?"

Latimer cleared his throat. Rasselas noticed that he was wearing his official ceremonial skydeacon robes. "It's about the storm."

"Yes?" Rasselas was tying his cravat now, raising his chin up into the air as he watched the skydeacon expectantly.

"I am going to speak with the other skydeacons about it, and I am afraid they won't be happy."

"Ah," Rasselas turned sharply to face Latimer, placing his hands on his hips. "Well, don't worry, old boy. I am sure everything is going to be fine." Whatever this man's problems were, Anodos was sure to fix them.

"*Erm,*" Latimer scratched his head nervously, "Have you seen Rook this morning? I was rather hoping to speak with him. He wasn't in his room."

"Well, I am sure he *wouldn't* be," Rasselas said quickly, "He's no doubt preparing for his grand entrance!"

"Grand... entrance?" Latimer cocked his head to the side. "Moonvine... is there something you know that I don't know?"

Rasselas was *dying* to tell somebody. He probably would have told just about *anybody* who walked into his room just then. Thank the Lights, it was Latimer!

"You bet there is!" Rasselas said brightly.

Latimer blinked expectantly. "Are you... going to tell me?"

"Yes!" Rasselas stood there proudly, hands on hips. Oh, this was going to be so great.

Latimer shifted his weight from one leg to another. "...yes?"

"Rook..." Rasselas declared, thrusting a finger up to the Heavens. His resolve weakened slightly, "*Uh...*" he stared at the Elf. Would Rook *want* him spoiling his surprise like this?

"Yes?"

"Uh, Rook is going to meet us in the throne room," Rasselas said anticlimactically.

"Oh!" Latimer brightened. "Alright, well, perhaps we should go then?"

"Yes, yes," Rasselas grumbled, throwing his green jacket over his shoulders. "Just wait for me."

Latimer tapped his foot impatiently, leaning over to peer out the window and check the Skies when Rasselas took a moment to polish his boots.

"It really is time to be there, Moonvine," mumbled Latimer, "We don't want to miss the—"

"Ready!" Rasselas declared. "Now come on, don't doddle."

Rasselas charged through the door, grinning. Latimer scrambled to catch up with him.

The throne room was lined with all the banners represented by the visiting delegates. Soldiers, skydeacons, priests, and other noblemen crowded the side rows, and there was a line of silk ropes forming an aisleway down to the throne. Down the aisle, the line of kings and princes waited patiently, standing together proudly. Rasselas was among them. He stood with his hands behind his back, smiling smugly, with Prince Tingo on one side of him and King Stathe on the other. He searched for Valley in the crowds but could not find her. Highlord Cato was mysteriously missing as well. Anodos wasn't there, but that was to be expected!

The oddest thing was the lack of Faeries in the room. This was a Faerie throne room, and Hanz had filled it with Humans. How disgraceful.

"So is Hanz planning on crowning himself? Or that Faerie Regent?" Tingo whispered cautiously into Rasselas' ear.

"Hanz isn't going to crown anyone," Rasselas whispered back. "Just watch. There is a little *surprise* coming."

Brassy horns began to play a clear, triumphant march. Then three figures entered the room, gliding ceremoniously down the aisle. Regent Hevel was at the front of the procession and held the Faerie crown on a pillow. Rasselas gasped. Hevel—there he was! Hanz was next in line, dressed in enough velvet to suffocate an army, and then was Captain Oswald, holding another pillow. On it rested the Faerex' scepter. It made Rasselas' blood boil seeing a Human holding something so sacred.

The procession moved down the aisle, until King Hanz and Regent Hevel were standing on either side of the throne. The look on Hevel's face made Rasselas feel a little uneasy. The man looked more unsettled than a cat on a boat.

"Friends of Mensa, leaders of Raqia," Hanz announced loudly, raising his hands to the gathered crowd. "Today, we will finally stabilize the throne of Arelle. We will bring prosperity back to our lands and end the famine! We will unite under one peace treaty. Today, a ruler will be crowned. Someone who can use the throne and its power for the *good* of Humans." Hanz turned to Hevel, gesturing with his hand toward him. "This Faerie is the Regent, the caretaker of the throne. He is the only one with the authority to pass the crown to a worthy leader."

"And I suppose Hanz thinks of himself as the worthy leader?" Rasselas whispered into Tingo's ear.

"He's really brought the Regent, Rasselas," Tingo whispered back. "Doesn't that mean something? Surely the regent knows the right person to pick. Why *can't* Hanz be worthy?"

Rasselas glanced at Tingo in disbelief. Did he *really* think it possible for a Human to sit on the throne of Arelle?

"Welcome, one and all," Hevel said in a shaky voice. His hands were vibrating as they plucked the crown from its resting place. "Today, the rightful king has returned!"

Rasselas' attention shot back in Hevel's direction. Yes—this was the moment. Anodos had no doubt spoken with him. Oh, Hanz was going to be so dumbfounded!

"There is only one man who can sit on this throne," Hevel said, his confidence rising only slightly, "Only one true king. And this?" He turned toward Hanz, "Is him."

Rasselas watched in disgust as Hevel placed the Faerie crown on Hanz' head. The Faerie crown! The first of the three imperiums given to the Faerex. It gave him authority over Faeries. Next was the throne, which Hanz moved to sit upon; the throne gave the Faerex power over the Land. Thirdly, there was the scepter—Oswald was walking it over to King Hanz slowly—it gave the Faerex judgment, and the power to kill. Only the true Faerex could wield those things. None of this meant anything if a Human tried to touch them. Even if an unqualified Faerie tried to use them, they would be as impotent as a corpse. What did Hanz think he was *doing*?

"My god," Rasselas muttered to himself. It was all a show! It didn't need to be real; everybody just needed to *believe* it!

Oswald passed the scepter to Hanz, who turned it proudly in his hands. There was a wide, greasy smile on his face.

"Long live the King!" Hevel cried. A chorus of voices resounded in response.

"Long live the King!"

Rasselas was aghast to hear the words coming from Tingo's mouth, and all the other Delegates. *Everyone,* save himself, seemed to be repeating it over and over.

"This is insane!" Rasselas' shout silenced the room.

He thrust a finger out at Hanz, and all heads turned to gawk at the disruptor. "He's not a Faerie! He is a pretender! This man has no authority, no power! Do you really think your lands will grow fruit now? Do you *really* think the famine is over? He's impotent, I tell you—*impotent!*"

"I," A new voice cried out authoritatively, silencing Rasselas, "Affirm this new rule." A man dressed in long, charcoal robes, with a long flowing train glided out to the center of the stage. Rasselas recognized him as Fellow Cassian, the head of the Mensa skydeacons. "The Lights have predicted this coming reign, and we pronounce that it is blessed by the Lights."

Hanz bowed his head to Cassian in thanks.

"No!" cried another voice. The faces in the crowd searched for its source. Rasselas held his breath, watching in horror as Latimer stepped out into the aisle. He strode courageously forward, then knelt before the King. He rose again.

"I..." his voice was shaky as a rope bridge, "I have studied the results of the last storm, and my findings..."

Rasselas slapped a hand against his own forehead. What was this man *doing*?

"Quiet, Latimer!" Cassian bellowed, "The skydeacons reached a consensus on that storm days ago. Step *back*."

"That's just it, sire," Latimer directed his voice toward Hanz. "The skydeacons didn't even get a chance to reach a consensus. There is... there is..." he turned to face the crowd. "There is a *warning* coming from the Skies!"

There was murmuring among the crowds.

"Listen to your elder," Hanz said to Latimer firmly, "stand down."

"I *must* say my findings," Latimer cried bravely, "The storm last week was not an anticipation storm, it was a *fury* storm! It does have a name, but it is not what you announced," he pointed an accusatory hand at Cassian, "It is called: *New Abomination*. And you know it, don't you?"

Cassian tipped his chin upwards, refusing to respond. Latimer turned to the Delegates who had assembled there at the front of the stage.

"The Skies are filled with dread and warning, there is something new and evil happening, and the Lights are angry. If King Hanz' skydeacons are trying to hide it, we need to ask why." He turned to face Rasselas now. "I think Prince Moonvine is right, friends, I think that Hanz is *not* the rightful King!"

Hanz stood, silencing the room. He took a determined step forward, then pointed his scepter at Latimer.

"Not the rightful King?" Hanz asked. His blue eyes seemed to glow.

"I am sorry," Latimer said weakly, "I must speak the truth. You are not the King....I think."

The scepter within Hanz' hand made a flash of light. He raised it upwards, then pointed it toward Latimer. Then all present gasped in unison, watching as Latimer's body was thrown backwards. His head hit the marble floor with a disturbing crack and then silence filled the hall. A dark red pool of blood began to form around where Latimer's body lay. Hanz lifted the scepter, then turned to the room.

"Impotent?" Hanz' booming voice filled the hall. It seemed to echo inside Rasselas' head.

"No..." Rasselas ran and knelt beside Latimer's body. "Impossible!"

"Impossible?" Hanz' voice bellowed again. "Not for the true King," he said. Hanz then lifted his hands into the air and spreading out on either side of the King's body, a magnificent set of four wings took form. On his right side were two glowing white wings, and on his left two as dark and as terrifying as the night. Hanz flapped his massive wings victoriously; they seemed to fill the room with their sheer size. The hall filled with gasps and cries.

Rasselas only gaped. A tear dropped from the corner of his eye as he studied the wings he remembered seeing as a boy.

"Two light, two dark," Hevel muttered from the sidelines, bowing reverently, "It is the King! Bow to the King!"

"You heard him!" Hanz cried, "Bow!"

No one was stupid enough *not* to bow. No one—but Rasselas. He jumped to his feet.

"You bastard!" Rasselas screamed, spit spraying from his mouth. "Those are Anodos' wings! Those are my brother's wings! You-you-you-you sick *monster!*"

"Silence. Brat."

"What did you do with Anodos? What have you done to his w—"

Hanz pointed his scepter at Rasselas. "Don't you know what happens to those who defy me and my rule, *Moonvine*?" Hanz said mockingly. "Bow."

"I will never bow to you, you monster!" Rasselas roared. "If I die—fell it—I die!"

"Die, then." Hanz gritted his teeth. His scepter began to glow, and Rasselas closed his eyes.

Then, there came a crash.

Rasselas opened his eyes and shielded himself with his arms as a hailstorm of stained glass rained down over him and everyone else in the throne room. Black shapes moved overhead, barreling in through the broken windows, and something knocked Hanz to the ground. A pair of strong arms grabbed Rasselas at the waist.

"Get off me," Rasselas cried as he tried to elbow his attacker away. But before he could fight anymore, he felt himself lifted up into the air. Rasselas let out a sharp cry as he looked down to see his legs dangling beneath him, kicking in protest as the ground shrunk away. Shouts and screams erupted from the crowd beneath him.

All around him, black wings flapped and swooped, messily carrying Rasselas higher. Down below, Hanz lay on the floor, and Rasselas could clearly see Anodos' wings springing from his back.

"No, no, no, no, no," Rasselas cried as he slapped the arms that carried him. "Put me down, put me down! Those are Anodos' wings down there! We have to do something—we have to save him."

The intruder carried Rasselas higher, until the Eight Stones became a small little building below them.

"It's too late," said a deep voice, "he asked me to save you, and save you, I shall."

"Put me down!" Rasselas shouted hoarsely. "Anodos, *Anodos!*" His hands reached out helplessly as his brother's beautiful wings grew smaller and smaller, fading out of sight. "Take me back!" He was crying now, crying like he cried the day he heard Anodos had been killed. Once again, his brother had been taken from him, and he was helpless.

"Hold on tightly to me," said the voice. "If you care for your brother, then honor his last wish."

Rasselas wiped his eyes angrily, then turned his head. He gasped, seeing a dark-haired Faerie with a black cloth tied around his eyes.

"Wh—" Rasselas found himself slipping, then threw his arms around the Faerie once it occurred to him just how high they were flying. "Put me down!"

"I cannot put you down until I do what your brother asked me to do. I must bring you to safety," the Faerie said darkly.

"You... you know Anodos?"

The Faerie said nothing.

Rasselas looked up, then swallowed when he counted the Faerie's wings. "I... I know who you are," he said at last. "Your name is Felix. You are the Faerie of Sight."

"I am."

"My brother spoke to you?"

"Climb upon my back," Felix said with a grunt. "You are heavy, and it is a long flight to Winter's End."

"Winter's End," Rasselas said quietly. "We cannot go so far when..." he turned his head, seeing now that Arelle was nothing more than a bright speck on the horizon, "when Anodos needs us."

"I need your eyes," said Felix, "I fly blindly westward. I need you to guide me to Aorist's home. I must speak with your father."

Rasselas wasn't sure what to say. His heart still pounded with anxiety, and his mind swirled with questions. He did as Felix asked and very awkwardly climbed onto his back while in midflight. He wrapped his arms around Felix's neck and lay between the massive wings, which found a gentle breeze and soared, outstretched like an eagle. There, caught up in the clouds with a total stranger, Rasselas dropped his head onto Felix's back and let out an angry, roar-like cry.

Felix did not speak with Rasselas for some time. Bells went by, and the landscape below them changed. From grass, to hills, to mountains.

"Where are we now?" Felix asked at length.

Rasselas sniffed, then lifted his head. Through swollen eyes he studied the mountain peaks. "Somewhere over the grey range. Veer left a little."

Felix adjusted his flight.

"I am sorry I did not come sooner," Felix said in a low voice. "I flew blindly to Arelle from memory."

"How..." Rasselas wiped his nose with his sleeve. "How did you know to come?"

"Hanz put my eyes in his body. I can see everything he sees."

Rasselas' stomach lurched. "He—what?"

"He has found a way to use the Faerie of Flesh to merge Faerie parts to a Human. Hanz wished to use the power of my far-sight. The Crimson Gate may only be used by me, and so he took my eyes so that he could use that, too."

"This man," Rasselas hissed, "Just when I think I know how evil he is, he—" Rasselas cut himself short, blinking. "So you see what he sees?"

"Yes."

"Does *he* know that?"

"I don't think so," said Felix.

Rasselas hesitated. "But... Anodos?"

"Rook knows that I can see what he sees. He called to me, knowing that I read lips. He asked me to save you."

"*When?*"

"Last night." Felix sighed. "Hanz threatened to kill you. Anodos was taken and..."

"Oh, *Hades,*" Rasselas muttered under his breath as the horror came over him. "Hanz cut off Anodos' wings... so that he could use the King's imperiums."

"Yes."

Rasselas was at a loss for words. What could be said? Hanz didn't need to kill Anodos to steal his throne. All he had to do was *become* Anodos.

"I've failed, Felix," Rasselas said at length. His body shook with another encroaching sob. "I came all this way to save Anodos...to save Faeries, and..."

"Rasselas," said Felix, "save your words. What is done is done."

"Take me home, Felix," Rasselas said in a muffled voice as he rested his face once more on Felix's shoulder. "Just take me home."

THE END

Epilogue

I RAN MY FINGERS DOWN THE LENGTH OF HER ARM. How smooth it felt—pure softness. Her head rose and fell gently against my chest to the rhythm of my breathing. It was one of those perfect moments. I had a lot of them in my life—perfect moments—and that was because *she* was my wife.

"We should do this all the time," I said through a yawn.

"We *do* do this all the time," came her response. I laced my fingers into her hair, running them along her scalp.

"Sure, but," I yawned again, "I mean like, just come out here and lay out a blanket on the balcony. Listen to the waves in the distance and just.... be."

"I know," she said with a sigh. "Just soak it up. Let's just be quiet and enjoy the silence while it lasts."

We both took in a deep breath, then let them out in unison.

"I've got a really great life," I said at length.

"You say that a lot."

"Yeah, well—I really *mean* it this time. I'm so happy, my love. I really do have such an amazing—" Then I felt it: the hole inside me. It was so empty, so cavernous; it was like the empty stomach of a starving man while he watched someone else eating greasy food.

"Oh, Lola," I sighed.

"What?"

"I…" my voice trailed off. *No, don't mention it to her. Don't ruin the perfect moment*—she looked so happy and peaceful lying there in my arms. It would be unkind to bring up that gaping hole, that bleeding wound. She missed him more than I did, if that were possible.

Unless…unless she was feeling exactly what I was feeling in this moment; the feeling that something was missing in our lives. Our son…*my* son.

"Leo," Lola said quietly. I felt her fingers graze my ribcage. I shuddered at the warmth I felt from it.

"Hmm?"

"Would you like your life to get…just a little bit…*more* happy?"

That was a loaded question. I blinked rapidly as I stared up at the Sky from where I lay on the outdoor terrace.

"Uh, sure…" I said brightly. "What do you—"

Oh dear.

I stiffened. "*Again?*"

Lola buried her face into my armpit. "Yes," she said in a muffled voice.

"Wait—*again?*" I said, louder.

"*Yes,*" came her muffled voice.

"Why are you hiding your face?" I said, tapping her shoulder playfully. "Lola!" I grabbed her arm and shook her, laughing, "Look at me!"

My wife lifted her head lazily. Her auburn hair was messily covering half her face. There was evidence of a cheeky grin, but it was hiding behind a bashful cringe. "I'm sorry…" she said.

"Sorry?" I laughed, sitting up very suddenly and pulling her with me. I tucked her hair behind her ear and laughed. "You've got nothing to be sorry about, you lovely, *wonderful* woman! But, are you sure? You're positive?"

Lola nodded bashfully. "Yes. I have suspected for a little while, but today, I am sure I felt it move." She placed her hand gently on her belly.

"Oh, my perfect Lola." I brought her face close with my hands and kissed it. Then, she kissed me back. We lingered there, taking in each other's scent, and then we both laughed.

"Five children," Lola shook her head as she gathered her hair to one side, "do you think it's too many?"

I leaned my arm on my knee and shook my head. "Nah. Though," I chuckled, "I think your father will have even more reason to be annoyed with me. I'll probably get some passive-aggressive letter telling me to give you some space."

"Oh, Leo," she rolled her eyes. "He would never say that."

"Oh, he might." I crossed my legs and leaned back on my arms, watching Lola as the wind blew some blossoms into her hair. "He has no problem telling me all the things I am doing wrong as your husband."

"Let's not talk about him right now," Lola mumbled, turning to look over her shoulder. Her eyes caught a glimpse of the grey coast, and the smile left her face. I reached out to touch her hand and brought her attention back to myself.

"Lola? Are you alright?"

"It doesn't matter how many children I have, nothing can ever fill the...I still miss..."

"Anodos. I...I miss him too, Lola."

"Mama?"

Lola and I both turned our attention to the balcony door that led into our bedroom. Little Beatrice, our two-seasoned daughter toddled into the room unevenly like a little peg-legged pirate.

"Hallo, little Bee!" Lola smiled warmly, then her eyes shifted towards me, and she whispered, "I thought you locked the door."

"Sorry..." I whispered back, "at least we weren't—"

"Oh, sorry Mama!" Cosette came bounding out onto the balcony. "We were playing hide and seek. I know I said I would keep an eye on her so you two could get some alone time."

"It's no problem," I said as I studied Cosette for a moment. She was getting so grown up and looking so much like her mother. My daughter—questioning already! It seemed like only yesterday that she had been born. "My goodness, Cosette. You're looking so old. You need to stop growing."

Cosette laughed. "Alright, Daddy. I'll do that. Bee? Come on, come with me and I'll tell you another story. Remember Mama and Daddy wanted to have some alone time?"

Little Beatrice, with her brown curly hair pulled into pigtails, made a little dissatisfied frown. "I want Mama!"

"We just want a little more time together," Lola said as she motioned for Cosette to leave. "Go on, Daddy and I have things to talk about."

"Why don't you let them stay?" I whispered. "You can tell them the news."

"I want it to be our news for a bit," Lola whispered back.

I nodded. "Alright." I turned to the girls. "You heard Mama, she—"

"Where is everyone?" A male voice called from the bedroom. Lola and I both leaned forward to watch as Momentum came walking out, eating an apple. He spotted us sitting on the balcony and placed a hand on his hip. "Family picnic? No one invited me."

Cosette whirled to face Momentum with a joyous smile. "Mama and Daddy want some alone time, Uncle Mo," she said, "why don't you come play with me and Bee?"

Momentum, wrapped in a neatly tailored dressing robe glanced at Cosette with a patient smile. "Perhaps later."

"Is something wrong, Momentum?" I cocked my head to the side. I could tell when there was something he wanted to tell me. He always had an impatient way about him, as though he were feeling a great itch.

"I am not sure if it is a good or a bad thing," Momentum said as he walked up to the balcony's ledge. Rather than looking westward toward the Sea, he turned eastward and pointed. "But someone is coming."

"Ooh!" Cosette gasped excitedly, then ran up to Momentum's side. "Who? Who is it, Mo?"

Bee followed Cosette and tried to reach up to look over the balcony. Momentum lifted her up by the waist and set her on his hip. "Look at that," he said, pointing out at the horizon. "How many wings do you see, Bee?"

That got my attention. I leapt to my feet and helped Lola up by the arm.

"Don't you dare get our hopes up, Momentum," I said with a fierceness that surprised even myself.

Momentum looked over his shoulder at me with a solemn look. "It's not Anodos, sorry."

Lola hugged my side, and I put an arm around her.

"Four wings," Bee said in a singsong. "I see four!"

Lola held me a little tighter. "Leo," she whispered, "It's... it's not him, is it?"

"Felix told me he wouldn't show his face here again," I said in a low voice as my eyes tried to focus on the four black flapping wings that seemed to be coming closer. "Plus, he's blind. How could he..." my voice trailed off as Momentum gave me a knowing look. "I mean," I cleared my throat, "He would only come here if he had a really good reason... right?"

"Oh, I can't see him, Leo," Lola whispered. "Unless..." she looked up at me with her wide green eyes. "Do you think he has news of Anodos?"

"I'll go to the landing platform," Cosette called as she shot a fist into the air. "Race you there!"

"Wait!" Lola called, reaching out her hand, but Cosette was gone in a flash. She huffed.

"I'll go," I said, "you stay here. I don't want you to have to—"

"No." Lola held up her hand. "This is probably important. I want to be there."

Momentum, Lola, Bee, and I journeyed up to the mosaic landing platform out at the center of Winter's End. The four large willow trees that sat at the four corners of the pavilion swayed in the wind, and the clouds moved fast overhead. The figure in the distance was much closer now, and he could see Felix's unmistakable four black wings flapping toward us. Once he was close enough for us to make out his body, we saw that he was not alone. He carried another man on his back.

I felt a surge of hope well up inside me. Could it be? Could he have found Anodos? Was he bringing him home to us? After fifteen long, terrible seasons of searching, would I finally lay eyes on my beloved Anodos?

"It's not Anodos," Lola whispered from beside me.

I looked at her. "How do you know?"

"I just... know..." she looked down at her feet, and I held her a little closer.

"Oh, *Hades*," Momentum said. He turned to give me a wide-eyed look, mouthing the words: *your son.*

I shook my head at him. He nodded knowingly. I shook my head again. He nodded again, looking annoyed. I shook my head faster. He pointed at the sky. I turned angrily, observing Felix as he grew closer. Then I gasped. He *was* holding my son!

Felix swooped down and landed at the center of the platform. The man on his back climbed down and dropped to his knee. He was motionless for a moment as he rubbed his eyes, then he looked up and rose shakily back to standing.

It was my son, my *other* son—when had he grown so tall?

"Rasselas!" I called, reaching out a hand toward him. "Rasselas, are you alright?"

Rasselas began to run toward me, pushing Felix to the side. I could see daylight reflecting off his tear-streaked face. The lad had been crying.

"Rasselas!" I released Lola to hold both arms out toward him. "Rasselas, what *happened*?"

Rasselas skidded towards me, hands outstretched, then passed me by, dove toward Lola with a fierce passion.

"Mother!" he sobbed, collapsing at her feet in a mess of moisture. "Mother, it was him! He was there! And–and–and–and *he* took him!"

"Oh, darling," Lola lowered herself to her knees, drawing her younger son into her arms lovingly. She pet his head, cradling it against her bosom as he wept. "There, there, darling. You're safe now." She had no idea where he had come from; why he had come with Felix; or why he was crying; but she was ready for him. She was, after all, the perfect mother–nay–the perfect woman.

I didn't take it personally when my son chose to weep into his mother's arms over mine. I was quite used to that. I walked to Momentum's side, and we exchanged curious looks. Then, saying nothing, we walked side by side up to Felix.

The Faerie of Sight was standing there stoically, posing like a statue. A black cloth was tied around his eyes, and he wore only a dark velvet tunic and basic sandals. His four wings seemed to catch the wind, swaying like the tops of pine trees, and he lifted his chin curiously as we approached.

"Is... Aorist here?" Felix asked in a steady voice. Momentum and I exchanged glances once more.

"I'm here," said Momentum dryly. He took bite of his apple.

"I'm here, too," I said, "Leo."

Felix rotated his head to the side, turning his right ear toward me. Then he nodded. "Leo," he said, "I am sorry to return after promising I would stay away... I... *she* isn't here, is she?"

"She's here," I said cautiously, "But please don't leave. I think Momentum and I would love to, uh... have a chat with you."

"You might be too blind to know this," Momentum said with a mouth full of apple, "But Leo is standing there in a dressing gown. I just wanted to bring you in on that fun fact."

I glared at Momentum, who was clearly the one in the dressing gown.

Felix rotated his ear toward Momentum as he listened, then turned it back toward me. "I would not have returned unless it were of dire importance."

Momentum and I exchanged more curious looks. "Felix," I said slowly, "What do you mean by that?"

"I flew your son here from Arelle," Felix said darkly.

"*Arelle*?" I shook my head, "But... Rasselas was in Celestia!"

"No," Felix said, still standing still in his statue-like pose, "He was not. He was in Arelle."

"Why was he—"

"Leo," Felix lowered his voice, then stepped closer, holding his hand out in front of him in search of me. I stepped forward, meeting his hand with mine. He felt for my shoulder, then grasped it and leaned in toward my ear, "Leo," he said again in a whisper, "Anodos has been found."

My heart turned to stone within my chest. I shifted my eyes, first noting Momentum's stunned reaction, then Rasselas sobbing within Lola's arms. I leaned away from Felix, holding my breath as a throbbing pain thumped through my entire being.

"Where?" I asked darkly, "Where is he?"

Felix lowered his chin to meet his chest. "King Hanz...has him."

Like a flash, I was marching to the armory. I was a blaze of fire and adrenaline, single minded, determined. I heard someone running after me, shouting, but I could not hear him. I swatted him away as he tried to slow me down. I kicked open the door to Momentum's weapon stache and threw open the case which held the Beatus Staff. I reached out to grab it, but arms seized me, pulling me backwards.

I fought whoever-it-was, throwing them to the side. He pulled me harder until I fell onto my back. Momentum wrestled me to the ground. I fought hard against him, surprising even myself with my own strength. He held fast to my wrists, finally managing to pin me downwards.

"Leo!" Momentum cried, finding my eyes, "Stop!"

"That bastard has my son!" I screamed. "I–I–I should have done it! I should have killed him all those seasons ago! He's taken him, Momentum! I *knew* it was him...I..." my strength was fading. I shook myself, refusing to let the anger subside.

"We will get him back," Momentum said in a strong voice, "Leo, we know where he is now. We will get him back!"

"I will kill that man!" I cried, "You can't stop me, Momentum. I will kill him!"

Momentum stared down at me with his glassy eyes. "I...I won't stop you, if that's what you want to do, but..."

I tried to push the Faerie off of me, but he had me pinned. I took a deep breath. That was a bad idea; the deep breath fueled not my anger, but the sadness that was hiding under it. The fire inside me began to turn cold.

"Momentum..." I blinked, my voice growing weak, "I need to find him. I need to find Anodos. I need to bring him home."

"Well," my friend sighed, "Let's bring him home, then. Come on. Let's find out what Felix knows, and—" he paused, "And Rasselas...we will do something about it. But Leo?"

I stared blankly into Momentum's face. "What?"

"Don't touch that staff. At least—not yet."

The trilogy reaches its exciting conclusion in…

Sky Fury I & II

and there will be more to come in…

A Series of Frigid Fragments

About the Author

NATASHA KENNEDY IS an author and illustrator based in Seattle, Washington. Living with a painful and debilitating connective tissue disorder, Natasha's writing reflects her belief that suffering and hardship can bring about beauty and richness. Her interests in ancient Near Eastern and Medieval Cosmology have inspired her to combine truth with symbolism in the fantasy world of Raqia.

Natasha has produced a variety of works throughout her career as both an author and an illustrator. She is best known for her illustration work in a children's book line called the FatCat series, produced by Lexham Press.

Earlier publications, combining storytelling with illustration, include:

Where I Go When I Sleep, a bedtime series written for her own children,
Maia of the Forest, a fantasy retelling of Thumbelina in coloring book form,
Reklas Abandon, a graphic murder mystery novel, her first work, and
Tempest: Volume One, the beginning of a graphic novel series released in 2020.

In the years following the release of *Tempest V.1*, Natasha began to rethink the graphic novel series. Realizing it would take too long to complete the story in graphic form, she chose to compose the entire narrative as a fantasy novel. That novel became *Firmaments*, and it led quickly to books 2 and 3 as *The Tempest Trilogy* came into being.

After finishing the trilogy, Natasha continued with a collection of smaller books, eight in number, which take place after the events of the *Tempest Trilogy*. This is called *A Series of Frigid Fragments*.